FICTION   Garcia y Robertson,
GARCIAYR   Rodrigo, 1949-

           Knight errant.

DATE			

Knight Errant

FORGE BOOKS BY R. GARCIA Y ROBERTSON

American Woman
Knight Errant

Knight Errant

R. GARCIA Y ROBERTSON

A TOM DOHERTY ASSOCIATES BOOK
NEW YORK

KNIGHT ERRANT

Copyright © 2001 by R. Garcia y Robertson

This book is printed on acid-free paper.

Design by Jane Adele Regina

A Forge Book
Published by Tom Doherty Associates, LLC
175 Fifth Avenue
New York, NY 10010

www.tor.com

Forge® is a registered trademark of Tom Doherty Associates, LLC.

ISBN: 0-312-86996-7

First Edition: November 2001

Printed in the United States of America

0 9 8 7 6 5 4 3 2 1

For Michelle

Knight Errant

PART 1

Wild Wales

What danger or what sorrow can befall thee,
So long as Edward is thy constant friend...
—Shakespeare, *Henry VI*

Robyn

She saw the knight come riding up as she stopped to rest. Setting down her Nike squirt bottle, Robyn retied her hiking boots and then stood up to stare. She had not seen a soul since crossing the BritRail tracks near Pandy. By now A465 out of Abergavenny was far behind her. She had been hiking alone along the Welsh border, a rolling green-gold landscape of heather-covered tops furrowed by ancient earthworks—a place impossibly old and unrelentingly pretty—dotted with standing stones, burial tumps, wildflowers and faerie rings, which made this knight on horseback's sudden appearance all the more startling. He had no lance or helmet, but mail-clad sleeves and plate armor showed beneath a mud-spattered surcoat decorated with blue-gold bars. His long, heavy sword hung from the steel hip nearest her. Passing strange, as the locals would say; weird and a half, to be precise. Something sure to go in her journal.

Where is he headed? she wondered. Halloween's weeks away. . . . Maybe Brits celebrate it early.

Even at first sight, and from a distance, he looked engaging. His outfit alone would make anyone take notice. Long tawny hair fell onto steel-clad shoulders, framing brash, boyish good looks, a face alert and friendly, with a likeable smile. To top it off, he rode well, as if he and his big, black warhorse were old friends out for a morning jaunt—that landed them in the wrong millennium. Not your normal random guy.

From a clump of hawthorn came the long breathless trill of a wren, ending in a strident *tit-tit-tit* of alarm. Then silence.

Good advice. Go easy, girl; don't forget you're in a foreign country. Her short stay in Britain had been a full-blown disaster, which did not need to be topped off by running afoul of some escapee from a Renaissance fair. Not that she had much choice. Robyn already guessed this young horseman would not easily be turned aside.

All morning she had hiked blissfully alone under leaden skies, happily sharing the trail with grass voles and fellow robins. Luxuriating in solitude, she did not stop until she reached the undulating ridgeline along the Anglo-Welsh border. Here she saw both halves of Britain, lowlands and highlands, tidy green farmsteads running right up against wild hill country. Eastward, neatly hedged Herefordshire crop-land looked like the Jolly Green Giant's garden; westward, the dark, untamed mass of Wales rose to touch the sky, lonely, exhilarating, and beautiful beyond belief. In a wet October, well past the tourist season, she had the footpath to herself—until this knight appeared atop his great black warhorse, wandering nonchalantly out of the Welsh hills.

By now she could use some company, even a touch of adventure. Splendid isolation became boring. But this broad-shouldered young horseman looked like more adventure than she needed. Deciding not to give a greeting, Robyn stood watching him ride up, looking very fresh and innocent to her, full of noble purpose. Good for him. She was mortally tired of men who had seen everything and knew it all. In place of a helmet, he wore a black velvet cap pinned with a white October rose. His warm, open smile said he was happy to see her.

Too bad she had already had her fill of handsome, self-assured Eng-lishmen. She had flown out from California to see one. Collin Grey, of the Dorset Greys, had swept her off her feet and into bed during an extended stay in L.A. Collin worked for Sotheby's in London, but his main business in America seemed to be showing her an amazing time. Cheerful, caring, and darkly handsome, Collin had a flair for adventure, a welcome willingness to take risks, even in love. He came from an old English family, complete with an old English manor in the Cotswolds. Back in the sixteenth century, a Grey had even been queen for a day—or more like a week. The Tudors were not amused. She ended up mounting the scaffold for an Elizabethan buzz-cut. "I pray you despatch me quickly," she told the headsman. Pert, learned, and polite—giving orders even at the block. Collin had inherited Queen Jane's sense of style and knack for pushing life to the edge.

When Sotheby's called Collin home, the affair continued via fax and Internet. Collin could be as sexy and imaginative on-line as he was in a hot tub—always beware when a man can be reached only by e-mail and cell phone. He mentioned his upcoming birthday party at his country home, "What a shame you can't be there." Robyn took time off from the studio, flying the Atlantic to surprise him, the sort of impulsive gesture that makes or breaks a relationship. When she got to the Cotswolds she was as surprised as Collin, finding he had more than an estate, stables, and a hound pack. He also had a wife and three young sons. Leaving little room for her.

Putting aside appalling thoughts of revenge, Robyn tried to make the best of the trip, visiting well-kept castles and hiking in the Welsh hills, aiming to walk out her anger and humiliation. And just to be by herself. Now that, too, was denied her.

As the knight topped the grassy ridge, sunlight parted the clouds for the first time that morning, shining splendidly on his steel hips and mail sleeves. Close up, she sensed an easy confidence, coupled with the alert eagerness of youth—a fetching combination. She guessed this particular youth had already seen a lot of adult life, and it did not daunt him.

He rattled up and reined in. Built like a college quarterback, the boy was a way better dresser. Fair hair, brown eyes, steel armor, blue-gold surcoat, black cap, white rose, knee-length riding boots, and tooled leather gloves all came together to breathtaking effect. She stared in absolute amazement. Here was the real thing—what football uniforms merely mimic. Swathed in personal colors and seated atop his warhorse, this young fellow required stable boys, seamstresses, saddlers, glove makers, armorers, bootblacks, a haberdasher, and a florist just to dress to go out. His horse fit the outfit, a big, black Friesian stallion with long silky fetlocks. From an ancient breed of cold bloods—ancestors to the English Shire horses—Friesians were strong, enduring, and loyal, the very mount Robyn would pick if she had something that heavy to carry. Whatever his fantasy, he took pains to do it right.

Grinning, he called down to her, "Ho, lad. Tell us the way to Llanthony priory."

Ho, lad, yourself. Robyn wore a borrowed man's jacket over bulky sweats, and she'd had her hair cut short the day before at a Bristol body boutique, exorcising demons by doing something for herself. But that was no excuse. First Collin took her for a ride. Now this grinning idiot took her for a boy. Where did Englishmen get their arrogance?

She started to set him straight. Then stopped. Sunlight glistened on the boy's honey-brown hair and broad armored shoulders. They were alone on the windswept ridge. Young Sir Handsome was not only weirdly dressed, but heavily armed. Besides his wicked long sword, he had an oversize dagger and a heavy flanged mace hanging from his saddle. Whoever forged his costume had worked overtime to make it real—and lethal. Maybe she should humor him. At least until they got closer to the motor road.

"What's the matter?" he asked, pushing back his velvet cap with a gloved hand. "Are you Welsh? Or just deaf?"

"I'm from Montana," she replied evenly, keeping her voice low, letting him jump to his own conclusions. "But I live in West Hollywood."

He arched an eyebrow. "Which Holy Wood?"

"In L.A. Next to Beverly Hills. Boys Town."

His smile turned quizzical.

"California, USA?"

Young Don Quixote laughed, like he never heard of L.A., or California, but decided it hardly mattered. Was he putting her on? Buoyant good humor lurked behind lively brown eyes with long soft lashes. "Sounds like neither of us knows the way to Llanthony. Well met, anyway. You have a voice as sweet as a songbird's, making these Welsh hills much less lonely."

Great. Young Sir Handsome was gay. Just her luck. Looking away she saw sunlight shining on grass tops, and clumps of blackthorn hung with blue sloe berries. Below the ridge lay Herefordshire, serene and distant. She looked back at him. "Did you say Llanthony?"

"Yes, the ancient Augustinian priory in the Vale of Ewyas, built round the chapel founded by Sir William de Lacey."

"Never heard of it," she admitted.

He smiled at her ignorance. "It has been there since the reign of William Rufus."

Right. Good old William Rufus, whoever he was. She studied her newfound knight in armor. Behind him rose the Black Mountains, the y Mynydd Du, wild Welsh hill country famous of old for feuds, bloodshed, incest, and other "inhuman acts and savage crimes"—the Ozarks of south Wales. Nowadays largely empty, the dark tangle of bare ridgelines and wooded vales had a few hardy inhabitants, and a couple of lonely tarred roads running through it. Not an outstanding spot for wandering off the beaten footpath with a well-armed and possibly lunatic stranger.

Happily all this smiling young horseman wanted was the way to Llanthony. Wherever that was. At least her knight was not the sort afraid to ask directions. She got out her map, determined to send Sir Handsome on his way. Sitting down, she spread the big, pink-covered Ordnance Survey Sheet over her knees. These Ordnance maps were a marvel, showing every farm, footpath, and patch of bracken for hundreds of square miles. Leaning closer, her knight seemed thoroughly amazed. "What a marvelous map you have. I have never before seen the like of it."

She shrugged. He could get his own in Abergavenny. She found the path forking off to Llanthony farther along the ridge. Standing up, she tried to show him where they were, and where Llanthony was.

He leaned farther out of the saddle, one hand resting lightly on his steel hip, not the least afraid of falling, fairly exuding grace and agility. Robyn bet with his build he could do handsprings in that armor. Looking from the map to her, and back to the map, he could not contain his astonishment. "How utterly incredible. Your map is wonderfully detailed, and you read it like a clerk."

"Thank you. Look, just past this old quarry you come to a small knoll—"

"What are you called?"

"Robyn. Robyn Stafford. The path is marked by a pile of rocks—"

"A stout name," he declared. "Any relation to his grace Earl Humphrey Stafford, duke of Buckingham?"

"None that I know." Since coming to Britain, she had found she had an old English name. There was even a county of Stafford not far to the north. Nothing was all that far away in a country the size of southern California.

"Too bad. Duchess Anne of Buckingham is my mother's sister; they are both Nevilles by birth. We would be cousins."

"An absolute shame," she agreed, pointing back to the map. "That pile of rocks is where the footpath forks off toward Llanthony—"

"A Stafford, but no kin to Buckingham. Who, then, is your lord?"

"I don't have one. Not at the moment, anyway. The path crosses the ridge and comes to a stone wall—"

"No lord? That is hard to credit."

Life is full of surprises. She tried to redirect his attention to the map, tracing the route with her finger. "Follow the path along the wall, and you will have no trouble finding the priory." Looking up, she saw he was ignoring the map, staring straight at her instead.

His grin widened. "Robin, you are a likely looking lad, smart and comely, and you read wonderfully well."

She stared back at him. They were no longer discussing the way to Llanthony. Conversation now centered on her present condition and future prospects.

"Show me the way to the priory, and I promise to reward you handsomely, even take you into my household. Such as it is." He said this as earnestly and sincerely as if it made sense.

Letting the map go limp, she looked about. Cloud shadows drifted slantwise across the ridge. They were absolutely alone on the bare top. She stared back at her knight on horseback, seeing a cheery over-armed teenager in plate armor fresh out of the Gutenberg edition of *Gentleman's Quarterly*—friendly, amiable, and attractive. Who thought she was a boy, but clearly had a crush on her. Who planned to reward her "handsomely"—ten guesses how—and then to take her home afterwards. Only in jolly old England. She sighed and asked, "Who are you?"

"Edward Plantagenet, earl of March." So much for a sensible answer. He said it with rueful pride, as if he knew the picture he presented, lost and alone in mud-spattered armor. Reaching down, he patted his mount's strong black neck, "Caesar will vouch for me."

Robyn had no ready reply. The earl of March? In October? Could you lord over a month? Like being Queen of the May? He looked awfully young to be earl of anything. Despite having absorbed two biographies of Princess Di, she knew next to nothing about British nobility. Just odd bits gleaned from *Braveheart* and a smattering of Shakespeare. Was the fortnight before Halloween the time for belted earls to ride about in full armor? Not terribly likely.

Reaching into a belt pouch, he produced a green twig. Breaking it in two, he put half in his mouth, offering her the rest. "Here, have some. It stirs the blood and freshens the breath."

She took it, sniffing suspiciously. A sprig of mint, a medieval Tic Tac. Did he mean to kiss her? She humored him, savoring the strong green taste.

Blue tits burst from the heather, scattering skyward, giving harsh scolding cries of alarm. She looked to see what set them off. A small, spotted brown bird of prey came bobbing along the ridge. Edward pointed at it excitedly. "Look there, see that?"

"That little hawk?" The tiny falcon hovered for a moment, leaning into the wind, and then shot off over Herefordshire.

"Yes, a hunting kestrel. I love them. They are so quick, clean, and graceful."

She gave the handsome young idiot a last chance to let himself off the hook. "Are you joking with me?"

"Not at all. I would know one anywhere. My mother kept kestrels in the castle mews. My father's badge is the falcon and fetterlock," he added proudly.

Of course, in the castle mews. Under ye olde falcon and fetterlock. Brits had such vivid imaginings. Collin's family were firm believers in witchcraft and faerie folk. His sister Jo called her daughter *changeling* when the girl would not mind, threatening to return her to the pixies. Just that morning a daft old woman in Abergavenny answered her plea for directions with a warning to beware of the little people, who lived under the hills and rode ponies the size of greyhounds. But the old woman had said nothing of knights on black chargers. "I mean this costume you are wearing." She nodded at the steel riding suit. "Where did you get the armor?"

"Made for me in Milan," young Edward answered proudly, "by master Italian smiths."

"But why? Are you part of some play or pageant?"

He straightened in the saddle, showing off the blue-gold bars on his surcoat. "Sorry," he grinned. "I am who I am. Edward, earl of March. At the moment I may not look it—but I am on the run, seeking sanctuary in the Vale of Ewyas. The monks at Llanthony will know me." Her knight did not seem the least insulted—after all, he knew who he was. Looking wistfully after the hawk, Edward added, "If I can just get down into Devon, I have friends who will see me to Calais. Or Ireland. Have you ever been there?"

"Been where? Ireland?"

"Calais. A great port town ringed with castles, full of fine wines and beautiful fabrics. Calais is the gateway to Flanders, and near to France."

"No, I've never been there." Calais was *in* France, but why quibble? He sounded like he had seen it. She sure had not.

"You will love it. I was born not far from there, at Rouen in Normandy."

She stared up at him, happily chewing his mint, totally at ease with the crazy masquerade. He had a fantastic act to go with his armor.

Men had lied to her before. Far too often. Collin had made a blithering lovelorn fool of her. And in Hollywood lying was a way of life. Actors thought they could get away with saying anything, and studio execs spun her absurd tales every day—but never with such brash innocence. Edward did not much care if she believed him. Why should he? He was a belted earl. He was not selling her a story. Or trying to get into her panties. Hell—he thought she was a *boy*. All he wanted out of her was directions to the priory. She asked softly, "What moment are we talking about?"

"What moment?"

"What year is this?"

"Why the thirty-seventh year in the reign of poor Mad King Henry."

Mad king who? It hardly mattered. The England she knew had a frumpy old queen. "Could you give me that in A.D.?"

He stopped chewing, staring blankly at her.

"Anno Domini?" she hinted.

"You mean since the birth of Christ?" Edward acted as if it were a trick question. He took a moment, ticking off years on gloved fingers, and then replied proudly, "One thousand four hundred and fifty-nine years, or thereabouts."

Right. 1459. Or thereabouts. Over five hundred years off, just about burying the needle on the bullshit meter. She shook her head, feeling suddenly sorry for this overgrown boy in armor. He thoroughly believed what he was saying, believed it so much he barely conceived she could doubt him. Edward was sincere, generous, easygoing, and totally off his rocker.

Sighing, she refolded her map, saying, "I'll take you to the priory." Why not? She had been headed that way herself. So what if he was gay? Or crazy? He was polite and likeable, and plainly needed her help. He wanted her for his household—whatever that meant—but despite being heavily armed and on horseback, he made no attempt to force or abduct her. Always a welcome sign. All in all, it had the makings of a cheap and easy first date.

Taking the lead, she set out for Llanthony and the Vale of Ewyas. According to her map, the priory was a ruin, but Llanthony had a church and a pair of hotels, though no bus service. Hopefully someone there would take Edward off her hands. He was an English problem, and they must have centuries of experience in dealing with genial madmen.

Strolling past hawthorns bright with ripe red berries, she listened to Edward's troubles. He said he was fleeing a lost battle; though he made it sound like an armed debate. Edward's friends and family—numbering in the thousands—had gathered on his family lands, not wanting to fight, hoping Mad King Henry would hear their grievances. The cannon and plate armor were just to get daft King Henry's attention. "We stood on our rights," he told her proudly, "facing down knaves that would profit off a poor mad king." But it was all for naught. "Now we are hunted fugitives, betrayed by Andrew Trollope—an aptly named pimp. Scores of good men are dead. Sir Thomas and Sir John Neville are taken. And all who would not submit to tyranny are now charged with treason."

What a story. He said it so simply and sincerely she could not help thinking it was true. She should haul out her journal and start punching in the story as he talked. Turn this into a treatment, and she could sell it to the studio. She asked where it all happened.

"At Ludford on the Tern." That was the worst of it, he told her. Ludlow Castle, the family home, had been abandoned. Left to be sacked. His mother, little sister, and two small brothers were at the mercy of men "wetshod in wine and bent on misrule." And Ludlow town was thrown open to rape, which especially angered Edward. He had that old-fashioned chivalry, and clearly did not like thinking of his mother and sister in enemy hands. Despite using words like *wetshod*—and saying women faced being "vengefully defouled"—Edward's speech seemed strangely normal. Way too clear, in fact. It was the big flaw in his act. If he really came from 1459, he should have a treacle-thick accent—as bad as Shakespeare's. But his English was no worse than what she heard in the London tube.

She still found it heartrending to hear how women and children bore the brunt of defeat. "How old are your sister and brothers?" she asked, ashamed for thinking she should exploit his madness.

He thought a moment. "Margaret is already a woman, thirteen or so. George is eleven, and Richard, seven. Or maybe six."

"And you?" she asked.

"Seventeen, or thereabouts." He made it sound old, but to her he seemed awfully young to be so utterly bonkers. "I was born on the twenty-eighth of April . . ." He counted on his fingers. "In 1442." Edward was proud to get the year right, though it made him closer to six hundred than seventeen.

Her pocket beeped loudly. She jammed her hand into her borrowed jacket, feeling for her cell phone. Robyn had forgotten it was on, and now someone was calling. Edward glanced about, "What sort of bird is that?"

She managed to silence the cell phone, drawing it out of her jacket. "No bird, just this." She held it up. The silly thing was a gift from Collin, so he could call her anytime.

"What is that?" Edward wanted to know.

"Hi, Robyn. You there?" asked the phone in her hand. She recognized Heidi, her assistant at the studio, a California blonde addicted to tight leather, skimpy tops, and dead white lipstick. Heidi sounded excited, a not unusual state for her. It had to be after three A.M. in L.A. What the hell was happening? She had been gone four days; couldn't the studio manage that without her?

"It's a phone," she explained, putting it to her ear. "Operates on a global hookup off the Internet—don't ask me how. I don't even get the bills." The phone seemed so romantic at first. Magic even. But it let Collin control the relationship, making her always available. Saving him from having to leave messages and risk her returning calls at the wrong time.

"Hi, Heidi. What's happening?" Something big to have Heidi calling in the middle of the night.

"We're having a luau." Heidi's voice sounded slurred.

"What?"

"A luau. You know. Tiki torches. Mai tais. Big, bronze surfer boys, like the one feeling me up."

Heidi was drunk off her ass, at some godawful party, on a Wednesday night. Actually a Thursday morning. A first even for Heidi. Robyn thought maybe she had her time zones crossed. Maybe it was not all that late out there. "What time is it in L.A.?"

"In L.A.?" Heidi sounded too drunk to make sense of the question. "How should I know?"

"See if your surfer has a watch."

"Nope, just string briefs. And he's about to lose them. Besides, a watch would not do any good."

"Why?"

"Cause we're on Maui."

Make that stoned and drunk. At least it explained the luau. Heidi had closed up shop and flown to Hawaii. Things were going famously without her. Working with Heidi was like being in touch with a wildly chaotic alter ego. Heidi had grown up in a tiny two-room in the Valley, raised by her mom, with no dad. Or rather with a succession of dads, some cruel and indifferent, others far too friendly. Heidi had needed smarts and guts just to survive puberty. Her dumb blonde act hid savvy judgment and a hard-drive memory—in a business that ran on good looks and joie de vivre rather than common sense, she pulled down enough to take snap trips to Maui, while buying Mom a bungalow in Santa Monica.

"Why are you talking into your hand?" demanded Edward, peering down from his high ornate saddle.

"How's Collin?" Heidi had a not-so-secret crush on Collin. The man had an absolute knack for collecting women.

"Dead, I hope."

"What?" It was Heidi's turn to be confused.

"Where is that voice coming from?" Edward was utterly fascinated by the phone.

"Look, I can't talk now. I'm entertaining an earl."

"Wow! An earl. Is he handsome?"

"Stunning." At least Edward the mad earl topped Heidi's sloshed surfer.

"Out of sight! Oops! Got to run, he's getting into my pants. Give my love to Collin."

"Fat chance." But Heidi had already hung up, leaving Robyn holding the phone.

"May I?" Edward leaned down to take the phone. Not seeing much danger, Robyn handed it up. Edward looked it over and then held it to his ear. "It has stopped talking."

"She found something better to do." Half a world away, Heidi was balling some surfer on a dark patch of beach—and Robyn had been worried how the studio would do without her.

Edward handed the phone back. "Astoundingly aweful!"

"So a lot of folks say." She had seen the downside to being always in touch, with a phone that followed her everywhere. Collin used it to keep her in his hip pocket. "It's got caller ID. Constant redial. Call waiting. Call rejection. E-mail. Takes messages, organizes my sched-

ule, and reminds me of appointments. Pretty much runs my life."
Right now she felt tempted to get rid of it.

"Is it witchcraft?" He did not sound overly worried by the supernatural.

"Not really. But like I said, don't ask how it works." Edward did
not look ready for the electronic age. He hardly looked ready for the
Renaissance.

They went a ways in silence, broken only by slow hoofbeats and
a low wind out of Wales rustling the grass tops. Dark skeins of
rain fell on Herefordshire. Without warning, Edward asked, "What
about you?"

"Me?"

"Yes, you. Robin Stafford of Holy Wood. What do you do when
you are not giving aid and comfort to fugitive earls?" He sounded
lighthearted given his family's plight, but even on short acquaintance
she could tell Edward believed in making the best of bad fortune,
assuming he would somehow set things right. Such youthful sureness
made her smile.

"I work for a movie studio," she explained. "Production work
mainly. Phone calls, fielding pitches, reviewing scripts, keeping over-
priced creeps happy—that sort of thing."

Edward looked thoroughly puzzled. "A moving studio?"

"You know, Hollywood. Show biz. We make pictures."

He plainly did not know. "You work for an artist? A painter? An
illuminator?"

"They are more like plays. I wanted to be an actress, but . . ." She
realized she had slipped. But it no longer seemed so important to
conceal her sex. For an armed madman, Edward acted pretty harmless. Very concerned and gentlemanly, actually. The whole pretense
of being a boy began to irk her. Why shouldn't she be honest?
Edward was.

He stared down at her from the saddle, still hopelessly puzzled.
"You mean like a mummer? Or in a miracle play? One of those boys
who puts a pillow in a gown and pretends to be the pregnant Virgin?"

"Sort of." She nodded glumly. This was getting nowhere. "It did
not turn out to be all that easy."

"I can well imagine."

Hardly. Crazy as he was, Edward could not hallucinate even half
of it. Acting lessons, casting calls, producer's parties, diseased pricks

she sucked up to but ducked going to bed with. All while waiting for her break. If she had smarted-off less and put out more, who knows what she would be now? Not just a glorified gofer with an oversexed assistant, that's for sure. But why burden Edward with her stalled acting career? He had troubles that went way beyond not getting a break in Hollywood. Or being dumped by a cad from Sotheby's. How could that compare to losing your mother, sister, and brothers? And the family castle? Not to mention your sanity. Still, it was nice he cared.

Climbing a small summit, with Edward clopping along behind her, she could make out Skirrid Fawr from the top. Green ascending ridgelines blocked her view of Abergavenny and Pandy. Nor could she see Hereford, Chepstow, or the big highway bridge over the Severn. Just farmsteads, sheepfolds, and bracken-covered tops seamed with ancient earthworks, as if the twenty-first century were slipping away, while she slid into Edward's world. Shaking off the feeling, she fished into her jacket for an energy bar—something reassuringly artificial. Tearing the plastic seal, she split the bar with Edward, telling him it had "Chocolate, honey, granola, figs, soy lecithin, and high fructose corn syrup. Terribly healthy."

Figs and honey, he knew about—but chocolate, granola, and soy lecithin were something new. Nor could he make sense out of "high fructose corn syrup." But he declared the taste combination "Absolutely aweful," asking if she had some more.

"Sorry." She shook her head. "I meant to fast. The bar was just for emergencies. Maybe in Llanthony."

"Yes, indeed." He licked his fingers. "So, on to Llanthony. Monks can work miracles."

Monks had nothing to do with it. Not wanting to shake his faith in religion, she set out in silence. Fall heather felt springy underfoot, bouncing back beneath her heavy boots. Descending past an abandoned quarry, they came on a small col between two tops. Here a path forked off toward Llanthony priory, crossing the ridge and slanting down into the wild remote Vale of Ewyas.

Robyn stopped. This was where they should part. She had no need to be there when Edward found his sanctuary to be a ruin-cum-tourist-trap. He rose happily in the saddle, peered down the path, and then turned gratefully to her. "Well, you need not be ashamed," he told her. "Not in the least."

"Really?" She already felt bad for the fun she had at Edward's expense. And for the letdown he faced.

"Yes. You would make a fine female, with your fair skin and quick wit. You have the face and voice for it. Pad your figure, put on a wig, and Holy Wood could not want for a better woman. Forsooth, I would fall madly for you myself."

How chivalrous. She grinned up at him, seeing how badly she misjudged his intentions. What she had taken for a gay come-on was warmhearted good humor. Edward Plantagenet, earl on the lam, lost in Wales, hunted by the mad king's men, his noble family fleeing or in custody—yet he took time out to cheer up a common roadside waif. A sexually confused lad, stricken with fits of talking to his hand. Whose biggest ambition was to prance about dressed like a woman. True noblesse oblige.

"Anything's possible," he insisted, "if you put your whole being behind it." She could see he really meant it. An earl at seventeen, rich and handsome to the hilt, but he truly meant to help her. "Come wear my livery," Edward begged. "I do not normally invite beautiful young strangers to commit treason—but you are an exception. Join the fight for justice. When we set England aright, you may get your wish as well. We will have you playing the Blessed Virgin at Coventry on Corpus Christi Day."

She could not help laughing. The mad earl of March with his sidekick, Robyn the boy wonder. Kingdoms set aright and damsels done in drag. It had a ring to it. A sort of Robin Hood meets *Tootsie*. Could really pack them in. Move over, Man of La Mancha.

"See, even the thought of it cheers you."

Too true. Edward was not just another happy armored maniac with a rose on his cap. He was a tonic, who had brightened her otherwise lonely walk. Instead of an annoying male presence, he had become a companion of sorts. Weird but friendly, a welcome diversion, putting her own troubles in perspective. Too bad he was bonkers. She felt touched—and sad. There always seemed to be some weird conservation of male energy at work, whereby guys who had it all together— sharp, caring, well-heeled, and handsome, without being completely full of themselves—were otherwise unavailable. Either married or gay, or like young Earl Edward, hopelessly deranged.

He broke off another sprig of mint, chewing happily and offering her some. She took it, looking wistfully at his magnificent horse. Every detail of his absurd fantasy was really artfully arranged, and she still hoped it was all an incredible put-on. If this turned out to be some elaborate system to get women's sympathy and attention, it was cleverly successful. Reaching up, she stroked the Friesian's black, velvety neck; carrying a man-size boy in armor was not even making the stallion sweat. His breath had that clean cut-grass smell. "What did you call him?"

"Caesar. Because he is the greatest of all time."

"He's beautiful, too."

"Really?"

"Exceptionally so." She ran her hands through his sable mane. Thoroughly horse-crazy as a teen, Miss Rodeo Montana, she still rode whenever she could—but she had never had a horse as big and fine as this. How did a young madman afford him?

"He is sweet and gentle as well," Edward assured her, "and you may ride him. If you come with us as far as the priory."

Hitting on the perfect bribe, Edward praised Caesar's easy gait and the wonders of the hidden Vale of Ewyas. "The Holy Fathers keep Ewyas free and wild, tucked away from the temptations of the world. So beautiful that they say Sir William de Lacey gave up war as soon as he saw it"—a supreme compliment from such an earnest young man-at-arms. "Deer and birds come and eat from your hand, and the air is so wonderfully healthy that disease is unknown. Were it not for love of God and hope of Heaven, monks there might live forever. They will gladly feed us, maybe more granola, chocolate, and soy lecithin, if we are so lucky."

She laughed at how easily he was corrupted by "natural" additives. Clearly they were at that carefree stage of "getting to know you" where everything was funny—even his wild tales about Ewyas, which her map said was just a slow spot on the back road between Abergavenny and Hay-on-Wye.

"Come to this magic vale for a ride and a rest," he insisted. "Mayhap there I will convince you to enter my service. Even though it be treason."

How could she resist such a witless winning smile? Not to mention his marvelous mount. "All right. I will go as far as Llanthony." Treason or not, she would see this to the end. You did not have to be Heidi to like a little excitement, to show your soul is not totally dead to adventure. And for some weird reason, she trusted Edward. Normally she liked her dates lucid and unarmed, but she felt strangely safe with this earnest young earl. She glanced at her watch, seeing plenty of time for a short adventure. Splendid. Today was a day to do as she pleased, and if it pleased her to play along with Edward, so be it. Whatever his problems, the boy was not boring. After Collin, he could be just what she needed.

"What is that on your wrist?" Edward asked. "More witchcraft?"

"Just a watch." Instead of trying to explain, she slipped it off her wrist, handing it up to him.

He puzzled over the digital readout. "This is really remarkable, the numbers change on their own."

"They also tell time."

"Fantastic. So you do not need to see the sun on a cloudy day."

"And at night they glow in the dark."

Smiling he handed back the watch. "I would dearly like to see that."

Sorry. No chance. She had a strict rule against spending the night with deranged teenagers, no matter how friendly and handsome. Especially when they expected her to be a boy. She slid the watch back around her wrist. "Just tell me you are not for real."

He raised an eyebrow. "Not for real?"

"Say this is just an act. Some mummery on your part. Won't you just admit to being a late entry in Ye Auld Hereford Days Rodeo?" It would make things infinitely easier. They could have a good long laugh, finish up their walk, and ride his huge horse around the old romantic ruin. Then relax over supper and a Welsh sunset. After that, who knows? If he would stop acting crazy, he might get pleasantly surprised. Llanthony had two hotels that offered bed and breakfast.

Edward smiled ruefully. "I am sorry, but I am what I am." He would not change his story—not even to please her. Admirable honesty, really. She was godawful sick of men telling her whatever they thought she wanted to hear.

Taking the turn toward Wales, she found herself no longer leading, but walking at his side. Gilded spurs shone in the sunlight. One of her feathered namesakes hopped along ahead of them. Looking up, she saw her knight errant was in wonderful spirits, smiling proudly, with tiny flecks of chocolate stuck to his cheek. The breeze in their faces smelled of heather and sheep dung. At that moment she wished the mad adventure did not have to end—at least not right away. Edward was excellent company in his oddball way. Maybe not her knight in shining armor, but close enough for now. His daft courtliness felt refreshing, bold and inventive, but not pushy. You always had to deal with off-the-wall male obsessions; imagining himself to be a earl on horseback was by no means the worst. Not by Hollywood standards.

What if they did discover some Welsh Shangri-la in the Vale of Ewyas? With five-hundred-year-old monks serving up ale and mutton. Or chocolate and granola? Would that be so bad? Or so impossible? The path under her feet had to be at least a thousand years old, running along Offa's Dyke, built by Saxons to keep out Welsh neighbors ages before Edward claimed to be born. Time and place were pretty relative. Right "now" Heidi was making naked love in the hot tropic night while waves broke on the dark sand, or so Robyn imagined. Finding themselves in the fifteenth century would certainly make Edward happy. She could feel herself willfully letting go of reality to please a newly met male, never a healthy sign.

Slanting down into the vale, the path ran along a stone wall made from stacks of dark split-stones crusted with golden moss and white lichens. Edward assured her sanctuary lay just ahead, hoping the monks might have word of fellow fugitives, "I lost Salisbury and Warwick during the night, and desperately need to rejoin them."

"Salisbury? Warwick?" Those were places not people.

"The Neville earls." He said it like she should know them. "Our last allies against the king. Now they, too, are gone. I awoke this morning without them; just myself and Caesar awaking alone. When I mounted up and tried to find them, the land seemed much changed, and I was sorely alone until I met you."

So was I, she thought, genuinely sorry she could not drag this out a little longer. But geography was against them; Llanthony loomed ahead, just out of sight down the path. Reality was about to bring this happy interlude to a screeching halt. By now she felt thoroughly guilty for lying to Edward. Here he was, about to have all his hopes smashed; she at least could be truthful. Why have him find out all at once that there was no priory, he was not an earl, this was not the 1450s, and she was not a boy? Better let him down easy. She could not do much about the priory and his earldom, but as for the boy part . . .

Robyn stopped and turned to him. "There is something I must tell you." She hated to tell him she had lied, even by omission. But Edward had been honest with her—maddeningly so at times.

"What's that, fair Robin?" Edward grinned happily, but the joke was going to be on him.

She sighed and shook her head, sticking her hands deep in her pockets, really sorry to dish out his first disillusionment. "Look, I am not—"

Before she could finish, a dark streak whistled down the slope. Leaping back in shock, she saw a black arrow land quivering in the grass between her and Edward. Startled speechless, she stared in open-mouthed astonishment at the feathered shaft sticking at an angle in the sod alongside her footprints. The word *justice* was written on the black shaft in neat white letters. A foot or so to the right and the message would have been buried in her side.

⊷⇒ John–Amend–All ⇐⊷

*R*obyn's mind reeled, feeling this absolutely could not be happening. She stared numbly at the black arrow sticking out of the bright green turf with JUSTICE written in white on its shaft. Having it thud into the grass at her feet astounded her more than Edward appearing in full armor. One amiable young madman might be acceptable—even amusing. But this was unbelievable, and thoroughly scary. At best it was a dangerous masquerade, some sick, outrageous prank. At worst . . . But now was not the time to spin worst-case scenarios. She stood stock-still, heart racing, breath clinched, tight, unreasoning panic gripping the pit of her stomach, watching her world slide alarmingly out of control. Shouting *"Wait!"* or *"Stop!"* would not do her a bit of good.

Edward drew his sword and wheeled Caesar about, putting himself between her and the threat. Thank God he took his delusions seriously. Crazy or not, she felt almighty happy having this brawny boy in armor and his big warhorse between her and where the arrow had come from. Hesitantly she peered upslope past the horse's flank, half expecting a second shaft would hit her between the eyes.

None did. Instead a bowman rose out of the heather at the top of the ridge with another black arrow nocked and ready. Trim and tall, the archer was dressed all in red, except for a white feather in his peaked Robin Hood cap. Alert dark eyes and a sharp spade beard made him look like the jack of hearts from an old-fashioned poker deck.

"Ho, knave." Edward pointed his sword at the stranger, suddenly seeming very much an earl on horseback, alert and upright, brooking no challenge, bred to command. Despite the bowman's distance advantage over his sword, Edward displayed utter faith in *l'arme blanche*, shouting, "Beggarly knave, drop your bow and give up your name."

Standing his ground, the scarlet archer called back, "You may call me John-Amend-All."

Edward rose higher in his stirrups, keeping between her and the next arrow. His sword arm stayed aimed straight at the archer's red breast. "Lower your arrow, or I shall call you dead."

John-Amend-All lowered his bow. Robyn took a wary breath, relief flooding through her. Seeing that second arrow aimed at the ground meant this might all end peacefully, possibly with a sane explanation—though that seemed a lot to hope for. Until something like this happened, you could totally forget England was a foreign country. They had first-run movies, network TV, and almost spoke the language—making Britain seem like some quaint out-of-the-way part of America. Western Canada, perhaps. But if you were not careful, you could abruptly find yourself in a wildly different world, with no easy way back. She heard the bowman call out, "I have a timely warning for the earl of March."

Edward settled back in the saddle, letting his point drop. "Give your warning to me. I will pass it along when next I see him." Both men smirked at that bit of male banter; neither doubted that Edward was who he claimed not to be. Right now Robyn barely doubted it—that black arrow had been sensationally convincing. If this was all staged, it had totally sucked her in. Once she somehow got safely away, she might question what she was seeing—but not here, not now, not with it happening in front of her.

"Tell Edward not to go down into the Vale of Ewyas," the archer replied, nodding at the path to Llanthony.

"Why?" Edward looked down the path into the narrow green Vale.

"Listen." The bowman cocked his head. Robyn listened hard, again holding her breath, trying to hear above her madly pumping heart. From the vale below came the high moan of a hunting horn, then a view halloo. Followed by fast hoofbeats.

"There is why." John-Amend-All pointed with his bow. Three horsemen burst from hiding at the head of the vale, riding full tilt at them, wearing blackened armor without crests or badges. Pounding up the path behind them came two dozen men on foot, carrying bows and dressed in hunting green, the foremost blowing the charge on a brass horn as he ran.

Warning delivered, John-Amend-All turned and ran, vanishing over the ridgetop.

She wished him luck. Were it not for his black arrow, she would have strolled down that path into the Vale of Ewyas, expecting nothing more disconcerting than priory ruins turned to a bed and breakfast. But that timely warning was not a plan of action. Should she turn and try to outrun a trio of horses? Or stoutly demand they stop this outrageous game immediately? Lest she notify the police in Pandy. Paralyzed by poor choices, she stood clutching the phone in her pocket, feet braced to run. But neither running nor punching 999 seemed likely to save her.

Strong hands in leather gloves grabbed her around the waist, jerking her off her feet. Blindsided by a black blur, she felt herself lifted up and away. Letting go of her phone, she seized hold of the arms at her waist, shocked by the cold hard feel of steel mail. Swung through the air, she landed with a jolt in front of Edward's saddle. In a single fluid motion he had sheathed his sword, turned his mount, leaned down, and scooped her. A smart bit of horsemanship. One hand held her hard against his breastplate, the other gripped the reins. "Stay still," he shouted in her ear.

Too veteran a rider to need that advice, she settled into her awkward seat, arms about his armored waist, doing her best to avoid the dangling mace. Steel sleeves held her in on either side. An arrow zipped by, and then they were pounding off along the ridge.

Wet clods flew at her legs. Hoofbeats rang in her ears. She felt like the heroine of a Sir Walter Scott novel, galloping along in the lap of young Lord Lochinvar, with Musgraves and Fenwicks yapping at their heels. Thrilling and terrifying at the same time. Welsh hills turned to a headlong blur of grass, heather, rocks, and hedges. Fortunately, she had no fear of horses ridden at speed, having been a champion barrel racer as a girl—with blue ribbons to prove it—doing hairpin turns so sharp her stirrups almost touched the ground, idiotically brave until she broke her leg.

Twisting about, she peered over Edward's steel shoulder, seeing the wild hunt leap into loud pursuit, shouting insults, shooting arrows, and blowing horns. Not a bit like barrel racing. No kids and rodeo moms cheering her on, just men in metal and leather chasing her with oversize cleavers or trying to nail her with arrows. English hospitality at its absolute worst. But would they actually harm her, when they were clearly after him? Her only sure way to find out was to throw herself at their mercy and see. Better take her chances with Edward. Swept up in something utterly unreal, she had to just hold on, hoping the huge warhorse did not go down, flattening her under mount and rider.

Yells and bugle calls faded. Arrows stopped coming. She saw the men on foot dwindle, unable to keep up. But Edward's mount was carrying double, and the trio on horseback were bound to catch them. Strong and brave, and willing as he was, the big Friesian did not have the legs to outrun three fresh horses. Not with her weight added to Edward's. What's more, they were fast running out of ridge. The mad gallop had carried them the whole distance they had come, and then some. Ahead she saw the summit where the ridge sloped down toward the BritRail tracks and A465. Worlds were going to collide. What would happen when they came pounding into Pandy, dodging traffic, with three black riders in tow?

She never found out. Without warning, Edward reined in. Sliding her off his saddle bow, he lowered her deftly to the ground. "Sorry, this is as far as we can run." He said it calmly and simply, as if he had been giving her a lift into town. Not like three berserks on horseback were bearing down on them.

Shaky feet found the turf. Stumbling, she managed to stay upright, mentally giving them both points for a perfectly timed dismount. Their bodies seemed remarkably in tune—like trick riders who had practiced this act for years—but the first time they so much as touched each other was when he scooped her up onto his saddle. Each impromptu impossibility just led naturally to the next, as neatly as if it made sense.

Looking up, she saw the three riders thunder toward them, strung out by the chase. Totally unreal. A nightmare situation. "Astoundingly aweful," as Edward would say. She clamped down the blind screaming panic inside her, coolly trying to guess what was the worst that could happen—and how to avoid it. Edward flashed her a brave smile, then turned to meet the attack. He did not seem smug, just godawful sure of himself. Hopefully with good reason.

Any woman who works late hours in L.A. lives with the threat of random mayhem. Drunken men prowl Hollywood nights looking for sex and not caring a lot how they got it. Once she had crossed a dark studio parking area, pleased with having delivered a promising pitch, without actually ending up in bed. Suddenly a car screeched up—a grinning man leaned out the driver's window, looking her over with glazed eyes and offering a ride. When she shook her head, he pulled a gun, a big ugly automatic, ordering her into the car. She kept walking, all the time imagining a bullet hitting the small of her back—but ready to die in that dark parking lot rather than submit. She remembered a friend of a friend whose waitress roommate left for work one night and never came back. Not ever. Flyers went up. Her folks flew in from Iowa. Weeks later cops found her powder blue Toyota with the keys still in the ignition. As she walked, Robyn clung to that image, refusing to let herself just disappear. When she got to the shelter of an all-night taco stand, the gunman called her a "snotty bitch" and roared off.

Harrowing as that walk across the parking lot had been, this was way worse. Daylight gleaming on razor-edged steel made bullets in the night seem pretty insubstantial. Afraid to take her eyes off the action, she saw Edward trot his horse a little bit toward the oncoming riders. Realizing he was trying to move the fight away from her, she retreated up the ridge, giving him all the room he needed.

Stopping at the windswept crest, she stared at the blue-gold bars on the back of Edward's surcoat, praying not to see them soaked with blood. The lead rider came roaring at him, lance couched, leaning into the charge, an awesome sight, more than a ton of beast, man and metal all concentrated behind a gleaming steel lance point. An avalanche of flesh and metal thundering down on them. She could see every detail of his black helmet and heavy plate armor—a stark contrast to Edward's gaily colored surcoat, velvet cap, and white rose. It occurred to her that these men were not in the least eager to proclaim their identities. Not a good sign. They probably meant to leave no witnesses.

As the black rider bore down with unstoppable momentum, Edward coolly unlooped the heavy flanged mace from his saddle bow. Letting his hand slip down the mace, until he held it right at the knob on the handle, Edward sat waiting in the saddle—not showing a nickel's worth of fear. Robyn tried desperately to read his thoughts. His calm handsome face seemed totally unruffled, like an actor who absolutely knew his part—as if he had been through this particular scene countless times and only needed to get it right. The black rider galloped at him, gaining speed.

At the last moment, Edward pulled on his reins, nimbly jerking his mount aside. Caesar danced sideways, and Edward leaned out of the way of the lance like a quarterback slipping a tackle. Caesar spun instantly about, positioning his master perfectly, showing absolute understanding between man and mount.

Edward rose in the saddle as the black rider shot past, swinging his mace through a tremendous backhand stroke, catching the hurtling rider right on the back of the helmet. Robyn saw shards of blackened steel fly from where the helmet met his neck. Losing his lance, the rider slumped in the saddle, hung for a second, and then bounced off his galloping mount to land with a great clang in the ridge grass.

He lay there without moving, limbs ungainly splayed, like a discarded mannequin in black armor. His frightened mount kept right on running, headed for the BritRail tracks and the village of Pandy. She hoped the poor beast stopped before reaching the motor road.

Not bothering to look back, Edward put spurs to his mount, bolting straight at the second rider. Caesar galloped full tilt into the enemy horse, nostrils flaring, teeth bared, like a king stallion attacking a rival. This abrupt change in tactics took the black rider by surprise. His lance point wavered. Weaving in the saddle, Edward ducked under the point just as their horses collided. His black velvet cap went flying.

Losing his cap, but not his balance, Edward rose in his stirrups, gleefully beating at his attacker with the mace. It sounded like a multicar crash, or a mad tinker pounding sheet metal. This time both horse and black rider went down, rolling together onto the turf. Only the horse got up, struggling to its feet, dazed and breathing heavy, leaving his master lying twitching in the grass.

Stunned by this sudden startling violence, Robyn watched the final rider rein in, staring through his helmet slits at Edward. The man's horse began to shy, crabwalking warily sideways. Neither man nor mount liked what they had seen, nor did she blame them. Young Edward, earl of March, sat atop his snorting charger, honey-brown hair whipped by the wind, grinning madly, mace in hand, looking like mighty Thor just down from Valhalla. Ungodly happy to take them on. One long look was enough. The black rider wheeled his reluctant charger and galloped back along the ridge, not caring to try his luck alone.

As his hoofbeats faded, Robyn realized the havoc was at an end. Utterly unbelievable. A hush fell over the ridge, as if nature were holding her breath. Everything had a sudden extra-keen adrenaline edge to it. Sunlight gleamed like liquid gold, colors shone brighter and sharper, grass greener, sky bluer, blood redder. Her heart beat alarmingly against her breast.

Forcing herself to breathe, she walked on wobbly feet over to where Edward's rose and cap lay, taking care to avoid the second rider groaning in the grass, making no attempt to rise. She picked up Edward's black velvet cap—the white rose pinned to it had not lost so much as a petal.

Edward cantered up, expertly hanging the bloody mace back on his saddle bow, not at all worried that the third rider might return. Or that the archers would come running up. He stopped next to her, breathing hard but otherwise unruffled. Numbly she handed the cap up to him. Thanking her, he set it rakishly back on his head. Then Edward leaned down, lifting her with incredible ease—showing his great strength in armor and steadiness in the saddle—setting her back on her seat in front of his saddle, facing him.

Steel arms surrounded her, amazingly reassuring, melting the numbness in her solar plexus. Her heart slowed, her breath steadied, and she relaxed into his grip, resting against his hard breastplate, realizing he was not treating her a bit like a boy. "Cry if you like," he told her, holding her tight to his armored chest. "It helps."

"Does it?" she whispered, looping her arms around his steel shoulders, laying her head next to his—too shocked for tears. Slowly, violence and tension subsided, senses returned to normal. Shock faded.

She felt his breath against her cheek, smelling of mint, and the horse moving slowly beneath them. Otherwise the world seemed incredibly still, floating free in space.

"It does. I cried at my first battle—at Saint Albans. I was thirteen, but I was wearing a helmet, so no one ever knew." He smiled and added, "Except you. You alone have I dared tell."

"Why?" What made her so special?

"Something about you makes me bold—too bold to keep secrets. And ready to take risks." Had he not stopped to scoop her onto his saddle, he might have gotten clean away. Making Caesar carry double meant facing three men who clearly meant to kill him—only the task turned out harder than they suspected.

"How long have you known?" she asked.

"Known what?" He tried to look chivalrously innocent.

"You know what." She refused to be teased, determined to make him say it.

"That you were a woman? Since soon after we started talking. I could tell by your voice, and by the way your face softened when I told you my mother and sister were taken."

"But you said nothing."

"I wanted your company and assumed you had reason for your disguise." Some disguise. Short hair, sweats, a bulky jacket and hiking boots. His own hair was like a golden-brown torrent, falling onto her face, smelling of wood smoke. She no longer doubted Edward Plantagenet, earl of March, came from somewhere very strange and distant. Somewhere that could easily be five hundred years away.

Taking off a blood-spattered glove, he tucked the soiled leather into an armor strap, then raised his bare hand to brush her cheek. His fingers traced the line of her jaw, smelling of sweat and leather—the first time their flesh had touched. No wonder knighthood was so romantic. Being cuddled by someone in a suit of armor turned out to be an awfully chaste affair. "And I did not want to scare you away."

He had been at best only semisuccessful. Though she did not much blame Edward, the last few minutes had scared her senseless. She had been more frightened than she could ever have imagined. More frightened than in that dark L.A. parking lot, or when she broke her leg barrel racing. She could never remember being so scared. "When you turned to face those three riders, I was sure we were dead. And instead—"

"We are whole and alive, and they are routed." Edward made it sound so simple, but it had been a miracle. A bloody miracle. Unbelievably gory and horrific. The most ghastly bit of personal mayhem she ever witnessed up close—yet it saved her life. His, too. Whatever happened to her from now on, whatever she made of herself, for good or ill, she owed it all to that terrible swift spasm of violence. Edward took it far easier than she ever could, asking her, "Is Robin really your name?"

She nodded. "Just like the bird, but it is spelled with a *y*. Are you really the earl of March?"

"Touché," he laughed. "You have an astonishing way of talking, Lady Robyn."

"Just plain Robyn." She wanted no more make-believe, feeling too drained for anything but unvarnished truth. All pretense and posturing had been scared out of her. Whatever was happening to her was deathly real.

"Once I've beaten Mad King Henry, I will have him make you a lady—a countess, even. It will not be the wildest thing he has done."

"Once you've beaten him?" It seemed a tall order, even for a boy whirlwind on horseback.

"I shall write it into the articles myself." He said it in absolute seriousness—being an earl at seventeen must make you wonderfully sure of yourself. Way too sure. This was all madness. The horse's swaying gait reminded her they were headed somewhere. Somewhere real. Not to his castle, since he no longer had one. Nor could she much imagine taking him home to her West Hollywood apartment— though the studio would give her one hell of a finder's fee.

She shook her head. "None of this is happening." But even she did not really believe that.

He laughed again, "You will see. I was not lying when I said I wanted you with me. And not as a lad in my livery. I want you for my lady love and constant friend. Though I know that is most self-ish. . . ."

"Selfish? How?" She could follow only half of what Edward said.

He sighed, suddenly seeming sad. "So long as you are with me, you are in mortal danger."

In more ways than one. She did not mean to fall for another mad, handsome Englishman. Not even for this fair-haired boy. For all she knew there was already a countess of March, tucked away in an Irish castle. She straightened up, looking him full in the face. "Why? Are you married?"

Looking startled, he vigorously shook his head. "No, my lady. I am not the least bit married."

"Why not?" Edward was a perfect catch—rich, courtly, handsome, as well as skilled in the saddle.

He smiled. "When I was four, they tried to marry me to a French princess, but nothing came of it. Now it is too late to force foreign royalty on me. When I marry, I swear it will be for love, and love only. Right now I have neither a wife, a lady, nor even a mistress. Until I met you, I was all alone."

Saying that, he kissed her, guiding her lips to his with his one bare hand, very deftly done for a lonesome, innocent young earl. Despite being seventeen "or thereabouts," he kissed like he meant it. Forgetting her doubts, she kissed back, surprised by how good it felt, and by his tenderness, no lewd urgency, just the intimate shock of first contact. His mouth tasted of mint—young, fresh, and clean. His steel arm pressed tighter at her waist; medieval children must grow up marvelously quick.

Caesar came slowly to a stop beneath a copse of pines. She sensed dappled sunlight out the corner of her eye. Edward's bare hand stayed where it was, cradling her face, making no attempt to grope her, taking love as honestly and seriously as he faced life, or battle, doing nothing to spoil the moment. Why rush things when you always got what you wanted?

Lips parted. She took a deep dizzying breath of pine scent and then looked her armored lunatic in the eye, telling him, "This is absolutely mad."

"Why so?" He acted utterly innocent. "Once I have brought Mad King Henry to heel, we can do as I wish. I will have whatever I want, and marry whom I please. My father will object, but I am his firstborn, and heir, an earl in my own right . . ."

Marriage? God, what was she getting into? For all his charm and ability, Edward had that teenage budding-male enthusiasm, wanting something as soon as he saw it. Now and forever. "Whoa," she told him, "slow down."

"Slow down?" He sounded shocked at the concept.

"Look, there is no King Henry, insane or otherwise. And no one is going to make me a lady. Or a countess." Pleasing as Lady Robyn Stafford might sound, none of this would happen.

"Henry is hardly a true king," Edward admitted. "But that did not stop him from making his bastard half brothers into earls. The royal will is an awesome thing, even when wielded by a half-wit."

"No. This is nonsense," she insisted. "Just beyond that hill are motorways, the BritRail, satellite dishes, civilization galore." At any moment her phone might start beeping with another breathless message from Heidi. Or a contrite call from Collin. She looked to see if there was a plane overhead, just to prove her point. All she saw was a buzzard soaring high over Herefordshire, mobbed by a pair of rooks.

Edward laughed. "You have such a way of talking. I suppose those men who attacked us were imaginary as well."

He had her there. How could she be sure that the twenty-first century lay just down the footpath? What if she had somehow wandered into the 1400s? Hardly likely, but no more impossible than being romanced by a boy earl in armor.

"No, the danger I have brought on you is very real," Edward explained, bringing her face back next to his. "Already I very much regret . . ."

She never found out what he regretted. Their lips brushed and suddenly they were kissing again. She tilted her head back, feeling his young athletic body strain against the armor; by now she sat astride the saddle bow, thighs resting against steel loin guards. The gloved hand at the small of her back held her upright, with their faces comfortably level. She finished up by licking flecks of chocolate from the corners of his mouth.

Edward laughed, looking at her with shining brown eyes. She wondered how far this was going to go. What was the age of consent in England? Did his seventeen "or thereabouts" make her a pedophile? Was it a crime for foreigners to molest handsome young earls on horseback? Some lesser form of lèse majesté, perhaps? He did not seem to mind—but did that make it legal? Or moral? But the intense rush of emotion overwhelmed her scruples, for the moment at least.

"There is something I must do," he told her. Letting go, he helped her slide gently to the ground. She stood waiting in the long grass, already guessing what he intended.

Glancing over his shoulder to be sure it was safe, he swung down beside her in a rattle of armor, moving swiftly and easily half-encased in steel. That much was just like in the movies. Pulling up a handful of heather he began rubbing down his horse with long slow strokes, showing the sort of barnyard efficiency you would expect in a real medieval earl. She joined him, helping rub the Friesian's big black flanks—an only child on a Montana ranch, she spent many lonesome hours caring for horses. And she owed a lot to this stallion, who charged so fearlessly and positioned his master perfectly. Totally new to mounted combat, she already saw everything depended on the horse. Barrel racing with edged weapons. Edward smiled, seeming to read her mind. "I wish I were half as brave as he. The best rider is helpless if his horse's heart is not in the fight."

Again he glanced over his shoulder, getting nervous now, expecting the archers. With their hands on the horse, instead of each other, they had time for sensible considerations. She asked, "Who are they?"

"If they would have us know, they would have worn arms and badges instead of blackened mail."

"But you must have some idea." Anyone this angry at him could hardly have escaped his notice.

"There are many at court who would happily see me dead." He continued to rub Caesar's black flank. "The queen, perhaps. Clifford and Somerset, for sure."

"Why?"

"My father killed their fathers." Seeing her look of horror, he added, "He did not kill them himself. Duke Somerset and Lord Clifford died fighting at Saint Albans—to their sons that is the same." Standing there, clutching a clump of heather, she sensed the weight he carried—born to ancient hatreds. And his fear of what could happen to his family. The men who just missed killing him most likely held his mother, sister, and younger brothers. She could see that at seventeen he was already living for others, fighting his father's battles, hoping to free his mother, taking on the kingdom's troubles. He told her, "Dreadful as it seems, we must part for now. I am what these men came for, and will just draw them to you."

There was no arguing with that; those black riders could hardly have been coming for her, a relatively inoffensive tourist who wandered onto the scene. "What about the other one—the archer in red who warned us?" Whose black arrow set the whole business in motion.

"The one who called himself John-Amend-All?" Edward shook his head. "I have never seen him until now, but if I see him again, I must certainly thank him." Reaching up, he took the white rose from his cap. Edward touched the flower to his lips and then handed it to her. "Please, remember me."

As if she could forget. Wiping heather off her hands, she took the rose, stunned to find this outlandish, impossible adventure suddenly at an end. With this boy, thought and action seemed the same. A hour ago her main wish was that he would go away; now she really wanted to see more of him, at least until she knew what was happening. Unreal as this adventure had been, her bond with him was real, surprising since they had just met, but she had never before met a man under such surprising circumstances.

He started to mount, but she stopped him with her hand, saying, "Wait." Like everything else today, this was happening far too fast. He stood there, puzzled and happy, one arm already on the saddle—but ready to do her bidding.

She made him kiss her again. It thrilled her to have this brash, egotistical young earl at her beck and call—if only for a moment. Power and excitement surged through her, knowing she could stop him with a word—when men in armor and flights of arrows did not even slow him. She refused to let go until he relaxed into a long, splendid kiss, a kiss that would have to last awhile. Maybe even a lifetime. She could already see she was going to miss him.

When she was done, he swung back into the saddle, looking wistful. "Robyn of Holy Wood, you are someone fantastically special, as bold as you are lovely. Be safe. When you hear that Edward of March has beaten the king, pray come to me. Then you shall be my lady. If you so wish . . ."

If you so wish? Forsooth. Who would not wish? She stared up at him. He was tender and gracious, and a belted earl besides, a splendid figure from a fairy tale, mounted on a magnificent charger. And if he beat the king, Edward Plantagenet would be running Merry Olde England. To top it off, he could be terribly romantic. He had fought to protect her, then had her in his arms, but all he asked for was kisses and remembrance, not trying to feel her up or suggesting they go into the thicket for a little on account. Instead he gave her a rose and graciously offered to make her a lady. His lady. Other Englishmen could well take lessons. He had driven Collin right out of her head. She felt sorely tempted to mount up behind him, to go where he was going, seated on Caesar's broad black crupper, seeing this mad adventure to its end. But that was absurd. She had things to do. She had her apartment in West Hollywood and her studio job. She had a life in L.A., sort of.

Looking equally reluctant, Edward turned and rode away, leaving her standing in the shelter of the pines, thinking she might have made a horrible mistake. At the crest of the ridge, he paused to look back and wave. Then he topped the rise and disappeared.

Evergreens bobbed overhead. She stared at the white blossom in her hand, the only tangible thing she had to show for it all, aside from the sore spots left by Edward's high hard saddle. She had to at least have another look. Walking up to the top of the ridge, she saw Herefordshire spread out before her—and no Edward. There were hoofprints in the wet earth, but she soon lost them in the heather.

Gallant, chivalrous young Edward had his male priorities firmly in place. One minute she was his lady love and "constant friend"—not to mention a countess-to-be. A moment later he was off on business that did not include her. Making a living, overthrowing a kingdom, landing on the moon—any excuse would do. Still holding the rose, she followed the path back the way she first had come, through the grassy banks of an ancient hill fort, past fields, farms, and hedges. Finally she reached a tarred road. She stood and stared at the black asphalt bordered by white bramble flowers. Holding a hand up under her nose, she sniffed the horse sweat and heather, reminding herself it had all really happened. Then she set off down the weathered sign of civilization, until she saw the BritRail tracks and the village of Pandy beyond. There she stopped, not wanting to be back in her own world. Cars buzzed by below. She heard the far-off drone of a jet. It seemed so safe and ordinary, so awfully confining.

Going back meant admitting her adventure was over and there was no handsome young Earl Edward wanting her for his lady. That she had nothing to look forward to but a plane ride to L.A. followed by work on Monday—and the awful task of telling everyone she had been thoroughly abused by Collin. Dumped again. God, how ghastly that sounded. She would rather be spitted on a lance. Robyn stared down at the rose in her hand. What sort of keepsake was this? Was she supposed to press it in a book? Or just moon over it until the petals fell off. She remembered why she had gone walking in the Welsh hills to begin with.

Cautiously she turned about and retraced her steps, back along the one-lane blacktop, then up the footpath. But this time there was nothing. No Edward, earl of March. No John-Amend-All. No riderless mounts. No black armored men lying dead or maimed in the heather. Not so much as a spent arrow. All she found was her Nike squirt bottle, where had she dropped it in the chase.

✦══ The White Rose ══✦

H *ere, have some of ours.*" Jo Anne Grey passed Robyn a cup of steeping breakfast tea. Earl Grey was "Our flavor"—a Grey family joke. Autumn rain lashed the windows, but the warm aroma of new-baked bread filled the tiny kitchen. The white rose sat in a water glass on the linoleum table, between the jam pot and the fresh-cut loaf. "You may be taking this thing with Collin too hard."

"I was taking it miserable hard," Robyn admitted. "But not anymore." She had lost any speck of interest in Collin.

"That is what I am afraid of." Jo shook her head. She had long, straight black hair and searching eyes. The family face that looked so handsome on Collin seemed severe on her.

So far, Jo Grey had been a lifesaver. The only good thing that had happened in England—until Edward came riding up. In that awkward moment when Robyn crashed Collin's birthday party, Jo swooped down and took Robyn under her wing. Refusing to let her go slinking off to cry herself to sleep in some shabby hotel, Jo insisted Robyn come home with her instead—walking out on her brother's birthday party with the American stranger he had wronged. Then staying up with her until dawn, serving tea and sympathy to that jet-lagged stranger. "It's not you," Jo told her. "It's Collin. He's done this dozens of times. When we were in school he shamed my best friend so much she never came round again. Infidelity is a disease with him. He cheated on you. He cheated on his wife. He'd cheat on himself, if he could only figure out how."

"This has nothing to do with Collin."

Jo gave her a so-you-say look. Jo had suggested the walk in Wales, and seemed to regret that attempt at amateur therapy.

Robyn disagreed. Admittedly Edward had brightened her self image, but that did not mean she made him up. If her subconscious aimed to stoke her ego, why not come up with a delusion slightly more believable? She had not even meant to tell Jo how the walk came out. On the train back from Abergavenny she mooned over her rose, determined to tell no one—aside from her Brentwood therapist back home. The entry in her electronic journal began, "No one is ever, ever going to believe this. . . ."

But as soon as she got up the next morning, Jo asked, "How did it go?" And Robyn told everything.

There was an otherworldliness about Jo that invited rash acts of confidence. The sole decoration in her tiny kitchen was a torn magazine page pinned to the wall, with a picture of that most famous Grey, Lady Jane. Queen Jane was not even an ancestor—the Tudors made sure she died childless—just a rebellious teenager who spoke her mind and treated adults as equals. Her parents tried to beat the independence out of her, before putting her up as queen. But it took a headsman's ax to silence her. Jo had made her into a sort of Protestant patron saint, a strange presence to have looking on each morning at breakfast. When Jo arched an eyebrow, you saw the resemblance. "Who did this knight errant say he was?"

"Edward, earl of March. Can you really be lord of a month?"

Jo sat down opposite her, elbows on the linoleum table, fingers laced together supporting her chin. "March means the Welsh Marches, the border country you hiked through."

"Oh." That made more sense.

Jo stared at the rose on the table, willingly giving even the wildest story an honest evaluation. Like Lady Jane, she paid for her honesty. Her brother had a London town house and a country estate. Jo lived with her daughter in a ramshackle two-and-a-half room cottage, divorced and disinherited. She had married "badly," then been deserted by the man for whom she had given up everything. Faded linoleum on the floor exactly matched the pattern atop her homemade table.

"But when you went back you found nothing. It might have been a put-on," Jo suggested. "A practical joke. You know men. Anything for a kiss."

Robyn shuddered, thinking of the swift ease with which Edward up-ended two armed men. "That fight was no prank. Edward knocked two men clean off their horses. Killing one for sure." There had been ample time for the footmen to come up and cart away the dead and wounded. "And the way he talked about his family was awfully real." She had dated actors in "Holy Wood." Some pretty talented and a couple whose names you know, men who got paid millions a picture to be convincing. None had been half as believable as Edward. "I don't blame you for thinking I'm crazy. When Edward first showed up, I thought he was crazy. As nuts as you think I am now. Worse even."

Jo shook her head. "I don't think you are nuts."

Overwrought. Under stress. Seeing things. Hallucinating scarlet bowmen and knights in armor. Making out with an imaginary young earl—but not clinically loony. Not yet, anyway. She still had that to look forward to. This mystery already wore on her. What if she never found out more than she knew now? Her meeting with Edward would live on in her memory, a big question mark hovering over her grip on reality. She could not just bury something so momentous inside her. If it sounded nuts at the moment, imagine her as an old lady—telling grandkids how she had been romanced by the earl of March. She had to get some closure or she would surely go batty.

Keeping her hands tucked under her chin, Jo raised a single finger to her lips. "What were the colors on his surcoat?"

"Blue and yellow." Robyn did not have to close her eyes to picture them.

Getting up, Jo opened a drawer and took out pencil and paper. "Can you draw the pattern?"

Robyn drew the pattern as best she could, shading the blue bars, leaving the yellow ones blank. "And there was this white space in the center, shaped like a shield."

Jo nodded. "The white escutcheon. Those are Mortimer colors."

"Mortimer?"

"Mortimers were the medieval earls of March."

Edward Mortimer. An odd name for her hero. She mentally tried the name out, Lady Robyn Mortimer. "But he called himself Edward Plantagenet."

"That just means he claimed descent from Henry Plantagenet, the grandfather of Prince John and Richard Lionheart. We Greys are descended from him as well. In those days royalty got about. The Mortimers were Plantagenet earls of March. They got about some themselves, one Mortimer earl married a Welsh rebel, another seduced a queen."

Jo stroked the flower with her finger. "And the white rose is a Mortimer badge. I can believe you might conjure up a knight on horseback. Or scarlet bowmen and black riders. But how did you conjure up the Mortimer coat of arms?"

Robyn had no ready answer. Those were just the colors Edward had been wearing. She had not thought to ask him what they meant.

Jo stared at the morning rain on the window, flowing in silvery rivulets down narrow panes. Outside the sun had yet to show on what was bound to be a very wet Friday. "Do you really want to find out what is behind this?"

"Fairly desperately."

Jo turned back to her. "There is only one way I can think to help."

"What's that?"

"You could see Widow Wydville."

"Widow Wydville?"

"She's a seeress." Jo said it lightly, as though the woman took in boarders—which also turned out to be true. "She runs a bed-and-breakfast, and a public house of sorts. A bit batty herself, but absolutely bound to have an opinion on anything this odd. It will mean a drive in the rain."

Robyn did not care if they had to swim. "What will this seeress do?"

"With a seeress, you have to go and see." Jo called to her daughter, who was in the bedroom dressing for school, "Dearie. Are you ready to go?"

She got a sleepy response. "Sort of."

"Don't bother with your books," Jo told her. "Just grab some jam and bread. It's home school today."

A muffled cheer came from the bedroom.

Jo rolled her eyes at the child's delight. Robyn pulled on her boots and borrowed jacket. As soon as the door opened, rain came flooding in. Jo grimaced. "Thank god we've got the navy."

Jo's car was a beat up old Bentley, 4.5-liter coupe, battleship gray—just like James Bond used to drive—called The QE by the family, or

Bouncing Bettie. Passed on to Jo by her brother, Bettie might have really been the Bentley Bond used to drive—she was that old. Worn shocks made for a lively ride, and the convertible top no longer converted, but that was just as well in the rain.

Jo's daughter, Joy, was a nine-year-old version of her mother, slim and lively, with long straight hair. Grave gray eyes looked even larger and more serious on a child's face. They even dressed alike in expensive hand-me-downs, fashionable mother-daughter outfits from another decade. Joy acted as if it were the most normal thing to leave her ramshackle home, pile into their beat-up car with some crazed American stranger, skipping classes and setting off into a howling storm to see a seeress—all in the name of home schooling. In fact she was ecstatic, bouncing on Robyn's lap. "Old Lady Weirdville. All right! What a corker! Will we be witches?"

"I can't promise anything," Jo cautioned.

"Oh, let's hope we'll be witches." Joy looked up at Robyn. "You'll love it. Really love it." Robyn was not nearly so sure, but Joy's enthusiasm was infectious. Something seemed bound to come of this, if only not to disappoint the nine-year-old. Squirming about, the girl reminded her mother, "It's Friday. There could be a Black Sabbath."

"We'll just have to see." Jo shoved the Bentley into gear. "And don't say Black Sabbath. It's not polite. The proper word is Witches Night."

"Last time I was the altar," Joy boasted. "They need a virgin for that. The cup feels cold on your naked tummy, but I held absolutely still!"

"Indeed you did." Jo sounded proud.

Robyn rolled her eyes, wondering what she was getting into—but it was a bit late to back out. Wheels whipped wet gravel off the drive, and they were under way. Big Marchal headlamps bored twin tunnels through falling rain. Joy sat on Robyn's lap, elbows on the dash, spreading homemade blackberry jam on homebaked bread, all the while praying they would be witches. The white rose rode in the glove box, wrapped in a frayed tea towel. Embossed on the glove box was what looked like a two-legged white dragon, but was actually a wyvern—a Grey family badge. Blue and white were the family colors, just like BMW's.

Past Cheltenham, Jo caught the M5 motorway, skirting Gloucester, headed south straight into the tempest. Robyn recognized the route; it was the way they had come from Collin's wretched birthday party. Greystone, the family estate, lay off to the right. South of Gloucester, they changed over to a primary road paralleling the motorway. Peering through the blinding downpour, Robyn made out the turn-off to Berkeley Castle, a local landmark. Jo took the opposite fork, climbing back into the hills, braving the blur of rain. Her face half an inch from the windshield, Jo worked the brake and clutch like a grand prix driver, skidding and sloshing through the turns, throwing up spray. Brake, shift, brake. Much as she might disdain her brother, Jo was clearly Collin's sister, sharing his willful sense of adventure at all cost.

Robyn winced as Jo spun through right-angle turns and then jammed the Bentley back into gear, gas pedal to the floor. Tossing a cheery, "Hold tight," over her shoulder, she roared off down the wrong side of an invisible rain-swept roadway.

Holding tight to Joy, Robyn tried to keep the would-be witch from flying through the windscreen. The girl in her lap went "Whoo" and "Whee," squealing at the turns, absolutely trusting her mother not to slam them into something solid. Clearly they had done this before.

Between breakneck turns Jo tossed off comments on the woman they were visiting. "Widow Wydville's given name is Jacquetta. But she never uses that. . . . Hang on here!" She spun the wheel, sending the Bentley slithering into another harrowing turn. "Widow Wydville is what she goes by. No one knows her maiden name."

"Because she's from Transylvania," Joy added eagerly.

"Tosh. Where did you hear that?"

"You can tell by how she talks," Joy insisted.

"Oh, really? What a linguist. Well, hang tight." They went tearing into the next turn. When they straightened out, Jo went on, "Wherever she comes from, she's terribly timid. Let me do the talking." Robyn nodded, holding on to Joy and clinging to the dash, trying to make sense out of the sodden landscape. They were somewhere in the southwestern fringe of the Cotswolds, where the hills trailed off into Avon, merging by degrees with the built-up areas around Bristol.

Bouncing Bettie jolted to a stop beneath a tall stand of oaks. Rain beat on the metal bonnet. More rain dripped from the trees. Grabbing her travel bag, Robyn got out and raced for shelter, with Joy running along under her jacket. Jo led them to a gaunt stone-and-timber cottage ringed by bare earth and thistles. Bounding up muddy steps, she beat on the door.

Water streamed from the thatched eaves. Suddenly the door swung open, revealing a bent, white-haired woman with a witch's long nose and prim wrinkled lips, welcoming them in a thick unrecognizable middle European accent. "Come in, come in."

Jo thanked her, "It's wet enough to do in a duck."

"Ja, ja." The woman nodded. Her hair was pulled back in a tight bun, showing a high forehead and wide, staring, heavy-lidded eyes. "Leave your damp things by the door. I'll light a fire." Her house looked like it had been furnished from the prize rack at a carnival shooting gallery. Every flat surface was covered with the wildest bric-a-brac, china spoons, terra-cotta angels, tin tea sets sitting on scraps of lace, porcelain pigs with wings, pearl buttons, wild peacock feather arrangements, a ceramic pitcher covered with painted-on magpies.

"Mrs. Wydville, I'd like you to meet Robyn—"

"Nein, nein." The old woman waved her hand and shook her head, turning away from them. "No Mrs. Wydville. Not here. Not today . . ."

"It's all right," Jo assured her. "Don't worry."

But the old woman disappeared into the kitchen, saying, "Nein. Nein. No longer here. She move away. . . ."

Joy giggled. Jo told Robyn, "Don't worry. She's just afraid of you."

"Me? Really?" Drenched and wilted by the ride, Robyn did not feel like much of a threat. Nonetheless, she turned around, ready to leave, not at all looking forward to another neck-or-nothing ride through the rain. This old woman did not want her in the house, and here she was uninvited, her travel bag in hand, dripping on the poor woman's floor, surrounded by an astonishing display of cheap trinkets and china cutlery.

Jo seized her arm. "It's nothing," she insisted. "Don't worry. It's just that you're a stranger."

"An American," her daughter added, as if that excused anything.

Mother and daughter hauled her deeper into the dark little cottage. "She's deathly afraid of being hanged for sorcery," Jo whispered.

"Or burned," Joy suggested.

"Give her time. She'll come around." Jo's upper-crust arrogance showed. She was Jo Anne Grey, of the Dorset Greys, born and bred in a centuries-old Cotswold manor, descended from dukes and kings, with a ne'er-do-well brother at Sotheby's. How could some funny old foreign woman turn her out of a thatched hovel? Feeling silly, Robyn followed Jo into the old woman's kitchen. Widow "Weirdville" had not asked them to go; she merely denied being herself. Stoutly refusing to admit who she was for fear of being denounced and burnt.

Robyn could see why. The kitchen was straight out of the fourteenth century, with a rough stone floor, tall homemade cupboards, and an open hearth. A kettle hung suspended from a chain leading up to a chimney hole cut in the roof. China cats chased china mice atop the cupboards, and the only plumbing was a cold-water tap, fed by a pipe coming in one window. Otherwise the place seemed untouched by modern times. A witch's wooden spinning wheel stood in one corner. Joan of Arc would have found the smoky hearth and cast-iron cookware centuries out of date.

The crone turned, at bay in her antique kitchen. "Nein, I told you, she not here."

"Show her the rose," Joy suggested. The girl had heard the whole tale of Edward in the car coming over, happily absorbing every inexplicable detail—taking her "home schooling" very seriously.

"Yes. Show her the rose." Jo slid the travel bag off Robyn's shoulder, setting it firmly on the stone floor, laying claim to a bit of kitchen. The whole business seemed more idiotic by the moment, but seeing no alternative, Robyn gingerly unwrapped the tea towel, laying the rose on the handhewn wooden table, the bloom looking as fresh and white as when she had first seen it on Edward's cap.

Widow Wydville cocked her head, staring hard at her, then at the rose. Little sky blue eyes gleamed in recognition. Without saying a word, she went to a cupboard, getting out fresh soda bread and tinned sweets. She put them down on the table alongside the white rose.

Jo grinned and then mouthed, "We're in."

Robyn sat down on a three-legged stool, chewing on a piece of soda bread and watching the witch putter about her kitchen. Jo dragged a chair in from the other room. Joy attacked the sweets. The Seeress went back to the cupboard that had held the sweets and soda bread, returning to the table with an ornately carved wooden box. Setting the box down on the table, her wrinkled hands carefully lifted the lid. Robyn smelled camphor. Expecting to see something magical, she saw instead a large blue butterfly and a pair of mothballs.

"Ooh," Jo breathed softly. "It's a big blue."

"Beautiful," Joy exclaimed. "It looks alive." But it was not. Robyn saw wing scales missing, and an antenna knocked off, lying beside the mothballs.

Jo shook her head. "Big blues have been gone from England since before you were born. I saw the last ones in Devon, when I was a girl."

"What happened to them?" Joy craned her head to get a better view of the butterfly. As if staring hard could bring it to life.

"Late in the last century, rabbit plague wiped them out. That plus the decline in sheep farming."

Joy looked up. "How could that be?"

"Big blue caterpillars, *Maculinea arion*, fed on wild thyme. They even looked like thyme flowers, which helped hide them from birds. When they got big they would crawl off the thyme plants into the grass. When foraging ants found them, the caterpillars secreted a sweet substance that the ants liked, causing the ants to carry them off to their nests, and care for them all winter. At the beginning of summer the butterflies would emerge from the ant holes, mate, and lay their eggs on thyme plants."

"Amazing." Robyn studied the blue butterfly. Mother Nature had witchcraft as strange as anything women had been burned for.

"But it all depended on wild thyme, a most sensitive plant. The decline in sheep farming and the dearth of rabbits let tougher grasses run wild, choking out the thyme. There is not enough left to support the big blue. They kept a single colony alive for a while in Devon. That's where I saw them. Now they are all in boxes or under glass."

Widow Wydville carefully replaced the lid. Robyn saw the carving on the lid was indeed a butterfly. Old and worn, but clearly a big blue. She looked at the old woman, surprised the witch had said nothing about the box or the butterfly—Jo had done all the talking. The witch nodded thoughtfully. "Yes. Displacing Spell. That is it."

"What is it?" Robyn asked. The cryptic remark had clearly been directed at her.

"Your young knight with the white rose. He is under a Displacing Spell."

Robyn stared. She had said nothing about Edward to the witch. No one had. She had merely shown this seeress the rose. And the witch replied with a butterfly. "Isn't she an absolute corker?" Joy exclaimed. "Mrs. Weirdville knows everything."

Smiling, Widow Wydville offered the girl another sweet.

"How did you know?" Jo demanded.

The old woman shrugged, turning back toward her cupboards. "It is what you came for, no?"

Robyn nodded. Just when she concluded her trip in the rain was a first-class goose chase, this seeress succeeded in astonishing her, half convincing her that Edward would be something more than a lifelong unsolved mystery. "What is a Displacing Spell?"

Rummaging through her cupboard, the witch returned with eggs, flour, oil, a cup of milk, sugar, and spices. She set them out on the table, saying, "The Displacing Spell does not hurt the victim. Does not put them to sleep or make them mad. It merely sends him somewhere else. Perfect for when the victim is protected from harmful magic."

Robyn watched her cream the sugar and butter. "So Edward was sent here from the Middle Ages?"

Widow Wydville did not answer, mixing in eggs and flour. Maybe she thought that much was obvious. She added a couple of pinches of soda, then some of salt.

"But shouldn't he speak Old English?" Despite words like *wetshod* and *forsooth*, Edward sounded so normal. He had barely had an accent, just enough to know he was English.

Joy laughed. "Old English is for Beowulf. Middle English more likely."

"Or Norman-French," her mother suggested. "Depends on the date."

"1459." Robyn remembered how proud Edward had been to come up with the correct calendar year.

"Humm." Jo reconsidered. "Forget the Norman-French. I think by then the nobility spoke mostly English."

The witch laughed. "Nein. That is not how the spell works." She added a pinch of nutmeg to her potion. "He is displaced not just in time and place, but in his whole person. He takes on the language wherever he lands. He breathes the air. He drinks the water. He speaks the speech. Give time, and his old world will fade completely."

That sounded semireasonable to Robyn—given what she had so far agreed to swallow. But a thousand other questions remained, some small, some huge and glaring. "What about John-Amend-All? And the black riders? Were they displaced, too?"

The witch poured in cream of tartar and then slowly added sour milk, mixing until she had a firm dough. "I do not know about your scarlet bowman. But those black riders mean someone wants him more than displaced. They want him taken. Or dead."

"So where is he now?" Robyn wished they had gotten a paper, to see if anyone had found a knight wandering the Welsh hills.

The witch shrugged. "Maybe here. Maybe there. It does not matter." She sprinkled flour on the table and began rolling the dough into long strips. It mattered to Robyn. Edward was out there somewhere, thoroughly displaced, with people out to get him. Or so it seemed. Unless this was all some wild flight of fancy.

"No matter, no matter at all," the witch muttered, cutting the strips into thin ribbons and then plaiting them, wetting the ends to make them stick.

Robyn looked helplessly at Jo. "It matters to me."

"Wait." Jo raised her hand, then turned to the witch. "Why does it not matter?"

Widow Wydville bent down, blowing on the fire and feeding in kindling. She straightened up, pouring sizzling oil onto the griddle. "Because the rose will bring him back."

Robyn looked at the rose, still lying on the table. "How?"

"Through magic," the witch replied. She started frying the plaited dough.

Of course—magic. Robyn found it all very hard to believe. "Back where? Here? Now?"

"No." The witch shook her head. "After the rain." She flipped the first batch of golden brown crullers onto a towel to drain, sprinkling them with sugar.

"That will be too late." Robyn could not afford to wait on the English weather.

"I told you," the witch replied, "we have the rose. It does not matter."

"It matters to me," Robyn insisted. "My plane leaves in the morning."

Widow Wydville patted a cruller to cool it and press out the excess oil; then she handed it to Joy. The girl took a greedy bite out of the warm brown pastry. Jo looked over at Robyn. "How much does it matter?"

That was the question. How much would she do to see this through? Could she just drop it here, get on an A.M. plane at Gatwick and fly back to Hollywood? Not hardly. Though she did not believe this daffy crone could really conjure up Edward, she could not turn her back on the chance. A couple of years after she left home for California her parents had been killed in a plane crash. One evening she had been talking with them on the phone, wishing them well on their vacation, excited and happy. The next day they were gone forever, without a chance to say good-bye. That arbitrary finality always seemed grossly unfair. If she had a chance to bring Edward back—however slim—she would take it.

Searching through the travel bag at her feet, she came up with the cell phone. What time was it in Maui? Late yesterday evening. At least Heidi would be up and around. She punched her assistant's private number, figuring the call would be rerouted.

Heidi answered on the first ring, a good sign. Robyn asked, "Are you sober?"

"Partly."

"I'm going to stay the weekend in England. Cancel my reservations, and get me a Monday night flight out of Gatwick."

"Sounds like things are happening."

"You would not believe the half of it. Call the studio in the morning. Tell them I won't be in until Tuesday."

"What shall I say is going on?"

"If I wanted to answer that question, I'd be calling them myself." She could not tell the studio that she was on a magic quest to conjure up a long-dead earl, not without sounding absolutely loopy. Whatever Heidi came up with had to play better than that.

Heidi giggled. "Aye, aye, Captain. Shall I beam you up a mai tai?"

"Just get it done; then have one on me." She hated to encourage Heidi's bad habits—but after having flown to Hawaii in the middle of the workweek, nothing was going to hold her back. Mai tais were hardly the worst thing Heidi would get into.

A sharp intake of breath, followed by a moment of silence, showed she was already smoking something with more kick than a Camel. Heidi hissed between clenched teeth, "How's Collin?"

"I'm dumping him for the earl." That should make her happy.

"Oh, goody." Heidi took another long drag. "I got dibs."

"He's all yours."

Heidi hung up, eager to be off the phone before Robyn could change her mind. It would serve Collin right to set Heidi on him, and Robyn toyed with the notion of giving her assistant Collin's address in England—not even a wife and kids could put the brakes on Heidi. But knowing Heidi, she already had it. Heidi might come off like a walking hairdo, but that was just protective coloration. Stoned or sober, the girl could be deadly efficient—when the need arose.

With nothing to do but wait on the English weather, they stayed for tea, which lasted so long it turned into lunch. Widow Wydville minced up mutton and onions, flavored with mushroom relish, Worcestershire sauce, pepper, wine, and oatmeal, and garnished with a boiled egg. This witch's potion turned out to be delicious, with a fine nutty taste. Not your normal overcooked English beef. Afterwards they braved the rain again, whipping over waterlogged country roads and then barreling back up M5, making it safely to Jo's.

Near to midnight, the rain stopped. Robyn was still awake, sitting cross-legged on the kitchen floor, her electronic journal in her lap. It being the witching hour, Jo had the tarot cards out, telling Robyn's fortune by candlelight. That was as close as they came to observing the Black Sabbath. Joy bounded in to say the drumming on the roof had ceased. "That means a ritual tomorrow. And we can be witches!"

Jo celebrated by spiking her Earl Grey with Glenlivet. A couple of sips and she was dancing around the kitchen with Joy riding barefoot on her toes. Lady Jane watched from the wall, wearing a martyr's enigmatic smile. Jo talked as she twirled, "You know Collin's wife will likely be there."

"Where?" Robyn looked up from her cards.

"At the ritual." Drink made Jo sound mischievous. "She is in Widow Weirdville's coven."

That was awkward, but probably could not be helped. "She won't make a scene, will she?"

"Hope not." Jo laughed, swinging her daughter around.

"Well, I am completely uninterested in Collin. Someone should tell her that."

Jo laughed again, high on Earl Grey and Glenlivet. "It would sound most convincing coming from you."

Fat chance. She shook her head, determined to put Collin and his loving spouse completely out of her mind. She would not let the woman who destroyed her relationship with Collin spoil her chance to see Edward again. Turning back to her journal, she started to punch in the three cards turned over for her. (She was recording her tarot cards, to see if there were any patterns, or if they were just random.) The first was the Wheel of Fortune. She knew what that meant: fate, destiny, the inevitable, and the unexpected. The other two were not so familiar. She called to Jo, "So what do these two mean?"

Jo waltzed over, Joy still riding on her toes. Pointing to the most dire-looking card, showing a woman bound and blindfolded, surrounded by eight swords driven into the ground, Jo told her, "Eight of Swords means crisis, calamity, conflict, treachery, and imprisonment."

Joy piped up, "But also rebirth, hard work, and new beginnings."

Jo spun her daughter about. "Just like you, my precious little reborn calamity."

How convenient, all the cards seemed to have double meanings. Magic was mostly misdirection anyway. Robyn picked up the last one, showing a naked child on horseback, crowned with sunflowers, carrying a flag, beneath a dazzling sun. "The Sun in Splendor," Jo called down. "It means joy, triumph, high spirits, maybe a happy marriage."

"Also loneliness, heartache, spoiled promise, and success delayed." Joy delighted in giving the reverse meanings.

Right. Robyn took a sip of spiked tea, holding the card higher. "Know who this child on horseback reminds me of?"

"Edward Mortimer?" Jo laughed—mother and daughter were both having giggle fits. "Don't set your hopes too high, dearie."

Shuffling the cards, Robyn put them back in their black cloth. Jo was right: she felt herself going way, way out on a limb. Setting aside job and rational judgment, just because some witchy old woman said she could bring back a boy who claimed to be a long-dead earl. Well, too bad. Putting down the tea cup and card, she typed into her journal:

Okay, so I'm hooked. Hopelessly. Possibly seeing Edward again excites me. (Please, don't let me fall for someone just because he's totally unattainable!) At absolute worst, it will be a spectacular bust, with nothing coming of it. No magic. No Edward, earl of March. At least I will have tried, and not just given in to impossibility. . . .

⊶⊷ Hetty Pegler's Tump ⊶⊷

Few places are more beautiful than rural England after a rain. Robyn awoke to see green gleaming countryside out the spare bedroom window, a perfect blue-skyed painter's landscape still wet from the brush, with lush, rolling meadowlands cut by dark hedgelines and dotted with sheep. In the near distance, she spotted a white church steeple, backed by stone-roofed farmsteads and tall copses of trees. After living for years in southern California's ferro-concrete chaparral, it constantly amazed her to wake up in *Watership Down*.

Joy was already perched on the bed, her small pink feet sticking out from under a white satin chemise that belonged to her mother—"Made exclusively for Victoria's Secret." Black hair framed gray child eyes, dancing with glee. "Oh, do! Oh, do get up! See what a smashing day it is?"

She sat up among the sheets, smiling back at the girl. Having no children of her own, she doted on other people's, enjoying all of them, without committing to any one, never worrying about discipline or spoiling them—those were someone else's problem. "So, I guess we get to be witches."

Joy nodded excitedly. "We are meeting the coven at Hetty Pegler's Tump!"

"Where's that?"

"Near Nympsfield. Below Coaley Peak. So, do get up!"

"I'm up," she told the girl, throwing back her covers.

"Yes!" Leaping to her feet, Joy pumped the air with her fist and then dashed off to tell Jo their guest was awake.

So who was Hetty Pegler? What was a Tump? The Queen's English "as she is spoken" was full of ordinary sounding words with no clear meaning. Joy returned with Earl Grey tea and tinned crumpets. Pouring into chipped Willow Ware cups, Joy invited her to have "Some of ours."

She accepted, sipping her tea and staring out at the church steeple. "So, tell me what a tump is."

"An ancient burial mound." Joy bit down on a crumpet. "Deliciously creepy."

"And how about Hetty Pegler?"

"Been dead for centuries. So don't expect to see her." Joy grinned over her crumpet. "Unless we get lucky." Tea parties in bed, then off to spend the day with witches trying to commune with the long dead. What a weird, magical upbringing Jo was giving her daughter. And Joy reveled in it, showing that absolute child's delight in anything adult and dangerous.

Finishing her crumpet, Joy hauled a heavy iron necklace out from behind her. Flanged lengths of metal hung from the chain, looking like oversize hand-beaten lock picks. "This is for you."

"For me?" Heavy metal accessories were not really her.

"I made it," Joy announced proudly. "In metal shop."

"Really?" The girl was only nine.

"Actually, in Uncle Collin's garage and stables. He home-schools me, too. I did not know who it was for until you came to visit. It is to keep you safe."

"That so?" She hefted the necklace, it felt heavy enough to use in self-defense.

"Swear to Hecate." Joy looked so sincere, Robyn had to accept, or else deny the girl's time and effort. Thanking her, she ordered the wild child out so she could shower and dress.

Jo had an aged coin-operated shower, turning bathing into a rare adventure. To save time—and give herself something to do—Robyn had laid out her clothes the night before, a sleeveless blue V-neck jumpsuit and a gold silk blouse. Comfortable, yet eye-catching in Mortimer blue and yellow. Edward would see her wearing his colors. And lace panties, no less—just in case. A gift from Collin—it would serve him perfectly if someone else got into them. Hiking boots, her borrowed jacket, and Joy's heavy metal necklace ruined the effect, but that could not be helped. Jo and Joy wore matching white smocks with flower wreaths in their straight black hair. Very witchy.

By the time Robyn finished giving her new short hairdo a quick brush, Jo had the Bentley running. A break in the English weather was not to be wasted. They set off again down M5, switching over to A38 south of Gloucester, an old Roman road leading into Bristol. Jo followed the Roman road south for a half dozen miles, then cut back toward the Cotswolds, just before the Berkeley Castle exit, saying, "Best to take the scenic route."

Down-shifting, Jo took to the back roads, avoiding Dursley, an old mill town where Shakespeare was once wanted for poaching. Twisting lanes climbed the Edge, the sharp west slope of the Cotswolds, a great limestone ridge stretching all the way up to Yorkshire. Green woodland wound atop the scarp, remnants of the vast deciduous forest that used to cover all of the uplands. Generations of Britons had cut back the woods, replacing them with scattered copses, open fields, grass leys, green hedges, and rose thickets. The warm buff-and-gray limestone beneath had been made into farmhouses and rock fences that seemed to grow right out of the ground, not competing with the landscape but completing it. Joy spotted a pair of yellowhammers as they whipped past, and a black-and-white stonechat, with its rust-colored breast. Named for a bird, Robyn took these as good omens.

Widow Wydville was waiting for them at her cottage door, dressed in an otherworldly outfit—a blue lambskin cloak trimmed with fire opals and glass beads, over a white ankle-length shift cinched at the waist by a wooden link belt. Bareheaded and barefoot, she wore white furry gloves. "They're catskin," Joy whispered.

And she had thought white smocks were witchy. Up till now she had been secretly telling herself nothing could really come of this Olde English voodoo. This was merely an excuse to extend her stay, getting Edward out of her mind before plunging back into the real world. Seeing Widow Weirdville dressed like Death done up for a holiday made the whole excursion less of a lark. She still did not think Edward was going to show, but now she began to worry about what actually would happen. Ending up the sacrificial victim of some crazed New Age coven would pretty much top off an otherwise insane trip.

She had no chance to question any of it. Jo and Joy kicked off their shoes, while Robyn got the rose from the glove compartment, still wrapped in its tea towel. She shed her jacket but kept her hiking boots—let the would-be witches go barefoot in the woods, she would keep her feet firmly in the real world. Widow Wydville guided them up a winding path into the trees behind her cottage. Joy bounded on ahead, while Robyn stayed with Jo, walking behind the witch. Soft ground gave beneath her boot soles, springing back with each step. Rainbow dew sparkled on rusty leaves and glistening strands of spider web stretched between the trees. Ahead she saw blue sky and the brow of a hill.

Civilization returned too soon. At the top of the woods they struck a paved road. Cars shot noisily by, blowing clouds of exhaust. They followed the asphalt road to the picnic area alongside Hetty Pegler's Tump. When first built, the white limestone burial chamber must have stood out against the local skyline. Over the centuries the tumulus had sunk into the turf and was now half-covered with sod. The tump's massive stone portal was blocked by a locked door, a gateway into the realm of the dead. This "modern" door and entrance had been installed sometime during the previous century—in the English countryside even the "new" stuff was old. Robyn liked that. She had spent ten years in L.A. and nearly every place she hung out at when she first arrived—every club, restaurant, coffee shop, and antique store she enjoyed—was gone now. Replaced by something newer and more expensive.

The coven had assembled in the picnic area, much to the delight of Korean tourists happily snapping their Nikons. Four would-be witches were waiting, all barefoot, wearing long white homespun smocks and flowers in their hair. The total effect was eerie—the stark stone burial chamber, the locked doorway to the underworld, the solemn flower-crowned women in homespun. She felt like she had taken a big step back in time. Even samurai paparazzi could not make it seem like the twenty-first century.

Widow Wydville had the key to the tump. Turning it in the lock, the witch swung open the door. Mice startled by the light shot into their holes. Coven members had to bend down, crawling on hands and knees after the witch, worming their way into Mother Earth's womb. As soon as Robyn crossed the new-old entrance stone, she was in the realm of the dead, a cramped megalithic crypt unbelievably ancient even in Edward's day, a limestone burial vault older than the Caesars. Older than Moses. The last coven member closed the door behind her, shutting out the light and tourists.

Crouched in quiet darkness, smelling damp earth and cold stone, Robyn heard the coven breathing around her. Even Joy was silent, not giving off so much as a giggle—she could be quiet when a spell called for it. Widow Wydville said a long, low prayer in a heathen language and then lit a tall candle using a flint tinderbox. Shadows leaped out. Light fell on the women's faces. Huge slabs of Cotswold limestone surrounded them, shining in the candlelight. The crypt air was so still and the witch's grip so firm that the candle flame stood stiff as a spear point. To her left Robyn saw a pair of empty chambers opening onto the main passage, forming dark, gaping caverns. To her right, another pair of doorways were still sealed. Joy had boasted that two dozen skeletons had been taken out of Hetty Pegler's Tump. More were undoubtedly buried behind those sealed doorways. Switching to English, Widow Wydville invoked the Gray Goddess who ruled over death and rebirth:

> Holy Hecate,
> Death Crone and Dark Mother,
> This is your place.
> Time out of mind
> You have ruled this tomb.
> We pray to you,
> Hear our plea,
> Unlock the past.

Hecate's invocation was followed by a ritual greeting, each member of the coven giving her first name, then her mother's, then her maternal grandmother's. Since Robyn knew all but one of the women already, the ritual replies gave her a moment to collect herself. She studied the ring of fire-bright faces.

Red-haired Marlene was the only woman Robyn had not yet met. She turned out to be grave, soft-spoken, and very Irish, with a thick accent, deep worry lines, and a pale British indoor complexion. Peggy and Nora had been at Collin's ill-fated birthday party, and were clearly a couple. Robyn had yet to see them apart. Peggy was stout and motherly, with frizzy blond hair, merry blue eyes, a Cockney accent, and an cheerful outgoing manner—as English as Marlene was Irish. Nora was tall and quiet, not nearly so outgoing, but obviously happy with herself, especially since she had Peggy.

Bryn was the beauty of the group, annoyingly slender, with big soulful eyes, a wide sensuous mouth, and shining chestnut hair. She was also Collin's wife. Robyn had not seen Bryn since that disastrous birthday party, when she discovered that her wonderful new boyfriend was Bryn's husband. Too bad in a way. During those first misunderstood minutes, when Bryn met her at the door, Robyn had liked her, liked her a lot. Feeling an instant intimacy between them, an immediate yearning to know this person better. Imagining Bryn to be a friend of the family Collin never mentioned, Robyn was struck by the genuine welcome she got. By how warmly she was invited in, as if Bryn had been waiting all evening just for her—an American stranger crashing the party. She laughed and apologized, thinking she had already made a friend. Guessing they had much in common—and not just their taste in men. Then they introduced themselves, and all hell broke loose. Though they now said nothing to each other, some of that special feeling lingered. She doubted she could ever easily lie to Bryn. Not with much hope of fooling her anyway. They were that close.

Jo, Joy, and Widow Wydville brought the coven up to seven—the number of days in a week and seas in the ocean. And the number of deadly sins. "A lucky number," the witch explained. "Now with you we are eight." Robyn felt a strange chill at being so swiftly and easily included in the circle. Wariness began to replace skepticism, making her uneasy. "And when Edward comes we will be nine," the witch added. "A holy number."

Holy for some, unholy for others. Edward was being cast in the role of the Horned God, the male member of a coven. The Devil in the Black Sabbath. A cheerful, fair-haired, brown-eyed devil, gentle in manner and deft of tongue, a skilled horseman very deadly with a mace. Six feet of happy young aristocrat who wanted Robyn to be his "lady." With the coven assembled, the circle cast, and Edward invited in, they crawled back out of Hetty Pegler's Tump, returning to the light of day, turning their backs on the realm of the dead.

Tourists greeted them at the entrance, snapping more pictures. Jo got annoyed with the hordes of sightseers swarming over the Cotswolds, calling them *grockles*. But Robyn never minded working to an audience—maybe it was the Hollywood in her. Besides, she did not take this "witchcraft" all that seriously, and even tourists needed to be entertained, shown something weird and unexplainable, something not listed in the Michelin guide. By now Robyn truly felt like part of the show—not just another uninvited visitor from over the ocean. Though this ritual was probably just an elaborate put-on, she at least had a purpose for being here, a mythic connection to the land going back centuries. That alone should thrill the tourists.

Heading into the woods, the coven began a high, clear chant, drowning out the traffic sounds. Trees closed in around them, dew sparkling like diamonds on dark mossy trunks. The tourists stopped at the first stream, which was swollen from the rain, with steep slippery banks. Robyn forded it easily in her hiking boots. Coven members lifted their skirts, stepping right into the swift icy water without missing a note. Feet and ankles came out dripping wet and white as parchment.

Ahead of her, the ground got steeper, turning from soggy to rocky. White and green lichen clung to outcroppings of warm honey-gold limestone. As she scrambled up a narrow, bracken-lined rabbit run, her phone began to ring. She felt silly for having brought the thing, for bothering to keep in touch with the world, even at a time like this. Snatching it out of her pocket, she whispered, "Hello." She could see Widow Wydville looking at her. So were Joy and Bryn, still singing away.

"Hi, Robyn. It's me, Collin. We should talk."

"No way," she whispered, desperate to avoid a scene.

"Oh, come now. Be fair, there are things I must tell you."

"This is not the time," she hissed back. He had not called her since his birthday.

"Please. Now is best. Bryn's not here."

"Oh, really?" His wife was a dozen paces off, singing along with the coven, but staring hard at her.

"Yes, she's off with her witchy friends. We could get together. Just the two of us."

Not bloody likely, as the Brits say. Robyn settled for a terse, "No."

"Please. Give me a chance to explain."

"No." It was hard to be adamant at a whisper.

"At least turn down the music. I can barely hear you."

"Not possible," she whispered.

"Look, I still love you. . . ."

She cut him off, folding the phone and putting it in her pocket. The perfect note to end on. She thought how thrilled she had been the first time Collin said "I love you." It nearly made her cry. Now his love was just an added annoyance. She could tell Collin would not just let things drop. Somewhere, sometime, she would be talking to him again.

Going over the same old ground. But not here, not now. Not with Bryn staring at her and the coven caterwauling away. The slope ahead leveled off. She came out of the trees into clear, blue-gold sunshine. Green farmland lay in front of her—hedged meadows, grass leys, and sheep pastures, sprinkled with houses and lined with stands of trees. A light, playful breeze caressed her face.

She was back on the Cotswold Edge. Emerald countryside fell away from where she stood, sloping down toward the silver loop of the Severn. She could see clear across Cam Long Down, the Vale of Berkeley and the Noose of the Severn, to the Forest of Dean and the dark Welsh hills beyond. Villages dotted the low ground by the river, with the M5 motorway cutting a sharp, crisp line between them. Berkeley Castle was hidden by the great green fold of the Cotswold Edge stretching south and west toward Bristol. Saying a short prayer, Widow Wydville recast her circle on the open hilltop, arranging the coven in a ring and then telling Robyn to sit in the middle. The witch had taken out her tight bun, letting her yellow-white hair stand out from her head, blowing wild in the breeze.

Heart thumping, Robyn sat cross-legged on the grass: Her moment had come, and even though it would probably not amount to much, she could not help being excited. The coven closed in around her, a wall of women cutting her off from the world. Jo and Joy looked more than ever like mother and daughter in their matching shifts. Redheaded Marlene and fair Peggy, tall, angular Nora and Bryn with her bright big eyes—they all stared in at her, their singing sinking to a sonorous chant.

"Take out the rose and hold it in your right hand," the witch told her. Unwrapping the tea towel, she held out the white flower, as magically fresh as when Edward had given it to her. An uncanny sign in itself. Every move she made seemed to take her closer to where she needed to be, leading her into forbidden adventure. "You need something from your world," Widow Wydville explained. "Something to hold in your left hand. Something to anchor you here."

Right. What to use? Her VISA card? The souvenir silver shilling Jo had given her? She felt the pocketed phone pressing against her breast. Collin's gift, tucked next to her heart, her link to the wider world. What could be better? She took it out, holding it hard in her left hand.

"Good, good choice," the witch whispered, drawing the circle tighter until the women were kneeling within arm's reach of Robyn, their singing sinking even lower. Only Widow Wydville stayed standing, raising withered arms to the sky like the horns of a waning moon, her white hair forming a windblown halo above her blue lambskin cloak. She said another long, heathen prayer and then told Robyn, "Let go of yourself, but remember to breathe."

She did, breathing deep and long. Determined to give the magic a chance, she cast aside her doubts, merging with the women's voices around her. It worked; she felt the singing chant surge through her, bearing her up, filling her with a delightful lightness of being. It reminded her of a sweat-lodge ritual she had gone to on the Crow Reservation in Montana. The rose in her right hand seemed like a breath feather, trying to bear her up and away. The phone felt cold and heavy in her left hand, tying her to the real world, a sort of psychic anchor.

"Let yourself go," Widow Wydville repeated. "The moment is here." Encouraged, Robyn let herself go deeper, forgetting her doubts, freeing her body, setting her mind adrift. She started to picture Edward, first his smiling face, then his full body, no longer in armor, but dressed in shining cloth-of-gold and wearing his black velvet cap. She pictured him coming toward her, grinning eagerly. Sunlight gleamed on his gold hose and doublet.

Her anchor came alive in a burst of beeping. The phone in her left hand had started ringing. She did not need to answer to know it was Collin. The absolute fool. She felt him dragging her back to earth, cutting her off from the chant. Edward faded away. Her finger searched frantically for the hold button.

Before she could silence the beeping, Bryn reached out, coolly taking the phone from her, saying tartly, "That will be for me."

As the phone left her hand, the landscape took a leap, changing in front of her. In that same instant the circle of women vanished, leaving her alone on the hilltop, staring into blue space where the coven had been.

⊷⊷⊜ Trumpet of Swans ⊜⊷⊷

Feeling like the Fool on the Hill, she saw a big blue butterfly dance in spring sunlight where Widow Wydville had stood. She watched the butterfly settle onto a tall patch of wild thyme that had not been there before. Unbelievable. By far, the neatest piece of amateur conjuring she ever witnessed. No flash of smoke, no mirrors or thick black curtains, real right-before-your-eyes magic on an open hilltop. Incredibly impressive, if wildly inappropriate. Instead of summoning Edward, Old Widow Weirdville vanished, taking her coven with her—leaving a butterfly in her place. Silly really, and somewhat scary. Why disappear? What was the point? Was it some sort of sign?

Wings beating, the blue butterfly rose up again. She realized it was not just any big blue butterfly—it was the big blue. *Maculinea arion.* Like the one Widow Wydville had shown her. The one not seen in England since sometime in the last century.

And it danced in spring sunlight. Wet fall morning had turned into a spring day. Fallen leaves had vanished, whisked away with the coven. Dew had disappeared from the grass, and the sun stood high overhead in the wrong part of the sky. Nearby a hawthorn bush sported may-blossoms, hardly likely in October.

She glanced at her watch, which seemed suddenly very out of place. 9:33:17 A.M., and still October. A huge chasm had opened between the cold, precise high-tech time on her wrist and the warm, bright landscape with its noon sun and spring flowers.

Looking anxiously about, she saw whole houses and farmsteads gone, along with the roads leading to them. Drystone walls and hedges had vanished as well, replaced by great unfenced fields scoured by dark plow lines. Until now she had seen only faint traces of medieval deep plowed fields, suddenly they filled the valley below, grazed by huge flocks of sheep, innumerable, white specks dotting the open fields, more sheep than she ever imagined. What had Jo said? Hordes of sheep *used* to crop back the grasses, giving wild thyme room to grow. Making a home for the big blue.

Fear crept down Robyn's spine, raising shivers, then coiling cold and heavy in her gut. She stared at the rose in her right hand—no longer feeling it lifting her up. Petals had started to wilt. A pair lay in the grass next to her knee, looking like bright white teardrops. Edward's magical rose was fading, returning to its natural state.

She stood up, straining her eyes, trying to make out the straight, sharp line of the M5 motorway cutting across the flats. No luck, nothing but hazy green countryside. The built-up area around Dursley seemed to have disappeared completely—vanished in the spring haze—something so clearly impossible it had to be an illusion, some trick of the shifting light. Horror battled with denial. She had gotten carried away by the weird ritual and strange surroundings. Trying to shake the horrible displaced feeling, she headed back toward the asphalt road and picnic area, eager to get to somewhere more familiar, putting these ghastly discrepancies behind her.

Trees loomed taller, crowding onto the crown of the hill. Plunging through the fringe between sunlight and shadow, she dodged low branches and tripped on tree roots. Halfway down the hill she stumbled on something that crunched and slid underfoot. Cursing, she managed to catch herself. Looking down, she saw a dead hedgehog, white bones showing through its spiky gray coat, like a giant crushed chestnut. She shivered and went on, finding the brook they had gone singing across—shrunk to a trickle, yet right where she remembered it. Somewhat encouraging, but nothing to shout about.

On the far side of the stream, she got her worst surprise. The two-lane asphalt road was gone. B4066 between Dursley and Stroud had become a pair of wagon ruts. She stared dumbly at the tracks, sure she had gotten turned about in the woods, which were way denser and darker than she remembered.

Looking up, she felt her stomach give a ghastly lurch. She could *see* Hetty Pegler's Tump above her on the bare ridge, restored to its ancient state. The picnic area had vanished, turned into a shallow gully choked with trees and brush. The Tump itself was completely grassed over, as sealed and mysterious as when Hetty Pegler first found it.

Closing her eyes, she prayed just to be lost in the English countryside. Disoriented, possibly even deranged. Temporary insanity—that was the ticket. Momentary madness, a stern warning not to dabble in magic, no matter how innocent seeming. Sunlight beat on her. She heard sheep bleating and a dog barking. Jamming fingers in her ears, she shut out the sounds as well, making desperate deals with herself. Set everything right, and she would give up anything tainted with witchcraft. No playing at spells. No horoscopes. No herbal remedies. She would throw away her tarot pack and not so much as visit a psychic Web site. Never ever again.

She opened her eyes. The tump was still sealed. B4066 to Stroud was still a wagon track. The barking dog and bleating sheep sounded closer. This was reality. Grim, unrelenting reality. What had Edward said? 1459. America undiscovered. Printing newer than the Internet. Witches burnt. Women in chastity belts. The Black Plague. Antibiotics uninvented. Painkillers replaced by bleeding. Tampax and toilet paper unheard-of luxuries. Dentistry done with a hammer. Sick anger rose up, making her want to scream.

Which she did, so sharp and loud it startled her. Feeling a second, louder scream welling up, she stifled it. Sitting down by the wagon ruts, she cried big racking sobs instead, bitterly berating herself. What a brainless fool she had been. Letting Jo Grey and Widow Weirdville play magical games with her life. She cursed Bryn for grabbing that phone. What a malicious heartless bit of revenge that had been.

"I don't want your goddamned husband," she shouted. "I did not even know you were married." Not that Bryn could hear. The vengeful bitch would not be born for half a millennium. By then I'll be long gone, she thought, feeling good as dead already.

"Why are you crying?"

Looking up, she saw a dirty-faced little girl, blond and big-eyed, wearing a berry-dyed homespun dress and leaning on a crooked staff, her bare feet black with grime. One glance said she did not come from anywhere near twenty-first-century England. Her clothes were hand-dyed wool, worn but neatly mended. Wispy-white hair had been bleached by the sun not by a bottle. The barking dog leaped and yapped at her side. Both were surrounded by sheep, a whole shaggy flock of them, filling the cart path, edging impatiently forward.

Getting no answer, the girl asked again, "Why are you crying? Whose husband don't you want?"

She stared in wonder at the talkative little girl. A real medieval shepherdess—crooked staff, sheepdog, and standing knee-deep in wool were sure giveaways. No more than nine or ten, she had the same bold, self-possession as Edward, totally at ease with just her dog and her flock, not the least bit afraid to ask a stranger's business.

Childhood here and now seemed to end at infancy. Preteen shepherdess or teenage earl, they acted absolutely undaunted by an adult task, be it tending sheep or toppling a king—yet each took time to hear Robyn's troubles.

Wiping her eyes, she told the girl, "I am lost." Literally true, though she had a fair idea where she was. Little blond Bo Peep had a sturdy upcountry accent, far thicker than Edward's—barely sounding English—("Whooze hosbound doon't yee wont?") But Robyn had no trouble understanding or replying. Like the witch had said, she was "displaced"—breathing the air and speaking the speech.

"Where were you going to?" the child demanded.

"Is there a cottage in the woods below here?" Widow Wydville's thatched hovel should be a short walk downhill. With its weathered stonework and ancient kitchen, the cottage had to be hundreds of years old at the very least. Something there could easily reverse the spell.

"Yes, there is a cottage. Just this side of the Nymph's Field." The shepherdess pointed down the wagon ruts. "But you ought not go there."

"Why?" Already it seemed absolutely natural to be asking a grimy-toed nine-year-old's advice.

"A witch lives there." She said it matter-of-factly, without a hint of superstitious awe. As if witches were a normal hazard of life, like straying sheep or a wolf in the fold.

But Robyn desperately needed a witch. Magic got her here; magic would get her home. That a witch lived there here and now was wonderful news—an occult link between the two eras. A godsend, given her situation. Just getting there might free her; bringing things full circle could easily break the enchantment. This could all turn out no worse than a waking dream. Getting up, she thanked the shepherdess, who replied with a steady attentive stare. Child's eyes recognized an adult bent on mischief. "Beware," the girl warned, "there are Swans about."

"Swans?" Robyn stood and stared. Maybe displacement did not work as well as Widow Wydville thought. She could swear the girl said *swans*.

The child rolled her eyes. "Yes. Swans. A whole lewd trumpet of them."

She had heard of medieval people fearing frogs and toads, but not water fowl. "What sort of swans?"

The shepherdess shook her head. "Really mean-looking ones."

"I will be careful," she promised. Maybe they were wild swans. This was, after all, a child. Medieval resourcefulness went only so far; flocks of four-foot-long birds could be threatening to a little girl alone in the woods. Robyn had way more important worries.

Heading downhill, she found the way changed. Sheep paths and game trails ran in all directions through a dense forest more thoroughly used. Dodging tree trunks, she tried frantically to remember anything Widow Wydville said about displacing spells. But she had not half believed the witch at the time—never pressing for details. Now that she was thoroughly convinced, she could no longer get answers to vital questions. How long did the spell last? How could it be reversed? She tried to remember everything she could about the ritual by the Tump, the prayers said, the songs sung. Oh, Hecate can you hear me, now that I really need your help?

Seeing no sign of swans, wild or otherwise, she found Widow Wydville's place, aided by a decent sense of direction and the fact that the stone cottage had not moved in five hundred plus years. It had merely gotten younger, looking almost new, with crisp-cut stonework, fewer windows, and the thatched roof no longer sagging under the weight of centuries—but it was still the same witch's cottage she had left a couple of hours and half a millennium ago. No smoke came from the chimney, and the door no longer had a lock, just a polished wooden latch. She lifted it and let herself in, calling, "Hello."

No answer. The inside was even more changed. Knickknacks were gone, along with the stopped clocks and light fixtures, replaced by beeswax candles and hand-sewn tapestries. The kitchen had a butter churn by the door; a wooden bucket and brass pitcher replaced the cold water tap coming in the window. Searching through cupboards, she saw dried herbs, bundles of feathers, carved figures, bits of stone, and unmarked bottles filled with weird powders. Widow Wydville had made it sound so simple—too simple. No eye of newt or hair of bat. Which stuff would work on her, which just cured warts? She had no way to know. And it was all thrown together in no special order. Amid the powder bottles lay a bone flute decorated with owl feathers. Beside it sat a curiously carved butter mold. Hefting the mold, she studied the carving. *Maculinea arion* with wings spread. Magic or just misplaced?

Hoofbeats sounded outside. She froze, frustration turning to terror. This was not going to be the coven coming to retrieve her, and she dreaded having to confront medieval strangers, trying somehow to explain herself—the swan-a-phobic shepherdess had been rightly suspicious of her. What could she possibly say? Her presence here was a horrible mistake. She just wanted to be left alone in her misery, to get out of this as best she could. But that was not going to happen.

She heard the hoofbeats come to an ominous halt, followed by male voices. Someone dismounted. She put the butter mold back down beside the bone flute.

Heavy footsteps came up the walk to the witch's door. Could it be Edward? That would be a lot to hope for—but no more amazing than what had already happened. The spell was supposed to bring them together—that was the whole idea. She picked up the rose, praying it was him.

Boots mounted the stoop. She listened intently. The latch lifted; the door creaked. Holding tight to the bedraggled white rose, she made herself trust in the spell.

Only to be bitterly disappointed. The man appearing at the kitchen door was not Edward. Not even close. Heavier and wider than Edward, he was far shorter, shorter even than her, with a grotesquely pocked face half concealed by a beard the color of cooked beef's blood. An astonishingly ugly combination. His black greasy jacket hung open to the waist, with thick curly chest hairs taking the place of a shirt. Slung across this naked chest was a coil of rope, one end knotted into a hangman's noose. His stained gray hose were tucked into hairy cowhide boots. Menacing and then some—but it did not stop there. Looped through his belt was a black silk executioner's hood. Alongside the hood hung the weirdest knife she had ever seen—a straight sheathed dagger with a long knobbed handle and a hilt made of two steel balls. Dangling between his legs, the hilt and handle stuck out like a steel erection. Stitched to his black jacket was big white cloth bird. A swan.

Dear God, what now? The sight of this hangman in black, with his noose across his chest and knife between his legs, summoned up every misgiving she ever had about the Middle Ages. Scaring her half to death—though she fought not to show it.

Suspicious pig eyes surveyed the scene in the kitchen, with its feathered bones and witch's powders, and then fixed on her. "Whoo're yee?" he asked in a high-sounding West Country accent.

"Robyn," she replied warily, managing a smile. Seeing no immediate danger in giving her name. "Robyn Stafford."

He grinned, showing off gray, rotting teeth, held together by hamhanded dental work done with gold wire. "And what do you here—Robyn Stafford?"

"Minding my business." Any answer she gave was bound to sound insufficient. She did not try to match his "whoot doo yee hee-ear" accent—keeping her responses curt and formal. Aside from a knot in her stomach, she felt totally numb, utterly appalled by what was happening, but unable to stop it.

"And what business have you in a witch's hut?"

"Private business," she insisted—not the least tempted to share her troubles. Neither his evil slovenliness nor his musty smell inspired her to exchange confidences.

"What is this private business?" He sounded like he had never encountered the concept—and immediately disliked it.

She stood staring him down, thankful he did not tower over her. The truth would do her no good, nor could she think what lie to tell. What innocent purpose led you into a witch's kitchen? "I cannot say," she told him—that much was true.

His ghastly grin widened. "You will say." He added philosophically, "They always do. Witches like nothing so much as to talk. When you put the question to them right." Motioning toward the door, he invited her to go "oot" into the yard. "Where my dog may sniff you."

She had no desire to be "sniffed" by anyone—least of all this villian's dog—but saw she had small choice in the matter, and it seemed absolutely vital to give him no excuse to touch her. Clutching her rose, she followed him into the sunlight, telling herself this was all temporary. A nightmare that could not last.

Horses snorted, slapping at flies with their tails. Two dozen mounted men and boys waited in the cottage yard, all wearing studded leather and carrying edged weapons—swords, dirks, daggers, and bows, making her escort's noose and knife seem like nothing. Dressed in red and black, they had that tough boot-leather look that did not bode well, like bikers on horseback, wearing gang colors and grotesquely armed. Each one had a big white cloth swan stitched to his metal-studded jacket.

Their blond-bearded leader called down to her captor, "*Bonjour*, Le Boeuf. What have you got there?"

Better dressed than the rest, the lead horseman wore a red silk surcoat trimmed in sable. His hose had the same color scheme, one leg red, the other black, tucking into red leather riding boots. His speech sounded more cultured, with a hint of French—you could hear the class difference between him and Le Boeuf. But he had a yard-long sword at his side, an oversize knife in his belt, and a shiny steel cap on his head. An alert, experienced brigand, cheerfully prepared to do violence if need be. Not someone she could count on for help.

Le Boeuf laughed. "A treasonous witch from the look of her. Soon we shall know for sure." He whistled shrilly through a gap in his gold-wired teeth, and a hound loped up, thin and black, wearing a chain-mail hood with holes cut for his ears, eyes, and snout. Her miraculous grasp of the language had not betrayed her; they were having a dog sniff her for signs of witchcraft—a fifteenth-century version of the dope-sniffing K-9s at the airport. Things had gone beyond strange, to straight out surreal. She did her damnedest to be nonchalant about it, smiling and keeping stock-still, calmly letting the dog run his wet black nose over her, acting totally unflustered. What dogs smelled was fear, not witchcraft. Careful not to meet the hound's eye, she let the beast take his time, nuzzling her hands, legs, and bottom—doing her best to make a favorable impression. When he got to her crotch, she fixed her gaze on the blond-bearded leader in red silk and sable, making him look at her, not at what the dog was doing, smirking at the absurdity of the test.

He looked straight back at her with hard blue eyes, not returning her smile, taking the idiotic dog-sniffing dangerously seriously. Managing to seem both sinister and silly.

Suddenly the dog started barking. Sharp, staccato barks sending shivers up her spine. Despite her admirable display of innocence, the witch hound backed away, growling angrily between barks. So much for dumb brutes being better than their masters. "She's a witch, for sure," declared Le Boeuf cheerfully, calming the dog with a couple of pats and a leathery bit of meat.

His absurd pride in the idiotic test made her laugh aloud. How totally second millennium. Men stared as if she were mad. Her sudden good humor did have an hysterical edge, but she could not stop herself—terrifying or not, it was way too ridiculous. Witch-sniffing hounds. Riding about with big white birds stitched to your shirt. Medieval backwardness was no excuse—any century should find this stupid.

Collecting herself, she looked up at the horseman in red silk, carefully matching his courtly accent. "*Pardon.* Surely you don't take this dog show seriously."

He looked startled by her speech, seemingly shocked she could talk. Robyn realized it was the way she easily matched his courtly Frenchified accent. Clearly he had expected something more like Le Boeuf's thick West Country falsetto. Not happy to hear his methods ridiculed—even in cultured tones—Le Boeuf leaped to his dog's defense. "See here, Barrister is a purebred witch hound. Who's sniffed out a dozen witches an seen near half of them hung."

Rolling her eyes, she refused to admit the dog had any power, especially over her. Insulted, Le Boeuf turned to his fellows for support. "She's a witch, I tell you. And a traitor to boot. Anyone can see that. . . ."

Waving the hangman to silence, the blond horseman in red silk leaned down for a closer look at her. "How can you find this so funny?"

"*Vraiment?* How could I not?" She saw he was deadly serious, but refused to give in, laughing again and laying on the accent—a bit of witchcraft working in her favor. Talk like a noblewoman and mayhap they would treat her like one. Audrey Hepburn passed for a princess in *My Fair Lady.* "Come"—she arched an eyebrow—"trailing after a dog, sniffing for witches? *Mon dieu,* you're more likely to find rabbits, or an old bone."

Le Boeuf protested, "A purebred witch hound!"

"But still a dog," the rider in red pointed out. "We need proof we can put before a judge." He turned back to her, plainly confused by her courtly accent. "What is your name?"

She smiled evenly up at him. "Robyn Stafford."

"Stafford?" He straightened in the saddle, eyeing the rose in her hand. "You are not by chance claiming relation to his worshipful highness the duke of Buckingham?"

His worshipful highness? The same question Edward asked—put more obsequiously. She would not give the same easy honest answer.

What she said could determine how this armed felon treated her. It was no time to be timid. Or trusting. "Not by chance, but by blood," she declared. "I am his daughter."

That got a good laugh all around. One of the men on horseback made a mock bow. "What a wild chance. I am Robin Hood, the good duke's long-lost aunt."

Shushing his men, the rider in silk stared hard at her. "Truly?"

"Yes, *monsieur*." She bore down on the French title, with its double meaning. "Earl Humphrey Stafford, duke of Buckingham." She said it the way Edward had, glad she could get it out without faltering—trying to look indulgent yet aloof, the way a duke's daughter would if she were caught larking about in a witch's cottage. "Who may I ask are you?"

Touching his steel cap, the horseman straightened up further, saying stiffly, "Gilbert FitzHolland, sergeant-at-law." Adding ironically, "At your service."

"*Enchanté.*" She had won the test of wills, feeling like Eliza Dolittle at the ball. Obviously words were her best defense—a courtly accent, a bit of French, backed by every ounce of bland self-assurance she could muster. Heaven knew what it would eventually mean—these people were not stupid, just surprised by her speech, and the penalty for impersonating a noblewoman must be hideous.

FitzHolland ordered one of the boys out of the saddle and then turned back to her. "If m'lady will please mount up . . ."

Le Boeuf looked disgusted. Men chaffed the boy who had to get down, saying, "Make way for Her Highness."

Ignoring them, she took the reins, thanking the boy in French, seeing she had made the right choice. Dangerous as these men were, she had to meet them head-on, playing the role she had been handed. This was the improv class from hell. Be the mythical Robyn of Buckingham—or die. Tucking the wilted white rose in a buttonhole, she concentrated on coping with the strange mount and high Spanish-style saddle, acting like she rode this way every day. Settling in atop the big bay gelding, she felt better—glad to be level with the men and seated on a horse that looked to have some speed. No match for Caesar, perhaps, but certainly carrying less than the men's mounts, giving her an even chance if she had to run—not that she was eager to put her barrel-racing ribbons to a life-or-death test. Leaning forward, she patted the big bay horse, whispering in his ear, "Carry me well, there is a carrot in it for you."

FitzHolland smiled. "When you next see your mother, Lady Margaret, tell her that Gilbert FitzHolland says her daughter sits passing well on a horse."

His tone warned her. Too smooth and easy—as if he were slipping something past her. Giving FitzHolland a cold glance, she strained to remember Edward's every word, saying, "My mother's name is Anne, Duchess Anne of Buckingham, born Anne Neville, and I doubt very much she knows you. Please tell me where we are going."

"To Berkeley," FitzHolland replied, plainly taken aback, having expected her to trip at the first snare.

"Then let us be off," she suggested, with just the right degree of indifference, implying she had a choice. At least she knew where they were going. Berkeley Castle was a half dozen miles away, mostly downhill. She had toured the castle the Sunday before with Jo and Joy. Le Boeuf mounted a led horse, calling Barrister to heel. The boy who had surrendered his horse to her scrambled up to ride pillion behind one of the men.

With a wave from FitzHolland they set off, threading through the trees, climbing the low ridge leading to Cam Long Down. Crossing the wagon track, Robyn saw little blond Bo Peep still herding her sheep. Giving her a quick glance, the girl whistled in her dog and turned away, driving the flock down the cart path toward Dursley. She had warned Robyn about the Swans and witch's cottage—and could not be blamed if the warning was wasted.

Atop the ridge they broke out of the trees onto the green sweep of Cam Long Down, leaving the Cotswold Edge and descending into the flats of the Severn, scattering flocks of sheep. She stopped worrying about anything but her horse—since moving to L.A., she had no horse of her own, so she was used to strange mounts, and riding was her only skill even remotely medieval. Her big bay proved easy to handle, even downhill, sure and friendly, not in the least skittish. Mastering him made her more confident, letting her imagine she *was* Robyn of Buckingham, riding with mailed escort on a vital errand, engaged in a life-or-death masquerade. Her first starring role. And she had to live the part, or it might easily be her last. Gilbert FitzHolland drew his mount alongside hers, saying she rode "shrewdly well, even for a duke's daughter."

She tried for the right degree of amused indulgence, as if it were comical that her identity could be questioned. "Of course."

"What brings you here?" FitzHolland pretended to take her claim seriously, to keep from sounding ridiculous.

"My father's concerns," she answered airily, trying to remember everything Jo told her about the Staffords. They had been dukes of Buckingham and earls of Stafford, descended from royalty—related by marriage to Edward, earl of March, through his mother's family, the Nevilles.

"What concerns were those?" FitzHolland sounded unconvinced.

"Private ones." Pitching her reply carefully, she implied secrets she could not divulge. She had seen the Stafford coat of arms—a red chevron on a gold field—so her wearing tailored pants and Mortimer blue had to be part of the masquerade. "That is why I am dressed this way."

FitzHolland arched an eyebrow. "I did assume there was a reason." She could tell he did not believe her, but she was making the game interesting enough to keep him at bay—at least until they got to Berkeley Castle. But what then? They rode on in silence, trailed by his trumpet of Swans. Pastoral landscape flattened into broad fields cut by streams coming off the Cotswold Edge. Farmsteads clumped at the bridges and fords, connected by crooked hedgelines sprinkled with spring blossoms. She found it eerie to see no sign of the huge M5 motorway. Even the air had changed, smelling fresher and greener, without an undertaste of burnt gasoline. Outcroppings of Old Red Sandstone replaced gray-gold Cotswold limestone.

South of Cam Bridge they came on a stretch of Roman road, looking like a wall lying on its side—one day it would become A38 out of Gloucester. Only yesterday she had hung on for her life while Jo raced down it in the rain. A mile or two of stone roadway led to a bridge, with its attendant cluster of houses—her first medieval village. Thatch and slate roofs lined both sides of the road, backed by barnyards and privies. Black timber framing and white lime-washed walls set in flowered gardens formed an eye-catching contrast, giving the village a simple pleasing beauty—not at all like the concrete and asphalt roadstops she was used to. Sheep, pigs, and cattle fed on nearby grass and stubble.

Halfway across the bridge she hit a wall of hot cow-patty odors. Here again, the Middle Ages lived up to expectations; this little one-street town absolutely reeked of Chanel #2. At the far side of the bridge FitzHolland reined in, barking a command to dismount. His Swans swung out of their saddles, alighting amid ducks and geese.

Robyn stayed firmly in her seat, least it look like she took his orders—nothing is more ennobling than being on horseback when others are afoot. Half holding her breath to keep the barnyard odors at bay, she surveyed the scene. Scores of people stood by the bridge. Men mostly—some with families—those in front having bows and white swan badges. She was most taken by the women, bright spots of color among the crowd, wearing handsewn dresses, simple yet elegant. Fearing the Middle Ages would be all grubby and ragged, she saw she had been judging the place largely by the men—and the wrong sort of men at that. Some of these women would have turned heads on Rodeo Drive. If these were peasants, what must ladies be like? She wondered just how far fair speech and decent looks would get her, especially in a sleeveless pantsuit. At least her shirt was gold silk.

Everyone's face turned at once, someone important had appeared. She saw a small cavalcade approaching from the opposite direction. FitzHolland remounted, looking gleeful. "Ah, my lady, the good Lord Scales is here, His Majesty's lord constable of the Tower of London. Doubtless his lordship is familiar to you."

"I have never visited the Tower," she replied frostily. Actually, she had toured the bloodstained old pile on her first day in England, killing time before Collin's ill-fated birthday party. Better to plead ignorance than risk getting tripped up—for all she knew there was no Lord Scales. This "constable of the Tower" could be another attempt to trap her in a falsehood.

FitzHolland answered with a crafty look. "Lord Scales also has concerns hereabouts."

She braced herself. Could she fool a lord? Someone who must know her supposed father? Lord constable of the Tower hardly sounded comforting. She pretended to busy herself by looking about. Where the stream bank wagon track met the Roman road was crossroads of sorts, with a small flagpole in the middle. A ladder leaned against the flagpole and a chopping block sat beside it. This could be her last chance to run for it. But that might be what FitzHolland wanted—to see her bolt and have the fun of running her down. Bowmen kept the crowd away from the crossroads; big men with huge arms from pulling bows as tall as themselves, looking sharp and proud in studded leather with their white swan badges. She bet they were deadly with those bows. Deadlier than that Hollywood drunk with a pistol. Better to brazen it out here than to try to run.

Her throat tightened as a knot of horsemen trotted her way. At the head rode a tall white-haired gentleman dressed in a cloth-of-gold gown. Huge trailing sleeves decorated with white scallop shells reached all the way to his stirrups, a dazzling outfit, shining like molten gold in the sun, making her silk shirt seem drab. Pity his face was not so promising. Beneath his velvet cap he had pinched features—a sharp keen nose, flaring nostrils, and tight lips—reminding Robyn of an old-time movie villian, an aging Basil Rathbone in some costume drama. His lordship reined in to look her over. Ignoring his chilly scrutiny, she made herself look him easily in the eye. She could well believe this was the keeper of the Tower of London. He seemed that dangerous.

Unwilling to risk a FitzHolland introduction, she plunged straight into her tale, begging his pardon and saying she hoped she was speaking to Lord Scales. "If so, you must know my father, Earl Humphrey Stafford, the good and well-beloved duke of Buckingham?" She tried to sound conversational, throwing in that "good and well-beloved" part. Fervently hoping the "good duke" and her whole newly adopted family were so totally beloved and respected that no one would dream of harming her.

Lord Scales nodded, "I do indeed know the well-beloved duke . . ." Hearing his cold certainty, her heart sank, expecting his next words would be, "And you are not his daughter."

Instead Scales paused, seeming to savor the tension between them, eyes alight, a ghostly smile on his lips. She could see he did not believe her, and her whole fairy-tale deception was coming crashing down.

". . . yet until now I never had the pleasure of meeting either of his daughters. How splendidly charming."

Relief flooded through her. Lord Scales got her warmest, most appreciative smile, her first truly heartfelt smile since discovering she had fallen into a five-hundred-year abyss. She could not imagine why Scales had taken her side, but was almighty grateful that he had. Glancing at FitzHolland, she saw that he, too, was grinning. Maybe she misjudged them. Riding about armed to the teeth trailed by witch-sniffing hounds did not actually make them "bad" men—or so she hoped.

"This is utterly astonishing," Lord Scales assured her. "What a delightful mischance. It will be vastly entertaining to visit with you. But first, let us to the task at hand." Taking station alongside her, he nodded to FitzHolland.

FitzHolland motioned to Le Boeuf. Slipping his black silk hood over a gap-toothed grin, Le Boeuf uncoiled the rope from his chest. A crier called the crowd to silence. Armed men with swan badges led out a priest and a hatless pudgy man wearing good clothes and a hangdog look—like a local Kiwanis president caught with his hand in the till. He had that prosperous-citizen-gone-to-seed look, well fed but semi-shaved, his torn taffeta coat and soiled silk shirt elegant but unkept. His stained hose had gold trim, but the fat pink feet beneath were bare.

Robyn stiffened in the saddle. She could tell by the looks on the women's faces something horrible was about to happen. The crier called out the man's crimes saying the wretched fellow, "having no love of salvation or fear of damnation in his heart, did turn a false traitor to his supreme and natural lord, the most gracious and illustrious King Henry, by the grace of God sovereign of England, Ireland, and France. Let his fate serve as warning to all who would fail in true love and obedience to King Henry and so traitorously defy their lord and governor." Each word was like a blow, making the man sag further, until his guards were holding him up.

When the crier finished, the priest began to pray. Bowmen stripped off the man's jacket, shirt, and hose, leaving him wearing only a white loincloth; then they dragged him over to the pole with a ladder leaning against it. Le Boeuf bound the man's hands behind him. His pudgy pink body, balding head, and adult cloth diaper made him look like a big baby, especially as he started to cry. Sobbing great wrenching tears, the man swore in a cultured version of the West Country accent that he meant no harm to his "good and gracious King Henry. Great men covet my property and slandered me to get it. Men who now sit in judgment on me mean to profit from my death."

She could not watch. Dropping her gaze, she stared at her hands gripping the saddle bow. But she could still hear it happening, the priest's mumbled benediction in medieval Latin—which she understood completely—then the man's complaints turning into incoherent pleas, followed by stumbling feet on the ladder and then sharp gasps from the crowd. Out the corner of her eye she saw people's faces, some aghast, some gleeful, some set and pale—all staring at the hanging pole. Except for Lord Scales, who looked straight at her, his cool gaze boring into her from a few feet away. Unconcerned with the hanging, the lordly vulture cared only for her reaction—gloating at her fear.

Looking away, she caught a quick glimpse of the action. The man still lived, feet kicking against the pole, his face going gray. She shuddered and looked back at her white knuckles. Every ounce of carefully hoarded courage vanished. Cold terror made her want to vomit, but she did not dare, not on horseback surrounded by suspicious armed men. How long would the wretch take to die? Minutes already according to her watch. She felt Lord Scale's gaze still on her, while everyone else stared at the struggling figure. Without taking his eyes off her, Lord Scales nodded to FitzHolland, who called out, "Cut him down."

She looked up to see Le Boeuf and his men dash to obey. The man was still alive. Not in the best of shape to be sure, limp and twitching, and gasping for air. But alive. Relief crept over her. She did not know who the man was, or what he had done, but she did not want to see him dead. Lord Scales smiled at her, as if he had done it all for her benefit—though that seemed fairly unbelievable. He told her, "A duke's daughter should absolutely rejoice at seeing justice done. False treason threatens us all."

She was not rejoicing at anything—least of all at his heavy-handed reminder that she, too, stood accused of "lying treason." But she was glad to have the horrible ordeal at an end. Then the crier called out, "Light the fire."

Far from being over, the ordeal had barely begun. She looked away again, seeing birds in the blue skies and smelling smoke. She stared at the trees, rooftops, and faces in the crowd, anything but what was happening in front of her. Or the lordly fiend beside her. Men-at-arms sat loafing in the saddle, happily enjoying the live horror show. Beneath her palfrey's feet, bright yellow-green dung flies buzzed about the fresh droppings.

Strangled cries rose up, hoarse shouts of terror followed by the sickening aroma of roasting flesh mixing with the barnyard smells, making her gag. She remembered being a teenager sitting in a darkened theater with her eyes closed listening to the last minutes of *Braveheart*. She had been a Mel Gibson fan, and her date thought the movie was "heavy"—but she had not wanted that last scene to go on and on and on. Not even in wide-screen make-believe. Now she was sitting on a bay horse in broad daylight, listening to the real thing. Hearing the shrieks as they tore his guts out and then roasted them right before his eyes.

Too much even for this hardened audience. Some humanitarian in the back of the crowd cried, "Take off his head." Others took up the chant, "Take his head. Take his head. . . ." The crier called for order, but could not silence the crowd.

She had never imagined beheading as an act of mercy, but now she, too, prayed for it. Anything to stop the agony. She sneaked a look at Lord Scales and was horrified to find him staring cheerfully back at her. Clearly the lord constable of the Tower of London considered this day's victim already dead—but with her, the game was just beginning. "What say you?" he asked jovially. "Shall we give them what they want?"

She fought to keep from screaming, while people about her chanted, "Take his head. Take his head. . . ."

"Shall we?" Lord Scales demanded. Clearly he meant to make the man suffer until he got what he wanted from her.

Tears fell down her cheeks, splashing on the saddle leather and her clinched hands. Only one thing would stop the agony. She whispered to Scales through tight lips, "Just do it."

"What did you say?" King Henry's lord high constable leaned closer, near enough for her to smell wine and cloves on his breath and for him to feel her fear. Scales would not stop the torture until she plainly asked for this man's death.

Her voice rose uncontrollably, "For heaven's sake, do it."

"Yes, for Heaven's sake," Scales agreed. He gave the crowd what it wanted. Robyn heard the meaty thunk as Le Boeuf's ax came down. Followed by another, and another—until it was finally done. She felt shamed and relieved, relieved that it was over, ashamed that Lord Scales had involved her in a ghastly act of murder. No matter what "treasons and falsehoods" this man had committed, he could not have deserved this—making it plain murder so far as she was concerned.

Yesterday if someone had told her she would be asking to have a stranger's head cut off, she would have thought they were psychotic, now she was going mad herself. Lord Scales flashed her a wry smile. "Today's entertainment is at an end, and alas I must away. But we will soon renew our acquaintance, then you may tell me all about your illustrious family. It should make an amusing tale." Scales was toying with her. He did not believe her any more than FitzHolland did, but was in no rush to unmask her. Not here and not so soon— it would spoil the fun. She had seen his type in Hollywood, full-out sadists who enjoyed playing with their victims. His long-faced lordship would drag things out for his private pleasure—enjoying her helpless attempts to save herself. In the end he would be twice as dangerous as FitzHolland. And ten times as cruel.

"FitzHolland tells me you have never been to the Tower?"

She nodded. Glad to slip one small lie past him—saving a little of her of dignity. Though she could not see how the lie would give her the least advantage.

Lord Scales grinned wider. "That can easily be remedied." Turning to FitzHolland, he complimented the sergeant-at-law—"A splendid find. Make her safe. No one so valuable should come to unintended harm." FitzHolland swore to do his best, and Scales cantered off, trailing his glittering retinue—headed on some new mission of mercy. Le Boeuf sauntered back to climb aboard his horse, still wearing his hood, bright flecks of blood shining on his hairy chest. All around her Swans mounted up, put in a fine humor by the hanging and beheading.

Women approached, offering the gentlefolk refreshment. Drained and shaking, Robyn saw she still must assert herself. Reaching down ahead of FitzHolland, she took the first cup held up to them—if she was not this man's social superior, then she was his prisoner. Surprised at how heavy the cup felt, she had to steady her hand, realizing it was hammered silver. The robust woman who had held up the cup stared at her, looking puzzled, wearing a rich red dress and starched white wimple, simple and pleasing. Making her blue jumpsuit and gold shirt seem all the more silly and outlandish.

FitzHolland explained with a smirk, "We have a lady with us, a duke's daughter." Puzzlement on the woman's face turned to plain disbelief.

Knowing she hardly looked the part, Robyn drank as calmly as she could. Expecting water, she got flat warm beer instead, spiked with fennel to give a licorice taste. After a couple of sips, she returned the shining cup with a soft, "*Merci.*"

Taking back the nearly full cup, the woman looked dubious. Robyn remembered this alewife's face in the crowd, watching blankly and then calling loudly for the show to end. Nothing happening here had been much to the woman's liking, but that did not stop her from offering licorice-flavored beer to her betters—in a silver cup, no less. FitzHolland laughed. "Her ladyship will be used to better."

The woman turned to stare hard at him. "She is not a lady, and you well know it. Just a poor mad lass. You do wrong to mistreat her so." As plain as her beer, this stout alewife had no need to make pretenses and did not fear to speak her mind—even in the shadow of a gallows pole. Robyn expected to find peasants more downtrodden. Here at last was someone who took her side—not to rescue some bogus fair lady, but because she so plainly needed help. Too bad the woman's sole role at the moment was bringing beer to her captors. Why couldn't she have been queen? Or duchess of something?

Searching through her pockets, she found her souvenir silver shilling. It had Queen Elizabeth's picture stamped on it, but that would have to do—it was a sure bet no one in this hellish place took VISA. Leaning down, she handed it to the woman.

The alewife shook her head, staring at the strange shining coin; then she looked up, saying, "God bless and keep you lass. I will pray for you, and for these men to do you no harm."

Someone needed to. She straightened up and took the reins. Her watch read 10:51:23. She had been in the Middle Ages one hour, eighteen minutes, and some odd seconds. And she had already been accused of treason and witchcraft, threatened with death and mayhem, and forced to witness hideous torture. And she had been given a horse to ride and warm beer from a silver cup—not to mention having asked to have a man beheaded. Hearing the priest begin another Latin benediction, she added her own silent plea, begging the powers that be to somehow put all of this centuries behind her. The sooner, the better.

Berkeley Castle

Hanging and beheading had cheered her captors immensely. Nothing encouraged hardened felons like justice gone awry—skipping them to fall on better men. She sat holding her horse's reins, ready to be off, sickened by the obscene congratulations showered on Le Boeuf's performance. "Did you hear the bastard bleat?" asked a mounted bowman. "Like a sheep quartered alive."

FitzHolland chuckled along with his Swans. "Traitors will be wearing out their knees, begging to kiss my lord constable on all four cheeks."

Liking these white trash on horseback less by the minute, she leaned forward in the saddle, ignoring the hilarity, patting her horse and then whispering in the palfrey's ear, "You did good. Really good." Her mount snorted sharply. She nodded. "I know. I know. You hate the screams and smell of blood—I'm not fond of them myself." Horses had more sense than men would admit. Already she felt like this one was hers. "Keep it up, remember the carrot." One of her cards in last night's tarot spread had shown her as a prisoner surrounded by swords, but never in a million years did she think the meaning would be this literal.

FitzHolland signaled lazily, and they set out, full of beer and merriment, leaving the somber crowd behind, headed south and west toward Berkeley. Barrister loped along at their heels. Leading his Swans off the stone roadway, FitzHolland swung through meadows and pasture, hard on spring crops, but easier on the horses. Roman roads were built for carts and foot traffic. And these men proudly traced their descent from the horse barbarians who trampled the Roman Empire beneath their hooves. Larks shot up out of the meadow grass as they rode past, singing their loud warning to the world.

Glad to be off, Robyn figured the farther she got from Lord Scales, the better. Now she somehow had to lose FitzHolland as well. By now she had had about as much of medieval England as she could stand. Edward's ardent courtesy had seriously misled her—not every man in armor was a charming young knight errant. Here less than two hours, she already found the Middle Ages unlike anything she ever imagined. If she thought of them at all, she had pictured downtrodden serfs and courtly nobles—an endless *Robin Hood* meets *Masterpiece Theatre* miniseries, with no-name actors, English accents, and limited commercial breaks—never for an instant thinking how real it would be. The English accents were here, but what they said was surprising. That alewife at the bridge boldly told her betters their business, standing a dozen paces from the mangled remains of a man they had hung alive and then cheerfully hacked to death. Coolly defying the men who did it, the alewife refused to be intimidated when she saw wrong done to a woman—even a weirdly dressed stranger accused of witchcraft.

Berkeley Castle appeared ahead, the ancient stronghold of the de Berkeleys set on its wooded ridge. High battlements of gray volcanic rock and Old Red Sandstone towered above green water meadows fed by the Little Avon. She already knew this beautiful castle with a bad reputation, having seen it the Sunday before, along with the house in nearby Wotton-under-Edge where the lords of Berkeley kept their mistresses—Joy had set the itinerary, determined to educate her American guest. The well-preserved relic she remembered had become a living fortress, formidable and forbidding, standing guard on the lower Severn. All annoying signs of modernity had vanished. No asphalt roads. No parked cars. Wide glassed-in windows were replaced by gray-pink stonework. The town had shrunk to a tiny hamlet, nestled in the shadow of its castle and great stone church.

Berkeley's evil reputation came from a single fourteenth-century incident. This was where King Edward II was murdered. Best remembered as the ineffectual gay prince in *Braveheart*, Edward II was the first English king to be deposed and done to death. Later kings were done in with fair regularity—usually in the Tower—but Edward of Caernarvon was the first. Folks at Berkeley lived off the story for better than six centuries. Jo and Joy had supplied the horrid details. Being gay did not absolve His Majesty from producing an heir, so Edward II married a teenage French princess, Isabella the Fair—a disastrous marriage, even by royal standards. Isabella grew up hating her husband and his boyfriends. Finally she took a lover herself—a Mortimer as it turned out—and overthrew her husband, having his latest lover hanged, after they cut off the offending member "that did usurp the queen's prerogative." She locked King Edward up in Berkeley Castle, aiming to kill him, too. But no one knew how best to do it, never having done in a king before. His jailers tried various forms of mistreatment, hoping to have it look like natural causes—serving spoiled food, making him wash and shave with moat water, and casting him into a cell with rotting carcasses "thinking the stench would kill him." It did not. Being gay did not make the king weak; all they got for their pains was a barrage of royal complaints. Despairing of subtlety, "they drove a red-hot poker up his bum—as fit punishment for his sins, and to leave no marks on the body." Marriage for the royals could be murder.

No such lurid reception awaited her. Instead she found a mini-Renaissance fair going on in the outer ward. Women beat at the castle washing in big wooden tubs, hanging out fine woolen homespun in Berkeley red and white. Villeins unloaded hay carts while pigs rooted through ultra-organic vegetables, and castle boys played king-of-the-mountain on the dung piles. What a weird upside-down place this was—part fairy palace, part populated barnyard. Doves cooed atop gray battlements. Serving women slopped the hogs in handwoven originals, and alewives gave free drafts from silver cups—but daily necessities like aspirin or a hot shower were totally unobtainable.

Stableboys came to take their horses. Dismounting, she told one "Pray get me a carrot," trying her best to sound like a duke's daughter. He bounded off, and she said good-bye to her big bay gelding, giving him the carrot when it came. Then she turned him over to the stable lad with a soft, "*Merci.*" Bowing, the boy tugged his forelock and took the horse. Her palfrey vanished into a stall, and FitzHolland led her through the huge interior gate into the inner ward, which held the great hall flanked by a chapel, kitchens, dovecotes, a buttery, and a brewhouse. Here he handed her over to serving women in red-and-white livery, who took her through the great hall of the castle, an immense three-story-high space big enough to play tennis in, with soaring five-sided arches supporting a saddle-beam roof. Servants were clearing the remains of a meal, carrying out empty trenchers, breaking down trestle tables, and tossing bones to the dogs. A Welsh bard tuning his harp gave her a curious look. Treating her with aloof suspicion, the women left her in a small side chamber with high narrow windows and a unicorn hunt tapestry on one wall.

Happily rid of FitzHolland, she studied her surroundings, seeing a red velvet day bed, a table, and a carved washstand with a pitcher, basin, and chamber pot. On the table lay a handsome book bound in crimson velvet, decorated with silver studs and gold-leaf roses. Beside it sat a jasper and onyx chessboard with heavy crystal pieces. Not at all like the dungeon she had been dreading, this chamber was bigger and far more pleasant than the cell where they had kept King Edward II—which she had seen that on her tour. Hard to tell if she was a guest or prisoner. The door had a latch, but no lock. In theory she could wander about the keep, even go back in the great hall and hear the bard. She could make out his harp through the door, backed by a tinny dulcimer. Listening intently, she realized she could even make sense of his Welsh. The displacement spell let her understand a totally foreign tongue through a thick oak door:

> **My choice is a maid,**
> **Wonderous slim and fair,**
> **High-minded and lovely,**
> **Her Welsh flows sweet as wine . . .**

Astounding. A week ago she had barely known the language existed, now she could sing along with the harper.

Best not to press her luck. Instead she looked longingly at the water in the washstand pitcher, having just ridden several miles on two sips of beer. Maybe it was not moat water, but that did not make it clean. She asked the serving women for boiled water—so far no one had brought any. What a looking-glass world this was. Handwoven tapestries, live music, cut crystal chess pieces, a gold and silver bound book—but a clean glass of water, out of the question. Pouring some of the water into a small metal cup, she put the rose in it. The flower had lost more petals, but it remained her last link to Edward—she meant to keep it as long as she could.

She turned out her pockets, to see what she had taken with her from the third millennium. Not much. She bitterly regretted leaving her purse locked safely in the Bentley. All she had brought on her impromptu expedition into the past were some fairly useless folding money, a pocket guide to the Cotswolds Way, two handkerchiefs, her electronic journal, an utterly useless VISA card, a plastic lighter, a tube of arnica cream, and an "emergency" tampon—she prayed this nightmare did not last long enough for her to need it. Along with her watch, this was all that remained of techno-industrial civilization.

Not a lot. Nothing to wow the simple natives, except perhaps the watch and lighter. Edward had been taken by the digital timepiece. She checked the lighter's fluid, finding it half full. She would not be tempted to start smoking again anytime soon—tobacco was a long ways off. Did they grow hemp in medieval England? Heidi would know. She missed being able to beep her assistant whenever she had a problem.

She glanced at her watch. 11:43:13 A.M. But that was third-millennium time. Here and now afternoon sun slanted through the high windows. She could not shake the feeling that time was passing at home. That Jo and Joy would be worrying about her. And if this dragged on, she would miss her plane on Monday. Actually, there was no plane on Monday. Or any other day. This was the Middle Ages. No one missed her in the least. Half a millennium had to pass before anyone would start to worry.

Losing interest in her troubles, she opened the big ornate book to the title page, finding it was a handwritten double volume, *L'Epistre au Dieu d'Amour* and *La Cité des Dames*—*Letter to the God of Love* and *The City of Ladies*—by Christine de Pizan. Intriguing titles, and even more amazing she read them easily. Idly she turned to a random page, trying a bit of text:

> . . . God wished to make woman his spouse and his mother, the temple of God conjoined to the Trinity. Women should be joyful and know they have the same body as her. God never created anything as upright as she, or as good—except for Jesus . . .

Admirable sentiments. And she read Medieval French as easily as she spoke it. All without a single lesson. Berlitz had a lot to learn from Widow Weirdville.

"Hela!" said a voice behind her. She spun about and saw a black-and-white bird had landed on her window. Crow-size with a black body, a dagger-shaped tail, and white on its wings and belly—an English magpie. Opening its beak, it cawed loudly at her, "Hela."

Make that a talking magpie. "Hello to you," she replied.

"Hela," squawked the bird. Was she able to talk to birds as well? If so, this magpie did not have much to say. Robyn looked back at the door. The music outside had ceased. Should she just lift the latch and go? But where? Back to the witch's cottage? She doubted they would let her out the inner gate. As she stood staring, the latch lifted on its own. The heavy oak door swung inward. Hopefully the chamber maid with her boiled water.

Instead a man entered, dark-haired and handsome, a long thin sword at his side. He wore tall leather boots folded down at the knee, chain-mail leggings, and a blue brigandine jacket studded with silver nail heads. But it was his face that made her give a surprised gasp, then ask soft and tentatively, "Collin? Is it you?"

He stared at her intently. If he was not Collin, he was his long-lost twin. Same face, same eyes, same spade beard and neat trimmed mustache. Even the negligent way he stood, hand still on the latch, looking her over, giving her his total attention, that, too, was Collin to a T. Glancing over his shoulder, to see if anyone had heard her, he carefully shut the door. His hand stayed on the latch. "Do you know me?" Even his voice was Collin's, concerned yet careful.

She marveled at the uncanny resemblance. "I do if you are Collin Grey."

"Sir Collingwood Grey," he corrected her. "Collin is what my sister calls me."

"And her name is Jo?"

"Yes, Joanna. How did you know?"

She had no ready answer. She was in sufficient trouble as is, without babbling about being from some undiscovered country in the far-distant future. No matter how much he might resemble Collin, this was not the same smooth cad from Sotheby's she had fallen for. At best he was a distant relation, a noble ruffian wearing a nail-studded brigandine, with a yard and a half of honed steel at his side and heaven knows what on his mind. Her ordeal by the bridge had taught her to be wary. "I feel like I once knew you. And that we were friends."

More than friends. But what she needed most was a friend, someone to pit against FitzHolland and the ghastly Lord Scales. Right now she did not have much to work with. She had just emptied her pockets and seen nothing likely to save her.

"Yet I do not know you." He, too, seemed wary, acting stiff and uncertain. She could not guess why—he was a man, in his own time, dressed like a gentleman and claiming to be a knight, armed and armored, able to go as he pleased.

"Then why have you come here?" Something had drawn them together. Chance alone could not have brought Collin's look-alike relative right to her door. The world did not work that way—not even in 1459.

"I heard a witch had been taken. A mad witch, who claimed to be a duke's daughter." He sounded guarded, like Collin used to when he had something to hide. What he said was not an outright lie, but not the whole truth, either.

"And you rushed right over to have a look at me?"

"I was coming south, and had affairs hereabout."

"Any that concern me?" She could see he was concealing something important. Collin liked to leave things out, to save having to lie to your face. Heaven knows what it was this time.

He looked from her to the bird still perched in the window. Was he worried the magpie might be listening? "I must honestly admit you are not what I expected to find."

She shrugged, sorry to disappoint him. Too bad—she genuinely wished he had come for her. Collin would not have been her first choice, but any competent rescuer would do.

Letting go of the latch, he relaxed a bit, asking, "Do you have a name?"

"My name is Robyn. Robyn Stafford." Stranger in a strange land.

"And you claim to be a daughter to good Duke Humphrey of Buckingham?"

"Yes." That's what she claimed.

"His own true child?" Clearly Collin did not believe her. Despite her courtly accent, every man seemed to find her claim to be a duke's daughter inherently unbelievable. Why? Was her acting so obvious? Collin eyed her coldly. "His legitimate daughter?"

"I suppose so." He acted so much like the Collin she knew, she felt tempted to tell him the truth, to beg his help in getting back where she belonged.

"This is no time for supposing. You are his true daughter, or you are not." He stared hard, searching for some hint of nobility, or plain good sense. "You act as if you have no notion what danger you are in."

"I guess I don't." She clung stubbornly to the hope that she was only visiting, that at any moment she would be whisked back whence she came.

He stepped away from the door into the room, sitting his mailed hip on the table that held the chessboard, idly swinging a boot while he looked her over. He shook his head at what he saw. "You were found in a witch's cottage, wearing men's clothes and Mortimer colors, with a white rose in your hand. Women have been burned for far less."

"That seems unbelievable." None of those things sounded like crimes, much less capital offenses—but given that horror show at the bridge, who knows?

"You had best believe it," Collin told her. "Treason is afoot. Estates from Ludlow to Worcester are ransacked and ravished, and the duke of Exeter's men search these parts for anyone said to favor Salisbury, Warwick, or the earl of March. . . ."

Mention of the earl of March gave her hope. It sounded like Edward was still at large—and making trouble. If she could somehow get word to him, he would come for her. Or turn out to be a really big disappointment. Too bad now was not the moment to ask where he might be, or how best to address the letter.

". . . Fine upstanding gentlemen are being taken out and hanged—if they are lucky. Yet you go about dressed in Mortimer colors compounding treason with witchcraft. Have you met the good Lord Scales?"

"Just this afternoon."

"Always a delightful experience. His Majesty's cousin, Henry Holland, the worshipful duke of Exeter, is rather worse. Mad actually. Runs in the family. They named the rack in the Tower after his father—the 'Duke of Exeter's Daughter'—which gives you some notion of the family's preferred amusements. Fall into his hands, and you will have no secrets. You already know his bastard half brother."

"I do?"

"Gilbert FitzHolland, sergeant-at-law and diligent witch hunter? Goes about with a dog and hangman? Difficult to miss."

"Oh, yes—him, too."

"Precisely." Collin toyed with a chess piece. A queen. "The only thing shielding you at present is a poetical claim to be the good and diligent Duke Buckingham's daughter . . ."

She thanked God for the momentary impulse that produced that lie. Her one right move so far.

". . . but impersonating a noblewoman is also a crime."

Naturally. More second-millennium thinking. Breathing seemed to be a crime, for however long you could manage it. She expected the

Middle Ages to be backward, with religious persecution and outhouse plumbing, but not some Shakespearean Afghanistan—a madhouse where whatever was not mandatory was illegal. And hideously punished. Nothing prepared her for this. Not Jo's offhand history lessons or Edward's ardent courtesy. In all the breezy talk of burning, hanging, and quartering, Sir Collin had yet to use the word *trial*. Clearly the Magna Carta was not all it is cracked up to be. "What is the penalty for impersonation?"

"How ever could it matter when you already face hanging and burning?"

"I am trying to plan my day."

"Trust me, my lady, the penalty is trivial compared to being a witch or traitor. If impersonation is the worst you must confess to, consider yourself truly fortunate." Collin sighed, looking down at the chessboard, trading the queen for a knight. "Thank goodness the worshipful duke—your father—is a true gentleman who might well have mercy on a wayward but repentant daughter, even one he has only just met."

"Really?" If so, she adopted herself into the right family.

He arched an eyebrow, "You must know him better than I."

"Of course," she corrected herself. "My father is the very soul of mercy."

"So I have heard. But you must see him to plead your case," Collin reminded her. "And he is now with the king, in Coventry. If Fitz-Holland or Lord Scales have their way, by the time my lord Buckingham hears your tale, you will be nothing but an amusing anecdote."

"Can I appeal to the lord of the castle?" Someone ought to be willing to hear her case.

"Lord Berkeley?" Collin laughed. "He lives in dread of such people as Duke Henry Holland of Exeter or Lord Scales. As does anyone with a dram of sense. The last Lady Berkeley so displeased Countess Margaret of Shrewsbury that Lady Berkeley ended her days in a castle dungeon. And she, too, was a Stafford. Pretty as you are, Lord Berkeley will not even want to see you."

He set down the knight and straightened up. "As you must well know, one of your good father's favorite manors is at Greenfield, on the far side of the Severn. FitzHolland has sent for a reliable Stafford retainer who knows both of Duke Buckingham's daughters."

She sank slowly onto the day bed, thinking she had better enjoy these accommodations now; the next place they put her would not be so pleasant. What a weird looking-glass world. She claimed to be a duke's daughter—apparently a crime—but no one demanded her identification, since no one had any. Not the duke's real daughters. Nor Buckingham himself. No fingerprints. No photo IDs. No DNA. No credit checks. You were who you claimed to be—for as long as you convinced people. Which was why her speech carried such weight. Especially amid such babble—since arriving she had heard a couple of West Country accents, Court English, as well as Latin, French, and Welsh. The Middle Ages could also be ultramodern, a complex civilization that did not run on print. Voice checks and coded speech were very third millennium. Just to prove her wrong, some hapless flunky had to get into a boat and row across the estuary, risking wind, tide, and whatnot, then hunt up someone on the duke's estate in Wales who had seen his real daughters—and convince this stranger to row back and have a look at her. No wonder they got upset at impersonation.

Collin noted the open book. "Christine de Pizan—were you reading her?"

"Yes." She looked up from the couch, alerted by his change in tone. Men are not naturally conversational—when they start to make talk it means they have something on their minds.

"Do you like her?" he asked, taking things awfully coolly, standing there in his blue silver-studded steel coat and knee-high boots, discussing French literature—but it was not his neck in the noose.

"What I have read, I like." Hard to tell from a title page and half a paragraph.

He nodded happily. "She is great. I met her, when I was very young and she was very old. In Paris—back when we had Paris." Reminiscence ended in a rueful laugh.

She stared hard at him, not sure how much to trust this friendly conversational Sir Collin. "What would you do? I mean, if you were in my place."

That made him laugh out loud—clearly Collin did not much like her chances. "I am serious," she insisted. "How would you deal with FitzHolland and Lord Scales?"

Collin sobered up, "First and foremost, I would be Duke Buckingham's daughter." She nodded flatly; that went without saying. "And for Heaven's sake," Collin urged, "stop striving to make matters worse."

"How do you mean?" She desperately wanted to make things better—not worse. But she saw no way of doing it.

"Stop doing things to provoke people." He sounded earnestly concerned, as if—despite appearances—he was genuinely on her side. Something Collin excelled at; no matter what you caught him doing, no matter how deep and involved the lie—it was "all for your own good."

"What sort of things?"

He rolled his eyes. "Asking them for boiling water. What in God's name made you do that?"

"I was thirsty." Could she manage to explain the germ theory of disease? Probably not without compounding her crimes.

"Then ask for beer, or a good Bordeaux," Collin suggested. "These silly maidservants thought you were preparing a potion."

"I will try to keep my requests within reason." Much more of this, and she would surely go mad.

"Good for you. And for God's sake, get rid of that rose. Having it sit there in a cup of water is an open admission of guilt." He reached back and lifted the latch, studying her intently. Collin had that knack for making you feel you had his full attention. He seemed to have something he wanted to say, but did not quite dare. Very understandable. Witchcraft was a communicable crime. As risky as AIDS, and far easier to catch. She herself had been sniffed out by a dog.

Seeing he would not say what was on his mind, she could not help asking, "Do you have a wife named Bryn?"

"Bryn?" He gave her a puzzled penetrating look and then shook his head. "No. I am unmarried."

An improvement. She stood up, wishing she could get him to stay—but short of telling the truth, she had nothing to hold him with. One obvious question occurred. "What is the month, day, and year—anno Domini?"

"You really don't know?"

"No," she admitted, "I don't."

"You are, indeed, a strange one. Today is Saint George's Day, and tomorrow is Saint Mark's Eve. Which makes it Wednesday the twenty-third of April, in the year of our Lord, 1460."

April 23, no wonder it felt like spring. And 1460. Months must have passed since Edward got lost in Wales—half a year at least. Would he remember her? Silly thought, but natural under the circumstances—at least from what Collin said, Edward was still alive. Had he made it to Calais? She did not dare ask. Any curiosity about Edward of March was dangerous to both of them.

"Is there anything else I may do for you?" Collin inquired.

She looked squarely at him, "I do certainly hope so. I very much want my freedom—to be able to leave here without fear of Fitz-Holland, Lord Scales, and the like." Not to mention grotesque monsters like Le Boeuf and his witch-sniffing hound.

"As do we all," Collin heartily agreed. "I promise you I will do what I can."

"Thank you. I am very much in your debt." The last words she ever expected to say to Collin Grey—any Collin Grey, least of all a medieval one.

"Think nothing of it," he told her. "You are the one doing me a favor."

"Really?" What did smooth-spoken Sir Collin plan to get out of this? She had gone through her pockets, and the results were unimpressive—all that left was her.

He grinned wickedly, "How often does a simple knight get to serve a duke's daughter?"

She returned his smile, nodding solemnly, "The entire Stafford family very much thanks you."

"Who could ask for better?" Collin bowed and backed out, closing the oak door behind him. The latch fell, and the magpie flew off as well, leaving her totally alone. But with a bit more hope. Here at last was true chivalry, a "simple knight" ready to do a good deed for a fair damsel—a duke's lost daughter, no less. Ridiculous. But what other explanation was there? She turned the problem around in her head. He did not seem to be lying—at least not about helping her. Nor about the date or about being a bachelor. That last part meant the parallelism was not complete. The similarities between this young nobleman and her Collin were not inexplicable. They looked alike because they were related—however distantly. And Collin and Joanna were Grey family names, reissued through the generations. But his marriage to Bryn was a chance pairing, not likely to be repeated.

Neat, but not near enough. Any such "natural" explanation sounded way too pat. Of all the men in medieval Gloucestershire, why did Sir Collingwood Grey come through her door? Hidden forces were at work here—but that went without saying.

She noted an immediate change of heart among the serving women, who so far had shunned her like the pox—afraid she would throw some spell over them. Or drag them to the stake with her. Now there was a scratch at the door. The latch lifted, and a curly-haired girl entered, carrying an iron pot. Putting the pot down on the table, the girl turned and vanished without a word. Robyn lifted the lid and sniffed. Beer. Just as Collin suggested. Pouring some into a cup, she found it warm but thirst-quenching. Stronger than the alewife's brew, and this time flavored with cinnamon.

Remembering the wine on Lord Scales's breath, it dawned on her that nobles drank only wine and ale. And maybe hard cider and brandy, if they could get it. No tea, no coffee, and definitely no water. An alcoholic aristocracy—a government that went about permanently hammered—no wonder England was in such bad shape.

She felt tipsy herself. Another serving woman entered, set down a change of clothes, and withdrew. An intriguing outfit—a long white silk chemise, then a loose yellow gown that slipped over her head, with sleeves that buttoned from wrist to elbow, cinched at the waist with a red leather belt. A sleeveless red jacket elaborately trimmed in cloth-of-gold went on top of the gown, buttoning tightly down the front. Elegant yet flattering—and she had feared ending up in rags. Collin must have picked it out. He always had an eye for women's figures and great taste in clothes. He had spent hours dress-shopping with her in Beverly Hills—which should have told her immediately that the man was married. But this Sir Collin claimed to be a bachelor. Forsooth. Perhaps he was a better liar than she thought. Or mayhap he was gay.

She slid Joy's clunky gift necklace inside the gown—not to ruin the effect. It had not saved her so far, but who could tell? She needed all the help she could get. Her yellow linen gown and the red wool gold-trimmed jacket layered her in Stafford colors. Crimson slippers completed the ensemble. Closing her eyes, she tapped the slippers together, saying, "There's no place like home." Nothing happened—but it never hurt to try.

She turned about, admiring her outfit, wishing for a mirror. Another knock came on the door; serving women returned with a meal of smoked fish, meat pie, and fig pastries glazed with sugar and honey. Also more beer. Strange how decent treatment could bring back your appetite—she felt hungry for the first time since that gut-wrenching scene at the bridge. So long as it looked properly cooked, she would give it a try.

The women complimented her on her dress and figure, helping to get the gown to hang right. "There, you look lovely m'lady. Doesn't she? Like a lady in a song, trim but womanly. How do you keep your figure so firm?"

"Yoga," she told them. "And three evenings a week at the health club. Dancing and rearranging furniture does the rest."

"Health club?" They stared at her, completely puzzled.

"You know, a gym." But they did not know, so she had to explain. The concepts were not so foreign—they knew the value of diet and exercise. And they had heard tales of Turkish harems, where women spent their days in steam baths, being massaged by sturdy young blackamoors, who had their privates sliced off "to make it decent."

They giggled and then told her, "When you said 'health club' we thought you had been beaten with a beauty stick."

"It can be like that, but I do not do the stuff that really beats you up. I cannot even stand jogging."

"Jogging?" Another futuristic concept.

"Running through the country for exercise. Hard on the legs, and I don't like it."

They agreed it sounded daft. "Running through woods and fields, tripping on your skirts . . ."

"Well, you do not wear skirts to jog." Happy to find them so friendly, she described a typical jogging outfit—shorts, sports bra, T-shirt, and running shoes.

Absolutely aghast, they asked where she came from. "Staffordshire," she replied cautiously, unsure where the Staffords had their home. It seemed a good enough guess.

"That cannot be in Avon. Or even in Herefordshire. No wonder she is so innocent—living way off in the hills like that." They cooed over her, patting her short hair into place and making last adjustments to her gown. "Listen lamb, the men hereabouts are not what you are used to. Begging m'lady's pardon, but none of them are blackamoors with their balls cut off. Any woman who goes out into our woods and fields bare up to her ass had better be an awesome shrewd runner."

She promised not to try jogging anytime soon. They left, still laughing. Later the curly-haired girl came back to change the chamber pot. Beer, good feeling, and cheerful service went to her head. She could well imagine herself a duke's daughter—or able to pass for one—with servants ready to hop to her needs. This was more like the Middle Ages she had heard of. Hollywood overflowed with women who remembered their past lives—every one having been Mary Queen of Scots, or Eleanor of Aquitaine, never a scullery maid or fishwife. Clearly people in the past all led interesting, pampered lives—with a couple of countesses for every serf and serving girl.

Having finally come down where she ought to be, she treated herself to more Christine de Pizan, flipping through the big silver-studded book:

> . . . reasonable men ought to appreciate, cherish, and love women. They should not have the heart to dispraise those from whom all men are born. For there is no creature in the world a man should love more than her. It is ugly and shameful to find fault with the one who should be most loved, the one who does the most to give men joy.
>
> By nature man without woman can feel no joy. She is his mother, his sister, his loving friend . . .

What had Edward called her?—his "constant friend." Pretty sharp for the second millennium. She dragged the table over into the light, along with the best chair and the washstand. Liking the room even better this way, she read on.

Dusk caught her by surprise. Looking up, she saw the rearranged room growing dark, and realized she had neglected to reset her watch. She tried to estimate when sunset would be, so she could tell how many hours off her watch was—fortunately April and October were half a year apart, so the days were roughly the same length. And daylight savings did not apply.

The latch lifted again. She looked up from her watch. The serving women had been polite and obedient, knocking and announcing themselves. This had to be a man. Maybe Collin. She looked forward to thanking him and showing off her gown.

When the door swung wide, she saw Gilbert FitzHolland, holding a large candle. An unpleasant surprise. Even worse, there was a stranger with him, wearing mud-spattered red-gold livery—Stafford colors. FitzHolland raised the candle to let the duke of Buckingham's man get a better look at her.

The Stafford retainer rolled his eyes and shook his head. "She is nothing like our gracious lord Buckingham's daughters." He did not look happy at being hauled out of Glamorgan on a fool's errand.

FitzHolland apologized to the disgusted underling and then turned curtly to her. "You will come with me."

Cursing them for being so diligent, she bundled up her clothes and hiking boots, along with the rose and some fig pastries—secretly snagging the steel cup as well. It belonged to the de Berkeleys, but her need was greater than theirs. How unfair that this fellow had gotten here so fast. Why couldn't her masquerade have lasted longer? She considered brazening it out, demanding to know how FitzHolland could take the word of a some nameless oaf over that of the duke of Buckingham's daughter.

Instead she said a silent good-bye to her little room, with its tapestries and chessboard. Wherever they were headed was bound to be less inviting. She would miss Christine de Pizan's simple pleas for love and understanding between the sexes. Too bad she could not take the book, but it weighed forty pounds and must have cost a fortune, with its hand-copied text, silver studs, and velvet-gold cover—when she got home she would buy the paperback. FitzHolland led her back through the great hall, now nearly deserted. Trestle tables stood stacked along the walls. She heard the ghostly rattle of night birds roosting above the dusty battle flags. Crossing the shadowy inner ward, they entered the big, brooding shell keep, the oldest, most bloodstained part of the castle. Atop the massive carved door she saw the Berkeley coat of arms—a white chevron on a red shield sprinkled with white crosses. Gules, a chevron argent, with crosses gules—the heraldic blazon popped into her head. She could now read coats of arms as easily as she read medieval French.

Horrified by where they were headed, she tried to appeal to FitzHolland, "This is all a terrible mistake. I really, really should not be here."

"Silence, bitch," FitzHolland barked, "or I will have you bound and thrown in the cesspit."

There was no arguing with that. Stone walls closed in around her, cloaked in huge flickering shadows cast by FitzHolland's candle. The oldest parts of these ancient keeps were incredibly cramped and close, like tunnels cut in living rock. Despite the narrow darkness, she knew where they were going. Ahead, at the base of a bastion tower, lay the most famous stop on the Berkeley tour, the King's Gallery, where Edward of Caernarvon had been kept. The cell's wooden door now had a huge iron lock.

She watched FitzHolland get out the heavy key—big but simply made, with two flat L-shaped tangs—a design she had seen before. Turning it in the lock, he lifted a latch and swung the door aside. Stinking darkness lay behind the door, black as a pit bottom and smelling like a latrine. Lifting the candle, FitzHolland made an "after you" motion.

Candlelight flooded a small wood-floored cell with a trap door at its center. Rats scattered at the light. A slim girl with long dark hair sat on a window seat, staring glumly through the bars at the dark courtyard outside. Her bare feet were pulled up onto the seat to avoid the rats. She had on a simple white shift and a crown of dried flowers—a woolen shawl lay in her lap. Looking up, she let light fall on her face.

Robyn stopped and stared, so surprised FitzHolland had to plant his gloved hand in her back and propel her into the room, saying, "This way m'lady." She barely heard him. The black-haired girl in white sitting on the stone window seat was Jo's daughter, Joy.

⋯⊷⊜ The King's Gallery ⊜⊶⋯

*B*linking in the candlelight, Joy stared past her, straining to see. Getting a good look at FitzHolland, the girl turned listlessly back to the barred window. Clearly Joy hoped to see someone else. Who wouldn't? Robyn was mortally sick of the man herself. He had persecuted her for no good reason since the first hour she arrived. What had she ever done to FitzHolland? They had never so much as seen each other before today. Never even shared the same century. Whatever problems these people faced could not logically be her doing. But FitzHolland had that toady, turnkey mentality, despising her for being different, for daring to impersonate his betters. He made a smirking bow. "This being a king's cell, a duke's daughter should feel at home."

She refused to take the bait. So her dad had not been the much-beloved duke of Buckingham; he was still better than FitzHolland. Better than Lord Scales. Way better than any of them. He had been kind, hardworking, and loving, and raised her to believe in herself, to be a "great lady." And she would play the lady to the bitter end, even if they killed her for it; going to her death with her head high—like Queen Jane—just to gall her captors. No matter how long his miserable life lasted, FitzHolland would always be someone's flunky.

Seeing she would not answer, the sergeant-at-law turned and left, taking the light with him. She listened as the lock clicked shut and the latch dropped. Bootsteps faded into blackness and rats scurried across the dark planks at her feet. Letting her eyes adjust, she dimly made out the barred window on the opposite wall. The girl slumped beside it was an invisible presence—a soft breathing in the blackness. Robyn whispered, "Joy?"

The darkness stirred. "Do you know me?"

Good question. Reaching into blackness with her free hand, she found the nearest wall with her fingertips, drawing support from the wet stone—wishing she could climb right up it to get away from the rats. "Is your mother Joanna Grey, sister to Sir Collingwood Grey?"

"She is," was the wary answer, in the same cultured court accent as Collin's. Puzzle pieces fell into place.

"Then I somewhat know you." Here was Collin's secret. He came to Berkeley Castle looking to rescue a female prisoner claiming to be a noble's daughter—only it was not her. He had come looking for his niece. Nothing else made sense.

Following the wall with her fingers, she stepped high to keep from kicking a rat, and carefully avoided the middle of the cell. Beneath the trap door in the center of the floor was a dank thirty-foot-deep pit for disposing of privy waste, animal carcasses, and unwanted prisoners. She had looked down the ghastly shaft during her tour of Berkeley, shivering at the thought of being thrown down it alive. Now it lay directly under her feet. Cold, horrible smells welled up, making her picture the pit uncovered, though she knew it was closed. But any time her captors tired of tormenting her, they could just fling back the wooden trap and toss her in, to die in stinking darkness. She never doubted they would do it. King Edward of Caernarvon had died here—who was going to much care what happened to her?

Just as she reached the dim window, a black-and-white bird burst from between the bars, cawing madly. Jerking back, she stifled a terrified shout, flinging up her hands to protect her face. Wings flapping, the bird flew at her head, screeching in anger. She hit back, trying to shoo it off.

"Let her be," shouted Joy. "Stop batting at her."

"Tell it to the bird," Robyn replied, keeping her hands in front of her face.

"I am talking to the bird," Joy protested.

Peering from behind her hand, she saw her attacker circle the cell in a flutter of wings, landing back on the windowsill, looking straight up at her. It was the magpie. The black-and-white bird cawed at her, "Hela."

"Hello again," she replied warily.

Joy giggled in the dark. "That's her name—Hela."

"Hela?"

"Hela," chorused the magpie.

"Named for the Queen of the Dead," declared Joy. "She only wants to protect me."

"Quee-een," chorused Hela. "Quee-een Hela."

"Then why didn't she attack FitzHolland?" Robyn suggested—instead of scaring her silly.

Joy giggled again. "Hela is a big coward."

"Naw, naw," the bird cawed indignantly. "Quee-een Hela."

"Shush, you boastful bird," Joy silenced her spirited pet. Dim light filtering between the bars glittered off the girl's tear-streaked cheeks. Above her smile, her eyes were hollow from crying. Otherwise the child looked exactly like the Joy she knew—which really strained coincidence. There had to be a whole hidden dimension here she was just not getting. "Are you really a duke's daughter?" Joy asked.

Setting her rose and metal cup on the windowsill, she sat down beside the girl, drawing her legs up off the floor, leaving it for the rats. "My name is Robyn Stafford—but so far as I know, the duke of Buckingham is not marching to my rescue."

Joy laughed ruefully. "That would be much to hope for." The magpie mocked her laugh, mimicking it, making it sound silly rather than rueful.

Too bad really—there had been the off chance that she, too, was someone's double. Why not? Collin and Joy certainly were. But the man from Buckingham's estate said she looked nothing like the duke's daughters. Just her luck if her long-lost twin turned out to be some hardworking Staffordshire milkmaid no one cared a whit about.

"I am a duke's daughter as well," Joy informed her, "the natural child of Edmund Beaufort, duke of Somerset. Which makes us cousins, descended from kings."

"Kee-ings," Hela cawed proudly.

No such luck. Robyn's royal descent was purely nominal—but the child plainly enjoyed having something in common with her. So she humored her cellmate, saying, "Well, cousin, any chance *your* father is coming to free us?"

"No chance at all." Joy shook her head. "My father is in Heaven. Killed at Saint Albans when I was small."

Robyn offered her regrets, really meaning it; a powerful father would have been a godsend. Joy said she, too, was sorry "though I only saw my sire on state occasions. I am his bastard." She said it without shame, in fact with a deal of pride. "He sent me glittering presents on Christmas—which is my birthday. That's why I am called Joy. Children born on the Lord's Day are always joyful. And can never be tempted by the Devil."

Handy attribute. Being a bastard might not be bad, if it meant growing up rich, pampered, and descended from royalty. But it had not kept Joy from ending up in a cell. "I do very much miss the presents," Joy admitted.

"Why are you being held here?" Robyn asked as gently as she could.

"For witchcraft." Not surprising. But it sounded heartbreaking from a half-grown girl. Particularly one so matter-of-fact about it, like a modern preteen saying "shoplifting." Darn, they caught me with a bracelet at the Bon Marche—my third time, too. Now they will burn me for sure.

"What about you?" the girl asked. "Why are you here?"

"Oh, witchcraft as well." She settled for the short answer, trying to match the child's nonchalance. "That and carrying a rose." Plus impersonation of a noblewoman in drag—it amazed her how many offenses she'd committed in less than a day.

"What color rose?"

"White."

"Why-ite," whistled the magpie, doing a little hop-step.

Joy grinned at the bird's antics. "That explains it."

"Not to me." The rose had been so terribly romantic when Edward gave it to her—and had gotten her into endless trouble ever since. Not unlike Collin's gift phone. "What does the white rose mean?"

"You don't know?" Joy had that precocious child pitch in her voice, shocked and pleased to find an adult so ignorant. "The white rose is a Mortimer badge."

"That much I know."

"The duke of York's supporters wear it to remind King Henry that the duke descends from the Mortimer earls of March, giving him as good a claim to the throne as King Henry. Better, some would say." Her voice dropped. Even sitting in a prison cell, facing hanging or worse, she hesitated to speak treason. "King Henry's grandfather killed King Richard, son of the Black Prince, seizing the throne for himself. The duke of York descends through the Mortimers from King Richard's eldest brother—his mother being a Mortimer. King Henry's lawyers say the claim is invalid because it comes through a woman." Joy sneered at that sexist quibble.

"I suppose they had to find some reason." Robyn pictured herself happily preening at the mirror, dressing herself up in Mortimer colors, not knowing it would soon be a crime. "So FitzHolland supports the king?"

"Kee-ing," Hela cawed. Him, too, thought Robyn.

"All the Hollands and FitzHollands support King Henry. So do the de Berkeleys and the Staffords, making it strange to see you championing York."

"I am an odd Stafford," she admitted, having not meant to champion anyone—or even be here. "Who do the Greys favor?"

"Ourselves, mostly. Lord Grey de Ruthyn and Sir John of Groby are King Henry's men. Grey of Powys backed the duke, but since the sack of Ludlow I ween he has seen the silliness of that. Nowadays only a fool favors York."

A fool like me, thought Robyn. Facing certain hideous death, even the despairing wretch at the bridge denied supporting York. "But some people must secretly favor him?" she suggested.

"Lord, yes." Joy nodded eagerly. "Everyone does. London loves the duke. So do the commons. Even some of the better sort favor him, like the Nevilles and Lord Clinton."

"Why?" What could be worth such heinous punishment?

"Because King Henry is mad." Joy said it casually, without a twinge of fear in her voice. Raised amid hereditary power, Joy was far more afraid to say the duke of York was descended from a Mortimer than to call the king a madman.

"Really?" When Edward talked of Mad King Henry, he had sounded flip and irreverent—making it seem like a nickname, like Good Queen Bess, or Old King Cole.

"Mad as a March hare. The poor pious soul cannot help it." Even an imprisoned witch-girl could pity a stricken king. "Madness is in his family. His grandfather was king of France and went berserk with a lance, killing four men before he could be subdued. They kept him confined in a palace, screaming in terror, raving that he was made of glass and would break if anyone touched him." Joy relished the details of royal tragedy—like episodes in an endlessly popular soap opera. "King Henry does not have it that bad—but there was a whole year when he did not know himself. For months he refused even to talk. And on his best days, he does not want to be king. You can tell just by looking at him."

"You have seen him?" Robyn had stood for almost an hour in London to see the queen drive past, but had not been able to tell much about Her Majesty's mental state.

"I saw him oftentimes in Coventry. He and the queen hold court there, since London will not have them. He dresses all in black and wears farmer's boots. Until someone says so, you do not know he is the king."

"Kee-ing," chimed Hela, striking a pose on the windowsill.

Joy had a child's eye for the truth. No matter what adults might claim, Henry's clothes said he did not want to be king. "Henry constantly gives away parts of his kingdom, mostly to friends and relations. He gave away our lands in France to get a young queen, and now she rules the country for him, overturning laws and squandering taxes on her favorites. Anyone who objects is judged a traitor. But the duke of York is the king's close kin and tried to keep King Henry from ruining the nation." Her voice dropped. "Secretly, nearly everyone hopes York will succeed. No one likes living under a mad king and a French queen. Whenever it comes to blows York wins—but in the end he always gives in. A mad king is still king." Joy made it sound like a national death sentence.

"Kee-ing," cawed Hela, thoroughly enjoying herself.

"So no one dares to complain?"

"Not now." Joy shook her head. "Not with York beaten. Not if they want to live. These are terrible times. Last May there was a bloody rain in Bedfordshire, and at Lamastide a Shropshire knight gave birth to a two-headed calf, then the king's army sacked Ludlow, driving out the duke, and now Holland's men scour the West Country for York's supporters. Have you seen Lord Scales?"

"I am afraid I have."

Joy shivered. "Lord Scary, if you ask me."

That's for sure. Leaning back against the barred widow, she stared at the darkness. No chance of getting a fair hearing here-and-now. Nothing she could say would set her free, least of all the truth—not when a mad king made honesty a hanging offense. Speaking your mind could cost you your head. Or worse.

"Where do you come from that you know so little?" Joy asked.

"America." Land of the blissfully ignorant.

"Where is that?"

"Far away across the sea." And then some. She unwrapped her clothes bundle, taking out a fig pastry. Breaking it, she offered half to Joy. The girl took it at once, stuffing it in her mouth; a sure sign they were not feeding her much. Robyn gave her the other half as well, feeling guilty for the good meal she had gotten—wishing she could give Joy a meat pie to go with it. "What of Edward, the earl of March?" she asked, giving the girl another pastry. How much hope could they pin on him?

"He is the duke of York's oldest son." Joy devoured the second pastry more slowly, breaking off part for the bird. Hela pecked eagerly at the offering.

How strange to actually be in Edward's time, surrounded by people who knew him. Or knew of him. Hoping not to hear anything bad about Edward from her opinionated fellow prisoner, she casually asked, "Have you seen him, too?"

Joy smiled happily. "Many times."

She need not have worried—Joy had plainly fallen for him as well. "What's he like?"

"He's wonderful. We used to visit him at Ludlow. He is so fearless and smart, and kind. He cares for everyone, noble or common, and always greets you with a smile. Never treats you like a child or thinks less of you for being female." That sounded like Edward. And being heir to the Duke of York meant he stood in line for the throne, if you thought the crown could pass through a woman.

Joy went on in hushed tones. "When he was my age, he led an army to free his father. Now he has grown up to be a great earl, the future of the House of York. People trust and respect the duke—but they love Edward."

Hearing such a heartfelt endorsement made her miss him all the more—wishing Edward had been here to greet her, instead of Lord Scales and Gilbert FitzHolland. What was the use of having a knight if he could not come to your rescue? "Where is Edward now?"

"In Ireland, visiting his father. He arrived this Saint Patrick's Day, much to the delight of the Irish." Joy got a kick out Edward's showmanship—but Ireland sounded like a long way off. Much as she might like to, Robyn could not just wait for her knight to come rescue her. Somehow she needed to get out of this cell on her own.

Seeing a child behind bars brought home the horror of her situation—more even than being there herself. Her own plight had such a huge tinge of unreality to it. For all she knew, the spell would suddenly whisk her away, taking her back to modern times. Or turning her into Mary of Scotland. Or Lady Godiva. But this girl was securely at home, condemned by her own time and people. Robyn could barely imagine what it was like to be nine years old or so, locked in a stone cell above a waste pit, only taken out to be scolded and tormented. Awaiting some mockery of a trial before men already convinced of her guilt— all in the name of justice and godliness. It made her want to scream.

Yet Joy herself seemed mainly bored by incarceration, taking to being a prisoner the way Edward took to knighthood; not as some impossible adult task, but as part of her being, something she meant to excel at. Personally, Robyn did not plan to make a career out of being a prisoner—especially in this stinking hole. She already had plans to get out; fingering the iron necklace hidden inside her gown, she felt the curious shape of the heavy flanges, picturing the key

FitzHolland had used to open the cell door. They seemed an obvious match. She tried to remember everything Joy—the other Joy—had told her about the gift. All Joy had said was that she would need the necklace, and it would help keep her safe. Not much to go on. But if it got her out of this cell, that was a giant step in the right direction.

Nothing could be done until the castle completely quieted down, so she set her watch to wake her at midnight local time. Or what she thought would be midnight. Impressed by the digital readout, Joy watched in awe as the numbers changed, whispering, "Are you really a witch?"

"Not exactly. I was in a coven for a short time—but that turned out badly, disastrous actually. This is just a clock."

"But the numbers change on their own and glow in the dark, and it fits on your wrist." And she had yet to hear it chime.

"I guess that is magic," Robyn admitted. "Why do they think you are a witch?"

Joy shrugged, "Because I am. We are all witches in my family, have been for ages. I took in witchcraft with my mother's milk." She tried to sound nonchalant, but it was a heavy admission to make in the dark chill of King Edward's death cell. "Not bad witches," Joy hastened to add. "Not most of us anyway. We do not worship the Devil or burn babies. But we still do sinful things."

"Like what?"

"Love potions. Witches Sabbaths. Legerdemain. Putting spells on our enemies. I tried to hex FitzHolland, but it did not take. He has some protection from spells, through Le Boeuf—or maybe from the dog." Barrister the baleful witch hound. Hela gave a scornful bark. Laughing, Joy stroked the bird, saying, "Hela is my familiar spirit."

"Hela." Happy at hearing her name, the bird hopped up on Joy's wrist, preening and repeating her call. "Hela. Quee-een Hela."

"How were you caught?"

"Our coven was uncovered in the midst of a Sabbath. Everyone got away but me. I tried summoning Uncle Collin here to save me—but that did not work either."

"Not by much." She told her how Collin had been there that afternoon—no doubt looking for her.

Gleeful to find that her spell even half worked, Joy sat up, saying eagerly, "We must get word to him somehow. They may suspect him, and mean to use me as bait. They already offered to free me if I named the adults in the coven."

"And you refused?"

"Oh, no. I gave them a great list of names. Headed by the countess of Shrewsbury, and the earl of Wiltshire, King Henry's rapacious treasurer, and his countess, who is the queen's lady in waiting. All are evil, with blood on their hands, and would not be much missed—though none to my knowledge are witches."

Robyn stared at her pint-size partner in crime, astonished at how medieval children were shoved into adulthood. At nine years old Robyn had been in the fourth grade—proudly starring in a traffic-safety video—not trying to bring down the government with charges of witchcraft or casually using words like *rapacious*.

"It did no good," Joy admitted wistfully. "They wanted to hear other names. But I kept insisting, and inventing details—spells said, curses cast, trips to Witches' Sabbaths. Eventually they stopped asking. Now I am just waiting, and praying for a church trial."

"Why?" Robyn had heard the usual horror stories about the medieval church, with its Crusades, Inquisitions, and human bonfires.

"Church courts are by far the best," Joy assured her. "No juries. And they usually only give out fines and penance. Several dozen Hail Marys could set us both free. Also they don't allow dog evidence."

Score one for the God squad. "Would regular courts let that witch hound testify?" She pictured Barrister barking at her from the witness box.

"Not if you get a sober judge. Unless it's a jury trial—then anything could happen. A lot depends on your lawyer. A smart Gray's Inn lawyer could get a jury to listen to a dog. A really litigious one can get testimony from a toad." Law had not changed a lot in five hundred years.

"It seems a really desperate witch like you should know a spell to get us out of this cell."

Joy laughed. "If I did, would I be here? On Sabbaths we go on Witches Flights, but they are journeys of the spirit—you return to where you started." No help there. Joy dropped her voice. "But it is possible to escape from here."

"Really?"

"King Edward did."

"I thought he died here." In grossly unpleasant fashion.

"He did," Joy whispered. "They caught him and brought him back. Escaping does not always mean getting away. Yet he did get out of this cell and out of the castle as well. Only he had help, a loyal servant had the key to that door, and a disguise. Once past the door, he slipped right out of the sleeping castle."

Once past the door. Robyn fingered the necklace at her throat. She had gone over the options—walls were solid stone, the window barred, the ceiling high out of reach, beneath the floor lurked the castle pit—if they got out, it had to be through the door. Her cellmate sighed, "Someone should send us a file or a key in a meat pie."

"Maybe someone will." She felt the flat tangs hanging from the heavy necklace, trying to judge their shape. "How long until the castle goes to sleep?"

"Not until midnight. When the matins bell rings in the church."

"Will there be guards?"

"Only a watch on the walls looking out."

That sounded way too easy. "No guards in the halls, or at the doors and gates?"

"Why should there be? No one needs to guard locked doors inside a stone keep. Unless Lord Berkeley fears being murdered in his sleep— then he might have men at his door." Despite horrific punishments, a wealth of edged weapons, and a slipshod sense of justice—this was an incredibly trusting age. No personal ID. No drug tests or breath checks. Archaic locks. Scant internal security. Castle walls kept the public out with minimum human supervision. Why keep watch over sleeping stone? First and foremost, Berkeley was a home and a fortress—not a prison—the cell they were in was just a makeshift lockup, a short stopover for unfortunates on their way to the pit or gallows. Even a king could not count on being lodged there for long. "What's life like in America?" Joy asked—plainly bored by talk of escape, when they could not even get through the door.

"America is a big place. The part I lived in is called Hollywood. It is warm the year around, and we make a business of entertaining— parties, feasting, putting on shows. I suppose that is why we know so little."

"It sounds heavenly."

Hollywood had its charms, especially compared to being locked in a dark stone cell above a cesspit. "It can be a lot of fun. But I was tired of it, you know, looking for something new. Something different." She had succeeded spectacularly. This was new and different, beyond anything she ever imagined.

"Is that why you came here?"

"Sort of. A miscarried spell brought me here."

Her cellmate sympathized. "If even one of my spells had worked, I would not be here, either."

To pass the time, she amazed Joy with tales of the future—music videos, Web TV, the home shopping channel, Euro Disneyland, whatever modern wonders came to mind. Her cellmate took it all as gospel. Being a witch-in-training, Joy was a devout believer in sprites, goblins, ghosts, faeries, and necromancy. She knew only herbal remedies and naturally assumed the sun went around the earth. She used words like *litigious* and *legerdemain*—but *science* was not in her vocabulary. Nothing the third millennium had to offer seemed outlandish—not missions to Mars, not no-cal soda. Halfway through her description of tomorrow, Robyn realized Joy had fallen asleep, slumped on the window seat, her shawl trailing off her lap onto the dark floor.

She marveled at how the sleeping girl resembled the Joy she knew. And how different her life was. The Joy she knew played at being a witch; this girl lived it, under appalling conditions, in the face of ghastly penalties. Shivering at what she had seen—or just heard—Robyn knew way more than she ever wanted to about hanging, beheading, and disemboweling. Yet this witch-child slept easily, her head resting on bars set in stone.

Making a pillow out of her denim jumpsuit, she slid it between Joy's head and the bars. Wedging herself onto the narrow seat next to the sleeping girl, she tried to go to sleep herself. A near impossible task. Way too much had happened. Way too much was still happening. Before she could even hope to sleep she had to decide where she should wake up.

She still held tight to the hope that at any moment she would be whisked out this spell. The longer things went on, the less likely that seemed. But it could happen—today had conclusively shown that anything was possible. Yet if she woke up anywhere but here, she would be leaving this sleeping girl alone in the cell. Already she felt responsible for the child, and could not bring herself to abandon Joy in exchange for some magical get-out-of-jail-free card. So she made a deal with herself—silly and nonsensical, since she had no real power over anything—but nonetheless an important personal commitment. "I can wake up here," she told herself, relaxing for the moment her absolute need to get home. "But once I get her out of this cell, then it's home as quick as I can." That settled, she lay back against the cold bars and went to sleep.

Her watch woke at the witching hour on Saint Mark's Eve. Shutting off the beeping, she sat staring into darkness with no notion where she was. For a few magical moments she was just plain Robyn Stafford again—on vacation somewhere, not due back at work until next week. But what sort of resort was this? Cold, dank, and incredibly foul? And why was she sleeping sitting up? Slowly the whole weird impossible day came back to her. The morning drive. Meeting the coven at Hetty Pegler's Tump. The disastrous ritual. Gilbert FitzHolland. Lord Scales. Sir Collingwood Grey. Her failed impersonation. And finally being lodged with Joy in the incredibly foul King's Gallery. Welcome to the Middle Ages.

Being whisked back home looked like the least of her worries. Groaning, she straightened herself out, feeling stiff and cold. Retrieving her cup and rose from the window sill, she tossed out the water, carefully tucking the bedraggled rose into her clothes bundle. Off in the darkness, she heard the matins bell toll in the Berkeley church tower. She had set her alarm two or three minutes early—not bad for a time sense five hundred years off. Maybe her watch was magic. Reaching over, she shook the sleeping girl, whispering for her to wake up. Joy stirred, asking, "What's happening?"

"Nothing yet. Do you think the castle is asleep."

"Of course, dead asleep." Just like Joy had been.

"If I got us out of here, is there anywhere we could run to?"

Joy sat up, rubbing her eyes with her fists. "Greystone is a couple of days north of here. Get there, and Collin will see us safe." Joy had infinite faith in her uncle.

"Do you want to risk it?"

Joy nodded eagerly. "Anything to get out of here."

Her sentiments as well. Reaching beneath her gown, she pulled out the heavy iron necklace. Handing it to Joy, she asked, "Have you ever seen this before?"

Joy could barely see it now, but Robyn could hear the clanking as the girl examined the necklace. "Not that I remember," Joy confessed. "What is it?"

"It might be the key to this cell. At least it looks like it could be."

"Where did you get it?" Joy whispered, fully awake and sounding excited.

"That is the weird part. I think you gave it to me."

"When was that?" Joy did not sound near as surprised as she should have.

"It was given to me by a girl named Joy—who looks exactly like you. Only she lives in the far, far future." Or she would live—a half a millennium from now.

Joy sighed, handing back the necklace. "There is something more to being a witch, something I did not tell you."

"What's that?"

"Please do not get mad or upset," Joy pleaded.

"I will not hold it against you," Robyn promised. What could Joy be hiding? They had already ruled out all the useful stuff, like invisibility and teleportation.

"We are immortal," Joy whispered. "Or at least, we do not die like normal people. If they execute me, I will be reborn. In the same body, but in another age." That explained a lot. If Joy was a witch and Collin a warlock, their reappearance half a thousand years hence might be unnatural, but not at all coincidental. It might even be planned.

"Then this girl in the future could have been you? Reborn in another time?"

"Seems like she would have to be me." Joy sounded immensely relieved that she did not take offense at a witch's immortality. "A lot of people get angry when they find out we live forever. But it is not as useful as it sounds. You still have to die—and with a witch they make that as unpleasant as possible. And when you are reborn, you are really reborn, as a baby. You don't come back knowing who you are, or who you were. I barely remember any of my past lives."

Robyn smiled. "In my time a lot of people think they have that kind of immortality."

"But with witches it is real. And we do not have to do anything for it. We don't have to be good, or pious, or give to the poor. It just happens. And we do not come back better, or worse, just the same. It is probably why people do not trust us."

"Well, I trust you." She hefted the necklace. "In fact, I am trusting that the future you 'remembered' is just what we need to get out of here."

"Thank you so very much." Joy leaned over and kissed her on the lips, showing that strange medieval mix of forwardness and innocence.

Time to attack the lock. She swung her feet down onto the rat-infested floor, feeling her way along the wall over to the door. Breaking and entering had never been her specialty, but she had twice gotten into a borrowed Mercedes after locking the keys in the ignition. Getting through this door could not be much harder, especially if she had magical help. She found the door in the dark, then the keyhole. Selecting the tang on the necklace that looked most like the key, she eased it into the lock, feeling for the tumblers. It took some twisting and turning; then suddenly she felt the lock turn. The bolt slid back. Eagerly she leaned against the door.

No go. The lock was open, but the latch on the far side was still holding the door shut. Damn. Telling Joy to hold on to the necklace tang to keep the lock open, she searched through the clothes for her VISA card. Sliding the card between the door and the stone, she felt for the latch.

And did not find it. Damn again. She pushed frantically on the card. She had the lock open, but the latch was keeping the door shut—and her VISA card was just too short to lift it. What a completely useless piece of plastic.

She took a deep breath. Calm down. You are almost out. Do not panic. Just get around this last little hitch. Taking hold of the necklace tang, she handed Joy the credit card, saying, "Your fingers are smaller. See if you can use this to lift the latch on the far side of the door."

Joy obeyed, pressing her slim fingers into the door crack. Robyn held the tang with sweating hands, praying this would work. Suddenly she felt the door give as the latch lifted, swinging outward. And she thought a credit card would not work in 1460.

Joy giggled. "Are you sure you are not a witch?"

"Only when it comes to locks." And foretelling the future.

Joy handed back the card. "What is this. It feels strange, smooth but stiff, not like wood or metal."

"A VISA card. Plastic money. Never leave home without it." Slowly she eased open the door. Outside, the cool dank hallway was blacker than the cell; bottom-of-a-mine-shaft black, and utterly silent. No wonder these people dreaded night. Back in L.A. evenings meant free time, dates, music, dancing, romance if you were lucky. It meant putting off deadlines and responsibilities until tomorrow. Clubs, coffee shops, freeways, and all-night supermarkets blazed with light. Dawn in the city could be downright dull and deserted. But in Berkeley Castle, night was still an act of nature. God had turned out the light, letting loose ghouls and demons, and "things that go bump in the night." Torches and candles were feeble and short lasting, and rightly so—the proper place for any decent soul was asleep in bed. Only witches and their ilk made use of the night. Which is what made those West L.A. candlelit "take back the night" marches so subversive. Women out at night have always been up to no good.

Collecting her things, she guided Joy out of the cell into the darkness. Closing the door behind them, she locked it and replaced the latch—leaving a mystery for the morning. Or next Friday afternoon, if they were callous about feeding prisoners. Let FitzHolland think they vanished into the night air—it might discourage pursuit. Holding on to Joy, she felt her way down the hall, with the lighter in her free hand—offering instant illumination if needed.

And ran right into pile of staves set against the wall, that fell with a crash and clatter you could have heard in Cornwall. Horrified, she crouched down, her heart hammering loud enough to wake the dead, expecting Berkeley Castle to be up in arms at once. But nothing happened—it had not been a burglar alarm, just careless storage, or someone's unfinished chore.

She set out again, soft-footed as she could, stepping over the fallen staves, with Joy firmly in tow. Every turn and stairway was right where she remembered—this was her third time through the keep, but the first time she had to find her own way in pitch blackness. It felt eerie, inching through the high dark castle, with no sound but soft breathing and the swish of skirts, fearing that at any moment she might blunder into someone. Following the left-hand wall, she found the chamber at the head of the forebuilding—where King Edward was finally done in, when the stench from the pit failed to kill him. Someone was snoring in the corner, fast asleep at the murder scene. She headed straight for the main door, with Joy at her heels, hoping no one had bedded down in the middle of the floor.

No one had. Coming to a stop against cold stone, she worked her way along the forebuilding wall to the massive wooden door. Naturally, it was locked—at least she did not have to worry about it being latched. Feeling about, she found the lock and went to work. Not having seen the key, she did not know which flanged tang on the necklace to use, making it harder. Working by touch, she tried different tangs, feeling for the heavy tumblers, freezing in fear when she heard the sleeper stirring. Joy crouched beside her, amazingly silent for someone so talkative. But this was the witching hour, and the girl treated lock-picking like a religious ritual.

Finally the lock gave, and the door swung open. She checked her watch—what seemed like an eternity had been less than twelve minutes. The Mercedes had taken longer. Guiding Joy out of the forebuilding into the courtyard, she shut the door behind them. It took more fiddling to lock it.

Straightening up, she found she could see again. Patches of pale moonlight illuminated the inner ward. Great hall, chapel, kitchens, and buttery all faced inward, casting shadows onto the lopsided quadrangle formed by the curving wall of the keep. She set out through the shadows, holding tight to Joy, going straight to the big inner gate. Soon as she reached the recessed gate, it was back to blackness. Here she had to use the lighter, flicking it on to find the lock. Picking the most promising tang, she put out the lighter and worked by touch, trying to move the tumblers. No luck. Wiping sweat off her hands, she changed tangs and tried again.

This time she succeeded, swinging open the big inner gate. Beyond lay the outer ward with the stables, barn animals, washing troughs, a low curtain wall, and a small single-story gatehouse. Locking the inner gate behind them, she led Joy straight to the outer gate—the last door between them and freedom. Followed by a straying cat.

She found the gatehouse dark and silent. Hopefully the porter was asleep. The final gate looked to be a simple affair, not as big or as fancy as the inner gate. With the castle cat rubbing against her legs, she fumbled through the smaller tangs until she found one that fit the lock. Sort of. None of the crude iron pieces was a perfect fit.

Hela came fluttering out of the dark to land on Joy's shoulder. Even the talkative magpie seemed to sense the importance of the moment, saying nothing for once. Instead, the bird tugged silently at Joy's long dark hair—seeming to be a signal between them.

"Someone is coming," Joy whispered. Robyn stopped struggling with the stubborn lock and listened, her heart hammering again. Heavy booted footsteps sounded in the barnyard behind them, headed for the gatehouse. Who the hell could that be at this hour of the morning? With her luck it had to be FitzHolland. Silently cursing this last obstinate lock, she pulled Joy away from the door, waiting in the shadows by the curtain wall. Footsteps entered the gatehouse and then stopped. A door scraped open. A couple more steps; then the door closed. Silence descended. Joy hissed, "He has gone to get the porter."

Leaping up, she attacked the lock again, having at most a minute or two to get it open. Bracing herself against the door, she put her full weight behind the tang, trying to shift the tumblers.

The tang snapped. She still had hold of the handle, but half the tang had broken off in the lock. Horrified, she dug at the lock with her nail, managing to extract the broken half. But what now? That had been her best-fitting piece. How unfair, she groaned in frustration, knowing it would take more than a VISA card to get them out now. Maybe they should just climb the wall. With something to use for a rope, they could find a stair leading up to the wall walk, slip through an embrasure, and lower themselves into the moat.

A door scraped open behind her. Bootsteps rang out, headed their way, accompanied by a light jingling. Shoving Joy behind her, she got out the lighter—not much of a weapon, but all she had. That and surprise. In the pitch darkness the flare of the lighter would be blinding. Then what? She hadn't a clue. Grab the man's sword and brain him with it? Better yet, put the blade to his throat and demand their freedom—that was what movie heroines did—but this was all too awfully real.

Bootsteps came closer, stopping right in front of her, so close she could feel the man's breath. He smelled of sweet lavender. She flicked on the lighter, thrusting it in his bearded face—at the same time shading her eyes.

Dressed all in red, the man had a sharp spade beard, a Robin Hood cap, and a big black bow across his back. She recognized John-Amend-All, the crimson bowman who had warned Edward of the ambush that first day in Wales. Grinning, he held out a gloved hand with a iron key in it, attached to a ring of similar keys. "Could you use this?"

She stared at him, surprised and looking silly, standing at the dark gate, holding up the fiery lighter. Lady Liberty in red-gold Stafford colors. As she took the keys, her finger slipped and the lighter went out.

When she flicked it back on, he was gone.

"Who was that?" Joy whispered.

"Tell you later." She jammed the key into the lock. It turned. The door swung open, and Joy let out a muffled hurrah, mimicked by Hela. As soon as they were through, Robyn closed and locked the door behind them, tucking the keys into her gown. Who knows when they might come in handy? Saying a silent, heartfelt good-bye to Berkeley Castle, she led Joy across the deep ditch and along the south moat, away from the village with its dogs and people. Skirting the moonlit water meadows, they climbed the wooded ridge and disappeared into the darkness under the trees. By the time the lauds bell tolled behind them, they had found the Roman road and were hiking north on dark worn stones laid down by the Caesars.

◆═ The Cotswolds Way ═◆

Birds chirped maniacally at first light from the trees by the road. Robyn felt dead tired. Roman roads were hell on slippered feet, and she had long ago switched to hiking boots. Despite being barefoot in the numbing cold, Joy proved surprisingly durable, so they made the most of these precious hours before anyone knew they had flown—following the road running north and east, straight across the flats between the Severn and the Cotswold Edge. Dogs in darkened villages barked at them, but they saw no other travelers.

By now they were miles from Berkeley, seven at least, maybe nine, and already beyond the Frome. But the girl was beginning to give out, and soon they had to get off the road. Sunrise on Saint Mark's Eve lay just beneath the Cotswold Edge. "A little farther," she whispered to Joy, "then we can rest."

Holding hard to her hand, Joy muttered, "Tease me not, I lack the strength."

"I know. We will quit the road and find a place to rest." That lightened the girl's spirits—but she had not said it just to please Joy. Pursuit would come trotting up this road, stopping travelers and inquiring at farmsteads, making the Roman road too dangerous by day.

Staggering along like this would certainly attract attention—a lady in a riding gown and hiking boots, dragging a half-awake child could not be all that common. She should abandon the road, get some badly needed rest, and then set out some way safer. But which way was that? To her left, dark open fields stretched out toward the Severn. On the other side of the road, beyond a flat bare fallow field, rumpled meadow and pasture climbed toward the high wooded Cotswold Edge, crowned by morning light.

Houses loomed ahead in the half-light. "Hela," cawed the magpie, who had already left the road, settling in a tall birch beside the fallow field. Thin bare branches stretched up into the paling sky. "Hela!"

"Hello," she called back, "we're coming." Taking the bird as an omen, she led Joy off the road into the fallow, doing her best to head due east, straight for where day was dawning over the Cotswold Edge. "We need to get away from the road," she told Joy. "Then we can rest."

"Right, rest," the witch-girl agreed sleepily, clinging to her for support. When she reached the birch tree, the bird flew off, leading the way. Beyond the bare plowed fallow a black stand of beech trees lined a stream dividing field from meadow. About a mile farther on the ground began to rise, blending into upland pasture. Here was water and cover, two of the things she needed most at the moment. Dawn song faded as the world grew light around her.

Half carrying the girl, she staggered over the last of the fallow field and into the trees—where she gratefully collapsed, lying down out of sight of the road. Robyn was determined not to be recaptured, but right now she desperately needed rest. Joy was already asleep. A fly landed on her, crawling about, licking her sweat. So what if it carried come horrible medieval disease; she did not have the energy to brush it off. Leaving the magpie to keep watch, she slid into an exhausted stupor, letting rustling leaves and the rippling brook lull her to sleep. Hopefully she would not wake up for at least five hundred years.

Hours passed. Dappled sunlight replaced the dawn chill. Above her the magpie cawed, "Hela, Hela, Hela . . ."

Her eyes flicked open. She heard sheep bleating in the background. So much for waking up at home. The bird was directly overhead in the smooth bole of a beech tree. "What's up?" she whispered. "Is someone coming?"

"Naw," replied the magpie.

She checked her watch, mentally adding the extra hours to make it medieval time—not yet noon. She had been in the middle ages for twenty-one hours, eighteen minutes, and fifty-three seconds—it just seemed like forever. Closing her eyes, she tried to sleep some more. No chance. She had way too much to think about. Had they discovered she was gone? Could they guess where she was headed? Would she ever get home? Clearly she would never get an ounce of sleep here and now except when utterly exhausted.

Sitting up, she looked around. Hela was right, there was no one nearby. Sheep grazed on the fallow. Farther off, a man on foot led a line of horses up the Roman road toward Gloucester. No sign of anyone looking for them. Thank heavens. For the moment she felt safe—a first for the Middle Ages. She was not being threatened, menaced, denounced, held prisoner, or stumbling through the night in her sleep. Leaving her free to deal with other problems—like thirst, hunger, and a desperate need to pee.

Joy lay curled alongside her, sleeping soundly, still wearing her crown of flowers in her long black hair. So let her sleep in. Joy was free. For for the first time in a long while she was sleeping in the open instead of in a cell—it would take more than sunlight and a rippling brook to wake her.

Getting up, Robyn found a secluded spot and relieved herself. Crouched down, with her head turned to keep a wary eye on the road, her new short hair fell across her face. She caught a whiff of the peach shampoo she used yesterday morning at Jo's—a tiny bit of the twenty-first century she had brought back with her. How strange to smell her own world from half a millennium away.

Luckily, girlhood in Montana helped prepare her for the Middle Ages, and not just by teaching her to ride. Gathering twigs and straw off the fallow, she used her lighter to start a fire. Filling her steel cup with stream water, she set it on the fire to boil. Actually, the cup belonged to Lord Berkeley, but she deserved some recompense for the trouble she had been through. While the water boiled, she gathered more twigs to feed the fire. A lot of work for a cup of warm water, but at least it would be clean.

By the time Joy awoke, brunch was laid out—the last fig pastry and a fire-blackened cup containing lukewarm water. Joy treated it like a feast—thanking her with a kiss. "This is amazingly aweful. First you save me; then you feed me. How outstanding!"

She smiled at the child's enthusiasm. "I have not saved us yet."

"You will," Joy assured her, confidently chewing. "Can I see the keys?"

Getting out the keys to Berkeley Castle, she gave them to the girl. Joy studied them while she ate, saying, "I must memorize their shape. Someday, I have to copy them."

"Someday far in the future." Robyn stared at the witch-girl, astonished at how much she resembled the Joy she knew at home. Pretty bloody amazing, as the Brits would say.

"Far, far in the future," Joy agreed. "Please let me see the necklace."

She gave it to her, and the witch-girl laughed. "What a pitiful copy." Joy held the keys next to the necklace. "This shows how hard it is to remember past lives." Clearly the future Joy had not known what she was making, or why.

While the witch-girl compared the keys to the necklace, Robyn got out her *Cotswold Way Guide*. When pursuit came, it would come up the Roman road to Gloucester, or up wagon tracks through Stroud and Painswick—but not along the Cotswold Way, a footpath that would not be laid out for another five hundred-odd years. She told the girl, "We have to stay away from the roads—it will be much safer using the Cotswold Way."

Joy looked up. Keys and necklace lay side-by-side in her lap. "What way?"

"The Cotswold Way."

"What is that?"

"A walking path, laid down in my time." Actually long before her time. "It runs from Bath to Chipping Campden, and right through Greystone. This guide lets us avoid the roads and towns." She showed Joy the map section nearest to them.

"Whoo," Joy whispered. "More witchcraft. Never have I seen a map so cunning and detailed, nor writing so neat."

"It is printing."

"I have heard of that," Joy declared proudly. "But I did not expect it to be so clear and crisp. How can a screw press be more perfect than a holy clerk's hand?"

"Must be witchcraft," Robyn admitted. "The path and waymarks will not be there, but land cannot have changed that much. The nearest landmark should be a tall wooded outcropping, with a ring fort at its crest—called Haresfield Beacon." Here less than a day, she was already in charge of finding their way. Hardly fair, but it could not be helped if they wanted to stay ahead of FitzHolland.

Burying the remains of the fire, she told Joy, "Time to go." Haresfield Beacon had to be somewhere above, so she set out on a footpath that wound up along the line of the trees. Someone must live upstream. Her *Way Guide* showed no towns in this part of the Edge—the nearest villages were Whiteshill and Randwick on the far side of Standish woods, no big places even by the third millennium. She could not be sure they existed here and now. Laid out to avoid towns and roads, the Cotswolds Way cut through the steepest, least peopled part of the Cotswolds, the scenic but unprofitable Edge—wild wooded tops better suited to birds and beasts than to people. Which very much fit her needs; the worst part of her strange new world was not knowing whom to trust.

Her mistrust was immediately tested. The footpath climbed past split-stone sheepfolds and empty shepherd's rests—but in less than a mile ran straight up to a little lime-washed cottage with black timber framing and roses twining by the door, becoming someone's garden walk. Washing was spread out to dry on the tangle of hawthorns that took the place of a hedge. Big spotted pigs slept placidly by the door. She turned to Joy, asking, "What should we do?"—sorely tempted to skirt the place.

"Knock on the door and see what is supper." The girl bounded up, pounding on the door. Inside a dog began barking. Hela barked back, alighting atop a hawthorn.

She braced herself, hoping Joy knew best. The cottage door opened, and a woman peered out, holding back a barking dog with sharp yellow fangs. She wore a floor-length dress beneath a blue wool cloak, and her graying braids were wrapped in tight Princess Leia–pancake coils. Pudgy white hands were speckled with blood. "Good noontide to you, m'ladies."

"Good noontide to you," Joy replied with a curtsy, swiftly crossing herself. "Pray, have you food for weary pilgrims?"

"Come in, come in," the woman ushered them into a soot-blackened kitchen, dragging the dog back by his leash and tying him in a corner. Half a gutted pig hung from the black rafters above a pot of hot barley. Big loops of stuffed intestines and bags of onions hung beside the half porker, whose grinning head sat on a sideboard amid white lumps of lard. Drops of dark blood dripped from the pig into the bubbling barley. Taken aback by this cheery soot-blackened butcher shop, Robyn left introductions to Joy—who seemed to be doing famously. Hela stayed outside.

"Where are you pilgrims to?" asked the woman, tossing her dog some scraps of pig meat to quiet him.

"Saint Albans," lied Joy with a smile. Saint Albans was a suburb of London, far off the other way from Greystone.

"Ach, so far, so far," the woman protested, swinging her pot off the hearth and laying out an iron griddle. "We have many fine and holy shrines hereabout. Painswick Abbey is just over the hill, and beyond that is Prinknash."

Joy shook her head. "Sadly, it must be Saint Albans."

"Hailes Abbey has the blood of Christ in a bottle."

"But we go to pray at the tomb of my father, who was killed at Saint Albans." That settled the woman, who turned out to be named Mary Margaret. Cutting slices of bacon, Mary Margaret laid the slices one by one on the griddle—enough for them, and her, and the dog, and anyone else who came along. Her blackened kitchen filled with the delicious sizzle of frying bacon.

"My father was the most well-beloved Edmund Beaufort, duke of Somerset." Joy was totally into her story, by now believing they were actually going to pray at his tomb.

"My Lord," mused Mary Margaret, selecting an onion, "the duke of Somerset. And you are his daughter?"

"His natural daughter," Joy replied proudly.

"Indeed," the farm wife nodded, cutting chunks of onion into the sizzling bacon grease.

"I am called Joy," the witch-girl added, "because I was born on Christmas Day."

"And your talkative friend?" Mary Margaret nodded at Robyn.

"She is my cousin, Robyn Stafford of Hollywood, and also a duke's daughter."

"The Holy Wood up by Coventry?"

"Oh, no," Joy shook her head, "a bigger and better Hollywood. Far and away, across the water, and much more miraculous. They live in huge glass houses and make moving pictures out of nothing." Amazingly, Mary Margaret took it all in, gladly serving them bacon and onions on big slabs of fresh baked bread, while chatting on about holy spots in the area. Her hands were bloody from being inside a pig, but the food was fresh off the fire and seemingly safe. By the time Robyn had washed the meal down with grainy ale, she felt pleasantly full and tipsy. Joy apologized to their host, saying they had to be going, "Saint Albans is yet a ways off."

Giving them bread to go, Mary Margaret kissed them both good-bye. On the far side of her house, past the tangle of hawthorns, the path reappeared, headed uphill. With wind and sun behind them, Robyn climbed the Cotswold Edge, getting a sweeping view of green pastures stretching away to the south and east, broken by patches of brown fallow and the thin line of the Roman road. Farther off, she saw the shining loop of the Severn, twisting totally about before becoming a flat silver sheet, merging with the Bristol Channel. Beyond it lay the black Forest of Dean, and the Welsh hills where she had met Edward. Or would meet him, centuries from now. Finally the path faded into pasture grass, leaving them alone in the vast landscape, with just the *Cotswold Way Guide* and her own good sense to guide her.

She had purposely not asked Mary Margaret for directions, to conceal where they were going—sticking to Joy's Saint Albans absurdity. Sighting a steep wooded promontory ahead that had to be Haresfield Beacon, she asked Joy if the girl knew the place. "It looks like Ring Hill," the witch-girl hazarded, "but I have never seen it so close."

Keeping the promontory to her left, Robyn plunged into the cool beech forest. Hela flew in ahead of her, dodging between the trees, calling as she went, seeming to know where they were headed. Trees parted, and at the crest Robyn saw the slumped wall and filled-in ditch marking the remains of a ring fort. Ring Hill. Just as Joy had said. And behind her Haresfield Beacon jutted out from the Edge, with a huge covered pile of cut timber stacked atop it. Literally a beacon, when lit it would be seen well into Wales. A surge of power swept through her, this place was strange, but not so strange that she could not find her way about. Even using a third-millennium map. Losing five hundred years had not left her helpless.

Joy was even more jubilant, with that child's impulse to make everything a holiday—even running from witch hunters—"Tomorrow is Witches Night, and we can dance to Hecate and summon her help—if we are not already home." Hela cawed happily overhead.

Maybe. Robyn meant to tackle the Middle Ages a day at a time. If she found food, clean water, and a place to sleep, she would be ecstatic—should that require supernatural help, so be it. On the far side of Haresfield Hill lay more woods; then they were back at the lip of the Edge, this time looking down into the Vale of Gloucester. Pastureland rolled away from the Edge in green waves, topped with white foamy flocks. Here and there, steeples rose above small clusters of thatched roofs—the Middle Ages were as religious as advertised. Joy pointed out the bell tower of Painswick Abbey and wanted to go begging, "As sure as God is in Gloucestershire we shall lack for nothing."

Robyn shook her head. "We did not escape to turn a profit. We need to make time while we are fed and rested." Joy looked disappointed, but Robyn had seen too many costume dramas with hapless extras burned at the stake. She was not about to turn herself in to the local abbot—not unless she was a lot hungrier. Keeping a low ridge between her and Painswick, she set off into the pastures, wading through flocks of bleating sheep.

Tired as she was, it felt delicious to have ten solid miles between her and Berkeley—a third of the distance to Greystone. With luck, she could be there tomorrow night. Walking through flowered pastures on a spring afternoon, surrounded by sheep and sunshine, hardly seemed like an escape from anything, unless it was the world outside. Bright wildflowers, green pasture, and brown plowlands formed a tremendous tapestry, decorated with tiny villages and tall abbey towers. Large sections on her map were marked off as "parks" and "ornamental grounds"—attempts to preserve some of this original stillness and beauty amid the hurly-burly of the third millennium. Seeing the cathedral town of Gloucester, shrunk to manageable size and lying by a loop of the Severn, she remembered what Joy had said—"As sure as God is in Gloucester." Even the witch-child thought of this as not just church lands, but holy ground.

At the next abbey, Prinknash, she broke down and let Joy go begging. The place was smaller, and less intimidating than Painswick, set on a wooded ridge overlooking Gloucester between Pope's Wood and Cooper Hill. Friendly openhanded monks offered them supper and lodgings for the night. She managed to turn them down, getting away with just bread, cheese, blankets, a joint of mutton, and a jar of cider, plus a little lantern and a stock of candles. Anything more would have been too much to carry. God's country indeed. Free food. Ready lodging. She could not remember a better Saint Mark's Eve—escape was almost too easy.

She passed the night in a shepherd's rest, between High Brotheridge and Witcombe Wood, a simple split stone lean-to, three walls and a slate roof faced away from the weather. Set right on the Cotswold Edge, it looked down on the Ermine Way—another Roman road running south and east toward Cirencester and the Vale of the White Horse. By building a fire on the open side, she was able to make it snug. Joy nestled in beside her, and she closed her eyes, lulled by a full belly and the sweet odor of dried sheep dung and wood smoke. This second night in the Middle Ages was a vast improvement over her first—which did not tempt her to stay. She had gotten Joy out of that cell—and so far as long-term survival went, she was just a drag on Joy's act. From the way Joy conned Mary Margaret and the monks at Prinknash, the witch-girl would soon be owning the place. She could go home with a clear conscience. Not bothering to set her watch, Robyn prayed for the fates to take her home.

"Hela, Hela," the magpie cawed at the new day, waking both her and Joy. It took only a moment to remember where she was—but for that moment she was home. She was Robyn Stafford, with a good job and a decent apartment. On vacation in England, greeted by a beautiful morning—with a day of hiking ahead. Then she remembered. Make that an extended vacation. She sat up and looked about. Time to carpe another diem—but for a moment, at least, she had been home—never doubt the power of prayer, not in God's own Gloucestershire.

Joy gave her a good-morning kiss. "Happy Saint Mark's Day, and a good Friday as well," the girl declared gleefully. " 'Tis the Goddess's Day, and tonight will be Witches Night." T.G.I.F. Thank Goddess It's Friday. This Joy was as much in love with magic as her modern reincarnation. And even more physically affectionate. Joy kissed her good night, and first thing on getting up in the morning—a trusting childish ritual Robyn went along with to keep the girl's spirits up.

She stared out over dewy landscape, wisps of hair blowing across her face, still smelling of peach shampoo, reminding her of home. High on the Cotswold Edge, she could no longer make out the Severn, lost in a heaving sea of meadow and pasture, broken by brown plowed islands of fallow. Already a connoisseur of medieval conditions, she decided that dawn in a dung-spattered rock pen beside a burnt-out fire completely beat awaking in a stinking cell atop the castle cesspit.

Two days ago, neither would have appealed much—now it made all the difference in the world.

Safe for the moment, and secure enough to think about personal hygiene, she had hopes for a bath. Whoever slept here last had fleas. It had been two days since her short immersion in Jo's clunky coin-operated shower. Since then she had walked or ridden almost thirty miles and slept in her clothes two nights running. The last time she so much as washed her face was in that little room with the unicorn tapestry off the great hall at Berkeley Castle. Her fellow fugitive sounded horrified. "A bath? Whyever for?"

"To get clean."

"But we are escaping," Joy protested, "flying for our very lives."

"So? I cannot wait until we are somewhere safe." By now she no longer counted on being whisked out of the Middle Ages at any minute. She saw medieval washing and flossing in her future. Unbelievable. "I feel like I have lice already."

"Lice are a sign of health. Cold and drafts are what kill."

"I can wait until the day warms up." It was too delightful a morning to argue disease theory. "First we need to get past the Roman road." The Ermine Way cut straight across their path. Beyond it lay the highest, most uninhabited part of the Edge, nothing but sheep, blue skies, and great swaths of woodland and high pasture. Birdlip Hill looked to be the best place to cross, where woods crowded down on both sides of the Roman road. She led Joy along the edge of Witcombe Wood to within a half mile of the road; then they plunged into the trees, where pigs rooted in the underbrush, breakfasting on grubs and tubers. She heard hoofbeats ahead—horsemen who left Gloucester at sunup climbing Birdlip Hill. Crouching amid the brush and pigs, she let the riders pass, waiting for the gap between them and the first of the foot traffic.

As soon as the hoofbeats faded, she took Joy's hand and dashed across the empty stretch of road into the wooded tangle on the far side. A deer broke cover, ambling across ahead of them—he, too, had been waiting for the road to clear.

North of the Roman road, she emerged from the woods onto an empty landscape, dotted with ancient burial mounds. Her bath came in a stream feeding into the River Churn, the most distant tributary of the Thames. Far downstream the tiny brook became the broad river flowing under London Bridge, which was always falling down in nursery rhymes. How weird to think that, but here it was, just a cold trickle in the Cotswolds. Naked and shivering, she remembered the scalding stream that came out of Jo's balky coin-operated heater. Had she known how long that hot shower had to last, she would have put every shilling she had into the silly contraption. She dried herself with a scratchy wool blanket. Even a simple morning bath had become a form of medieval torture.

Folding up her chemise and linen gown, she put on her pants, boots, and gold silk shirt, topped off by her red sleeveless jacket. A strange mix of the modern and medieval—but she felt fairly comfortable, and semiclean, making this day's hike even more of a lark. She gave her crimson slippers to Joy, who was delighted, despite their being several sizes too big. Sitting down, she hauled out her electronic journal and wrote:

Friday, 25 April 1460, Saint Mark's Day
　Just typing the date chills me, it seems so mad. Totally ridiculous, really. But here I am, sitting on a bank above the River Churn, which is really a stream. And I have been in the Middle Ages . . .

She called up the exact figure from the journal.

. . . 46 hours, 57 minutes, and 22 seconds. All without a bath—until now. But I am not mad—not yet, anyway. This would be some sick joke, if it were not so relentlessly real—with no bloody end to it in sight. Suppose we get to Greystone, what then? Find Edward in Ireland? Guess so. God, I hope he remembers me. Who else is there to appeal to? Good Duke Buckingham? Lord Scales? Sir Collin? Part of me is totally repulsed by the question. Having goals means admitting I might stay beyond the weekend.

Packing away her journal, she checked her map and then set out. Only Sudeley Castle stood between her and Greystone. Thanks to the good monks of Prinknash, they had enough food and cider to get them to Greystone—leaving her with naught to do but enjoy her stroll through gorgeous spring countryside and grand sweeping views. Joy went running ahead, her new slippers flapping at her feet. Each time they came to a tumulus or long barrow, the witch-girl knelt down to pray for the ancient dead. This was the Goddess's Day, with Witches Night ahead.

Dusk found them crossing Cleeve Common, the highest part of the Cotswolds, a wide tree-ringed top dotted with juniper thickets and tufts of wild thyme. Rabbits came out to feed in the fading light, right on cue, making it seem more than ever like *Watership Down*. This was as far as she meant to go today. Below the edge of the common lay Sudeley Castle—with Greystone a half dozen miles beyond that—potentially the most perilous part of the trek, leaving the high wastes for more populous bottomlands. Worse yet, FitzHolland might well guess where they were headed. Greystone was Joy's home, her surest safe haven. If FitzHolland meant to lay a trap, it would be in the half-light ahead. Better to lie up here on the moor until morning, when she could more clearly see her way. She had done well enough to come this far in two days, and to still have food for tomorrow.

Another tumulus sat at the far side of the high heath, and Joy went down on her knees to pay her respects. Robyn walked on to a gap in the ring-wood, where she could look down on the Vale of Sudeley with its pastures, parkland, church, and castle. It was almost all down-hill from here to Greystone. Her *Cotswold Way Guide* called Sudeley Castle a "fortified manor"—but it was castle enough for her, with towers, battlements, and a big double gate. Beyond it on the far bank of the Isbourne she could see the old Saxon village of Winchcombe. Staring down at the castle, she had no idea who Lord Sudeley was, or if he was friends with the Greys. Or how he fit into the fight be-tween York and the king. Or even if he was at home.

Beyond Winchcombe lay an empty immensity of air, hanging above the River Isbourne and the floodplain of the Severn. According to the *Way Guide*, the remains of a Roman villa lay right on the slope in front of her, but she saw no sign of it. Vespers bells rang in the castle church, sounding low and sonorous from two miles away. Lights shown in the castle. Down there, people's days were ending. Hers might as well, too. When she got back to Joy, the girl was standing beside the long barrow—the biggest they had seen so far. Grabbing her hand, the witch-girl dragged her toward the dark burial mound laid out along the Cotswold Edge. "This is Belas Knap," Joy told her. "I have been here a thousand times. We are home!"

"I hope so." Home for her would be the thump and roll of her return flight touching down at LAX. Trees ringed the Edge behind the

mound, falling away toward the flats. Belas Knap meant "Hill Beacon" in Saxon. According to the *Way Guide*, the long barrow was
five thousand years old, with better than a score of corpses inside,
some showing signs of sacrifice.

"Home is right there." Joy pointed over the mound, to the north
of the setting sun, smack at where Greystone lay—though the manor
could not be seen because of trees, distance, and fading light. The
witch-child brought her hand down to pat the mound. "My family is
buried here."

Robyn could believe it. According to Joy, witches had lived here
forever, covens of women who figured descent on the mother's side,
marrying into each wave of new arrivals—Normans, and Saxons, and
Romans, and Britons before them. "And you, an absolute stranger
found our way here, through the wildest of the Cotswolds." Joy made
it sound magical, but the witch-girl was prone to see the supernatural
everywhere.

"Thank the Gloucestershire Ramblers Association and the Ordnance Survey Guides—I just followed the map." It was what lay between here and there that worried her. "What do you know about
Baron Sudeley?"

"Baron Sudeley?"

"His castle lies between here and Greystone."

"Oh, you mean Uncle Boteler. He is neighbors to us. A hero from
Old King Harry's time, who made his fortune in France. He kept a
French admiral prisoner in one of the towers, paying ransom until
Sudeley was complete."

"He sounds favorably disposed." Unless you had the misfortune to
be French and rich.

"Oh, Lord, yes," the child laughed. "He loves me, and treats me
like a princess whenever I visit him."

But would he shelter them now? Maybe. Even against the likes of
Lord Scales? Better not to take the risk. Having come this far on their
own, she very much wanted to get to Greystone in one swift dash,
starting at first light and getting there in time for lunch. For that they
needed food and sleep. But when she offered Joy bread, the witch-
child shushed her, taking the bread but making a sign for holy silence.
Saying a prayer as the sun went down, Joy placed the bread on the
long barrow as an offering to the dead. Hela, feathery Queen of the
Underworld, flew down and began pecking at the bread.

"It is Witches Night," the girl reminded her for the upteenth time, gathering dead branches from the edge of the wood. "Set your magic clock for midnight—I am going to call on Mother and Collin." Seeing no chance of talking the girl into getting a sensible night's sleep, she set her watch, started a fire, and ate bread, bacon, and onions—then lay down for some badly needed rest. A midnight ritual followed by a dawn wake-up made for a very busy Witches Night.

Again her watch woke her at the witching hour. Shutting off the beeping, she looked about. Joy was already up, putting more dried branches on the fire, breathing life back into the glowing embers. Soon the fire by the burial mound blazed up, throwing sparks high into the midnight sky—though they were supposed to be in hiding. Below them, the matins bell rang in the church, and Joy again made the sign for silence. Robyn obeyed, listening as the witch-girl began a low crooning chant that started softly, almost like a lullaby, then grew in volume, rolling outward, full of longing, calling power out of the blackness and raising hairs on the back of Robyn's neck. She barely believed a child's lungs could make such eerie sounds.

Hela joined in, mimicking phrases, filling gaps with raucous bits of harmony. Then the witch-child started to dance in the firelight, her head thrown back, eyes half-open, limbs twitching and jerking in time to her keening. Hela cawed louder, and the chant spiraled upward. Joy spun about, faster and faster, doing a wild tarantella in time to her singing. Her clothes started to come off. First her shawl flew into the darkness. Followed by the blanket she had been wearing for warmth.

Her weird aria rose to a new crescendo as she whirled about the fire in frenzied gyration, her white shift spinning outward, her bare feet flashing. Wild abandon shone in her eyes as she whipped off the shift and threw it away, dancing nude before the flames, wearing just her crown of flowers. Sweat gleamed on the girl's thin bare body and spindly limbs. With her howling mouth wide open, and eyes shut tight, she leaped directly through the flames. Once. Twice. Three times. Then, giving out a low moan, she sank into a faint.

No wonder they burned witches. She stared at Joy curled into a fetal ball between the fire and the burial mound, never having seen a show like that, especially put on by a child. Hollywood liked to think it was unshockable—but when it came to witchcraft, clearly the movies had much to learn. Gathering up the wool blankets and the girl's shift, she laid them atop the sweaty sleeping child, to keep her from catching a chill in the cold night air. Wrapping herself in the shawl, she lay back against the mound, watching the fire burn down. Slowly she dozed off.

Suddenly Joy was awake and on her feet, hugging the blankets to her thin body, bubbling with excitement. "We did it! We did it!"

"Did what?" She helped the shivering child back into her shift, pulling the thickest blanket around her shoulders.

"A Witches Flight. I never did it before all on my own. But it worked. I was home with mother in Greystone."

Robyn stared into the darkness, north and east, toward where Greystone lay. She saw a far-off spark of flame in the night. A bonfire? A signal beacon? An answering witch fire?

"Not in body," Joy explained, "but in spirit. I never really left here—but I was there with her. I told her we were here at Belas Knap. They will come for us in the morning."

She certainly hoped so. Like Joy said, the witch-girl had not actually gone anywhere, but had been in an exhausted trance brought on by the weird frenzied dance. It could easily be a delusion, a fever dream concocted out of a very real desire to be home and safe. But Joy absolutely believed it. And Robyn was in no condition to doubt it, sitting beside Belas Knap at the edge of Cleeve Common, five hundred years in the past. Was that, too, a delusion? If so, she had long ago stopped pinching herself.

She settled for getting some food into the excited girl. "If they are coming for us in the morning, we should get some sleep now." Grudgingly Joy agreed, but the lauds bell was tolling below before the witch-girl got to sleep. Off toward Greystone, Robyn could still see the spark of flame. She fell asleep watching it, her head resting on the burial mound.

"Hela! Hela!" the magpie cawed at sunup. This time there was no doubting where she was—no precious sleepy moments before she remembered. Joy's blackened fire lay in the lee of Belas Knap. Cleeve Common stretched away to the west, and the Humblebee Woods were below her. It was dawn on Saturday, April 26, 1460. She could hear a dog barking on the common.

"Hela! Hela! Hela!" The magpie flew in furious circles overhead, then settled down on the burial mound, loudly mimicking the dog barks.

Leaping to her feet, Robyn shook Joy awake. "Wake up, wake up. Someone's coming."

"Mother?" The witch-girl looked sleepily about.

"Not unless she's bringing a dog." The barking was coming from behind them on Cleeve Common—Greystone was miles away in the opposite direction. It might be some stray hound, but already Robyn expected the worst.

"We need to get into the woods." Grabbing up their meager possessions, she bundled them in her gold riding dress, hustling Joy into the trees. Tall beeches and low evergreen thickets closed in about her. Branches whipped at her face. Roots tried to trip her. Dodging between trees, she herded Joy ahead of her, trying to keep headed downhill without going head over heels. Despite its Winnie-the-Pooh name, Humblebee Wood didn't seem the least bit friendly—a steep, overgrown tangle, far bigger than pictured in the *Way Guide*. But so long as they kept going downhill, they were bound to come out on the pasture below. Then what? She wished she knew. Every time she looked back, all she saw were trunks and branches, and the dark spaces between them.

Dewy pasture appeared ahead. She had reached the far edge of the woods. She stopped, chest heaving, letting Joy catch her breath. The child clung to her, eyes closed, breathing hard. The two-day hike, followed by her Witches Flight, had exhausted Joy. Being jerked awake at dawn had not helped, either.

What next? Open pasture stretched off toward Sudeley Castle. Much as she might want to, they could not just wait here to see if they were really being pursued. The Cotswold Way veered off to the left toward Winchcombe. Greystone lay father east; heading that way meant crossing Beesmoor Brook, then climbing back up the Cotswold Edge. She looked at Joy. "Can you keep going?"

Joy nodded, not too convincingly. The girl had lost one of her red slippers and seemed to favor her bare foot.

"Are you hurt?" she asked.

Joy shook her head, still too winded to talk.

She scanned the pasture. Less than a mile off was another stretch of woods along Beesmoor Brook. Once they got across that open pasture they could go to ground among the trees and then decide where to head next. "See those trees?" She pointed to them, and Joy nodded. "Can you get to them?"

"Yes," Joy hissed between breaths, her first word since they stopped to rest.

"Good. Let's go." She pushed the child ahead of her. Joy took off her remaining slipper and ran. Hela went winging on ahead. Robyn waited, listening for signs of pursuit, giving Joy a head start. Nothing. No barking, no hoofbeats, no crashing in the undergrowth. They could easily be fleeing from phantoms, exhausting themselves in the morning chill.

But she refused to risk ending up back at Berkeley—that would be too incredibly disheartening. Determined to die rather than go back to that hole, she set off running behind the bird and the girl. Wet grass tops whipped at her pant legs. She kept stopping to look back, letting Joy set the pace. Almost at the tree line, she turned for a last look and saw her pursuers. Silhouetted against the sky—framed in the gap in the woods near Belas Knap—a half-dozen horsemen looked down from the Cotswold Edge. Several had tall lances. They surveyed the scene; then they began to descend the Edge.

Redoubling her efforts, she yelled for Joy to run. Joy ran, though her steps were flagging. Catching up with the girl, she seized her hand and sprinted into the wood. Joy could not climb the Cotswold Edge and run the final five or six miles to Greystone—not with horsemen at her heels. Time to change directions. She steered Joy downstream. When she got to Beesmoor Brook, she snatched up the barefoot girl, splashing across in her boots, carrying Joy.

Setting the girl down on the far bank, she asked, "Do you know where you are?"

Joy nodded downstream, "Sudeley Castle lies over that rise. Winchcombe is beyond that."

"Good." She gave the weary girl a pat on the rear. "Run as fast as you can to Sudeley and pray they take you in. Understand?"

"What about you?"

"I'll be right behind you."

"Don't let me hold you back," the girl pleaded. "Remember, I cannot really die. I will be reborn; that makes me immortal."

Right. Immortal. Too bad the girl was not inexhaustible, as well. Or invisible. "Just run for it. I'll be right behind you." Off Joy went, with Hela winging overhead. For now the woods would cover them, but there was at least a mile of cleared pasture and water meadow between them and the castle. Men descending the Edge could not help but see them. When she broke out of the trees, she looked back to see the horsemen were partway down the Edge, level with the bottom of Humblebee Wood. As she watched, they changed direction and picked up speed, heading her way, making it a straight-out chase. She put down her head and ran, catching up with Joy, seizing her hand again, saying, "Come on, they have seen us."

Hand in hand, they ran. Sudeley Castle rose over the low ridge ahead, on the far side of a park dotted with oaks. That brought on a burst of speed. But the horsemen could easily see where they were headed, and angled to cut them off. She ran flat out, fairly dragging Joy along with her. Pasture dipped down toward a small stream.

They splashed across, but on the far side Joy stumbled and gave out, bare feet folding beneath her. "Leave me," she pleaded. "You can make it. I cannot really be killed."

She hauled Joy up the far bank with might and main. Looking back, she saw the lead riders reach the bottoms about a half mile back. Strung out by the chase, they rode bent down, going hell-for-leather to catch her before she got to the castle. Hela circled overhead, crying, "Naw! Naw!"

There was nothing left to do but carry the girl. Dropping her clothes bundle, she picked Joy up and started to run with her. Which turned out to be terribly hard; the girl weighed more than she thought. Pain shot through her arms. Breath came in sharp gasps. She concentrated on the castle, seeing it draw closer, determined to throw herself at the mercy of Baron Sudeley—Uncle Boteler, who always treated Joy like a princess.

Hoofbeats sounded behind her. She glanced back to see the lead horseman crossing the pasture stream and entering the oak park surrounding the castle. He wore a colorful surcoat, rode a beautiful bay horse, and had his sword in hand. In seconds he would be upon her.

She tried to run faster, legs pumping, lungs laboring, arms aching. Sudeley Castle's square towers seeming to bob about as she ran. She heard a call from the battlements and saw the main gate swing open. Her heart leaped; if she could she would have cheered. Instead she made straight for Sudeley's opening gate. Despite the hoofbeats at her heels, she was going to make it. "Naw! Naw!" Hela cried above her, sounding overly defeatist with the castle finally in reach.

Bounding out the open castle gate came a black beast with a silver head. She immediately recognized the four-footed horror. Barrister the purebred witch hound raced toward her, his chain-mail coif shining in the sun. Behind him came men on horseback, with big white swans on their steel-studded jackets. The lead horseman had on half-armor, steel plate from head to hip, with big turned-down leather boots covering his feet and legs. He had his helmet visor up. Her old friend Gilbert FitzHolland grinned to her in greeting.

She stopped, sinking to her knees, stunned by misfortune, clutching Joy to her breast, too tired even to cry. They were trapped. Witch hunters had driven her like a frightened deer, straight into a snare. No safe haven waited in Sudeley Castle—just FitzHolland, his ghastly Swans, and his beastly dog. She had nearly killed herself running right into their hands. Groaning in heartfelt despair, she could not believe her bad luck.

Barrister took a running leap at her, teeth bared, totally pitiless. Holding tight to Joy, she struggled to her feet, reeling back against a tree. As the witch hound came snarling at her, she lashed out with her hiking boot, hoping to connect with the mailed head. She missed, and Barrister got hold of her heel, biting down hard, trying to tear the boot off her foot. She jerked and kicked, but could not free her foot. With Joy clinging in terror to her arms, she had no hope of fighting off this savage steel-hooded dog, backed by FitzHolland's armed pack.

PART 2

The Irish Sea

Ride a cock horse to Banbury Cross,
To see a fine lady upon a white horse.
Rings on her fingers and bells on her toes,
She shall have music wherever she goes.
—Mother Goose

Trial by Combat

Horrified, she grappled with Barrister as FitzHolland cantered up, visor tipped casually back, with Le Boeuf right behind him, grisly as ever with his beef-blood beard and botched dental work. Both were in marvelous spirits, grinning broadly. More Swans reined in around her, happy as if they had been to a hanging, laughing as Barrister bit at her heel. FitzHolland called down, "My dear Lady Stafford, how delightful to see you."

Screw you. She thought it but did not say it. It was impossible to think up really witty repartee with a shaking child in your arms and a savage witch hound chewing on your boot. Only the solid Gloucestershire oak at her back kept her upright. Joy clung hard to her, eyes clamped shut, arms locked around her neck, spent and helpless, sobbing in terror. Hela cawed in the dark branches above, barking back at Barrister.

Unable to use her hands, she wrenched her foot free, kicking at the witch hound. Her boot bounced off the dog's chain-mail hood, only making Barrister madder. FitzHolland laughed at her struggles. "Pray do not tease the hound—he has a temper."

Backed against the tree, surrounded by hideous uncaring horsemen, she felt her strength ebb. Joy got heavier. And none of FitzHolland's Swans were going to help her; sitting happily in their saddles, applauding the dog's antics and making malicious suggestions, waiting for her to drop the child. She cast a despairing look at Sudeley Castle. Fairytale walls and towers stared serenely back on her. Men sauntered through the open castle gate, headed her way. Frantically she searched their faces, seeing a white-haired old man followed by a half-dozen younger ones, all splendidly dressed in fur-trimmed gowns with fashionably slashed sleeves. And all strangers. She saw no one she could call on. Not Edward. Not even Collin. And none of them seemed in any great hurry to halt FitzHolland's vicious amusement.

Without warning a horseman thundered out of the pasture behind her, bursting into view atop a beautiful bay horse, turning everyone's head, even Barrister's. Parting FitzHolland's startled Swans, the stranger reined in right in front of her, throwing up dust. She recognized the bright embroidered surcoat and long shining broadsword of her lead pursuer—totally forgotten until now.

Having FitzHolland's Swans issue forth from Sudeley Castle made her forget she was running *from* someone. Here was the first of the horsemen who chased her off the Cotswold Edge. In his teens or early twenties, he was clean shaved and bareheaded, with bowl-cut bangs in front and long hair in back. Close up, she could see his colorful surcoat was made from several coats of arms quartered together. Beneath it he wore stylish particolored hose and long leather riding boots turned down at the knee. *Très chic.*

Leaning out of the saddle, the newcomer gave Barrister a swat with the flat of his blade, sending the surprised witch hound yelping off. Swords leaped from scabbards, FitzHolland's Swans showing steel teeth. Le Boeuf howled, "Whoreson, that is my dog!"

"Then call him off," advised the cultured young horseman in the multicolored surcoat. "Ere I have to carve him in half."

Le Boeuf swung down out of the saddle to protect his whimpering hound, shouting, "Do not dare to harm my dog!" He might gleefully torture men to death, but hated to see a good hound mistreated.

The bareheaded young horseman laughed, supremely confident despite the odds against him. He had clear heavy-lidded eyes and a wry smile. "I am Sir Anthony Wydville, heir to the well beloved Baron Rivers. I shall have your dog for dinner if it so pleases me." Hela imitated his laugh.

Wydville? As in old Widow Weirdville? Curiouser and curiouser. Was this self-assured young stranger a relative? And a witch or warlock himself? Warlock or no, he worked wonders. Whoever the well beloved Baron Rivers might be, his name had visible effect. Le Boeuf shut up. Even FitzHolland looked taken aback. Swans sank back in their saddles, lowering their swords. She wondered if Joy knew this bold, handsome boy, but the girl was too wrung out to be grilled for information. She just had to assume that anyone who batted Barrister about must be a friend.

More riders clattered up, winded from their dash down the Cotswold Edge. All were armed, a couple carried lances. Dogs bounded about the horses' legs, barking at Barrister. Hela barked along with them from the branches above, happily adding to the cacophony. One of the new arrivals wore half-armor—a breastplate, gorget, bevor, and sallet covering his chest and head. His arms had steel sleeves, but he wore gloves instead of gauntlets, and had nothing below his loin guard but chain mail tights and big leather boots. His tall gray warhorse had hardened leather armor shaped to fit the head, neck, breast, and flanks. Reining in, he tipped back his sallet visor, smiling grimly at her. It was Collin.

She was never happier to see him—not in this millennium or the next. FitzHolland had twice as many men at his back, but Collin counted for a lot. If this Sir Collin had even half his descendant's instinct for wiggling out of tight corners, they were home free. Slowly letting Joy down, she gave the tired girl a look-who's-here nudge, getting her to open her eyes and see the good news. Joy whispered happily, "I told you he would come."

FitzHolland's Swans parted again, this time for the white-haired gaffer strolling over from the castle. He wore a gorgeous green-gold fur-trimmed surcoat with slashed and flowing sleeves over gold hose and green pointed shoes. This overgrown leprechaun had to be Lord Ralph Boteler, Baron Sudeley—Joy's Uncle Boteler. Sir Anthony saluted with his sword. "Good morrow, my Lord Sudeley."

Lord Sudeley nodded amiably. "Good morrow, good Sir Wydville."

Appalled by this bonhomie, FitzHolland turned in his saddle, appealing to Lord Sudeley's sense of justice, "Good and kindly my lord, I beg you, help see the law is carried out. These two witches are in my custody; I have warrants for their arrest."

Lord Sudeley looked askance. "When you spoke of warrants to serve, you did not say they named my neighbor's niece. That may do in Devon or London, but thanks be to God we are in Gloucestershire."

Caught attempting a fait accompli, FitzHolland none-too-gladly confessed. "I only hoped to spare your lordship trouble."

"To spare me?" Lord Sudeley arched an eyebrow, "From what, pray tell?"

FitzHolland tilted his head toward Collin, sitting atop his gray leather-armored charger. "From complications such as this."

Baron Sudeley smiled grimly. "Your kind intentions are for naught. Now that Sir Collingwood Grey is here, I fear he will not let you have his niece—not unless you will fight him. Or do they do things differently in Devon?"

Collin grinned in agreement. Behind his bravado, Robyn bet he wanted things ended without a fight. Given the easy way, Collin would take it. She heartily approved, not wanting to see her freedom put to some silly test of arms, especially one Collin could lose. For once, FitzHolland agreed. He thought single combat silly as well, protesting such "wanton disregard for the king's law. These women are witches. The younger one freely confessed to black magic and abominable acts and goes about with a familiar spirit in the form of a black bird."

"Hela, Quee-een Hela," came from the branches above.

FitzHolland pretended not to hear. "Yet, seeing she is Sir Collingwood's niece, he may have custody of her—until her case is heard in court."

Glad not to have bloodshed, Robyn turned to take Joy to Collin. Much as she might like seeing FitzHolland spitted on a lance, this felt better. Well, surer and safer, at least.

"Wait," FitzHolland called out. She saw the sergeant-at-law's steel finger pointing at her, backed by a look of pure loathing. "Not you. You are no one's niece."

FitzHolland truly hated her. She had twice made a fool of him, first by her silly lie about being Buckingham's daughter, then by escaping from Berkeley Castle. Having ridden all the way to Gloucestershire to get her back, he was not the sort to let her just waltz away again.

Lord Sudeley looked to Collin. "Is this woman any relation of yours?"

"She is not," Collin admitted. It is never a good sign when armed men blandly refer to you in third person—as if you were an object, without rights or opinions of your own. Clearly Lord Sudeley's neighborliness did not apply to her. Collin was free to make off with his niece—but if he wanted her, as well, he had to fight, risking death or defeat for someone he barely knew.

"She is a traitress and impostor," FitzHolland declared. "Deeply involved in diabolic acts against the crown." Diabolic acts against the crown? She had barely arrived in Mad King Henry's England, and already she was plotting to overthrow the monarchy by magic. For a mere sergeant-at-law, FitzHolland had a splendid imagination. Coming on like Cotton Mather preaching to the heathen, he warned Collin that "to protect a traitor from the king's justice is itself treason to the king."

"Kee-ing," Hela cawed.

"I served my king in France, and more lately at Saint Albans and

Blore Heath," Collin replied levelly. "Even a sergeant-at-law cannot turn that into treason."

"And what about your Lord God?" FitzHolland demanded. "You protect this witch at peril to your own immortal soul."

"Do I?" Sir Collin raised a doubting eyebrow. Born to a family of witches, he must be accustomed to giving them aid and comfort.

"So help me God," intoned FitzHolland, hoping to see the chastened sinner back down.

"Then let Our Lord God be the judge." Collin crooked a gloved finger, and one of his horsemen offered him a lance. He hefted the ash shaft, testing its weight and feel; then he held it straight out at eye level, sighting down it like it was a giant steel-pointed pool cue. Dissatisfied, he asked to see another. If he was indeed a warlock, Collin took the judgment of God awfully coolly.

FitzHolland tried to sway Lord Sudeley in lawyerly fashion—flattering and threatening at the same time. "My good and gracious Baron Sudeley, place this woman's case before a lawful court and a proper judge, and I swear to abide the outcome. She was taken in a witch's cottage with witch's things; then she used black arts to escape from a locked cell at Berkeley Castle. Siding with her puts you in peril, both here and in the Hereafter."

"Which is why I leave the decision to God," Lord Sudeley retorted, raising elegant slashed green sleeves to show he had empty hands. "Let the Lord witness that I side with no one—seeing only that the fight is fair. If you mislike that, let him have this woman and pursue your case diligently in the courts."

FitzHolland's witch hunters might have the law squarely behind them, but Baron Sudeley would not side with a mere sergeant-at-law against a knight and neighbor—not in the shadow of his own keep. Behind the kindly old hypocrite stood the tower where he had kept a French admiral prisoner for ransom, happily profiting off feudal law and his own personal power. It heartened Robyn to see medieval injustice and class prejudice finally working in her favor—what was the use in obeying laws that led to wicked ends? FitzHolland opened his mouth in protest, but Baron Sudeley silenced him. "Attend to our weapons. If you beat Sir Collingwood Grey, I will see you leave with your prisoners. If he hits you as squarely as he is wont, women will be the least of your worries."

Lord Sudeley told his people to pace off a tilting field "forty paces by forty paces of flat, firm ground, without stones or stumps." Obedient flunkies eagerly paced out the lists between two stands of oak. Boys scrambled to clear away stones, happy to see live combat, while others raced back to the castle, shouting the news ahead, wanting no one to miss the show.

FitzHolland turned to her, his face twisted with scorn. "You have made no end of trouble. When you are bound to your stake at Smithfield, I will happily kindle the fire."

What do you say to someone who wanted to see you burned alive? Who could not wait to light the match? Not much. She merely asked, "Why will you not just leave me be?"

His lip curled in contempt. "Thou shall not suffer a sorceress to live. So said Our Lord to Moses."

"Exodus 22:18," Le Boeuf added in Latin. Robyn bet he memorized every verse that favored burning, stoning, beating, and rape. Le Boeuf was just the type to turn the Bible into pornography. Joy tugged on her hand—not liking the tone of the conversation. She let the little girl lead her over to where her uncle was choosing a lance. Win or lose, their fates were joined.

Collin finally settled on a lance, saying, "This will do for a sergeant-at-law." Men had dismounted to work on his armor, tying steel tassets to his loin guard, and strapping plate armor around his thighs. The horseman beside him had big steel gauntlets ready to go over his hands. He smiled down at her and Joy. Half his face was now hidden by his steel bevor, so you had to know Collin to tell he was smiling. Stripping off a glove, he took Joy's hand, saying, "Do not worry, your mother is at Greystone. She sent me to get you."

"When will I see her?" whispered Joy.

"You will sleep there tonight," he promised. Amen, thought Robyn, maybe even in a real bed. Collin looked over the girl's head at her. "*Bonjour*, Lady Stafford. It is most cheering to see you again."

She would see how *bon* the day was in a bit. Suppressing reasonable misgivings—like, "Are you sure you can do this?" Or, "Do you really want to risk death for a stranger?"—she settled on a simple, heartfelt "Thanks. Cheering to see you, too."

"Thank you for finding my niece when I could not." Collin never minded letting you go him one better—giving him an excuse to do you a favor in return. He gladly gave others the credit, so long as things went his way—and right now he had everyone relying on the man he trusted most, himself.

She wished she shared that trust. She was rooting for Collin, of course—at the moment she was about his biggest fan. But way too much depended on him. And Collin looked tired, while his big gray was winded from chasing her down the Edge. Horse and man must have left Greystone after midnight to be on Cleeve Common before dawn. Despite his exertions, Collin acted unnaturally confident—like he meant to close a difficult business deal. Only he would close it with his body. Her old Collin, back in L.A., had been athletic and tolerably brave, liking to ski and rock-climb—but that had all been in fun. He was a firm subscriber to the postmodern brain-body split. Bodily risks were for recreation; you worked only with your brain. Unless you were a steelworker or a running back. Or an aspiring actress.

His men handed up a small shield bearing a silver wyvern—the same dragonlike beast embossed on the glove box of Jo's old Bentley. And on the spoons in her tiny kitchen. Letting go of Joy, he slipped the shield onto his arm and then took the girl's hand again, saying, "In a moment I must meet this man. When I am done, we will go home to Greystone. I swear."

"Knock him senseless," Joy murmured weakly. "He set his dog on us."

"Whatever you wish." He patted his niece's hand, as if he had promised her a pony ride.

"We called you," Joy whispered, including Robyn in last night's spell, though she had no real part in the ritual—except as an amazed spectator. Joy had her uncle's habit of gladly sharing credit so long as things went her way.

"I know." He nodded to his niece. "You did splendidly. That is why I came. Now go with Lady Robyn, while I meet this man." Collin handed the child back to her, adding, "I hope this goes quickly. I am short a night's sleep, which slows my arm, and throws off my eye."

Joy's arms went tightly around her waist. Here was the moment to make peace with Collin—in minutes the man might be lying on the greensward with a lance in his gut. While she was hauled off to the stake. She started with an apology. "I am sorry I ran from you this morning." All this could have been avoided if she had waited to see who was chasing them. Or just trusted in Joy's spell.

He looked surprised. "What? That? Do not worry about it. That wicked little chase woke me up."

She smiled a weak thanks, afraid he merely meant to cheer her. Joy tugged on her blouse, whispering, "Give him your favor."

"My favor?" She favored Collin immensely at the moment, especially compared to FitzHolland. She felt Joy's hand in her pocket, pulling out her handkerchief—a bright neon green souvenir from Euro Disneyland. Another gift from the future Collin. Joy gave the kerchief to her uncle.

Sir Collin stared at the handkerchief, looking mystified, "What color is this?"

"Kiwi."

"And who is the smiling mouse wearing a dress?"

"Her name is Minnie."

Collin grinned and tied the kerchief to the gorget about his neck. Slipping on his steel gauntlets, he took the lance and turned to his men, saying, "I will soon be back. This sergeant-at-law could not unhorse my grandmother."

"Yes," agreed the squire who had held his gauntlets, "but Old Lady Grey was uncommon good with a lance."

Laughing, Collin spurred his gray charger, riding over to where Baron Sudeley stood. She had heard in college that feudal lords exercised power "personally"—now she knew what that meant.

Lists had been paced off, marked with colorful little pennants stuck in the ground. Sir Anthony had dismounted to confer with Lord Sudeley, acting as a second. Where did Collin find such a useful young fellow so quickly? Trust Collin to ride up in just the right company—this had all the signs of careful planning—too bad she had beat them down from atop Cleeve Common.

FitzHolland was ready as well, encased in steel from head to toe, set to take injustice into his own hands. An excited mob of men-at-arms, squires, stable boys, and hangers-on in bright Sudeley livery ringed the cleared ground, eagerly awaiting the fight. Women and children watched from the castle battlements. Hela flew down to land on Joy's shoulder, acting wary of the throng. Robyn did not blame the bird. It was an amazing scene, right out of *Ivanhoe*, with her in the Elizabeth Taylor role, waiting to see if she would be saved or burned.

"Oyez, oyez, oyez," cried Lord Sudeley's herald, quieting the boisterous crowd. He sternly warned the spectators, "Let no person of great or little estate, no matter what their nation or condition, come nearer than four feet from the tilting ground, and let no one speak, cry, make continence, or token, or noise by which one combatant may gain advantage—upon peril of life and property."

Having cowed the crowd, the herald turned to the combatants. "Do each of you swear you are armed with nothing but lance, sword, and dagger? That you have no other daggers and knives, no other instruments or engines, no charms or herbs, or experiments or enchantments? That you trust in nothing but God, your body, and your rightful quarrel?"

They so swore. Her old Collin had been barely religious. This new Sir Collin invoked God whenever the need arose, acting like he had the Almighty in his armored pocket. Did he really think God was on his side? A warlock defending witches from a sergeant-at-law in the king's service? Apparently—since he was about to stake his life on it.

She watched the herald examine the weapons—long lances, big ballock daggers, and huge hand-and-a-half swords—measuring them against each other and then pronouncing them fit to kill. White-haired Baron Sudeley motioned for the combatants to lower their lances. "I will make one last appeal, for love of peace and our good king's law, set aside your quarrel so the day may end sans bloodshed."

Neither of them spoke, sitting silently in their tall saddles, lance points touching the ground. Lord Sudeley motioned again. A splendidly dressed flunky stepped forward, handing him a big, two-bladed ax. With a couple of ceremonious swings, he chopped the steel points off the lances, along with the last foot or so of shaft. Giving back the ax, Lord Sudeley announced loudly, "Let all witness that I begged them to desist, and when they refused, I blunted their lances. My herald stands ready to separate them if one becomes helpless or disabled. No matter what the quarrel, I will not continence plain murder. The rest remains with God." They saluted him with shorn lances.

Cutting off the lance points was a neat bit of theater that reduced Lord Sudeley's liability—but they still had wicked long swords and sharp, deadly daggers. Risk had merely been reduced, not eliminated. And her own peril was real as ever. Whether they fought with beanbags or blunted lances, her life was still the prize. She watched as the combatants turned and trotted to opposite ends of the lists. Collin stopped within easy earshot, but she heeded the herald's warning and said nothing. What could she contribute anyway? Until this out-of-control trip to England, the closest she ever came to armed combat was girls' field hockey.

Collin's eyes stayed fixed on his opponent, studying him keenly. Then he brought his sallet visor down, and she could see nothing. He might as well have been a suit of armor sitting on a gray horse. Horses were brought for Baron Sudeley and his herald, so they could view the coming fracas with dignity. Front row on horseback was the best height for watching just about anything—and Baron Sudeley was plainly used to the best. He lifted his hand, and his herald called out, "Lessiez les aler"—"Let them rest awhile." No one seemed ready to rest, least of all the combatants, facing off on horseback, like boys in the playground waiting for someone to say, "Ready. Set. Go!"

"Lessiez les aler," the herald called out a second time. Both lances came down, each pointed straight at its opponent's chest. Tension increased with each call for rest. Robyn had to remind herself to breathe. The herald looked to Lord Sudeley, who nodded his head.

"Lessiez les aler et fair leur devoir de par Dieu," the herald called out. Which meant something like, "Let them go do their duty in the name of God." She was learning medieval French magically, word by word as it was spoken. Distracted by the totally irrelevant realization that Gérard Depardieu's last name must mean "name of God"—it took her a moment to realize that this meant "Charge!"

Collin spurred his gray charger and shot forward, her kiwi green Minnie Mouse handkerchief streaming from beneath his steel sallet. FitzHolland did the same, hurling himself and his horse at Collin. As Collin's gray charger and FitzHolland's big dun warhorse pounded over the cleared ground, she whispered a hurried prayer for Collin, and for herself.

Lances level, faces hidden by helmets, the two horsemen thundered at each other, eating up the gap, meeting with a crash that made her flinch. She saw Collin lean into the collision, tilting his silver wyvern shield upward, throwing his body into the impact as he steeled himself for the shock—something that took incredible agility and timing. FitzHolland's lance struck Collin's tilted shield and bounced upward. Collin's own lance slipped past FitzHolland's shield, slamming into the man's armored midriff. Bowing on impact, the blunted lance lifted FitzHolland right out of the saddle.

FitzHolland seemed to hang in the air while his dun charger ran out from under him. Then the sergeant-at-law came crashing down.

Landing hard, FitzHolland hit, bounced, and lay still. Seeing Fitz-Holland sprawled on the ground, having lost his lance and shield, Robyn foolishly thought the fight was over.

Collin reined in. Then to her absolute horror, she saw FitzHolland lurch upright, drawing his big hand-and-a-half broadsword. Throwing down his lance, Collin did an armored dismount, getting set to face the sergeant-at-law on foot. Far from being over, the fight had gotten more deadly, with honed steel replacing blunted lances.

Before Collin could draw sword, FitzHolland was on him, rushing up, swinging to kill. Holding tight to Joy, Robyn heard the crowd around her cry foul, but Lord Sudeley's herald moved too timidly to stop the offending sergeant-at-law. She gasped as Collin brought his shield up at the last instant. FitzHolland's blade rang against it. Striking again and again, a vicious flurry of blows battered Collin to his knees. Swans cheered FitzHolland on.

Unable to get out his sword, Collin inched backwards, his wyvern shield buckling under FitzHolland's assault. Collin kept retreating on his knees, until he fetched up against his own lance, lying where he had tossed it. Grunting in triumph, FitzHolland swung harder, holding the huge sword with two hands, hammering at the blue-and-silver shield. People around her shouted to stop the fight. Her own heart hammered horribly, sure she would see Collin hurt or killed, and then be handed over as a prize to FitzHolland and his happily celebrating Swans.

Stung by the crowd, the herald urged his horse forward. But the fight was over before he got there. FitzHolland brought his sword down in a terrific cut, trying to cleave Collin in two. Instead, Collin rolled sideways, avoiding the blade and seizing up his own lance. Swinging the huge spear around, he landed a ringing reply on FitzHolland's helmet.

FitzHolland fell face forward, limbs twitching convulsively, this time showing no sign of getting up. Thank heavens. She was safe. And Collin looked unhurt as he got to his feet, cheered wildly by the crowd. Slowly she let her breath out. Never a fan of blood sports, she shied away from bulldogging and found TV football too violent. Her heart always went out to the men hurt on the field. But not to FitzHolland. He meant to do horrible things to her, and she would be glad if he never got up. She had never wanted anyone dead before—but no one ever scared or mistreated her so much.

Collin remounted and did a victory lap as the crowd roared in approval, shouting, "God is with Gloucestershire." And, "Take that back to Devon with you." She joined in the cheers. Along with Hela, calling from Joy's shoulder.

Tipping his blunted lance to the hometown fans, Collin trotted over to where Baron Sudeley sat waiting. Sir Collin saluted his neighbor. "Thank you, my most gracious Lord Sudeley for a fair fight and a most sporting morning. With your leave, I will take what is mine and go."

Baron Sudeley nodded, saying Collin could go where he willed, expressing the pious hope "that you may now take your case to court and acquit yourselves of these grave charges against you."

Collin promised to take the case to court, "as soon as it is most convenient." A polite fiction to appease his neighbor's conscience. Collin was no more eager to face FitzHolland in court than she was—the whole point of the trial-at-arms had been to get around the law.

He cantered briskly over to where she waited with Joy. His squire took his sallet, lance, and battered shield, saying, "Splendidly done, sir. He went down like a whore's drawers."

Still shaken from seeing Collin on the ground, fighting for both their lives, she asked, "Are you hurt?"

Collin grinned. "Not gravely, though my shield arm will surely ache sorely on the morrow."

She promised to massage it, happy to have brought her tube of arnica. His hurt had been all for her. Thoroughly revived, Joy let go of Robyn's hand and reached up to her uncle, alive with excitement. Stripping off a gauntlet, Collin pulled his niece onto his horse's leather-armored crupper. She hugged his armored waist, shouting happy congratulations in his ear. "You knocked him senseless, just like I begged you."

"I try to please."

"You did. You did." Joy bounced on her hard leather seat.

Robyn congratulated him as well, adding, "I am immensely in your debt." With scant hope of repaying him.

"And I am equally in yours." Collin patted Joy's knee. "For returning my favorite bastard niece to me."

Joy pounded him on the back armor. "Your only niece you mean."

"But still my favorite," he insisted. Uncle and bastard both laughed. This was a whole new side to Collin, the concerned and courageous family man—as good with children as he was with a lance—putting life and limb on the line for a stranger he had just met. She liked this Sir Collin much better than the smooth cad from Sotheby's with too many secrets.

Sir Anthony strolled over, offering congratulations. "Shrewdly done. You are a sorcerer with a lance, even from your knees. I doubt ever to see a sergeant-at-law better served."

Collin acknowledged the compliment, then did formal introductions, "Robyn Stafford, meet Sir Anthony Wydville, my cousin-in-law and fellow troubadour."

Cousin Anthony declared himself to be *"enchanté,"* acting polite and poised, on top of being brave and athletic. Horsemen enough to beat his companions down the Edge, he had ridden right into the midst of FitzHolland's Swans, head bare, sword in hand, with nothing to protect him but a heraldic surcoat, trusting in his nobility to carry the day.

Warning, "We must be off," Collin ordered up a horse for her; a beautiful gray-blue gelding, with sad brown eyes and long soft lashes. She liked the look of this new horse, and this new Sir Collin—so at ease with his wits and his body—but then she had liked the old Collin, too, and look where that had got her. She pulled herself gingerly into the saddle, a lot having happened before she usually had her morning coffee. When they were on the same level, she leaned over and kissed Collin thanks. No easy thing to do unless you have had practice necking in the saddle. Collin looked both surprised and pleased. Joy giggled behind him. Squires cheered.

"That was for saving me," she informed him.

"Really?" He grinned. "I would do it more often."

Hopefully not. She talked quietly to her new mount, saying hello, letting him get to know her voice, asking Collin, "What is his name?"

"He is called Plunket, because of his color."

She patted the horse lightly, "A pretty color and a pretty name. Come, Plunket, let's be friends. There's a carrot in it for you."

Collin's retainers had picked up her dropped clothes and belongings. Searching through the bundle, she found the keys to Berkeley Castle gone, but everything else seemed there—including the rose. No sense going back for the keys, which could have fallen out anywhere between there and Cleeve Common, and belonged to Lord Berkeley anyway. So they set out, Joy riding pinion behind her uncle. Passing the tilting ground, she saw FitzHolland on his feet, groggy but upright. Feeling guilty for wanting him dead, she told Collin, "I am glad now you did not kill him."

"Kill who?" He sounded as if he had already put the fight out of his mind.

"FitzHolland."

"Oh, him. I have never killed anyone—not intentionally. Why start with some overly lewd sergeant-at-law?"

"Admirable sentiments." And strange. So far she had never seen Sir Collin unarmed, and the way he leaned into the impact must have taken plenty of training. "Yet you are very skilled with a lance."

He shrugged. "Not skilled enough, for I have killed men I did not mean to. But never on purpose, only through mishap."

"How many of these fatal mishaps have there been?"

"Three." He did not sound pleased. "Twice in tourneys and once in battle."

"How unlucky."

"More for them than for me," Collin observed.

Curiouser and curiouser. Here was yet another side to Sir Collin. The Collin she knew did not easily own up to his mistakes—being as forgiving with himself as he was with others. This Sir Collin was more ready to confess his sins and call on God. Perhaps he needed to be. These were dangerous times, when even a dedicated pacifist in armor could not get by without killing "by accident." All this made her tremendously glad to be with someone she semi-trusted. For the first time since arriving in medieval England, she was totally free. Not in prison. Nor in custody. Not even on the run. Charges of witchcraft and treason hung over her, and she was horribly dependent on Collin's generosity and protection—but she had a beautiful spirited palfrey beneath her and the promise of a bed to sleep in.

Riding up the Vale of Isbourne, along the base of the Edge, she passed between a great huge tithe barn and the village of Winchcombe. Clouds were rolling up the Severn, threatening rain, but even a downpour could not dampen her spirits. Past Winchcombe they picked up the line of the Cotswold Way, cutting across the lower Edge, headed for Hailes Abbey, where the Cistercians had Christ's blood in a bottle.

Orchards and fish ponds surrounded the Abbey. Collin ordered a halt, dismounted, and stripped off his armor before entering hallowed ground. She insisted on massaging his shield arm, rubbing arnica into the stiff, bruised muscle, wishing she could do more. His arm felt far stronger than her Collin's had, hard and corded from exercise. She wondered how it would feel against her back. A giddy thought, but understandable under such outlandish circumstances. She would have to take care not to get carried away with gratitude. Collin seemed vaguely amused by her concern—thanking her when she was done and then donning a blue-white doublet and gold hose provided by a page.

Her pantsuit raised eyebrows, but the monks set out a royal breakfast in the great hall of the abbey, starting with roast mutton, smoked fish, dried fruit, herbs, nuts, cheeses, and boiled vegetables, accompanied by tankards of ale and sweet, grapey half-fermented wine that stained anything it touched. Medieval meals were not as drear and deadly as she had feared. The man who served her had clean hands, and they ate with their fingers off slabs of bread, so there was no worry about unwashed dishes and silverware. She passed over anything that looked disease ridden or insufficiently cooked. But at Hailes Abbey, there were plenty to choose from, as the courses kept coming—smoked lamprey, pickled sheep-tongue, dried apples, French beans, and fish aspic. She was surprised to see other wayfarers eating with them, as well as whole families that apparently lived in the abbey. Old folks, well-to-do couples, servants, beggars, and children all shared the monks' board in the great hall. Along with assorted pets—dogs, cats, pigs, and birds. Hela got into a cawing match with another magpie, exchanging bird and human insults, clearly calling each other "shrew" and "hussy." Vivid costumes, plain trestle tables, and loud friendly chatter made it feel like a masquerade-cum-church-picnic. Women asked where she came from.

"Hollywood."

"Up near King's Heath?"

"No, another. Across the sea."

"How do you speak such fine West Country?"

"I have a good ear," she confessed.

"But a bad appetite. You have not touched your eel. Here, taste the pig's feet." Despite being loud, smelly, and plague ridden, the people at Hailes perked her up. You could not judge the Middle Ages by Fitz-Holland and Le Boeuf. Or Lord Scales. Even the way they pushed tainted meat at her reminded her of home. Meals had been a big deal for her small family, especially in the dark depths of a Montana winter. When strangers dropped in unexpectedly, the meals turned into feasts.

She hated to leave Hailes just when she was starting to feel the least tiny bit at home—but Collin insisted they push on before pursuit caught up. "There are woods and tops between here and Greystone where men might easily lie in wait." Leaving the abbey, the little cavalcade climbed Salter's Lane, an ancient track leading to the Salt Way. Turning off the lane into the orchards, they rode beneath apple and pear trees, emerging onto bare slopes topped by an overgrown ring fort sitting squarely on the Cotswold Way. From the slumped grassy ramparts she got a sweeping view of the Vale of Isbourne. Hailes Abbey lay directly below her, huge even at a distance, surrounded by gardens, walls, hedges, barns, and outbuildings. Behind her, she made out the blue line of Cleeve Common where her day had begun. Heavy gray clouds were blowing up the Severn from a storm in the Bristol Channel, dragging dark streaks of rain.

Setting out again, her elation turned to anxiety. Without the edge of hunger to keep her going, weariness overwhelmed her. Drained by days of hiking and nights spent sleeping in the open, she could not believe the unfairness of her situation. What had she done to deserve this? Absolutely nothing. This all began with a day hike in Wales—now she was impossibly lost, cut off from home, living in mortal dread of death and mutilation. Dark masses of trees covered this part of the Cotswold Edge, and here if anywhere they could expect attack, though she could hardly tell that by her companions. Collin and Joy joked together. Having taken off his armor to eat, Collin did not bother to put it back on. Sir Anthony got out a lute and began to strum, pausing every so often to adjust the tension on the catguts. Was she overly cautious or merely crazy? Peering between the trees, she imagined shadowy movement and the glint of steel.

Suddenly, Sir Anthony burst into song, his voice sounding clear and young—like Edward's:

True Thomas lay oer yon grassy bank,
And he beheld a lady gay . . .

She straightened up, thinking, What an accomplished lad. Sir Anthony could win a downhill steeplechase, confront a score of armed felons, second a duel, and sing a song, all in a single morning.

> She turned about her milk-white steed,
> And took True Thomas up behind,
> And aye wheneer her bridle rang,
> The steed flew swifter than the wind . . .

Sir Anthony's singing soothed her—keeping her from starting at sounds in the woods—even though the theme was disturbing. "True Thomas" was whisked off to "Elfland" and forced to stay there for seven years and a day, and to always tell the truth. Not at all the fate she hoped for.

> He has gotten a coat of the elven cloth,
> And a pair of shoes of velvet green,
> And till seven years were past and gone,
> True Thomas on earth was never seen.

When he was through, she thanked the knight troubadour, telling him his singing had done wonders. Sir Anthony smiled, saying, "All music is a miracle of God. Song nourishes the soul, inspires joy and tranquillity, stimulates healing, aids digestion, cures melancholy, and is an antidote to poison." Centuries-old Sir Anthony sounded very young and New Age, a lad ahead of his time. She asked if he knew "Greensleeves."

"Greensleeves?" He gave her a questioning look.

She sang the refrain

> Greensleeves was all my joy,
> And oh, Greensleeves was my delight . . .

Sir Anthony instantly recognized the tune, and began to play, then to sing. His words were completely different, but the familiar melody lifted her spirit, making her think she might survive all this—if she could somehow hang on to her sanity.

At the top of the woods, trees gave way to bare green hillsides. They were back on the lip of the Edge, riding along the Cotswold Way, with the village of Stanton a mile or so below. She recognized Greystone Manor ahead, surrounded by walls and outbuildings. The place had changed mightily in more than five hundred years, but she knew it by the turrets atop the main hall and by the shape of Shenberrow Hill behind it—the land had changed a lot less than had the buildings on it. Blue banners flying over the battlements bore the same silver wyvern as on Collin's shield. She had found her safe haven, or so she hoped.

⊷⟞⟝⟞⟆ Greystone ⟆⟞⟝⟞⊷

Greystone *had changed tremendously* since Collin's ill-fated birthday party. Floodlit gardens had surrounded the embattled medieval hall with its corner turrets and two grand wings, one built during the regency of George IV, the other under Queen Victoria. This impressive pile—the newest parts of which were nearly two hundred years old when she first saw them—fronted on a circular drive at the end of the tarmac road leading down to the village of Snowshill. She could still picture the wrought-iron gate and ivy-covered porter's cottage.

None of which existed in the here and now. Both grand wings were gone, along with the gardens, the gravel drive, the wrought-iron gate, the porter's cottage, and the tarmac road to Snowshill. All she saw of the Greystone she knew was the great hall itself, shorn of its nineteenth-century wings and tall Tudor windows. Three stories of windowless stone stared down at her through tiny arrow slits. Though topped with turrets and battlements, the hall had no moat or towered curtain wall—just a small walled bailey enclosing stables, kitchens, pigeon lofts, rabbit hutches, a rose arbor, and witch's herb garden— making Greystone a "fortified manor" and not a proper castle.

But it was castle enough for her, riding in front of the rain, feeling the first drops as she passed the bailey gate. Plunket went straight to the stables and stopped at the mounting block. Collin swung out of the saddle and then turned to help her down onto shaky legs. "Welcome to Greystone, my lady. We are most glad to have you here."

"No gladder than I to be here." She breathed in the beery smell of straw and horse piss, hearing the double gate shut behind her, feeling safe for the moment—unless her outlandish abbey breakfast proved fatal.

Giving her a reassuring squeeze, Collin turned to see to the horses.

She liked this new confident, unmarried Sir Collin, who risked body and soul for her—without being afraid to bring her home afterwards. His warm, easy welcome was infinitely superior to the shocked look she got from the old Collin when she crashed his birthday party. Despite dire circumstances, this second visit to Greystone was starting out way better than her first. She approved the new emphasis on simplicity and protection. The walled bailey and windowless facade fairly exuded security—a heartening sight considering how her day had started. Narrow stone steps led up to the second-floor entrance, not the big, sweeping stairs and indefensible French doors she remembered. The first floor was blank stone, without so much as a firing slit, and there was a small sideways drawbridge at the top of the stairs. Lift the narrow bridge, and not even a stoop remained to cling to—terribly handy when creditors called.

Oak doors flew open, and Joanna Grey dashed across the plank drawbridge and then down the narrow stone steps, trailing clouds of blue silk. Joanna had her daughter's long black hair, and the same wild manner and stern mannish face Robyn remembered. Before Joy could dismount, her mother lifted her from the saddle, shrieking in delight. Hela flew around them, enthusiastically echoing their cries.

Obviously this new Jo did not know her. Hugging and kissing Joy in rapturous rain-soaked reunion, Joanna Grey of Greystone utterly ignored Robyn—these witches barely remembered their past lives, and saw even less of the future. Collin had to step in and introduce them, telling his sister that Robyn had gotten Joy out of Berkeley Castle. "I gave her the keys," Joy explained gleefully. "Not this me, but a future me." Joy showed off the iron necklace, the real keys to Berkeley having been lost in the mad dash down the Cotswold Edge.

Jo immediately threw wet arms around her, giving her the same heartfelt welcome that the third-millennium Jo gave her at this very manor five centuries from "now." That was more like it. Consistent if eerie. "Come join us at supper," Jo demanded. "Joy is my life. Ten thousand thanks are far too few."

Who could say no? Not this penniless fugitive from the future. Jo lead her up Greystone's narrow steps, across the upper drawbridge, and into the shelter of the great second-floor hall—followed by Collin and Sir Anthony. Huge south-facing windows were gone, replaced by narrow firing slits. Servants scurried about, laying out food. More tired than hungry, she still appreciated the effort; when they were not setting dogs on you or threatening your life, people in the Middle Ages were incredibly hospitable. You could not knock on a door without being offered tainted meat or a lice-infested place to sleep.

Jo insisted she make an attempt to eat—sitting her down before a plate of smoked stockfish with green ginger, cheese, figs, and almonds. Jo even cracking the almonds for her with a brass nutcracker. "Joy says you are a daughter to the much-beloved duke of Buckingham."

"Joy exaggerates. My name is Robyn Stafford, but so far as I know, I am no relation to the much-beloved duke."

"Of course Joy exaggerates." Jo hugged the girl to her. "She is my daughter. Have I not taught her well?"

"Very well," replied Robyn, thinking of Joy dancing naked by the bonfire at Belas Knap—some would say too well. "Without her, I would not have known what to do once we got out."

"She is displaced," Joy explained, "from a far-off land in the distant future."

"Displaced?" Jo looked at Collin. Her brother stared back at her, in a bit of silent sibling communication. "Which makes you an even more special guest," Jo decided, cracking another almond.

Robyn wished she were more ordinary. "Unwillingly displaced," she told them—hoping they would take the hint and offer her a way home. This Jo was a full-fledged witch and must be better than the amateurs who landed her here.

Brother and sister both laughed. Collin asked with an air of innocence, "Is there any other way?"

"I hope this displacement can be reversed, and I can be sent home." The sooner the better. She tried to delicately impress on these people that she had absolutely no desire to stay in their century—in fact she would happily put their whole millennium behind her.

"There are ways," Jo assured her, "but it is not so simple. Besides, you have only just gotten here."

"Stay the night, at least," suggested Collin. From the way he said it, she knew she had absolutely no hope of being gone by morning.

She gave in to medieval hospitality. "I would be glad to stay the night, and gladder still to rest right now." Her day had been nonstop from the moment she awoke to barking on Cleeve Common.

Jo rose and took her hand; medieval women could look so graceful doing the simplest things. "Come see my favorite place to lie down." She led her over to the stone stairs at the north end of the great hall.

Joy went, too, with Hela perched on her shoulder. On the cooler west side of the stairs was a big stone buttery, and on the east side a large pantry. The stairs themselves led up to the third-floor living quarters—just below the battlements.

Jo took her to a carpeted room in the northeast turret, saying, "This is the kitchen tower—and my own special roost." It was obviously Jo's room, having the same shabby-elegant air as her future Cotswold cottage. Instead of Queen Jane's portrait, a tiny shrine faced the canopy bed with a miniature of the Virgin blessing doves inside, lovingly hand-painted. Alongside the bed sat a pile of books and manuscripts, topped by an oil lamp. A pair of chests, a washstand, and chamber pot finished out the furnishings. Light came from cross-shaped arrow slits spaced around the walls. Sitting down on the bed's silver wyvern coverlet, she thanked Jo profusely. So far she had slept in a cell and a shepherd's rest, in a stubble field, and beside a burial mound. A feather bed would be a welcome change.

"It is I who owe thanks," Jo protested. "And I will do whatever I can to repay you." Jo keenly felt a debt—one reason she always lived so sparsely. For a tower room in a manor house, this place was amazingly spare, having neither a chair nor a table. Rain spilled in one of the stone slits wetting the elegant hand-woven carpet, reminding Robyn of the rain-streaked windows and linoleum floor in Jo's little third-millennium kitchen.

Hating to sound ungrateful, she told her host, "The best thing you could do for me would be to send me home."

"I will if I can," Jo promised. "How were you displaced?"

Robyn told her story—abridged edition—leaving out her affair with the future Collin. No sense giving Sir Collin downstairs ideas. She felt far too deeply in his debt already. She also went easy on Edward, making him into a nameless knight errant wandering out of Wales. Only a fool showed Yorkist sympathies nowadays. She felt foolish enough showing off her rose—still wrapped in a tea towel from Jo's little future kitchen—looking very bedraggled and missing more petals. Jo cupped the wilted flower in her hand, listening intently. It took some time to explain what a cell phone was—and Joy insisted she show Jo the watch. She recited as much as she remembered of the ritual at the tump, and finished off with her finding the witch's cottage again.

Jo shook her dark head. "This spell can be lifted, but not by me.

Someone has brought you here; I do not know why. Someone whose name is best not said, lest saying it should alert her." Jo stared straight into her eyes, trying to communicate with more than words.

Wonderful. Whoever sent her here was a witch so powerful even Jo feared to say her name aloud. That same Jo who was so utterly fearless in life and love, whether behind the wheel of a Bentley or raising her bastard daughter to be a witch. Not reassuring. "How can you be sure who brought me here, just from what I told you?" None of this made much sense, not that medieval magic was supposed to.

"You will know when you see her," Jo prophesied. "But first you must become more adept at spellcraft, before you can confront the power that brought you here."

Great. Loosening her boots, she lay back onto the big bed, staring at the ceiling, wondering, "Why me?" Exhausted before the conversation began, she now felt totally spent.

Dragging a book out of the pile by the bed, Jo opened it to the title page. It was a bound manuscript—Christine de Pizan. Putting the rose inside, she closed the book, saying, "We should save this." Shoving the book back down under the pile, Jo told her, "Sleep now. Were it a simple thing, I would send you back home at once."

"I know you would." Jo would indeed help her, even at some cost to herself. And Jo would be truthful with her—far more than she herself dared be. But that was Jo. She felt ashamed, taking advantage of such generosity, though at home she was the same way. There were some women she would do anything for, without really knowing why—like Heidi, whom she had hired despite flashing warning signs. She looked across the bed at Jo. "You have always been so really, really kind to me."

Jo laughed. "The immortal's curse. Someone will say, 'I knew you in King Arthur's day, and you were just that way.' Usually it is a lie. Witches seldom remember their past lives so exactly. But with you . . ." Jo stared at her in intent speculation. "With you it is totally true. You really did know me in the distant future. Not as I was, but as I will be."

She nodded sleepily. "To me it seems only a week ago that we first met, right here in Greystone." A bigger and electrified Greystone, with great glass windows and a gravel drive—but still the same stonework, only not nearly so sharp and crisp, worn smooth by time. And scarred inside and out by fire—she had seen burn marks at the birthday party that did not exist here and now. Some time between now and the third millennium, Greystone would burn, but why worry her hosts?

"How completely wonderful." Jo leaned over and kissed her full on the lips. "You must tell me all about me. But sleep first, we can talk when you wake."

Joy climbed up on the bed and kissed her good night, saying, "We promise to do our best."

She thanked them both, kicking off her boots. There was one clear difference between Jo then and now. In the third millennium, Jo never felt the need to kiss her good night. Medieval women seemed less restrained about casual affection—another thing she had not at all expected. "What about Sir Anthony?" she asked. "Is he a, ah . . ."

"Warlock?" Jo arched a mischievous eyebrow. "No. Sir Anthony Wydville is a most Christian knight, devout and honest. But he can nonetheless be trusted . . ."

"The women in his family are witches," Joy explained cheerfully.

"Some of them," her mother objected.

"His mother and sisters are."

"That is so," Jo admitted primly—clearly Joy had said more than Jo wanted. It must be devilish hard keeping secrets around the girl. "Sir Anthony treads a fine line between family and conscience, as do many in these troubled times. And even though he is not a witch— you must be."

Robyn grimaced. Everyone seemed determined to make a witch out of her—Joy, Jo, even Gilbert FitzHolland. "Must I be?" she asked wearily. Could they not just have her soul instead.

"Only if you wish to return home."

Which she did. Witchcraft got her here. How else did she plan to get back? She nodded solemnly.

Jo gave her another good-night kiss, saying, "Now I must go. Do not worry about your past and future; just be my friend and companion for now."

"And afterwards . . ." How long could she live on Jo's hospitality?

Jo shrugged, "By then you mean to be home, do you not?"

"That I do," she agreed sleepily. Jo and Joy departed, leaving her alone, listening to rain patter on the stone slits as the room grew dark. Evening was coming on. What a nonstop full-tilt day it had been. How many more lay ahead? Not a lot, she hoped. Jo had been somewhat encouraging. The spell could be reversed. Just knowing that was like being halfway home—desperation had her totally trusting the unsup-ported word of a newly met medieval who claimed to be a witch. Jo even knew someone who almost certainly could send her home; the trick would be to make that happen.

Without getting up, Robyn unbuttoned her tight red jacket. To-morrow she could do laundry and have a bath. Tonight just getting undressed would do. Slipping off her pants, she slid under the coverlet, suspecting the linen was not very clean—but any bugs in the bed be-longed to Jo, who looked tolerably healthy. Whatever the state of the sheets, this was incredibly better than where she had been sleeping. She was coming up in the medieval world, lodged in a castle turret instead of the dungeon, not that it stopped her from wishing to wake up at home.

She awoke not knowing where she was. Her eyes opened and she looked around the chilly tower room. First light fell through the arrow slits, and the rain had stopped. Someone breathed beside her on the big feather bed. Propping herself up on an elbow, she peered over the pillow. Jo lay curled on the far side, sleeping soundly. Strange. Jo had a guest bed in her cottage. Then she remembered, she was not in Jo's little cottage; not even in that century, not even in that millennium.

Closing her eyes, Robyn dropped back onto the pillow, telling her-self she was somewhere safe, and she could actually imagine going back to sleep. But it was hopeless. Too much hung over her. And something crawled in the bedclothes beneath her. She craved a bath and clean underwear more than sleep. Lying with eyes shut, breathing deeply, she marveled at how real this all was. Dank moldy smells welled up from wet stone walls. Jo's warm weight felt heavy on the bed. All that remained from her own world was the faint odor of peach shampoo in her hair. Turning her head, she opened her eyes, looking across the pillow at Jo. She had not shared a bed with another woman since college—unless you counted the times Heidi was too bombed to drive home. Sometimes Heidi made it to the couch, but when Heidi passed out on the bed, it was either lie down beside her or sleep in the couch herself. Heidi would always be up before her—fixing eggs with a phone in her ear, getting messages. Acting like her staying over was planned ahead of time. Which perhaps it was.

Now she was stuck in an endless sleepover. In an age with no notion of privacy. She had been here four days, two of them spent hiking through one of the least inhabited parts of England, at a time when the population was minuscule to begin with. But since dusk on the day she arrived, she had hardly been alone. And had never gotten far without people wanting to know who she was and what she was about. Offering food. Or a night's lodging. Or both. Or just deciding to take her into custody.

Bells chimed in the damp gray air. Prime. She must have slept through the bells at matins and lauds. Small surprise. Jo rolled over, opened her eyes, and smiled. "Good morrow, Robyn Stafford. I trust you enjoyed your night at Greystone?"

"Very much," she assured her host—though that had not stopped her from wishing herself centuries away.

Sitting up, Jo pushed with her foot on Joy, who lay at the bottom of the bed. "Wake up, dear. That was prime."

Joy groaned and got up. Keeping a blanket wrapped about her, she stumbled sleepily to the door, pulled back the wooden bolt, and then pushed it open. Seeing Robyn, she smiled and waved, then disappeared down dark, winding stone stairs.

Yawning, she asked Jo, "Can I get a hot bath before breakfast?"

"What?" Jo sounded shocked. "A bath before Mass?"

"That is what I was hoping."

Jo sounded scandalized. "Spurning God on this our Lord's day in order to plunge yourself into water on a cold morning? That would be begging for a fever or worse." For a witch who taught her daughter to dance naked on Friday nights, Jo seemed awfully wary of Sunday baths.

Joy reappeared carrying a candle, followed by serving women with fresh clothes. Jo got up and played Lady Bountiful, presenting Robyn with a clean white chemise and a wine-dark satin dress, topped off by a matching jacket with buttons down the breast and sleeves. "This was made for me, but will probably fit you. We are nearly of a size."

Robyn protested that she could never repay her. "You have already," Jo replied. "Besides, Collin had it made for me. He has the land and income, I am but his unmarried sister with a bastard child." Everything it seemed came from Collin. Jo said it nonchalantly—like small talk among friends, rather than a shameful secret. Immortals must measure their lives differently.

Serving women helped her dress, doing on-the-spot alterations. To her surprise, she found the clothes not only clean, but warmed by a fire as well. Hose and garters came with the outfit; so did white gloves trimmed with ermine. Over it all went an elegant pearl headpiece and a white surcoat embroidered with little red birds—making her feel regal. Dark Ages or not, people here knew how to dress. She just had to show them how to bathe.

Descending the tower stairs, she found serving men in blue-white livery waiting to escort them to Sunday morning Mass. She had never been to a Catholic service before—but this was the Middle Ages. Christianity was compulsory. Standing on religious principle was a sure way to end up bound to a stake waiting for someone like Le Boeuf to kindle a fire. Even a genteel witch family had their own chapel and priest—which must have been handy when it came to confession. Entering the chapel, she copied Jo's curtsy to the altar, and to Collin. Both felt strange. Being neither Catholic nor accustomed to bowing to men—at least in public. Especially one she was no longer seeing; but Collin had been bumped up from former boyfriend to her new lord and master. He nodded to acknowledge their bow as they settled into a front-row pew.

Mass began at once—it must have been waiting on them. Her first Catholic Mass was made even weirder by the way she understood every word of medieval Latin. Better even than the priest, whose memorized monotone was riddled with misplaced words and obvious gaps. Hiding behind pressed palms, she took her cue from Jo and Joy, who threw themselves into the ceremony, sinking to their knees and praying devoutly. Joy's face looked as transfixed as it had during her wild dance at Belas Knap. Medieval Christianity must still be close to its pagan roots, at least in this corner of the Cotswolds.

Sir Anthony was on his knees the whole time as well. Collin took Mass more lightly, sitting in the lord's pew, talking to underlings when the priest's back was to him. She watched out the corner of her eye, wondering what to make of him. Jo was fiercely happy to reward anyone who gave aid and comfort to her daughter. But what of Collin? Yesterday he could have saved himself a deal of trouble by turning her over to FitzHolland. Instead he called on God to judge and risked his life for her. Now here he sat on the Lord's day, coolly conducting business during the service. Stewards and bailiffs knelt at his pew, giving brief reports and getting terse orders. Sometimes he merely listened and nodded. But when the priest came to the rail with the Communion bread, he was kneeling there, ready to take a piece on his tongue.

So was she. As Saint Augustine says, "When in Rome . . ." The first thing she had for Sunday breakfast was the body of Christ. Whose blood was in the priest's wine, and in a little bottle in Hailes Abbey. Miracles seemed pretty commonplace here and now; no wonder Jo and Joy so readily believed her story.

After Mass they filed into the great hall to breakfast on hot spiced wine, pancakes, and—swear to God—roast peacock pie sprinkled with cinnamon sugar and boiled eggs, an incredible combination she barely touched. She sat on a cushioned seat at a raised part of the table, along with Collin's family and Sir Anthony, separated from the rest of the household by an ornate silver saltceller. Those sitting on benches "below the salt" breakfasted on bread, bacon, and ale, enjoying themselves nonetheless, laughing and joking as they lifted their tankards.

Her own goblet felt warm and heavy, and smelled of cinnamon. Hot sweet wine went down surprisingly well on a cold Sunday morning. Avoiding the peacock, she sneaked some bacon to go with her cinnamon pancakes. Her server's hands were clean, and medieval manners were immensely better than the movies made out; there was even a boy called a "sewer" who went about with a washbasin and kettle of hot water. Collin apologized for his preoccupation at Mass. "I have been on our king's business instead of my own. God will understand. Anyone who made the world in seven days knows what it is like to be rushed."

"Six days," Sir Anthony corrected him. "On the seventh day, even the Almighty rested."

Collin shrugged. "Being Almighty, God could afford to rest. Mere mortals often find the week too short. Times are terrible hard, with castles and manors sacked, and King Henry's enemies, both real and imagined, being hanged and beheaded." And a witch hunt under way as well. Collin did not say it—out of deference to Sir Anthony—but she could hear it in his tone. Plainly Collin was worried for his niece and sister, and for her as well. And for those enjoying beer and porridge "below the salt." Every looted manor meant more than some lord punished by the king—it meant plain folks losing their livelihoods, and worse, being raped or killed for their master's mistakes. No wonder Collin was careful about his politics, opposing the king's sergeant-at-law, but not King Henry.

"We have antagonized FitzHolland." Collin frowned at the

thought. "And he can bring his half brother Duke Holland of Exeter down on us—a fate too terrible to tempt." Heavy silence hung over the high table. She remembered what Collin said in Berkeley Castle, how the torture rack in the Tower was called the Duke of Exeter's Daughter.

"And now his grace Henry Holland is admiral of England," Sir Anthony added sourly, finding this especially galling. Sir Anthony had some special hatred of Lord Admiral Holland, which Robyn could only guess at—but it made him a ready ally against FitzHolland, the lord admiral's bastard brother.

"Much good it may do him." Collin lifted his glass in a mock toast. "Holland aims to blockade York in Ireland, but will have trouble aplenty from Welsh pirates and the wild Irish. I doubt Duke Holland will prove a match for Owen Boy O'Neill, much less Warwick, or the Duke of York."

Jo joined in her brother's toast. "May Duke Holland's enemies be many and nasty."

Everyone lifted glasses to that, even Robyn, the newest and least deadly of Duke Holland's many enemies. No one said what she could contribute. Or even how she could pay for her keep. Which was good, because she owed these people a lot and did not have much to offer beyond personal effects. Unless you counted the wisdom of the ages. Despite their casual air, she could tell when men expected something of her; they could not keep it out of their voices—that hint that you ought to be grateful. Somewhere there lurked a quid pro quo, and it did not seem to be sex. So far Collin and Sir Anthony had acted like a couple of Sir Galahads in training. Which really worried her. Sex she could deal with; the unknown scared her far more.

Coming from the impossibly high-tech future, she ought to have some way to repay them. Heck, she ought to own the place. Hollywood time travelers usually wowed the natives by inventing gunpowder or predicting eclipses. But these people already had gunpowder, and they hardly needed any help killing one another, being rather too handy at it already. And if an eclipse was coming, she sure did not know about it. High tech just did not translate well here and now. How could she invent something labor-saving and useful in a world without electricity or even running water? Three of the four people at her table were supernatural immortals, so whatever she did to impress them had to be really outstanding. Like maybe discovering America?

There were two whole continents out there that no one knew about. Even Collin would be impressed.

She planned to start with simple hygiene. But it turned out Jo knew all about Sunday baths—Jo just did not believe in bathing before Mass. After breakfast, Jo had sheets hung in a passage off the kitchens and told the cooks to boil water. Then Robyn, Jo, Joy, and several of the serving women took turns steaming in a big basin behind rose-scented sheets. Cooks kept hot water coming, making her forget Jo's old balky third-millennium shower.

Bathing turned out to be a group effort. Serving women helped her undress, and everyone made friendly comments about her body—how soft yet strong it was, how young she looked. "Comes from not having children," they told her. Spanning her hips with their hands, they assured her she would make an absolutely splendid breeder. "And it will fill out m'lady's breasts nicely, too, give you something more on top." So much for privacy. She asked Jo who Duke Holland was and why he hated them so much.

"He hates everyone," Joy interjected, industriously helping her rinse the last of the peach shampoo out of her hair.

Jo agreed with her daughter. "Duke Henry Holland is vain, vicious, and dangerous, and King Henry's closest cousin-male. He has the family madness. While King Henry's madness is the meek and incoherent sort, Duke Holland's is violent and deadly. When King Henry had his yearlong fit, Holland and Lord Egremont seized the city of York, declaring that whosoever supported them need not pay their taxes. A most popular proposition, but not enough to make Holland king. The duke of York put down their rebellion, imprisoning Holland in Pontefract Castle. When King Henry returned to what passes for his right mind, he ordered Holland released."

"And nine months in Pontefract only made the good duke worse," declared the serving woman bringing towels.

"If that were possible," Jo observed tartly, passing out the towels. "Now Duke Holland has imprisoned every Venetian merchant in London, for refusing to lend their fleet of galleys to keep York pinned in Ireland—an adroit piece of diplomacy that has enraged the foreign merchants without adding a single ship to Holland's fleet. Duke Holland is already hated by the London commons for hanging mercers and apprentices—now he has turned against the Italians as well. It is no small feat to make enemies of both the Londoners and the Italian merchants, since the two despise each other, competing fiercely and having nothing in common—not even speaking the same language. Yet Holland has united them against him." Never underestimate the power of hate.

Her hair now smelled of roses. Drying herself, she asked why Sir Anthony disliked Duke Holland so much—being neither common nor Italian?

"Sir Anthony Wydville's father, Baron Rivers, was lord admiral," Jo explained, "but he lost the office when Sir Anthony, his father, and his mother, the duchess of Bedford, were all taken prisoner by the rebel earls at Sandwich and whisked off to Calais, whereby Baron Rivers lost his fleet and his office. Sir Anthony was paroled by Warwick and Edward of March, but he hates Duke Holland for profiting from the family's misfortune."

When Robyn was dry, she got more warm clean clothes to change into. Afterwards she hung about the kitchen, noting how food was prepared, seeing what was washed and what was not. Things were not as bad as she feared, nor were they as good as she wished. Dogs and cats slept on the kitchen floor, but at least they kept the rats at bay. All ingredients were natural, and most relentlessly overcooked. Doubtful meat was shredded and then boiled in sugared wine and ginger until it was not only safe but palatable. Some food was killed alive in the kitchen, ensuring freshness, but making for very gross moments—raised on a ranch, Robyn had still never seen a pheasant drowned in its own blood before. When women asked why she winced, she explained that she was used to eating "frozen birds flown in from Arkansas." Which only provoked questions like "Where is Arkansas?" And "How can the birds fly if they are frozen?" Any attempts at true sanitation were totally hit and miss. Common stew simmered for hours in ultra-sanitary conditions, only to be ladled into bowls washed with bilge water. Cleanliness was next to unknown. Washing hands was for "Ladies like you, ma'am."

Curiously, the reverse was true. At Greystone the lower you ate, the better. Kitchen help had only their own germs to worry about, but the lord's meat passed from hand to hand—and Collin in turn gave "special guests" tidbits off his plate. Having your dishes washed for you was a dubious advantage when done by unclean hands in infected water. And while simple fare was safe but dull, the really deadly dishes were those fit for a king. Like roast swan gilded with egg yolks, with its feathers pasted back on. Yuck. It amazed her that royalty survived such meals. Of course, some did not. Dysentery, she discovered, was a great killer of kings. Mad King Henry's father died of it. So did bad King John in Robin Hood's day. And Henry I succumbed to a "suffet of oily lampreys." Double yuck, as Heidi would say.

But she could get boiled water to make herb tea. Mint. Chamomile. Fennel and anise—having a witch's pantry to choose from. Insisting on doing her own dishes, she only ate meat she cut herself. Folks thought her weird, but her cheerfulness and willingness to work won over the kitchen staff. Milkmaids saved her the skim milk they would otherwise throw to the pigs.

Jo gave her a *Babee Book*, to teach her better manners, mostly how to address Collin and how to do a proper curtsy. And how to have pleasantries on tap, for when her lord "does bid you be merry." It was chock-full of useful advice, like "Do not wipe your nose on the table-cloth, nor pick your teeth with your knife." It warned her to be a "dear darling, not a shrew" and not to watch men wrestling or shooting-the-cock "for that is what strumpets do." Luckily, neither sport much tempted her—especially the latter, which involved nailing a live bird to a tree as a target. She read to Joy from the section on raising children: "Never curse or scold if they are misbehaved, but take up a rod and beat them until they beg for mercy. They will love you all the more for it. . . ." Joy hooted at that, saying it would take more than a caning to get her to beg. Clearly, child psychology was in its infancy.

Next morning she awoke knowing exactly where she was. No longer expecting to be whisked home at any time, she gave in and reset her watch, severing her last electronic link to the third millennium. Who cares what day and hour it was in the far-distant future? Propped in bed beside her, Jo watched, all agog at the glowing digits. "What does MON 4-28-60 mean?"

"Monday, April twenty-eighth, 1460." Edward's eighteenth birthday—making him legal. Much good it did her, with him in Ireland and her here in bed with Jo. Still, it was nice to think of him—wondering how he had changed in half a year. Hopefully, he still thought of her, when not cavorting among the colleens. Half a year might well seem like half a millennium to a teenager. She wished she had some way to send Edward a letter, but it was treason to send anything of comfort to the rebels in Ireland. Especially love letters. At least she would now know how to address him, and do a decent curtsy—if she got the chance.

"Marvelous." Jo liked the idea of having the date and time on your wrist. To Jo the day was "Saint Catherine's Eve, two days until May Eve."

"May Eve?" Robyn looked over at her bedmate.

"A most special date on the witch's calendar."

But of course. Spring orgies and all that. How much more of this could she take? She resented the easy way Jo said she "must" be a witch. How unfair. She was a stranger here who should be treated with respect—even reverence—considering where she had come from. But from the moment she arrived, she had been hounded by witch hunters and accused of heinous crimes. Even her "friends" insisted on dragging her into feuds with powerful lords and diabolical acts punished by burning—seemingly intent on proving FitzHolland right.

"Come—you will like it. Maybe even enjoy it," Jo insisted. "And it is not too soon to get ready."

She immediately shocked everyone by asking to have another bath. "But it is only Monday," Jo protested. "Please, do not punish yourself so—you have done naught to deserve it. Inordinate washing shows guilt, a sign the soul is unclean." Just like Lady Macbeth. Jo could be right, maybe she was trying to wash the Middle Ages away.

"Perhaps she merely likes to show her body," a gap-toothed cook suggested. "It is wonderous beautiful." Yes, they all agreed, she was indeed an eyeful. "But why waste your nakedness on us? Save it for the men and May Eve. They are the ones who will most enjoy it."

She said she would gladly bathe alone, but they took it as an insult, hastening to soothe her, humoring her weird desire. "Dear heart, do not despair, we are heating the water. Here, let us help you with your clothes." By the time her bath was done, she did feel better; it was impossible not to. Everyone was so friendly toward her, and so full of May Eve, she would have felt like a spoilsport, acting sour and wanting to be pampered. Young women were especially happy, vowing May Eve was the gayest holiday of the year, "When all the rules are overturned. When we do as we wish, picking and choosing among the men."

Older women laughed at their youthful enthusiasm, while admitting "it was useful to have one day out of the year when you are not married." When Robyn asked what that meant, they giggled slyly, saying, "You will see."

Everyone had the May Eve fever, from the lowliest milkmaid to Sir Collin himself—whom she had seen but little, aside from at Mass and meals, and never alone. Collin became a distant presence, always seeing to his lands or exercising his squires, while keeping a wary eye out for armed men making awkward demands. Which irked her a bit. She felt thankful to Collin, and not just for saving her from burning— but she missed being included in his concerns. She found it hard not to think of this semi-stranger as her Collin. Someone she used to have available at whim—not in the least her lord and master.

But after breakfast he came around, asking if she wanted to ride out and "see to the dairy herds. Mayhap you will remark something done better in the far future." Mayhap she would, having grown up on a cattle ranch—though the biggest advances in dairying were mechanical milking and refrigeration, things she was not up to inventing. But his pretext hardly mattered; this was a transparent offer to trade her morning chores for a ride with him, to see his herds and lands, and to listen to his troubles. Breakfast was particularly unhygienic, so all she had in her was burnt toast and mint tea—not the best basis for a morning on horseback. Still she leapt at the chance to go lollygagging with her lord.

Collin already had Plunket saddled, a sign he was not used to household women saying no. In fact, her lord seemed happy and confident, riding along the Edge toward Buckland Wood, inspecting herds of small dark Welsh heifers and angular medieval cattle—also noting fences, sheep pens, and fish weirs on the Isbourne in need of repair. Most of Collin's land was let out to tenants, but he had great herds of sheep and cattle, and enough cropland to feed his household. Calving was well along, and she listened to milkmaids complain how they lacked fodder for breeding cattle. Something she could well believe; many medieval animals looked seriously underfed—the rest, merely lean. She had yet to see a fat one.

"It is the rains." Collin turned in the saddle to study clouds above Lidcombe Hill—more rain off the Bristol Channel, drifting up the Vale of Severn. "A wet spring makes everything harder, and I fear summer will be worse." He told her how rains had played havoc with woodcutting, manuring, and hay-making, adding to his problems. Collin had to be his own weather bureau as well as estate manager. He promised the milkmaids more hay, "and parsnip tops, which make the milk sweeter."

Everyone laughed, knowing Robyn drank the skim milk usually slopped to the pigs—it amused Collin vastly that people in the future thought it especially healthful to live on vegetables and pig slop. "Like those monks that live on figs and water. Your Holy Wood is indeed most holy."

"Not half as holy as here." She looked over the stone steeples rising from the green Severn Valley. Abbey lands touched Collin's on three sides. She sensed the peace lying over the land, the myriad shared tasks, the closeness to the soil—not at all what she expected. Collin told the maids he would have the reeve get them their fodder, and men to clean the byres and to cart water—that dairying was women's work did not make it less important. Cheese laid up now would feed everyone in winter, as would the pigs raised on skim milk. When they rode on, she asked, "Do you know about vaccination?"

"Vaccination?" Collin clearly did not.

"Milkmaids get an illness from the cows, called cowpox, that saves them from getting smallpox." This was her one bit of medical knowledge that might make a big difference here and now. The word *vaccination* even came from the Latin *vaccinus*, meaning "cow"—her Latin vocabulary had grown enormously of late. "Cowpox is not so bad, and whoever gets it is safe from smallpox."

Collin's face lit up. "So that is why their skin is so soft and clear; I thought it was all the cream they drank." Anything that saved you from the deadly pox while softening women's skin had his instant approval. "You are a witch after all."

"Not really." Not yet, at least; Jo meant to change that.

"But you do know the future?"

"Some of it." Not near enough. Life right now felt like some nightmare final exam that she had totally forgotten to study for. She could not tell anybody what would happen next month or next year. In 1492 Columbus would discover America—but that was three decades away.

"Joanna says you knew her and Joy many centuries from now."

"I knew two like them."

That got a happy laugh from Collin. "Like them? My sister and niece are like no one else I ever knew. How could it be anyone but them?" She admitted his point.

"And what about me?" he asked.

"Yes, you, too." Knew him and then some. They were entering ticklish territory.

He looked at her intently. "That was why you thought you knew me that first day?"

She nodded.

He thought on that, then asked, "Did I have much to do with bringing you back?"

"Not directly." He had not been with the coven on that hilltop, but Collin had come to Los Angeles, appearing out of nowhere in her life, convincing her they were eternal soul mates. True, he had not tried to get her to come to England—in fact was horrified when she arrived. But without him, she never would have come, especially not to this out-of-the-way corner of the Cotswolds.

"But I did have a part in it?"

"Yes, you did. Or someone very like you."

"*Mon Dieu*, I wish I knew what my motives were." He stared ahead, as if trying to see through the centuries, pondering what his future self could have been up to. She had not thought of it that way before, but it did make sense. He must have come to Hollywood to find her. But why? He turned back to her, smiling artfully. "Aside from the obvious reasons, fair lady."

"The obvious?" Nothing about this seemed the least obvious.

"You are passing fair and pleasant to have about. Had I not done what I did then, you would not be here now." Everything could be turned to Collin's advantage, from cowpox to her own cosmic catastrophe. "How do you get cowpox," he asked, "in order to be saved from smallpox?"

"Same way the milkmaids do. From milking. Or from cow pus, especially if you prick yourself with it on a needle."

Neither appealed to Collin. "Pricking yourself with cow pus? And you claim not to be a witch? That makes my sister's worst potions sound palatable—there must be another way."

"Perhaps," she admitted. "Some of them must get cowpox from close physical contact with other milkmaids."

"There, that sounds pleasanter." His smile returned. "Good health does not have to hurt."

Maybe the Middle Ages was not ready for modern medicine. And certainly not modern agrobusiness. Every task, no matter how detailed or difficult, was done by people, or their animals. Not just farming and dairying, but also the shearing and carding, and a lot of the spinning and weaving in what was a great wool-producing area. Here every nail and every pin was handmade by someone. On Collin's manor, pins and nails were forged by a pair of brawny female smiths—who gave every sign of being same-sex-oriented, something accepted with small comment. Sex here and now was a private pleasure, and very often a sin, but not a national calamity. No one thought England would be ruined because Joy was a bastard or because two blacksmiths shared a bed. Life under Mad King Henry left them with more real worries.

Most tenants were working families, farming their own land as well as Collin's. Those who tilled his land or grazed flocks on his pastures paid him rent, though this was not always the case. "For centuries we farmed our lands and ran our own flocks using labor services from our tenants." Collin talked of centuries past like he had seen it. "A silly system. Forced labor rewards dodgers and shirkers. Now tenants work the land as they will—ten times harder than if a bailiff stood over them with a stick."

"And pay you for the privilege?"

"Exactly." He grinned mischievously. "But I charge them less than they would charge each other—and they well know it. Turn Greystone over to some grasping baseborn landlord out to make his fortune, and half these families would be driven off land their great-grandparents tilled. And there would be no one to throw a feast or to appeal to in hard times. Or to tell tales about. So I am a hero, instead of hated."

"So I noticed." Collin was genuinely popular. Being the lord, men had to tip their hats and give him good-day—but no law said the women must look at him how they did. He was every dairy maid's prince charming. Handsome, chivalrous, and unattainable.

"And I did away with the most obnoxious of the lord's prerogatives," he told her, "like heriot. When a tenant died, the lord used to take the family's best beast."

"How horrible!" A private tax on widows and orphans.

"*Exactement.* No money could make up for the ignominy of walking off with some grieving old woman's prize cow."

"What about droit du seigneur?" The lord's ancient right to a bride's "first night." She meant to pierce his smug chivalry.

He laughed. "You do have a tongue. Here we call it merchet."

"And it still exists?"

"But, of course." He looked aghast, as if to say who would let something so useful slip away?

"And is still practiced?" Perhaps Sir Collin was not that unattainable after all. Just busy.

"My lady, we are civilized nowadays, and wash our fingers before we eat with them. A money payment is substituted."

"How unromantic." Money could already buy almost anything.

"How true, still I try to observe the spirit. If I approve the marriage, I give the money to the bride as a wedding gift."

"And if you disapprove?"

"I hold the money to see that she and her children do not become a charge on the parish. It helps people take marriage seriously." Sir Collin shrugged off the cost to him. "These are small fees, paid once in a lifetime. I have wide holdings and can afford to buy goodwill." There were hard lords and easy ones, and it well behooved a warlock to be an easy one. "Besides, I live cheaply enough, having so far avoided that greatest expense of all."

"What expense is that?"

His mischievous grin returned. "Having a wife."

But, of course. Marriage here and now was a serious business decision—for many, the most serious business decision. Everyone was Catholic, so divorce was rare. And the Church absolutely backed a woman's right to choose: Girls married off as infants could refuse at the "age of consent." Teenagers saying their own vows were married in the eyes of Mother Church, needing neither priest's nor parents' permission. Women could be picky, and often married "beneath them" if the man had other attractions. Even a wealthy gentleman like Collin could not count on finding a "suitable" wife—since he was expected to marry an heiress or a woman of property, adding to the family holdings.

She liked this unmarried Sir Collin, who was generous and clever, without being pushy, a welcome combination in any man. How happy not to have him snapped up—still free to go riding with her. And he felt safe. Unattainable was not so bad after the scares she had suffered. This was Collin, someone she felt like she knew. He had risked his life for her, given her shelter, and never tried to take advantage of her.

Leaving only the nagging question of why he had not tried to take advantage of her. What's the matter? Was she not pretty enough? Other guys seemed to think so.

When time came to kiss good-bye, Collin pulled her firmly to him, holding the kiss extra long, showing he meant it. Not at all like the kisses he gave Jo. Woozy from riding on an empty stomach, the kiss went straight to her head. When their lips parted, he whispered, "You feel thin—pray do not starve to death on us." She promised not to, wondering what the kiss meant. Mayhap Sir Collin was not so safe after all.

⋯⇒ Robin and Marian ⇐⋯

She came back from her ride to find that her fellow mice had done Cinderella's chores for her. "And there is something for you on the bed," Jo announced when they got back from dinner—a noontime meal here and now—where Robyn put dubious fish cakes and doubtful pork-raisin pie on top of her morning toast, with no excuse except that she was starved. Lying on the bed was a bolt of fine blue satin. No parchment note came with it. Totally Collin, a necessity disguised as a present. Still a charming gesture, if one that rooted her even more deeply in his world.

She put it to immediate use—designing and cutting out a riding dress, to be trimmed with some of Jo's cloth of silver. Next time they went riding, she could be wearing Collin's colors. Tired of hand-me-downs, she was happy to go from mending other people's cast-offs to designing her own outfits. Throughout her "acting career" she often settled for stage manager or costume designer. Now in her biggest role ever, mundane skills like hand-sewing were suddenly essential. Dress up was no longer a game, but a necessity—every day here and now seemed like Halloween.

May Eve was more like Halloween than most, starting with the sound of piping and the phallic sight of Collin and his men erecting a maypole. Some wore fanciful masks: wolf faces, pig snouts, a giant mouse head, or grinning skulls. All of them were happy, and there was constant joking back and forth, a lot of sly looks and giddy talk. May Day seemed to be that kind of holiday.

Coming in from setting up the pole, Collin winked at her. She replied with a smile. There were advantages in flirting with your lord. Or so she heard. Group baths were an education in more ways than one. Since she was not "a fit object for marriage," all Collin could offer was love and excitement—which she was free to accept or reject. Short of violence, he had no way to sway her. Church, law, and society all supported her right to say no—even encouraged it. And if a lord was indiscreet enough to offer marriage, Mother Church was there to make it real. Curiously, the landed heiress or rich widow had more to fear. Women of property could be abducted for their lands and coerced into forced marriage, consummated by rape. But with her, what would be the point? What you saw was what you got.

She spent the day getting ready for the morrow, sewing on costumes and pounding boar meat. Under Jo's supervision, she mixed the pulverized boar meat with eggs, pinecones, and raisins, frying the resulting concoction in fresh grease spiced with pepper, ginger, cinnamon, saffron, sugar, and salt. She poured the mixture into a raw pastry appropriately called a *coffyn*—then the cook "planted" the coffyn with dates, raisins, small birds, and hard-boiled eggs, glazing the whole mess with egg yolks and saffron, before putting it in the oven to bake—along with special May Day cakes. On festive occasions the medieval diet could be thoroughly imaginative. For doing this and her other chores, Jo paid her pennies a day, though it was clear that all money came from Sir Collin. She did not feel slighted—everyone worked for silver pennies in the West Country's piggy bank economy. Gold nobles were rare and worth a month's wages. Shillings and pounds existed only on paper. Her Hollywood salary would make her a duchess here and now. Instead she was finding out how Heidi felt, working for a lenient but eccentric boss lady.

Despite the winks and smiles, when night fell the sexes separated. Everyone retired to their respective beds, or so Robyn assumed. She for sure did. Her watch read WED 4-30-60—one week in the Middle Ages. Seven days she would not likely forget. She was doing well just to have survived them. But she needed to do better than that. Way better.

Well after the witching hour, she was awakened by girls' excited voices. She sat up and found the tower room full of women. Wash-

erwomen, cooks, and dairy maids—not all of them, but enough to fill
the room. Serving girls stood giggling with Joy. She had to recognize
them by their voices because most were masked, and all wore green
gowns, green-dyed cloaks, and flowers in their hair. A similar outfit
was laid out for her, including a wreath of buttercups. Women
laughed at her changing under the coverlet, saying, "No need for
shame. 'Tis May Eve. No one worries about being bare-assed on Beltane."

No one expects to be dragged out of bed, either. Beltane was the
Celtic name for May Eve. Were they drunk? Tipsy for sure, from
drinking beer at breakfast, dinner, and supper. At times like this, the
Middle Ages was really like being back in college. Sleeping three to a
room. No one having regular jobs. Endless lessons in medieval history,
punctuated by beer parties. Apparently at all hours. She looked at her
watch—3:07 A.M.

"Come, it will be immense fun." Jo hauled her out from under the
coverlet. "This is May Eve. From now until dawn tomorrow there are
no lords and ladies, no Church and king. No rank and no marriage.
Just women and men, free to do as we will." May Eve might have no
rank, but Jo was clearly in charge of this romp. Being a knight's sister
and a gentlewoman witch counted for something, even on Beltane.
"Come along." Jo pulled her off the bed, crowning her with buttercups. "We dare not waste a moment of the day. We will start with
song and prayer, to welcome in the May before the men are up."

"When the men are up, twill be too late to pray," a milkmaid called
out. Others laughed in agreement. "And we will all sing another
song." That's for sure. Robyn foresaw a wild day at Greystone, with
plain Jacks and Jills running things, unaided by Church and law.
Winding their way down the tower stairs and out into the bailey, they
joined more women, carrying torches. Firelight cast dancing shadows
on the blank stone face of the fortified manor, turning women into
fantasy shapes. Surprisingly the bailey gate stood wide open—a black
hole in the firelight—letting in the night.

Night was still night here and now, day's dark twin, and the Devil's
domain, non-streetlighted blackness inhabited by footpads and walking dead. Jo meant to start the day of lawlessness by defying a primal
taboo. Taking a torch from a big smiling blacksmith, Robyn joined
the snaking line of green-gowned women filing towards the dark gate,
singing:

> **We come all so still**
> **Where our Mother was,**
> **As dew in April**
> **That falleth on the grass.**

A week ago she had been skulking about Berkeley Castle, remembering "take back the night" marches, now she was in one—and totally thrilled. Her fears did fall away, beginning with the absolute hopeless terror that haunted her since she first realized she was in the Middle Ages, her fear of never getting back. Filing through the gate, singing along as best she could:

> **We come all so still**
> **To our Mother's bower,**
> **As dew in April**
> **That falleth on the flower.**

Terror still lurked in the night. Not imaginary ghouls and goblins, but witch hunters, and the very real night riders that preyed on the West Country. Yet each singing step put her fears further behind her. Yes, there was danger. But not here. Not now. Nor on the morrow. For the morrow was May Day. And there would be neither laws nor outlaws. Folks would live as they willed, without fear and without want. As they were meant to. And these women meant to make the most of it.

Lauds bells rang as they climbed Shenberrow Hill, meeting another line of torch-bearing women coming up from Stanton; together they spiraled in toward a great brush pile at the crest of the hill, with an open butt of ale nearby. Circling in around the pile, they tossed their torches one by one into it, setting the brushwood alight. Flames leaped up, shooting huge sparks at the sky.

Throwing her torch onto the pyre, Robyn saw an answering glimmer from out toward Broadway Hill. Looking south past Lidcombe, she spotted another fire. Up and down the Cotswold Edge, people braved the night to light bonfires, welcoming in the May. Joy seized one hand, a tough-handed blacksmith took the other, and they all began circling the fire, singing:

> **Of the Maiden sing,**
> **She that is makeless;**

King of all the Spring,
The babe at her breast.

Another line of green-clad women, circling in the opposite direction,
answered back:

Mother and Maiden,
Was never none but she;
Well may such a lady
God's mother be.

Robyn felt awed, surrounded by women who had welcomed her,
listened to her stories and accepted her foibles, not holding her
strangeness against her, trying against all odds to make her feel at
home. Singing subsided, and dancers took time out to visit the ale
butt, pledging and toasting each other from a common cup. As the
fire burned down, women began jumping over the flaring embers,
some alone, some in pairs, leaping hand in hand through the last of
the flames. As they jumped, they called out wishes for the coming year.
Easter was New Year's here and now, so for them the year had just
begun. Robyn could still not shake the feeling that this was still late
October. Halloween costumes and all. The year should be wrapping
up, not just beginning. But she leaped happily when her turn came,
shouting, "Take me home!"

First light showed over the Cotswolds. May Day was dawning, and
she did not want the magical night to end. She stood with her breath
misting in front of her, seeing people moving in the gray May morning, coming up from Stanton and Snowshill. Youths and maidens
mostly, some wearing masks or crowns of flowers, headed for Lidcombe Hill and Littleworth Wood, to gather greenery. And to wash
their faces in the first dew of May.

Having shouted out her wish to leave, she made a pact with herself—she would spend this day totally in the Middle Ages, putting off
all thought of going home until tomorrow. Otherwise how could she
be truly free? Not by moping about wishing she were somewhere else.
She refused to be the only one at Greystone stubbornly unwilling to
celebrate life. She would drink from the common cup and stop ob-
sessing about being trapped in a world without microwave popcorn.
Giving herself this one day to enjoy, to do what she willed, partaking

in whatever pleasure appealed to her—so long as it seemed tolerably safe. How often were you granted a day of freedom? Who knows when one would come again?

Women began to file back down toward Greystone. Men came up to meet them, blowing on pipes and beating drums, wearing stick antlers and wild costumes—whether she willed it or no, May Eve was ending. Now "the men are up" and the dance would be different. Ale on an empty stomach made her light-headed and happy, not yet ready to go back to Greystone. Treating herself to a little more total freedom, she headed for Lidcombe instead, to help young folks "bring in the green."

Lidcombe Wood was full of dark leafy crisscrossing trails, alive with laughter. Half the countryside was up and carousing. This was May Morning, a day out of time. No rank. No law. No Church looking over your shoulder. She met a masked trio, two boys and a girl coming the other way, arms linked and looking flushed, wishing her a "Happy May." One of the youths grabbed at her green gown, hoping to make it a foursome. Smiling, she slipped his grip, continuing on her way, looking for fallen green boughs to bring back. May Day or no, she could not bear tearing them from the living trees.

She emerged triumphant from the wood on the west slope of Lidcombe Hill, arms full of fallen greenery. Steep bare pasture fell away at her feet, bounded by Gallop Wood a couple of hundred yards below. Beyond Gallop Wood she could see all the way to Bredon Hill, and deep into the low green Vale of Evesham, where the spire of Evesham Abbey rose above a loop of the Avon. Closer in, she recognized Stanton, and Toddington by the Isbourne—this tiny corner of medieval Britain was becoming thoroughly familiar.

Hoofbeats sounded behind her. Spinning about, she saw Collin reining in atop a palfrey decked with daisy chains. He wore a green feather mask and a long stylish green jacket slashed up the side to show off tight green hose, a well-muscled leg, and knee-high boots. Swinging easily out of the saddle, he wished her "a most happy May."

Here was an appealing pleasure—but was it safe to partake? Resisting the impulse to curtsy, she wished him a Happy May as well. Until dawn tomorrow they were equals, and a little voice inside urged, "Make the most of it."

Collin stepped closer, stopping when they were near enough to touch. He took off the mask and smiled. For once she enjoyed the tension between them, feeling in complete control, knowing she would not do anything she did not want to do. How nice to have him as her equal—no longer lord of the manor, and now totally unmarried. Very much the Collin she had been madly in love with. Not only had he never betrayed her with Bryn, but this Sir Collin had in fact saved her life. That alone deserved a kiss. She leaned up to do it. He looked happily surprised.

Laughter broke out around them. Children and teenagers had crept up in the undergrowth, spying on their nominal lord and his curious guest. Seeing the kiss coming, the youngest could not hold their giggles, and their elders joined in the chorus of laughter. Collin winced and rolled his eyes. Today he could not order them away. And it was going to cost him a kiss.

More people poured out of the wood, men and women as well. Before she could protest, Robyn was surrounded and separated from Collin. Sturdy hands seized her and would not let go, hoisting her up off her feet into the air. Shocked at being manhandled—even in fun—she saw they meant to put her on Collin's palfrey. Surprised and scared by the rough familiarity, she felt safer mounted, hastily scrambling aboard the horse.

People cheered wildly as she clung hard to the saddle. She was ringed by tenants and servants, some masked, some not; all decked with greenery and thoroughly enjoying their day of freedom. Plain Jacks and Jills would run things for a day, but it never occurred to Robyn that their plans might include her. Apparently they did, because men took the reins on the palfrey, and women fell in beside her, and they paraded happily back through the green lanes of Lidcombe Wood—gleefully robbing their lord and master of his horse, his companion, and his kiss. Leaving Sir Collin to make his way back to Greystone on foot.

Lurching along atop the palfrey, her own day of freedom had come to a swift end. So much for doing "only what she willed." She was as much in these people's hands as she had been in FitzHolland's; hopefully whatever they had planned for her was not something humiliating. Or dangerous. Or unsanitary. Because she had no hope of saying no. Parading her back to Greystone, they picked up more youths and maidens returning from the woods decked with green leaves and crowns of flowers. Robyn realized these people must have done this every May for eons—DNA lineages in these little English villages had been traced back to the ice ages. Lord knows how many women they had led down this slope.

At the bailey gate the triumphal procession met the Lord of Misrule and his court. His lordship Much the Miller was dressed in a wild harlequin costume sewn with playing cards, wearing a belled fool's cap and donkey ears. He had a tankard for a scepter and his first unofficial act had been to throw open the manor brewery. Much's court consisted of Devils, Saracens, kettle-helmed knights, and wild men wearing horns and body suits covered with horsehair. His spiritual adviser was the Abbess of Unreason, one of the blacksmiths wearing a hooded robe over her green gown. She sat perched atop a beer barrel, balanced on a goat cart, holding a crown of gold leaves. Her "monks" wore goat horns and straw boots, and they cavorted with pregnant nuns. Among them were real monks and clerks from Snowshill and Stanway, come to Greystone for a secular May. One wore a bishop's miter but was otherwise stark naked. On May Day folks were free to scoff at their betters, satirize religion, even speak the truth—crimes normally punished by hanging, burning, and dismemberment.

People parted, making a path to her palfrey. Wondering what this all meant, she watched from the saddle as Jo stepped forward, holding an ornate russet gown of crushed velvet, embroidered with cloth-of-gold leaves. Joy bore a great green mantle to go with the gown. "Come," Jo called up to her, "Lord Much of Misrule wants you for Marian, Queen of the May."

"He does?" She could not fathom why. What had she ever done for Much, besides eat his bread? When she did not burn it trying to make toast.

"Everyone does." Jo swung her arm to indicate the motley throng. Plain Jacks and Jills shouted their agreement, giving a ragged cheer, followed by a chant of, "Marian, Marian, Marian . . ."

"See, you are too good a chance to let pass," Jo declared. "How often have enchanted strangers from far-off lands come this way?"

Now the chant changed to, "Holy Wood, Holy Wood, Holy Wood . . ."

How amazing—they liked her. She had made a hit without knowing it. Absolutely shocking, since all she had done was work night and day to ingratiate herself; listening intently to what anyone told her, giving the fairest answers she could, copying their customs, and diligently studying her *Babee Book*. Trying desperately not to be too much trouble—all the time thinking herself a thorough pest, knowing nothing about anything, but wanting everything done her way.

Blunt dirty hands helped her down off the palfrey. Women surrounded her, raising green boughs to screen out men's gaze, while Jo and Joy helped her change into the May Queen's gown. Then the Abbess of Unreason draped the green silk mantle around her shoulders, saying, "Do not fret, my dear. We will help you with your answers." Her answers? They meant her lines. She had landed a speaking part.

Women formed an arch with their boughs, and out stepped Marian, Queen of the May—née Robyn Stafford of Hollywood—head high, crowned with a circlet of gold. Cheers rang out. Ahead she saw her chariot, drawn up by the bailey gate, a hay cart strung with flowers harnessed to a huge pair of spotted hogs. She boarded proudly, to be drawn by giant swine through the green-boughed bailey gate to wild applause.

Within the walled bailey, she presided over the maypole dance from atop her chariot—which was good because she could never have managed the steps. Women and men danced around the maypole, hands clasped and arms linked, laughing and singing, while keeping time with their feet, facing the pole and treading in place when they sang the chorus, then galloping off around the pole with each new verse. Standing with her in the chariot, playing lady-in-waiting, Jo whispered, "Be ready."

As she said it, the Lord of Misrule started a new song around the maypole:

> **Come all you gallants brave, and listen a while,**
> **With a hey down, down, an a down**
> **For of Robin Hood, that archer good,**
> **His song you shall hear . . .**

Right on cue, Robin Hood himself appeared, bow in hand at the bailey gate, dressed in Lincoln green with a red feather in his cap, backed by a band of outlandish merry men wearing hides and blowing horns. It was Collin.

Who picked him to play Robin? Much the Miller might be Lord of

Misrule, but she wondered who else had a hand in it. Whoever did, the choice was popular. Folks around the maypole cheered, continuing their song while Collin mimed the actions, strutting about and bending his bow. Bringing more cheers. She marveled at how easily he made fun of himself, and how funny he was at it. Collin had the good sense to enjoy being lord of the manor—rather than letting it go to his head.

"He will come to woo you," Jo warned, "but do not give in—not until he has won you as well."

Right. Do not let everyone think she was too easy. She was Maid Marian, Queen of the May, womanhood personified, and no man could win her just by strutting about and making a fool of himself. She had standards to maintain. So when Collin bowed, hat in hand, before her, and the singing proclaimed his love, she got to be deliciously condescending. Coyly she pretended not to get his meaning, while using every sitcom double entendre she could dredge up—even the oldest ones were new to 1460—putting the crowd in stitches.

Jo giggled whispering, "Very good," in her ear. Robin Hood withdrew crestfallen, and a new suitor entered the list. Sir Anthony rode through the bailey gate in full armor, wearing red and silver Wydville livery. He reined in before her and did a deft, armored dismount, going down on a metal knee to ask for her hand. "Remain true to Robin," whispered Jo.

Totally into the role, she turned Sir Anthony's suit aside with more sweet malapropisms, trying to hit the right tone—somewhere between burlesque and soap opera. Everyone howled to see a baron's son on bended knee, being hilariously turned down by the May Queen they had crowned. Sir Anthony remounted and rode off, followed by hisses, catcalls, and cries of, "Go back to Grafton."

Next the May play went from flirting to farce, requiring her to go back behind a screen of boughs and emerge dressed in Robin Hood drag, to everyone's vast amusement. Then she went in search of the lovelorn "Robin"—finally finding her jilted outlaw in the stables. Collin pretended not to know who this "boy" was, and they fought a mock battle balanced on a beam above a water trough, flailing away at each other with inflated pig-bladders tied to quarterstaves in a life-size Punch-and-Judy show. Following the script, the flailing ended with Collin going toes over tail into the horse trough—to howls of laughter from his servants and tenants. From her place on the beam, she called down to Collin, saying an "infamous knight" had dared play court to his "lady love." Then she retreated behind her screen of boughs to change back to the Queen of the May, putting on her crown and finery for the final scene—a joust between her suitors.

Returning to her hog-drawn chariot, she presided over a farcical reenactment of the fight at Sudeley Castle. Aside from cloistered nuns under vows of silence, everyone from here to Wales had heard of Collin's fight with FitzHolland. But only a handful outside Sudeley had actually seen the joust. His tenants and servants must have felt cheated. Now they would get their chance to see him perform. First came a clowning parody by squires mounted on donkeys, armed with broomsticks, wearing pot-and-kettle armor—common folk ridiculing lordly pretensions. But when Sir Anthony and "Robin" rode into the lists armored cap-a-pie, even the clowns fell silent. Here was the main event. Collin had traded his own livery for Lincoln green, and looked like a different person with his sallet closed and a hunting horn on his shield. She was already learning to judge a knight by his colors. Only the kiwi green Minnie Mouse scarf streaming from beneath his sallet said this was Collin.

Both had blunted lances, but she sensed a delicious shiver going through the motley throng, knowing they would see something thrilling and dangerous, done by their betters for their amusement. Modern times and the Middle Ages had this much in common—when else did you get to see millionaires bang away at each other to amuse the masses? Here and now they just did it on horseback. Having already seen way more mounted combat than she ever meant to, Robyn thanked heaven this fight was between friends—making it somewhat less dangerous, though Collin had never killed anyone except by accident.

Trotting to opposite ends of the bailey, the knights turned to face each other, lances held high. Jo whispered, "You must signal the charge with your arm." She did not want to do it, seeing no reason for men and horses to throw themselves at each other. Much less two men she liked. Reminding herself this was a play, and a role—that she was no longer Robyn Stafford but Marian, Queen of the May— she raised her hand high, calling out, *"Lessiez les aler"* like Lord Sudeley's herald. Everyone looked to her. She called out, *"Lessiez les aler,"* again. Their lances came down. Once more, Robyn had to remind herself to breathe.

She let her hand drop. *"Lessiez les aler et fair leur devoir de par*

Dieu." And they charged, thundering at each other. She winced as they slammed together in a ringing collision that bowed both their lances. Neither man toppled from the saddle; neither lance broke. They rode on and turned about, preparing for another charge.

"Two more passes," Jo whispered, "unless one of them is un-horsed."

She raised her arm again. By now she well knew what havoc dropping her hand would bring, and suddenly it thrilled her, thrilled her completely. She was mortally tired of living in fear of what armed men might do to her. How they might hurt her, or kill her, or just throw her into a cell because they did not like her pert replies or because she wore pants. For once she had the upper hand, and the crowd on her side. By dropping her arm she could send these two high and mighty males galloping at each other, each trying to unseat the other. All for her, Marian, Queen of the May. So why not enjoy it? They were here by choice. Collin and Sir Anthony were absolutely enjoying themselves, as was the crowd. Even the chargers had to be willing—neither man was the sort to ride a warhorse that would shy from a charge. So far as she could see, there was the only one person here against her will, "*Lessiez les aler et fair leur devoir de par Dieu.*" She brought her hand down hard.

Again they came crashing together. Again she winced. Both lances shattered explosively, flinging chunks of wood at the cheering crowd. Both riders reeled in the saddle, but neither lost his seat. They merely rode to opposite ends of the bailey, where squires on stilts, dressed as Welsh giants, gave them new lances. When they had their lances couched and their horses looked ready, she raised her hand for the third time.

Having shards of wood hurtle past her head took the thrill out of jousting. Though it was done in her honor and at her command, this was still a man's game—one that made pro linebackers seem like sissies. So she did like Collin, leaving it up to heaven, saying a short prayer for no one to be hurt and then bringing down her arm.

They hurtled at each other for the third time, Sir Anthony in Wyd-ville white and red, Collin in his Lincoln green. At the moment of impact, Collin leaned into the blow, like he had done against Fitz-Holland, at the same time tilting his hunting horn shield. Sir Anthony's lance bounced upward, but Collin's hit square on the Wydville's red-and-silver shield. Only to shatter uselessly. People ducked as the largest part cartwheeled into the crowd. Too bad. Despite her pious "let heaven decide" attitude, she secretly hoped Collin would win. He was Robin Hood, Marian's true love, and she was only putting him through these trials to test his devotion. He was not supposed to lose.

So why was everyone cheering? All around her antlered men and green-gowned women were shouting and throwing flowers. Robin's merry men blew their horns and shouted a view halloo. She could hardly believe they had all suddenly turned on their hero. Jo leaned close to her ear. "Prepare to give him his reward."

"Give who a reward?"

Jo looked surprised. "Robin Hood." Who else? "Collin," Jo added hurriedly, least Maid Marian totally flub her lines.

"But his lance broke?" Disintegrated, actually. Even now he proudly showed the stub to the crowd.

"That is good," Jo explained. "If no one is unhorsed, the prize goes to the one who breaks the most lances." Sir Robin wins on points. Tipping back his sallet visor, Robin Hood came trotting toward her, nonchalantly holding his shattered lance, his Minnie Mouse scarf snapping in the breeze. He drew rein beside her hog-drawn chariot, smiling impertinently at his Queen. And she felt like his Queen; at this moment they were Marian and Robin, the Queen of the May and her outlaw consort.

She leaned out of the flowered swine cart and kissed her lord and outlaw on the lips, basking in the cheers of the crowd. Collin had gotten his kiss. Plain Jacks and Jills just made him work for it, and do it in front of everyone. On a spot where Queens of the May had been kissing their Kings for centuries—maybe even millennia. She imagined that long line of women, some of them real queens, some queens for a day like her. Bestowing their kisses on whatever local hero proved himself most worthy. One moment in the Middle Ages she would not have missed for anything.

Robin and Marian parted lips, and the crowd hooted its approval. An easy audience to please. Lord Much of Misrule proclaimed games and feasting to celebrate the nuptials. Welcome news. She had been up for hours without eating, going on ale and adrenaline. Her audience dined heartily on beer and bread—big round May Day loaves baked before dawn—along with the boar's meat pastries and May Day cakes. But she was a player, Queen of the May, on stage or on her chariot. So she nibbled May Day cakes while watching the games. Some were serious contests like running, jumping, wrestling, stone-putting, and shooting-the-cock. Others were less so, like dueling on stilts, or chasing a greased pig, and bowling-for-kisses, where maids on milking stools took the place of pins. Back in his Lincoln green jacket and tights, Collin won the archery contest as easily as if he were really Robin Hood.

With no day's work to do, everyone retired to the manor hall for more feasting, music, and dancing. She found the smell of green boughs in the windowless hall intoxicating. So was the dancing. And the wine, which was fortified with brandy. Food and drink lay on trestle tables spread around the hall. Today there was no high table, and no one seated "below the salt." Men and boys put on displays of sword dancing, springing into the air and twirling about, blades flashing, doing wild jigs and extravagant leaps.

Carried away by the music, she danced with her Robin Hood. Neither knew the other's steps—but it did not matter. Knowing each other's minds instead, they moved gracefully together, his body fitting comfortably against hers, taut as a lute string and totally in tune. This was their night. Everyone made way for Robin and Marian, applauding as they whirled about the great stone floor with never a stumble or misstep. For once she felt wonderfully at ease in the Middle Ages, happy even—though this was not in the Middle Ages, not really. May Day was timeless, tied to all the May Days that had been and were to come. And she was not even herself; she was Marian, Queen of the May, and the only "Robin" around was the one in her arms. She knew she would be dancing with this same Robin Hood—or a reasonable facsimile—five hundred years from now. On a head full of fortified wine, it was easy to believe that they were lovers eternal—Marian and Robin—now and in the centuries to come.

He, too, looked happy to be someone else for a day. No longer lord of the manor, with its myriad cares, threats, duties, and obligations. He looked glad just to be Robin Hood, an outlaw with a lady in his arms. Lutists and minstrels played on behind them for as long as they wished to dance.

She never wanted the night to end, not if it meant going back to the dreary and dangerous Middle Ages. When the matins bell rang and the other revelers were abed, she was in Collin's tower room—for the first time ever—getting a personalized tour. His room was built to be a twin to Jo's on the opposite side of the keep, but more than the length of the manor hall separated them. Jo's room was spare yet messy; Sir Collin's was sumptuous and tidy, with Persian carpets on the floor, Flemish masterpieces on the walls, and a huge cloth-of-gold canopy bed. She felt like she had stumbled into Aladdin's cave, saying, "This is amazing, incredible, really."

"Yes, it is." Collin sat draped in a gold-studded chair, idly swinging a boot. "Would it were mine. Alas, it is too big to steal. Though these studs will most likely come out." He pried at one of the bits of gold embedded in the chair, totally in his Robin Hood character, even when it was just him and her. Days began at dawn in the Middle Ages, which made it still May Day. Collin, too, meant to stretch this out as long as he could.

She stood looking at one of the paintings, a Flemish court scene, the Burgundian court at picnic. Everyone was dressed all in white with gold trim, from noble ladies and the Duke of Burgundy to the meanest gross valet. Yet each person's costume was different, and each face, a portrait in miniature. A scene, an allegory, a statement about life, all set on a fairy backdrop—something Sotheby's would love to sell.

Hands settled lightly on her shoulders. Without a sound Robin Hood had risen from Sir Collin's chair and come up behind her. "Does my lady care to dance some more?"

She did. So they went spinning about the carpet to no music but their own, on heads full of fortified wine. "Have you ever wanted to be someone else?" Robin asked her. "Even for just a day?" He clearly did.

"Of course. No woman comes to Hollywood unless she has dreams like that."

"This Holy Wood must be a wonderful place."

"And then some. You are immensely popular there."

"Really?" That caught him off guard, and he looked to see the catch.

"Robin Hood is always popular. A really sought-after role." Fairbanks, Flynn, Connery, and Costner all played him, along with who knows how many others. Her studio was currently working on a remake. There was something about the story that was always appealing—maybe it was all those May Days.

"And Marian? Is she popular in Holy Wood?"

"Absolutely." Where would Robin be without Marian? Audrey

Hepburn played her, so did Olivia de Havilland. And now Robyn Stafford. "And they always live happily ever after." Not always—look what happened to Connery and Hepburn.

He waltzed her over to the big gold canopy bed. "Well, this is our last chance."

"To live happily ever after?" That seemed a tall order, even for May Day.

"To be two people we are not." With that, he kissed her. Reminding herself that this was her day to do as she wished, she kissed back, full of fantasy and fortified wine, determined for one night at least to be the lady of the manor, not some hunted, frightened fugitive—but Queen of the May, able to have whatever she willed.

When their lips parted, he warned her, "We will be different people on the morrow."

"Is that a promise?" Waking up a different person held no terrors for her. She very much wanted to wake up somewhere else, in another life. Being catapulted back in time had taught her to treat each day anew, filled with infinite possibility for good or ill. Right now she was Marian, Queen of the May, and Robin was her eternal mate, now and in centuries to come. Tomorrow she had to wake up as someone else. Hopefully as herself, at home.

He laughed. "I do swear it," Collin said, pulling her down onto the bed. This Robin Hood felt warm and familiar, but brawnier than she remembered, with stronger arms and tighter thighs—from all those workouts with a lance. When they were naked, she reached around to pull him closer and felt a long, jagged scar running down the back of his ribs. She was shocked by the size of the scar—something very much not in her fantasy—blowing the fortified wine out of her head. She might be Marian, Queen of the May, Robyn of Holy Wood, or the duke of Buckingham's long-lost daughter—but what she was doing right now was very real. And dangerous, as well.

⟿ Ride a Cock Horse ⟿

For the first time in the Middle Ages she woke up alone, and in Collin's gold canopy bed, no less. Surrounded by his splendid room, another medieval first. Lest she forget how this happened, her green-and-russet Queen of the May costume lay strewn on the floor. Dim dawn light angled through the arrow slits, shining off the cloth-of-gold. My God, what have I gotten myself into? Lots from the look of it. She tried desperately to recapture her mood from the night before. She was Marian, Queen of the May, womanhood personified, while Collin was Robin Hood, her love eternal, now and in the millennium to come.

Good luck. Try telling that to Friar Tuck, who by now was back mucking the Snowshill stables. None of that seemed very real, not alone and hungover on a gray May morning. She remembered Collin's promise that she would wake up a new person. Well she had, and then some. She had meant her stay in the Middle Ages to be mercifully swift and utterly sexless. Brief, safe, and celibate was her motto. At absolute worst—if by some macabre mischance she were truly trapped here—she might reluctantly become countess of March, should young Edward prove loving, chivalrous, unswervingly faithful, immensely wealthy, and not opposed to hygiene.

Yet here she was, a week into the Middle Ages, back in bed with Collin. A new unmarried Collin, brave, athletic, and more loving than she remembered—but nonetheless Collin—whom she had been trying to escape ever since her fateful walk in third-millennium Wales. Fill her head with fortified wine, change her name to Marian, and all her firm resolve flew out the manor window.

Giggling servant girls came in, picking up her discarded finery and bobbing under the bed for the chamber pot, making the room presentable before Sir Collin got back from breakfast. They laid out a gown for her—one of Jo's—and then departed, grinning happily. And she thought the Middle Ages would be a dour place. She stared at the sable-lined royal blue dress, its bodice speckled with silver shooting stars. Alongside lay a long chemise, hose, garters, and a gold-trimmed coif—not too subtle hints that she ought to get up.

She felt like she had been seduced by the whole manor. She tried to give Collin a simple kiss of gratitude, and the good folk of Greystone turned it into a huge production with songs, scenes, and contests—giving her a whole new identity, filling her head with fancies, and declaring her queen for a day. Making Collin beat a baron's son just to get her kiss, then getting her drunk and telling her extravagant lies. After a date like that, how could she not end up in his gold bed? It was what everybody wanted. Robin and Marian must have started as fertility figures, whose spring union ensured the harvest. After last night it should be a bumper crop.

Fertility, what a ghastly thought. Pregnant in the Middle Ages had an absolutely appalling ring to it. How could she have been so foolish? She kicked off the covers. Nothing to do but don her borrowed finery and face the music.

Downstairs at breakfast, Collin flashed her a warm smile from his seat at the head of the high table, nodding to acknowledge her curtsy. Nothing in her lord's look said this was different from any other morning. People innocently asked what kept her. "May is not a month for lying abed. You nearly missed your burnt bread and boiled grass." More medieval good humor. Collin held aloof from the ribbing, but he seldom made fun of her strange habits—aside from wanting her to put on weight. What he thought was impossible to guess. Of all the many male masks, the warm, confident smile was always the hardest to see through, especially in 1460.

Talk around the table turned to other things, like the pressing need to spread more manure or weed the winter wheat. Or the latest outrage at court. Or how the rains were playing hell with the harrowing. She kept watch on Collin out of the corner of her eye, seeing if he was looking at her. He seemed totally engrossed by Greystone's problems. Sadly, Sir Anthony had to get back to Grafton, his family's seat. Collin offered him an escort as far as Banbury, "If you will but wait and keep the feast of Holy Cross with us?"

Sir Anthony piously accepted, not wishing to travel "on the Feast of the Holy Cross, nor on the Holy Sabbath." People here and now were often their own bosses—and not shy about giving themselves holidays, coming up with all kinds of religious reasons to put things off, celebrating the most obscure saints and apostles. Half the days on the calendar seemed to be saints days or some special event in the lives of Jesus and Mary.

Collin looked happily about, as if to ask, "Anything more?" His eyes met hers and his smile widened; then his gaze moved on. No one spoke up, so he offered a final toast, to Holy Mary, seeing as it was Friday. Everyone took to their tasks as if May Day had never happened. Collin and Sir Anthony went hunting. Jo reminded her that Friday meant Witches Night. "And the morrow is the Feast of the Holy Cross, with a special Mass." And the day after that was Sunday; a most holy weekend loomed. Which must be prepared for now— once May Day was paid for. Cleaning, baking, and mending took up most of the morning, while she tried to put last night out of her mind. No longer Maid Marian, she had to go back to being just Robyn— who had troubles enough of her own.

Not so easy to do. Worries mounted about what last night would "mean." She wanted nothing holding her here, not even brave, handsome, unmarried Sir Collin, though he was more or less the man she had been hopelessly in love with—only better. There was no Bryn here and now, just Collin being an incredibly loving lord of the manor. And going home meant abandoning this new Sir Collin completely, returning to the dull, safe third millennium, where Collin was some British bounder and Edward did not exist. Yet what did she really have to offer Sir Collingwood Grey of Greystone? Certainly not marriage or lasting love. Not even honesty. She had not said one word to him about Edward—her other gentleman "friend."

Just when work started to distract her, Jo "remembered" the serving girls were to change Collin's bedclothes. "And he will return soon from hunting." Robyn was the reason the sheets were not changed, and the serving girls had mysteriously vanished. Another bit of medieval humor, making Maid Marian strip the bed. In that splendid tower room, stripping back the golden coverlet, memories of last night welled up. Was it right? Was she in love with him? Or just charmed and thankful? If not, should she have slept with him? Bundling up the bedding, she closed her eyes and took a deep breath, smelling sex in the bedclothes and thanking the cosmos for an amazing May Night. Then she resolved to put it out of her head . . .

. . . and promptly collided with Collin on the stairs of the keep, coming face-to-face with the consequences of last night. She had her arms full of their soiled bedding, headed for the wash tubs. Collin was coming in from riding, wearing hip boots and a russet doublet. He stopped and smiled. She bobbed a curtsy, without letting go of the bedding, giving him her most innocent, "Good day and Godspeed, good sir."

On the narrow stairs they could not help but be close. Rising from her curtsy, she found herself right in his face. Lips inches apart. With nothing between them but the sheets they had made love on. She smelled the sweat and horse leather on his doublet and realized she hoped he would kiss her. Who cares if it was May 2? She could tell he wanted to; she could read it in his face. He wanted to kiss her and then pick her up in his arms, bedding and all, carrying her back up the stairs to his tower room, ruining the clean sheets she'd just put on the bed. But he did not, and when his lips finally moved, it was to say, "May Day is over and done with."

His blunt certainty hurt her. What a Robin Heel! She had gone through mental gymnastics all morning, wondering what to do about last night. Was it love? Was it right? Sir Collingwood Grey had no such qualms. Having had his delight filled Night of May, his mind was now on other things. This bold new Sir Collin had wined, dined, and bedded her, then decided once was enough—for reasons of his own that did not require consulting her.

"And forgotten as well?" she asked, managing the same innocent tone as her greeting.

"No," he whispered, "not in the least forgotten. Last night will stay with me so long as I live." Maybe longer, if you counted future lives. Then he did kiss her. No mere peck, but not like last night, either. After all, they were standing on the manor stairs, the only passage between the great hall and living quarters, used by maidservants, porters, children, dogs, and cats—the whole Greystone extended family. Finishing the kiss, Sir Collin went on up the stairs to change out of his riding boots . . .

. . . leaving her standing on the steps with a hollow ache in her chest, stunned to be dumped by Collin yet again. Stewards jostled past, followed by a gang of pages going the other way. So far as Sir Collin was concerned, last night seemed to have no consequences— good or bad. Blame it on May Day. Or on Robin Hood. Anyone but him. He had satisfied his curiosity by bringing her to bed; now he had other things to do: affairs to manage, an estate to run, his king to serve—and a million other male excuses.

How grossly unfair. She had fine, solid reasons for not pursuing this medieval one-night stand. What was Sir Collin's excuse? Maybe she was not marriage material—thank goodness. But he was lord of Greystone manor, for God's sake, and no one here and now stopped him from doing pretty much as he pleased. And it pleased him to steal an enchanted evening with her as Robin Hood and then end it there. Leaving her to see to the soiled bedding. Not very flattering, but about what she deserved.

What a silly fool. Until this moment the sole advantage of being in the Middle Ages had been that this new unmarried Collin had not seduced and betrayed her. Indeed they had not even been intimate. Fate had given her a chance to correct that third-millennium mistake, to have an honest nonsexual relationship based on respect and friendship. In a little over a week, she had put relations with Collin right back where they had been.

Feeling that all eyes were on her, she took Collin's linen down to the washtubs between the stables and the kitchen. Washerwomen greeted her jovially, recognizing Sir Collin's sheets and giving her a gentle ribbing. She did her best to return the good-natured greetings; to them she was still the mysterious stranger from far-off Holy Wood, the Queen of the May who had captured their lord's heart. She stood with her eyes smarting in the sunlight, staring at blue skies and green treetops above the bailey wall, hearing the cries of children and the thump of laundry bats. May Day was indeed "over and done with," and the natural order, restored. The swine who had drawn her chariot lay sleeping in the mud, waiting to become ham and sausage.

Seeing women at work and children playing around the gaudy may-pole, she marveled at men's incredible capacity for making you feel common, especially once you slept with them. She had thought herself someone special, centuries ahead of all this, but Sir Collin's chivalrous condescension certainly put her in her place. Yesterday she was Queen of the May, showing Collin her favor, a week before that she had been plain Robyn Stafford with a Jeep four-by-four, a poolside apartment, a time-share condo in the mountains, and an e-mail address; today she was just another female dependent at Greystone, working to earn her pennies a day. Someone must wash Sir Collin's sheets, pound his boar meat, and gut and pluck the birds he killed. No wonder magic and fantasy were women's special realms, full of wonder and awe of what the world might be—jealously outlawed by men, who stood ready with the rack and burning stake to see female imaginings did not go too far.

Loneliness and humiliation welled up within her. At least this Collin had not lied to her. He told her plainly May Day was "time out" when normal rules did not apply. And she had happily gone along, making love as "Robin and Marian" not Robyn and Collin. What an utter idiot. One more reason to get home as quick as she could, as if she needed new ones. Thank the Goddess this was Friday, with Witches Night ahead. She fixed her mind on the forbidden magic that might actually get her home. Much more of this and she would surely go mad.

When the witching hour came she was sitting on the carpeted floor of Jo's tower room, eyes closed, breathing dark night air, listening to the matins bells toll. She wore a plain white shift—like the one Joy wore that first night in the dungeon of Berkeley Castle. Jo and Joy breathed beside her in the darkness. The rest of the manor was asleep. A week ago she watched Joy dance naked by the bonfire at Belas Knap. Tonight she would take part in person.

Tolling bells fell silent, and Jo led them in a prayer to Darkness— "that surrounds us always. Darkness before. Darkness after. Darkness of sleep. And the darkness of death." Then, with a click, Jo lit a candle placed between them, using Robyn's lighter. It pleased Jo to have fire at her fingertips—"Not every novice brings something so amazing with her."

Light flared up. Robyn saw a candle and a wine goblet standing in the center of the white triangle formed by their bodies. Neither candle nor goblet had been there when the lights went out. Joy squealed at the burst of flame from the lighter, one of her favorite bits of third-millennium magic. Hela mimicked her excited cry.

Raising a finger to her lips, Jo signed for holy silence and then turned to Robyn. "You are luckier than most novices learning the Witches Flight."

"Why is that?" As soon as she said it, she realized she had broken her silence.

Jo merely smiled. "You are already far from where you should be." Obviously. She was living proof that the Witches Flight worked; otherwise, how could she be here? Emboldened by her predicament, she threw herself into the ritual, giving it total attention—watching as Jo intoned a short prayer and poured fine gray powder into the goblet.

Putting the cup her lips, Jo took a deep sip and then offered Robyn the cup.

She took it, drank, and then passed the goblet to Joy—finding the wine strange-tasting even by medieval standards. What was that gray powder? And how could she so nonchalantly give drugged wine to a nine-year-old? Bit by bit she felt herself going totally native. Children here and now drank small beer for breakfast and went off to their morning tasks all the happier for it.

"Close your eyes again," Jo ordered, "and let yourself relax." Jo began a low keening chant, like the one her daughter used at Belas Knap. Closing her eyes, Robyn smelled the clean soapy fragrance of her well-washed body, mixed with night air and hot candle wax. "Feel the magic flow through you," Jo told her. Sinking deep into the chant, Robyn let herself relax, muscle by muscle, starting with her toes, slowly moving up her calves and thighs, through her abdomen and along her spine, to her shoulders, neck and head. She felt the chant lifting her up, like Edward's rose had lifted her up during the hilltop ritual that landed her here. Her head started to swim.

"Now let yourself go," Jo commanded, the same words the Widow Weirdville used on that third-millennium hilltop above Cam Long Down.

Eyes closed, she let herself go, rising with the chant, feeling herself floating free in the night air. She pictured Jo and Joy beneath her, chanting away before the candle flame. She even pictured herself at the third corner of the triangle, chanting along with them, while her spirit hovered overhead. Suspended between her body and the cosmos beyond.

Slowly the chant subsided, fading into a whisper. She settled gently back into her body. When the chant ceased, she opened her eyes. Jo was smiling. "Did you feel yourselves letting go?"

She nodded happily, as did Joy—who was already an old hand at such exercises. "Good," Jo declared, pleased by her novices' success. "We have done well this Witches Night." Robyn agreed. Despite her fears, this dose of real medieval witchcraft was vastly encouraging, not in the least bizarre or frightening. Imagining herself floating about the room might seem trivial, but it was a start. She felt herself making real progress on the near impossible task of getting home, instead of just sinking deeper into this medieval morass. They finished off with a closing prayer to the Virgin Mother, and to the Discovery of the

Holy Cross. Later, lying on Jo's canopy bed, she imagined herself floating upward as she drifted off to sleep. That night she dreamed of home. Her apartment in Hollywood was full of people she knew, friends from college, Heidi, a couple of old boyfriends—but not Collin. They all wanted to know, "Where have you been?"

Next morning at a special Mass for the Holy Cross, she knelt between Jo and Joy, whispering along with the priest. It seemed strange to go from Witches Night to morning Mass—but no one else acted the least bit bothered. Seeing their heads bowed together in prayer, Robyn realized that whatever they privately believed, Collin and Jo had to be public Christians. And not just from fear of burning. They owed it to Collin's servants and retainers, who could not be cut off from the Church just because their master was a warlock. When the priest placed the host in her mouth, she closed her eyes, imagining herself hovering beneath the chapel's painted ceiling, looking down on herself at Communion. Throughout that morning and afternoon, she practiced out-of-body imagining, pretending to watch herself move through the day. Pretty easy to do, when her day was so absolutely weird to begin with.

Monday after breakfast a small cavalcade assembled at the bailey gate to see Sir Anthony as far as Banbury, a day's ride to the east. Surprisingly, she was finding herself able to get up at first light, cheerfully, and without coffee. Another medieval miracle. It was the full night's sleep that did it. She had never slept so completely, with no late night TV, DVD, or Internet to distract her, just utter exhaustion and absolute silence—aside from the night birds and tolling church bells. Collin had a whole traveling household: favored pages, prized cooks, squires, and valets, plus two serving women for Jo, and one for Joy. It amazed Robyn how much it seemed like a big happy family departing, with everyone laughing, joking, and giving parting kisses. Half the mounted servants were underage. Aside from Sir Anthony's squire and valet, these "children" were young people who lived, worked, ate, and slept together. They bowed to Collin, called him *sir* and obeyed his commands, but otherwise rank was a sometime thing. She saw teenage squires pay far more deference to a pretty serving girl than to a ten-year-old page—though the boy was a baron's son learning to behave. The serving girl was as common as they come, yet she was free to leave the household if she thought she could do better. But the baron's son had nowhere to go but home to his parents.

Buoyed by her out-of-body success, she felt caught up in the holiday outing mood—it was, after all, Cinco de Mayo, though she was the only one who missed the peach margaritas. And she got a fine white mare to ride, along with Plunket the gray gelding to be her sumpter horse. She wore her brand-new silver-trimmed riding dress, made from the bolt of blue satin Collin had given her. No longer queen of the manor, she was still plenty popular, and squires crowded about her, trying out their French and angling for a kiss. She managed to mount despite their assistance.

Collin looked more than usually barbaric wearing his blue nail-studded brigandine, with a huge hand-and-a-half sword slung at his waist. Sir Anthony wore mail beneath his heraldic surcoat, and squires held their helmets and lances. These days the West Country was a dangerous place—with not a Bobby in sight. Collin ordered the bailey gate swung wide, saying, "If we are at Broughton Castle by dusk, Lord Saye will give us lodging for the night."

Setting out briskly into the dawn, they headed down between Litt-leworth Wood and a pair of burial mounds; past Collin's closest neighbor, the limestone manor of Snowshill, belonging to the Abbey of Winchcombe. Bells on her borrowed saddle rang softly as she rode along. Climbing Burton Hill, boredom got the better of her pique, and she spurred her mare, catching up with Collin and Sir Anthony at the head of the column, showing she could ride as well as any second-millennium barbarian.

Infuriatingly pleased to have her at his side, Collin pointed out sights, offering a running commentary on the countryside. They had not said two words to each other since their kiss on the keep stairs, but Collin acted supremely confident, with none of the wariness he showed when they first met. Clearly he held no grudge. Why should he? Sir Collin had gotten what he wanted from his mysterious visitor. And no doubt figured he could get it again, if the need arose. All was right in Greystone, and with her lord and master, Sir Collingwood Grey, knight-troubadour, king's man, and warlock.

Well, she was learning to be a witch. When she mastered the Witches Flight, Sir Collingwood Grey would be the one trapped in this benighted era. She might condescend to come back and visit Sir Collin now and again, just to rub it in. Sitting higher in her jingling saddle, she looked about, seeing more of medieval England every time she turned a corner or topped a hill. When she got home, people would want to know what it was like, assuming anyone believed her. Farms and villages spread out before her, more plentiful than along the Cotswold Edge, fading into the hilly green horizon. She waved to shepherdesses and women in the fields, who smiled and returned the greeting, plainly wondering why the lady on the white mare was waving at them. From atop Burton-on-the-Hill, with its big tithe barn and long barrow, she could see all the way to Warwickshire. Ahead of her lay the heart of England—the traditional center of the country being a stone cross on the green of the Warwickshire village of Meridian. Curious about their night's destination, she asked, "What is Lord Saye like?"

Collin considered, then replied, "Thoughtful and cautious, a man who has done well and avoided trouble. It is hard to know the human heart, but he has no reason to love Lord Scales, and he considers meddling bastards like FitzHolland beneath contempt." Lord Saye at least had taste. "That is why I chose his keep for our night's lodging, and also because his castle is awfully beautiful, set in a flat shimmering lake. Being our guest, you deserve to see the best the West Country has to offer." That was pure flattery, since even she knew the best West Country castles were to the north; Warwick Castle was up that way, and Kenilworth. But it was nice he still felt the need to flatter her. Beyond Burton-on-the-Hill the land dipped down toward another Roman road, the Foss Way. Armed men on the march were headed up the road toward Coventry, carrying bows and big wicked-looking axes—they wore red-gold livery and marched behind a banner of a streaming silver star. "The earl of Oxford's men," Collin told her, "coming late to the dance again." Seeing her quizzical look, he added, "His lordship John de Vere, earl of Oxford, was a day late to Saint Albans, whereby we lost the battle. He is amiable, stout-hearted, and cares for the public weal, but is inclined to be slipshod and tardy."

On the far side of the Foss Way, Collin showed her the Four Shire Stone, where Worcestershire, Gloucestershire, Oxfordshire, and Warwickshire came together. Climbing a ridge, they left godly Gloucestershire behind, following an ancient path along the Warwickshire-Oxfordshire border. She saw a dead body lying beside the path, on the Oxfordshire side, a thin old man with bare feet, showing no outward sign of violence. He might have been sleeping, but for the great flock of crows that scattered as they rode past. Collin got out his sallet and shield, and Sir Anthony traded his lute for a lance, saying, "Here the land is wilder." Collin added that robbery was a real fear, "Especially for those not armed and ready to take immediate offense." Neither said a word about the corpse.

South of Long Compton, they came on a circle of ragged standing stones set in the grassy ridge, positively reeking of witchcraft, faerie rings, and the Old Religion. "These are the Rollrights," Joy told her gleefully, "the stone remains of an ancient king and his men. He met a witch on this ridge, who told him to take seven long steps, then:

If Long Compton thou canst see,
King of England thou shalt be.

But when he took his seven steps, he found the view of Long Compton blocked by a mound of earth, and he and his men turned to stone." Some story—the King's Stone, standing closer to Long Compton than the others, struck a commanding pose, a giant phallic mushroom reminding Robyn of Rodin's *Balzac* rearing out of the sidewalk on Wilshire in front of the L.A. County Museum. Farther on, Joy pointed out a second group of stones on the Oxfordshire side of the ridge, backed by burial mounds. "Those are the Whispering Knights, who plotted treason against their king." They, too, ended up stoned. Robyn marveled at what it must be like for Joy, growing up a witch-child in a magical landscape, where kings stood turned to stone and bodies lay beside the road. Bells jingled on her saddle bow as she set out again.

At dusk they reached their day's destination, Broughton Castle, set on an island in a lake, an elegant double-walled fortress at the end of a narrow stone causeway. Swans swam amid lilies beneath the castle walls. "Beautiful," she sighed, sitting back in her saddle, happy to end the long day's ride in such a lovely spot.

"I told you it would be," Collin agreed. "The Broughtons dammed up Sor brook to make the lake—but the place was only a moated manor in those days." He said it as if he had seen it, making her wonder how much of his past lives Collin remembered. "When the Broughtons died out, Mauduits and Hungerfords lived here as well—but the Fiennes have it now. Lord Saye's father was king's treasurer, well able to leave his son a magnificently furnished castle." It said a lot about Mad King Henry's rule that folks naturally assumed the royal treasurer died rich.

Sir William Fiennes, Lord Saye and Sele, met them at the square embattled gatehouse. Curly haired and clean shaved, he had a lordly concave nose and Cupid's-bow lips, and he feasted them regally, offering wine, music, and a roast swan. Remembering the lovely birds in the moat, Robyn settled for the fish and nuts. Sitting over brandy at the high table, talk turned to politics, and Lord Saye asked Collin if he had been at the fight in Staffordshire "where Lord Audley was killed."

Collin nodded gravely. "I did, indeed, see Lord Audley die. And it is a terrible tale to tell." Lord Saye still wanted to hear it. Staffordshire was two counties off, a long way when news went by hand-carried letter, or word of mouth. Travelers' stories around the dinner table were the nearest thing these people had to the evening news—everything here and now was gossip, or firsthand accounts, skipping print and going straight to the Internet.

Intent and serious, with none of the cavalier "let God decide" attitude he had shown FitzHolland, Collin told how last fall he had been serving the queen—"in Chester, where King Henry had granted a great livery of swans. Word came that the earl of Salisbury was headed for Ludlow, bringing troops and guns to aid the duke of York. Strong-minded woman that she is, Her Majesty did not wait for King Henry, but marched us at once to stop Salisbury. We had with us a great mass of Cheshire men, many of them deadly archers, but all of them raw, quarrelsome, and unused to battle. Lord Stanley made fair promises to join us, but never did."

Collin toasted Lord Stanley's caution and then went on: "Sunday, the twenty-third of September, we caught the earl of Salisbury near Mucklestone, on the road to Market Drayton. His battle was drawn up behind Hempmill Brook on Blore Heath, protected by stakes and ditches. We had more men and the king's authority, so our leaders, Lord Audley and Lord Dudley, told Salisbury he could not pass, saying he should lay down arms and submit to the king." Lord Saye stared hard at Collin, as did Sir Anthony, and she sensed them putting themselves in his place, wearing heavy sweaty armor, with wicked-edged weapons in their gauntleted hands, staring through narrow helmet-slits at steel-jacketed men across a ditch, knowing there were friends and family on the far side. All because Mad King Henry could not get along with his cousins. "Salisbury seemed to waver, calling his men from behind their ditches. Which proved our undoing. Seeing them falter, Lord Audley attacked. All ahorsed, we tried to gallop across the brook, to get at Salisbury ere he could escape. It was a trap. Salisbury met us with cannon and flights of arrows. It took two charges to get across the Hempmill, and in the end we had to dismount, leading our horses over."

He painted a horrible picture of men in armor dragging reluctant mounts up the slippery banks of the muddy brook. Arrows fell on them and stone cannonballs crashed in their midst, "shattering into pointed shards that beat like hail on our armor. Before we could remount, Salisbury's footmen were on us, heathen northerners howling in hideous Yorkshire, swinging big halberds and brown bills, cleaving plate and mail. Her Majesty's Cheshire men scattered like frightened swans. I hardly blame them—a halberd took the head off my horse, a most ghastly sight. Half a thousand of our horsemen surrendered outright, going over to Salisbury's rebels. Lord Audley was slain halfway down the slope, fighting valiantly—if not well. Lord Dudley was lucky enough to be taken."

"And what of you?" Saye asked.

Collin winced. "There was no honor to be had, and I managed nothing of note." He stood up, opening his blue-white doublet. "I was with the vanguard that got across the brook. Borne over by the rush, I was unhorsed and rolled back down the stream bank, forced face-down into the mud, nearly drowning me in my helmet. Struggling to my knees, I got a blow from behind that laid open my corselet." Lifting his shirt, he showed a red scar running down the back of his ribs. The scar Robyn felt on May Night.

Closing his doublet, Collin finished his dismal tale. "My squire pulled me from the press. I would have been captured, but I had a kinsman on the rebel side who pretended to take me for ransom, but left me behind when Salisbury fled to join York at Ludlow." Collin told how he lay all night bleeding onto cold dark ground, while a mad monk fired off one of Salisbury's abandoned cannons. Like he said, there had been small honor to be had, and even the victor Salisbury was now a hunted rebel, his life and lands forfeit. Edward had been looking for him the day they met in Wales.

Lord Saye called out a toast to Collin, who had served his king and gotten nothing but a nasty scar. Sir Anthony added a second toast, "to your unnamed kinsman." They all drank to this nameless rebel against the crown—who was not even true to Salisbury since he let

Collin get away. Sir Anthony set down his goblet, saying, "At least your luck has not changed."

Collin grinned ruefully. "My record remains unblemished."

Seeing her puzzled look, Lord Saye leaned over to say, "My esteemed neighbor has been in a score of battles . . ."

"Four, actually," Collin corrected him. "It only seems like more."

". . . and lost every one."

Collin ticked them off on his fingers, "Formigny and Castillon—those were in France. Saint Albans. And now Blore Heath. Every one a lost cause."

She arched an eyebrow at her lord. "So you have never been in a winning battle, and never killed a man—except by mischance?" An admirable record in its way.

"Not in this lifetime," Collin conceded. He lifted his goblet, saying, "To yet another lost battle." They all drank to his latest defeat.

Otherwise Lord Saye showed scant sympathy for the rebels, saying "The duke of York has a pleasant enough exile in Ireland, but because he defied King Henry, Ludlow was stripped to the walls and the town thrown open to rape. I would flee to France rather than see that happen here."

"York was a fool," Sir Anthony observed, "who dragged helpless innocents down with him."

"What about a king who makes war on his own subjects?" Collin asked. "Who, then, is the greater fool?"

Sir Anthony smirked, this being a question it was treason to answer. "I am on parole, barred from such taking sides."

Saye asked, "What parole?"

"Part of the price of my release from Calais." Sir Anthony revealed that he, too, had been a prisoner, captured by the rebels in a Christmas raid on Sandwich and carried off to Calais along with his father, mother, and most of the royal fleet. Baron Rivers, it appears, had put in a shocking bad showing as King Henry's high admiral, getting hauled off to Calais along with his ships. No wonder the Wydvilles hated Lord Admiral Holland for profiting off their misfortune, hoping to see him do no better. Sir Anthony told them that "until my ransom is paid, I may not honorably bear arms against the rebels." They all toasted Sir Anthony's timely release from politics.

Having drunk wine with dinner, and all the toasts that followed, Robyn finished off the evening by collapsing onto a strange bed that already held Jo and Joy. Happy Cinco de Mayo. Was this how Heidi felt, passing out on her bed in Hollywood? If she was ever made countess of March, she dearly hoped to get her own room. Or at least her own bed.

Gray clouds hung over next morning's departure. Servants in Lord Saye's livery helped her mount her white mare, and she trotted across the castle causeway past swans who had escaped the stew pot. Bells jingled softly on her saddle bow. She asked Jo, "Which side is Lord Saye on?" She had seen him drink to King Henry's health, and to the royal army's defeat at Blore Heath.

Jo glanced over her shoulder at the square stone gatehouse, "Lord Saye has more reason than most to be cautious. His father was King Henry's treasurer—and roundly hated for his extortions. Ten years ago, when Jack Cade's rebels took London, Lord Saye's father sought safety in the Tower. Seeing the whole city in arms against them, the constable of the Tower turned Saye's father over to the rebels, who were happy to lay hands on the king's chief tax collector, giving him a hasty trial and then beheading him." Having seen his father's head stuck on London Bridge, for faithfully—and profitably—serving King Henry, Lord Saye must be considering his position carefully. "And the man who gave his father over to the rebels still holds his post in the Tower." She realized Jo meant the delightful Lord Scales.

"Who is this Jack Cade?" Robyn asked.

Jo gave her a significant look. "An Irish rogue, you might know, who raised a great Kentish mob against the king's misgovernment. He dressed all in red, and called himself John Mortimer. Or John-Amend-All."

From the way Jo looked at her, Joy must have told her mother about the man in red who gave them the keys to Berkeley Castle. Robyn asked, "What happened to him?"

"He defeated the king's army and was given a pardon and promises of reform. When London turned against him and threw out his Kentish rebels, Cade's royal pardon turned out to be as worthless as any of Henry's promises. Sheriffs killed him, or so they say." Jo gave her a thoughtful look. "Some swear he lives on, at least in spirit."

Very much in spirit, if it was the same John-Amend-All Robyn knew. But these were witch's secrets, not to be bandied about on horseback far from home. At Banbury, she saw the huge stone Banbury Cross reminding her of the old nursery rhyme:

Ride a cock horse to Banbury Cross,
To see a fine lady upon a white horse.
Rings on her fingers and bells on her toes,
She shall have music wherever she goes.

What a strange, strange land this was, with its fairy-tale castles and places out of Mother Goose. It made her feel like Alice in Wonderland. Or like that fine lady on her white horse.

Here they said farewell to Sir Anthony. His home was Grafton, in Northamptonshire, a half-day's ride to the east. Beyond Banbury the land was more settled, and Sir Anthony could expect to be home before dusk—while Collin needed to get back to Greystone. She got a pleasant kiss good-bye; then he was gone along with his valet and squire, headed east on the Towcester road. Seeing him go, she mentioned to Jo how it might be nice to see Grafton someday—hopefully in the third millennium; she did not plan to extend her stay by sightseeing. "Most likely you will see Grafton," Jo told her as they turned back toward Greystone.

"I will?" She misliked the certainty in Jo's voice.

"Grafton is the home of young Sir Anthony's mother, the Duchess of Bedford, high priestess to our coven."

"Really?" Why had Jo not told her sooner?

"*Absolument,*" Jo assured her. "I would have told you beforetime, but I did not want you doing anything to betray your knowledge. Duchess Wydville is cunning and powerful, and for your sake, I would not overly alert her. I want you welcomed into our coven before she guesses where you came from. When dealing with Duchess Wydville, it is best to keep back secrets, since she will be more hospitable if she hopes to gain by it." How lovely. Jo did not trust her coven's high priestess, the woman best able to send her back.

Rain slashed down west of Banbury. Drenched to the skin, she got back to Greystone feeling more like a dunked harlot than a fine lady, fearing that she must find her own way home. Two days in the saddle strained muscles she forgot she had, but as soon she had dried off, she threw herself into preparing for Witches Flight. Sitting alone in Jo's tower bedroom, eyes closed, she imagined herself moving through the manor, going down the keep stairs, picturing each worn stone step, past the pantry and buttery to the great hall, and then into the kitchens. When she could put herself in any part of the manor, she tried going outside, redoing the entire two-day trip in her mind, going past Snowshill manor and Burton-on-the-Hill, past the Four Shire Stone and the Rollrights, to Broughton Castle, and then Banbury Cross—and back again. Emboldened by success, she pushed her flights of fancy farther, back to the day she arrived, to the witch's cottage with its thatched roof and polished wood latch. Lifting the latch, she let herself in, smelling the dust and beeswax, examining the witch's curios one by one—powder bottles, bundles of feathers, an ancient clay Venus, the bone flute and wooden butterfly butter mold. Cutting off her imaginary visit before Le Boeuf arrived, she made the bigger leap of imagining the cottage, not as it was now, but as it would be five hundred years hence, when she first visited it—literally seeing the future—replacing the wooden bucket with a cold-water tap, trading bits of candle for terra-cotta angels. She smelled the fired crullers and the mothballs, and stared into the wooden box at the big blue, with its missing wing scales and broken antenna. All without leaving Jo's room.

Friday morning, lying abed, waiting for the manor to wake, she brought herself full circle, back to that windswept top in Wales, standing knee-deep in heather, setting aside her squirt bottle, and bending down to retie her boots—the ones now under Jo's bed. She saw the laces in her fingers, felt the knot draw tight, then stood up, seeing Edward riding toward her, in his muddy blue-gold surcoat, a broadsword on his hip, and the white rose on his black cap, the same white rose now pressed in a book by her bed. She figured she was ready.

That night she put it all to the test, sitting on the floor with Jo and Joy, staring at a tall black taper. Jo made the sign for holy silence. "Today is the ninth night of May, triply blessed. And the coven will initiate novices. You will be presented to the high priestess—Lady Jacquetta Wydville, duchess of Bedford. There is no high or low on Witches Night, but she is second only to the queen among noblewomen, and well nigh the most powerful witch in Christendom. Show her utmost respect." If you value your head—Jo did not need to say it; you could hear it in her tone. Robyn nodded obediently.

Jo cast the circle, placing a big two-handed potion cup in the center. They took the draft in order of age, youngest to eldest. Joy drank first, then handed the goblet to Robyn, who drank and passed the potion to Jo. As soon as the cup passed, Robyn heard a roaring in her ears, and her head began to spin. Jo raised the potion cup over her head, saying a prayer to Hecate, Goddess of Death and Rebirth. Then Jo drank, set down the cup, and started to chant. They all joined hands, and the roaring grew with the chant.

Wind whipped up from nowhere and blew out the candle. Jo's chant expanded, filling the darkness. No longer feeling the floor beneath her, Robyn held tight to her companions' hands. Greystone vanished around her, and she felt lifted up, floating off into the night, carried along by the rushing spirit wind over the dark rolling midlands. She pictured the black landscape below, both what she had seen and what she imagined, feeling herself flying over the Rollrights and Banbury Cross, headed for that dark horizon hiding the heart of England.

Jo's sonorous chant subsided, and the spirit wind faded, losing its power. Robyn heard branches rattle above her and felt soft turf beneath her feet. She had landed, and was no longer sitting in Jo's tower room, but standing out in the open. Jo and Joy stood with her, backed by a grove of black trees, still holding her hands. Despite being barefoot, dressed only in a linen shift on a cold May night, she did not feel the least chilled. Warmth welled up within her.

Before her stood a little blond-haired girl about Joy's age, looking amazingly out of place—all alone on Witches Night in these dark woods. Like a scene out of Goldilocks and the Three Witches. Jo gravely took the little girl's hand, placing it in Robyn's, saying, "Robyn Stafford, of Holy Wood, California, this is your sister initiate Beth Lambert, daughter to John and Amy Lambert of West Cheap, London. Tonight you will enter the coven together."

Little Beth Lambert did a deep curtsy and came up smiling. Joy grinned back at her. Seeing this child about to join them was a shock—especially with little Beth's parents nowhere in sight. Wherever this dark wood was, London looked to be a long way off, and the question "Does your mother know what you are doing?" popped immediately to mind. But that was not the sort of question you could ask, not on Witches Night. Amy and John Lambert were probably piously asleep in West Cheap, thinking their daughter was, too.

Holding tight to Beth and Joy, she followed Jo through the trees. Darkness lifted. Ahead a spark of light pushed back the night. Careful not to let go of the girls, she walked toward the light, seeing it grow to become a bonfire, throwing sparks into the blackness above. By the light of the fire, she recognized the familiar outlines of an Iron Age ring fort with a wide V-shaped ditch and low, slumped ramparts built by ancient Britons. Jo led them through a gap in the ditch toward the fire.

Women and girls formed a ring before the bonfire, most in simple shifts, some in gaudy gowns, surrounding a rough-hewn ironstone altar with tall black candles at its corners. An ancient green-bronze knife and an offering of pomegranates lay on the altar. Behind the altar stood a woman in a black flowing robe, wearing a horned headdress like the High Priestess in a tarot deck. Puzzle pieces tumbled into place. Her Grace the duchess of Bedford, second only to the queen among noblewomen, and high priestess of Jo's coven, was a younger, more striking version of Old Widow Weirdville, the same witch who sent her here. And who could, hopefully, send her home.

Robyn stood surrounded by the women who brought her here—Jo and Joy, and now "Widow Weirdville." Or at least their medieval incarnations. Or dream images thereof. She half expected Bryn to pop up from behind the altar—and was almighty thankful that she did not. But why did they do it? What was she to them? or she to Hecate, that they should bring her here? She could not believe this was merely some colossal cosmic accident. The longer this medieval nightmare went on, the more she believed she was brought to this ghastly era for a purpose. Heaven alone knew what it was. Jo and Joy could not tell her. Maybe this high-priestess-cum-duchess would. So she set out to please, doing a deft obedient curtsy, still holding the little girl's hand. Even in a witch's dream, it paid to be polite. She still felt very much like Alice in Wonderland, hoping this horned duchess would help her, and not turn her in to the mad king and wicked queen who were chopping off people's heads for daring to wear a white rose instead of a red one.

Raising her arms, the high priestess called out in a clear commanding voice. "Who are the new spirits who have come to our coven?" From behind her women answered in a weird ritual tongue that did not sound like French or Latin, and certainly was not English. Medieval Greek? Maybe. Hebrew? Hardly likely. Hungarian? Early Indo-European? Whatever it was, thanks to the Displacement Spell she understood every word:

Hecate's daughter,
Priestess of light,

**Here is the pair,
Come to coven with us
this Witches Night.**

Two women wearing crowns of flowers stepped forward, dressed in white and looking enough like Duchess Wydville to be her daughters; both had her long gold hair and Sir Anthony's heavy-lidded ice-blue eyes—now demurely downcast, making them look sly and sinister. Humbleness hardly suited the daughters of a regal duchess and powerful witch-priestess. The older daughter motioned for Robyn and Beth to kneel before the knife and pomegranate. Robyn felt immediately wary, sensing a magical link with Duchess Wydville's oldest daughter that might bode well or ill.

Holding on to Beth, Robyn obeyed. It felt comforting to have tight grasp of the little girl's hand. Beth squeezed back, seeming not half as scared as she—though the girl must be miles away from her bed in West Cheap. Childhood was so incredibly short here and now. Children left home, started careers, got betrothed, and became kings when they should still be in grade school. Sometimes preschool. Little Beth Lambert—looking to be about ten—was becoming a witch. Which seemed appalling, but at her age Edward had led an army on London.

The high priestess took the bronze knife and pomegranate from the altar. Holding the fruit over her head, the duchess called on Hecate, Queen of Death and Daughter of Night, Protector of Children and Innocents, saying in the same unknown tongue, "Pray have this pair into your keeping." Plunging the knife into the pomegranate, she let the red juice drip onto the altar. Then the high priestess split the fruit in half, holding it out with reddened hands, saying in heavy accented English, "Eat from the food of the dead, that you may be reborn."

Beth eagerly seized her half pomegranate. "Arise," the duchess told the girl, "and be reborn in Her service. Your Goddess name is Jane." Little Beth-Jane rose up, clutching her piece of fruit, happy with her new name. Robyn realized that she would be getting a new name as well. What would it be?

Duchess Wydville turned to her, holding out the half pomegranate. "Arise and be reborn in Her service. Your Goddess name is Diana."

Diana? Not bad. Especially when every other woman here and now was an Elizabeth, Margaret, or Anne. At least her new high priestess had a knack for naming. Surprised and pleased, she rose up, taking her cue from Beth, gravely thanking the duchess for the new name and the half pomegranate.

Bending over, she helped Beth pry some seeds out of her half. Smiling wide, the child trembled with excitement, obviously overjoyed to join the coven, greedily swallowing her seeds, then licking at the red juice running down her fingers, unconcerned by any dire consequences. Not nearly so brave, Robyn dug several seeds out of her piece, saying a private prayer to Holy Mary, the Christian version of the Death-Virgin. Having covered her bases, she ate the seeds, tasting acid juice on her lips and tongue. Nothing from now on would ever be the same.

Her naming seemed a signal for rejoicing. Women rose up singing, starting to dance around the bonfire, led by the duchess's two daughters. Jo beckoned her to join them, which she did, bringing the two little girls with her. Whirling about in time to the chanting, first with Joy and "Jane"—then with Jo—she was reminded of "women only" dances she went to in Hollywood. There was a comforting simplicity to single-sex dancing. You chose partners as you pleased, with no men to be wary of, or compete over. And no worry about what men might see or think. As if to prove the point, women started to strip off their shifts, tossing them onto the bonfire, dancing naked before the flames. Burning shifts wafted upward, borne aloft by the heat, white flaming ghosts flying into the May night. Even Hollywood dances seldom got that comfortable.

Closing her eyes she spun faster, turning tighter and tighter circles, hands above her head, happy with her new sense of power, pleased with her new secret name. Witch-princess Diana. Two weeks ago her situation had been hopeless, blundering about Widow Weirdville's cottage, searching desperately for something useful, and finding only feathers and carved butter molds. Now she was a witch-in-the-making, able to fly by magic, already halfway home.

Suddenly the chanting ceased. Opening her eyes, she found herself back on her knees in Jo's candlelit room in Greystone, her head still spinning. Jo and Joy grinned happily at her. Beth Lambert was gone, hopefully back to her parent's in West Cheap. But Joy must have eaten some of Jane-Beth's pomegranate seeds; tiny red flecks showed in the corner of her mouth. Looking down at her own hands, Robyn saw they, too, were red with pomegranate juice.

⊹⇒ Kenilworth ⇐⊹

Witchcraft worked. Despite its total implausibility and horrific inherent dangers, witchcraft worked, even worked wonders. She had the proof on her hands. She thought her Witches Flight would be purely imaginary, some form of mental projection—like she had diligently practiced. Robyn had not expected to "go" anywhere. Not physically. But there was nothing mental or imaginary about the pomegranate stains. She had actually gone somewhere and brought something real back with her. Hollywood, here we come. She desperately wanted to know what was in the gray powder Jo put in the potion. Wing of bat? Eye of newt? Whatever it was did the trick.

Jo would not say, responding with an enigmatic look. Damn her witchy secrets. Wheedling got nowhere. Jo claimed the powder was not important. "What matters is you, and your abilities. You are a very apt pupil, though it does help that you come from a different time and different place. Your ties to this world are not so strong."

No kidding. She hated washing the pomegranate off her hands, wondering how things were with "Jane" Lambert, her sister-initiate. It chilled her to think how easily the child made herself a witch, gaily putting herself beyond the law, seemingly without thought of penalties and dangers. According to Jo, Beth-Jane's Father, John Lambert, was a full member of the Mercers' Company, one of the merchant corporations that ran the City of London. "One day he will be an alderman, maybe even Mayor of London. And she will always be your coven sister, which could become a fortunate connection, when she grows older." Without a doubt. Only Robyn hoped to be gone long before Beth-Jane got any older. No one seemed to think ten years old too young to start making your way in the world—least of all little Beth Lambert. Greystone was full of stable boys, milkmaids, turnspits, serving girls, and squires, all somebody else's children—fostered or apprenticed by their parents. Some as young as seven, but few showed signs of missing home. None of these parents actually needed to sell off their kids; Greystone's pages included a baron's younger son, and the serving girls were wool merchant's daughters. Only peasants and the poor raised their own children.

"Parents are too easy on their children," Jo told her, "look at how badly I spoil Joy."

Point taken. "So why not foster her out?"

"We tried," Jo sighed. "Hecate knows we tried."

Later she got the full story from Joy, who was not the least ashamed to talk about it. Joy had been fostered to the household of Sir John Fortescue, a Cotswold neighbor on the manor of Ebrington just past Chipping Campden, a few hours' ride from Greystone. A spectacularly bad choice. "They mistreated me sorely," Joy complained, "getting me up before dawn to cook porridge and polish the chamber pots, beating me and making me sleep in the kennel when I said nay. Nor would they let me off for Witches Nights. Naturally, I revenged myself."

Naturally. Joy's petty revenge included giving the meanest dogs mange and making the cook's cakes fall. Her choice of victims gave her away, and they sent her back to Greystone. "Rank injustice," Joy insisted, "since they had no real proof."

Witches had to take a long view of the law, adopting the third-millennium assumption that lack of evidence was the same as innocence. Robyn asked, "What happened then?"

"They got proof," Joy admitted sulkily, pained to say she had underestimated adults. This neighbor, Sir John Fortesque, was King Henry's lord chief justice, and a Devon man by birth, friend and ally of the Hollands. Having a suspicious mind—even for a lord chief justice—Fortesque set FitzHolland and his witch-sniffing hound to seeing what was afoot. FitzHolland surprised the local coven members at a midnight ritual, and all the women got away except for Joy—which was how the girl ended up sitting in a cell in Berkeley Castle, praying for a Church trial.

Hearing Joy's story left Robyn puzzling over her own role in all this. Her arrival had been most convenient—for everyone but her— leading to Joy getting free and Jo getting Joy back. Without her lock-pick necklace and VISA card, Joy would still be in FitzHolland's hands. And while her arrival seemed to be a complete surprise here and now—in the far-off third millennium there lived another Jo and Joy, who were prime movers in getting her here. How much had they known about their past lives? Enough enough to guess that Robyn

Stafford would be almighty useful in 1460? If so, her usefulness should surely be at an end, so no one could object to her going home.

Rain returned in buckets. Aside from her sewing, rainy day amusements included cards, chess, and backgammon. Card decks here and now were like tarot decks, with suits of swords, clubs, cups, and coins. The cards were King, Queen, Knight, and Knave, then the numerals one through nine. Plus a pair of Fools that looked like Jokers, but counted for nothing. She amused everyone by continually thinking the aces and Fools outranked everything. Despite this handicap, she got a great reputation in cards—finally discovering something where the third millennium had a clear advantage. All their games were kids games—or close to it. Jo and Joy played Bataille, what modern kids called War, and Trente-et-un, a form of blackjack played to thirty-one instead of twenty-one. Since Bataille by any name is a bore, and Trente-et-un interesting but terribly limited, she taught them to play Crazy Eights and Old Maid, which mother and daughter found "Wonderfully fun."

She tried to explain they were not her games, but that was hopeless. With rain pouring down outside, "Robyn's games" were an immediate hit—played throughout Greystone, mostly for ribbons, kisses, and quarter-pennies. Half pennies for the big bettors. People immediately came up with inventive variations. Crazy Eights became "Crazy Kings" and Old Maid the "French Queen." Signs of the simmering political unrest.

On Sunday a surprise arrived. Out of nowhere came a letter for her. Seeing the magnificent parchment package sealed with wax and ribbons, Robyn's first reaction was—"For me?" Must be some mistake. Medieval England had no post office, no stamps, no ZIP codes, not even street addresses—giving ample chance for error. Aside from crown messengers, everything went in private hands. People carried letters for each other, or trusted them to travelers. Common carriers acted as a pack-pony UPS. Anyone bringing mail to Greystone could expect at least a meal, and usually a night's lodging. But who here and now would be writing to her? Edward, she hoped, though how would he know she was here?

Ripping off the ribbons, she opened the packet, reading through the archaic wording. It was a summons to attend court at Kenilworth Castle in Warwickshire, written by a fair-handed clerk, but signed by the duchess of Bedford. It was weird to see her name penned on parchment in medieval script—"Damoiselle Robynn Stafford." Impressive even when misspelled.

Jo knew what it said as soon as she saw the seals on the packet. "Duchess Wydville wants to see her new novice in the flesh."

"What should I do?" Duchess Wydville had the power to send her home—but that was hardly why she was being called to Kenilworth. What did the duchess want with her? Did she dare just put herself blindly into the witch-priestess's hands?

Jo consoled her, "Fortunately you have no choice. Duchess Wydville is our most powerful protector. You must go whether you will it or no. Come, you have never been to court—we shall all go, and it will be fun. You shall see."

That was what Jo had said about May Eve, and look how it turned out. She felt an instinctive terror of being dragged deeper into medieval England. The overnight trip to Broughton Castle and Banbury had been a bit of a lark—but she nearly drowned getting back. Court at Kenilworth would be totally different; that would be the heart of the beast. Far safer to stay at Greystone, venturing out only on Witches Flights.

Collin, of course, sided with his sister. "Better to go straight away, seeming eager, making the best impression. Without the Wydvilles good lordship we have scant to put against the Hollands or Lord Scales." Much as she hated it, he was right, they must put themselves in the hands of Duchess Wydville, under the dubious proposition that the "enemy of my enemy" was a friend.

Jo immediately dived into details, telling Collin what they must pack for a trip to court. Living with Jo was like having a roommate totally addicted to dress-up and costume parties. Jo soon had her brother going over her wardrobe and talking fabric—satin versus taffeta, and how to get the newest sleeves to hang right. Robyn could not help smiling at these bold, manly knights like Collin and Sir Anthony—heavily armed dress designers, wearing wool pantyhose, feathered berets, and knee-length gowns, trimmed in lace, ribbon, and pearls—human peacocks, whose greatest ambition was to be Knights of the Garter. Her own collection of homemade gowns and hand-me-downs made her feel like a poor relation hoping to better her chances at court.

Two days later the rain let up, and they headed north with Collin's traveling household, past Buckland Wood and Broadway Hill, aiming to show they appreciated Wydville "good lordship." Descending the Cotswold Edge at Saintbury, a little stone-roofed village with a pretty Norman church and stone cross, Robyn saw the low green Vale of Evesham spread out before her. She felt uneasy at leaving Greystone, though Kenilworth was only two days' ride away. But, who knows—if she made a smashing impression on Duchess Wydville, all her problems might be solved.

Pushing past Mickleton and Mean Hill, they crossed the Stour at Clifford Chambers, reaching the Avon at Stratford, where they passed the night. It perked her up to be in Stratford-upon-Avon a hundred years ahead of Shakespeare—finding it a graceful riverside village, full of gabled half-timbered houses. No one but her thought Stratford the least bit special—most found it a little too ordinary, eager as they were for the sights of Kenilworth. The cramped, dirty inn where they spent the night was indeed a pit, a big comedown from Lord Saye's storybook castle. She heard rats gnawing in the clay wattle walls, and everyone laughed when she refused the ill-cooked meat and vile wine. She told them she was fasting.

"What for?" they asked.

"In honor of Shakespeare." Your yet unborn national bard.

"Who is he?"

She quoted the twenty-ninth Sonnet, always a favorite, and rather apropos:

> When, in disgrace with fortune and men's eyes,
> I all alone beweep my outcast state,
> And trouble deaf heaven with my bootless cries,
> And look upon myself, and curse my fate,
> Wishing me like to one more rich in hope . . .

They all stared, surprised to hear her suddenly spout poetry. Warming to her act, she nodded from one to the other as she recited:

> Featured like him, like him with friends possess'd,
> Desiring this man's art and that man's scope,
> With what I most enjoy contented least . . .

That brought laughs all around, especially from the younger squires, and those she nodded at. Just for devilment, she finished up looking right at Collin, though she was actually thinking of Edward:

> **Yet in these thoughts myself almost despising,**
> **Haply I think of thee, and then my state,**
> **Like to the lark at break of day arising**
> **From sullen earth, sings hymns at heaven's gate;**
> **For thy sweet love remember'd such wealth brings**
> **That then I scorn to change my state with kings.**

They all applauded. "Hunger makes her a poet," someone suggested. "A good one at that. Take her food away."

"The words are not mine," she quickly admitted. "They come from someone named Shakespeare."

None had heard of him, but all agreed, "This Breakspeare has a fine tongue."

"His name is Shakespeare. William Shakespeare."

"As you like it. By any name the fellow's a wordwright, so you need not starve yourself for inspiration."

Truth was, nothing tempted her, not the moldy cheese, nor a particularly deadly-looking liver pie. Hela picked at her untouched platter. Even beer would just make her use the privy, something she had sworn not to do. No one else seemed to mind. Boatmen fresh off the river tore at the lethal liver pie with their fingers, and foot peddlers set down their shoulder bags, taking time out to tell lies and tip back a tankard—all of them badly needing a bath. Which did not stop the local women from giving them kisses to go with their meat and ale. Something she never expected from the Middle Ages was how forward women would be. Hollywood waitresses regularly flirted with customers, but how many kissed each man as he was seated, and again when he got up? Free to be as forward as they liked, women knew if some drunk tried too get physical, the other patrons would cheerfully beat him senseless in exchange for another round of kisses. Far from being scornful of her for living well off a man who was not her husband, women grinned, asking if she knew witchcraft.

"Give us more," the drunk squires cried. "More of your Shakespeare." Why not? How often do you get to quote the Bard in his hometown? She gave them one of her favorite pieces, Puck's epilogue from *A Midsummer-Night's Dream*:

> **If we shadows have offended,**
> **Think but this, and all is mended,**

> That you have but slumber'd here,
> While these visions did appear.
> No more yielding than a dream . . .

She had long given up thinking this might all be a dream, but she did mean to vanish from these people's lives, hopefully leaving fond memories behind. Reaching out, she took the hands of those on either side of her:

> . . . So, good night unto you all.
> Give me your hands, if we be friends,
> And Robin shall restore amends.

Everyone applauded, urging her to eat. None of them wanted to see her vanish. But rank smells still assailed her from around the room—sweat, sour wine, burnt cloves, and cook smoke. She could have found her way to the privy with eyes shut, if she were the least inclined to use it. Inns here and now were not at all like the dark impersonal bars on the Hollywood dating circuit. Young and old laughed and talked over tankards of cheap ale, buying each other rounds and singing off-key—but that did not make the food any safer, or tempt her to use the facilities. The Middle Ages seemed most tolerable when she was in a castle or manor house, or living off the country, able to have things how she wanted—semi-clean and thoroughly cooked—making her feel like she really was a duke's daughter reborn. Or the princess in "The Princess and the Pea."

Kenilworth was far more to her liking, a magnificent double-walled castle, with red sandstone towers soaring above the treetops, surrounded on three sides by a huge artificial lake, a hundred acres of flat still water dotted with swans. Definitely what the Middle Ages was supposed to look like. She crossed the lake on a long walled causeway with gatehouses at each end, what Collin called the "Tiltyard," telling her, "Tourneys have been held here for a hundred knights at a time." He sounded wistful, as if he sorely missed crashing headlong into half-ton of armored man and beast.

Passing through the double-towered gatehouse at the end of the causeway—called the Mortimer Tower—she entered the spacious outer bailey, barely believing what she saw. King Henry's court was in nearby Coventry, but Kenilworth was his military headquarters, his seat of power—and a world unto itself, walled off from the rest of England. Kenilworth had its own market and mill, courts and gallows, bathhouses and brewery, stables, kitchens, pleasure gardens, and gay pavilions. Today was market day, and half of Warwickshire had come to trade and sell, and drink King Henry's flat spiced beer. Knights and ladies in white satin rubbed shoulders with visiting Spanish diplomats and wild Welsh chieftains, perusing stalls selling wool cloth, steel cutlery, beads and bangles, leatherwork, silver filigree, and imported wine, highlighted by a pig auction and horse show—all surrounded by an artificial lake and miles of parkland and hunting preserves.

That was just the outer ward. Towering above her—looking down on this Camelot-cum-country-fair—stood the inner ward, set on high ground behind walls eighty feet tall, enclosing banquet halls, churches and chapels, a broad inner courtyard, and a central keep that was a good-size castle on its own. Inside were the royal apartments, plus private residences for powerful dukes and duchesses with their own stewards, butlers, pages, maidservants, and armed retainers—forming a city unto itself, a nation within a nation, populated by the rich and privileged. Twenty-foot-thick walls cut them off from the outer ward, which was, in turn, walled off from the world. And this was just King Henry's military camp—no wonder king and court seemed a tad out of touch.

That afternoon Joy took her on a revealing tour of the inner ward, declaring the castle was impregnable—"In the days of Edward Longshanks, Kenilworth withstood the entire might of England. The garrison left the gates to the Tiltyard open by day, showing the king that Kenilworth could not be taken." Robyn believed her, looking out over walls, gardens, gates, horse paddocks, banquet halls, and then more walls, and the vast sheet of water, ringed by green woods. To the north—the one direction not defended by water—lay Coventry, King Henry's de facto capital, where Lady Godiva once rode naked through the streets, seen only by Peeping Tom. Lady Godiva had always been one of her heroines, if only because she did it on horseback. Just west of Coventry was Meridian, the village that marked the middle of England. But rather than being in the middle of things, Kenilworth had a sense of splendid isolation—far from London, far from the sea, and far from foreign lands, cut off from the world by miles of placid countryside. Hela hopped about on the stonework, cawing at crows.

On the way down, descending narrow circular stairs, she met a man coming the other way, dressed in black and wearing peasant boots. He had a white pinched face, a long nose, big sensitive eyes, looking like a castle clerk, or someone's aging groom. Stopping her on the stairs, he gently asked her name.

She made a curtsy—not that easy on narrow stairs—saying, "Robyn Stafford." He declared she must be new to court, and she agreed. "New everywhere it seems."

He nodded in agreement. "We are in this world but a brief time." She said a hearty amen—the briefer the better—pleasing him mightily. "It is good to hear one so young awed by the brevity of life. Are you a true daughter to the church?"

"I try most diligently to be." No one gave her any choice, least of all this inquisitive cleric. They chatted a bit more; then he took his leave, without trying to bless her or even get a kiss good-bye. He just encouraged her to be good, praised her piety, and shuffled off up the stairs acting like he owned the place.

Turning back to Joy, she saw the witch-child was down on her knees. Joy nodded toward the boot steps retreating up the tower stairs. "That was the king."

"Kee-ing!" Hela fluttered down to land on Joy's shoulder. So that was Henry VI—a man Shakespeare wrote three plays about—claiming to be King of England, Ireland, and France. Incredible. Just seeing Henry explained a lot, a shadow king, wandering unattended, talking like a cleric and lecturing wayward young women, dressed in bad boots and sackcloth amid all this splendor. Not so much a monarch as a walking cry for help. Robyn certainly felt sorry for him, realizing he desperately needed to be protected from the murder and mayhem done in his name.

But she had problems of her own. That night she would be presented to Duchess Wydville in the flesh—much more frightening than inadvertently chatting up the king. To prepare her for the evening presentation, Jo literally sewed her into a glittering cloth-of-silver creation with graceful hanging sleeves, and the Grey barry of six blue bars on the bodice. Jo told the Wydville story as she sewed, keeping Robyn from making ignorant mistakes. "Duchess Wydville was born Jacquetta of Luxembourg, and descends from a water sprite named Melusine, who still watches over her family, appearing whenever death is near. For a dowerless Burgundian noblewoman with naught to offer but youth and beauty, she married astonishingly well, wedding His Grace the duke of Bedford, King Henry's uncle, a widower twice her age—and the man who burnt Joan of Arc." Jo grimaced at that last part, showing even a witch can be scandalized. Joanna Grey might be an unwed mother with a bastard daughter, but she is far above marrying a man who burned women for witchcraft.

"Was Joan really a witch?" Robyn asked. Jo ought to know. The teenage martyr who turned the tide in the Hundred Years War was another of Robyn's heroines. Ingrid Bergman played her in *Joan of Arc*—but she much preferred Jean Seberg in Preminger's version of Shaw's *Saint Joan*. Both actresses had gone to the stake proclaiming their innocence—giving very convincing performances, even if Seberg had the better lines.

"How else could she have beaten us?" Joy demanded. The young witch-in-training had infinite faith in the Black Arts. "She beat them all, including Lord Talbot and Lord Scales."

"For which Duke Bedford burned her at the stake," Jo tartly reminded her daughter. "Men are not much amused by being beaten at their own own games."

Too true. Any teenage girl who bested her betters at war and diplomacy was plainly guilty of witchcraft or worse. Medieval men invented the Madonna and Whore complex. And Joan, that most wayward of teenagers, totally embodied the concept. To the French she was "the Maid," pure and virginal, God's rebuke to a sinful world. To the English she was the witch and whore portrayed in Shakespeare. Chivalry was a two-edged sword. The same chaste sense of honor that brought Collin to her defense justified turning Joan into French toast. Any woman who repaid men's courtesy and protection with rebellion was irredeemably wicked—an unnatural traitress, for whom burning was much too good. Yet that did not actually make Joan a witch. She told Jo that in her day Joan was a saint. "Next to the Virgin, she is the most famous female saint on the modern Christian calendar." A strange fate for a fifteenth-century peasant lass, who heard voices telling her to dress in drag and lead men into battle.

"Who knows what lies in the human heart?" Jo concluded, the very words her brother used about Lord Saye. "Witch or no, Good Duke John of Bedford burned Joan alive. Two years later Duke John himself died, most likely worn out by a young wife and the war in France—

though I like to hope Jacquetta poisoned him." If she did, it was a poor career choice, leaving her a childless and penniless widow—"But still dowager duchess of Bedford," as Jo brightly pointed out, "and King Henry's aunt by marriage. The Royal Council brought her back to England in state, giving her the manor of Grafton to live on." Robyn pictured the witch-priestess playing the brave young widow of the heroic Bedford—that able killer of witches and Frenchmen—black velvet perfectly setting off her fair skin and golden hair; with no jewelry to mar the effect, just a thin circlet of diamonds showing she was a duchess. No matter how demure and downcast she acted, her black gown and circle of diamonds proclaimed her fit for a king's brother.

Jo sighed, taking in Robyn's borrowed gown as they talked, "She did not need be a sorceress to have knight-troubadours panting to put a smile back on her face. In a year the inevitable happened, and the bereft young widow was with child." That was what comes from everybody being Catholic. Contraception here and now was really in the Dark Ages.

"She had secretly married a handsome squire in her retinue named Richard Wydville," Jo explained, stitching on the form-fitting silver bodice. Secret marriages and betrothals were big among the nobility—not to mention bastardry—half the time there was no one good enough for them to marry. Edward was probably being pretty quiet about his rash promise to make her countess of March. Jo told her the Privy Council took Grafton away, "Vowing that if Squire Wydville wanted her so much, he should keep her." Two poor-but-beautiful young social climbers had made the colossal mistake of marrying each other.

Jo stepped back, checking the hang of the sleeves. "Luckily, they had not lost their power to charm. Duchess Bedford won the favor of the Beauforts and shared in the rewards King Henry lavishes on his relatives—both real and imagined. Grafton was restored, along with Duchess Jacquetta's dower. Squire Richard Wydville is now Baron Rivers, Knight of the Garter and a Privy Councillor himself." King Henry had a passion for promoting anyone who by marriage or bastardry could claim to be his kin.

"A happy ending?" Robyn asked, guessing there were those who hated seeing the Wydvilles go from the squirearchy to the Privy Council in one ungainly leap. Jo, too, had "won favor with the Beauforts"—Joy's father having been Edmund Beaufort, duke of Somerset. All Jo had to show for it was a delightful bastard daughter.

"Mayhap." Jo's voice dropped, though the three of them were alone, and Kenilworth's walls were ungodly thick. "Duchess Jacquetta is not the first witch to marry into the royal family."

"Really?" Robyn never suspected this was such a problem.

"*Certainement.* Half the women who have married into the royal family of late have been witches, a scandalous ill-use of love potions that does us all disrepute. Mad King Henry's grandfather married a Basque witch, Queen Joanna of Navarre—who I was named for," Jo added proudly, doing a mock curtsy. "Two of his sons, Duke John of Bedford and Duke Humphrey of Gloucester married witches. All three were married in their prime, at the height of their power—two had been widowers and one divorced." Do we see a pattern here? No wonder Scales and FitzHolland were so paranoid. First a teenage witch defeats them in France; then two more witches wed the young king's uncles. Had anything happened to frail fey King Henry, England would have had a Witch Queen—instead of a French one.

"All save one of the witches were discovered," Jo noted sternly, lest her two novices be tempted by power. "Queen Joanna spent some years in prison. Eleanor Cobham, who made herself duchess of Gloucester, died behind bars, and the Witch of Eye, who aided her, was burnt. It is misuse of magic," Jo warned her witches-in-training, "to just find the richest most powerful man you can, then make him marry you." Luckily Jo did not know her elder novice had been necking with an underaged earl. "Of all these witches only one remains undiscovered and unpunished, still a duchess, confidante to the queen—and married to a man she wanted."

What a story. Absolutely made for the movies—magic, sex, and politics, all feeding off each other. And tonight she would see the sole surviving social-climbing sorceress—neither imprisoned nor burnt, but living as duchess of Bedford, with dazzlingly plush apartments in King Henry's castle at Kenilworth, and her husband on the Privy Council, while her daughter attended the queen. Plus the stalwart Sir Anthony Wydville for a son. Who says you cannot have it all? Witchcraft looked like an insanely tricky business, a human lottery with huge rewards and horrific punishments, and her only ticket home.

"So, see you mind your manners," Jo warned when they had finished sewing themselves into their gowns. "Curtsy deep and show your dimples, for we dearly need to please this duchess."

She promised to abide by all the rules in her *Babee Book*, and curtsy to the floor, doing her best about the dimples. Entering the reception chamber, Robyn did her lowest curtsy, not lifting her gaze, waiting for Duchess Jacquetta to give her leave. Out the corner of her eyes, she saw silk trailing on soft carpets, a cascade of colors, backed by bits of carved wood paneling.

She heard, "Rise, Robyn Stafford," and looked up to see Duchess "Weirdville" in the flesh, done up like Queen Elizabeth's grandmother, only grander, wearing her circlet of diamonds and a bright blue gown with gold fleurs-de-lis and clouds of lace—making Robyn's own home-stitched finery seem tawdry. Duchess Jacquetta's high bodice and long trailing sleeves were decorated with Wydville magpies—much to Hela's delight. With her was her eldest daughter, Lady Elizabeth Grey, the cool poised blonde who assisted on Witches Night—wife to Lord Grey of Groby, and lady-in-waiting to the queen—the girl whose birth brought down the wrath of the Privy Council, doing quite well with a life begun in disgrace. "Come, my dear," Duchess Wydville commanded, "tell us about yourself."

Right. Now she wanted to know her. When they first met in modern England, the witch pretended not to know her—but had known all about Edward, and the Displacing Spell, probably because her own past self had put the spell on Edward. Widow Weirdville even showed her the damned blue butterfly, the first thing she saw here and now. But how much did this Duchess Wydville know? Not near as much. Since this was a "witches only" private audience, Robyn told her story—abridged edition—acting as if she did not know who this wandering young knight might be, leaving out their kiss at the end and his promises to make her his "lady." Blaming all her current problems on vain curiosity—being at best half-convincing.

Listening intently, the duchess seemed puzzled, if not totally disbelieving. At the end, she gave Robyn a curious look, asking, "Why then would I have sent you here?" Duchess Wydville spoke with the Franco-German accent of her native Luxembourg. ("Vy den vould I haf sent you here?") What the future Joy mistook for Transylvanian.

Robyn took care not to copy it, saying in court English, "It did seem like an accident at the time."

"Nonsense." The duchess dismissed that notion out of hand. "It is no accident. I do nothing but for a reason. *Nein?*" That Robyn could well believe. She had been brought here for some still unknown purpose—but right now neither of them trusted the other enough to really try to find out why, hiding behind polite bewilderment. Duchess Wydville touched a finger to her lips, staring hard at her. "Well, now that you are here, what will we do with you?"

What, indeed? She dared to be blunt. "I want most of all to go back."

"Before we even know why you have come?" Duchess Wydville recoiled from such an unthinkable breach in etiquette. "*Nein!* Nonsense. You are here for some purpose. Look at you—young, smart, and pretty, and you have already done the Witches Flight. And you know the future. You were sent here for a purpose, an important purpose. I just wish I knew what my reasons were."

So did Robyn, hiding behind a superglued smile; but she did not trust this duchess enough to tell her the whole truth, much less sort through clues together. Clearly nothing would come from this séance.

Duchess Wydville looked her over carefully, as if closer scrutiny could solve the problem; then she shrugged. "No matter what my motives, I take responsibility for my actions. You are welcomed into my household."

Dumbfounded, she did not know what to say. She came here hoping to be sent home, not to enter the Wydville household. In all her lurid imaginings, she honestly never pictured this predicament. Hopelessly naive of her, really. Now that she thought about it, being taken into the Duchess's "protection" was what she should have most feared— far more likely than being clapped directly into a dungeon, and nearly as scary. She had a thousand serious objections to serving the Wydvilles, none of which she felt like voicing.

Luckily, Jo spoke up for her. "Please, my gracious Lady Bedford, may she not bide with me awhile, at least until Michaelmas. I owe her that much for saving my daughter."

Not the least pleased to see Jo leap in, Duchess Wydville nodded slowly. "Yes, *natürlich*, until Michaelmas, then."

Finding her voice, Robyn enthusiastically thanked the duchess, secretly thanking Jo even more. Duchess Jacquetta had the power to send her home, but plainly wanted her here. Robyn did not aim to just give herself over to whatever purpose this amoral witch-priestess came up with, not if she could help it. To seal the deal, Duchess

Jacquetta gave her a purse with a dozen gold half-nobles. Magic coins, worth half a year's wages at what Collin had been paying her. "Here, child"—the sinister duchess suddenly turned kindly—"hire yourself a decent seamstress."

Curtsying low, she exited, uneasy at being dependent on some of Edward's most vigilant foes. Weirdville, indeed. All that could be said for the duchess was that they had enemies in common. Faced with choosing between the Wydvilles and Duke Holland's witch hunters, she would gladly take the duchess, but she thanked Jo profusely for saving her from making the choice.

"Only until Michaelmas," Jo reminded her.

"When is that?" She felt silly not knowing the simplest things. Michaelmas might be next week.

"At the end of summer."

"Good." She could not possibly be here that long.

During her stay at Kenilworth, she saw King Henry a few more times at magnificent feasts in the huge banquet hall. Built by Henry's great grandfather, the hall was nearly a hundred feet long, with tall sculpted windows, huge fireplaces, and a great raised dais for the high table. Earls, barons, and Knights of the Garter stood in solemn attendance. Ushers with long white wands cleared the way, looking like walking jokers, wearing floppy caps and stiff tabards emblazoned with lions and lilies. Then came the great Sword of State and the chancellor, Bishop William Waynflete, followed by Henry himself. Obviously uncomfortable in all this splendor, he managed to look out of place in his own hall.

Not so his queen, Margaret of Anjou, who looked totally in her element, pretty and animated despite her heavy robes and crown—happy to have lords serving her beer. Henry's two Tudor half brothers were also in attendance. She supposed they must be some relation to the Queen Elizabeth Tudors, which did not bode well for King Henry's own little Prince of Wales. Jo told her that these half brothers were products of yet another secret marriage—this time between King Henry's widowed mother and a Welsh squire named Owen Tudor. Despite scant proof the marriage even took place, King Henry made his half brothers royal earls, promoting them past almost all the nobility in the land. Only dukes outranked them.

"Royal titles mean royal lands," Jo pointed out, "and royal income, as well." Henry had showered gold on his overextended family—some of which was now in Robyn's purse—so much gold that his government was bankrupt, and dared not ask Parliament for more taxes. Or even hold court in his capital. Folks expected the king to live within his income, and were not happy to hear he had given his income away, whether it went to bastard Welsh relations, or royal ne'er-do-wells like Duchess Wydville, who spoke with an accent and had scandalous habits.

Living within his income seemed to be the last thing on Henry's mind. Kenilworth was a fairy-tale place, where men-at-arms outnumbered stable hands, and lords were so plentiful they waited tables. Washing with distilled rosewater, Robyn was confronted with incredible fare, a typical menu might include:

FIRST COURSE	SECOND COURSE	THIRD COURSE
Roast Peacock	Cokyntryce	Plover
Fillets in gelatin	Ox-tongues in tripe	Curlew
Heads of Boars	Capons with pickled eel	Snipe or small birds
Heron in carp sauce	Suckling pig stuffed with	Blood pudding
Mutton tarts	steamed crabs	

Followed by sugared custards sprinkled with silver foil, all washed down with barrels of wine and ale. Half of it she would not have touched under torture. Cokyntryce was a pig and a capon cut in half and then sewn together to make a half-pig, half-bird, which was stuffed with eggs, breadcrumbs, pepper, and mutton suet, glazed with ginger and saffron, then roasted whole on a spit. When she first saw a spitted saffron pig staring at her, wearing a bird's butt and waiting to be sliced, she almost lost her mutton tarts. Picking through these outrageous feasts, searching for anything semi-edible, she caught King Henry's attention; seeing her reticence, he sent her tidbits from the royal platter—roast kidney with lamprey. Yum. Which she had to force down with a smile, or create a royal uproar. Each outlandish dish came with harping and singing, or Italian tumblers, or dramatic recitations, or comedy skits and dances by "savage men" in wild costumes.

All for a weekday dinner away from court. Small wonder the country could ill afford King Henry. She could see up close the staggering gulf between plain West Country folk at Greystone, wearing homespun and breakfasting on bread and beer, and the gay rarefied life of their rulers. Common folk—like her—only came to Kenilworth if they had something to beg or sell. And by most standards she had done amazingly well, getting money in her purse and the duchess's promise of a position. King Henry even fed her off his plate—but she could not say the experience had instilled any great sense of loyalty to the crown.

Coventry was more fun, more lively, too small to be a real city, but still noisy, crowded and dirty—a wild open-air flea market with noxious eateries. Mercers sold the "true blue" cloth that is supposed to hold its color, and she saw Saint Michael's Cathedral, destroyed by German bombers in World War II—she had already seen the rubble on a future "home schooling" trip with Joy. It felt very witchy to stand in front of a massive building, knowing exactly when it would be leveled, in fact having already "seen" the ruins. Alongside the cathedral she talked through a little barred window to a woman walled up in a stone cell. Not a prisoner but a volunteer, piously protesting the evils of the world.

Staying for Witches Night, they left next day before noon. Collin rode through the Sabbath to get back to Greystone fast as he could, by a different route, with a different crossing of the Avon—just to be safe. Robyn rode past Warwick Castle, a splendid edifice with long walls and lofty towers on a low escarpment above the Avon, belonging to Richard Neville, earl of Warwick—but now "in the king's hands." The Neville earls of Salisbury and Warwick were the duke of York's only powerful allies, and were now both in Ireland with Edward. Seeing their huge brooding castle standing near empty so close to Kenilworth brought home to Robyn how badly divided England was.

She got back to Greystone late Sunday, at twilight on Saint Theodotus Day, with the Feast of Saint Dunstan due on the morrow. Saint Theodotus was the patron saint of barmaids and innkeepers, but she was happy not to end his day in an inn. When her feet touched down in the dark rammed-earth bailey, she could not suppress the "home again" feeling. Back to being part of the Grey household and Collin's extended family, learning good serving manners, needlepoint, and spellcraft.

What if that was all? Now and forevermore. Witches Night at the Wydvilles had been another disaster. Yet magic was still the answer; she just had to do it without the duchess. But first some sleep . . .

19 May 1460, Feast of Saint Dunstan, Greystone

After almost a month here and now, seeing 1460 still makes me cringe. It is so absurd. And unfair. Right now it is the middle of the night, between lauds and prime. 3:43 according to my watch. Dawn is not far off, and Greystone is quiet. Something woke me, and I cannot get back to sleep, so I am sitting up in bed writing. Witches Night at the Wydvilles was as weird as I feared it would be. All I could do was hover out of body above the cast circle, afraid to let go. But Duchess Wydville has the power—I could feel it. Too bad she will not help me.

Kenilworth was incredible, outrageously aweful, but it did not get me home. Or even measurably closer. Greystone is not home, but it is my haven, which I would be helpless without. Thanks to Jo I did not have to give it up. Yet. I hope I never leave again, except to go home. I just want to sit here and sew, especially now that I have the money for satins and lace. Court gowns made us look shabby. Staying simple and tasteful, trying not to stand out, was a big mistake. Being plain only attracts attention when you live among peacocks. Just look at King Henry.

In Coventry I saw a woman walled up in a cell attached to a church. Her cell has a narrow window opening right onto the street, so she can speak to passersby. At first I thought she was a prisoner—I had heard of prisoners in the Southwark "Clink" begging alms from their cell windows—but this woman was a volunteer, a religious mystic. An "Anchoress," according to Jo, who says she can never leave that cell—living a life of prayer, penance, and meditation. She may not talk to men, engage in trade or barter, or keep any pet but a cat. But she is allowed to give advice. Seeing Jo and Joy, she praised motherhood, "That proper love, wisdom, and charity shown by a mother for her child, is what we get from God, who is mother to us all." Amen.

Jo told me that if all else fails I could become an anchoress, saying King Henry greatly favors them. Food and drink, solid lodging, time for prayer and contemplation. Watch the world go by your window. No thanks. Being walled up for the rest of my life is too much like what FitzHolland has in mind. Just Jo's twisted Brit sense of humor. Medieval career opportunities? What a ghastly thought. Where is Edward? He promised to make me a countess . . .

She stopped, listening intently. Her hand hung above the mini-keyboard, about to complete the sentence. Candlelight came from a burning stub by the bed. Somewhere in the walled bailey outside a dog barked. She listened harder, hearing a muffled bang, sounding like an explosion, followed by a cry of alarm and running feet. Then came a second blast, louder than the first. Definitely an explosion.

Switching off her journal, she leaped out of bed, finding her lighter and another candle. Her watch said 3:55. Why did things always have to happen at three in the morning? First light was not far off. Jo sat up in bed, looking wide-eyed. Joy was still asleep. From beyond the door came loud shouts and the smell of sulfur smoke. "What has happened?" Jo demanded.

"It sounded like a bomb." Two bombs actually. She lit her candle.

"A what?" Jo stared dumbly at her.

"A bomb. Explosives." She could not shake the twenty-first-century notion that a terrific bang followed by smoke meant an explosion. It had not sounded like a cannon shot, and could not be a truck back-firing. "Wake Joy," she suggested, fearing the worst.

Jo shook her daughter. Holding the candle before her, Robyn opened the bedroom door, seeing nothing but tower stairs spiraling down into darkness. Silently, she stepped out onto the stairs, edging her way down one wall to the stone landing at the base of the tower; here a big oak door opened onto another landing, and the straight flight of stairs descended between the buttery and pantry into the great hall—the same stairs where she collided with Collin while carrying the May Day washing. Easing open the oak door, she heard more shouts and the clash of steel coming from below. Holy Hecate, a battle royal was going on in the great hall. What a horrible thought. She peered down the stairs, too frightened to go farther. Suddenly a man in a steel helmet stepped into view below, holding a big shiny halberd and looking up at her, grinning so wide she could count his teeth by candlelight. Stitched to his quilted brigandine was a large white swan.

The Golden Valley

Suppressing a scream, she dashed back into the tower, slamming the thick landing door behind her, dropping the bar into place. Booted feet sounded on the stairs, followed by a halberd banging on the far side of the oak door. Racing back up the tower stairs, she slammed into Jo coming down, with Joy hanging onto her mother's nightshirt. Mother and daughter looked horrified, both asking at once, "What is happening?"

"Enemies in the great hall; I saw a swan badge." She stood on the stone steps, breathing hard, seeing Jo and Joy seeming to waver in the candlelight. Hela flew back and forth, cawing unneeded warnings; by now they knew all too well what was happening. Below her the banging grew louder. More than one halberd beat on the heavy door; soon armed men would be coming in, whether they willed it or not. "We should best get dressed," Robyn suggested. Jo nodded—whatever came next, better not to face it in a nightshirt.

How do you dress for a housebreaking? The men below had on steel-sewn brigandines—studded with nail heads—stylish yet practical. But they had known what was coming; Robyn had to make do, picking the pants outfit she came in topped off with her tight red jacket—this was no time to be tripped up by a dress. Tying on her hiking boots, she heard the door below splinter. In minutes the invaders would be storming up the stairs.

Opening her saddlebag, she grabbed anything that looked useful— or too valuable to part with. Her lighter, herb teas, spare clothes, boiled water, her new blue-and-silver riding dress. The attack Collin feared was here, coming faster than she ever expected. Someone had broken into Greystone—Swans for sure, FitzHolland most likely. That pair of explosions had blown in the bailey gate, then the main door to the keep, filling the great hall with smoke and witch hunters. Hopefully Collin was up, organizing a counterattack. Until then, she, Jo, and Joy were trapped in this tower—whose only door was the one being beaten in below.

Leaving them just one escape route. When she finished stuffing her saddlebag, she started ripping down the bed curtains. Jo and Joy had already torn blankets and linen off the bed and were pulling more bedding from the linen press. Bundling up the bed curtains, she threw the saddlebag over her shoulder. From below came the crash of splintering wood, followed by a ringing cheer as the door burst open. She turned to Jo and Joy, standing with possessions slung over their backs and their arms full of bedsheets. "They have broken in," she shouted in French. "Get to the top of the tower."

Carrying curtains and bedsheets, they dashed up spiral stairs, taking steps two at a time by wobbling candlelight. Booted feet rang on stone behind them. At the top, Jo threw back the wooden trap. Cold night air whipped down the stairwell, blowing out the candles. Hela fluttered up into the gray square of predawn sky showing overhead. Pushing Jo and Joy ahead of her, Robyn scrambled through the trap onto the open top of the tower. Black battlements showed against the lighter sky. Rolling clear of the trap, she helped Jo slam it shut. Joy shot home the bolt. More bangs and curses came from below as men beat at the trap with their halberds.

Robyn got up and looked out through an embrasure at the back of the tower, seeing nothing but darkness below. She spun about, still speaking French to confuse the foe: "We must get down before they think to put men at the base of the tower."

Jo nodded silently, sitting on the trapdoor, tying sheets together. Joy tested each knot by heaving on it with all her might. Robyn joined in, turning the pile of bedding and curtains into a makeshift rope. The men on the far side of the trapdoor thought they had their prey penned atop the tower—but to truly cut off escape, the witch hunters had to send someone back down the stairs, through the smoke-filled great hall, out the blown bailey gate, and around to the back of the keep. Hopefully they could all rappel down the tower before anyone thought of that.

Kneeling atop the trapdoor, Jo tied the bedsheet rope to the bolt, tested it, and then shouted, *"C'est bon!"*

Winding the sheets once around a battlement, Robyn flung the loose end through an embrasure, a fluttering white snake disappearing into blackness. Jo jumped up and gave her a quick kiss, saying, "You go first. I will send Joy down, then follow after." Up close, Jo trembled slightly, though her voice stayed calm—but it was not herself Jo feared for, having freely chosen to go last. Saying a swift morning prayer, Robyn seized hold of the bedsheet rope and swung out through the embrasure. Her hiking boots found the wall and she started down, fast as she could. Luckily she could only see up. Above her the tower battlements stood out against the lighter sky, but the drop beneath her was totally black, hiding how far she had to fall.

Boots slipped on the dark stone, and she swung wildly, banging hard against the tower. Pearl gray sky spun about her, and she hit the tower again, her boots scraping for a toehold. Shoulders aching, fingers locked in terror, she held on, got her footing, and kept on going.

Abruptly, her feet hit solid ground—she was down. Joy came next, followed by her mother. Snatching up fallen possessions, they skirted the remains of an ancient hill camp, plunging into the wooded hollow on the far side of the hill. Hela flew ahead of them, dodging between the trees. Black leafy branches closed in overhead, cutting off the lighter sky. Robyn could not see where to put her feet; luckily she did not need to, with Jo and Joy pulling her along. Crashing through the hollow, they dragged her into a cleared space between the dark hollow and the black line of Gallop Wood, stopping there to catch their breaths. "I wish Collin were here," whispered Jo, glancing back in the direction of Greystone.

Amen. But by now Collin could be in the hands of the witch hunters, or worse. White frightened faces of mother and daughter showed plainly in the predawn light—they were out, but very much on their own. Robyn asked, "What do we do now?"

Before anyone could answer, Hela cawed a warning. Barking broke out behind them, coming from the far side of the dark hollow. Jo rasped, "We run!"

Right. Robyn took off running across the cleared ground toward Gallop Wood, with Jo and Joy going hand in hand ahead of her. Dogs were after them. Curtains and bedsheets hanging from the back of the tower told right where they had gone, and with daylight showing already, dogs would have all day to run them down. But beyond Gallop Wood was a spring and a shallow stream; if they got there ahead of the hounds, it might hide their scent. A slim hope, but she could not think of anything better.

In seconds, she crossed the clear space, crashing into the dark wood, raising an appalling racket. Tripping over tree roots and ducking to

avoid black branches, she lost sight of Jo and Joy. They knew Gallop
Wood far better than she, but she could not call for them to wait, so
she plunged blindly through the bracken, headed downhill, her saddlebag over her shoulder. Hopefully they would guess the horrible din
behind them was her.

Without warning Gallop Wood gave way to steep pasture dotted
with trees. Stumbling into the open, she stopped, surprised to have
run out of wood—and to find herself totally alone. She looked left
and right, seeing no sign of Jo or Joy, or their raucous magpie. She
stood on the edge of a slanting sheep pasture about halfway down the
Cotswold Edge. Below her was a black patch of woods, bordering a
gully; the spring and stream should be off to her right somewhere.
Shouldering her saddlebag, she made for the stream at a labored run,
breath coming in ragged gasps, boots feeling heavy on her feet. What
if she could not find Jo or Joy? Trying to make her own way across
medieval England did not have much appeal. Where would she go?
To Ireland, to find Edward? That sounded awfully daunting, alone
and faced with a vast dawn landscape. At least she no longer heard
the dogs—just the long musical morning call of a thrush. Which suddenly turned into a fast *tchick-tchick* alarm call.

Riders burst from the wood behind her, a pair of them, wearing
steel-studded jackets and white swans on their breasts. Dawn light
gleamed on their lance points. Seeing her, one gave a spirited cheer,
elated at the prospect of riding down a fleeing woman. His companion
answered with a view halloo, and they both spurred their horses toward her.

Weariness evaporated. Spinning about, she dashed straight downhill, making for the wooded brake, hoping to draw her pursuers away
from Jo and Joy. Hoofbeats sounded behind her, twin sets, getting
louder. Flinging aside her saddlebag, she put her head down and ran,
desperate to reach the line of trees.

Only to run straight into another armored rider, appearing right in
front of her, materializing from the dark wood as if by magic. One
moment he had been half in shadow, hidden beneath the trees; then
suddenly there he was there, on a horse, solid and real, blocking her
escape. Horrified, she stopped dead, mouth agape. How had he gotten
ahead of her? This made three of them, all on horseback, against one
of her. Totally unfair. A swift glance over her shoulder showed her

the other two were almost upon her. She turned back toward the lone rider. Dodge past him, and she still might make the woods. Feinting left, she dodged right, and then cut back left.

"Stay still," the fellow called down to her, sounding exasperated. "Let me pass, and I will see to them."

It was Collin, mounted atop his gray charger, wearing his steel sallet tipped back to see more clearly. Silver nail heads on his blue brigandine jacket sparkled in the dawn light. He had his lance held low to keep from snagging it on the trees, and as he trotted past, he lowered his sallet and raised his lance. Ignoring his command to stay still, she kept on running, not turning until she reached the trees. Discretion was needed in obeying a lord's orders; no doubt if Collin had thought about it, he would have told her to take shelter—then watch in safety.

She said a quick prayer as Collin urged his charger up slope, going from trot to canter. Caught by surprise, the dawn sky at their backs, her pursuers did not see Collin emerge from the dark wood ahead. Coming at them obliquely, he burst out of the shadows, crouched behind his silver wyvern shield, lance level. The lead rider barely got his mount turned to meet the charge before Collin's lance caught him in the midriff, hurling him from the saddle . . .

. . . landing him smack in the path of his fellow. Collin played the pair of Swans perfectly; the first rider's fall made the second swerve and rein in, lest he ride right over his companion. Doing a barrel-racing turn, Collin brought his horse around, aiming at the second Swan's flank. Before the fellow could react, Collin's lance plucked the second Swan from the saddle as neatly as the first. Coming down with a thud, the fellow rolled several times—then stopped.

Collin finished off by rounding up their horses; then he came trotting back to her, leading both mounts. Reining in, he tipped back his sallet, saying tersely, "Take your pick, my lady."

Both were bays; she decided to take a chance on the mare, pulling herself into the saddle, at the same time pointing up slope. "My things."

He stared at her over an armored shoulder. "What things? Where?"

"Let me have the reins, and I will show you." Collin tossed her the reins, and she urged the bay mare up slope, back the way they had come. Her mount went easily enough, foolishly supposing they were headed home. Passing Collin's downed opponents, she was glad to see they looked alive. Collin's lance was a blunt jousting pole, like those stacked by the bailey stables, fit for *à plaisance* but not *à outrance*. She asked how he ended up armed with a jousting lance.

Collin shrugged. "I was in the bailey when the gate was blown, and this was all I could lay hands on. But things are going ill enough, without adding a pair of killings." Why start a couple of blood feuds that could be avoided? Able to take on two men at once, uphill and with a blunted lance, Collin could afford to be generous to his enemies.

When they got to her saddlebag, he caught a strap loop in his lance, handing it up to her. She thanked him and pointed toward the stream. "I think Jo went that way. We were hoping to lose the dogs."

"Dogs?" Collin asked, looking about. "What dogs?"

She realized she no longer heard the dogs—not that she missed them. In fact, she had not heard their baying since leaving Gallop Wood. "The dogs we were running from."

Guessing that was all the explanation he would get, Collin headed off toward the stream. She followed, keeping a sharp lookout behind, but seeing no sign of pursuit. One of the men Collin hit was on his feet, attending to the other. Her mare looked back as well. Did the horse realize she had changed owners? Catching up with Collin, she asked if he recognized anyone in the attack. Collin nodded, "That misshapen cur with the witch-sniffing hound."

"Le Boeuf. But not FitzHolland?"

"No, just his hangman." Collin told her he had been up on the bailey wall, roused by a barking dog, when the outer gate blew in. "They came charging through, going straight to the keep door and blowing that in as well. By then I was down the stable stairs, getting my horse and lance. When they rushed into the keep, I charged out, surprising the guard left at the gate. Circling around Gallop Wood, I came right here."

"Why?" How happy for her that he did, but it seemed awfully forseeing, even for a warlock.

"Jo and I agreed that if Greystone were ever surprised, she should go down the back of the tower, and we would meet on the far side of Gallop Wood."

Sensible plan. Woods along the Edge offered scores of hiding places, numerous escape routes, and sweeping views of the flats below. Finding the spring and stream, she saw no sign of Jo or Joy. Her mare started to shy, not liking where things were headed. Patting her horse's shoulder, she told Collin, "We should work our way downstream." That is the way she would have gone.

He nodded tersely, leading the spare horse over to the north bank while she and her balky mare stayed south of the stream. By now the sun was almost up, and she could clearly see ground that had been utterly black when she first looked down from the tower. "Hoofprints," Collin called across to her. She saw them, too, fresh hoofprints, with sharp crisp edges, made this morning. "Dog prints, too," Collin added. There had been dogs, and not just in her horrified imagination. He traced the line of tracks with his lance, saying, "These prints lead back up the Edge. . . ."

"Maybe they gave up the chase and went back to loot." She tried to sound hopeful, knowing this had to be hell on Collin, losing Greystone to his enemies and unable to find his family.

"What is that there?" He pointed his blunted lance at a patch of color on her side of the stream.

She rode over to look. It belonged to Jo, a white-and-blue silk bag—she had last seen it over Joy's shoulder. She swung down, picked up the bag, and tied it to her saddle; then she started searching for the girl's footprints. Joy had run right past here, probably Jo as well. She spotted Joy's bare footprints, just the toes and balls of her feet, pressed deep in the mud. Running in full-tilt panic—no wonder Joy dropped the bag.

Farther along she found another cloth bag, the one Jo had been carrying, heavier, made of red velvet—she tied that, too, to her saddle. Downstream lay a trampled section of bank, where horses had crossed and recrossed the stream, and riders had dismounted, striding about on booted feet. Here the tracks ended. Horses, dogs, and riders had found what they were seeking. She got down and examined the ground, spotting Jo's slipper prints amid the jumble. Dropping to her knees, she searched through the brush along the stream, lifting each branch to look beneath it. Behind her, the sun came up over the Edge, dawning on the Feast of Saint Dunstan.

Collin called down, "It is far too clear what has happened. What are you looking for?"

"This!" She held it up triumphantly, wringing one small victory out of the debacle. The leather bag was right where she guessed it would be. "Jo's potion bag."

"There's a good chance." Collin sounded impressed.

"No chance to it," she sighed. "I knew Jo would keep it to the last and try to hide it if they seized her." Jo had been "holding" as Heidi would say, and the natural impulse was to stash it, rather than have it found on her. Which meant Jo was taken for sure. Somehow they would have to find a way to free her and Joy. She asked Collin, "Do you think they took them back to Greystone?" Familiar surroundings and loyal tenants would make a rescue easier.

Collin shook his head grimly. "No. Not back to Greystone. Look." He pointed with his lance.

Dense black smoke billowed up beyond Gallop Wood, blotting out the low sun. Greystone was burning; nothing else was so close and so big. What a catastrophe—Greystone was not just taken, but gone. Her safe haven in a hostile era had vanished, and everyone she had lived with and gotten to know was homeless. Or in enemy hands. And there was nothing she could do for them. This time FitzHolland had come in overwhelming force, with the law squarely behind him. Calling out Collin's tenants to resist would just make them targets, too. She remembered the fire marks she had seen the night she crashed Collin's third-millennium birthday party. They had seemed so old then, like a part of the rock—she never thought to see them made.

Heartsick himself, Collin tersely told her to get mounted. "There is naught to do here, and much to do elsewhere." He was right: they must gather allies, call out the Greys, and alert the Wydvilles—for whatever good that would do—and the sooner the better. Hanging about here would only add two more prisoners to the bag. She pulled herself back into the saddle, shivering from the morning cold, for the first time feeling the full immensity of what had happened. She had lost Jo and Joy, her most constant companions, her roommates, and partners in spellcraft. With them went her best chance of getting home—also her hot baths and clean clothes, her chance to see how her food was cooked, even her *Babee Book* and the white rose Edward gave her; all gone up in smoke along with Greystone. How would she survive?

And where were they headed? She had no notion. Not back to Kenilworth, or to Sudeley Castle, or Lord Saye at Broughton, or anywhere else she had been before. All those places lay in different directions. Collin led her due west, off the Edge and onto the flats, crossing the Cotswold Way between Stanway and Stanton; ahead lay the green hilly Vale of Isbourne, and beyond that the wide floodplain of the

Severn. She looked at Collin, who was having a hard morning himself, having lost his sister, niece, and manor hall, not to mention his Flemish paintings and gold canopy bed. And his people were homeless and scattered as well. How many of them had been hurt or killed? How many women raped? Horrible images assailed her. She cringed to think of that singing circle of women who danced with her on May Eve, now in the hands of Le Boeuf and his like.

Her mare started to balk again, bringing her back to reality. Her mount was having the day from hell as well—dragged from her cozy stall for a cold, wet night ride, bombs going off, her owner knocked from her saddle, and suddenly she was the property of some stranger, headed who knows where. Leaning down, she spoke softly to the mare, telling the horse not to worry. "There is a warm stall waiting for you. With fresh hay and a bag of barley." Or so she hoped.

Collin turned in the saddle, letting her catch up. Stripping off a glove, he reached out and brushed her cheek. "You are crying," he told her, wiping away tears.

She nodded silently. "I was." Then she asked, "Where are we going?"

"Tewkesbury." Collin nodded at the green hills ahead. "A dozen or so miles to the west."

"What is there?" Tewkesbury rang a bell, but she did not know if it was from now or from the future. Or maybe from Shakespeare.

"A ford over the Severn."

So they were heading into Wales. Her horse was not going to like that. "And after Tewkesbury?" she asked.

He smiled at her insistence, the first smile she had seen all morning—aside from the crazed grin on that Swan with an ax. "You ask so swiftly and answer so freely, I could almost believe you were an Englishwoman—except that you sometimes miss the simplest things. I have family in the Marches. Grey of Powys will give us shelter, and Grey de Ruthyn is my uncle."

"Could we not go straight to Kenilworth?" she suggested. Naturally Collin meant to make for his uncle's and cousin's castles—the Greys were marcher lords, Anglo-Norman nobles given wide liberty by the crown, so long as they held down the Welsh. But the Welsh Marches sounded bleak, and her sole visit to court had been smashing. Duchess Wydville had wanted her for the ducal household, and King Henry fed her offal off his own plate, making her feel like a prize Pekingese—

but still she made an impression. "Friends there could put our case before the king."

Collin replied with a grim smile. "Just the two of us? With nothing to our name but a spare horse?"

Stolen, at that. She saw his point. King Henry's court ran on money and power, and right now they had neither. How could they hope to stand up to FitzHolland, backed by Lord Scales, and Duke Holland, admiral of England, King Henry's closest cousin-male? Strong, wise kings might give justice to the powerless, but Henry was not that sort of monarch. Not by a million miles. Collin shook his head. "No one at court will pay us heed until we have something to offer. Something they need. Or something they fear."

"Like what?" She tried to imagine what could move that crowd at Kenilworth. Nothing easy came to mind. Edward's father had given up trying, and resorted to arms.

"I do not know," Collin admitted. "But I will find something. Or else . . ." He stopped.

"Or else what?" She studied the angry horseman beside her.

"Or, Heaven help me, I shall bring them all down. Every one of them. Holland and Henry, and Lord Scales, and that damned witch-duchess." For a moment Sir Collin's cool, confident mask slipped, and he spoke straight from the heart, not caring how it sounded, not deigning to hide his feelings. "They all think they cannot be brought low, but believe me, I will do it if need be. I want my sister back. And my niece." She did not doubt he could do it. Collin never boasted, yet whatever he cared to do—from jousting to making love—he did it remarkably well, seeming to somehow draw on his past lives. Politics held no appeal to him, and he had stayed loyal to King Henry—but give Collin sufficient excuse, and he could play that game, too. If Sir Collingwood Grey had been leading the duke of York's rebellion, King Henry would have been sent packing long ago.

She tried to soothe him saying, "Somehow this will be made right. We know for sure Greystone will be rebuilt and restored." Greys would be living there five hundred years hence—she herself had seen it.

He looked at her and laughed, the old Collin confidence returning. "Yes, you are the living proof of that."

She got a sharp feeling for how strange these witch families were, yet how well they fit in here and now. Here was Sir Collingwood Grey, lord on the lam, having lost his family and manor serving a mad king, and yet serenely sure the family fortunes would be restored. Why? Because a woman from the future told him so, a footloose seeress with no name or prospects and no fixed abode. It mattered not a whit that what she said was totally true—no one but a medieval would believe it.

Fording the Isbourne, they climbed the low grassy hills to the west. She kept looking back over her shoulder, expecting to see dogs and horsemen, but all she saw was the Cotswold Edge sinking behind her. Beyond Bredon Hill, she entered terra incognita, parts of England she had never been in before, not now or in the future—unless you counted glimpses out a train window or breakneck trips up and down M5, clinging to the dash with Jo at the wheel. Ahead lay Herefordshire and the Marches, Mortimer country, where Edward had lands and followers, now lying very low. And beyond the Marches rose the great dark mass of Wales, where she had met Edward and this whole weird business had begun.

Seeing no sign of pursuit, Robyn relaxed her guard. Hunger started to gnaw. Her usual herb tea, toasted bread, and fried-egg breakfast was not much by medieval standards; but she missed it. Having been on the run before, she knew to do the small things first, finding food and water, staying dry and warm. Otherwise your big problems just got bigger. Convincing Collin to stop at a farmstead, they bought deliciously fresh bread, hard cheese, and flat beer, celebrating the Feast of Saint Dunstan in the saddle.

Past Priors Park, on Gupshill Manor, she saw the tall square towers of Tewkesbury Abbey on the far side of the Swillgate Brook, rising above the trees along the Avon. Then she remembered that bit of Shakespeare:

> **We are advertised by our loving friends**
> **That they do hold their course toward Tewkesbury. . . .**

The funny use of *advertised* stuck in her head, though she could not think who said it. Or in what play. It was how people here talked— advertising was not a business, but something loving friends did for one another. Crossing downstream at Lower Lode ford, where the Avon flowed into the Severn, she left Gloucestershire behind, riding through flat green Worcestershire floodplain. All cried out and having food inside her, she relaxed, strangely reassured to see rural England around her, with folks working away on their organic family farms, with no time for politics and witch hunts. England as it ought to be, a hand-tilled green landscape dotted with flowers. She asked Collin, "Have you an idea where we will sleep?"

"Tonight?" Collin looked at her like it was way too early to tell. "In Herefordshire, I hope."

"And then?" Wales was still a ways off, out beyond Herefordshire, and she had only a vague idea where Powys and Ruthyn might be. The nearest part of Wales to here was the Black Mountains, the famously desolate district where she had gone hiking with Edward.

Collin, hesitated, then confessed, "I have friends in Herefordshire, friends who can see us safely into Wales." From the way he said it, she saw a whole new side to Collin opening up. These "friends" did not sound like family, or neighbors, or normal political allies, yet he trusted them to take him in a crisis—and get him safely into Wales.

Which naturally made her curious, "What manner of friends?"

"Those that may be trusted. Though, alas, their names are a secret." Suddenly she was seeing the same old Collin, always holding something back. Sensing her disappointment, he protested, "I swore an oath not to reveal it."

"Really?" Robyn arched an inquisitive eyebrow.

"*Précisément*," Sir Collin assured her. "An absolute oath, on my knees, in Hecate's name, no less."

"But I will know where it is when we arrive?" How could he conceal their destination once she was there?

Collin shrugged. "That cannot be helped. Hecate will have to forgive me—but if I tell you beforehand, I will be forsworn."

Convenient. How do you keep an idiot in suspense?—Tell you tomorrow. The Middle Ages would easily drive her mad, if she let them. Crossing the straight north-south line of the Malvern Hills, they passed the night in Ledbury, a tiny one-street town just inside Herefordshire—where the inn, for once, was not half bad, more like staying in an alewife's home. And she got a room of her own. Another medieval first! And boiled water. Totally unexpected after the morning's catastrophe. Certainly heartening. Thanking Saint Theodotus, whose day had just passed, she took this moment of safety to go through Jo's possesions, seeing what she had to work with. As she hoped, the potion bag contained a packet of Jo's Witches Flight powder, along with dried mushrooms, herb bundles, and a bone talisman—no doubt useful, though she did not yet see how. She turned to the heavy bundle Jo had been carrying, which had all kinds of useful stuff, traveling clothes, some silver pennies—Jo was broke as always—a pair of slippers, a sturdy knife and metal cup, spools of spare thread, and Jo's sewing kit: just what Robyn would have packed.

Joy's pack was pathetic. Seeing the child's carefully hoarded treasures choked her up—ivory buttons, a rag doll, the lock-pick necklace, hawking bells, and several changes of clothes, all too small to be useful. When she turned up Joy's pebble collection, she broke down completely, sobbing over the idiocy of turning the whole huge apparatus of persecution against nine-year-old girls. It summed up the ghastly absurdity of her situation. Neither she nor Joy had done anything to harm the king, but with treason everywhere, mere suspicion had become a crime. Curling up, she cried herself unconscious, worrying over where Joy was sleeping.

Things looked better by day. So much so that Collin insisted she wear her blue-and-silver riding dress, saying it "most suited a May morning." She humored him, realizing she had become a household of one, and might as well match her master's mood. So said her burnt *Babee Book*. After many weeks of trying to fit in at Greystone, while working to get home, suddenly she was neither at home nor at Greystone. She was nearly on her own, paired with Collin, of all people. But without him, she would just be Robyn Stafford, stranger in a strange land, everyone else who knew her being impossibly far away or currently in custody.

Herefordshire spread out before her like a rumpled green blanket, bunched up against the Welsh mountains. Riding side by side, playing knight and lady, they followed the Wye Valley almost to Wales, crossing the Wye at Bredwardine and climbing the hill there to see Arthur's Stone, a massive twenty-ton capstone teetering atop lesser boulders, forming a polygonal burial chamber way older than King Arthur. She expressed some third-millennium skepticism: "This had to be ancient when Arthur was a boy."

"It was." Collin said it like he knew for certain, like he had seen that stone set in place. "But that does not mean Arthur was never here."

Touché. Why not? She was here, and with far less reason than Arthur. Before her lay the Golden Valley and the village of Dorstone with its squat church tower. To the west the Black Moutains rose in green tiers toward Waun Fach. Straining her eyes, she searched for the bare ridgeline between Hatterrall Hill and Hay Bluff, above Llanthony Priory—where she met Edward. Life had come full circle. Centuries from now, she would look down from that ridge in exasperation, staring out over Herefordshire, unsure what to make of the young knight errant's weird tale. Now she was smack in the middle of the story, with no idea how it would end.

Vespers bells rang as they descended into the Golden Valley. Ahead she saw a farmstead through the trees. Welsh greyhounds came running out to greet her, leaping, bounding, and looking curious—but not barking or baring their teeth. Giving welcome, not a warning. She could tell they knew Collin. Reining in before the main house, a long thatched cottage with broad bay windows and low gables, Robyn saw the door open and a slim smiling woman step out, wearing an gaily embroidered dress and holding a copper basin. It was Bryn.

Sitting atop her stolen mare, she stared down at Bryn, seeing what a first-class fool she had been. There was no mistaking it—this must be her. Bryn had been Welsh to begin with, and this woman had the same face, the same wide, sensuous lips, big almond eyes, and shining chestnut hair, cut short and decorated with spring blossoms. Seeing Bryn standing on the cottage stoop—as thin and beautiful as ever— brought a hollow ache to her chest. And explained a hell of a lot, including Collin's easy indifference, not just to her, but to the women at Greystone and Kenilworth, as well. Here was Collin's trusted "friend" in Herefordshire, whom he was loath to talk about. Who was neither family nor neighbor, and not some noble ally. All that left was love.

Good thing she had given up on Collin—in this or any lifetime; they were clearly not to be. She could tell this Bryn did not know her, seeing the puzzled way those light brown eyes looked from her to Collin, searching for clues to who this strange woman was, wearing her man's colors. This was as much a surprise to Bryn as to her. And much more of a mystery, since Bryn could not see the future. Well, good—it would put them on equal footing for once.

Collin swung out of the saddle, stepped up to the stoop, and kissed Bryn over the big basin full of water—without spilling a drop— which required practice. Bryn set the copper basin down at Collin's feet, helped him take off his boots, and then started washing his feet.

Collin called up to her. "Get down and doff your boots. I will introduce you."

She slid down, let the curious greyhounds sniff her, then knelt and
untied her boots. Kicking them off, she stepped barefoot up to the
basin, lifting her dress hem. Collin introduced her—"Robyn Stafford
of Holy Wood, this is Bryn Awyr of Glyndyfrdwy."

Curtsying low, she stuck out her foot, determined that this time
things between them would be different, refusing to have another fight
over Collin. Bryn smiled up at her. *"Bore da, Arglwyddes Stafford."*

She answered back, *"Bore da, Arglwyddes Bryn Awyr,"* surprising
the smile off Bryn's face. Robyn wanted it clear from the start that
she spoke Welsh. She always felt Bryn was someone she could never
lie to, and she did not intend to try. This was a new century, and a
new start with Bryn, and Robyn wanted to do everything right.

Without another word, Bryn took her foot and dipped it into the
warm water, washing it all about and drying it with a cloth. Then
Bryn waited patiently on her knees while Robyn changed feet. What
a novel way to meet the "regular girlfriend." One that could well be
copied at home—whoever gets the guy has to wash the loser's feet.

Actually the wash was merely a ritual Welsh greeting, and an invitation to stay, ending in an eruption from inside the cottage—
women, men, children, and dogs, all happy to see them, and all Welsh.
Men had long beards and Conan the Barbarian cloaks trimmed with
fur, worn over simple homespun tunics and leather vests. Women
showed more color, wearing dresses made from brightly dyed English
cloth, with gay hand-stitched designs. This tidal wave of well-wishers
dragged her inside, where she was assaulted by a Welsh feast, already
in progress. Half an ox turned over the fire in a huge hearth, an organic banquet all on his own—no hormones, steroids, or testicles.
Sitting down on green rushes spread on the dirt floor, she and Collin
were offered sheep's cheese, flat bread, and *coch yr wden*—which she
recognized as hung goat. Everyone else sat about watching them eat,
as if they were the floor show, not minding that she only sipped boiled
vegetable broth out of her own bowl. Water came from a dirt well
dug right into the cottage floor; women lowered leather buckets into
it and brought up cool clear water—which Robyn asked to have
boiled. Her hosts thought this scandalous, claiming hot water would
harm her teeth, but they indulged her anyway, tickled to hear her

speaking Welsh, immediately recognizing it as a miracle coming from her "Saxon" mouth. Like last year's bloody rain or the sinful knight who gave birth to a calf.

Young women harped and sang to entertain them, with children joining in, not just singing along, but each taking different parts, all coming together at the end in perfect B-flat harmony. No wonder the Welsh were called Singers. She asked why no one else was eating, and Collin explained, "This is the way of the Welsh. Strangers off the road are fed first. There are no beggars in Wales—just guests." He told her these were Bryn's cousins, and the farmstead belonged to Bryn's aunt who lived in Monington. Bryn stayed here to be close to him, but the crisis in Collin's family had kept them apart. Now the crisis had consumed his family—and Collin was thrown back on Bryn. His secret second life had become his real one.

Bryn wanted to know how she spoke Welsh so well, "As if you were born in Glyndyfrdwy."

Determined to stick to the truth, she confessed she was "under a spell, a Displacement Spell."

Bryn nodded. "I thought as much. You get so you can tell." That their hostess was a witch went without saying. How else would Bryn be here? Bryn asked where she was displaced from.

"A far-off land, in the far-off future." Whatever way she said it was bound to sound mysterious.

"Yes," Collin joined in, "Lady Stafford comes from a fabulous future land where they fly to the moon, and bathe three times a day—a very world of wonders." So wonderful, in fact, she could not wait to get back. "Listen, and you will learn."

"Tell me about this future." Bryn sounded intrigued, showing a witch's sense of seeing beyond the moment—coming from being reborn so often. "What is it like?"

"Much like now," Robyn admitted, "only different. Bigger and smaller at the same time—with whole nations and continents unknown to you, that double the size of the world. Yet we can get anywhere in less than a day. Vastness replaces distance. But the land is still the same. Wales is still Wales. Just this afternoon, I thought how I walked over Hatterall Hill toward Llanthony five hundred years from now."

"And have the people changed?" Bryn asked.

"Not so much." Some, like the woman with her, were amazingly similar. "But we are freer to get into trouble. There are no laws against witchcraft. No religious crimes at all."

Collin smirked. "They are so civilized they even make us Saxons seem savage."

"Saxons are savages," Bryn replied primly.

"Savage or not, in the future we are all more or less the same. Nobility no longer matters." Just money, she thought to herself. "There are still Welsh and Saxons, but people live where they wish and marry who they please." More or less. She had to add that last—knowing it was bound to be on Bryn's mind.

With an approving nod, Bryn told Collin. "You are right, we could learn much from them."

By now the ox was done, and everyone joined in the feast. Roast beast smell got the better of Robyn, and she broke down, eating several well-cooked pieces of roast ox, while Collin told how Greystone was burned and his sister and niece were abducted. This made Robyn feel guilty for gorging herself—you could bet Jo was not being wined and dined right now. Bryn repeated the tale in Welsh, so everyone would know her knight's plight. His hosts were sympathetic, if not particularly outraged—taking sides in "Saxon" quarrels inevitably led to disaster.

Afterwards, people sat about cleaning their teeth with hazel shoots and bits of wool while the local bard sang of Owain Glyndwr—whom the English called Owen Glendower—the last native prince of Wales. He sang of Glendower's magical powers, his love of singing, and his victories over the Saxons, telling how he freed all of Wales, three times driving King Henry's grandfather "bootless home and weather-beaten back." The ballad ended with Glendower eluding the Saxons one last time and then going to live in the Golden Valley. What the bard left unsung was how Glendower ended his life on the run; the last native Welsh prince may have escaped capture, but Wales herself was firmly in Saxon hands—something his audience did not need to hear sung about. He followed up his ballad with a love song, then a rollicking comic ditty, closing with a hymn.

Women laid a lumpy mattress stuffed with rushes alongside the trench where the ox had roasted. Robyn watched appalled as people piled in, all wearing their day clothes, crowding together for warmth under a single stiff blanket. Collin allayed her concern with a laugh.

"There are rooms upstairs for special guests." Bryn led the way up narrow stairs, candle in hand, to a tiny loft bedroom. Collin asked if it would do, sounding guilty for not warning her about their destination.

"Absolutely." Her little closet looked clean and remarkably rodent-free—and anyone who gave her safe haven from witch hunters would not get any complaints.

"Good." Collin looked relieved. "You will need sleep. We have to be gone before noon. This place is undefended and known to our enemies. Bryn will be coming with us. I am a horrible knave for not telling you about her. . . ."

"But I knew that already," she replied lightly. Inwardly she was furious at him for having led her on, though in a way, she understood. Collin loved an "unsuitable" woman and kept the affair secret. Who could blame him? Bryn was clever, competent, and beautiful—if hopelessly Welsh. Caught between love and prejudice, Collin lacked Edward's teenage optimism. He could not openly make Bryn his "lady."

"You did?" Collin looked surprised.

"Not about Bryn." Not here and now, anyway. "About you."

Conscience-stricken, Collin protested, "Bryn was the one who insisted we keep our betrothal secret. She is a granddaughter of Owen Glendower. Her family is devilish proud, and at feud with mine for ages. She does not want it widely known that she is wedding a Grey— folks hereabouts neither forgive nor forget."

Betrothal? Wedding? This Welsh language Romeo and Juliet had gone farther than she thought. Bryn was getting to marry her marcher knight. She asked cattily, "Won't the truth come out when you wed?"

"It is not truly a betrothal," Collin corrected himself yet again, "more what the Welsh call a trial marriage. Like a betrothal, only better." You bet. Collin's sheepish grin showed he could not wait to get some more of that better. Despite being Catholic, medievals made room for sex—and not just on May Day. "If all goes well, in a year we will marry for good," he explained piously. "By then Bryn will be sure she wants to live with the shame of marrying a Grey—even penniless Welsh witches can be impractically proud." Giving her a quick good-bye kiss, he left to be with his lady love.

Despite all their hokey chivalry, the Middle Ages were made for men—but what else is new. Feeling "impractically proud" herself, she dragged the thin rush-filled mattress out into the hall, preferring to sleep wrapped in a blanket rather than share a bed with lice and fleas. Happily, Collin and Bryn would be having their romantic reunion atop a lumpy bed of vermin. No doubt they would barely notice, but it made her feel better.

Lying on the cold plank floor, wrapped in her Cotswold blanket with her possessions for a pillow, thoroughly dejected, she tried to imagine how to surmount this latest disaster. Once again she was going to sleep alone; only this time really alone. Even when she lost Jo and Joy, there had still been Collin, sleeping within call. Chivalrous to a fault, paying the bills, and never asking for more than she was willing to give. Now she knew why. Without warning she had been demoted from knight's lady to the sole serving woman in Collin's new household. Not that Bryn would expect her to wait on them—the woman had introduced herself by washing Robyn's feet. But from now on she could no longer count on Collin, everything would be filtered through Bryn. She could no longer be sure of him being there when she needed him, his loyalties being divided at best—making her more alone than ever.

⊷⊨⧉ Bryn ⧉⊨⊶

She awoke stiff and sore, frozen on one side, aching on the other, from sleeping alone on hard boards with only a blanket for covers. And sad as well—miserably sad—not since that first terrible day when she found herself in the Middle Ages and in the hands of FitzHolland's Swans had she felt this utterly alone. Ever since her first night here and now she had had Joy with her—a delightful burden, in her bed and in her life, often amusing, at times unwanted, but always around and about. And after Joy came Jo, and then Greystone—lorded over by this new unmarried Sir Collin. She made friends there, and she was learning the magic that would take her home. Now her safe little world was all gone, ripped apart in a single vicious stroke. The emptiness it left was frightening.

On top of that, she now had to play second fiddle to Bryn in a very small traveling band. Just when one small part of the Middle Ages seemed tolerable, her world got turned upside down again. She supposed it was a warning—do not get comfortable where you do not belong.

Loneliness vanished as soon as she made her way down to the breakfast fire. Welsh swarmed around her, eager to do her bidding, glad to share what little they had, tickled at the chance to serve a "Saxon lady that speaks so fair." Warmed and loosened by the fire, she taught the two girls serving her how to make toast. Kenilworth could learn a lot from Welsh hospitality. Seeing these girls eagerly presenting her with half-burnt pieces of bread contrasted sharply with the ritual pomp and hollow honors at court. Unwilling to win people's love, the self-indulgent Court was content to rule through fear, while Mad King Henry fed pretty strangers off his plate. Collin had served his king at home and in France, suffering repeated defeats and a grievous wound—only to see his manor burnt and his people assaulted.

Being Collin, he made the best of it, coming down late for breakfast with a smile on his face and Bryn on his arm—in a hurry to be on his way, now that he had what he wanted. "Pursuit will be coming up the Wye Valley; we need to recross the river and be in the Welsh hills by nightfall."

Robyn found she was not the only serving woman in the newlyweds' traveling household. Bryn brought with her a formidable companion, a childhood nurse named Agnes, though Bryn called her by her Welsh name, Nest. Nest was a Welsh giantess, near to sixty, iron-haired, and taller than Collin, weighing "fourteen stone, and strong as a troll," according to Bryn. As a girl, Nest had gone to Ireland and been a camp follower in the army of Art MacMurrough, king of Leinster, fighting in the battle of Wexford. Besides being Bryn's nurse-bodyguard, Nest was a blacksmith, boot maker, and boatbuilder. "We came down from Glyndyfrdwy alone," Bryn boasted, "Nest being all the protection we needed. She can out-row men, run down mares, and beat the local boys at wrestling, two falls out of three."

Recrossing the Wye, they rode up the Roman road through Letton, stopping at Eardisley to dine at Baskerville Hall, where they were treated like visiting heroes. Surprised at the easy way people invited them in, she asked Collin, "Are we still fugitives, or not?"

"So we are," Collin assured her, "but there were Baskervilles in Eardisley—making their own laws—when the Plantagenets were mere counts of Anjou. Sir James Baskerville cares more for the good feeling of the Greys than for the opinion of a mad king. Most hereabouts would declare for York, were it safe to do so."

"And none of them cares that you fought for King Henry?"

"Mad, or no, Henry is their king, too. That is the great advantage of being for King Henry—though Lord knows there is little other. Even the most hardened rebel holds that Henry is king and must piously accept me doing my feudal duty. A rebel caught in arms can be hung and quartered. But killing a king's man is still murder—thank the saints. Making it far safer to be on Henry's side."

Which favor Collin tried to return by not killing his opponents. What a strange rebellion indeed, where the rebels honored Collin's loyalty and service more than the court he served. Baskervilles escorted them to Hergest Court, a moated manor belonging to the Vaughans— safe within the Welsh Marches—where she got her first bath since leaving Greystone, and a decent enough bed to go with it.

Next day's ride was up the line of Offa's Dyke, through misty Welsh foothills, cutting back and forth across the border, with Collin and Nest leading. Nest knew the way, and had a big Welsh longbow, which she used to keep trouble at a distance and bring down game for the pot. Neither Collin nor Nest spoke the other's language, so they made do with nods and grunts. Robyn dropped back to be with Bryn, finding her in buoyant spirits, happy to be with Collin again, demanding more stories about the future. Robyn tried to oblige, skirting dangerous subjects—like her relations with Collin—which still left plenty to talk about, the future being a very big place. When Collin was around they spoke English—but being alone, they lapsed into Welsh.

Her tales of the future got mixed reviews. Bryn did not see any need to replace bards with boom boxes, or for Wales to be swallowed in a United Kingdom and a European Union. "We are the last true Britons," Bryn informed her. "And still look to see Merlin's prophecies come to pass. The Saxons vanquished. Foreigners driven out, and Britain restored."

Good luck, she thought. When she was a girl in Montana, there were still people trying to dance back the buffalo, and not just on the Res. But this was sacred land to Bryn—the land of Arthur and Merlin. Robyn hastened to reassure her, saying, "Land like this is least changed." Superhighways did not run along the Welsh border, and the big cities were safely off in the flats. "These hills are less wild, with more people, and a lot better roads—but you could still get lost in them." She sure had.

"That is a comfort," Bryn declared. "I do not grudge people easier lives, just so they do not hunger for possessions and power. Family, land, and freedom are what matter. And freedom matters most. Nothing else—not life, not honor, not fealty, not our sworn word—matters so much as freedom. Which enrages the Saxons. They have beaten us in battle, taken our land, stolen our sovereignty, forced oaths of submission on us—and still they do not have our hearts. We persist in doing as we please. And they know that at any time we could all rise up demanding our freedom, as we did in my grandfather's time. Then the whole battle must begin again."

Bryn smiled conspiratorially. "We Cymry are like women in that way. No matter what vows or oaths they force on us, no matter what laws bind us, what our hearts want we will have, not much counting the cost." Cymry was what the locals called themselves—*Welsh* was a Saxon word; like *Sioux* and *Crow*, it was a name handed down by their conquerors, and like the Sioux and Crow the Welsh were learning to live with it.

Robyn marveled that she would give up her freedom to marry. "Sir Collingwood Grey is the reason," Bryn replied. "He is immensely strong and brave, with a deep sense of fairness and justice that sees beyond noble and common or Cymry and Saxon. I love him all the more now that we are married."

Who could argue with that? Hearing Collin praised so honestly and succinctly hurt. Five centuries had not changed much; all Collin's marvelous qualities were directed at Bryn. Even Collin's newfound faithfulness—marred only by May Night—was all for Bryn. Robyn could not help adding, "He saved my life." It had become her sole claim on him, the one sure sign Collin cared for her. "Risking his own life to do it."

"Yes." Bryn nodded thoughtfully. "Collin told me. He can be perilously gallant—a most endearing Saxon trait. I pray you thanked him well."

Was that a Welsh dig? Just how binding was this trial marriage? Certainly it did not cover May Night. She told Bryn, "I did my best."

"Good." Bryn acted like she knew just what happened—if it were put to her, Bryn could probably have named the date. "Men expect to be repaid. When they do not get their due, it can lead to wild imaginings and thoughtless acts."

She nodded in silent agreement, not admitting anything. Looking pleased, Bryn leaned over and patted her leg. "Now we must get you what you want, to lift your spell and send you home. Much as we will miss you." Clearly Bryn wanted Collin to herself, and if that meant sending her rival centuries away, so be it. It was what the future Bryn had done—and tomorrow was Witches Night.

Bryn was her immediate link to the world of witches and witchcraft. Collin was a man, excluded from coven secrets. Worst yet, in his heart of hearts Collin did not want her to leave—not being the type to wish a woman away for being inconvenient or because he had already bedded her. Collin liked her being here, even if he could not have her. Bryn, on the other hand, had both means and motive. Bryn was a witch in her own right and a granddaughter to Glendower, the Welsh wizard, who could walk invisible among his enemies and call on wind and storm. Or so the bards say. And Bryn must know there was something between her and Collin; if not now, then sometime in the past or future. Bryn should be glad to see her gone. Terribly ironic, yet totally fitting. Bryn's wanting Collin to herself was what threw her back in time; and now it might send her home again. Closing the circle. How weird to think this could all be over in a moment. She might never see these people again. Never be reunited with Edward or know what happened to Jo and Joy. Even the best outcomes had their downside.

Powys Castle sat guard over the gap where the infant Severn issued forth from the Welsh hills. On the far side of the river Offa's Dyke ran along the base of Long Mountain, separating Wales from Shropshire. Once home to the princes of South Powys, Powys Castle was now shared by two marcher families—the Tiptofts and Greys. A shared castle sounded strange, but according to Collin, "Sisters inherited the castle, and now their sons hold it together. The outer ward belongs to John Tiptoft, earl of Worcester, and the inner to Lord Grey de Powys. Fortunately both lords favor the duke of York, so the castle is not at war with itself—thus far."

She passed the night in a room in the outer ward, decorated with paintings sent from Padua by Earl Tiptoft, who found the Italian climate more inviting—his wife being a Neville, and Edward's first

cousin. And since the sack of Ludlow, Grey de Powys had made submission to Henry, making them all king's men. But while there was a
good deal of patient affection for Mad King Henry, Robyn had yet to
meet anyone with real love for King Henry's court—aside from Lord
Scales, or Gilbert FitzHolland.

Castle roosters woke her. The novelty of sleeping alone had worn
off, and she missed waking up with Jo and Joy, or at least seeing them
in the morning. Raising her arm, she stared at the glowing digits on
her watch—FRI 5-23-60. One month in the Middle Ages. Happy anniversary. She got out her journal, propped it on her knees, and typed:

Friday, 23 May 1460, Powys Castle, Wales
   Today I have been here a month. Unbelievable. A month of running, and hiding, and living off others. Boiling my water and watching
whatever I eat. (When I can.) Deathly afraid of getting so much as
the sniffles. No wonder it seems like an eternity. I no longer expect
to be whisked away at any moment. Damn! Damn! Damn! Worst of
all, seeing the date no longer makes me cringe. A creepy sort of
normalcy is settling in. Getting back is no longer a matter of life and
death. The worst happened—I lost Greystone—and here I am, still
alive. Having survived a month, I could live on for months more.
Maybe even years. Ghastly thought—but no longer totally unthinkable. What first seemed like a sure death sentence looks more like
life imprisonment.

Her emergency tampon was long gone. Nowadays being "on the
rag" was not just a figure of speech. At least she was not pregnant
and carrying Collin's bastard child—that would have been a real test
of Welsh hospitality. Tonight was Witches Night—her first since the
loss of Greystone—hopefully it would get her closer to home.

At Powys she got a fresh mount, a long-necked palfrey with a high-
flying Arab tail. Powys was famous for its stud herds, bred from Spanish stock brought over by the earl of Shrewsbury centuries before. This
meant getting used to a new and spirited mount while negotiating deep
narrow footpaths twisting through dark woods and steep pastures.
Climbing out of valley of the Upper Severn, they crossed over to the
valley of the Efyrnwy, then to the valley of the Cain, then the Tanat.
Fording the Tanat, they stopped in the tiny Welsh village of Llanged-

wyn—a place the Renaissance had not yet reached—finding lodging in a freeholder's hall, built of rough-cut stone, with an open hearth and smoke-stained rafters. They just rode up and introduced themselves. Surprised hosts hurried about finding food, serving them golden mead made from wild honey, while young girls harped and sang to them. Typical Welsh hospitality, though this time she had to wash her own feet.

When the last song was sung and their hosts had snuggled into the household bed, Byrn gave the witches sign, then rose and put on a cloak. Robyn did, too. So did Nest. Witches Night was here, and there was no wife or mistress or nurse—just three witches slipping out together into the night, leaving Collin to await their return. Night air felt cool, and Robyn heard the river running over rocks below the little village. Bryn and Nest led the way up a low wooded ridge, while she stumbled through the blackness behind them, trying to preserve a holy silence. She had no idea how Welsh spellcraft worked, but anything was possible. Even if Bryn did not send her home, she might find out what happened to Jo and Joy, or somehow contact Duchess Wydville, the one person here and now who she knew had the power to help. Whether the high-priestess-cum-duchess would help her was another question, but the attempt must be made.

Topping the dark ridge, she heard music in the air, a faint familiar melody, like the memory of a song. Having heard so much singing of late, it was hard to get it out of her head. Beyond the ridge the sky brightened, lit by a low soft glow which she thought must be northern lights. Black invisible ground sloped down beneath her feet, headed toward a stream that ran into the Tanat. After much thrashing through the bracken they came on a footpath, following it upstream. The ethereal glow got brighter, and the singing got louder. She could hear harps playing, pipes skirling, bells tinkling, and high-pitched voices singing in Welsh.

What sounded like a Welsh hootenanny turned out to be something far weirder. The dark footpath ended in a high mound ringed by a moat and topped by a walled manor, with a great gatehouse and drawbridge. Light shown inside the walls, where the manor hall was ablaze with torches. Sparks from the lord's hearth rose high overhead, like faeries dancing in the moonlight. No guard stood by the gatehouse, the drawbridge was down, and the great gates were flung wide. She heard laughter, as well as singing, and the slap of bare feet on an earthen floor—but they did not go in. Instead, Bryn stopped by the gate, kneeling in the darkness to croon softly in B-flat harmony. Nest sat down on the end of the drawbridge itself. It made Robyn feel like a poor relation, not invited to the party, but allowed to sit on the stoop and hear the harping. She rose on her toes, trying to peek inside, seeing dancers spiral past the gate, one a lady in white with lit candles in her headdress.

Without warning, Nest spoke. Words tumbled from the massive nurse's mouth as Nest sat immobile on the drawbridge, weird behavior from someone who almost never spoke. And it was not Welsh, either. Or English. Just an incoherent string of syllables. Robyn realized that for once she could not understand somebody's speech—an unnerving surprise. Nest's babbling was like baby talk. Babies here and now made the same cute sounds Robyn was used to; she did not magically understand what they were saying, no more than she understood Nest now.

But Bryn understood, and stopped singing to kneel beside her nurse, listening intently, lips moving with each misshapen syllable, repeating Nest's nonsense back to herself. Making sure she had it right. Slowly the syllables trailed off, and Nest's huge frame slumped forward, as if drowsy with sleep, threatening to topple off the drawbridge. Bryn grabbed her nurse's broad shoulders and gave Nest a tremendous shake. Then another, twice as violent. Bryn kept shaking the big woman, until Nest's eyes popped open. Nest asked in Welsh, "What happened? Did I speak?"

"Like a singing spring," Bryn told the nurse. "I thought you would never cease."

Bryn and Nest sang a closing prayer in Welsh. Robyn did her best to join in, though she felt pretty thoroughly excluded—and not just from the party inside. Clearly she had just been here to watch, and was not going to learn any Welsh magic tonight. Between Duchess Wydville, whom she did not trust, and Bryn who did not trust her, Robyn had no ready teacher. Could she teach herself witchcraft? Hardly likely. She missed Jo miserably.

Turning their backs on the moated manor, they picked their way back up the ridge by the light of the party. She kept looking over her shoulder, wondering whose manor was keeping such a raucous Witches Night. No doubt some of Bryn's witchy relations. Maybe Bryn just did not want to be seen with a Saxon. As she crossed back into the Valley of the Tanat, light and singing faded into the night. Following the rushing water upstream to their night's lodging, they found Collin waiting by the last embers of the fire. Bryn greeted him happily. "We are in luck. You sister and niece are alive—and all may be made well."

How Bryn got that out of Nest's meaningless ramblings, Robyn could not guess. Collin asked softly, "Where are they now?"

"Ebrington Manor," Bryn told him, "Away to the south and east, in Gloucestershire." Collin nodded, saying he well knew where Ebrington was. Nest's ravings were marvelously specific. Robyn knew Ebrington Manor only by reputation—it belonged to Collin's neighbor, Lord Chief Justice Fortescue, and was where Joy had been sent in a doomed attempt to teach her etiquette.

Bryn turned to her. "And you are not safe in England. Nor in Wales. You need to put yourself beyond the reach of king's law."

Tell us something we don't know. Robyn wanted to be well beyond King Henry's reach—like back in her Hollywood apartment, eating Moroccan take-out.

"Duchess Wydville wants to aid your escape," Bryn added.

"Escape? To where?" Hopefully home—that was where these witches should send her.

"To Ireland."

"Ireland?" Why was Duchess Weirdville suddenly eager to send her to Ireland, of all places? "Why Ireland?"

"Nest did not say," Bryn replied.

"She did not say any of this, so far as I could hear." Excluded from the ritual, Robyn had no reason to trust it.

"And you have such a good ear," Bryn laughed mockingly. "It merely takes training. I have listened to Nest all my life, and to me she sounds clearer than Saxon."

No doubt. She needed to see something tangible before she could believe Bryn. "Perhaps Ireland seems safe," Collin suggested. "FitzHolland could never get you there. The duke of York rules Ireland—if anyone can be said to—and the last fool King Henry sent to Dublin to arrest him ended up in pieces."

And not just the duke of York, either. Edward was there, as well. Half the reason she could not believe this was because it sounded too good. She asked, "How am I supposed to get there?"

Bryn had her answer ready. "A ship will be waiting for you in Conwy harbor."

"A ship? Really?" Waiting for her? It did not even sound possible—much less likely.

"A Saxon ship," Bryn added.

"How much more was there to this message?" Or was Bryn making things up as needed?

Bryn shrugged. "That is all. Duchess Wydville knows of your plight and has a ship at Conwy to take you to Ireland. And Her Grace warns that if you fail to heed her, you will fall into the hands of Scales and FitzHolland."

Again, marvelously specific. She could not shake the feeling Bryn was saying all this just to send her somewhere—and Ireland seemed sufficiently far and away. She asked Collin, "Where is Conwy Harbor?" She had only a vague idea of how big Wales was—they had been riding for days and had not seen half of it.

"On the north coast of Wales," Collin told her. "A day's ride from my uncle's castle at Ruthyn."

"Then we could go see?" Either the ship would be there, or it would not.

"Yes, we could." Clearly Collin's mind was more on Jo and Joy at Ebrington than on sending her off to Eire. "There might, indeed, be a ship. Duchess Wydville has ships at her will, her husband Baron Rivers having been admiral of England. But first we need to get to Ruthyn, and before that we need sleep."

Gloomy black stairs led to a low loft in the back of the hall, high and warm and away from most of the smoke—the guest suite. Despite a dismal month in the Middle Ages, Robyn had an encouraging new destination—Eire. With the chance of finding Edward. Taking that as a good omen, she drifted off to sleep, dreaming she was dancing to a harper's tune in a torch-lit Welsh hall.

Anxious to see if a ship really was waiting, she saddled up early, and they left little Llangedwyn and the valley of the Tanat. Mounting the ridgeline to the north, she looked for the moated manor from the night before—only to be greeted by bare ridgelines. Strange—but she might have gotten turned about in the night. Following what seemed to be the same footpath up the same stream, they came on a high mound strewn with rubble, ringed by a half-filled moat, and crowned with the blackened ruins of a gatehouse. There was no sign of the drawbridge Nest had sat on, but this was clearly the torch-lit manor from her weird Welsh Witches Night, looking a lot worse by morning light. Aghast, she asked Collin, "What ruins are these?"

"Sycharth," he replied, "the principal hall of Owen Glendower."

She stared at the ruins, picturing them full of life and song. Weird but encouraging. Clearly Bryn had not been lying about Nest's Witches Night babbling. No self-respecting Welsh witch would seek out the ruined home of her princely grandfather just to perjure herself. Not on Witches Night, with the faeries looking on. Not just to fool some footloose Saxon "lady" from the future. Robyn was witch enough by now to know that. If Bryn wanted to be rid of her, there were easier ways than lying on her dead grandfather's hall. A word to Nest would no doubt do it.

"Sycharth was big," Collin ventured. Especially for Wales—Collin did not have to say it, but she could hear it in his tone. The place had not been Kenilworth—or even Greystone, the "last true Britons" being poets, not builders. "Within the moat there were barns, a salt house, a church, and a mill. . . ."

"And a spicery, a pigeon house, and rabbit warren," Bryn added. "Also fish ponds and vineyards."

It had all been burned, even the church—a long time ago, from the look of it. She doubted either of them had seen the place whole, unless it was in another life. "Who burned it?"

"Good King Harry," Collin told her, "who killed all those French at Agincourt." That was King Henry's father, Henry V, the much-beloved warrior king who conquered half of France and took a French princess to wife—only to die young, leaving a baby-king carrying the hereditary insanity of the French royal family. King Henry's heroic father was revered throughout England as the last good king. "If only he had lived," was the weary refrain from folks who had seen France lost and the nation bankrupted. But to Bryn's people, Young King Harry's short belligerent career had been a disaster. The blackened stone atop this grassy mound showed the huge chasm between Collin's world and Bryn's—as well as the risks Bryn took. Should their "trial marriage" fail, she would be the one who was shamed. No wonder she wanted it kept secret.

Leaving the ruins, they headed deeper into emerald hill country, with few inhabitants besides little black cattle and small tan-faced

Welsh sheep. Green Welsh hills rolled off in all directions, topped by tall cottony thunderheads blowing off the Irish Sea. Riding over empty tops on trails known only to the Welsh, she saw why the Saxons never caught Glendower. By now she was better used to her mount and more able to enjoy the views. Wales might be wild, but she was also wonderfully wet and lush, with thick gleaming grass beneath her horse's hooves and hawks circling overhead. Descending a pass, they watered their horses at Llanarmon Dyffryn Ceiriog, a stop on the drovers road to Shrewsbury smaller than its name. "We have crossed the watershed," Collin told her. "From here to the Dee is mostly downhill."

Collin was in better spirits now that he had evaded FitzHolland and gotten home to the Marches. Freed to act and having Bryn at his side—and in his bed—he seemed confident he could free Jo and Joy, as well. She asked him about the feud between the Greys and Glendower, knowing something of the Glendower story, but not how Collin's family fit in.

"My family started the feud," Collin admitted sourly. "My grandfather Reginald Grey de Ruthyn coveted Croisau Common, a undistinguished stretch of moorland, seizing it from Glendower and evicting the Welsh—but Glendower took him to court and won back the land. When King Henry's grandfather usurped the throne, he bought my grandfather's support by giving him a warrant to despoil Glendower in the king's name, charging the Welsh with "treason"—a silly charge, since Henry's grandfather had just deposed, imprisoned, and murdered the rightful King Richard. At worst, the Welsh were inconveniently loyal, clinging to our lawful king longer than we ourselves did. Glendower's true crime was beating my grandfather at law."

From the very beginning, Mad King Henry's dynasty had to barter justice for political support—but this time they sold out the wrong man. "Grandfather marched on Sycharth and just missed seizing Glendower. Seeing he would get no justice from the new king, Glendower raised the banner of revolt, declaring for the old king, or if he be murdered, the Mortimer heir—a boy held prisoner at Windsor for the high crime of having a better claim to the throne than the king. Amazingly, Glendower nearly did it all. Welsh rallied to his banner. He crowned himself prince, holding Parliament and negotiating treaties. French allies and the Percys of Northumberland fought alongside him. He captured one Mortimer and married him to his daughter. And he nearly had the remaining heirs when their aunt, Constance of York, spirited them out of Windsor and got to Cheltenham before being caught." Cheltenham was within a day of the Welsh border. Glendower came near to having an independent Wales, with himself as prince and his grandchildren holding a claim to the English throne—all over a scrap of moorland. She could see a lot of him in Bryn.

"In the end, Prince Harry brought Glendower down. Besides burning Sycharth and Glyndyfrdwy, he captured Harlech Castle along with Glendower's wife and two of his daughters—one of whom had three daughters of her own by Edmund Mortimer, who died in their defense. These women and girls all met unknown deaths in the Tower of London." Collin's tone accused a national hero of child-murder. The three little Welsh girls were doomed by their Mortimer blood, which put them closer to the throne than Good King Harry himself—but murdering children, even half-Welsh children, was so repugnant it must be done in secret. "Long before that, Glendower brought down my grandfather, sacking Ruthyn and holding him for a ruinous ransom. Grandfather emerged from captivity burdened by debts he never paid off, though he lived another thirty years. And the great prize of Glendower's lands went not to him, but to the Beaufort earl of Somerset." King Henry's bastard relations were continually rewarded at the expense of the older nobility.

Blasphemous as it might sound, Robyn thought Good King Harry had been a disaster to just about everyone, massacring the French and Welsh, saddling England with an unwinnable foreign war, an empty treasury, and an insane heir. The Welsh were just the only ones smart enough to see it. Strangely, the only person she knew besides Bryn whose family suffered at Good King Harry's hands was Edward—his grandfather having been executed for treason. A weird link between two people otherwise totally different—separated by class, nation, language, sex, and religion—showing what a strange tight little island this was.

Skirting the east slopes of the Berwyns, she urged her shying palfrey down steep winding paths to Glyn Ceiriog, a delightful little river valley carved by the Afon Ceiriog. Climbing out past white water roaring down forested slopes, they struck out over the tops, reaching the Dyfrdwy—which Saxons called the Dee—at Glyndyfrdwy, Bryn's birthplace. There they spent the night among her kin, who were Welsh in every way.

On Sunday she saw the other side, riding out of the Valley of the Dyfrdwy past Llantysilio ridge to Ruthyn Castle, with its English town huddled beneath the red walls. Greys had held this land against the Welsh for almost two hundred years, thanks largely to Ruthyn Castle, which let them defy local opinon with impunity. Standing in its cavernous hall, surrounded by serving men wearing de Ruthyn's black ragged staff, she realized Collin did not cut much of a figure, having lost his manor and his sister—showing up with two young women and no retainers, aside from an immense Welsh nurse. Edmund Grey de Ruthyn was like Collin's grandfather Reginald, another in the line of ruthless lords of Ruthyn, with a gallows attached to his timber-frame courthouse. Hearing his nephew's woes, he swore astonished oaths while committing to nothing. Like many scheming egoists, Grey de Ruthyn recognized honesty in others, and no doubt planned to put Collin's loyalty to better use than King Henry had.

Grey de Ruthyn dismissed her as an odd bit of baggage, of no immediate use, which suited her perfectly, not wanting to be of use to anyone. None of this appealed to her—not Lord Grey de Ruthyn or living on the run or being an uninvited ghost in Bryn and Collin's love fest. She desperately wanted to get to Conwy Harbor, to see if there was a ship waiting to take her to Ireland, and Edward. Fortunately Bryn was equally desirous to see her off, and Collin could hardly stand against the combined will of the last two women left in his life. So they set out the next day, the last Monday in May, Memorial Day, as warm and sunny as any she could remember from home.

Conwy town and castle stood on a spur of rock, protecting a sheltered anchorage with a half dozen vessels swinging idly at anchor. Blockades of Ireland and Calais—the prime overseas parts of the realm—had turned merchants into smugglers and trade into treason, slowing the flow of goods and making everyone involved criminals, unless they bought exemptions. Declaring their occupation a crime—then demanding bribes to let them make a living—did nothing to win the hearts of merchants and sailors. One more Alice-in-Wonderland aspect of Mad King Henry's government. Only someone banqueting on sugared peacock in Kenilworth could think it would work.

Riding to the river's edge, she scanned the banners snapping in the sea breeze. By now she was used to looking for colors and badges. There it was—a field argent, with a fess and canton gules—the red and white flag of the Wydvilles, flying from the largest ship in the anchorage, a floating castle with painted wooden battlements on the bow and stern. Black cannon muzzles poked out from the quarterdeck, and the main yards ended in hooked blades meant to cut an enemy's rigging. Sailing the Irish Sea looked to be serious business, but seeing this big bark waiting at anchor for her was magic, as wonderful as anything she had seen on Witches Night. She turned excitedly to Collin. "Do you know this ship?"

Leaning forward in the saddle, he studied the vessel's lines. "She is the *Fortuna,* belonging to Baron Wydville. I sailed in her to France." Bryn smiled smugly at being proved right. Hiring a boat, they had Bryn's brawny nurse row them to the ship. Weary from yet another day in the saddle, Robyn looked forward to being done with riding, more than willing to give a sailing ship a try. They met the master in his cabin, a fat Kentishman, speaking with a southeast accent that she had never heard, but understood perfectly. He had letters for her and for Collin. Opening one with Wydville seals done in red wax, she found it was from the duchess, with an elaborate greeting followed by an apology for being unable to shield the "newest cherished member of our household." The only solution according to the letter was to send her to safety in Ireland. She was to go to Waterford, an English colony in southern Ireland. With it came a letter of credit worth six months' wages, and the names of some "reliable" women in Waterford and Dublin—who were certain to be witches. Also an impressive letter of introduction bearing a lion seal.

She showed Collin the crest. He told her, "That is the seal of the countess of Shrewsbury. Waterford and Wexford belong to the Talbot earls of Shrewsbury. I mentioned Countess Margaret of Shrewsbury on the day we first met."

"You did?" She tried to remember what Collin said on her first day in the Middle Ages, in that little carpeted room at Berkeley Castle with its unicorn tapestry and high windows. But so much happened that day, and in the days since.

"Countess Margaret of Shrewsbury is the woman who had Isabel de Berkeley thrown in a dungeon to die—because they had a quarrel at law over the ownership of Berkeley Castle. Ironically, the law sided with the Berkeleys, doing Lady Isabel little good. Countess Margaret stands high enough with King Henry and the queen to have gentlewomen murdered with impunity."

Oh, of course, that countess of Shrewsbury. It shook her confidence to realize that her sealed letters of introduction came from a murderess, even a highly placed one. Maybe she should somehow lift the seals and read the letters herself? But who would bother sending her to Ireland just to have her killed?

Collin showed her his letter. "According to this I am to see you safely to Waterford." She scanned his letter from the duchess—it was true, Collin was humbly entreated to take her safely to Ireland. And any humble entreaty from a witch-duchess with a husband on the Royal Council had to be obeyed. Happily, Collin made an excellent traveling companion—brave, generous, and resourceful. Having him along made it ten times likelier that she would even get to Ireland.

Bryn did not look pleased, having found the ship Nest foretold, only to discover the *Fortuna* was taking Collin, too. Collin did his damnedest to comfort her, taking Bryn in his arms, swearing he would not be gone long. "Wait for me at Glyndyfrdwy. I will come there for you swiftly as I can." Robyn felt another stab of jealousy, seeing Collin hugging Bryn to him, promising her a swift return as soon as he discharged this unwanted duty. After all she and Collin had been through, both here and in the future, it pained her to see him lavishing affection on Bryn. While she was a mere nuisance, needing to be sent elsewhere.

When the two of them untwined, Collin asked how long the crossing would take. The ship's master promised to have the *Fortuna* ready to sail in a couple of days. "We can be in Waterford by the end of the week, and back here by the first week of June." Which satisfied Collin—if not Bryn.

Tuesday, 27 May 1460, Saint Bernard's Eve, Conwy, Wales

Have spent two nights in a shabby little Conwy inn, just off High Street—between the river gate and the Hospital of Saint John. Enjoyed the worst inn meal yet. Lumps of lard on moldy bread, served with rotting fish and stale beer. Yum. Bet I have lost ten pounds so far, without hardly trying. Breakfast was oatmeal smothered in saffron. When I get home I will market the "Medieval Diet"—cheap, easy, and totally efficient. Sprinkle a few rat feces on dinner, and the pounds just melt away.

When not harping or speaking in tongues, Nurse Nest rarely says a word, and always in Welsh. But by watching her eyes, I can see she understands English, and some French—but tries not to let anyone know. Nest is Welsh to the core: cunning, secretive, and fiercely protective of her nursling, and deeply suspicious of anything Saxon, including Collin.

Less than a fortnight ago the witch-duchess of Bedford invited me to join the jolly Wydville household. Jo stepped forward and got me a reprieve until Michaelmas much against Duchess Wydville's wishes. Since then Greystone has been burned, Jo and Joy abducted, and I have been hounded halfway across Wales, until my best hope is to take ship for Ireland at the duchess's bidding. Less trusting souls—steeped in medieval superstition—would see magic at work. But to what end? If Duchess Wydville wanted me so badly—for whatever reason—why let me leave Kenilworth? Why send me to Ireland? Why not Grafton? Yorkist Ireland makes no sense, unless it truly is for my safety. Ireland is rebel territory, beyond the reach of King Henry's minions, no matter how powerful. Which sounds great. With the added advantage of Edward.

So I would be an idiot to turn it down. Right. Well, I am going—the chance of seeing Edward is too much to turn down. But somehow, someway I fear I will end up paying for the trip. Duchess Wydville did not get where she is by giving free rides to footloose females. She is scary smart, and sees things that I do not. C'est la vie. God, I am starting to think in French. Welsh, too. What I would not give to hear a New York accent. Or even a southern drawl.

Bryn saw them off at the quay, giving Collin a kiss good-bye, passionate enough to have him hurrying back. Turning to her, Bryn took a big double-edged saxe knife from Nest's broad leather belt. "Here." Bryn reversed the knife and handed it to her. "Take this parting gift."

Surprised to be handed such a weapon, she stammered her thanks—Bryn with a blade in hand was hard to say no to. "Thank you, thank you ever so much. I do not know if we will be needing—."

Bryn smirked at her naiveté, "You are going to Ireland, my dear, and will be needing a good heavy knife before you know it." Then Bryn kissed her good-bye on the lips, though it was nothing compared to the kiss Collin got.

Fortuna's bilges reeked of rotten fish and stagnant brine, but her huge white mainsail proudly bore Wydville colors, a wide red stripe at the bottom and a big red square in the upper right corner. Back to being a knight, Sir Collin got the master's great cabin on the quarterdeck, while she got a smaller one across the companionway, and the master bunked with his men in the forecastle. She did not mind the cramped accommodations, since she hoped for a swift passage with no time to get comfortable. Wind and tide were right to make for Menai Strait, cutting across Conwy Bay instead of hauling clear around Anglesey. Passing Lavan Sands, she saw Beaumaris Castle to starboard, big, square and solid—backed by the green hills of Anglesey, called Môn mam Cymru by the Welsh, meaning "Mona the Mother of Wales." Beaumaris was where King Henry's aunt, the duchess of Gloucester died under perpetual imprisonment for witchcraft. Here Conwy Bay shrank into the narrow Menai Strait, running between the Isle of Anglesey and the Welsh mainland, where the great mass of Snowdon glowered down on her, backed with gray clouds rent by blue streaks of sky. At the far end of the strait stood Caernarvon Castle, birthplace of the ill-fated Edward of Caernarvon, the king whose cell she shared in Berkeley Castle.

As the *Fortuna* entered broad Caernarvon Bay, she got a real feel for a wooden sailing ship at sea. Deck boards heaved beneath her feet, and the first full roll sent her reeling, as *Fortuna* reared and plunged, plowing through the swells by sheer weight and wind power. Sails thumped and rigging sang, hull timbers creaked and groaned, sounding like the opening of an off-key symphony, played over and over again. Not at all like skimming along in a fiberglass catamaran or partying on some producer's yacht—where the only risk of seasickness came from waking up drunk in the captain's waterbed.

Presently the favorable east wind died and the big Wydville mainsail hung limp. She saw the last patches of blue disappear behind the gray-black blanket overhead, sensing the calm before a storm. When the breeze picked up again, it was strong and from the northwest, accompanied by stinging spray. Putting on sail, the *Fortuna*'s master ran south and west, clawing for sea room before the storm struck.

Retreating to her tiny quarterdeck cabin, she felt the storm building, realizing they had scant hope of making Ireland, now almost dead to windward. The *Fortuna* would do well not to be driven back to Wales and racked up on the lee shore. Roaring in off the ocean, the norwester was broken somewhat by the invisible mass of Ireland, lying between them and the Atlantic. Wind shrieked in the rigging, and the hull timbers moaned a dismal warning. She felt the deck press hard against her feet, then drop suddenly away as the ship plunged down the side of a wave—she seemed to gain and lose forty pounds with each new pitch and roll. Hours went by. Wet and scared, unable to eat or sleep, she could hear waves breaking over the waist. Water cascaded across the tilted decks and out through the scuppers. An especially big blow would bring the *Fortuna* to a dead halt—as if she were swamped and about to go under—then the ship would bob back like a cork in a whirlpool, shedding water as she went through yet another wild gyration, making Robyn wish for a nice safe saddle. At dusk, she heard a banging on her cabin door. At first she took it for the storm; then she heard Collin shouting on the far side of the thin door, barely audible amid the howling gale. Lifting the latch, she looked out. His face looked soaked and frightened. "You had better come out on deck."

"Why?" she yelled back, being wet and battered enough already, on deck it would only be worse.

Collin shouted above the screaming the wind, "You need to be on deck. The ship may break apart."

Break apart? Scared as she was, she had not thought things were that bad. Hastily wrapping herself in a blanket, she fought her way out onto the quarterdeck, keeping her back to the wind and spray. Through fading light, she could see a line of breakers to leeward. Collin shouted in her ear, "Those are reefs off the Penrhyn Mawr. We are being blown into them."

Drenched by flying spray, she saw men aloft struggling to reef the mainsail, reducing the area exposed to the wind, keeping the *Fortuna* from being blown over onto her beam ends by the gale. Other men were down in the waist, hauling buckets up from the hold, bailing for all they were worth. She heard a sharp crack overhead and saw a line part, whipping across the deck to stand straight out in the wind, pointing toward the line of breakers.

Clinging to Collin for support, she watched the white line slip away to port, replaced by a tall cliffs looming out of the blackness. That had to be the Lleyn Peninsula, the western shoulder of Wales. As the *Fortuna* wallowed downwind, she watched the cliffs grow taller. In minutes they would be pounded to pieces at their base. She glanced up at Collin and was shocked to see him grinning. Was he looking forward to being reborn in some more hospitable century? Collin pointed downwind, shouting excitedly. All she could see was the line of cliffs, ending in a big black hole that threatened to swallow the *Fortuna*. "What is it?" she yelled.

"Bardsey Sound," he shouted back through the spray. "We are saved." She saw the cliffs fall sharply away to leeward, opening up as they rounded Braich y Pwll. Quarterdeck planking heeled beneath her, and the *Fortuna* came about, running before the wind into the broad dark waters of Cardigan Bay. Smiling, exhausted faces on the sailors told her Collin was right—the sea had failed to kill them.

Shaken but relieved, she retired to her cabin to change into dry clothes and get some desperately needed sleep. As night fell, the storm blew on into Wales and the Cotswolds. Lying in her cabin, she felt the wind slacken and swing around to the northeast. *Fortuna* rounded the south end of Ynys Enlli, clawing her way into Saint George's Channel, headed for Ireland. Exhausted and seasick, Robyn went to sleep, not waking until they made late morning landfall on the Wicklow Coast.

Hearing, "Land ho," from the topcastle, she went up to the quarterdeck rail, looking out on what only last night she had never expected to see, the wild coast of southern Ireland with its shallow bays, sandy beaches, and low green hills. Beyond the beaches, misty mountains rose up, cut by bleak boggy glens, all of it looking godawful empty. How was she supposed to find Edward in this wilderness? The place hardly looked inhabited. Long dark galleys drawn up on the sands were the only sign of life. She pointed them out to Collin.

"Irish pirates," he replied cheerfully. "Wicklow means 'Viking's Meadow'—give them half a chance, and they will come swarming out to greet us. That is what the cannon on the quarterdeck are for, to see they get a proper reception."

Cold and hungry, she went below, for her first real meal since coming aboard, barley bread, smoked fish, boiled eggs, dried fruit, and herb tea. Lulled by the pitch of the ship, she slept again, only to be jerked awake by a cry from the masthead, and the thump of running feet on the deck above. Something had come undone—she could feel it. Slanting sunlight poured in her cabin window, meaning it must be well into the afternoon. Wrapping herself in a cloak, she went to see what was amiss. Helmsmen had one of the stern windows open, and were peering out, paying no attention to her. Whatever had happened must be serious. Mounting the stairs to the half-deck, she saw men clumped at the end of the stern castle, staring astern. Collin was there, and she asked what was happening. He guided her to a wooden embrasure and pointed dead astern. "That is what is happening."

Looking to where his gloved finger pointed, she saw three long dark lines on the sea following in the *Fortuna*'s wake. They had no sails, but she made out the rhythmic flashes of oars catching the afternoon light as they rose and fell. She asked, "Are those galleys?"

Collin nodded. "War galleys, coming down from Wicklow in our wake."

"What do they want?" she asked. Their movements were so purposeful that they had to be following the bark.

"Whatever we have that is worth taking."

"Pirates?" No wonder Bryn said she would be needing a knife.

"The lead galley is flying the Red Hand of the O'Neills." Collin acted as if that were answer enough. He was dressed in his blue brigandine, showing he expected trouble.

"Will there be a fight?" she wondered, watching the galleys come on.

Collin considered. "Not if we can get into Wexford ahead of them. The wind is still strong from the north, which favors us. They have no sails and a long stern chase will tire their oarsmen." But he was still wearing his brigandine—just in case it came to blows.

Straining her eyes, she made out two more galleys farther back. Making five. More were no doubt behind them, hull down on the watery horizon. Galleys rode so low they could not be seen at any distance. She had noted at least a dozen drawn up on that beach to the north.

"Fortunately for the *Fortuna*, we are not far from Wexford."

How long had she slept? Hours, according to her watch. God, she felt groggy. What the Middle Ages needed most was coffee. She would gladly trade printing for caffeine any day. "How far is not far?"

He looked at the sun sinking toward the green hills of Erin. "We should be there before dusk. Which is well, for there is a bar at the harbor mouth I would hate to attempt in the dark. We just have to hope the wind holds; so long as it remains strong they will be hard put to catch us." *Fortuna*'s master put on every stitch of canvas to get the most speed out of his ship, calling for double bonnets on the mainsail and even rigging up the ship's boat sail on the half deck, to supplement the mizzen. The wind stayed strong, whipping up waves that made the galleys bob and pitch, oars flailing at the heaving sea. One by one they fell behind, getting less and less distinct in the fading light. But they persisted, keeping their bows to the waves, fighting to make headway—acting nothing like the indolent savages of popular English imagination.

Passing Cahore Point, the *Fortuna* ran down the coast toward Wexford—until a call came from the tiny two-man castle atop the mainmast, "Shoals ahead." Turning toward the bow, she saw a slick patch of water shining in the last of the light; beneath it lay a sandbar blocking the harbor entrance. *Fortuna*'s master ordered leadsmen into the main chains, where they started frantically swinging weighted lines. One of them cried out, "Four fathoms."

"What bottom?" demanded the master.

"Sandy," the bow replied. "And a half three." The sandy bottom was shoaling up beneath them.

Cupping his hands, the master shouted down to the tiller, "Hard a starboard." *Fortuna* turned toward the shore, her big mainsail flapping loudly as it lost the wind. Feeling the ship slowing beneath her, Robyn looked back over her shoulder, seeing no sign of the galleys struggling in their wake. The smooth slanting line of a sandbar slid by to port, little swift spinning whirlpools streaming from its landward side.

"Three fathoms," cried the leadsmen. Only eighteen feet of water— the bottom continued to shoal. How much did the *Fortuna* draw? Two fathoms at least, with its high masts, deep hold, and heavy bow and stern castles. The light Irish galleys probably drew less than a fathom.

"And a half twain!"

Less than a fathom lay under the keel. "Stand ready with the bow anchor," shouted the sailing master. Sailors in the forecastle got set to heave the heavy anchor over the side.

"Two fathoms!"

She saw the last rays of sunlight reflecting off a wide smooth patch to port. Little choppy ripples radiated out from shallows to starboard. The master called in sail, but the ship kept going, carried forward by her momentum and the incoming tide. Collin reached over and took her hand, saying, "Brace yourself, we are hitting bottom."

She felt a jarring shiver as the keel scraped on the sand. "Drop anchor," shouted the master. The heavy bow anchor went crashing into the water, and the *Fortuna* swung sideways, still bumping on the bottom. The sailing master gave another order, and the stern anchor plummeted into the sea. As the sun sank into the hills, *Fortuna* came to rest against the side of the sandbar, her bow to the oncoming tide.

Welcome to Eire. She looked at the darkening shore. No sign of help there, no sign of anything. In Wales things had seemed so simple: get to Ireland, get word to Edward, and hopefully he would come for her. Just getting here had been way more of a struggle than she imagined—Atlantic gales, lee shores, Irish pirates, shoals and sandbars—all combining to trap her within sight of her goal. Collin conferred with the sailing master, deciding to send the ship's boat into Wexford for a local pilot, familiar with the bars and shoals. She felt a sharp, sudden urge to be on that boat. If she just got ashore she would be safe—after all, she spoke the language, or would speak it when she got there. And she would be in friendly territory, ruled by Edward's father. Collin looked aghast at the suggestion. "You must be mad!"

"Maybe." Almost certainly at times. But that was her business, not his.

"Have you ever tried to make a night landing on a strange and lawless shore?" Collin inquired. "In an open boat? With a half-dozen pirate galleys prowling about?"

She was forced to admit that she had not.

"I thought not. Leave such things to mariners, who are learned at such risks." Sailors swung out the boat, and the master detailed a helmsman and half a dozen seamen to man her. Seeing how the boat heaved in the chop, she had to admit Collin's point—though a true time-traveling Hollywood heroine would have insisted on taking the tiller herself, amazing the natives with her seawomanship. Watching the boat thrash off into the darkness, she felt a pang of regret, still wishing she were aboard. She stared after it until she could no longer see the white splashes, sure she had badly missed the boat.

"Look," Collin pointed to starboard, taking her attention from the departed boat. Sparks of fire appeared against the dark mass of the land, low flickering lights level with the sea.

"Who is that?"

"Our Irish friends, and not far off. Knowing we cannot get into Wexford until morning, they have drawn their galleys up on a beach or sandbar to wait for first light."

"What will happen then?" Nothing violent, hopefully.

He shrugged. "That depends on wind, and weather, and when the boat comes back. With a pilot and a sea breeze, we can sail right in with the tide, galleys or no. That is what I hope for."

"And what if that does not happen?"

"Then we fight." Collin did not sound enthusiastic. "We have wooden walls and cannon; they have speed and numbers. With luck we can keep them out of the ship." Even she could see the danger there. Keeping the Irish at bay did not get them any closer to Wexford. If the galleys kept up the attack, the *Fortuna* would eventually run short of shot and arrows; then only the strength of her crew could keep the Irish out. When that was exhausted, the ship would soon succumb.

Collin ordered the sailing master to put up boarding nets and extinguish all lights. "Tell the crew; no singing, no talking, and to sleep under arms at their stations." Deathly stillness settled over the *Fortuna*, broken only by the ghostly creak of cordage and soft sounds of the sea. Sentries strained their ears, silently listening for the splash of galley oars.

Still wishing she had gone with the boat, she retired to her dark little cabin. Tonight was Friday, the Witches Night she hoped to spend in Eire. Instead it would be her first Witches Night alone—stuck on a sandbar, on a boat full of men, ringed by Irish pirates—it hardly seemed fair. But none of this did. Setting aside Jo's potion bag, she decided to save the Witches Flight powder for when she really needed it. That did not mean she skimped on the ritual. Changing to the blue-and-silver gown she had made from Collin's gift—hoping it might hold some May Day magic—she closed her shutters and draped dark cloth over the window, sealing off her little space. Burning a black candle in spite of the blackout, she took extra care casting her private circle, saying a heartfelt prayer for assistance, begging the Goddess to guide her steps. Then she cleared her mind completely, opening it to the night.

All she heard was waves lapping at the hull and the slosh of water in the bilges as the bark rocked at anchor. Incoming tide had lifted her free of the bar, and she was swaying in the swell. Such trivial sounds could be maddening when you were trying to let your mind drift—no wonder stone castles were so suited to Witches Flights, blocking out the world beautifully. But not here, not now. Why could she not concentrate? Because she was on her own? Nonsense—she spent hours alone doing out-of-body practice. She wondered if she should use the potion. Of course not. More maddening distraction, worrying about what she might be doing when she should just let herself go.

Another sound rose up to annoy her, a far-off splashing, followed by a stir overhead. Boot steps headed for the stern castle's starboard ramparts. Splashes grew louder, accompanied by the creak of oars. Heavy scraping sounds from the quarterdeck told her the iron breech-loading cannon were being dragged around to take aim at the threat. That killed it; she could not compete with cannon. Hurriedly saying a closing prayer, she snuffed the candle, putting an end to her first, very own Witches Night. A fairly dismal failure.

Finding her way onto the quarterdeck by feel, she discovered that the wind had died. Damp darkness surrounded her. She made out men crouched over their cannons, trying to peer into the murk. One of them called out, "Light to starboard."

She heard a who-goes-there hail from the half deck, and spotted a glint of light bobbing about like a lantern in the prow of a boat. A cheerful voice out of the darkness returned the hail in English. Cheerful and familiar. Pulling alongside, the boat bumped against the *Fortuna*. Someone shouted, "It is the boat, coming back with the pilot." Sailors hastened to throw them a line.

Amazed that the boat could have found them, she peered over the quarterdeck rail. By the light below she could see it was the *Fortuna's* boat, but the men at the oars were dressed in blue and purple livery. Someone, probably the pilot, stood in the bows holding up the lamp. Beside him stood a tall nobleman in a gold-and-white gown with long billowing sleeves and a sword at his side, his face hidden by a floppy velvet cap. As soon as the boat was secure, the nobleman scrambled up into the dark waist of the ship, plainly eager to be aboard. Neither his sword nor his billowing white-gold sleeves gave him any trouble going up the narrow ladder. Collin called for a light.

Some obedient crewman lit a lantern, casting a dim half circle of lamplight onto the quarterdeck. She heard the noble's boots on the steps leading up from the waist. He topped the stairs and stepped into the light, shining in cloth-of-gold and grinning broadly, looking fresh and clean and young, with light brown hair falling from his cap to his shoulders. "I did hope to discover you here," he told her happily. It was Edward, handsome, beaming, and extremely pleased to see her.

⊷⇒ Owen Boy O'Neill ⇐⊶

*S*he could barely believe it was happening, but here was her mischie-vous *beau sabreur*, proud and happy in his white-and-cloth-of-gold surcoat with angel-wing sleeves. His velvet beret sat at the same jaunty angle, above the same confident smile. Light from the lantern sparkled off gold trim, making Edward seem like a shining white-gold appari-tion stepping out of the night—putting her simple blue-and-silver gown to shame. He bowed low, "Lady Robyn, how astonishingly wonderful to see you again."

"And I you." She curtsied back. So much for Edward not remem-bering her. His easy bravado stirred her like a brisk sea breeze whip-ping away the fog of a failed Witches Night, filling her with confidence—reminding her how good it felt when they held each other on that far, far future day in Wales. She feared she did not make near so fine an impression. After days at sea, her hair must look a mess, and she had not even managed a decent curtsy.

Edward did not care. Ignoring the ship full of nervous enemies, he strode happily over to her, saying, "My lady, you look magnificent, more elegant even than I remembered."

He was teasing—the last time he saw her she was wearing a man's jacket and hiking boots, having just fled from armed felons. Torn between delight at seeing him and fear for his safety, all she could say was, "Why have you come here?"

"Because I missed you, more than I imagined possible. It seems centuries since we parted."

She smiled at that—since, of course, it had been. Did he know? or was it a chance remark? With Edward it was hard to tell; he liked to joke, but had a sharp eye for whatever went on around him—she remembered how keen he had been to see her watch and cell phone. "But how did you know I would be here?"

His smile widened. "Yesterday in Waterford, I got the sudden no-tion to ride to Wexford and meet a boat, hoping to find you on it."

And she should have been on it. What a colossal fool she was, mooning about her cabin, lighting candles, and praying for advice—when an inner voice already told her to be on that ship's boat. She had gotten the direction she begged for, but ignored it. Even worse, she let Collin talk her out of it. So much for being open to the cosmos. If she had done what her soul had urged, Edward would have been waiting when she stepped ashore. They could have been celebrating their Witches Night reunion somewhere safe and warm in Wexford. Heaven only knew what would happen now; her stupidity could easily be Edward's death sentence. Oblivious to the danger, Edward went on happily explaining how they had been drawn together. "When I got to Wexford, I found this boat seeking a pilot. So I came out to see who was aboard, secretly hoping to discover you here. What amazing good fortune . . ."

Bootsteps sounded behind her, coming down from the stern castle. She turned to see Collin stepping into the quarterdeck lantern light. Mail showed beneath his brigandine, and he wore steel on his knees, sleeves, and elbows. Only his head was bare. Behind him came a half dozen men in mail, wearing Wydville surcoats. Collin bowed slightly. "My lord of March, how happy it is to see you."

Edward acknowledged the bow. "And how excellent it is to see you, Sir Collingwood Grey."

"My lord knows me?" Collin politely asked his prisoner.

"All England knows your lance. I have been in awe of your ability since I first saw you in the lists."

Collin seemed surprised and flattered. "You saw me joust?"

"At Bristol when I was a boy. On Saint George's Day—you won a hawk, a hound, a horse, and a ring from a lady's finger. But that was before bad feeling turned tourneys into battles."

Despite the friendly banter, she saw Edward's hand had slipped to his sword. Her stomach tightened. The two men she most cared about stood facing each other across an invisible line, the same line that divided all of England, separating those who served Mad King Henry from those who believed in something better. Collin thanked him for the compliment, saying, "If my lord of March would care to accompany me, I would be glad to offer refreshment. It must be a cold, wet row out from Wexford."

"Indeed, it was damp." Edward sounded as if he only now noticed the wet night air.

"Come, then, my lord. Warm brandy will dry you out."

"Lo, the very thing." Edward turned back to her, full of his usual bounce, saying, "Who would have thought a stranded ship contained such wonders?"

Bowing low, Collin indicated the way to the great cabin. Edward strode over to the door, acting as if he owned the ship—which, in a way, he did, since the *Fortuna* was in Irish waters, and Edward's father was still king's lieutenant in Ireland, despite being attainted for treason. Edward's cool confidence was heartening, but when she tried to follow, Collin stopped her. "I will be pleased to present your regrets, but this is men's business."

Armored men cut her off from Edward, opening the door to usher him into Collin's cabin. She started to call out. Before she could, Edward looked back over his shoulder, caught her eye, and winked. Then he disappeared through the door. She did not try to follow. Edward knew what he was doing, or at least thought he did. If she made a scene, what could he do? Cut his way through six armored men to get to her side? Not very practical or pretty, particularly in a small space. She had failed him once by not going with the boat—had she done that, all this would have been avoided. Now Edward was playing nonchalant, trying to take his capture in stride. She should follow his lead and not force his hand.

Collin directed her to her own door, but she refused to budge, saying, "See no harm comes to him."

Collin stood between her and Edward, silver nail heads on his blue brigandine gleaming in the lamplight. "Right now his life is in his own hands. He will be harmed only if he resists."

"Do you swear to that?" she demanded. Whatever Collin promised now, Edward was likely to suffer a good deal of harm if he fell into the clutches of King Henry's court. Edward would not even get a trial, having already been condemned to death in absentia—along with his father, the Neville earls, and numerous others—by the "Devil's Parliament" convened in Coventry after the sack of Ludlow.

Collin's voice dropped to a whisper. "Come now, I know he seems likeable and is an excellent judge of jousting, but he is a condemned traitor—of course we have to take him."

"Oh, yes, of course," she retorted sarcastically. "You planned this from the beginning. You knew I was coming here hoping to see Edward, and you meant to take him."

Collin sighed. "How could that be? You never told me it was in your mind to see this man. Wind and storm drove us here, along with Irish pirates. I sent that boat into Wexford harbor hoping to find a pilot. How could I know it would return with the earl of March?"

"How, indeed!" She glared contemptuously at him. Only one person here and now knew about her connection to Edward, the person who "displaced" Edward to the future to begin with, the very same witch-duchess Wydville who supplied the ship. Either Duchess Wydville's innocent concern for a stranger lost in time had just been wonderfully repaid, or this had all been planned in advance, a well-laid trap, with her as the bait.

"First and foremost," Collin reminded her, "I have been taking you to Eire, where you very much wanted to go. But I never renounced my allegiance to King Henry or promised to abet attainted traitors. Naturally, if a chance appeared to lay hands on the earl of March, we would have to take it, though that hardly seemed likely beforehand."

"Naturally," she snorted. She knew this chance did not just appear. "Edward did not just happen aboard that boat. He was drawn here by witchcraft. . . ."

Collin cut her off, "If we must talk this way, let us take the conversation into your cabin, before it becomes unlawful."

She, too, did not want to thrash out their differences in front of Duchess Wydville's men, so she retreated into her cold, dark cabin. Her blackout curtains were still up, and she relit the candle with her lighter, setting it on the washstand. Collin looked about, sizing up his surroundings—this was the first time he had been in her cabin.

Too angry to play the proper hostess, she told him straight out, "You know there is magic behind this. Edward was drawn here, just as I was dragged out of my own time."

"Mayhap that is so," he admitted. Any other conclusion would make him look silly, which Collin hated.

"Mayhap, nothing," she snapped back. "You know witchcraft is at work." More than a month into the Middle Ages, she had almost despaired of the spell bringing her and Edward together—the way "Widow Weirdville" originally promised—now here they were, together with a vengeance. It was plain she had been used to trap the Yorkist heir. Anything else was too much of a coincidence.

"These are women's secrets," Collin observed dryly, "lying beyond the ken of men. Luckily, I have naught to do with them."

"Really?" Even when you came to Hollywood and swept me off my feet? Which was how this whole farce started. How she ended up here, at the wrong end of time. Had Collin's later self come to L.A. looking for her with this end in mind?

Collin sighed wearily. He, too, had endured a hard couple of days. "I swear on my immortal soul, I knew nothing of this beforehand."

She stared evenly at him. So you say. And maybe you even believe it. But centuries from now his later self would come to "Holy Wood" and seduce her—which then went smashingly with the family plans. Was that why she had been brought back in time and given this fabulous free trip to Ireland? She bit her lip with worry. "What will they do with him?"

Collin shrugged. "For that, you will have to ask Baron Rivers, or Her Grace, the much-beloved duchess of Bedford."

She replied with a scornful look; how like a man, anxiously keeping his hands clean. Collin may not have cast the spells, but he was not above reaping the benefits. He sighed again. "Greystone has been burned and sacked; my sister and niece are in the hands of witch hunters. I did not ask for any of that."

"Then why put up with it?"

Collin cocked his head. "What do you mean?"

"Why do you put up with a mad king, and a court that bankrupts the nation, then lines its pockets by putting justice up for sale?" Collin was right, she could not speak her mind without spouting treason. "Then when someone like Edward stands up against tyranny, you hunt him down and turn him over to his killers. Next time you sit down with your lordly neighbors to complain about the excesses at court, remember you are getting the government you deserve."

"What do you care?" Collin inquired contemptuously. "You are going home to your wonderful perfect future, where such things do not happen. We, alas, have to live here."

How unfair. She never pretended the future was perfect. In many ways the bad old twentieth century, with its World Wars and Holocausts, had been much worse than 1460. King Henry's crimes might not compare to Auschwitz and Hiroshima—but that did not mean they should go unpunished. Or that Collin needed to be an accomplice.

Collin cocked his head toward the great cabin. "Bringing back Edward of March will make life a lot easier for many of us. Lord Rivers and Sir Anthony were taken by March and the Nevilles, costing them the admiralty and a crippling ransom. Now we have the means to get some of that back. Or better yet, we can barter him for Joanna and Joy, people you should be concerned about, though they live in this poor benighted century." Seen from Collin's viewpoint, it made hideous sense. Baron Rivers, the duchess, even Jo and Joy all stood to gain by Edward's capture, and there was Collin as usual, making it all happen. Of course, he, too, would be rewarded—for bringing in the heir to the House of York, Mad King Henry would make him a lord.

Worse yet, she owed it to them. These people had taken her in, feeding and clothing her, when she had small hope of doing it herself. Lodging her in mansions and castles. And she repaid them by taking sides with a traitor. She reminded herself that they had brought her here to begin with, and right now stood to profit handsomely at her expense. Her smug "I'm from the future" superiority was neatly punctured; backward savages had taken her in, finding her entertaining, and now useful. And would no doubt discard her if she proved tiresome. "At least let me talk to him," she pleaded.

Collin shook his head. "That would do no one any good."

"So you say." By now she vastly regretted May Night.

He looked hard at her. "We have been good to each other. You freed my niece, and I have done my best to pay you back. But I very much need the earl of March and cannot give him up just to please you."

"Then go and please yourself." Collin had betrayed her again, though this was far worse than just seducing her while being married to Bryn—twice.

"As you wish, my lady," Collin bowed and left. She slammed the bolt home behind him, a futile gesture—but meant to claim at least this small space. She was thrown back on her own resources, at the moment horribly meager. Sitting down on her narrow rope sea bed, she took stock; she was alone at night, with Edward under heavy guard on a ship full of armed men, surrounded by dangerous shoals and sandbars in pirate-infested waters. Hopeless and then some. She could neither get to Edward nor leave the ship, and appealing to Collin had gotten her nowhere. Waves lapped against the dark hull as she stared into the candle flame praying for guidance.

Witches Night was still not over. Somehow she must use that—it being the one thing still in her favor, the sole advantage she had not totally blown. But how? She fingered Jo's potion bag. Who could she appeal to? Jo and Joy were prisoners who could barely help themselves. Duchess Wydville was the enemy. Bryn would like as not side with Collin. Which left things very much up to her.

Having doubted herself once this Witches Night—with disastrous results—she refused to make that mistake again. She had wanted to be on that boat, but feared the black, heaving swells, doubting her ability to make a night landing on a strange shore from an open boat. Now she would jump at the chance of nothing but a wet dark boat ride to be safe with Edward. Fate had offered her that, but she turned it down. Or more correctly, she let Collin talk her out of it—no danger of that now. Doffing her blue-and-silver gown, she donned a white linen shift and then recast her circle. This time her prayers were not just correct, but heartfelt and contrite—this time she would be truly open, listening with all her being, grateful for any help she got. Nor would she hold anything back. When the proper moment came, she poured all the gray powder into the potion cup.

Her head swam as she repeated the chants Jo taught her. Closing her eyes, she let go of the tiny cabin, letting her consciousness drift outward into darkness. Cold, clammy night enveloped her. She could feel the sea heaving beneath her, but not the deck she knelt on. Letting go even more, she opened herself to the blackness. She could smell salt spray and sense the depths beneath her—but all she saw with eyes shut tight was colored sparks dancing in the blackness behind her eyelids.

Slowly one of the colored sparks—a red one—began to grow. As it grew, it drew closer, becoming a flickering and expanding point of fire, like a red candle flame. Dancing flame coalesced into the image of a man dressed in crimson. She recognized the scarlet archer who called himself John-Amend-All—striding toward her out of the darkness, a smile on his bearded face, his bow and black arrows slung across his back. He met her just above the waves, with flecks of spray hitting her bare feet. The crimson Jack of Hearts made a mocking bow, "My Lady Stafford, pray come with me."

"Where to?"

"To where we may do some good."

"Where is that?" she wondered, amazed by the way she hovered over an invisible sea.

"Come and see," he suggested. "I swear it will do you well."

Reminding herself to be open, she told him, "I will come." And they went. As he led her through the darkness, she asked, "Are you Jack Cade, the John-Amend-All who led the revolt against King Henry's court?" Or more correctly his ghost?

He found the question funny. "Yes, I am Jack Cade—but I am also John Mortimer, and Dr. Aylmer, and those who died with him, and those who were hunted down and hung afterwards, and those who stood in the crowd and watched them die, while wishing them well in their hearts. Better to say that I am their spirit."

"What are you doing here?"

"Watching over Edward, earl of March—who embodies the hopes and dreams that did not die with us." All manner of folks had high opinions of Edward. Hopefully he would get a chance to live up to them. Looking down, she made out the white tops of breakers below, and she sensed the heavy mass of land ahead. More sparks of light appeared, this time low down, and strung in a ragged line. She recognized the Irish campfires she had seen at dusk. As she got closer she could see their galleys beached beside the fires.

"Here lie the O'Neills," explained the scarlet ghost, "awaiting first light. If someone told them where Duchess Wydville's ship was anchored, they would be on it at once, before the tide ebbs."

"Someone should tell them?" she suggested. Anything that kept the *Fortuna* from sailing was to Edward's advantage—even an Irish attack.

He laughed. "That I was born in Eire does not mean I speak her language." She had heard that Jack Cade was Anglo-Irish, but thought it merely an attempt to blacken his name—many considered the English settlers as bad as their Irish neighbors. "O'Neills have heard us shout English at them for centuries, and profited from it hardly at all. But no Irishman figures he can lose by following some strange beautiful woman into the night. Especially if she speaks fair Gaelic."

Buttering her up, but it worked. If anyone was going to bring the Red Hand of the O'Neills down on the *Fortuna*, it must be her. She tried moving toward the shore, bare toes treading just above the wavetops. It worked. John-Amend-All hung back, giving her room to work. Ahead she could see the Irish strung out along the beach, their galleys drawn onto the sand, each with a watchfire and sentries wrapped in tawny cloaks. Spears and iron-rimmed shields lay at their sides. The rest were asleep, looking like bundles of wash abandoned on the beach.

As she reached the shore break, consternation erupted. Sentries leaped to their feet. Hounds bayed, and she heard cries of, *"Bandraoi! Bandraoi!"* Meaning, "Witch!"

Taking that as a compliment to her entrance, she tried out her Gaelic, spreading her arms and calling to them, *"Uí Néil, Uí Néil,* why do you sleep? When the Saxons sail at break of day."

Even the dogs fell silent. Men stood staring, spears clutched in their hands, bearded faces agape in disbelief. Encouraged by the crowd's amazement, she tried again. *"Uí Néil, Uí Néil,* why do you sleep? The Saxons sail at break of day."

One of them stepped forward—a prosperous-looking felon with a braided blond beard that shone in the firelight. He wore a steel cap, a dark embroidered tunic, and a cloak pinned with a gold broach, and he held a pair of silver-studded spears in his right hand. Blue eyes wide with wonder, he strode down to the water. Wading cautiously into the shore break, he stopped when it reached his knees, introducing himself as, Éoghan Boy Uí Néil—Owen Boy O'Neill, or Blond Owen O'Neill—naming ancestors going back to Niall of the Nine Hostages, who was king of Eire in Roman times. His Gaelic was way better than hers—even awakened by a midnight apparition and standing knee deep in the surf, he managed to address her in intricate flattering verse:

> **Woman of fate, whom heroes would fight for.**
> **Who are you? Whom high kings would woo.**

"A friend," she answered, hoping that was so. She meant to do the O'Neills a favor—but if she merely got a lot of them killed for no good result, they were better off where they were.

Owen Boy O'Neill waded deeper into the break, to get a closer look, asking her:

> **Why have you come to us,**
> **Flickering over the dark water,**
> **Like white fire on the waves?**

"To show you the way to the Saxon ship." She slowly backpedalled as she spoke—the more aloof and mysterious she was, the more likely they were to follow. Men could never resist a woman just out of their reach. She beckoned as she backed away, singing, "Follow me, follow me . . ."

Blue eyes alight, Blond Owen started to do just that, wading into the surf past his waist. Suddenly remembering his galleys, he spun about and sloshed back up onto the beach, shouting commands to the O'Neills. There was debate. Not every O'Neill thought that thrashing off into the night after a ghostly woman in white was the tactically sound alternative—but Owen Boy saw a legend in the making. Even on short acquaintance, she could tell this O'Neill had a poetic soul. After some browbeating and spear-brandishing, the O'Neills got all headed in the same direction, pushing their galleys into the surf. Blond Owen stood on the prow of the biggest, shouting orders to the rest, not all of whom liked where they were headed. Unsure herself, she looked over her shoulder and saw John-Amend-All receding behind her, dwindling like a red spark in the night. She backpedalled to keep the spark in sight.

And the O'Neills came after her, their galley oars rising and dipping like gulls' wings, sending them gliding over the water, sliding over sunken bars and rippling shoals. Keeping the galleys in sight, she followed the receding red spark toward a low glow in the east. Witches Night was fading. She made out the *Fortuna*, her black masts and castles backlit by a low band of first light spreading along the watery horizon. Robyn looked back to see the O'Neills winging along behind her, with Owen Boy's galley in the lead.

Suddenly she was back in her dark cramped cabin, staring at a little puddle of black wax with a bit of candle wick burning in the middle. As she knelt watching, the bit of wick went out, plunging her into blackness. Witches Night was over. She could feel the ship rocking gently beneath her. Nothing seemed to have changed. Was it all a potion-induced dream? Might John-Amend-All, Owen Boy O'Neill, and his reluctant band of Irish pirates just be products of her over-wrought imagination?

She hurried to dress in the dark, wriggling into her blue-and-silver gown. Trumpets blared as she pulled on dry slippers, and she heard orders bellowed from the half-deck, followed by shouts, oaths, and feet drumming on the planks overhead. Then came the sharp report of cannons, and gun smoke wafting under the door—the O'Neills had indeed arrived, unannounced and unwelcome.

By Hecate, she had done it. Who would believe it? She was a witch—flying through air, talking to spirits, foretelling the future, and conjuring up Irish pirates. Until now, witchcraft had been a wild ride, with someone else always in charge. Jo, Joy, Bryn, Nest, the duchess—anyone but her. But this had come from her, and her alone, once she threw her whole being into it, going right to the edge and then giving in to the cosmos. Philosophical implications alone were frightening, not to mention the practical applications. Still a wild ride, but one that came from within. She thanked Hecate again.

⊷⥲ Wexford Bay ⥬⥬⊶

*S*traightening her blue-and-silver gown, she slipped carefully out of her cabin, clutching the saxe knife Bryn had given her, just in case. A cannon banged on the quarterdeck, spewing smoke. Shouts and howls came from above. No sentries stood on guard outside the great cabin. She tugged on the latch, finding it lashed down with a length of rope—a good sign—Edward was alone and alive inside. Why else tie the latch? She sawed through the rope with Bryn's saxe knife—mentally thanking the witch, who had foreseen her need. Not yet in Ireland, and she already had it out.

Lifting the latch, she pushed open the door. Edward sat at Collin's window seat, looking relaxed in his gaudy gold-and-white surcoat, his honey-brown hair ruffled by the morning breeze, studying the excitement in the half-light outside with amused interest. His black velvet cap lay on the seat beside him. Seeing her, he smiled broadly, "Good morrow, m'lady. Again I hoped it would be you."

And it was. She smiled back, slipping the saxe knife into her belt, closing the door behind her, and sliding home the bolt—grateful to have that thin bit of wood between her and the chaos on the quarterdeck.

"Week before last I dreamed of you," Edward sounded totally unconcerned with the mayhem outside. Or his perilous condition. All he cared about was seeing her again, which was flattering, if somewhat insane given the circumstances. "You were in Kenilworth, with a bevy of women. Some pretty, but none so much as you. All were praying and chanting in weird tongues"—Two weeks ago was Witches Night at Kenilworth. What a simpering fool she was! She thought nothing had happened at the séance, but Duchess Wydville had been feeling out her connection to Edward, using her to invade his dreams. Not that Edward minded—"A most radiant vision. And when I was drawn toward this ship, it seemed a silly chance that you would be aboard. Yet now . . ."

He stopped, looking at her, amazed to have gotten his wish. She felt that wordless gulf between them, full of fear, excitement, hope, and wonder. He might be an earl, heir to a duchy, and the "best hope of England," and she might be from the impossibly high-tech future, but with both of them adrift on the Irish Sea, surrounded by their enemies, none of that mattered much. Life-or-death danger was awfully leveling. What mattered was that she found herself mercilessly drawn to this boy she barely knew. She wanted to forget their differences and take the heir to the House of York in her arms, picking up where they left off half a millennium hence. He wanted it, too—she could see that in his eyes—though he was too much the young gentleman to say so. Why else would a busy boy earl take a wet, dark ride in an open boat?

Cannons banged on the quarterdeck, breaking the spell. Edward turned back to the window. "Who is attacking the ship? O'Neills? I thought I saw their Red Hand banner." He stared wistfully at the sea battle outside—going merrily on without him. "I wonder who leads them."

"Owen Boy O'Neill." She did not bother giving Owen Boy's fanciful pedigree.

He looked surprised. "Tall and blond? With a braided beard? Spouts incomprehensible poetry at the sight of a pretty woman?" She nodded again, he had Owen Boy to a T. "Splendid," Edward declared. "The very O'Neill we need. Whatever could have brought him here, just when we could most use him?"

"I did," she replied modestly.

Edward looked happy and amazed. "However did you do it?"

"Magic." She meant to be honest with Edward, no matter what. If she could not trust him, then things were truly hopeless. Gun smoke drifted in the window, smelling of brimstone.

Far from being appalled, Edward made a bow. "Robyn Stafford, you are an absolute wonder." He sounded fascinated. "When first we met I thought you might be a witch—with your talking box and magic clock."

She had long ago lost the phone, but the magic clock was still on her wrist. "When first we met, you thought I was a boy," she reminded him.

He grinned sheepishly. "And never was I so pleased to be mistaken. Was it magic that brought you here as well?"

"Yes." Though she doubted he realized just how far she had come. This was not the moment to bring up the third millennium. "And you, too."

"Me, too? What do you mean?"

"I mean you, too, were brought here by magic. There is a spell that brings us together." Edward certainly deserved to know that much.

"Truly? Spellcraft brings us together? Thank God for that." Stripping off his gloves and tucking them into his belt, he took her hands in his. "For I have missed you much."

Hard warm hands sent an exciting tingle through her, a surge of nervous longing that had nothing to do with being aboard a floating castle besieged by pirate galleys. "I know," she whispered. "That is part of the spell." She had missed him, too.

Edward arched an eyebrow. "Is that so?"

"Yes." Her fingers moved on their own, interlacing with his. Holding hands with the hope of England felt incredibly thrilling. She had known from the start that this boy would not be boring, but she had not expected quite this much excitement—with cannons banging in the background. "I did not put the spell on you, but I know the witch who did." And it was a good bet she meant him to be falling in love with someone else.

"Who is this witch?"

"The duchess of Bedford."

He looked shocked. "The very same duchess of Bedford I only just entertained in Calais? Why would she do this favor for me?"

She smiled, holding tight to his hand. "She did not do it for you. Believe me, this was not at all her intention."

"Then I am most pleased her spell miscarried."

From outside the cabin came a splintering crash, followed by a high-pitched scream and a dull thud. They both looked toward the door. Another cannon went off. Edward rolled his eyes and sighed, "I ought to do something about that."

"By all means." She was not sure what he could do. Summoning the O'Neills to save Edward had seemed like such a stroke of genius. Now she had no idea how to turn them off.

He shook his head. " 'Tis a pity neither of us speaks their heathen tongue."

"But I do."

"Do what?"

"Speak Gaelic."

He stared at her. "How is that possible? Is this Holy Wood you come from in Eire?"

"It is the spell," she explained. "I am Displaced. Out of my normal space and time. I speak whatever language is spoken to me."

He cocked an eye. "*Vraiment?*"

"*Absolument,*" she assured him.

"*Incroyable!*" They laughed at their spontaneous burst of French. He stopped laughing and stared at her, suddenly unsure and awkward, the first time she had ever seen him at a loss. "Alas, I very much fear that I need my lady's aid. I need to confront the O'Neills, who are in truth my father's vassals. However little they show it. But . . ."

"Being their true and rightful overlord does not mean you speak their language?"

His smile returned. "*Exactement!*"

She expected to be talking to the O'Neills again. How else would they get out of this? Yet she found it touching that he hesitated to ask—hating to put her at risk. He grimaced as a cannon boomed on the quarterdeck. "I abhor those iron monsters. Far better for everyone if they had never been devised."

Amen. But it seemed a tad late to uninvent gunpowder. And this century's little iron breechloading cannons were popguns compared to what fifteen-year-olds in L.A. carried tucked in their waistbands. She glanced over her shoulder at the door, saying, "Shall we go and face them?"

"Yes, but first . . ." He pulled her closer, so close she felt hard steel under his surcoat—love spell or no, her hero had come dressed in mail. He kissed her, a kiss so intent and passionate it nearly lifted her off the deck. He did not let go of her hands or try to grope her, but his mail thigh pressing against her hip made her silver-trimmed gown and lace petticoats feel remarkably thin. All this with his back to a ship's door while a battle royal raged on the other side.

Slowly she opened her eyes. He grinned happily, asking, "Are we ready?" You bet, ready for anything. After a kiss like that, stepping out and stopping a battle should be a snap. She merely nodded.

Reaching around behind his back, Edward slid the bolt and stepped through the door, still holding her hand, keeping his armored body between her and the action. Beyond the shade of the stern castle, gray dawn spilled over the quarterdeck. She winced to see a wounded sailor curled against a bulwark, a steel dart sticking through his thigh—the crash she heard had been him falling from the half deck, tangled in a section of rail. She hated to think of the seaman being hurt. Duchess Wydville's men served an unjust cause, and the O'Neills had come south from Ulster looking for mayhem and plunder. But the sailors were ordinary mariners, only meaning to take her safely to Eire. She tightened her grip on Edward's hand. Even his armored presence was no sure protection. Galleys had them surrounded, and a dart or spear could come winging at her from any direction. Still it felt good to have him close.

Stepping onto the quarterdeck, Edward ordered the sailors to cease fire. They stared up from their cannons, startled by his sudden appearance. Seeing their hesitation, he let go of her hand and seized the nearest keg of powder, hurling it over the side, to splash between the *Fortuna* and one of the Irish galleys. "Cease your firing," he shouted, "in the name of Good King Henry. I am earl of March, and son of the lord lieutenant. I will be obeyed."

She smiled to hear him so willing to use the king's name when needed—but it worked. Hearing one of their betters invoking King Henry, they naturally obeyed, hoping to Heaven he knew what he was doing. Silence descended, broken by moans from the skewered sailor and heathen cries from the O'Neills across the water. Morning breeze swept the gun smoke leeward, and she could see all eyes had turned to her and Edward. Sailors whispered to each other, " 'Tis the earl o' March, I tell you. York's son—the good duke's heir. Thank

Heaven fer that." None of them seemed to care that he was an attainted traitor, condemned to be hung, drawn, and quartered by the
Devil's Parliament.

Looking cautiously over Edward's armored shoulder, Robyn was
relieved to see that except for the wretch groaning in the bulwarks,
hardly anyone seemed hurt. Bows and cannons had kept the O'Neills
at a distance, without doing much damage. The little smoke-spewing
cannons were noisy and frightful, but not very accurate, having no
sights and no way to change elevation. Cannoneers had to rely on the
ship's roll, firing when the angle felt right. But after a couple of volleys
the air was too full of smoke to see the target, anyway.

Collin called down from the stern castle, wondering why the firing
stopped. Getting no answer, he leaned out an embrasure to see for
himself, grimacing at the sight of Edward on the loose, with her alongside him. Collin's plans were clearly coming undone. Edward called
up to him, "Why do you molest my father's vassals? You have gotten
them sorely excited."

Collin yelled angrily back, "We have none nothing to provoke
them. This is a wanton attack."

"Nonsense," Edward replied, "I will not believe that. They are
the gentlest of neighbors. Here, I will show you." Striding over to the
quarterdeck rail, Edward shouted a cheerful English greeting to the
nearest Irish galley. "Ho! Gentlemen, good morrow! What brings you
all the way to Wexford?"

He got a thrown spear in reply. Robyn ducked as it sailed over their
heads, thudding into the deck boards behind her. Jeers in Gaelic accompanied the spear. So far she had kept Edward between her and
the O'Neills, uncomfortably aware that she was the only woman
among several hundred men in a testosterone frenzy. To stop the fighting she had to risk her neck, putting her uniqueness to use—not an
appealing task. Stepping from behind Edward, she called out a greeting in Gaelic, begging to speak to Éoghan Boy Uí Néil.

Jeers ceased, replaced by astonished silence. Now it was the
O'Neills' turn to be taken aback, seeing her suddenly appear alongside
Edward. She saw their lead galley row cautiously closer, a huge sixty-
oared longship with the Red Hand of the O'Neills fluttering from her
sternpost. In the bow stood Owen Boy O'Neill, peering at her over
the top of a silver-rimmed shield, wild-eyed and breathing hard, but
with his beard still neatly braided. By dawnlight he looked bigger and

blonder, wearing gleaming scale armor under his cloak and a broad sharp sword slung at his hip. She repeated her greeting, adding how glad she was to see him again—"Here is the fine, brave ship I promised you."

Owen Boy shouted over his shoulder to back oars, and the galley glided to a stop, riding even with the *Fortuna*'s waist. He called back to her, "My fair lady, we hoped for a friendlier reception."

She translated for Edward. He grinned back at her, "Tell them it was but a misunderstanding." Which she did. "And invite the O'Neill aboard," he added, "with my promise of a truce." Edward called down to the sailors below, telling them to come up out of the waist, saying the Irish were about to board.

They hastened to obey, scrambling up onto the forecastle and quarterdeck. O'Neills gave a pagan cheer and came gleefully aboard, whooping and capering, with Owen Boy in the lead. Edward turned to her. "Tell them not to molest the mariners, and stay off the forecastle, but say they can have whatever they want from the hold or cabins, as recompense for their troubles."

She translated, and got another cheer in Gaelic. Laughing like drunk leprechauns, the O'Neills proceeded to loot the ship. Disappearing into the main hold, they emerged with kegs of wine, barrels of salt-beef and ship's biscuits, even canvas and spare cordage slung over their shoulders, along with iron bolts, spear staves, drinking cups, and soup kettles, anything not nailed down, plus a good bit that had been.

Collin called down a protest from the stern castle. Edward shouted back, "A thousand pardons, but she is my ship now, a prize of war to use as I please. And these good guests are my father's vassals. You are free to lodge complaint with my father's court in Dublin—but do it politely. Eire is *corporate de luy mesme* by act of an Irish Parliament. Any appeal to English laws prejudicial to the customs and privileges of Eire is good for a thousand-marks fine. Loose accusations of treason can get you hanged, drawn, and beheaded."

Collin swallowed his complaints. Outnumbered, outranked, and trapped on the half deck, there was little he could do but watch Duchess Wydville's ship being stripped. She felt sorry for him, but she had given Collin a chance to go along with her, and he refused. Now he must take his lumps.

Owen Boy O'Neill bounded up the steps to the quarterdeck, where he saluted her—but not Edward, son of his nominal overlord. Lest that lead to trouble, she hastened to introduce them, in English and in Gaelic, "*Éoghan Boy Uí Néil*, please meet Edward Plantagenet, earl of March."

"Tell him we have already met," Edward suggested, "at my father's Castle of Trim."

No need to translate. She could tell Owen Boy O'Neill well knew who Edward was—he just did not much care. Any right-thinking Irish brigand felt more beholding to a "beautiful, brave and well-spoken lady"—as Owen put it—than to the English heir to Ulster. Owen smiled wide at her, saying, "Fair spirit, you did not say Prince Richard's son would be aboard." So far as the Irish cared, Richard, duke of York was a prince of the blood and more to their liking than the current "Saxon" king.

"I promised you a Saxon ship," she reminded him, spreading her hands to show she had delivered. "I said nothing about who would be aboard."

"Which cabin would be yours?" Owen asked. She told him, and the O'Neill ordered his men not to disturb it. Instead they emptied out the great cabin, taking the cushions off the window seats and the feather mattress off the bed, along with Collin's spare clothes and belongings—acting so deft and polite about their plundering, it felt like they were doing a favor, helping strangers lighten ship amid the treacherous Wexford shoals.

"See," Edward told her, "treat the Irish decently, and they are decent to you. Though it pays to keep your guard up."

Edward turned to the crew, bunched onto the quarterdeck and stern castle along with his own men who rowed the ship's boat back from Wexford. She could see the sailors were torn between their duty to the Wydvilles and their hope that Edward would save them from the Irish. Thanking them for their patience, he commended them on weathering last night's gale. "You have brought my father a stout ship, for which I thank you. In exchange, I have brought a pilot to guide you safely into Wexford. On the morrow we set sail with the earl of Warwick for the narrow seas. For those who come along, I promise regular pay and rich prizes, under whatever officers you choose."

Heartened by the prospect of serving under a veteran pirate like the earl of Warwick—famous for sacking German and Spanish ships—they gave three hip hoorays for the duke of York, and three more for his admirable son. Collin and the ship's master stood isolated on the stern castle, along with the Wydville retainers. Any objections, and they would end up trying to tread water in armor. She prepared herself to plead for them.

Owen Boy O'Neill bowed and said his good-byes, inviting her to visit him in Eire. "Ours is a magic isle, green all year round, with neither snakes, frogs, toads, scorpions, nor dragons. Her holy soil is so inimical to poison that sprinkling it in your cup will keep you safe, though you sup blindfolded with your deadliest foe." She promised to remember that and to look him up when she was next in Ulster. Owen beamed, then bounded up, ordering his men back over the side and into the galleys. They obeyed, struggling under the weight of their loot, and soon the galleys were wallowing off toward the Wicklow coast, leaving the stripped and battered ship behind.

Collin came stiffly down from the half-deck, surveying the carnage. Her heart went out to him. Having only meant to do her a favor, seeing her safely to Ireland, Collin now faced yet another defeat, having lost not only a battle and a ship, but also his best chance of getting Jo back. But it did not have to be a defeat, and she told him so, "I am so sorry, but I had no choice. What Duchess Wydville did was wrong, as wrong as the way King Henry governs. Here is our chance to be with the people standing against that." She meant to take that chance; he could, too.

Collin smirked at her. "It must be splendid being from a far off neverland where answers are always so simple. We must live in the times we are born in. I have a family to think about, a sister and a niece." Clearly Collin cared more for them than who was ruling England. Robyn did not blame him. She would like to say she boldly chose to oppose tyranny—truth was, Duchess Wydville did not give her much choice. Tyranny had been fairly tolerable when it held out the hope of sending her home.

Collin turned to Edward with a nodding bow. "What now, my lord?" Collin was not without resources, still having his talented sword, backed by the armed Wydville retainers on the half-deck.

Edward blandly acknowledged the bow. "When we get to Wexford, I wish you would dine with me; then you are free to go where you will."

Collin looked suspiciously for the catch. "At what ransom?"

"None whatever." Edward enjoyed being magnanimous. "All I ask is that you talk of jousting at the table. And also that if ever I am in need, you will think kindly of me."

How could he not? Collin nodded grimly to the younger man, "That I will." She did not doubt it. Collin valued his freedom and disliked being in anyone's debt. Taking his leave, he went below to see what was left of his cabin. Watching him go, she thought how much had happened since Saint George's Day at Berkeley Castle—when he was the man in armor and she was the hapless new arrival headed for a rat-infested cell. She had not meant to turn the tables on him so decisively—but realistically, she had nowhere to go but up. She just wished her freedom did not have to come at Collin's expense.

Edward took possession of the stern castle so his pilot could stand on the half deck, calling orders down to the tiller. Leadsmen were back at work in the bow. She went up to join him, feeling suddenly shy—for the first time ever they would just be together, without being confused, menaced, pursued, or held captive. Faced with such normal, nonthreatening circumstances, they might have nothing much in common, considering he was a medieval earl and the highest title she ever held was Miss Rodeo Montana.

But being together and out of trouble was not so bad as she feared. Edward's happiness at having her with him was so warm and unforced, she could not help feeling heartened. She thanked him for his generosity toward Collin, which showed amazing leniency, since Edward himself lived under a death sentence that Collin came close to having carried out. Edward shrugged off his clemency, as though it were beneath him to hold a grudge. "I have always admired Sir Collingwood Grey, in and out of the lists. I am just lucky he did not have a lance."

"Did you know he has sister, named Joanna, who has a natural daughter called Joy?" Joy was the only person she had ever dared talk with about Edward.

Edward nodded. "An aptly named child. Whenever her mother brought her to Ludlow, she always made me smile."

Joy would have been happy to hear Edward remembered her. She told how Greystone had been sacked, and Jo and Joy taken prisoner. "I think Collin hoped to trade you for them."

Edward looked off toward the Irish shore, saddened but not angry. "I can well understand. If my mother, sister, and little brothers could be freed, and all I must do was give my enemy over to the king's justice—I would be hard-put to say no. Having to make such choices at all is the real wrong." How true. Edward asked, "What is his Welsh wife like?"

How did he know Collin had a secret wife? Edward must have excellent sources of information, far better than hers, and she had been living with Collin for more than a month. "Her name is Bryn, and she is so beautiful she makes your gaze blur."

His smile returned. "No mean praise coming from you." Edward even managed to turn Bryn's beauty into a compliment to her. Skirting the sand bars, the pilot rounded Raven Point, leaving Saint George's Channel, entering the wide green waters of Wexford Bay. Shore birds wheeled over fens and mudflats. Edward leaned through a stern castle embrasure, pointing out the tall embattled tower of Selskar Abbey and the walled town of Wexford—"which has streets so narrow you can shake hands across them."

Listening to his stories, she felt weirdly at ease. When she was actually with Edward, things were so natural, their differences seemed trivial. So what if he was young, rich, idealistic, and handy with a mace? Seen in the right light, those could actually be advantages. With Edward she felt like she had someone who was fully on her side, someone with no secret agenda—except to get her into bed. Someone from whom she did not have to hide anything. Hecate knows why—must be the spell at work. Too bad she had to leave him. But leave him, she must. Her first solo Witches Night had been an astounding success, having contacted a spirit, gone on a Witches Flight, and won over the wild O'Neills—all in one night. And all on her own. Absolutely amazing. At this rate she would be home in no time. Pushing back her sleeve, she checked her watch, wondering if they would be in Wexford in time for breakfast. What did the Irish eat before they had potatoes? She would soon know. 7:23 A.M., medieval sundial time.

Looking up, she saw Edward staring at her wrist, watching the digital readout tick off the seconds. He asked softly, "So, is it really true that you do not come from here?"

She raised an eyebrow. "From Wexford? No, never. This is my first time in Ireland. Truth to tell, I look forward to seeing the place."

They both laughed; then he turned serious. "I mean your Holy Wood is not anywhere nearby."

"No, it is not of these isles. Not in Ireland. Or in England. It is far across the Atlantic, in an undiscovered country called America."

"America." Edward rolled the strange name around on his tongue. "I do remember you saying that—it sounds Italian."

"That is because America was discovered by an Italian. Or rather it will be discovered, some thirty years from now."

Edward looked more than a bit unbelieving. "You not only speak French and Gaelic, and carry a magic clock, but can also see into tomorrow?"

"Because I was born in the future." Would Edward believe her? He was not an immortal witch like Jo or Collin, steeped in magic his whole life. She slipped the watch off her wrist and handed it to him, showing him how to adjust the digital display, at the same time she gave him the short history of the future, concentrating on England and America, leaving out the really unbelievable stuff, like Internet sex and talking toilet bowl commercials. While she talked, Edward played with the digital display, turning it on and off, making time run forward and backwards. Finally he slipped the watch back on her wrist, taking the opportunity to run his hand over hers, setting off another excited tingle. Every time they touched, her heart beat harder.

"Well, do you think me mad?" she asked. If he thought she was nuts, it was no go—in more ways than one. It might seem cute to plunge into a relationship with a guy who thinks you are totally crazy, but she had no time for that. She needed someone who believed in her, and in whom she could believe.

He smiled wryly. "No madder than I. The day we met was passing strange. I awoke alone that morning, with Warwick, Salisbury, and all my companions gone, as was the farmstead where we had been staying. Caesar and I were on a bare hillside." She pictured him waking up alongside his tall black Friesian stallion, staring at the empty Welsh hills, both horse and man wondering what happened in the night.

"Caesar and I went in search of my companions, finding you instead; for which I am forever thankful. But then we were attacked, and it seemed best to separate, something I would not have done except that the need was dire. Yet when I rode round to the Vale of Ewyas, I saw no sign of the men in black armor. All was as I expected, monks at Llanthony took me in and helped me find my companions. We made it down into Devon, and there Sir John Dynham and his family hid us and found us a ship that took us first to Guernsey, then to Calais."

She could tell Edward did not believe he had been in third-millennium England, and she had no way of proving it. "To me it was the same," she admitted. "I went back to where I was staying, and everything was as I remembered, except for the rose you gave me." And now that, too, was gone, burned when Greystone was burned. She had done her level best to make sense of their meeting in Wales, since her whole life turned on that moment. She still firmly believed that on that first day in Wales Edward was the one out of place. Somehow she was caught up in the spell—and not by accident, either. Jo, after all, had planned that hike for her in detail, talking her into it in the first place, plotting out her path, even lending her the jacket. "Someone cast a spell on you," she told him. "Most probably the duchess of Bedford. A spell that took you out of your own time, to a place many years hence, where they waited to capture you."

"Why go to so much trouble as that?" he wondered. "Why not turn me straight into a toad and be done with it?"

"Witchcraft does not work that way. You are under a protection that does not allow you to be harmed by magic." She told him about last night's talk with John-Amend-All, and how that ghostly archer was watching over him. "Whatever was done to you had to be something harmless and agreeable. So instead of hurting you, they brought you forward to my place and time—England in the far, far future, where men waited to take you. But John-Amend-All appeared and warned you."

And when that did not work, she was sent back as bait, to lure him into yet another trap. Or so it seemed. She did not like the implications of that—it meant Edward was, indeed, under a love spell, as well. Another "not harmful" way of getting control of a man, particularly a young, headstrong, and energetic lad like Edward. But why her? Was he fated to fall in love with the first woman he met? Or had she been part of the plan from the start? Whatever the answer, it had certainly made a mess out of her life. She could feel herself really falling for this brave, caring fair-haired boy—but at the same time desperately wanting to be home, even if it meant leaving him.

Edward took her hand, pressing it prayerfully between his palms. Alert brown eyes looked hopefully into hers. "Robyn Stafford from Holy Wood, in America, I have never before owed my life to a woman. Except, of course, my mother." What could she say to that? They had not even spent a whole day together, and already they had twice been in dire straits, forced to come to each other's aid under desperate circumstances. She could not honestly keep track of who had saved whom—and when.

"Will you come with me to Calais?" Edward asked, smiling like he knew her answer. "I mentioned it when first we met, saying how much you would love it." Indeed he had. She remembered him saying he was headed for Calais, or maybe Ireland. At the time she thought he was mad, or maybe lying. Now she was about to step ashore in Ireland—after a wild battle-at-sea-saved-by-Irish-pirates second date. His grin widened. "I would not be so forward and abrupt, but Earl Warwick's fleet sails from Waterford for Calais with the morrow's tide. If we are to see Calais, we must sail with them."

"Yes," she agreed. "I will go with you to Calais." How had he described it? A fabulous port city ringed with castles—"full of fine wines and beautiful fabrics." How could she resist? He was who she had come here to see, and if he was going to Calais, then she would go with him. Seeing his absolute heartfelt delight at her answer made her smile, amused by such obvious enthusiasm. Edward was far too young and straightforward to conceal his happiness or even to want to hide it.

●

PART 3

The Heart of England

Bring forth that sorceress, condemned to burn.
—Shakespeare, *Henry VI*

⤙⤚ Inglorious First of June ⤙⤚

S he sailed from Waterford aboard the *Trinity*, the broad-beamed flagship
of the earl of Warwick—leaving Eire behind, bound for Calais.
Trinity had a bulging swan's-breast bow, a towering spread of canvas,
and sumptuous accommodations between decks. From the carrack's
stern gallery, she could see the small fleet of warships and transports
fanning out on either beam under blue skies. Sailing on the *Trinity*
was Earl Warwick's mother, the Countess of Salisbury—with Robyn
attached to her household at Edward's request. Crusty old Countess
Alice—the only woman attainted for treason by the Devil's Parliament, and Edward's aunt by marriage—was white-haired and well
upholstered, with none of the duchess of Bedford's supernatural
beauty. Fifty or so, and prematurely old, Countess Alice had a comfortable broken-down appearance, and a pudding-and-cream complexion. She had several grown sons—one an earl, another a bishop—
and a half-dozen younger daughters.

Charmed by her smooth young nephew, Countess Alice accepted
Robyn happily—"Such a well-spoken young woman is godsend, surrounded as we are by these wild and witless Irish." Robyn hid her
smile behind a deep curtsy, amused to hear this white-haired Saxon
countess unconsciously parroting Owen Boy O'Neill's praise. Edward
told his aunt she was an orphan—true. From a good Staffordshire
family—false. Who owned their farm in freehold—true. And she recently served in the households of Sir Collingwood Grey and Lord
Grey de Ruthyn—partly true. Assuring his aunt that she would be a
splendid addition to her household-in-exile—hopefully true. Seeing
how easily Edward got his way with old Countess Alice was a bit
disconcerting. Was she being charmed as easily? Hopefully not.

She did her absolute best to please the countess, taking charge of
the old noblewoman's gold-embossed chamber pot while giving out
the latest Kenilworth gossip. After months in exile, the entire household was starved for news of home. Any gaffes she made or gaps in
her narrative—things she should have known—were glossed over as
the result of her rural upbringing in Staffordshire. Certainly no one
thought she was from some far-off horribly advanced future, just a
bit slow and forgetful.

Standing on the stern castle, emptying out the enamel chamber pot,
she watched the world-circling Ocean swallow up the Emerald Isle.
Owen Boy O'Neill was right: Ireland was magic. In her one-day stay
she had not seen a single snake, toad, scorpion, or dragon. Nor did
she see much of Edward, whose time was totally consumed in getting
set to sail. For company she got one of those "wild, witless Irish" a
dreamy redheaded half-Welsh half-Irish teenager named Deirdre—
"Just like the sad lady in the sagas." Deirdre had come from the
household of the exiled Lord Clinton, a handsome fair-haired ally of
York, and one of the poorest members of the baronage, forced to sell
off his serving girls—even the pretty ones—just to make ends meet.
Hired to be her chambermaid, Deirdre believed in all manner of amazing things, like blond leprechauns that lived underground, and that
barnacles grew on trees, spending part of their lives as birds. "Serving
a well-born witch is not the maddest thing that has happened to me,"
Deirdre assured her. "Not by a Saxon mile."

Startled, she asked the red-haired serving girl, "What makes you
think I am a witch?" Or well-born, for that matter?

"O'Neills claim to have seen you flying over the wavetops on
Witches Night—but that could just be strong drink talking. It is your
speaking such good Gaelic that is proof for sure."

"How so?" she asked. When they were alone, she always spoke
Gaelic with the serving girl—though it was, in fact, illegal for "English" to use that language.

"Only magic could make a stranger speak so well. Most Saxons
could easier fly through the air than get out a single sentence." She
said nothing, not wanting to lie to Deirdre or involve the teenager too
deeply in her secrets. Just starting to admit to herself that she was a
witch, she was not the least ready to tell the world.

Deirdre hastened to reassure her, "Have no fear m'lady. I would
not tell on you." Indeed, Deirdre could not. Irish could not give evidence against Saxons or appeal to English law. And since it was high
treason to submit to Irish law—the Irish were born outlaws. It was
also treason to marry an Irishman or nurse an Irish child. Likewise it
was illegal to wear Irish clothes, take a Celtic name, graze Irish cattle,
or listen to Irish music. King Henry's court ordered Anglo-Irishmen
to shave their upper lips, lest they be mistaken for Irish. Deirdre's
impoverished parents committed a crime just by creating her—making
her illegitimate in every sense of the word.

In fact, during her one-day stay in Ireland, Robyn found herself forced to commit all manner of crimes and misdemeanors. Merely by giving justice to all and not enforcing such outrageous statutes, Edward's father made himself immensely popular. So popular locals joked that "the wildest Irishman in Ireland will soon be sworn English." When the clan chieftains got secret letters from King Henry telling them to rise up against York and the English settlers, they passed them on to the duke with expressions of astonishment. Having finally appointed a lord lieutenant who listened to them, the Saxon king now begged the Irish to kill him. Deirdre certainly had naught but good to say about the duke and his handsome sons. "Especially his oldest, the one you have put a *geis* on." By that Deirdre meant a love spell. Was it that obvious? Hopefully only to Deirdre.

She told the girl she had never put a spell on anyone—yet. Deirdre looked dubious but did not argue, happy just to have a chance, "to see the wider world."

"And you assume I am someone to see it with?" Robyn asked archly.

"But, of course," the girl answered.

"How do you know?" She hated taking responsibility for the teenager—much as she might need the help and company.

"Because you have the magic." Deirdre broke into a smile. "Even an *eejit* could see that. I would not find your like again in a thousand years."

At least. "What about your family?"

"I have none," Deirdre replied cheerfully. "None that can care for me. Why else would I be washing and cleaning for foreigners?"

"Neither do I," Robyn admitted, and took the girl with her, paying her out of the money Duchess Wydville gave her. Deirdre knew English, Gaelic, and a good bit of Welsh, and was adept at finding her way in a world that considered her completely out of place. She did the washing, slept in the corner, told outlandish tales, and eagerly ate anything Robyn refused—an absolutely perfect traveling companion.

On the first day of June, the little fleet rounded Land's End and the Runnel Stone. Blue skies and billowing white clouds stretched over the entrance to the English Channel. Crossing the wide mouth of Saint Michael's Mount Bay, they rounded the Lizard, and land fell away to port—the broad expanse of the English Channel opened up before them. Beacon fires sent up columns of smoke from Lizard Point and Black Head, showing they had been spotted by coast watchers.

Hearing a cry of, "Sail ho," Robyn looked leeward, recognizing the triangular sail beating toward them as Warwick's scouting carvel, tacking furiously, bringing urgent news from downwind—a sure sign of trouble. When the carvel got closer, a trumpet blared, signaling they had something to say. Seamen raced to take in sail, and the *Trinity* slowed, letting the carvel come alongside. The call came across the water, "Sails to leeward. Fleet ahead."

She took the news below to Countess Alice. Presently the *Trinity* put about, and the whole fleet hove to into the wind. Another trumpet sounded, this time from the flagship's stern castle, "Captain's call." Boats set out from each ship, converging on the *Trinity*, and Earl Warwick met with his captains in the admiral's cabin, directly above the women in the great cabin. Robyn waited by the cabin door for the council of war to break up, listening for Edward. Hearing boots on the stairs, she slipped out into the companionway.

Edward looked cheerful, but was already in armor, wearing a back-and-breast, loin-guard, tassets, greaves, and steel sleeves—another bad sign. Over his armor he wore a surcoat bearing his personal colors, royal blue and the purplish-red mulberry color called murrey. He told her, "Duke Holland's fleet is standing out to leeward, putting themselves between us and Calais. Fishermen say he has fifteen sail with more than a thousand men-at-arms aboard. Unless Holland turns aside, there is bound to be a battle." He sounded very matter-of-fact, but he always talked that way about fighting. At first she thought it was teenage bravado, but she was beginning to see Edward truly did not think fighting was so important. Or all that dangerous. It was merely something he had to do, and do well. His idea of a good fight was their taking the *Fortuna* without a man being killed. She was the one who worried. Was heavy steel armor the best thing for a sea battle? She supposed so, Edward not being the type to fall overboard. There was even a certain chivalry in it, since the greatest threat to the women and noncombatants aboard was that the ship might sink. Edward's armor said he refused to survive failure.

Trumpets sounded above, calling the crew to battle stations. Kissing him for luck, she let Edward go.

Unable to just sit below and wait, she went up to the quarterdeck with Deirdre, finding a spot at the port rail with a good view ahead and landward. The ship nearest to windward was the *Fortuna*, now in Earl Warwick's service, close on their port beam, blocking her view of ships farther back. Calls of "Sails, ho" came from the topcastle. Leaning hard on the rail, she peered forward, shading her eyes, seeing nothing but blue horizon and the coast of Cornwall. Gulls glided idly by, looking for lunch in their wake.

Slowly a mass of sails appeared ahead, standing out from the coast. She tried to count the masts, and gave up at a dozen. It had to be Duke Holland's fleet.

Lookouts in the topcastle called down, *"Grace à Dieu."* Meaning they had spotted the royal flagship, the *Grace à Dieu.* Men began stringing bows and rigging boarding nets, laughing and joking—showing none of the hesitancy or nervousness she had seen in the crew of the *Fortuna*, whose master had filled out his ship with landsmen, impressed boys, and Welsh shepherds. Warwick's men were experienced mariners, accustomed to winning at sea, turning handsome profits off piracy and rebellion. Even the seasick Welsh aboard the *Fortuna* were happy to join them.

Leaving Deirdre on deck, she dashed down the steps to the countess of Salisbury's cabin. Dark, cool between-decks closed around her, shutting out the clamor on the stern castle. Her countess's cabin was a whole other world, with a cut-down purple velvet canopy bed, a day couch, and a cupboard cushioned with red velvet, holding silver plate, crystal bowls, gold ewers, and filigree goblets—all tied tightly in place to protect them from the ship's pitch and roll. Sea chests contained silks, furs, and satins, along with the altar clothes, jeweled crosses, candlesticks, and vestments for Countess Alice's private chapel. If it came to a sea fight, a single stone cannonball could do untold damage.

Women crowded around the cabin windows, trying to see what was happening—without much luck. The windows were small and poorly placed for seeing the action, low down and looking right aft. They could see where the *Trinity* had been, but not what was up ahead. Countess Alice sat on her great cushioned day couch, wearing fur-trimmed velvet and an old-fashioned steeple headdress with silk streamers—hardly the outfit for a sea battle, or even a day on the water. Seeing her appear, the countess acknowledged her curtsy, asking, "What goes on above? A boy claims they saw the *Grace à Dieu.*"

She rose swiftly from her curtsy, "My lady, not just the *Grace à Dieu*, but a dozen sails besides."

Women at the windows turned to listen. Countess Alice sighed, "I suppose it is too much to hope that it might be the Venetians."

"Or the Norwegians," suggested a giggling lady-in-waiting, half amused, half afraid.

Robyn shook her head. The Venetian galleys of Flanders fled to avoid being dragged into the fight, and no one really thought it was the Norwegians. "It is His Grace, the duke of Exeter, trying to keep us from getting to Calais. Fishermen say he has fifteen sails in all, and more than a thousand men-at-arms."

Countess Alice straightened the velvet folds on her gown. "If it is indeed the duke of Exeter, then will you please go back above and tell us how His Grace is faring." Leaving Countess Alice to face the sea fight in the sturdy upholstered cabin, she raced back up to the half deck, taking steps two at a time. Deirdre looked excited, watching as great castle-like Saxon ships prepared to grapple each other. Robyn was not at all thrilled to be dragged into yet another sea battle, not so soon after her first.

Minutes blinked by on her digital watch as the two stately fleets drew closer, propelled magically by the wind. It was like watching a fascinating slow-mo collision, seeing each movement gradually unfold, but unable to stop it. Edward's happy-go-lucky "nothing will happen to me" attitude about battle lulled her into trusting him. He was sharp, athletic, and quick on his feet, and had been fighting battles since he was thirteen, claiming he had never been scratched. But that was pure gambler's fallacy—any run of luck was bound to end—one horrible moment could make up for all his escapes. Edward believed in leading by example, and an arrow could find a chink in his armor, or he could step in the way of a stone cannonball. Cheerfully taking chances did not make the risk any less real. She pictured awful things happening while she watched helplessly.

Duke Holland's fleet began to come about, turning closer into the wind, prows swinging around to meet Warwick's smaller fleet head-on. Warwick's sailors were confident, but only because they had already seen unspeakable horrors at sea, things she would rather not witness, much less be part of. Seeing it was Sunday, she prayed, closing her eyes and pleading with the Almighty—not for victory, but to avoid the whole bloody business—seeing no reason to mar this pleasant first

Sunday in June with death and mayhem. Oh, Lord, this is your day, keep it sunny and peaceful. She swore to burn a dozen candles to the Virgin if they got to Calais without a fight.

Holland's fleet kept on turning, sails flapping limp and then filling again, prows swinging totally around, going over onto a port tack. Distance between them began to open. Holland was headed back toward Devon, to a chorus of catcalls from the rebels aloft. She marveled at their jeers, given the numbers against them. If Warwick himself came about and bore down on Holland with the wind at his back, it would have drawn cheers from the men in the rigging, outnumbered though they were. To them the royal fleet was just a flock of rich prizes, wallowing along and ripe for the taking. Hearing the cheers and seeing the fleets separating, Deirdre turned to her. "Do they not mean to have a battle?" She could not believe the Saxons meant to cheat her and not crash these wooden castles together.

"Hopefully not." She hurried back down the steps to tell the countess of Salisbury. Women looked away from the windows as soon as she entered, knowing now they could learn more from her than they could ever hope to see. "Does His Grace not mean to stop us?" asked Countess Alice, seemingly disappointed by the Duke's lack of initiative.

Robyn shook her again. "Not from what I have seen."

"But you said Holland has more ships?"

"They have more ships, and bigger ships, but I doubt they have the men to really man them." She told them how Edward talked the *Fortuna*'s crew into rebellion. "None were willing to lay down their lives for Lord Rivers."

"Why ever not?" the countess asked.

Because they had bankrupt masters who barely paid them, expecting them to work for cuffs, sneers, and love of the king—but she guessed Countess Alice might not like to hear that. "I imagine their hearts are not in it."

Countess Alice thought it a thin excuse. To mollify her, Robyn admitted she did pray to Our Lord, and promise twelve candles to the Virgin just before Lord Holland turned away. Old Countess Alice looked pleased. "See girl, there is always a sensible explanation. Thank your Lord above for the miracle." And people called this a superstitious age. Countess Alice gave her some pennies to pay for candles at the Church of Saint Mary's in Calais.

Night fell, and Duke Holland retired to his lair in Devon, leaving the way to Calais open. By dawn the next day they had the Channel to themselves, aside from a few fishing smacks and foreign sails making for the French coast—lest they be dragged into an English family squabble. Unable to count on King Henry, Warwick paid his Calais garrison by raiding foreign shipping. Hearing "Land, ho!" from the masthead, she turned to see the French shore curving to meet them; ahead lay the Strait of Dover, the "twenty miles of open sea" that stopped Napoléon and Hitler. She pointed out the coast of France to Deirdre—who would have nodded just as gravely if she had told her it was Tibet.

Calling it France did not make it any more familiar. She knew France had to be in the Middle Ages, too—but to see nothing but fishing villages dotting the coast still shocked her. No highways. No resort hotels. No yacht harbors. Nothing but sailboats on the water. Europe was dotted with tiny peasant villages connected by dirt roads, more backwards than Paraguay. No autobahns. No Eiffel Tower. King Henry's crazy relatives living in the Louvre. Absolutely amazing. Yet the sails on the water looked beautiful, gliding along with just the wind. There was a whimsical charm to a world where you had to ride or sail to get anywhere.

Past Cape Gris-Nez, the land curved back to the east. By now she was in the Pas de Calais, coasting along sandy French shoreline, threading between dangerous shoals and off-shore currents that could sweep a fleet into the North Sea. Calais seemed to rise out of the sand. Coastal dunes ended in a tall round tower guarding the harbor entrance, where curving jetties led into a narrow anchorage right under the turreted walls of Calais. Blue sea, white sands, and flat green fields surrounded the fortified port, forming a stunning panorama, as spectacular as Edward claimed. Windmills sat in the low fields, their giant fanlike arms flailing at the breeze, and flying over it all was King Henry's lion and fleur-de-lis banner, a little bit of England on the coast of France. Deirdre sighed, "You Saxons do know how to build big." If this girl thought Calais was something, what would Deirdre say to London? Or Paris? She hoped she had done the right thing, bringing her out of Wexford.

Warwick's fleet sailed between the jetties, dropping anchor beneath the walls. Just coming ashore was a scene, with all Calais turning out to greet them; wool mongers and dockworkers, street urchins, seamstresses, and washerwomen, knights, ladies, and soldiers of the garrison, all lined up behind the mayor and comptroller in their heavy robes of office, and the Merchants of the Staple in their resplendent livery. Waiting by the gangway were Lords Fauconberg and Audley in red, silver, and gold. Fauconberg was a lesser Neville—Salisbury's younger brother. Audley was son to the Lord Audley that Collin saw killed at Blore Heath, a curious recruit who came to Calais to fight the rebels and ended up joining them.

Calais was the only bit of England the rebels controlled—even if it was in France—so they aimed to make the most of their return. Without morning papers or network news, people here and now had to make repeated public statements, even if it was as simple as church on Sunday, or wearing a lord's livery, or a lady's colors. She liked that about the Middle Ages. All politics was personal. Edward and the Neville earls had returned to Calais. Henry Holland, duke of Exeter, and all the king's ships had not dared to stop them. To show how happy and humbled they were, the returning heroes marched straight up through the water gate to the Church of Saint Mary's, showered with flowers from the rooftops. And she went with them, cheered all the way to the church—as if they had conquered Holland, instead of merely avoiding him. At Saint Mary's they all got down on their knees—the countess, the rebel earls, the captains, knights, and commoners—all enthusiastically thanking Heaven for their safe return from Ireland. With Deirdre kneeling next to her, Robyn lit the dozen candles she promised to the Virgin for getting her to Calais without another sea fight.

She walked about afterwards, getting her land legs back. Deirdre cooed at the shops and cloth marts, saying, "Ooh, what a wonderful place. How good to be somewhere that does not rock beneath you. Or threaten to drown you in your sleep."

Calais turned out to be an intoxicating mix of the familiar and exotic, English for over a century—the last vestige of King Henry's once vast holdings in France, Britain's window to the wider world, the only part of England bordering on continental Europe. She heard English, French, Flemish, Latin, Venetian, and Danish spoken in the markets. With no peasant hinterland to oppress, Calais lived off trade and commerce; almost everyone had something to do, and from what she could see, did it well. Merchants sold pickled herring, Gascon wine, Italian lace, and Louvain gloves, taking Scots guilders, Louis d'Or, and Venetian ducats, then weighing out change in Dutch groats or English pennies. Most of all they sold cloth and wool; everything from fine crimson damask to sturdy washables, like unbleached Dutch linens, fustian, and cloth of Rennes. Normally all exported English wool was sold through Calais by the Merchants of the Staple, who had a royal monopoly—but now Calais was embargoed and blockaded, making new Cotswolds wool a rarity, smuggled in at inflated prices—"M'lady, this fine cloth is of the very best Gloucestershire wool, coming all the way from the Cotswolds."

She shook her head, saying, "So did I."

"You did?" The clothier looked taken aback. "But you speak Walloon so well?"

Walloon? Was that what they were speaking?

"Does my m'lady like silk?" the cloth-seller asked. "This came all the way from Far Cathay."

She ran her hand over an African-looking cotton print, saying, "Where does this come from?"

"Brasil," he replied proudly, holding up the cloth for her to see.

"Brazil?" She wondered if she had misheard him—they were, after all, speaking Walloon, a language she never knew existed.

"Yes, a big island in the Atlantic. Have you not heard of it?"

"Yes." She was just surprised that he had, thirty years before Columbus. Deirdre hung on her arm, wide-eyed with wonder.

Her second day in Calais, she fell sick—something she had dreaded every day since she arrived here and now. She and Deirdre had been given a room in the countess of Salisbury's town house. Duties were light, and she saw little of Countess Alice, who now had her husband's household-in-exile to manage, no longer needing to make do with half-Irish serving girls and strangers from Staffordshire. Which was well, because she awoke on Tuesday morning deathly ill, and with no good reason. She had conscientiously boiled her water, bathed every day she could, lost a dozen pounds picking through her food, and been merciless toward ticks and fleas, killing every one she could find.

But it had done no good; she found herself flat on her back, weak, feverish, and frightened out of her wits. Worst of all, she did not know what it was—more than a cold for sure; otherwise, who knows? Cholera and dysentery came with diarrhea, which she did not have, thank goodness. Whatever it was, even Deirdre's wild optimism could not cure it. Though Deirdre tried, offering up Irish remedies, made from dirt, bread mold, and boiled rose hips. As a sign of how desperate she was, she actually swallowed the mess—which only made her feel worse.

Edward came to see her, looking concerned, the first she had seen him since leaving Saint Mary's the day they landed. Their tête-à-tête by the stern castle stair with Holland's fleet bearing down on them had been their most personal time together since leaving Ireland. And now, on his first visit to her place, she lay in a shift and blankets, flat on her back, feeling like death warmed over.

She asked what the symptoms were for plague. "Black rotting pustules," Edward announced cheerfully. "Under the arms and around the privates, oozing foul-smelling pus."

Good to hear. She had seen nothing like that. And she did not smell foul, just sickly.

"Followed by bleeding boils and black blotches, along with terrible pain and . . ."

She raised a weak hand. "Enough, enough." So it was not the plague. For all she knew, she could probably die of a head cold here and now.

"It is all those baths you take," Edward suggested. "Wetting yourself all over on cold mornings."

Deirdre disagreed, while ladling clear warm vegetable soup down Robyn's grateful throat. It perked her up a bit to hear them arguing over outlandish treatments—debating the virtues of a sweat bath to bring down her fever, versus swabbing her naked body with brandy—Edward's idea—half in Gaelic, half in Latin, and all hilariously unhelpful. Edward came back two more days in a row, by which time she still did not feel any better. "Do your best to live," he suggested, "at least long enough to come to Bruges with me."

"Bruges?" She had never heard of the place.

Edward described a serenely beautiful city of canals and stately mansions, "the Venice of Flanders. I must go there soon, and I would that you will go with me."

Nice thought. But Bruges sounded a long way off, especially when she could barely get out of bed. However, he wrung a promise out of her to think about it, and went away pleased, clearly expecting her to live. But being an earl did not make Edward a doctor.

Next night was Witches Night. Sick and exhausted, with no one but Deirdre to help her, she decided this Witches Night would just have to pass without her. Drinking another of Deirdre's Irish concoctions, she lapsed into a deep coma. Only to dream furiously. She was back in her Hollywood apartment, lying on the couch. Heidi was there, phone in her ear, making calls and cooking something in the kitchen. Suddenly she was hungry, feeling like she had not eaten a real meal in weeks. But when Heidi brought the food over, it was the very worst sort of medieval fare—quail eggs and eel pie in fish aspic, crawling with lice. Heidi knelt beside her, trying to spoon-feed her this mess. Nauseated, she threatened to throw up all over her living room couch. "Thank goodness." Heidi heaved a happy sigh, upending the eel pie and aspic into the garbage disposal. "I am a production assistant, not a nurse."

"Why not order out?" Robyn begged.

"Of course," Heidi picked up the phone and started to punch. "Kenilworth's having a boar's-head special with blood pudding. But it is hard to beat the Cokyntryce and ox tripe at Trader Vic's. Do you think they deliver?" Robyn gave up, slipping gratefully back into her coma.

For the first time in weeks, she woke up wondering where she was, lying in a big feather bed instead of her apartment couch, staring about the town-house bedroom, with its ornate fireplace and leaded glass windows looking out on Calais. In place of Heidi, she saw a red-haired young girl in a green dress tending to the fire, singing snatches of Gaelic to herself. Understandable Gaelic at that. Deirdre looked up, smiling to see her awake. That happy Irish grin brought it all back—her trip to the past, her flight to Wales, followed by Ireland, Calais, and then her fatal illness; home and Heidi had been a dream.

"Doing better?" Deirdre asked. Amazingly, she was. Her fever had vanished, replaced by ravenous hunger, which Deirdre fed with fresh bread and Irish stew. She had survived her greatest fear since arriving here. Dying of some dread medieval disease had been her most fixed expectation since coming to Merry Olde England. Burning at the stake was spectacularly fearsome, but fear of disease dictated everything she did, what she ate, what she drank, how often she washed, even where she slept. Surviving this bout of sickness was another Witches Night victory—as big as any that had come before. She went shopping to celebrate her recovery, buying silks, satins, and fine woolens, designing fanciful outfits in her head, starting with a pantsuit for riding, and matching jackets, Deirdre's in green velvet, hers in Edward's murrey and blue.

Two days later the pantsuit was done. Deirdre had gone to do a wash, but came bounding back up the stairs and into the room, swearing, "There is a great white horse waiting by the kitchen gate." Going down to investigate, she found a beautiful pure white mare in the alley behind the town house, blowing clouds of steam in the cold morning air. Her saddle and bridle were crimson leather, and her reins were held by a young page in murrey and blue.

Going down on his knee, the page offered her the mare's reins, saying, "Please m'lady, a gift from my lord Edward of March."

"Why ever?" was all she could say.

"My lord Edward wants to go riding," the kneeling page explained. "He waits by the Milk Gate."

For a teenage exile, Edward had style. As did the mare he sent, looking to be part Arab, with an arching neck and high tail, but acting more amiable than any Arabian she ever knew, standing patiently among strangers in a narrow alley, waiting to see what these humans wanted. Telling the page to wait, she raced back up to her room to change. While she did, Deirdre scurried about, packing bread, cheese, figs, and apples into a saddlebag. Good idea. She had not had breakfast, and it was too much to expect that Edward would think of it. That fantastic gift horse below was about the best you could expect from a man—food, too, was out of the question.

Giving Deirdre a grateful hug and kiss, she bolted out the door. Back down at the kitchen gate, the page looked shocked by her murrey-and-blue pantsuit, but that could hardly be helped; besides the boy left home to get an education. Instead she concentrated on the mare, stroking her and talking to her. When the horse seemed ready, she hoisted herself onto the crimson saddle. The mare looked curiously back at her, not seeming to mind. Good enough. Splendid, actually. It was weeks since she had been riding—an amazing change from her days on the run, when she and Collin lived in the saddle. Reaching down, she accepted the reins from the page, saying, "Take me to your earl." They set off down the alley toward the Milk Gate behind Saint Mary's, the mare's iron shoes ringing on the cobbles.

Edward waited at the Milk Gate atop Caesar, bareheaded and smiling broadly—but wearing half-armor, a shining back-and-breast, steel sleeves, loin guards, gauntlets, and big riding boots with the tops turned down. His steel sallet, gorget, and bevor hung from his black charger's high saddle, and he had a lance in his right hand, and a sword at his side. Some picnic. And the page had thought her pantsuit strange. "How do you feel?" Edward asked.

"Better than ever," she happily admitted, thrilled to be atop such a gorgeous horse.

"I thought you might live. How do you like your new mare?"

"She is outstanding, an incredible delight. How can I—?" She felt silly. This white mare was a wonderful gift she could not hope to repay—but one he could well afford. Even in exile, stripped of his lands and income, he still had hundreds of horses and men at his command.

Edward's smile widened. "Her name is Lily. What use is there in riding if you are not well mounted?"

What use, indeed? Horses were for riding. Life was for living. She reached down and patted Lily's warm white shoulder, amazed at how solid and real her new mare felt. Edward never seemed to count the cost of something he wanted, an admirable if reckless trait. Making the armor he wore today all the more ominous. Tactfully, she asked if he expected a battle—"Or just a joust?"

His look turned apologetic. "Calais is under siege. Leave her walls, and we must be prepared for anything."

But, of course. And by now she felt pretty much prepared for anything; still, it would be nice to have a date with Edward that did not begin or end with a battle. Trotting out the Milk Gate, she liked the look of the Calais pale, seeing sunny water meadows, sleek peaceful spotted cattle, and a stone church dedicated to Saint Peter. Wet ditches were choked with lush grasses, white water lilies, and bright yellow blossoms. Windmills turned in the wind, keeping low dyked fields from flooding, while peasants cut flax and hay, working to stay ahead of the rain—a vibrant Brueghel landscape, waiting for the artist to be born.

She relaxed, riding stirrup to stirrup with her knight, chatting happily. What a fantastic feeling this was—to be able to say what she pleased without being watched or overheard. She had learned to take medieval ways for granted—to sleep, dress, and bathe with someone beside her. Even privies hardly ever had separate stalls. Privacy lay somewhere in the far future. Yet for the moment, they were completely alone. No ship full of sailors. No noble household. No crowded mini-city under siege, just them and their horses.

Edward pointed out the fortified bridge at Newnham, guarding the road to Boulogne. "Last month the duke of Somerset came up from Guines to take it, but failed." Henry Beaufort, duke of Somerset—Joy's legitimate half brother—held out for King Henry in Guines Castle, just to the south. Past Newnham Bridge they were in disputed territory; with Guines and the little swamp-ringed castle of Hammes in enemy hands, regular raids and counterraids took place across the green "Pale." Edward had picked the most convenient means to be alone with her, picnicking in no-man's-land.

Halting on a patch of high ground, near a huge creaking windmill, Edward dismounted and then helped her down. Flat green countryside shone like polished jade. Edward pointed out the towers of Hammes and Guines poking above the marshes. Deciding it was safe, he loosened the straps on his armor, taking off his gauntlets and unbuckling the tassets on his loin guards so he could sit more easily. A knight's saddle is so high and stiff, he practically stands in his stirrups. Pulling a bag off his mount, Edward proudly announced he had brought a wine sack and meat pastries. She smiled, showing him the cheese, figs, bread, and apples she brought, sure that breakfast would be up to her. For a teenage noble, Edward could be marvelously thoughtful. As he unslung his sword to sit, she took it from him, saying, "May I?"

Edward nodded, and she drew the big blade from its scabbard. Held two-handed, the sword was not near as heavy as she thought it would be, feeling like a sharp steel wand shining in the sun. She took a practice swing, slicing empty air.

"Good," exclaimed Edward, "only keep your shoulders level and pivot from the hips, putting your whole body into the swing. She swung harder, letting the sword carry her around, like it was a living thing. "*Très bon.*" He clapped his hands. "Try to straighten your right wrist more. Swing the sword instead of letting it swing you."

She did not mean to become expert at it—witchcraft was more her forte. Why play a game men would win? Witchcraft was how women leveled the playing field—so naturally it was loathed and illegal. Besides, Joan beat them in battle and was burned, anyway. She took another swing. "I just wanted to see how it feels. You know, experiencing male authority firsthand." This was an age when men literally wielded power, with their own arms, against each other's bodies—but hopefully not against hers. "This is one way you are centuries ahead of us." Light-years, actually.

"Really?" Edward seemed proud to put one over on the future.

She slid the sword back in its sheath. "You know how to fight the right way, settling your differences with blades and arrows. Mostly." Scary as Edward's sword was, it was infinitely better than a .357. Not to mention a nuke.

"How do you settle your differences?" Edward had every boy's prurient interest in weaponry.

She settled down beside him, to share the food they had brought. "I would rather not talk about it. Let us just say those popgun cannons you use get a lot worse." The Middle Ages could be rightly proud of its primitive weapons, which made war much safer and everyday life less of a risk. Two great modern killers, handguns and traffic accidents, were completely eliminated. Every so often people here and now went on berserk rampages—like Mad Henry's French grandfather—but how many innocent bystanders can you actually get with a lance?

Sitting on the grass, eating figs, he asked, "What is your England like?"

"My England?" She licked fig juice off her fingers.

"Yes, this far-off future England where you say we met. To me, things seemed very much the same, though I was well lost until you appeared with your wonderful map."

Staring off over the Calais pale, she tried to summon up modern England—not as easy as it should have been. Was the Displacement Spell stealing her memories? "It has many more people. And many more things. And goes way faster. Horseless wagons made of steel race along monstrous tarred roadways, taking people from city to city. And the cities are huge. Bath is twice as big as London is today. And London is enormous. One solid city from Dartford almost to Windsor, holding many more people than in all of Britain and Ireland today."

She glanced over at Edward to see how he was taking this—not over well, from the look of it. Hoping to soften the blow, she offered bread and cheese to go with the figs, using her saxe knife to slice it. "But the biggest change is in the way people think. There is still royalty and nobility, but it is the common people who make the laws and see they are carried out. Weapons are banned—only the police and army can carry them. There is no private war, no trial by combat, no livery and maintenance."

Edward chewed thoughtfully on his bread and cheese, clearly not looking forward to his country's future. "What a passing strange place."

"Not really." She split a new fig for herself.

Edward arched an eyebrow. "How so?"

"Much of it already lives in the hearts of your people, especially the women, who are weary of misrule and private war. Everyone dislikes being robbed and beaten by men wearing a lord's livery, or seeing justice perverted, and juries bribed and intimidated. Everyone I talked to just wants justice for all, and the freedom to live their lives as they will."

"That is what we are fighting for," Edward insisted, "for freedom and justice, and an end to misrule."

Words like *freedom* and *justice* came easily to a fair-haired boy raised in privilege, bowed to every day, and loved by all, one sure things would always go his way. "I mean justice for everyone," she told him, turning the fig inside out, "not just for nobles and ladies. Freedom for the lowest turnspit and washerwoman, to do what they wish and dwell where they would."

Edward shook his head. "You speak boldly, Robin Stafford."

She shrugged, tearing at the fig with fingers and teeth, trying not to make a mess. "Women in America speak as we please." Within limits.

He looked down at her riding pants, done in his blue-and-purple livery. "And dress boldly, as well."

"We also dress as we please." Particularly in Hollywood.

"Here, women must be more circumspect," he reminded her. "In Rouen where I was born, they burned the Maid of Orléans for making magic, wearing men's clothes, and talking back to her betters." By the Maid of Orléans, he meant Joan of Arc.

She looked him straight in the face. "I also talk to spirits in their own tongue." Not exactly the same as Joan's saintly visions and voices, but awfully close.

"Are you not afraid?" Edward asked.

Sure, but she did not mean to show it. Boys in armor were not the only ones allowed to be brave. Finishing her fig, she put down the husk, wiping her hands on the grass. "Need I be?"

He shook his head. "Not so long as you are my lady. I swear I will give even my life to save you from harm." Edward was not one for empty words, having so far done everything he said, short of subduing the king.

"Thank you most mightily, my lord." She meant it—what good was speaking your mind if it merely got you burned? She was glad to have Edward's protection, and he was clearly her lord. She depended on him and even wore his livery—her position in the countess of Salisbury's household being mere convenience; handsome unmarried earls in exile did not need pretty serving women. For all its bawdy barbarity, it was a curiously innocent age, pious and churchgoing, but prone to secret scandal—sin was frowned on rather than punished. Divorce was difficult, but bastardry rife.

He reached over and took her hand. "And what does Lady Robyn most want?"

"To go home." She had sworn to be honest with him.

"Happily, that is one thing I cannot do for you." He raised her hand to his lips, licking the fig juice off her fingertips. She felt the tingle all the way to her toes. "For I would miss you most grievously."

"And I would miss you, as well." Her body tensed against desire. She had not come to the Middle Ages to fall in love—in fact, she had not meant to come here at all. Staying alive, and a step ahead of the witch hunters, was far more urgent. Having this handsome, headstrong teenager for her lord and master was an amazing novelty, but she felt the need to warn him—"My lord, it is not enough to want me. You must want all of me, my mind and heart as well as my body."

He grinned at her over her hand, which was still at his lips. "My lady, I would not have it any other way. You are my window into tomorrow. I find everything about you fascinating." He said it simply and sincerely—not flattery, just how he felt.

We shall see. That could just be the love spell talking. Or mayhap male hormones. Edward's lips went from her hand to her mouth, but all they did was kiss—being in half-armor made him very manageable. Had he been wearing less steel, he might have gotten farther; a lesson for all young knight errants in love. This was their first date where they were not in a sea fight, facing capture, or just being chased by mystery bowmen and black riders. She meant to take it slow for a change, resisting any temptation to tear off his breastplate and get at the chain mail underneath.

Instead they sat on dewy grass, with huge windmill blades creaking overhead, talking about hopes and dreams between kisses—her stalled acting career, his need to free England from court tyranny. Edward wanted to know all about her growing up in Montana, and what it was like to be a teenager in America. "Montana," she admitted, "was a lot like here. Not flat like Flanders—in fact the name means 'mountains'—but I grew up on a cattle ranch with few neighbors and not many kids nearby."

"But you had brothers and sisters?"

"Nope"—she shook her head—"an only child. Of course, I had TV and the Internet—the whole world at my fingertips. Got to chat with folks from all over the planet. You know, teenagers from Trinidad. Chinese child-molesters who liked saying nasty things to little round-eyed girls—that sort of thing. But not what you would call real friends." Edward sympathized, though he clearly only took in half of it—but he really did want to know her, not caring if it was not easy.

"Oh, I made up for it," she assured him, "overcompensating all I could, riding competitively, going to college, becoming Miss Rodeo Montana, moving to L.A. Hollywood was going to make a big star out of me."

"In those Holy Wood passion plays?"

She nodded. "But then my parents died, and in some ways I ended up more alone than ever. We lived in different states, but we talked a lot, and I would go home for Christmas. Suddenly, I had no one I was close to. Except for Heidi." And Collin.

"Heidi?"

"She called me from Hawaii that first day in Wales—remember? You thought my phone was a bird. Heidi is kind of wild, but loving to a fault. And thinks the world of you, by the way. Hopes we hit it off famously—your original born optimist."

Pleased to hear that, Edward took her hand again. "This Heidi has your best hopes at heart. My family will be your family. You will love them all. I have my father, the duke; a most wise and pious mother; a half-dozen brothers and sisters—and my mother was born a Neville, so I have a whole army of cousins." Literally. "All the relations you could want, really."

And more. Marrying Edward meant marrying his whole extended clan-cum-armed-rebellion. What woman would not want to think it over? Rains came, putting an end to the picnic. She helped buckle the steel tassets to his armor, and tightened the straps on his back-and-breast; then she mounted Lily and they rode joyously back through the downpour. Their best date yet. She got home to Deirdre drenched but happy, finding her serving girl already had a fire going. Stable boys saw to her new mare, while Deirdre helped her undress, toweled her dry, and then slipped her into clothes warmed by the fire—all the time demanding "details" in Gaelic. Wishing some lord would send her, "a great Saxon horse and an invitation to go riding."

Having the luck of the Irish, as well as the Welsh, Deirdre got her wish. Days later a horse arrived for her—this time a chestnut gelding. Edward evidently gave away horses like Elvis gave away Cadillacs. With the gelding came an invitation for them to accompany Edward to Bruges, as guests of Lord Gruthuyse, whoever that was. Flurries of packing followed, plus riding lessons for Deirdre, who had ridden plow horses and Irish hobbies, but not a lady's palfrey.

Then they were off, riding through flat Flemish countryside with an escort of men-at-arms and mounted archers and protected by a safe-conduct from Philip the Good, duke of Burgundy—the first time she had set foot out of English-ruled territory, though she had been to Wales, Ireland, and France. Crossing at tidal fords, they threaded their way past colorful Gypsy caravans and through herds of swine headed for the Calais markets, giving the trip a holiday air. Edward amused Deirdre by attempting gallantries in Gaelic, mangling phrases heard during his stay in Ireland. Watching him struggle to compliment a serving girl in a language few English deigned to speak—which it was a felony even to use—showed how much he had the common touch. Edward might have been born in France, but he was still a hayseed earl from the Marches—who had never been formally presented at court. She liked that, and told him so.

He shrugged at the compliment. "Not many of the nobility support us." Edward merrily ticked off his enemies on gloved fingers: "Beaufort, Clifford, Holland, de Vere, the Percys, Pembroke, Stafford, and Lancaster, all arrayed against us, the finest and greatest nobles in the land, save only my family and the Nevilles." House of Lords for Mad King Henry. Edward never bothered to belittle his enemies, always giving them their due. Nor did he stoop to hating them—a wise policy when he had so many. He had a fondness for Owen Boy O'Neill, an outlaw and rebel against his father, and he let Collin go free, asking only that Collin someday return the favor. "So," Edward concluded happily, "we cannot but love the commons, for if we do win, it will be because of them. And the Church," he added. "That is why we are going to Bruges, to meet with Bishop Coppini, the pope's legate, who plans to settle our English differences peacefully."

Lots of luck, she thought. Pope Pius's legate better have miracles up his golden sleeve. Bruges—which meant "bridges"—was as spectacular as promised, built on riverbanks and canals, the ancient capital of Flanders and now a great wool mart and banking center. Arching bridges connected "islands" crowded with tall mansions, covered markets, and soaring stone churches dedicated to Saint Christopher and Saint Peter, to the Virgin, and the Holy Savior. She and Deirdre got an ornate bedroom in a palace-mansion at the end of the Djiver canal. Light and airy, the room had a huge walk-in fireplace, and paneled walls hung with priceless paintings by Flemish masters—breathtaking landscapes done in vivid colors, deft textures, and stunning detail. Outside her tall stone windows lay the town and country that inspired the paintings, dominated by the massive castle of the counts of Flanders, with its turreted walls and fortified bridges.

Here she had her first Witches Night since that strange Hollywood fever dream in Calais. Deirdre would have been glad to help, but she waited until the girl was asleep, having already drawn Deirdre too deeply into her troubles. Setting her watch to wake her, Robyn left the closed canopy bed to cast her circle alone on the floor. She did not attempt a Witches Flight, merely reaching out to Jo, trying to make contact—hoping to find where Jo and Joy were held. Kneeling in silence, broken only by Deirdre's soft breathing, she reached out to Jo, trying to the point of total collapse, but she could not break through. Something walled her off from Jo, something as heavy and tangible as stone, a massive wall so real she could feel the rock and mortar.

Her host, Louis de Bruges, Seigneur de Gruthuyse, was a friendly, cultured nobleman in his thirties, pious looking, with thoughtful brown eyes, bowl-cut bangs, and a long elegant nose. He entertained them with feasts, music, dancing, and hawking, choral odes and masquerades. At a *danse macabre* she met the object of Edward's mission, Bishop Francesco Coppini, the papal legate, a small excitable Italian. Skeletal dancers dressed like Death wound about the floor, pulling knights, ladies, pages, and servants into the dark dance—while the pope's legate preached the virtues of peace, begging Edward in Latin to "cease civil strife and accept King Henry's good lordship."

Edward swore he would, "If there is any good lordship to be gotten."

"Will you make peace with King Henry?" The Italian demanded a direct answer. "Putting aside all thoughts of vengeance?"

"If King Henry wills it," Edward replied evenly. "He is my liege lord. How can I can have peace unless he so desires?"

She did not hear how the legate answered, because at that moment she and Deirdre were touched by Death and swept up into the dance. Not until the dance was done and the pope's man had left, did she get Edward alone. Walking together in Louis of Bruges's torch-lit garden, she asked how things had gone with the talkative Italian.

"He hopes to make a peace between King Henry and us." From the way Edward said it, she could tell he thought the chances were slight.

"That is what everyone hopes." With the exception of monsters like FitzHolland and Le Boeuf, everyone she met in England hoped King Henry could settle things peacefully. "Being a priest must make him want peace all the more."

Edward laughed at her naiveté. "He wants us to make peace in England so we can all join in a grand crusade against the Turks, or perhaps the French." So much for Pope Pius II's good intentions. She had hoped the Church might somehow broker a peace—now it appeared the pope merely wanted a wider war.

"That is why Philip the Good supports him," Edward explained. "Burgundy is already near to war with France, and Duke Philip loves to think himself a new Jason, leading his Order of the Golden Fleece up the Hellespont to free Constantinople from the Turk."

"And what do you think?" She hoped Edward was not the least tempted by a Crusade against the Turks—holy wars had no appeal for her.

Edward smiled ruefully. "One war at a time is sufficient."

She squeezed his hand in agreement. "His Holiness is right, even if for the wrong reasons." Seeing his questioning look, she told him, "Not about attacking the French and the Turks. About making peace at home. Everyone in England wants peace, and the sooner the better." She was speaking for the people she knew, serving women and alewives, sailors and milkmaids, not to mention the nuns praying in their cloisters and knights like Collin, who had seen enough war to be sickened.

He smiled at her. "Do you realize that you called England home?"

Another medieval first. She tried to dismiss it by saying, "Only because we are in Calais."

"Bruges," Edward reminded her, tickled by her slip.

"Home or not, England prays for peace." She would not let him change the subject.

He turned serious. "What if peace means keeping Mad King Henry on the throne?" Edward sounded as if he did not know the answer himself.

"Especially if it means keeping King Henry," she insisted. "What matters is how England is governed, not who happens to be king. People cannot wait about for the right king to be born, they need good governance now and in the years to come, no matter who sits on the throne. Henry is a fine figurehead, and that is what England needs—a nonambitious, not too bright king, well able to take orders. Henry could easily be that." The Royal Council would run things anyway, and with a figurehead king, the Council would have to answer to commons—particularly if they wanted to vote taxes. Not a true constitutional monarchy perhaps, but a start.

He looked askance at her. "I suppose this is how things are in America?"

"Not at all—we have been doing fine without a king for a couple of centuries." Or making do with an elected one.

"So what would you have us do?"

"Just what His Holiness wants." Except for the part about fighting the Turks. "Let the Church negotiate a peace between you and King Henry, a peace that people can live with."

Edward surprised her by saying softly, "That is what I will say to Warwick and Salisbury."

"Really?" She was shocked to have won him over so easily.

He held tight to her hand. "Yes. And this must be a secret between you and me. I think it would be mad to make my father king by putting a bloodstained crown on his brow. So long as Henry will serve, we need no other king." As his father's oldest son and heir, Edward was renouncing the crown for himself as well—a remarkable sign of sanity. "Peace and compromise can get us what we want, while wanton killing will lose us all." His rueful smile returned. "And we cannot lose by being generous, since whatever offers we make, Her Majesty the queen will instantly reject them."

So why not offer the Moon? In her heart she knew it was true—but the queen was just one woman, a foreigner like her. Summoning up her courge, she told him, "Take me with you."

Edward looked taken aback. "Take you where?"

"To England when you go." All Calais knew "the lords" were planning a descent on England. And soon. One of Edward's tasks was to talk Bishop Coppini into coming with them.

"Please, my lady, ask anything else of me." Clearly Edward planned to keep her in Calais, away from the fighting. Picnicking, trips to Bruges, and a pair of gift horses had all the signs of a charm offensive, softening her up for tearful surrender on his last night in Calais.

Nice try, but she was not born in 1460. He was not going to get a tender good-bye in the sack just by sailing off to war, leaving her waiting faithfully by the water gate. It was all of her, or nothing. "What I want is to go with you."

"Why?" He looked genuinely puzzled. "What would you do there?"

"I would watch over you and keep you safe." And honest as well, she added to herself. Two months ago she just wanted the Middle Ages wiped away, thrown back into the pit of the past. Now she cared about these people and their lives—more so than was safe. Must be the spell at work. "How can England ever hope to be my home if you leave me in Calais?"

Edward's smile returned. "And I did want to keep you safe." Edward, who never feared for himself, worried for her, just as she worried for him. Despite their vast differences, she had never felt such immediate sympathy with any man, never known a man whose concerns were so close to hers—who held honor, love, and family above all else, whose favorite sport was dancing and whose ideal in a woman was her. That he was young and she from the future made them both new to this world, able to see things not just as they were, but as they might be; an England freed of her ancient quarrels, with justice and mercy for all. She leaned forward and kissed him, giving him something to take his mind off his fears, whispering in his ear, "Together we can do it right."

Faced with an argument he could not resist, Edward gave in. "It appears I can deny you nothing. Let us hope we are not sorry."

One of the fun things about Edward was how he instantly responded to her touch. She could always get this brash young earl's attention, feeling his excitement whenever their skin made contact. He defied the Royal Council and rebelled against his king—but he listened to her.

She twined her fingers in his. "So long as we are together, I do not think we will be sorry." Parting would be the hard part. They rode back into Calais late on midsummer night. Saint John's Eve bonfires burned across the Calais pale, supposedly to keep the flat countryside safe from dragons. But tonight marked her second month in the Middle Ages, and by now she was witch enough to know that those fires were themselves the worldly incarnations of dragons, the all-devouring fiery death worm from pagan funeral pyres.

⊶⊷ The Glorious Fourth ⊷⊶

*E*dward kept his word. She and Deirdre got a small cabin aboard his own ship, a Flemish coaster purchased for the occasion and given an English name, the *Swallow*. It felt good to be on Edward's ship with no Nevilles peering over her shoulder. No Countess Alice to keep happy. She and Edward could do what they willed. For so long as they lasted. Which did not look likely to be very long. Even to her untrained eye, their forces seemed remarkably meager—a handful of ships, a couple of thousand men-at-arms and archers, an amateur attempt to make a medieval epic on a shoestring budget, and with England's fighting nobility set to give the Lords of Calais a heavily armed greeting.

Alone with her in the master's cabin, Edward shrugged off the odds, his booted feet propped on the pilot's table—refusing to stand on ceremony aboard his own ship. "Wool merchants have advanced us a minor fortune to restore trade between London and Calais. If we do not do something soon they will want their silver back, much of which is already spent." Who says medieval men were not practical? Or money minded.

Clearly happy to have her with him, he acted wonderfully confident, making this seem like a day trip on the water, a kind of low-rent Carnival cruise with bronzed sunbathers replaced by a couple of hundred knights and bowmen, and a dozen horses. Very much a moment worth stealing, a special chance to be together on Edward's own ship, to talk, to share ideas, even to dine privately in his cabin without worrying about lordly interruptions or being watched over by servants. If it took a week to get to England, that was fine by her. "God is on our side," Edward piously reminded her. "He must count for something." They had talked Bishop Coppini into coming with them, swearing to be "peaceful and obedient"—if Henry let them. Submitting to the august authority of His Holiness Pius II, they promised even to fight the French or Turks, if their king and the Holy Father so willed. That last idiocy did not worry her much—there being little danger of Pope Pius and Mad King Henry agreeing on what day of the week it was, much less on war with the Turks.

She told him, "Heaven will be with us, but only if we let it be." The pope's promise was not nearly enough.

He gave her a puzzled look. "What do you mean?"

"Heaven will be with us only if we really and truly put an end to killing. That is what ordinary people pray for, to live their lives without fear. And to have a government whose purpose is not to line its own pockets."

His brow furrowed, but his boots stayed on the table. "When murder is done by King Henry's men, it is those commoners you so love who cry most loudly for vengeance."

She knew he was right. Word from England had gotten worse. King Henry had declared anyone who aided the rebels to be traitors themselves, and Lord Scales had been turned loose on the Berkshire town of Newbury. Upright citizens were hanged, drawn, and quartered for the heinous crime of paying their rents and wearing their lord's livery. All property was confiscated, and the victim's families turned out to starve. Newbury had done nothing to deserve this, but similar treatment had been promised in Kent, Surrey, Sussex, Middlesex, Essex, and Hertfordshire—threatening another "Harvest of Heads" like the hangings and beheadings following John-Amend-All's rebellion. Faced with imminent invasion, the court's immediate impulse had been to alienate the citizenry with judicial murder and random terror, giving southern England every reason to wish the rebels luck. If people did lay hands on the executioners, they were unlikely to just forgive and forget. "Is that how you live in the far, far future?" asked Edward. "Always forgiving your enemies?"

"No," she admitted, "we do not. But as time goes by, we have found fewer and fewer reasons for killing each other." Thank goodness.

Her worst fears were confirmed as they set sail. Standing with Edward on the *Swallow*'s stern castle, she watched Earl Warwick's sailors behead three prisoners on the beach at the harbor entrance, beside the Rysbank tower. A ghastly omen to begin on. She had disliked Warwick from the first, a touchy, self-important pirate, needlessly cruel and too smooth by half. She did not need to be a prophetess to know Warwick would come to a bad end; his arrogance absolutely demanded it—hopefully he would not take Edward with him. Sailors in the *Swallow*'s rigging cheered each stroke of the ax.

Appalled at the spectacle, she told Edward, "Who is going to join us, if this is what we have to offer?" Here was why she had to go with him—win or lose—she would not let him go to war with only Warwick for a guide.

Stricken by her concern, Edward vowed, "I will do my uttermost to see no one suffers merely for opposing us or for obeying King Henry's orders. Punishment will be for real crimes. After fair trials. Our hope is to someday live together when this is done." She believed him, despite what she had just seen on the beach. So far as she could tell, Edward had never lied to her, never seeming to need to, nor did he ever doubt her outlandish tales. Sometimes they seemed so in tune that no falsehood could pass between them—she never felt that way about a man before—not even one in her own time.

"Even Lord Scales need not fear us," Edward added significantly. Even Lord Scales—lord constable of the Tower and the Butcher of Newbury—he, too, could expect a pardon. Not for his own sake, but for the peace of the realm.

Setting sail from Calais with a south wind at their backs, she saw the queen's ships at the harbor mouth, tacking leeward, keeping between them and the open Channel. For once she had a perfect view of things, standing on the half deck beneath the stern awning, with Edward at her side. "Will you go below?" he asked—still worried for her safety. "If there is a fight?"

"Of course," she agreed, slipping her hand in his, reassuring her nervous knight—"If there is a fight." He was wearing armor, and she was not, but he did not use it as an excuse to order her about. She mentally offered another dozen candles to the Virgin, who watched over wayward women in love.

Holding her breath, she waited to see what the opposing crews would do; none of these bold knights could get at each other unless the sailors agreed. Queen Margaret's ships drew closer, close enough to see the queen's bright daisy flower banner, flying alongside the lions and lilies of England and France. One by one, the approaching ships came about, sails flapping and then filling again, going over onto the opposite tack, falling away leeward—leaving the way to England open. She owed Our Lady another dozen candles.

Wind blew steady from the south, and the *Swallow* lived up to her name, skimming across the straits. Porpoises leaped and plunged ahead of the ship, blowing plumes of spray. Too soon Robyn saw the white cliffs of Dover rising out of the narrow sea—so much for the slow romantic route. Life was about to go into high gear. Rounding the South Foreland, the little fleet entered the Downs, the stretch of sea between the coast of Kent and the Goodwin Sands. White chalk cliffs sank down, replaced by shingle beach and then sand flats. Ahead she saw Sandwich nestled in the low coast, walls and church towers thrust above the surrounding fields; William Neville, Lord Fauconberg, had seized Sandwich harbor to secure a landing spot. Beyond that there was not much to count on.

"Will they welcome us?" Edward wondered as they stood together on the stern castle, watching the sandy coastline come closer. He was not talking about Sandwich, already in Neville hands. He meant England as a whole. Edward and the Nevilles were staking everything on a single roll of heavily weighted dice. With the high nobility solidly against them, even lackadaisical King Henry could easily field ten times their numbers—nothing short of an immediate national uprising could save them from execution. Nine months before, Edward had seen his father beaten down by the king's name and forced to flee to Ireland; now Edward meant to do better, with a tiny fraction of the force that failed his father.

"Women will welcome you," she felt sure of that.

"Really? Now that is a start." Edward sounded pleased.

"Yes, indeed." She thought of the women she knew. Darling Deirdre, whose mere existence was a crime. Jo and Joy imprisoned for being themselves. Brazen, calculating Bryn, daring to love above her station. Or the Little Bo Peep shepherdess who warned her to beware of the Swans, and the alewife in red homespun who spoke her mind to FitzHolland. She thought of witches at their dance and the young harpers who sang for her from the Golden Valley to Glyndyfrdwy. "I bet there is barely a woman in England below the rank of baroness who did not yearn for justice, peace, and good government." If their men would but listen.

Edward's grin widened. "That is gladdening." He meant it; Edward looked happier and was hardly the sort who ignored female opinion. What other Saxon earl would dig up odd bits of Gaelic, to impress his lady's serving girl? "If the women are with us, we are halfway there."

"Only do not disappoint them," she warned.

Edward looked a little shocked, clearly he had not planned to disappoint anyone, least of all her. "How so?"

"By not changing anything. This cannot be just about replacing one gang of nobles with another. Women are not looking for a change in the king's livery; they are looking for a change of heart."

Edward's confident grin returned. "I am an earl, descended of kings." He made it sound like a burden, not a boast. "King Henry is my cousin, so is Somerset. Holland is my brother-in-law. Your much-beloved father—Humphrey Stafford, duke of Buckingham—is my uncle by marriage." She had told him how she tried to pass as Buckingham's daughter, and he teased her about it. "But if I meant to please the fairest families in the land, I could best do it by tying myself to an anchor and leaping over the seaward rail. Adversity has taught me to much prefer the opinions of commons, bowmen, sailors, mercers, artisans—and women."

"Even women?" she mocked his breezy assurance.

"Especially women," Edward laughed, no longer looking worried by what reception he got. Bare feet beat on the deckboards as sailors took in sail, bringing the *Swallow* about. Sandwich was two miles up the shallow winding River Stour, but the tide was with them, and the ships were able to crawl upriver under sweeps, dropping anchor below the town. Cries of "A Warwick, a Warwick" showed the Nevilles were ashore. The Lords of Calais had landed.

All of Sandwich turned out, and though the place was not big, their enthusiasm was heartening. By the time Robyn got mounted, she and Edward were surrounded by a cheering throng of fisher families, market women, and men in mail, wearing sallets and waving brown bills. Deirdre scrambled up onto her palfrey, happy to get aboard a horse, saying she had never seen "so many Saxons all together." And so excited.

Edward started working the happy crowd, giving a fair little speech thanking them for showing up. Until coming to the Middle Ages, Robyn never realized how much politicking it took to be a lord—she'd assumed lords gave orders and serfs shuffled off to obey. Not at all the way things were done in Kent. These were the people who routed a royal army at Sevenoaks during John-Amend-All's rebellion—you had to earn their obedience. Fortunately, Edward was up to it, calling to men in the crowd by name, then leaning down to clasp their hands, thanking them for "this safe harbor and hale welcome." He had not lied about knowing and liking commoners, combining his liking with an uncommon ability to connect names and faces. Local magnates, men from the Calais garrison, veterans who fought at Saint Albans—all came pushing up to bask in Edward's recognition. She had been flattered by the way he held her memory fresh after months apart. Now she saw he remembered nearly everything and everyone. Being a boy born in a backward age had not kept him from being brilliant.

Word went back through the press, spreading through an excited hush—"March, March"—rising louder and turning to a chant. "March, March, March . . ." Someone started singing:

Send home, most gracious Lord Jesus most benign,
Send home thy true blood into his proper vein . . .

More and more voices joined in. One by one the song named the exiled lords, urging God to send them home. When they got to Edward's name, everyone was singing, loud enough to be heard in London: "Edward, Earl of March, whose fame the earth shall spread . . ."

Heady stuff, but Edward handled it, acting neither arrogant nor embarrassed, just glad for their affection, as if people sang hymns to him every day. With this sort of welcome, there was no need to wait about in Sandwich, testing the waters. Bishop Coppini, the papal legate—a man of peace toward anyone but Turks—settled down with his entourage to wait events. Everyone else took the road west toward Canterbury.

Streams of armed able-bodied men joined the column as they made their way across Kent. Lords Cobham and Bergavenny turned out, with their retainers. So did scores of children, cheering as the march passed farmsteads and crossroads. Whenever Robyn turned in the saddle to look back, the line of marchers had gotten longer, and when they got to Wingham manor—halfway to Canterbury—she could no longer see the end of it. More men piled out of a pair of inns, the Dog and Red Lion, drunken smiles on their faces and longbows slung across their backs. Some thirsty fellows fell out of line to take their place at the bar, but most kept pressing on toward Canterbury, not wanting to miss this mighty adventure.

Holy Canterbury came next, birthplace of British Christianity, and site of her holiest shrine. From here Saint Augustine began the conversion of Britain to Christianity, and here England's most famous martyr, Saint Thomas à Becket, Archbishop of Canterbury, was murdered in his cathedral at vespers. She spent the night in Saint Augustine's old Church of Saint Martin outside the town walls, sleeping, praying, and lighting her dozen candles to the Virgin. Inside Canterbury, King Henry's captains sweated and dithered—watching the numbers grow outside—until they finally had to throw open the gates, adding their own men to the throng. When the gates opened, Robyn trooped in with Edward to pray in the huge cathedral before the gold bejeweled tomb of Saint Thomas à Becket—for they were a godly army, and wanted the whole world to know it.

Of the many religious moments during the last couple of months, this was the most magnificent. She walked the whole length of the tremendous ornate cathedral, big as Yankee Stadium and smelling of must and incense, with its stone pillars and soaring Gothic arches. Vast hollow spaces lit by tiny candles dwarfed the long line of penitent rebels. Marching past the spot of the archbishop's martyrdom and ancient altars dedicated to various saints, they crowded into Trinity Chapel kneeling before the tomb of Saint Thomas of Canterbury, killed in this cathedral on the orders of another out-of-control King Henry—three hundred years earlier. Symbolism that was obvious to all. Kneeling before the martyr's golden jewel-encrusted tomb, Robyn prayed her heart out, not for a moment doubting that this was a desperate enterprise with slim chance of succeeding. And if they failed, good and kindly King Henry would be merciless to anyone who was not an actual relative. As she prayed, she stared at a huge red ruby set in gold upon the tomb—a jewel so famous it had a name, the

Regal of France. They emerged from the great cathedral to be greeted by masses of cheering townspeople.

That night was Witches Night. Which she celebrated in private prayer. No doubt there were witches marching with them, though none were known to her, and Deirdre would have been willing, but it was bad enough hauling her off to live among Saxons without making her a witch, as well. And they were spending the night in a cloistered abbey courtesy of the Benedictines. Jo claimed the notion that magic did not work on hallowed ground was Christian superstition, but Robyn did not want to press her luck or insult her hosts—so she used only the goddesses' Christian names in her prayers; Saint Anne for Hecate, Mary for the Mother, and Saint Joan for Diana.

Then it was on to London. Half of Canterbury came with them, along with armed contingents from Rye and Winchelsea, led by the town mayors. She looked back on what had to be the biggest outpouring from Kent and the south counties since John-Amend-All's rebellion. Past Canterbury came the rains, curtains of water threatening to drown the marching columns. Despite the deluge, the march pushed on through Rochester and Dartford, stopping to pray at churches and shrines, picking up more recruits, becoming a moving city. Mostly male, to be sure—but there were women, as well. Nuns from Canterbury, footloose alewives, runaway serving women, and whores from the Sandwich brothels. Young wives came along, who could not bear to be parted from their husbands, bringing their babies and children. Would-be wives came as well, assuming this mass of brave and goodly men would be the place to look. She and Deirdre rode with the small mounted knot in the lead, a few hundred at most—lords, ladies, knights, prelates, and men-at-arms—with thousands upon thousands trailing behind them, chanting and singing in the spring rain, carrying weapons and crosses. It is hard to hold down a countryside where every yeoman has his bow and every gentleman, his suit of armor. By the time they got to Blackheath, they outnumbered every city in England—save only London herself—and all who joined the march were putting their necks in a noose.

At Blackheath, the rains let up. Robyn saw the remains of John-Amend-All's great camp: trenches and earthworks thrown up by the men of Kent when they last marched on London. "Ten years ago this month," a woman told her significantly. Kent had a long memory. But what would happen now? What would London do? London was crucial. Confined to Kent, the rising could not survive. John-Amend-All's rebellion broke up when London closed its gates to the rebels, fighting them off in the Battle of London Bridge. If the same thing happened now, the huge march would lose momentum, melting away in the downpour. During two months in medieval England, she met only two Londoners—one she liked a lot; the other scared her silly. The one who horrified her was Lord Scales, King Henry's constable of the Tower, and the one she liked was her sister-initiate, little blond "Jane" Beth Lambert. Two more different people were impossible to imagine—making it difficult to judge the city as a whole. At Canterbury, a delegation had come down from London to say the city had royal orders to resist them. A week later, here they were at Blackheath in their tens of thousands, not nearly so easy to dismiss. Edward sounded confident—but no more so than usual—sometimes she feared he would die confident.

Her first sight of London was Southwark, the south-outwork of the city, London's bridgehead south of the Thames. Created by the roads leading up to London Bridge, Southwark was a city in itself, with stately mansions, famous inns, stinking tanneries, Dutch breweries, and bear-baiting arenas, all ruled over by the bishop of Winchester. The unwalled borough had a floating population of upright citizens, transients, pleasure seekers, peddlers, and cutpurses. Shakespeare's Globe Theater would be built just upriver, in the part of Southwark called Bankside; she had seen the modern reconstruction on the day she flew in from L.A. to surprise Collin.

Despite dreary skies, Southwark turned out to greet them behind crosses and bishop's banners. Rising in her saddle, Robyn saw people pouring out of the city, cheering and singing, some in armor, but most just ordinary Londoners, coming out to see the rebel earls. Floating over the crowd were the banners of the bishops of Exeter and Ely. "What are they saying?" Deirdre demanded, leaning forward in her saddle, frustrated at seeing English history being made, but hardly speaking the language.

"It does not matter what they are saying. What matters is who says it." London's city fathers had sent George Neville, bishop of Exeter, to welcome them—Warwick's younger brother and Salisbury's son; clearly London was theirs. "We are in."

Deirdre sighed and sank back in her saddle, looking sorry she learned to ride. Victory could be merciless as defeat. Lady and serving girl desperately needed rest, suffering from days in the saddle, and from going down on their knees in every church and cathedral between here and Canterbury. Except for the riding dress she had worn two days running, everything Robyn owned in the world was wet. Still, she was on display, so she sat through the bishop's welcome, and various fulsome responses. In a world where nearly every word was spoken or handwritten, people thought nothing of riding half a week and then taking hours to say, "Hi, glad to see you, come on in." Especially when they had an eager audience. Every event was in real time, and politicians spoke straight to the people, since the nearest thing to news media were the bards singing for their supper.

Edward trotted back from the conference, happily announcing a triumphal entrance into London tomorrow. By now the sun had broken through, shining off his armor. Great news. Fabulous, in fact. Too bad by then she had gone beyond exhaustion, into terminal paralysis, and she told Edward if she did not have a dry, safe place to sleep she would surely go insane. Her knight let nothing dampen his enthusiasm. "Luckily, I know the very place."

"In truth?" She could barely believe it. Southwark would be full to bursting, and his family's London home, Baynard's Castle, had been taken into the king's hands, making Edward as homeless as she. The masses around her were already settling down to camp on Saint George's Field. But the boy had proved adept at doing the impossible. Working his way through the adoring crowd, Edward led her and Deirdre up Long Street, to where a huge mansion thrust above the jumble of rooftops, taking up half a block—tenement shops lined the street in front: an inn, two bakeries, a chandler's, hoser's, and haberdasher's. Shopkeepers, patrons, barmaids, and baker's boys turned out to greet them. Seeing Edward, they gave a wild cheer, struggling forward to touch him. Stripping off his gloves, he leaned down, smiling and clasping hands, asking, "Is the master of the house within?" Atop her white mare, surrounded by well-wishers, Robyn saw she had to get used to being cheered wherever she went—so long as she was with Edward, anyway. It did feel thrilling to live at the eye of the storm, seeing England changing right in front of her, hopefully for the better.

Pushing through the press, a well-dressed fellow went down on one knee, introducing himself as Christopher Hansson, estate agent for

John Paston, the Norfolk gentleman who owned the huge house. Edward begged safe lodging for female members of his "retinue," and Hansson fell all over himself inviting them in. Deftly disengaging from his admirers, Edward escorted her in. Behind its great gate, the manse had a spacious entrance court with stables and kitchens, including a buttery, larder, pastry, poultry mews, bathhouse, and dairy barn. Edward nodded to her. "Does this place please my lady?"

Pronouncing herself thoroughly pleased, she dismounted amid geese and chickens. Hansson showed them up wide steps to a main hall big enough to play handball in, if you cleared out the carved oak furniture, tapestries, battle flags, and gold plate. Grooms in blue-gold livery showed them past the private chapel and into the great parlor, where afternoon sunlight flooded through a big windowed bay, falling onto fine carpets. Baker's boys brought fresh rolls from the pastry kitchen along with butter from the buttery.

"Whose house is this?" she asked, seeing Italian sculptures and walls hung with weapons and armor, trying to imagine their owner. Surrounded by such opulence, she could barely believe that moments ago they had been homeless traitors-in-arms at the head of a rain-soaked insurrection.

Edward broke open a roll, buttering it with his thumb. "This is called Falstaff's Place," he told her, licking the butter off his thumb. "This mansion and much else belonged to Sir John Falstaff, a veteran of Good King Harry's wars in France."

"Falstaff?" There was a Sir John Falstaff in Shakespeare, a companion to young King Henry V, who appeared again in the first part of Henry VI—Orson Welles played him in *Chimes at Midnight*. It would be too much of a coincidence for them not to be the same person, but she never pictured Shakespeare's fat, cowardly tippler owning such a palace.

"Most valiant and lucky, Sir John Falstaff married a rich widow in Castle Combe," Edward explained. "And got still richer in the French Wars. Alas, he died last November on his estates in Norfolk."

"So who is letting us use it?"

"Sir John's lawyer, John Paston. He hopes Falstaff's many properties will now come to him—according to a will he drew up. Powerful lords at court covet Old Falstaff's properties, giving us enemies in common."

That did not surprise her. She had long ago lost track of how many enemies she had made in just two months in the Middle Ages. "Which enemies?"

"His lordship, the much-feared Henry Holland, duke of Exeter, hopes to get hold of this place." Edward spread his hands to indicate the elegant surroundings. "And who could much blame him?"

Who, indeed? A mansion like this, in a bustling suburb of London, with stables and tenements attached—in her time it would be worth millions, even without plumbing and cable.

"Another of Paston's enemies is the much-esteemed and gracious Lord Scales." Paston, indeed, had need of friends. "Until we arrived, these lords had charge of London. Merely by coming to Southwark we have made Paston's and Hansson's lives much more rewarding, and so as long as you are here, the place is under my protection. Falstaff's Place was nearly sacked the last time Kent rose up." She told him about Shakespeare's Falstaff, how the Bard had made Sir John into a drunken buffoon and coward, an easy-go-lucky loser that generations of people had laughed at. Edward was horrified—"He was in no way like that at all! He was a valiant knight who beat the French at the Day of Herrings—and fought at Agincourt with Good King Harry—a pious, tight-fisted old warrior with a keen eye for any advantage, never forgiving an insult or forgetting a debt." Edward looked askance, asking, "Did this Shakespeare lie a lot?"

Apparently. "Poetic license," she told him. Shakespeare's Falstaff could not have beaten the French, except to a bottle. But one look at this place showed Sir John to be no drunken ne'er-do-well. She saw hand-woven tapestries of hunting scenes, and the Adoration of the Shepherds, the Assumption of Our Lady, the Siege of Falaise. His private chapel had a grisly display of holy relics, including an arm of Saint George—the right one—and a finger of John the Baptist. Not a place some unthinking souse would just stumble onto.

She spotted a faded banner decorated with a crowned white hart on a gold chain, and the motto—*Dieu et Mon Droyt*—"God and My Right." The blue-white background was sprinkled with red roses, reminding her of the white rose Edward had given her—incinerated along with Jo's copy of Christine de Pizan. In college she had stage-managed a production of Henry VI, Part I, which had a scene where powerful nobles chose sides by plucking roses off a garden bush—one side picking white roses, the other side, red. Coming up with rose bushes was no easy feat in the middle of a Montana winter. "Hath not thy rose a thorn, Plantagenet?" Who said that? Edward was a Plantagenet. She furiously tried to dredge up the dramatis personae of a long-lost junior college production. The duke of Somerset! Joy's father? Or her half brother? Probably. And Warwick was in the scene, as well. Red rose versus white. The Wars of the Roses. How did the Wars of the Roses come out? Who won? Who lost? Would be nice to know. Shakespeare might have made some things up, but he was writing about history. His history, and he knew what came next. She wished she had a decent copy of the Bard's complete works.

Instead she got a wonderful garret room looking out on London and the river, furnished in that marvelous medieval mix of impossibly elegant and outrageously primitive. Her canopy bed had a quilted feather coverlet, embroidered with Falstaff's coat of arms—a bush of feathers supported by twin angels, ringed by a blue velvet belt with the gold buckle of a Knight of the Garter. Beside it stood a plain wooden washstand supporting an iron basin and a gold-trimmed pitcher of Thames water not fit to wash her feet in. The Middle Ages had a knack for sturdy elegance—it was simple stuff like clean water they could not manage. Deirdre ran straight to the window, leaning out and going, "Ooh" and "Ahh" at the rooftops of Southwark, and London across the river. "And I imagined Calais to be grand."

Over her serving girl's shoulder, she got her first look at old London. City walls seemed to rise right out of the far bank of the Thames, surrounding a forest of steeples dominated by the great stone spear of Saint Paul's pointing straight at Heaven. After seeing endless green countryside—with motorways reduced to muddy ruts and towns turned to tiny hamlets—such towering stonework amazed her, so many churches, all these dwellings, shops, and people, crammed so close together that houses were in danger of falling into the river. Her first medieval bath had been in the furthestmost trickle of the Thames, by Birdlip Hill in the Edge Country when she first broke out of Berkeley Castle; now here was the broad river rolling before her. Part of the city cut right across the river—at first she thought the Thames took a jog, but there was nowhere to jog to. Shops and homes ran from bank to bank atop a score of stone arches striding across the river. London Bridge—another scene from nursery rhymes. She stared dumbfounded at a beautiful stone chapel sitting atop the arches in midstream and flanked by timber-framed houses jutting out over the

Thames. No wonder there were so many songs and stories about London Bridge and this city across from Southwark.

She felt a mailed arm go around her waist. Edward had stepped up behind her, pulling her to him, a bare hand on her hip, his body pressing against her back. "From Dartford nearly to Windsor?" he asked her.

Looking about, she saw they were alone—aside from Deirdre, staring rapturously at the city. Hansson was gone, and Edward had closed the door without her hearing it, no mean trick for a man in plate and mail. The closest thing to privacy all day. She leaned back against his arm. "What do you mean?"

"You said London would one day be all city, from Dartford to Windsor." Edward was appalled by her descriptions of the ferroconcrete monster London would become. Now she saw why.

How sad to think of this bustling brawling faerie city, with its teeming shops and one-of-a-kind homes, covered over by endless square miles of steel and asphalt. "It will. And so wide you cannot see the green fields beyond."

His grip tightened. "Thank Heaven I will never see it. Here is the London I love." He preferred dirty old London town and her plain common people to the vast third-millennium metropolis, sight unseen. And why not?—look how this London had welcomed him. What a day it had been, and what a place to end it in. Sinking back against Edward's mailed chest, she wished just for once her knight were not in armor. Deirdre had her back to them, leaning well out the window, studying the city—as though she were trying to count the houses. He whispered in her ear, "Tell me what will last."

"What do you mean?" she asked.

"What in the London we see will last until your time?"

She tried to remember her single day's tour of the city proper. "Part of the walls. Some of the churches." But not Saint Paul's. And not the Bridge. "The London Stone, a few inns. Houses here and there." It did not sound like much. "And, of course, the Tower," she added.

Edward nodded. "Yes, of course, the Tower." Who could forget the Tower of London? "The much-esteemed Lord Scales holds the Tower for King Henry." She looked past Deirdre at the grim stone pile downriver. So the constable of the Tower was in residence. Too bad. She had hoped Lord Scales was somewhere far away, with King Henry at Coventry, perhaps. Or on a mission to Mongolia, trading torture tips with the Great Khan. "He has a number of nervous lords and ladies with him, including my older sister, Anne."

"Your sister is in the Tower?" He never talked much of his older sister.

"Yes, she is countess of Exeter."

"Your sister is married to Henry Holland?" Holland was easily Edward's most rabid enemy. Sometimes the Wars of the Roses ran right through the middle of a marriage bed.

"Alas, the was union not as lucky as we had hoped," Edward admitted.

She smiled at his family troubles, leaning back against his arm, letting him support her tired body. Edward was a pleasure to listen to, always speaking from the heart, never trying to impress her with talk or order her about. And he listened as well, really listened. Of all the people she had met in medieval England, only Edward gave a serious hearing to her outlandish notion that this world could be made better. And he meant to risk everything to do it. Others complained, but Edward acted. If she were not so tired—and Deirdre were not there—she would have made him take off his silly armor and show how much he loved her. This was the day for it. She asked him, "Will you show me?"

"Show you what?" Edward looked to see if she was serious or flirting.

"Your London." She nodded at the city outside her window.

"*Certainement,* starting on the morrow, first the Bridge, then Saint Paul's—the Tower must wait."

"That is okay." She sank deeper into his grip, shuddering at the thought of seeing Lord Scales again. "I have already seen the Tower."

Saying he must go to sup with the Nevilles, Edward surveyed the simple little room, asking, "Will this be suitable for you? I can make them find better."

"More than suitable," she assured him, sorry he was leaving, but happy to have this little space to share with Deirdre. It might not look like much to the earl of March—but if he meant to love a commoner, he had better learn to like the little things.

Letting go of her, Edward stepped back and bowed, "If you need even the slightest assistance, send word to me at once." He himself would be camping with his people on Saint George's Field; they had put their lives in his hands, and he took that charge seriously.

As soon as the door shut behind him, Deirdre spun about, a wide Irish smile on her face, asking, "Is he not wonderful?"

"No, not in the least," Robyn laughed. Her simple Irish serving girl had not been dazzled by the sights of London. Deirdre had been leaning out the window, listening to the goings-on behind her, getting an earful and an English lesson. "Come," she told her eavesdropping maidservant, "let us go down to the kitchen and see what's fit to eat." She followed the meal with a steamy bath, a change of clothes, a bout of prayer in Falstaff's private chapel, then a much-deserved sleep.

Next morning Edward made good on his vow to show her London Bridge and Saint Paul's. Despite days in the saddle, Robyn was never happier to be on horseback, pushing gingerly through the throng jamming Long Street, caught in an appalling press of people eager to see the rebel earls enter the city. As usual, Edward and Warwick had picked their moment for maximum impact—ten years ago to the day, John-Amend-All had crossed this span in triumph, his sword borne upright before him, wearing gold spurs taken from King Henry's commander at Sevenoaks. He had stopped in midspan to cut the drawbridge ropes, declaring the city his. After three days of looting and lawlessness, London threw him out. This time Edward promised her, "We will do it better."

Keeping as close as she could to Edward, Robyn urged her white mare up onto the narrow pitted roadway of London Bridge, telling Lily not to worry—"These people are friends, no matter how many and how loud they are." Men-at-arms on foot fell in behind them, those closest to her wearing red surcoats bearing the white Neville saltire. Crossing London Bridge on a rainy Wednesday morning was like trotting on horseback through a packed open-air mall flung over a river. The Bridge was a tiny neighborhood, with its own market, bakeries, inns, and church. People born in these homes often lived their whole lives in this one-street town, with London and Southwark for suburbs, watching the world parade by their doorways—pilgrims and peddlers from afar, visiting potentates, beggars and archbishops, conquering heroes and captive kings, even a woman from the distant future. She saw scars on the roadway from the Battle of the Bridge, when John-Amend-All's Kentishmen were forced back across the Thames.

Below her, boatmen shouted to each other as they shot one of the Bridge's nineteen arches. At the second arch, she passed though a massive gate, and at the seventh she crossed the drawbridge. Atop the Drawbridge Gate, human heads stared down through sockets pecked clean by crows, letting loyal Londoners see the price of rebellion. Halting here, the earls ordered, "Take down the heads."

Cheers went back through the crowd as the heads were brought down for Christian burial at the Church of Saint Magnus the Martyr—then the procession lurched forward again. Keeping Lily calm, Robyn concentrated on the roadway ahead, trying not to lose Edward in the press. Flower petals rained down on her from the upper stories of shops and houses lining the Bridge.

Halfway across, she heard cries and shouts from some trouble behind her. Looking back, she saw a mob of faces pressing forward through a storm of petals, propelled by irresistible pressure from behind. Whatever had happened could not be helped. Struggling free of the Bridge, they crossed Thames Street and turned onto Candlewick Street, where cheering Londoners pelted them with more flowers. People hung at Edward's stirrup and kissed the hem of her dress, carried away with excitement. Passing Saint Swithin's and the London Stone, they made for Ludgate Hill and the great stone tower of Saint Paul's Cathedral, topped by its gilt weathercock. There they were greeted by the mayor and aldermen, along with the masters of the chief guilds, the Mercers, Grocers, Drapers, Goldsmiths, Tailors, Vintners, Ironmongers, Haberdashers, and Dyers. Dismounting, they entered the giant cathedral to bow before the archbishop of Canterbury, giving heartfelt thanks for having made it to London and for finding London so forthcoming.

Afterwards, she left Edward to meetings and conferences with nervous magnates, riding back to Southwark through what looked like a flower-strewn battle zone. There was no looting, like when John-Amend-All's rebels took the city. This rebellion believed in paying its way—and was more likely to borrow than loot. But there was blood on the roadway, and bodies in armor had been taken off London Bridge. Thirteen of the bishop of Exeter's men-at-arms had fallen in the crush. Weighted down by their armor, they were trampled by hordes of commoners trying to get a better view—the first casualties since leaving Calais.

She did not venture back into the city until Friday, the Feast of Saint Martin, when she joined a huge rain-soaked crowd gathered at Saint Paul's Cross to hear a letter the papal legate was sending to King

Henry. Rain on the Feast of Saint Martin supposedly meant a wet summer, but that was here already. Full of pious self-justification, the letter claimed Coppini had come to act as a "faithful shepherd, nuncio, and mediator"—making no mention of war with the Turks. He begged King Henry for love of God and in pity for his people, to let the rebel earls come before him and peaceably state their case, warning the king that to take up arms without trying to make peace would be wicked and contrary to God's will. Coppini ended by begging for a "speedy reply because the danger is imminent and does not brook delay."

People roared approval into the rain. If there was any chance for peace, it had to come now. So far, the rebellion was more like an election campaign than a war. Edward and the Nevilles had marched from Sandwich to London, gathering support, giving speeches, issuing proclamations, and kneeling at every stop to pray. Women even offered up babies for Edward to hold and cuddle—which he did quite well. And the only casualties had been Bishop Neville's knights, trampled to death by overly enthusiastic Londoners—but that was bound to change.

She was not the only one who thought so. Word spread that the Common Council had voted to support the earls, lending them horses, carts, and money. Knowing what King Henry would think of this, the Council also decided it prudent to seize the king's cannons, which were kept in Whitechapel, ordering them hauled down through Aldgate for the defense of London. Lord Scales sent word through a monk from Saint Katharine's by the Tower that he and the other holdouts in the Tower wanted to shop for food—a sign Scales had not stocked the Tower for a siege. Hopefully he had his hands way too full to make mischief. By the time she rode back toward Southwark the rain had stopped, and the summer sun was setting upriver, shining red on the water. Impromptu celebrations had begun. Innkeepers hauled butts of ale out onto the street, selling to passersby at a penny a tankard. Musicians played and people danced as London declared her independence from King Henry's court—picking the perfect day to do it. Today was Friday, the fourth of July. All it lacked was fireworks. She alone saw the irony; to everyone else the fourth of July merely meant the Feast of Saint Martin, and a promise of more rain.

To top things off, it was Witches Night, as well. When she reached the Bridge, revelers blocked her way, and she reined in to let them stagger past. Stepping out of the shadows by the bridge, a small girl tugged on her stirrup, saying, "Sister, I have been waiting for you."

She started to say she was no one's sister, but stopped, staring at the girl holding onto her stirrup, seeing she did have a sister after all. Little "Jane" Beth Lambert, her sister-initiate, smiled up at her, saying, "Sister, is this your mare?"

"Yes," she confessed, "she is mine," embarrassed by the easy way Edward gave her the magnificent mare. "Her name is Lily."

Beth reached up to her with both arms, saying, "Will you take me up?" Thinking the child was lost, she lifted the little blond girl up onto the front of her saddle. Sitting half in her lap, Beth happily petted Lily's silky white mane—"She is so beautiful. I saw you riding her this morning at Saint Paul's Cross, and Wednesday, when the earls entered the city." Far from being lost, Beth had been keeping close track of her. "You were riding with Lord Edward, earl of March. Is he not handsome? Do you know him well?"

"Yes, he is most handsome," she admitted. Clearly Edward had made another conquest. "And yes, I know him well; he gave me the mare."

"I am so lucky," Beth congratulated herself, "having a sister-initiate who leads such an astounding life." Astounding and then some. "Would Lord March give me one like her?" Beth asked, already envying her sister's success.

"Mayhap." So far as she knew, Edward had never met Jane-Beth Lambert, but they would doubtless get on famously.

"So long as you were on your mare," Beth explained, "I knew you must come back by way of the Bridge."

She looked down at the little blond witch-to-be in her lap. "You have been waiting for me?"

"It is Witches Night," Beth soberly reminded her. "And you have been cut off from the coven. When I saw you among the earl of March's retainers, I knew I must be with you this Witches Night." What else were sister-initiates for? That Beth was ten years old at best barely mattered; Jane-Beth saw her duty and did it, as any good child would. Jo's loss and High Priestess Wydville's betrayal had thrown the coven into confusion, pitting natural leaders against each other. Sensing this perilous vacuum above, Beth looked to her for direction, making the childish mistake of assuming adults knew what they are doing.

Guilty for not even thinking of Beth since coming to London, she told the girl, "I, too, am incredibly lucky to be your sister-initiate." Beth beamed up at her, immensely pleased.

Beyond the bridge, Bankside was busy drinking itself silly, celebrating a most glorious Feast of Saint Martin. Apprentice boys with white roses in their caps called out their love as she rode past. Too bad, but she already had a boyfriend. What a weird children's crusade this was, with its teenage hero and adoring witch-girls-in-training thrusting her into being the "responsible adult"—with these girls and with Edward. Even Warwick, the presumed adult in charge, was barely into his thirties, and already eclipsed his father, Salisbury. This was a war of generations. Mad King Henry was close to forty, and under the thumb of an even older court—people like Duke Buckingham, Lord Scales, Baron Rivers, and Duchess Wydville, many of whom served his famous father. King Henry's generation had squandered the nation's wealth and lost the war in France. Edward's watched them do it. Back at Falstaff's Place Deirdre demanded to know everything that happened in the city. Introducing Beth Lambert, Robyn did her best to translate events into Gaelic. Deirdre got the drift. " 'Twill be your handsome young lord against his daft king." Being Irish, Deirdre saw nothing wrong in it. Bad kings were a blight on their people—and it was a hero's duty to correct that.

"Hopefully they can come to peaceful terms." Robyn still held out for a miracle, but right now she had Witches Night to deal with. There was no way she could wait for Deirdre to fall asleep, not on a night like this. And not with Jane-Beth here. They would just have to have their Witches Night together. Deirdre was ecstatic, throwing arms around Robyn, kissing her in gratitude; the girl's complete trust in her was painful to see. She had tried valiantly to maintain a lady-and-maid relationship, but Deirdre would not have it. No wonder the Irish made such poor servants. Not satisfied to be a maid, Deirdre aspired to be a "companion"—like she had been Jo's companion—part and partner to the "astounding life" her lady lived.

And like Beth, Deirdre dived headfirst into witchcraft, heedless of the danger. To Deirdre, life was one big dare; born a mongrel orphan, the serving girl could not imagine magic making her life anything but better. But Deirdre had not been hounded by witch hunters. Twice.

Despite her determination to be the adult in charge, it felt strange to be the one casting the circle, lighting the candle, and saying the prayers, lapsing into American English, the language she still thought in—sounding impossibly weird to her Irish and Cockney witches-to-be. Conscious of her two novices, she did not try to beat against the wall between her and Jo, letting herself drift lightly instead, hovering protectively over her charges. She could feel them both starting to let go. Jane-Beth had already done the Witches Flight, and Deirdre had a far-and-away look in her eyes, as though she were already seeing into the Beyond.

"Listen," Deirdre broke the holy silence, cupping her hand to her ear, "a night bird is flying our way." Robyn listened, hearing a faint rushing in the darkness. Beth, too, strained to hear—but clearly lacked Deirdre's country-girl ear.

Bolted window shutters flew open. Flying into the room, a black-and-white bird landed on the floor between them, cawing as she alighted, "Hela! Hela!"

Deirdre gasped, "Oh, my, 'tis a magpie."

"Hela!" Hela announced proudly, candlelight gleaming on her black-white feathers. "Com wit Hel-la." Taking off again, the magpie flew three times around the room, then back out the window, calling, "Hel-la! Hela! Com wit Hel-la!"

"Follow the bird," Deirdre shouted, never having seen Hela before, but easily recognizing an omen. Beth obeyed, and Robyn felt her sister-initiate's spirit winging off after the bird. She had to follow, maintaining contact. Leaving Falstaff's Place behind, she felt herself flying over a riotous Southwark, then over dark waters, following Beth and Hela. Deirdre was nowhere about. Suddenly a familiar stone wall reared in front of her, the same stones that had stopped her in Bruges, cold, dank, and forbidding. She was still walled off from Jo. Unable to either batter through the wall or worm between the stones.

But this time Beth and Hela showed her the way, instead of trying to batter through, she flung her soul at the sky and flew over it. What she saw as limitless stone was actually the south wall of the Tower facing the river, near the Traitor's Gate. The Tower of London is not a single tower, but a walled castle, with a score of towers and turrets arranged in concentric rings. She flew over the Tower Green to the White Tower, the oldest part, the whitewashed stone inner keep laid down by William the Conqueror. Hela banked ahead of her, flying sideways through a dark arrow slit. Following Hela in, she stopped her flight, finding herself in a stone tower chamber, windowless except for the arrow slit and sealed by a heavy wooden door.

By the dim light of a tiny candle stub, she made out the gaunt happy faces of Jo and Joy. Mother and daughter were huddled over the candle, looking half starved and deliriously happy. Excited smiles made their surroundings seem all the more surreal—a small stone cell whose only furnishings were a straw mattress, a sheaf of grain, and a side of uncooked bacon. "How gladdening to see you," Jo rose to greet her.

"Also you, Jane," Joy added, seeing Beth was not slighted.

Acknowledging their greetings, Robyn realized why they looked so happy. Jo and Joy must have been alone in this horrible dank cell for heaven knows how long—then on Witches Night, friends appear. Two novice witches they initiated, coming at last to their aid. "And you did not need any potion to get here," Jo pointed out, proud of her novice's progress.

Jo was right. Two months ago, she begged Jo for the secret of the gray powder, now she had forgotten she ever needed it. Still horribly uncertain how to use this new power, she asked, "What can we do for you?"

"Get to Collin," Jo told her without hesitation. "Something blocks me from speaking to him. Tell him Lord Scales has us here in the Tower. He must—"

She never found out what Collin must do. Suddenly a shattering boom shook the air around her. She smelled sulfur. Another boom followed the first, and another whiff of brimstone. Looking around, she found she was no longer in the Tower, but back in Southwark. She was kneeling in her room in Falstaff's Place, holding hands with Beth and Deirdre. From behind the bolted and shuttered window came a hollow distant booming.

"What happened?" Deirdre demanded. Not having made the Witches Flight, Deirdre knew nothing about the trip to the Tower, or the aborted visit with Jo and Joy.

Beth piped up, "We followed the bird, out the window, and into the Tower."

"But the window is shuttered," Deirdre protested. And bolted, too. No real bird could have come in, and no one could have gone out. A mental gulf opened between what was "real" and what was not. Robyn felt as if she had flown to the Tower and back, but she had no real proof. No talkative O'Neills to confirm her flight. Her real body felt weighty as ever, not about to fly around the room, much less soar across the Thames, and the window was, indeed, bolted.

Signing for holy silence, she got her bickering charges attention, pointing to what lay alongside the candle. Shining in the candlelight was a single black-and-white feather. Beth and Deirdre both fell silent, staring at the feather and then at the window, two realities bringing the gulf back together. From the far side of the shuttered window, dull booming sounded again.

Getting up, she went to check the bolt and see what caused the booming. Shutters were latched tight, just as she left them. Drawing the bolt, she flung back the shutters. Night air streamed in, blowing out the candle. Big booms came from down river. She looked toward the Tower for the source of the sound. Spurts of fire leaped from the fortress ramparts, flinging incendiary projectiles, sputtering and trailing sparks. Huge Roman candles, whose booming broke her link to Jo. Fear and death sent hurtling out of the Tower onto the roofs of London. Crashing in among the close-packed wooden houses, the flaming bombs exploded, throwing embers in all directions. Bells began to toll in the city, calling for firefighters and bucket brigades to bring up Thames water. Newly captured king's cannon, sited in Southwark, banged at the Tower in reply, filling the night sky with smoke and flame. This was a Fourth of July London would not soon forget.

What Robyn kept remembering were Jo and Joy's gaunt faces and the sheaf of grain and side of bacon fat she had seen in the cell. Some Feast of Saint Martin. She remembered a story Bryn told her in Wales, how Bad King John had captured Lady Maud de Braose from a great marcher family. He put Lady Maude and her oldest son in a cell in Windsor, with a sheaf of grain and a flitch of uncooked bacon, then did not open the cell until they were dead. No doubt it suited Scales's sense of justice to conserve the Tower's food supply by starving his prisoners. It was just like Jo not to mention she was in want—and to simply call on Collin.

⊶⊷⊷ Northampton ⊷⊶⊷

*R*obyn *slept no more* than a nightingale that Witches Night, totally obsessed with getting Jo and Joy out of the Tower—at once, before they starved. But how? Who could she appeal to? Edward? Gallant and willing, to be sure, but what could he do, even with a big eager army at his back? She had felt the heavy stone walls of the Tower; by the time Edward battered his way in, Jo and Joy could easily be dead. Duchess Wydville? No doubt the good duchess could get them out—but would she? Not likely, not unless Robyn had something to offer in return.

Up and fretting when the lauds bells chimed, she concluded she must find Collin. Just as Jo said. Collin would know best what to do—whether it took wits or magic. Deciding that, she dozed a bit, but was up and dressed before prime. Leaving Beth and Deirdre sleeping off Witches Night, she went cloaked to the stables and had her mare saddled. Determined to see Edward, she left Falstaff's Place in the half light, headed for London Bridge, with early morning rain falling around her.

Last night's pleasure seekers lay sprawled before the tavern doors. Bored "Winchester Geese" waited for customers under the eaves of the public bath, making love for a living on a cold Saturday morning. Southwark was the London seat of the bishop of Winchester, who got both fines from the courts, and rents from the baths. A tidy arrangement, not just for His Grace the bishop, but for the women as well, who plied their trade in a bathhouse instead of a back alley. The bishop did not allow bath owners to beat or abuse women, or confine them to the stews, or live off their earnings—each woman had to have a place of her own where she could eat and sleep away from men. And in the baths, men were at least washed. Sex here and now had a curious medieval innocence. No AIDS. Not even syphilis. And a bishop watching over it all—if you must have a pimp, it paid to have him be rich and celibate. Much worse than the baths-cum-brothels were the bear pits, where beasts were forced to fight to the death and men teased blinded bears with whips. That was the real shame of Southwark.

Guards at the Drawbridge Gate let her through. Edward's orders—the immensely popular earl of March had made it clear "Lady" Robyn Stafford had the run of London and was not to be kept standing about in predawn drizzle. Smiles beneath the men's sallets showed what they thought her early morning visit was for—why she was so eager to go into London and see their young lord. Let them think what they liked; she had bigger worries than a dubious reputation.

No one leaned out their windows to cheer her now. Crows and ravens cried angrily overhead instead, while tidewater roared between the stone arches and men with nets fished off the supporting piers. From downriver came the dull hollow boom of cannons, as batteries in Southwark banged away at the Tower. Beyond the Bridge, London was just beginning to stir beneath dripping eaves and wet rooftops. Lamps were out and cookfires lit. Boatmen called to customers, "Go you hence?" Baker's boys cried "Hot buns!" and "Honey on the comb!" Edward was right: London seemed just the right size, small enough to be explored, but big enough to surprise—a city where you could walk everywhere and be always amazed. Even the boom of cannons was getting lost in the day's clamor.

In keeping with the pious nature of their rebellion, the earls had their headquarters at a house of God, Grey Friars, a massive church on Newgate Street. The rebel army was camped just beyond the walls, by the Smithfield cattle market, where FitzHolland had hoped to have her burned at the stake. Not so big as Saint Paul's, Grey Friars was still imposing, an immense church with spacious cloisters and a fine paneled library built by Dick Whittington, with reading desks and a vast supply of bound manuscripts. Halls were filled with monks and men in armor, and the warm smell of baking bread. Ovens throughout the city were turning out the big hard loaves that soldiers ate on the march.

Edward had impressive bachelor digs. He, too, had a room of his own, bigger than hers and more sumptuously decorated, but without her sweeping view of the city and river. Up before dawn—his table littered with parchment documents, muster rolls, and the remains of a plain English breakfast of bread and beer—he wore Mortimer colors like when they first met, a blue-gold surcoat tied with silk ribbons, over yellow hose and soft glove-leather boots. Men dressed so elegantly here and now, when they were not at war. Rising to greet her, Edward exclaimed, "How wonderful. I wanted to see you as soon as you were awake."

"And here I am." Having hardly slept a wink. He took her in his arms, for once unarmed and unarmored, and she felt warm solid flesh beneath the costly fabric—too bad they were in a house of God. Tired and scared, she very much needed comfort and support; just having him hold her made things immensely better. She rested her head on his shoulder, thinking of how throughout this whole outlandish ordeal, Edward had been the person most consistently on her side, the one man she could totally count on. Only Jo had been as honest and caring toward her—and now Jo was in desperate straits.

Seeing her seriousness, Edward's smile of welcome turned to worry. "What has happened? Why are you anguished?"

She told him. Not about the Witches Flight—one astounding story was enough by now—besides, that was a woman's secret. She merely said she had learned by magic that Jo and Joy were in a Tower cell, with a sheaf of grain and a slab of bacon fat for company. She had to get them out as fast as humanly possible.

Edward's puzzlement vanished, replaced by eager determination; given a problem, he immediately started searching up solutions. "Salisbury and Cobham have the King's Cannon from Whitechapel set up in Southwark, and may hopefully batter Lord Scales into a more peaceable frame of mind." But that could take forever—so far as Jo and Joy were concerned. Edward saw that, too, saying, "I will send word this very morning to Lord Scales, that he is responsible for the lives of Joanna Grey and her daughter. Whatever happens to them will happen to him. If they go free, so does he. If they are harmed, he will pay with his head." And Lord Scales had best believe it. So far things had gone much as Edward promised, with no mass reprisals against King Henry's henchmen. There had been some swift trials at the Guildhall for those accused of real crimes—followed by a few equally swift executions in Cheapside. English justice was vigorous and direct, with an emphasis on speedy trials, and not overcrowding the prisons. But there had been no spurious "treason" charges against men who merely obeyed their king. Not yet.

"And if Salisbury cannot blast his way into the Tower," Edward added, "we will bring King Henry himself back to London to order the Tower opened. Word has come that the court plans to secret King

Henry in the fens—on the Isle of Ely." Ely was an island in almost trackless marsh, where neither a fleet nor army could get at him. "Lord Fauconberg is already headed up Ermine Street with his men. We are getting ready to follow."

He was all set to do right, not just for her, or for Jo and Joy, but everyone in England, cheerfully taking on the hopes and troubles of an entire people. God, she wished him success, envying his boundless energy. She did not doubt he would do his damndest to scour the swamps for King Henry—but that, too, would take time . . . days for sure, maybe weeks, or even months. Only magic had the speed she needed. She whispered to his silk shoulder, "I have to go."

Edward's worried look returned. "Go where?"

"To find Sir Collingwood Grey. He will know how to free his niece and sister." Or so she fervently hoped.

Edward sighed. "I very much thought you would say that." His grip relaxed, and she could feel him working something off his finger. "I presume there is no hope of stopping you?"

"This is something I absolutely must do." She could be as resolute as he was when the need arose.

"Where is Sir Collingwood Grey?" Edward asked.

"With his uncle Lord Grey de Ruthyn. Either in Ruthyn or maybe Coventry." She could not picture Collin following the king into the swamps of Ely.

"Will you need silver? Horses? An escort of men-at-arms?" He made no attempt to stop her, though it was easily in his power. From the very first Edward had treated her as someone to be cajoled, flattered, or seduced, but not forced. "You know you can have whatever you want."

She shook her head. "Just the pair of horses you have already given me and my maid." She still had a some of the duchess's gold half-nobles, and an armed escort would attract unwanted attention.

"Then take this." He slipped a silver ring into her hand, still warm from his finger. "If you need anything, send me this token, and I will come at once, with ten thousand bowmen at my back." But, of course. She remembered the story Joy told her in the King's Gallery at Berkeley Castle—about how when Edward was nine or ten he had come to his father's aid with ten thousand Welsh border troopers, raised in his earldom of March. Now that he was eighteen, anything was possible.

Holding tight to the ring, she kissed him chastely on the lips. Edward responded just as delicately. They were, after all, in a church. When their lips parted, he whispered, "You have given me a new respect for religion."

"Really?" She thought she was a very impious influence, with her witchcraft and future ways. "How is that?"

"By bringing home to me the words of the godly Saint Bernard. He said, to be always with a woman, but not to have her is harder than raising the dead."

She smiled at his predicament, saying, "It can be hard on the woman as well."

"Next time," he told her, "it will not matter that we are in a house of God."

"How so?" Did he plan to get a dispensation from ever-friendly Pope Pius?

"Because next time I get you in a church it will be for our betrothal."

Betrothal? Impossible. This is what comes of having beer for breakfast. The boy was as mad as when she first met him—but she did not say it. Why part on bad terms? They were headed into danger and might never see each other again, so let Edward think what he liked. If something happened to her, or if he was killed in battle, their last memory should not be rejection. Better to make it romantic, even if wildly impractical. Much as she might love Edward, marriage was out of the question when what she wanted most was to get back to the third millennium. Whatever they had must be temporary, so why not keep it happy and light? With no heavy scenes.

She took the silver ring, giving him another virginal kiss good-bye—not saying yes, not saying no. When she got to the Grey Friars stables, she still had the ring in her hand. Turning it over, she found it too big to fit her finger, but embossed on the surface was a silver rose. She stood amid the straw and manure, next to the beautiful white mare Edward had given her, staring at the rose on the ring. Tears welled up. He did really love her, no denying that. This lovable young earl, who could have any woman in the land, wanted her. She felt touched and at the same time saddened.

Mounting up, Robyn rode out of the steamy stables into the morning drizzle. When she got back to Falstaff's Place, she found the girls up and dressed, with Hela stalking about, looking as solid and real on Saturday morning as the feather she left on Witches Night.

She told Deirdre to pack and get ready to ride, "You are going to get to see the West Country."

But first they had to return Beth to her home in West Cheap. As they neared the Mercery, the stone arcade where the Mercers sold their fabric, she heard the cry that gave Cheapside its name, "Great cheap of cloth." When they got to the covered market, the cries turned to Cockney cheers as people recognized the "Lady from Calais" who rode into London with Lord Edward; anyone the least connected with reopening the Calais trade was an immediate heroine in Cheapside. Beth's parents were both there—John and Amy Lambert—surprised and pleased to see their daughter riding in the lap of a woman from Edward's household. As she let Beth down, people crowded around her, asking, "Does Lord Edward of March know that women and babes were murdered last night?"

Wildfire from the Tower had killed civilians and set fires, a special terror in this tinderbox city. Were it not for the rain, the whole city might be in flames. West Cheap did not like having women and children thrust into the front lines, while the only knights killed so far had died by accident. The Tower had never fired on the city before last night, and Londoners never wanted it to happen again; they were calling Lord Scales a murderer—but that was nothing new. Falling naturally into a Cockney accent, she assured them, "Lord Edward knows what the wildfire has done, and he is going to bring King Henry back to London, to have His Majesty put an end to murder from the Tower."

Hearing their cheers, you would have thought she reopened Calais single-handed, and now would deliver Mad King Henry. West Cheap was ecstatic to have its needs heard by someone "close" to the Lords of Calais—not caring if her closeness came from carnal dallying with their betters, in fact, rather hoping it did.

Robyn left the city, riding north up Watling Street with Deirdre beside her and Hela flying ahead, figuring she had best just follow the bird. Two months into the Middle Ages and she was riding off on a snow-white mare, following a magpie into danger. Some joke, but what choice did she have? Troops were also headed north—clumps of horsemen followed by covered carts, kitchen wagons, and great lines of bowmen slogging through fresh mud. They wore red tunics and the white ragged staff, a Neville badge. Pushing straight up Watling Street, past Bushey Heath, she stopped at Saint Albans to breakfast at Chequers across from the market—just down Saint Peter's street from the Castle Inn where Joy's father, the old duke of Somerset, was killed. She lit a candle at his tomb in the abbey, fulfilling the promise she and Joy made to Mary Margaret—who fed them when they escaped from Berkeley Castle. Then she went on up Watling Street, along the soggy green banks of the Ver, heading north and west toward Coventry—which King Henry and his court were vacating. If Collin was not there, she would scour the Marches looking for him, if she had to go all the way to Ruthyn. Beneath her rain-sodden cloak she wore the red-gold riding outfit Collin had gotten her that first day at Berkeley Castle. In the West Marches these days, Stafford colors were far safer than Edward's murrey and blue.

When the rains relented, she wrung out her drenched cloak as best she would, tying it to her saddle. Deirdre brought her attention back to the road ahead. "Look, my lady, Saxon knights."

Mounted men-at-arms trotted toward her down Watling Street, their armor gleaming from the rain. She scanned their banners, which bore the patriotic cross of Saint George—but not King Henry's swans or the Neville saltire, or roses of any color. Whoever was coming took pains not to let anyone know which side they favored. She tried to seem equally neutral, a lady out riding with her Irish maid. At wartime. In the rain. As they drew closer, she recognized the lead rider—it was Collin's friend, Sir William Fiennes, the curly-haired, cupid-lipped Lord Saye, who put her up in his fairy-tale castle-on-a-lake near Banbury. The man whose father Lord Scales had sacrificed to the London mob during John-Amend-All's rebellion. He recognized her as well, and they exchanged good-days. She asked when he had last seen Collin.

"Last I saw him he was with Lord Grey de Ruthyn in Coventry," Lord Saye replied. "But that was better than a week ago."

She asked how he looked. "As well as any of us," Saye told her. "These are difficult times. Sir Collingwood Grey has his king in danger, his cousins in revolt, his manor burnt, and his sister accused of witchcraft, but with all that, he still seemed to do splendidly. We could all pray for his fortitude."

She thanked him and then said cordial good-byes. Lord Saye and his retainers rattled off down the Roman road toward London. Plainly Lord Saye had learned from his father's fate—and was not trotting down the Saint Albans road to rescue Lord Scales from the Tower, but to join the rebels besieging it.

Past Dunstable and the Chilterns, she entered Brickhill Wood, emerging at Fenney Stratford, where a long stretch of Watling Street led straight to Stony Stratford. She and Deirdre spent the night in Stony Stratford, in an inn with the Sign of the Bull. Exhausted as she was, she still had trouble sleeping, for the inn was poor and the place seemed strangely ill-omened. Being a witch could be a serious burden, forcing her to keep odd hours, make strange trips, and constantly listen for calls from afar.

Church bells woke her the next morning, and they rode to Sunday Mass through a weeping drizzle, praying for peace along with the local congregation. Then she started on up Watling Street toward Towcester, Daventry, and the ironstone country. From there she could take the road west to Coventry, where Lord Saye had last seen Collin. Hela got in front of her, cawing, "Naw! Naw!" She ducked as the magpie flew at her face, squawking and screeching. "Your bird does not want us to go this way," Deirdre observed.

Robyn reined in. "She is not my bird." Deirdre merely shrugged. No matter whom Hela belonged to, the omen was plain—the bird did not want them following a week-old trail up Watling Street—and without Hela, they were flying blind. Another narrower, muddier road ran north through fields and woods toward Grafton and Northampton. Robyn misliked the half-submerged little lane, but she turned her mare toward it. Grafton was the seat of duchess Wydville—that alone might draw Collin this way. Hela winged on ahead, cawing happily.

Hela could fly above the muck, but Robyn had to flounder through swollen streams and wade flooded fords, walking Lily, who was still tired from yesterday's long ride. Deirdre tramped happily along beside her, claiming such fine weather made her homesick, reminding her of Ireland, "where we hardly have three sunny days in a row." Robyn decided to skirt Grafton and not face Her High Holiness until she found Collin. Hela did not object, but the detour added to their difficulties. It took the whole day to travel the dozen or so miles between Stony Stratford and the ironstone village of Hardingstone with its huge stone Eleanor's Cross. Calling at the first prosperous-looking farmhouse, she paid a boy to feed and stable their horses; then she accepted two seats at the hearth from a friendly farmwife wearing blue homespun. Big and motherly in her linen apron and white wimple, the woman had a dimpled grin, gaps in her teeth, and graying hair—but was probably not ten years older than Robyn. "Would m'lady like some porridge?"

She shook her head. But Deirdre eagerly accepted pork-scrap porridge straight from the kettle. Robyn asked for boiling water, making herself mint tea and drying her soaked cloak by the fire. Warm inside and out, she never wanted to leave this kitchen, and asked if they could have lodging for the night. "My, yes, m'lady," replied the farmwife. "But you will not want it."

"Oh, we would be most pleased, I am sure." She was not so much of a lady as the woman thought, and this tight, clean farmhouse, smelling of baking bread, appealed to her more than any inn. Outside the rain had stopped, but that hardly tempted her to leave. She could have curled up in a warm corner and gone straight to sleep.

"Well, m'lady will be sharing her bed with a dozen of m'Lord Egremont's border savages, filthy, booted, and fit to be hung."

"What?"

"Harbingers have been here, m'lady."

"Harbingers?"

"Yes, m'lady." She ladled more porridge onto Deirdre's plate, floating with lumps of lard. "Men in Percy livery have come to every farm and inn, speaking atrocious Northumberland and buying up every bed. They are lewd, dangerous men, and no one dares deny them. You and your maid will be far safer in the abbey with the good sisters to watch over you."

No wonder the woman had bread in the oven and a huge pot of peas and pork tripe on the fire. Men were about to descend on this farmwife en masse, and not just any men, either, but armed retainers of Thomas Percy, Lord Egremont, second son of Henry Percy, earl of Northumberland. Most famous for trying to ambush the earl of Salisbury and old Countess Alice on their way home from a wedding at Tattershall Castle—Robyn had heard the whole grim story aboard the *Trinity*. Now Lord Egremont was coming to Hardingstone, either tonight or on the morrow. Nor was Hardingstone happy about the visit. The best silver was buried, and the young women were in hiding. Though Egremont's harbingers had promised payment, these villagers expected the worst; to them, northerners were a breed apart, bandits and cattle thieves, speaking unintelligible Northumberland and stealing whatever they could carry. "Cattle lifting is in their blood," the farmwife told her. "And to them clean linen is like cloth-of-gold; how can they not covet whatever they see?"

She was still warming herself at the hearth when horses came splashing into the yard outside. Men called to each other in broad Northumberland. This was the first time Robyn heard it spoken, but thanks to the spell, she understood it perfectly—the old Anglo-Saxon dialect was actually more purely "English" than the Midlands speech, less infected by French and Latin, with a rhythmical lilt to it. A fun language to speak, full of weird words and unexpected syllables.

Fists beat on the kitchen door. Seeing the farmwife cringe, Robyn answered the knock, opening the door and asking in Northumberland what the men wanted.

She found herself facing an astonished border reiver, a big scar-faced ruffian in leather and mail, wearing a steel bonnet and a white Percy crescent. He stepped back, startled to hear his native North-umberland so far from home. More riders crowded around the door, all wearing the white crescent along with russet and yellow—Percy colors. They had wild names like Mary's Jock, Sweet-milk Selby, Bangtail Bell, and Black Dick Nixon—and were all happy to have found a pretty woman who spoke their language. She welcomed them in, saying they could spend the night, but warned they must pay for whatever they needed. "This is holy ground belonging to Delapré Ab-bey, and the theft of even a pin will surely be punished, both here and in the hereafter."

That last was pure invention—she had not the slightest idea who owned the land. But these border reivers took it as gospel, glad to find "an honest-looking lass speaking fair Northumberland so far and away from home." They besieged her with questions, asking, "What county would this be? Tell us true, m'lady, are we in Wiltshire yet? Or mayhap Surrey?"

"We were promised the loot of Wiltshire for our troubles," Bangtail Bell explained. "Also Kent and Essex," added his mates. "And Surrey, and Sussex, and Hampshire."

Her heart sank on hearing this. Half of southern England had been offered up for loot, and no doubt rape and murder, as well. These men could not wait to begin. Until now she had clung to the hope that King Henry could be theirs as peacefully as they had won Lon-don. Holland's sailors refused to fight, and she saw lords and commons rally to their cause, making her think Mad King Henry's army might go over to them, as well. Now she saw the court had found men who cared nothing for causes, or the rights of commons, having come south for what they could steal.

"So, is this Wiltshire?" they demanded. "The locals do deny it, but we do not believe them. Fingerless Will was in Wiltshire once, and says it did look much like this." Fingerless Will put his good hand to his heart, swearing this was so.

She hastily assured them that Wiltshire was still two counties to the south. "This is Northamptonshire. Indeed that is Northampton itself, there beyond Delapré Abbey." She pointed out the church towers of the Midlands wool town rising above the trees on the far side of the Nene. There was no mistaking the place—she wore Northampton-made riding boots, and had been hoping to get them resoled.

Their disappointment showed. "We have come a sore ways south already," Bangtail Bell explained. "And it is hard to hear we have still a ways to go for our reward."

Hard to hear, indeed. She thought of the thousands of southern bowmen marching north, Kentish archers and Calais veterans, their quivers full of clothyard shafts. These folksy felons on horseback did not have to go anywhere near Wiltshire to find their reward. Sickened by the carnage to come, she dragged Deirdre away from the porridge pot, saying, "We are overdue at the abbey." Violence hung heavy in the air. So far the men had molested no one—but a teenage serving girl and two fine horses might be more temptation than border moss-troopers could manage. At the big Queen Eleanor's Cross between the town and the abbey, she saw more mean-looking horsemen in leather jacks and rain-stained mail. Not all of them looked willing to wait for Wiltshire. Hela alighted atop the tall stone cross, cawing happily, showing a grim sense of humor, even for a magpie. Like the Eleanor's Cross at Saint Albans, this one was actually an intricately carved gothic momument, with arches and statues, and a huge stone cross on top. How typical that the most impressive edifice in this tiny hamlet was a memorial to a woman whose funeral cortege passed through here two hundred years ago. Seven hundred so far as Robyn was concerned. But who's counting?

Ringed by parkland, Delapré Abbey included a three-hundred-year-old Benedictine nunnery, dedicated to Saint Mary de Pratis, sitting on the south side of the Nene, where the rain-swollen river made a wide sweeping curve to the north. From the nunnery gate she could see the London road and the bridge leading to Northampton. Tents were pitched along the river, and laborers had dug a ditch and rampart to connect the two ends of the river loop. An armed camp was going up just across the Nene from Northampton.

Nuns swarmed out to greet her, veils blowing in the breeze, hustling them to a bench by the kitchen fire, happy to have female visitors in a place filling up with armed men, anxious to preserve a tiny island of peace and security against the rising tide of war. "God willing, you will be safe here," they told her. "We already have a knight and his lady in residence."

God better provide, a single knight sounded like thin protection. Young women from Hardingstone were hiding there, as well, making it a very nervous nunnery. Novices hung up her wet clothes to dry, excited by the feel of satin drawers or a silk chemise—"Oh, so soft and gentle. No wonder your skin is so white and smooth."

Deirdre whispered in Gaelic, "They wear itchy hair underclothes, and sleep on boards under scratchy blankets." No doubt. The abbey seemed tolerably clean, but awfully spare, full of well-swept bare corners. Little girls peeping out from behind the black habits no longer surprised her. No more than seeing some nun sitting in the corner, looking sad and pregnant. Convents could be very worldly places, especially in wartime. "Those rings mean they are married to Jesus," Deirdre whispered. "If they disobey, the abbess can beat them, or put them in the stocks." Asked how she knew so much about nunneries, and the girl turned smug. "I escaped from one. Twice."

Bells tolled, and nuns hustled them into chapel for vespers. Joining them on her knees, Robyn heard the hush of Sunday vespers broken by the sound of boots on stone. Peeking out the corner of her eye, she strained to see if the knight was wearing Percy livery. Instead she saw a blue-and-white surcoat bearing the black ragged staff of Lord Grey de Ruthyn—it was Collin.

She could barely believe it. Bryn was at his side, her short brown unbound hair hanging loose above the shoulders of a blue gown with Collin's silver wyvern embroidered on the breast. With them was Nurse Nest, tall and silent, but not wearing her longbow out of deference to the nuns. No wonder Hela had been so insistent they take the road north from Stony Stratford. Bowing her head, she thanked God and the black-and-white bird that brought her here.

Between prayers she took repeated peeks over her shoulder, making sure she was not imagining this, and to see how Collin looked. As Lord Saye said, he was bearing up well, considering all Collin had suffered. He did not look haggard or worn, and he gave her a swift smile. Sunday vespers in a nunnery was always one of his favorite places to be. If anything, adversity had honed him. He looked fit and alert, less devil-may-care, paying more attention to his prayers.

Bryn looked thoroughly pleased with herself, wearing Collin's silver wyvern on her breast, hands pressed in prayer, smiling her slim secret smile, with the man she wanted at her side, in her hand, and in her bed. "Good for you," thought Robyn, giving Bryn a reassuring smile—she felt like the proverbial bad penny, showing up in North-amptonshire after Bryn had seen her shipped safely off to Eire. Good for Collin, too. She was glad Collin had someone; bit annoying to have it be Bryn again, but that seemed to be their fate. Happily, it was not hers.

As soon as vespers were done with, Robyn rose and crossed herself. Bryn was waiting when she turned around, giving her a kiss of greeting, speaking Welsh so Saxon ears could not hear. "*Gadewch i ni eistedd a sgwrsio,*" suggesting they go somewhere to "sit and talk."

"*Ble?*" She asked, "Where?" slipping easily into Welsh.

Bryn took her and Deirdre to sup with her and Collin in a little private bedroom with a brick fireplace, canopy bed, tall windows, and a simple spread of bread, salt fish, cheese, carrots, peasecods, pippins, and a pot of green ginger set out on the table. Robyn asked for boiled water to wash the fruit and carrots, and make her herb tea. Collin took one look at the light repast and called for a joint of beef and a flagon of wine. Hela stalked about the table, pecking at the food, and adding her caws to the conversation. Being witches, no one found that weird.

Collin said he stayed in convents whenever he could, "Convents always cheer me. Nuns have next to nothing, yet they take in travelers, tend the sick, and make homes for widows and girls too feeble-minded to get husbands. Convents around Oxford are the best, and always have the liveliest nuns; comes from rubbing up against those learned young clerks in the colleges." Right. A little too lively in the case of that downcast nun sitting in the kitchen corner. She told Collin that Jo and Joy were prisoners in the Tower.

"So, they have given her up to Scales." Collin's easy self-assurance disappeared. "Those shameless idiots. I never thought they would be so needlessly cruel."

"What about Duchess Wydville?" Robyn asked. Having passed so close to Grafton brought her naturally to mind. "Will she not help?"

Collin scoffed, "Duchess Wydville cares only about currying favor with the queen. She has convinced Her Majesty that keeping Jo prisoner gives them a hold on me, preserving Joanna's life, but keeping her locked up. Secretly, the duchess likes it that way. With Joanna a prisoner, she has more power with the coven and with the queen."

Not an easy combination to beat. "It may not keep Jo and Joy alive for long." She told Collin about the siege of the Tower, and the sheaf of grain and slab of bacon fat.

Putting down his salt fish, Collin stared grimly at the food on the table. "This makes my decision much easier." He looked at Bryn and then at her. "I came this far with King Henry, hoping he would listen to me—away from Holland and the queen. But hapless Henry cannot speak for himself. Duke of Buckingham speaks for him, and Buckingham thinks he needs Holland and Scales more than he needs me. Which makes it past time for the much-beloved Duke Buckingham to find out how badly he is mistaken." Here was yet another Collin, coolly determined to bring down the greatest nobles in the land to get what he wanted. She looked over at Bryn—who was keeping her face blank. If Bryn knew what was coming, Bryn would not show it. Deirdre sat nibbling cheese. Nest eyed the Saxons carefully, saying nothing. "On the morrow," Collin told her, "King Henry arrives in Northampton with his army, and my uncle, Lord Grey de Ruthyn, commands the royal vanguard. If the rebel earls march north to press their demands, I will see that my uncle sides with them, against Buckingham, Shrewsbury, and Egremont."

Treason hung in the air—a charge that medieval law never took lightly—to oppose Buckingham and Egremont meant to oppose King Henry. To speak it was a crime. To hear it spoken and say nothing left you tainted. Even idle talk around the table could get you hung, drawn, and quartered—or burned if you were a woman. And this was much more than idle talk.

Sharp raps at the door startled everyone. Robyn imagined mailed fists with Scales's white scallops on their sleeves. Bryn signaled to Nest, who got up and answered the door, one hand on the knife in her belt. Nunnery servants stood in the doorway, bearing meat and wine; Collin's roast had arrived. Serving girls laid the joint of roasted meat on the table, supported by a magnificently carved platter. Nest set the wine down beside the roast, which was royally done, still sizzling from the spit. No one moved to touch it.

Nest saw the servants out, then closed and bolted the door. Collin stared across the table at Robyn, ignoring the joint he ordered. She and Collin had become more than just friends and sometime comrades in adventure. Two armies lurched toward collision, with Grey de Ruthyn commanding King Henry's vanguard and Edward leading the rebel advance. Collin was Grey de Ruthyn's favored nephew. She was Edward's "lady" and confidante, which meant the coming clash might be decided not before Northampton, but at this nunnery table. Collin chose his words carefully. "My uncle cannot give his support for nothing. He expects to be rewarded."

"Rewarded how?" Robyn herself had nothing to offer, and she could not see herself urging Edward to do anything dishonorable.

"For now he will want Edward and Warwick's good lordship in his land dispute with Lord Fanhope."

She did not know who Lord Fanhope was, or what his dispute was with Grey de Ruthyn—but it seemed a trivial point with the fate of England at stake. Robyn merely nodded.

"And should all go well," Collin added, "he seeks to hold higher office."

"What higher office?" Having met Grey de Ruthyn, she could not imagine what political ambitions the man could have. Anyone who would sell out his king merely to get the better of Lord Fanhope in a land dispute could hardly be very interested in running the country.

"I believe my uncle aspires to be treasurer of England."

Merely the most lucrative office in the land. Robyn shook her head. "You must know I cannot promise that." Who was she to make royal appointments?

"It is merely his hope," Collin explained.

"Then let him live in hope." Surely if Grey de Ruthyn saved them from fighting a battle, Edward and the Nevilles would find some way to reward him.

"Good." Collin nodded. "That will do for my uncle." That was far too easy; knowing Collin, there had to be more. He leaned forward, hands clasped in front of him, putting his full weight on the table.

"But for me there is something else, something I must have. Something you must swear to." Here came the kicker. Collin was not going to commit treason just to short Lord Fanhope on a land deal or to make his rich uncle more wealthy. "I must have Joanna and Joy alive, and out of the Tower. That is the only reason why I am doing this."

"But, of course." That was why she had come here—the only reason why *she* was doing this.

He shook his head. "It is not so simple. As soon as we Greys change sides, Joanna will no longer be of any use to her captors. She could be immediately killed—or worse." To the medieval mind, immediate execution could easily be considered merciful. "Joanna's release must be certain, sure and swift. I must have your absolute assurance on this."

"You have." The two things she wanted most at the moment were for Jo and Joy to be freed, and Edward to win with an absolute minimum of bloodshed. This was her best chance at both.

"And Edward's as well?"

Reaching into her purse, she took out Edward's silver ring and slid it across the table—with the rose showing. Collin picked up the ring, turned it over in his hand, and then looked from the ring to her. "Have you been to bed with him yet?"

"What does that have to do with it?"

Collin smirked. "From what I know of young Edward—everything."

"No," she shot back. "I have not been to bed with him." Not even on May Day—but she bit back that last dig, for Bryn's sake.

"Good," Collin concluded happily, "then we can be sure to have Edward's complete attention and consideration."

How dared he be so smug? But, then, a warlock willing to live outside the law, commit treason, even betray his king in battle must dare just about anything.

Collin relaxed, letting go of the ring, leaning back in his seat. "All we need now is a way to get this message to Edward."

"That I can do." It meant another ride through the rain—at least as far as Saint Albans. But she had been ready to ride all the way to Wales looking for Collin, and this time Edward would be waiting at the end.

Collin lifted a warning finger. "That I cannot allow." He seemed dead set on making her sorry she had found him.

"Why?" She was the obvious choice for getting a message to Edward.

"We need you here," Collin told her. "You are my best link to Edward. If the first message fails, we may need you to carry another. Besides, betraying King Henry does not ensure Joanna will be safe. We may have to brave the duchess of Bedford in her lair, and I would not want to do that alone."

Who would? She could well understand, having just passed on a chance to go to Grafton herself. Collin's point was clear: she would get what she wanted up front—an easy win for Edward. He was trusting her to do the near impossible in exchange. So how to get the message to Edward? She could not take it, nor could Collin. That left Bryn, Nest, Deirdre, or Hela—bringing in anyone else would widen the conspiracy, and the risks. Undoubtedly Hela could do it best, but she could not see putting all her hopes on a bird, no matter how magical and talented. That left Bryn, Nest, and Deirdre. Bryn would do it gladly, for Collin's sake, but Bryn was all wrong for the part. For one, Edward did not know her. Bryn would be some Welsh stranger—granddaughter to a notorious "traitor"—trying to see the earl of March in the midst of a desperate military campaign. Not too likely. And coming from the enemy camp, her story would be rightly suspect. Most objections to Bryn applied tenfold to Nest.

That left Deirdre. Everyone knew the red-haired serving girl-cum-chaperone seen with Edward and his lady. As soon as Deirdre appeared, Edward would want to see her. Any message Deirdre bore would be instantly believed—by Edward at least, and he was the one who counted. Reaching out, Robyn retrieved the ring, saying, "Can I speak to my serving woman alone?"

"But, of course." Collin bowed and left, taking Bryn and Nest with him. Hela remained, strutting about the table, picking at food the humans seemed to have forgotten.

She hated dragging Deirdre deeper and deeper into Saxon troubles—first into rebellion, then witchcraft, now into outright treason. Fingering the ring, she asked Deirdre, "Do you understand what is happening?"

"Most of it, my lady." Deirdre looked thoughtful. "Who is Lord Fanhope? And how has he angered Sir Collin's uncle?"

"No idea," Robyn admitted.

"But you want to send a message to Lord Edward anyway?" Deirdre asked eagerly.

"Yes." Her hand tightened around the ring—she dearly hoped she was not holding this girl's death warrant. "The message must go to Edward himself; no one else can be trusted."

Deirdre nodded gravely. "I understand." But did she? If anyone remotely connected to King Henry heard the message, their plan would be uncovered and Deirdre would be put to death—in the most painful and degrading manner inventive minds could devise.

She had to be sure the girl understood completely. "It will be a crime to carry this message, and death if you are caught."

"Of course, m'lady." Being Irish born, Deirdre knew all too well how English law worked. It had been a high treason for her parents to marry. The Gaelic lullabies her Saxon father sang to her were illegal, making Deirdre's whole life a compound felony.

"But you will do it anyway?" Incredible loyalty for the few pennies a week Deirdre got paid.

"Of course, m'lady." Deirdre did not even hesitate.

Much as she needed the girl's aid, she could not help asking, "Why?"

"Because the message is between you and Lord Edward. You are my lady, who has taken me into her service. And Lord Edward is the brave, kind son of the only Saxon prince to give us simple justice." Steeped in Irish myth, Deirdre understood instinctively—the mad king, a magic ring, a message between two noble lovers, and a serving girl to carry it. Deirdre was named for a woman in the myths who loved a rebel and died rather than submit to an unjust king—now her namesake was finally living the legends.

Robyn shook her head in amazement. "Does nothing worry you?"

"Yes, indeed, m'lady." Deirdre knelt down at her feet, clasping Robyn's hands. "I worry for you."

"For me?" Robyn was astonished.

"Yes, m'lady." Deirdre looked up at her, tears showing in her eyes. "Without me, you will be alone among the Saxons—and that worries me mightily."

"Well, I will do my very best to stay out of trouble."

"Oh, do, do, m'lady. Promise me—at least until I get back." She swore to be on her best behavior, so long as her serving girl was gone.

Deirdre seemed satisfied, giving her hands a grateful squeeze and then rising from her knees. No wonder the English were so homicidally incensed at the Irish—when even their half-breed ladies maids insisted on treating them as equals. She drilled Deirdre both in Gaelic and English on the message to give to Edward. It was not enough for the girl to learn it by rote, she had to understand it completely, in all its implications.

King Henry's army was coming to Northampton, and not just to see the Eleanor Cross and stock up on leather boots. They were already moving the mud about, throwing up defenses. And Henry had brought down northern troops, knowing southerners would not kill and pillage their own people. What southern and western troops Henry had were increasingly unreliable, so much that Lord Grey de Ruthyn was ready to desert in exchange for trivial considerations. When the rebels arrived, they could count on aid from King Henry's own vanguard—anyone wearing the black ragged staff of Grey de Ruthyn would be a friend. She had Deirdre draw the ragged staff on a piece of parchment, so there was no mistaking friend and foe. Then she gave her the ring, saying, "This is the token given me by Edward—keep it hidden. If they will not let you see Edward, have them show him the ring, and he will see you at once. Otherwise give it only to him, as proof of what you say." Kissing the hand that gave her the ring, Deirdre thanked Robyn profusely for the chance to prove herself.

She bid her serving girl rise, saying, "That is nothing. I fear we shall all be getting chances to prove ourselves."

Deirdre would have left at once, but Robyn insisted the girl get a night's sleep. England's troubles were not going to go away overnight. Instead she saw Deirdre off at dawn, under gray skies, escorted by a half-dozen of Lord de Ruthyn's riders, stripped of their ragged staff badges. Deirdre's escort knew nothing of the plot, and so could not betray it. All they knew was they must take this Irish lady's maid safely to London—or face the wrath of their lord.

She and Collin rode as far as Grafton, seeing she got past the Percy outriders and the duchess of Bedford—if she was in residence. After Grafton they parted, giving hugs in the mud and rain. Deirdre left wearing a big Welsh all-weather cloak borrowed from Bryn. She had been an unfailingly cheerful companion, stouthearted and amazingly level-headed, despite her belief in ghosts, leprechauns, love spells, and flying barnacles. Deirdre had Edward's youthful optimism, his feeling that if the world were not as it should be, then something should be done about it. Their attitude did buoy one up. And now neither of them was here.

Riding back through the rain, she thanked Collin from the uttermost depths of her heart.

He looked askance. "What for?"

She told how she had been dreading this upcoming battle. Seeing Egremont's moss-troopers made her realize England teetered on the verge of all-out civil war, north against south, nobles against commons, past against the future. But King Henry's swift capture—alive and unharmed—could end the fighting practically before it began. "You have given us a chance to take King Henry with the least amount of bloodshed."

"What if I came over to the side of good and right on that wretched ship off the Wexford coast—like you begged me? None of this would be happening," Collin reminded her. "Joanna and Joy would most likely be dead. And I would be another spearman in Edward's army, facing an uphill battle on slippery ground." Collin had certainly picked a prime moment to see the light. "Do not believe I am doing this for Edward, or England, or even for you. I am doing it for my family. For Joanna and Joy. And for my uncle, who expects to be well rewarded."

"Of course." She understood completely, kissing him anyway. Collin had betrayed his king, risking a grisly ignoble traitor's death, all for others—asking nothing for himself. There was nobility in that.

On the way back Collin turned aside near Hardingstone, saying he needed somewhere to pray—which sounded strange since they were staying in an abbey. He led her to a slumped overgrown ring fort at the edge of a wood, where she was astonished to see a square iron-stone altar block, standing before the burnt circle left by a bonfire. Déjà vu all over again. A closer look showed that the four corners of the altar block were covered with black candle wax. Here was where she had been intiated into the coven, after her very first Witches Flight. Where she had met Jane-Beth and Duchess Wydville. She looked about in amazement, trying to match it to her memories, while Collin prayed silently at the wax-spattered altar, the first time she had seen him actively participating in the Old Religion. No longer an interested onlooker or a semi-Christian, but a devout warlock kneeling before Hecate, goddess of death and rebirth. She whispered her own prayer for those who had been there with her, Jo and Joy, and her sister-initiate, Jane-Beth Lambert of West Cheap, London. When Collin was done, she asked what place this was, and he replied it was called Hunsbury—"a place where ancient dead are buried, and where witches dance on dark hallowed nights." She said nothing about being here before in spirit, since that was a woman's secret.

⊷⧉ King's Tent ⧉⊶

Going back to the room she shared to get dry clothes, she selected a green satin gown from her chest of borrowed outfits. Beneath the gown lay a dead kingfisher, a tiny mummified bundle of feathers pressed between layers of silk and satin. Deirdre put it there to give the clothes a pleasant odor and to ward off moths and snakes. Life without Deirdre meant fewer such surprises, but it also meant doing for herself. Boiling water, washing dishes, drying clothes by the fire, and cooking scones on a hot griddle—something Deirdre had taught her how to do. She had done all these before, but two working together went through tasks so much faster. Plus, she'd had someone to talk to.

Collin had no such difficulties, being deft at getting the sisters to do whatever he wanted, one of the many conveniences of staying in convents. He liked to sup with the abbess in the main hall, a tall stately nun who enjoyed sharing her table with men, drinking wine, and listening to droll tales. Collin's flirting with the abbess did not bother Bryn; their "trial wedding" was probably more secure than most modern marriages. So long as both parties were of age and freely consented, the medieval Church considered almost any betrothal a valid marriage contract. If it had been consumated—and Bryn's contented smile said it had—breaking such a betrothal could be more difficult and expensive than your standard third-millennium no-fault divorce. Bryn sat at a window seat, sewing and mending for hours at a time, speaking Welsh or English as the mood moved her, claiming to be completely happy—and very much looking the part, being unfairly beautiful and blissfully in love. Nurse Nest was in constant attendance, all the help Bryn ever needed.

And in the wet meadow between the nunnery and the River Nene, the king's camp continued to grow as men added ramparts and sharpened stakes to the ditch cut across the river bend. Tents in livery colors dotted the loop between the fresh-dug ramparts and the river, and more armed men marched down from the north as King Henry's army arrived en masse. By Monday noon, lions and lilies were flying over the camp, showing Henry himself had come to Hardingstone Field, sending the Sisters of Saint Mary into a tizzy, furiously telling their beads.

When asked what had happened, the nuns reported dreadful news from the king's camp. "His Holiness, the bishop of Winchester, has resigned, giving the great seal of the realm back to King Henry." They moaned that the "most holy voice for peace is gone from the king's camp." Robyn sympathized. By all accounts, William Waynflete, bishop of Winchester, chancellor of England, and overseer for the Southwark brothels, was a peace-loving man, and the main advocate of giving Edward and Warwick a fair hearing rather than a fight. Apparently he had not been heeded—and now had to go back to tending his Winchester Geese. Those whom the Gods would destroy, they first make mad—if poor, daft King Henry listened only to his warriors, he was in for a rude surprise. Just because a man is willing to kill to get his way does not mean he could be trusted. As proof of that, Collin donned his armor and set off to greet the king he agreed to betray, taking Bryn and Nest with him and leaving Robyn knocking around the nunnery with Hela and the Sisters of Saint Mary de Pratis for company. She hoped Edward was headed her way.

Rains returned. Among the nuns it was now official: this was the rainiest summer they could remember. "Heaven weeps to see England at war with herself," Sister Perpetua told her. "These rains will not let up until the land is healed." In lieu of a National Weather Service, heartfelt sentiments had to do. Sister Perpetua certainly believed it. When not badgering Heaven with pious advice, the nuns fussed over Robyn, especially the younger ones, gladly doing her washing just to get their hands on silks and satins—and hear stories from beyond the walls. However much they snapped at each other, they were always nice to her. Some were plainly never meant to be nuns—like Perpetua,

the obedient doe-eyed daughter of a local landowner who decided to
save on a dowry by marrying her to God. Trying hard to make the
best of it, the poor girl took the name of a third-century martyr, Perpetua of Carthage—but her heart was clearly not in it. Small and
defenseless, Sister Perpetua complained that the worldly abbess who
flirted with Collin abused them mightily—calling them beggars and
harlots—tearing off their wimples and pulling them about the choir
by their short hair. Rather than devote rainy afternoons to prayer,
Perpetua preferred to tag after her, helping with chores, happy to hear
stories about Calais, London, and L.A.

Come Wednesday morning, Perpetua announced that a delegation
of bishops had come to the king's camp pleading for peace, headed
by the bishop of Salisbury. Robyn saw Edward's wry humor in the
choice of ambassadors—nine months before, the bishop of Salisbury
was King Henry's envoy to the rebels at Ludlow, the prelate who
dictated terms to Edward's father. Now Bishop Salisbury was telling
Henry to lay down his arms. Sister Perpetua beseeched Heaven to have
King Henry heed his bishops. None of these nuns thought there was
any good reason for Christians to kill one another—or anyone else,
either. Smiting the infidel Turk might appeal to Pope Pius—but these
Sisters of Saint Mary were all for peace. Had it been up to King Henry,
they would have been home free. Seeing his bishops file in must have
cheered Henry immensely, and he no doubt listened happily to the
notion of everyone shedding their armor and sitting down to a peace
conference headed by him—but it would not be up to King Henry.
Having seen Lord Egremont's riders looking eagerly about for someone to plunder, Robyn could not picture them turned back by anything but force of arms.

Nuns returned from noon prayers even more agitated—a curate
accompanying the bishops having brought them bad news. Seizing her
hand, Sister Perpetua told how the bishops had gone to the king's tent
and begged Henry to accept Church mediation, suffering the rebel
earls to come into his presence. According to the curate, King Henry
listened in kindly fashion, but Humphrey Stafford, duke of Buckingham, bristled at seeing the bishops backed by men-at-arms, saying,
"You come not as bishops to treat for peace, but as men of arms."

To which the bishops retorted, "We come thus for surety of our
persons, for they that be about the king be not our friends."

Fighting back tears, Perpetua told her Duke Buckingham replied with a mighty "Forsooth"—the only oath King Henry allowed in his presence—adding that, "The earl of Warwick shall not come to the king's presence, and if he comes, he shall die." Sister Perpetua clung hard to her hand, saying this Duke Stafford of Buckingham "must be demon-hearted, indeed" to be so opposed to peace.

When she first arrived, Robyn tried to con folks into half believing she might be Duke Buckingham's wayward daughter—now she knew she could do much better than having this touchy homicidal duke for a father. She told Perpetua, "Having King Henry chair a prayer fest on the woes of England would turn the fight into a popularity contest. One Buckingham is bound to lose. He has to fall back on force." That was what those northern troops were for.

"We must pray for him, anyway." Perpetua dragged her down onto her knees. There was nothing to do but pray for the soul of Duke Humphrey Stafford, her sometime father. When their impromptu duet to the Almighty was done, Sister Perpetua insisted on "helping" her to her feet, giving her a gentle hug that swiftly became an embrace. She felt the nun's small hands searching for skin beneath those fine silks the Sisters of Saint Mary de Pratis much admired. Perpetua was so deft and matter-of-fact that it hardly seemed like sex, much less an assault. "Are you scared?" Perpetua whispered as her fingers found flesh.

Not that scared. She politely disengaged, extracting the nun's hands from her clothing, protesting that she was practically betrothed to an earl—though she no longer had the ring to prove it. Sister Perpetua would just have to take her word that she was way too engaged to be fumbling about with a nun, not even in a moment of national crisis.

Without protest or apology, Perpetua tighted her habit and adjusted her wimple, as if the whole thing had not happened. Robyn almost doubted it had until she saw the buttons on her bodice were undone. When it came to getting inside women's clothes, this nimble-handed nun had Edward totally beat. Neither of them said a word more about it. Sexual tension must run fairly high in a convent, and Robyn had no desire to report Perpetua—and have her disciplined by an irritable abbess who beat nuns for nodding off in prayer. Heaven knows what the punishment was for feeling up a guest.

By vespers her noble boyfriend had arrived. Rebel bowmen and men-at-arms waded up the muddy road from Stony Stratford, driving Egremont's border riders out of their warm beds in Hardingstone.

Deirdre had gotten through. Edward was most likely with them, being the vanguard commander, and a boy who favored swift, decisive action. Sensing she might be aboard the *Fortuna*, he had boarded the first available boat. Having heard that she had found King Henry at Northampton, Edward would not sit about dithering over his options, but would be here as fast as mud and rain allowed. Excited at the thought of seeing Edward, she ransacked her borrowed clothes chest, regretting that she had left her murrey-and-blue gown in London. She settled on a red riding dress and a gold-trimmed jacket of Bryn's with tight buttoned sleeves—Stafford colors. She wished she had a mirror, as her borrowed jacket refused to fit quite right. Fortunately she and Bryn were less than an inch or two apart. Collin liked his women to be just so—no more, no less. Hela hopped about the stone windowsill, cawing raucously at the Percy riders rushing past, retreating in the rain toward King Henry's fortified camp.

Sister Perpetua came bounding back from vespers. Putting the nun's passions to use, Robyn had Perpetua help adjust the jacket. With a hopeful look on her face, Perpetua happily tugged and pulled, getting the jacket to sit straight. Stepping back, the nun acted as Robyn's mirror, checking sleeve length and seeing the dress hung right.

Boots mounted the stairs outside, spurs ringing on stone steps; then a steel gauntlet rapped on the door. She marveled that Edward had found her so quickly. Getting a final ecstatic nod from Sister Perpetua, she went to the door, lifted the latch, and swung it open.

Collin stood in the doorway, wearing his blue brigandine over chain mail, carrying a sallet under one steel arm. "Magnificent! I forget how unbelievably lovely you can be."

Even though she hoped to see Edward, she could hardly be disappointed by such a heartfelt compliment, especially from a man so recently betrothed. She spun about, showing off the riding dress, thinking how nice it was to finally have Collin on Edward's side, no longer dividing her loyalties. Sir Collin nodded in appreciation. "Wonderful. And in Stafford colors! Perfect for being presented to King Henry."

Shocked, she stopped her spin. "King Henry?"

"King Henry of England?" Collin arched an eyebrow. "Camped in the meadow below? You have no doubt seen the tents; we are wanted there at once."

Her face fell. Collin meant it. He wanted her to come to King Henry's camp immediately—without even seeing Edward.

"Why the frown?" he asked. "Because Edward is here and you will not see him?"

"Is Edward here?" she asked hopefully.

"You know the boy as well as I. Better even. My bet is he will be pounding on the nunnery gate within the hour. So we must be off at once.

"Why?" What was the rush?

"Buckingham may be a fool, but he is not an idiot like King Henry. If he hears that I tarried to talk with Edward of March before taking my place beside the king, Buckingham will wonder what was said. We must come dashing in, with Edward's foreriders yapping at our heels, or we shall have hard explaining to do."

She considered stalling, even demanding to see Edward. But Collin was right—and she owed him cooperation. Hurriedly packing a saddlebag, she pulled on her boots and headed for the stables. Sister Perpetua came, too, carrying her cloak and saddlebag. Every trip, short or long, dull or adventurous, started in the stables, with the warm beery smell of straw and horse piss. Even with armies about to collide, and the kingdom at stake, she still had to start by greeting her mare, seeing Lily was fit and fed, and ready to ride. "How are the nuns treating you, girl? They have been nothing but nice to me." It beat the hell out of living in airports and staying in hotels.

Bryn was there, seeing her mount was brushed down properly, using good brushes and broad, even strokes. Nunnery stable hands were never the best. Nest was with her, keeping a watchful eye on Bryn while seeing to her own mount. Clearly Bryn was not going back to the king's camp; Collin was depositing her in the nunnery for safe-keeping. And Bryn was not at all pleased about it—not liking being left behind while her man went off with another woman, yet again. Collin did his best to mollify his bride-on-approval, giving Bryn a tender and loving good-bye, which bothered Robyn far more than it should have done. Much as she might want Collin and Bryn to be happy, it disturbed her to see Collin so caring, using words and gestures that used to be reserved for her.

Her own good-bye to Bryn was more perfunctory: a swift kiss on the lips and a soft "God keep you." Which Bryn returned with equal care. While not actual enemies, they were not best of friends, either. Bryn said nothing about the borrowed gold jacket.

Sister Perpetua's good-bye was much more heartfelt and tender, full of promise, with tears brimming in her big brown eyes. Nor did she kiss at all like a nun, making it a mighty effort for Robyn to get untangled and onto her mare without having a scene. Collin grinned at her predicament. As they cantered out the gate into the rain, he leaned over to say, "I am glad to see you enjoying your stay. There is no need to be lonely in a nunnery."

Ignoring the gibe, she assumed an air of innocence, asking, "Why is Bryn not coming with us?"

If he could accuse her of dallying with a nun, she felt free to needle him about leaving his betrothed behind. But Collin was no easy man to needle. He matched her assumed innocence with an air of knightly competence. "Bryn will be safe among the sisters. You have a role to play in King Henry's camp, and Bryn does not. Besides, Bryn can tell Lord Edward where his lady love has gone—no doubt the boy will fight all the harder for it."

"What role?" Why was it so vital that she be in the king's camp?

"No time to tell you now." Collin nodded over his shoulder. Rain-soaked horsemen were coming up fast from Hardingstone, their mounts' iron-shod hooves throwing up spray. Expecting them to be wearing Percy blue and gold—she instead saw Edward's murrey and blue. Her first impulse was to rein in, but she did not get the chance. Collin had his sword out. Shouting, "Get going!" he gave her mount a swat on the rear with the flat of his blade.

Lily leaped into a gallop, and she had to hang on, head down, wet mane slapping her face. It was hard for her to think of Edward's men as the enemy—but there they were, pounding through the rain, trying to run her down before she got to King Henry's camp. Luckily, her pursuers' mounts were winded from the long ride up from London, while hers and Collin's were fresh. Racing flat out, she beat them easily. One moment she was galloping head down with the rain in her face and Edward's armored riders at her heels; then suddenly she was reining in among wrought-iron cannons blocking the North-ampton road.

Cheers greeted her. Men wearing the black ragged staff of Lord Grey de Ruthyn reached up to help her dismount. Collin was right behind her, sword still out, making sure that Edward's riders turned back. Which they did. Then he, too, dismounted, his uncle's men clapping him on the back. "Three cheers for Sir Collingwood," someone called out. "He's been to the nunnery and brought back a lady. Heh-heigh! Heh-heigh! Heh-heigh!"

Coolly acknowledging the applause, Collin helped her walk their horses across a plank bridge thrown over the watery ditch, and through a narrow gap in the dirt ramparts. She was in King Henry's camp. Looking about, she saw long straight lanes of gaily colored tents sporting each lord's livery. Banners hung limp and wet, and between the lines of tents lay upended wine casks, broken pike shafts, and trodden horseshit, showing a hearty male sense of decor. Collin hustled her into his tent and then went to see to the horses. She had the tent all to herself, finding it big and comfortable, and full of Bryn's things. Partitions divided the interior into an entrance way and two sleeping areas. She selected the one that had been Bryn's, finding that it contained a cloth mattress stuffed with straw, a clothes chest, table, and chamber pot. She had brought boiled water with her, and food enough for a day or two. Hopefully it would all be over by then.

Returning at dusk, Collin shed his armor and broached a wineskin, complaining it was, "Damp enough to drown a duck." He looked worn and nervous, not near as cocky as usual. She lit an oil lamp, casting big, weird, smoky shadows on the tent walls, perfect for a novice witch and a notorious warlock. Now that they were alone, she asked why she absolutely had to be here; the notion of spending the night in an armed camp had her wishing she was back in the convent fending off Sister Perpetua. Taking a swig from the wineskin, Collin was careful to talk at a whisper. "If all goes well on the morrow, we will send this fine army flying and capture King Henry. But we very much want poor mad Henry safe and whole. He was wounded at Saint Albans, and Henry hurt or dead at our hands would be an unimaginable disaster."

She nodded. Poor, daft King Henry had become the national security blanket, one life standing between England and total war. She, too, very much wanted him alive—and not just to avert a bloody free-for-all. A weak king would inevitably lead to a stronger people. England had to be governed by someone, and keeping Henry on the throne ensured that someone would never be the king.

Collin took another swig. "Even with my uncles' aid, your boy Edward will have to hack his way into King Henry's presence. Buckingham is overproud and pigheaded, but nothing if not brave. And Lord Egremont is a violent fanatic who will go down swinging, taking unwary bystanders with him. Worse yet, there are those in the rebel camp who would very much like to see Duke Richard of York made king—it would be handy for them if Henry were to die here, while York is in Ireland and could not rightly be blamed. We need someone to be with Henry, to see he is safe, and that someone must be a woman. A man might just draw an attack. But the sight of a woman will most likely bring any man up short, long enough to explain that this is King Henry and he is not to be harmed."

It made gruesome sense, a peaceful female presence in Henry's tent might make all the difference. "But why not Bryn?"

"Bryn wanted to do it," he assured her. "Bryn was the one who insisted we needed a woman." Collin was enjoying this too much for it not to be true. And it sounded like Bryn's reasoning; why send a man when you could send a woman?

"Then why not her?" And as she had said for two months now— why me?

He grinned. "Bryn does not have your knack with words. Being a poor heathen girl from Wales, she speaks Welsh like a song and English with a charming accent. But nothing else, unless you count Gaelic. Some thick-headed Northumberland man-at-arms might not know what to make of a Welsh accent—no matter how charming. And Nest would insist on being with her." Heaven knows what would happen if they tried to bring a heavily armed Welsh nurse into King Henry's tent. Collin's grin turned wicked. "But there are no such problems with you. You are a witch from the fabulous future, with the time on your wrist and an enchanted tongue that speaks to anyone. Whoever comes through King Henry's tent flap, Yorkshire night rider or Flemish mercenary, that man must know at once that this is the King, and worth an amazing ransom so long as he is alive. Who better to tell him than you?"

No one. He knew he had her. She searched for some witty comeback, but none came. No wonder Bryn had been so furious in the stables. Bryn had created the part, only to be pulled for her unwanted Saxon understudy.

"Besides, Henry knows you, and he does not know Bryn, making you easier to get in." But not any easier to get out. Collin dropped his grin, making a serious appeal. "Help keep the king safe and alive, and you keep England from tearing herself apart. Here is your chance to stand up for that peace you so love."

"Right. In the middle of a battle?"

"The absolute perfect place to stand for peace." He saluted her with his wineskin. Declining the wine, she stared at the dancing shadows on the tent fabric. How incredibly absurd—but backing out was hardly an option. Not in an armed camp at night with a hostile army on one side and a rain-swollen river on the other. Better to forge ahead, praying for a break.

"Worried?" Collin turned solicitous.

She nodded wearily. How could she not be?

"If you were going to worry for anyone, you should worry for Edward," Collin suggested. "Slogging across flooded meadows with Buckingham's cannons smashing through plate and mail, blowing men to bloody rags. He will be leading the van, you know. Especially when he finds out you are here. He will be up those ramparts like he went up the side of the *Fortuna*." Collin took a drink in honor of Edward. One of the truly ghastly truths about battle was that it did bring out the best in men. Faced with a messy death, Collin did not envy Edward or anyone else. Real peril put you beyond petty concerns.

"I worry for Edward," she admitted. "And for you."

Collin stared at her over the wineskin. "I do not doubt that you do. You are so like Jo in that way, always worrying for others. No doubt that is why you two get on so famously."

"And you?" she asked. "What does Sir Collingwood Grey get out of all this?"

"Touché." He took a drink in her honor. "I am doing this for Jo and Joy. And my family. And for you." He took another drink in her honor.

"For me?" He had a strange way of showing it.

"This is what you wanted, is it not? Edward and I, fighting together, both on the side of right."

She admitted that was so, "Though I did plan to see it at a safer distance."

"We all had that hope. Yet here we are, in the very thick of it, and only the morrow will tell how deeply. Mayhap Buckingham will listen to the pope, bishops, and people—then the worst we face is prayer and speeches." With that pious hope, he retired to his part of the tent, and she did the same. Somewhat surprisingly, she soon found herself asleep.

Dawn brought gray skies, but no rain. Collin was already up and gone, so she breakfasted alone on fruit and scones. At midmorning Collin returned, saying Warwick had sent a herald with another peace offer. "Warwick said he would come naked to present his case before the king—if hostages are given to assure his safe coming and going."

By *naked* Warwick meant unarmed and unarmored—but she enjoyed the amusing picture of the high and mighty Neville groveling before Henry in the nude. "What did King Henry say?"

"Heaven alone knows what King Henry would have had to say, but Buckingham sternly refused. Warwick would have had more chance proposing marriage to the pope."

"So, what now?" She could tell her cue was coming up.

Collin glanced at the open tent flap. "We pray for rain."

A safe request of Heaven—it had rained for days, soaking every inch of the surrounding countryside. "Why?"

"Best weather for battle is a downpour," Collin told her happily. "Rain dampens bows and ruins powder. War is so much nicer when arrows fall short and cannons will not fire." Then all you need worry about is some six-foot fellow encased in steel taking your head off with a two-handed cleaver. Collin donned his own armor, wished her luck, and then went clanking off, leaving her alone again.

She took Collin's advice and prayed for rain. Having had plenty of practice praying of late—she could now pray in Latin or English, or even French or Welsh if she felt like it. She was not sure how much she even believed in God, though everyone around her certainly seemed to. No one here and now was able to get through a day— much less a battle—without badgering the Almighty for advice or favors. But whatever her doubts, she found it surprisingly easy to pray with thousands of men in armor about to descend on the camp beneath a storm of shot and arrows, swinging axes and war hammers. There are no atheists in plate armor.

No rain came. Was this going to be the first dry day in weeks? She kept up her prayers on and off throughout the morning, between nervous peeks outside. Around noon she heard the first drops patter down on the tent. She prayed harder. As she did, the drops grew louder, becoming a downpour. She thanked Heaven for its weeping, hoping to drown out the battle. But in an hour, Collin rattled back through the rain with dismal news. "Earl Warwick has sent his final message, at two hours after noon he will speak with the king, or else die in the field."

No need to ask which choice Duke Buckingham preferred. She hurriedly looked at her watch. 1:17 P.M. Less than an hour to go. How come Collin had not told her earlier? Probably to give her less than an hour to worry. "What now?" she asked.

Stripping off his gauntlet, he held out a hand. "Time to call on King Henry."

She pulled her cloak about her, took his hand, and followed him out into the rain. King Henry's camp had become a bog. Horses had all been sent to the rear. Men in armor were massed against the high ramparts, trying to keep out of the mud while awaiting the rebel attack—reminding Robyn of the boys at Berkeley Castle playing king-of-the-mountain on manure piles the day she first arrived. Most were bowmen, waiting behind pointed stakes. Many wore Buckingham's rope badge, twisted into the Stafford knot. With them were northerners wearing the Percy crescent, or Clifford colors, blue-gold checks with a bright red bar through the middle. Rusty half-armor and tattered livery made the northerners look like beggars in arms next to the southern knights—no wonder folks assumed they came south to steal. What a weird American Civil War in reverse: rural northern border reivers invading the more urban, commercial south of England.

King Henry's tent was easy to spot, twice as big as any of the others, with a cook wagon drawn up alongside containing the royal stove and pantry. And an altar wagon as well, carrying the king's chapel—both up to their wheel hubs in mud. Men-at-arms in Stafford colors stood guard beneath the tent fly, happy to have duty that kept them out of the rain.

Collin was right. Her presence was like magic. Stafford men-at-arms stepped aside at once. A man's intentions would have been questioned, but no one stood in the way of a woman seeking shelter, especially one wearing Stafford red and gold and a grateful smile. What better place for a woman to find shelter in a battle than the tent of mild, pious King Henry notorious for never having a carnal thought, even toward his queen? In fifteen years of marriage, his wife was with child only once. Significantly Henry's complete catatonic breakdown coincided with her pregnancy—but psychiatry here and now was best represented by Bedlam Hospital. Without even a clear line separating sainthood from schizophrenia, Henry's case was pretty hopeless.

And he looked it. Sitting inside his huge tent, forlorn and uncomfortable, King Henry wore a full suit of armor, beneath a surcoat proclaiming him king of England, France, and Ireland. In place of a helmet, he wore a steel neck guard and a small gold traveling crown, studded with emeralds. In armor up to his chin, covered with that grandiose coat of arms, and wearing a cut-down crown, King Henry VI seemed more than ever like an aging groom done up to play the part. Several real grooms stood in attendance amid a clutter of clerk's tables, wardrobes, and clothes chests.

King Henry's eyes lit up as she did a low curtsy; clearly he remembered her. Collin, down on one knee beside her, had his story ready, saying she had been chased into camp by rebel riders—lawless fiends bent on rapine—"and cannot now get back among the Holy Sisters at the abbey." With the Nene overflowing its banks and the roads blocked by men and cannons, she had dire need of His Majesty's protection—at least until the rebel army had been sent packing.

Henry lifted a slim pale hand. "Worry not, Robyn Stafford, you have our protection. Come sit in our sight, so you may be safe from any unchaste word or deed." Henry was a great worrier when it came to women, always afraid lest they be used for lewd purposes. For Henry, a bared breast was far worse than a bared blade. She settled down on a camp stool, as close as she could get to the king. Henry turned weary eyes to her companion. "And Sir Collingwood Grey, you have our leave to go."

Humbly thanking the king he was about to betray, Collin rose and backed out the open door flap into the rain, leaving Robyn to entertain King Henry. Heavy silence hung over the tent. Minutes passed in agony. What did you say to a king whose cousins were in arms against him? Whose capital had gone joyfully over to the enemy? Whose vanguard commander was about to do the same? Knowing King Henry's bent for religion, she mentioned her stay at the abbey and how the sisters took loving care of her (though a tad too loving at times). Happy to hear of so many women locked away from temptation, King Henry promised to visit the abbey, and "endow lands for support of the sisters." She thanked King Henry profusely in the name of the holy sisters—hoping he would take the hint and endow some lands in support of her. Henry was plainly in the mood. War often made men generous, as well. But Henry could be maddeningly obtuse, and merely beamed happily, saying how glad he was to have her here. "For you are joyous company on an ill day."

She thanked him again. "Your highness is too utterly kind." It felt terrible to double-cross this gentle, addled man. But being addled did not make Henry any less dangerous. Things done in his name had twice driven the country to full-blown revolt.

"You are far better company than Duke Buckingham," he told her. "That other Stafford does turn down some of our best ideas." Henry never could get his dukes to behave—and now Duke Buckingham had bullied him into having a battle, which Henry always hated. Despite his horror of sex, King Henry much preferred the company of women. Or better yet, monks. He had long ago given his wife charge of family affairs, even letting her command his armies. The absolute irony of the situation was that Henry would have gotten along famously with Bishop Coppini and Pope Pius, happily ruling over peace at home, while all these warriors went off to smite the Turks. But Buckingham would not allow it.

"And our bishops have deserted us," Henry complained. "All but the bishop of Hereford, who is our confessor. And our chancellor has left us, as well."

She looked about. Where was Buckingham? Where were the bishops? She glanced anxiously at her watch. 1:41 P.M. Less than twenty minutes before the battle was to start, and no one was coming to confer with King Henry—their nominal commander-in-chief, and God's anointed leader, to boot. He might as well be a groom in armor for all the attention they paid him. Yet this poor little man claimed to be king of England, Ireland, and France. "Why is it," Henry wondered, "that you are not married?"

Why, indeed? If they went too deeply into her private life, King Henry was bound to disapprove. She settled for a safe answer, saying, "I am betrothed." Sort of.

"To whom?" asked the king.

"To a most noble young man." Who was even now preparing to storm the camp. "But his name must remain secret until he has his father's permission."

"And you have been chaste with him?"

Remarkably so, given the circumstances—aside from some French-kissing in Calais. Like a lot of prudes, King Henry was inordinately interested in other people's sex lives. Serving women at Kenilworth told how he used to employ special windows to spy on female guests, lest they corrupt his household. Until the queen put a stop to his peeping. She checked her watch. 1:53 P.M. Warwick's deadline was minutes away; surely Henry had more important things to think about. "We have set aside our passions," she assured him, "waiting for the day when we wed."

"So, you are still a virgin?"

That was a stretch. "I am as innocent now as when I first arrived in this world." By which she meant the Middle Ages. Aside from her May Day fling—which by popular custom did not count—she had a completely blameless past. Her serious sinning lay in the far, far future.

Henry was happy to hear that. "And even when you wed," he advised, "do not let your husband use you unseemingly, but only sparingly, and with serious and grave concern." Henry's royal chaplain used to advise against marital intercourse, incensing a population desperately hoping for a legitimate heir—finally the chaplain's own congregation rose up and hacked him to death.

She promised to do her absolute best. Though to be honest, if Edward ever really laid hands on her, married or not, all bets were off—he was not a boy to do anything "sparingly"—the only "serious and grave concern" would be of their breaking the bed.

Trumpets blared. Her watch read 2:07. Warwick was late. Begging King Henry's permission, she went to the tent flap to see what was happening. Henry's tent was well sited, considering they were camped in a sinkhole. From the front flap she could see the full sweep of the camp defenses, and Delapré Abbey on the higher ground away from the river. People were crowded about the abbey park, nuns, bishops, and ordinary bystanders, not minding the rain so long as they got a good view. Craning her neck, she saw citizens thronging out of Northampton, lining the far bank of the Nene. Commoners treated the coming battle like a grand tournament. The leaders of the land had donned armor to decide their differences by force of arms. Who would miss that? It was like the president and the White House staff suiting up in steel to fight it out with the senate—every network on the planet would kill to cover it. No one seemed afraid of civilian casualties. Londoners were amazed and indignant when Lord Scales fired on the city, and if any cannonballs went astray today, plowing into spectators, there were sure to be more cries of murder.

Almost a mile away, alongside the Towcester road, she saw the wet banners of the rebel earls, hanging limp above dark masses of footmen. Without warning, the rebel army began to move. She watched in eerie fascination as the squares of footmen rolled forward across the Towcester road. Leading with its right, the rebel host came on with Edward indeed in the lead. As they came closer, she made out his blue-and-murrey banners overhead, sprinkled with white roses, along with his father's falcon and fetterlock. Thank goodness there was no gunfire—the rebels having no cannons, and the king's guns being half submerged. Arrows arched upward, but did little damage, wet strings and fletching taking away much of their sting. Like Collin said, you could not ask for better weather for a battle, except perhaps a blinding snowstorm.

But the king's camp was still well defended, fronted by a ditch full of waist-deep water, backed by tall slippery ramparts bristling with sharp wooden stakes. It hardly seemed possible that men in armor could wade that ditch, much less scramble up the muddy slopes and cut their way through the wall of stakes—not while men above hacked at them with brown bills and halberds.

King Henry called out to her, asking what was happening. Too awestruck to answer, she watched the armored mass roll toward them out of the rain, gleaming with honed steel. High ramparts kept her from seeing what happened when the rebels reached the ditch. But as they did, Grey de Ruthyn's men surged forward, mounting to the top of the ramparts. There they broke down the line of barricades, pulling up stakes and tossing obstacles aside. She saw them reach down and help the first of Edward's men up to the top of the ramparts. King Henry's loyal followers stared in stupefied amazement as their vanguard changed sides. Seeing Edward's men pouring through their impregnable defenses, archers stopped firing, throwing down their bows and streaming for the rear, kicking up mud as they ran. Letting fall the tent flap, she sat back down near the king, merely saying, "The battle is joined."

"Fear not," Henry told her, "Buckingham will turn them back. He has promised us this, sworn to do it absolutely."

She nodded silently, not thinking much of Buckingham's promise.

"And if he does not," Henry added, "we will see you are not harmed."

She smiled weakly, "Thank you, Your Majesty." Actually she had come to protect him—hopefully they would both succeed. From outside the tent came the crash of edged steel on plate armor. She heard someone cry, "A Warwick! A Warwick!" Meaning Warwick's men had followed Edward's into the camp.

"Did you know we were wounded at Saint Albans?" King Henry asked nervously.

She nodded again; everyone knew—that was why she was there.

"The day was hot," Henry explained, "and we had opened our bevor and doffed our helm. An arrow struck us in the neck, hurting horribly. Blood ran everywhere, but we did not swear," Henry added proudly. "Except to say, forsooth, you do foully to so smite an anointed king."

Forsooth, indeed. No wonder he wore that steel neck guard. Sounds of fighting came closer, rising to a crescendo of rain-soaked curses, screams, shouts, and cries, until the constant shattering ring of steel on steel blotted out every other sound, like being in a car crash that kept on happening. Looking around, she saw the king's clerks and grooms were gone. She and King Henry were alone in the big tent, with the ghastly clamor of battle beating on the fabric. Slowly the sounds started to fade as fighting moved away from the tent. Now was when someone would think to look inside. She braced herself, ready to step between Henry and whoever came through the tent flap.

Suddenly the flap flew open. Light spilled into the tent. King Henry rose from his chair, ready to defend her. Slowed by his heavy plate armor, he had no real chance; she was up ahead of him, halfway to the entrance before Henry was even on his feet. She found herself facing a startled bowman who wore a wide-brimmed steel hat and Edward's murrey and blue. He stood staring, sword drawn, not sure what to make of her.

She did a swift curtsy, trying to sound as courteous as she could, "Robyn Stafford, at your service. Who may I ask are you?"

"Henry," the startled bowman replied. "Henry Mountfort."

There was no need for any fancy accent after all—he was neither Flemish nor Northumbrian. Keeping an eye on his bared blade, she flashed him her warmest, friendliest smile, saying, "Henry Mountfort, meet Henry Plantagenet. And get set for your fifteen minutes of fame. You have just captured the king of England."

His point dropped, and Henry Mountfort bowed to the king he had taken prisoner, looking almighty pleased. King Henry looked shaken but relieved, happy to see the bowman bowing to him rather than running him through. Pretty shaken herself, Robyn suggested to Bowman Henry that he guard the tent flap, "Lest someone try to steal your fame."

Mountfort immediately took station at the entrance, already counting the fortune he could expect to collect. Sounds of fighting had died away completely. King Henry sat back down on his chair, badly confused. "Who is this man?" he asked. "What does this mean?"

She wiped the smile off her face, not wanting to gloat. "Your Majesty, this man means you are safe—but that my Lord Buckingham is beaten."

"Beaten?" King Henry mumbled the word, barely able to believe it. "Surely it is too soon for that? We cannot be beaten already." He could believe he was beaten, but not that it had happened so fast. She consulted her watch. 2:31 P.M. The "battle" had lasted hardly half an hour.

"We were beaten at Saint Albans, too," Henry confided, as if to tell her it would not be too bad.

Boots splashed through the mud toward the tent entrance. She looked up, praying it would be Edward.

And it was. He sauntered cheerfully into the tent, wearing badly dented armor, his sallet under his arm. With a single look he took in the whole scene, smiled wide, and clapped the bowman on the shoulder, saying, "Henry Mountfort, thou art, indeed, a hero." The bowman blushed, happy that his young lord so readily remembered him.

Edward turned his smile to her. "And you, Robyn Stafford, thou art an angel. An angel from tomorrow, come to save us today."

"Do you know this young man?" King Henry asked her, still badly confused.

Ever polite, Edward dropped to his armored knees, saying, "Your most high and gracious Majesty, I am Edward, earl of March, come to swear fealty to my king."

Earl Warwick and Lord Fauconberg entered, and King Henry stiffened, seeing two Nevilles that he knew all too well. They, too, fell to their knees, craving King Henry's forgiveness for taking up arms, swearing their loyalty. Mad and beaten though he might be, Henry was still their king. Grudgingly Henry accepted their apologies for fighting their way into his presence. This was the second such offense for Warwick, who had been forced to ask forgiveness from the wounded King Henry five years before at Saint Albans. Henry accepted Warwick's apology, with a pained look that said please don't do it again.

Then Robyn watched in fascination as Edward—who had come of age in conflict—did his first formal homage to his king. Stripping off his gauntlets, he put his bare hands between King Henry's hands, pledging fealty to his king, swearing on his knees to be Henry's vassal and to support him against all his enemies, both living and dead, and to faithfully give Henry aid and counsel to safeguard the king's person, rights, and possessions. Seeing Edward kneeling in dented steel, swearing obedience to King Henry in his spotless armor and grandiose surcoat would have made her wonder who really had won—if she had not been there to see it all happen. With equal formality, Henry accepted Edward's homage, raising the young earl to his feet and kissing his cousin on the cheek. Edward then repeated his oath, holding a martyr's tooth that Henry happened to have handy, confirming before God and all the world that he was Mad King Henry's man.

⊷⊶ Duchess Weirdville ⊷⊶

Riding her white mare through the rain, she returned in triumph to the nunnery of Saint Mary de Pratis with King Henry on one side of her and Edward on the other. Henry had commanded it, saying, "Ride with us, that we may see you safe among the sisters." So they all trooped up to the abbey, with Earl Warwick riding on King Henry's right, followed by mounted knights, lordly prisoners, mailed footmen, and a great mass of wet, excited spectators. Poor Mad King Henry had lost his army, seen loyal lords slaughtered, and ended up in the hands of attainted traitors—but he still had her, a triumph of sorts. Robyn had been put in his safekeeping, and Henry swore to return her to the Sisters of Saint Mary. Despite her claim to be betrothed, Henry obviously thought her a walking temptation, and would not feel right until she was locked safely back up in the nunnery. In King Henry's mind that was a victory, won over wantonness and womanly temptation, if not over the Nevilles.

She gladly humored the mad monarch, feeling guilty for helping ensure Henry's defeat, even though the battle had been swift and nearly bloodless. Out of tens of thousands on the field, only a few hundred had been killed, mostly drowned trying to flee across the swollen Nene in armor. Thanks to steel plate and sodden weapons, overflow from the rains killed more men than bills and arrows. Neither side had much hate for the other—witness the way Grey de Ruthyn's men casually changed sides in midbattle, welcoming their so-called enemies into camp. Edward and Warwick gave strict orders not to kill any common soldiers, "only lords, knights, and squires." Their rebellion was as much a popularity contest as a power grab—and since they meant to rule with the consent of commons, the earls did not plan to start by slaughtering constituents. Armor made that easy. In fact, Italian knights fought entire battles where no one was killed. Robyn very much liked the notion of wars without casualties—particularly civilian casualties—here the third millennium had much to learn from the Middle Ages.

But the first thing she saw on leaving the king's tent had been a mud-spattered body in battered, bloodied armor, draped in Stafford colors. Duke Humphrey of Buckingham—her sometime father—lay facedown in the mud. King Henry's bishops had pleaded for a peaceful resolution, but Buckingham preferred the test of battle. She could not shake that image. Lord Egremont was dead as well, along with Viscount Beaumont and the earl of Shrewsbury. Lords had stood and fought when shire levies and border reivers fled. Understandable, since the lords had more to die for—it being their quarrel to begin with.

Ecstatic despite the downpour, Edward leaned close to her, saying, "First I feared never to see you again, then Deirdre brought me your message." Rain pattered against his armor, like drops hitting a tin roof. "We marched here from Saint Albans through the mud, pleaded with Buckingham to let Henry and his bishops decide the issue, then had to fight this miserable sodden battle. And then, then . . ." Words failed him, dissolving into a rain-soaked grin.

And why not? When they parted she was headed on a dubious quest

to find Collin. Edward was marching off to beat the fens for King
Henry. Four days later, there she was in King Henry's tent standing
watch over his prize. And Edward had wanted to leave her in Calais.
"Unutterably astounding." He shook his head in wonder. "Coming
upon you in Wales was the most marvelous thing that ever happened
to me." High praise from someone who had just won a kingdom. She
thanked him primly, thinking herself marvelously lucky. But how long
could her luck hold? Hopefully long enough to get Jo and Joy out of
the Tower alive.

Archbishop Thomas Bourchier of Canterbury led them to the abbey
gate, along with the bishop of London. The great sodden mass of
spectators stood watching as King Henry and his new supreme lords
temporal rode into the abbey courtyard. If Sister Perpetua loved her
when she was just a pretty vagrant lodging with the sisters—what
must the nun think now? Seeing her escorted into the abbey court by
a pair of bishops, riding between King Henry and the handsomest
young earl in the land? Even Warwick acted pleased with her. Normally he ignored her or treated her like a gaudy plaything, proof that
Edward was but a boy after all, while Earl Richard of Warwick was
the man in charge. Today he condescended to be decent, even turning
some of his famous charm on her.

King Henry told Edward to escort her over to where the sisters
waited under the abbey eaves—plainly pleased to be ordering his powerful new vassal about. Eagerly complying with his sovereign's first
formal order, Edward dismounted, removing his gauntlets and helping
her down. "Be you good, Robyn Stafford," King Henry commanded.
"Stay sweet and chaste, and obedient to the Lord."

She gave a low, grave curtsy in the rain, to show her gratitude. King
Henry truly thought he had kept her safe, though a disastrous battle
raged about them. Buckingham and Egremount had failed hideously
so far as their king was concerned, and paid the price of failure.
Henry, however, had delivered her to the good sisters, whole and unmolested, making his part of the fight a thumping success. King Henry
loved doing things for people, giving dukedoms to his bastard relations, provinces to the French, small fortunes to charity, silver pennies
to servant boys. He enjoyed sending people away with a pious homily
and coin in their pockets, even if it meant emptying the treasury. Rev-
eling in the easy perks of monarchy, because the actual task of king-

ship was totally beyond him—he was her living, breathing argument against hereditary monarchy. Any name lifted at random from the local manor rolls could have done better as king. Or certainly no worse. And now it was no longer a capital crime to say that out loud. Not that she did. Henry had always been good to her.

Edward took her hand and led her across the rainy courtyard to where the nuns stood gawking like a flock of starlings huddled under the eaves. When they reached shelter, he stopped and took both her hands in his. "You did it," he told her excitedly. "I sent you off, fearing never to see you. Next I know, you have found King Henry and delivered up his vanguard to boot. Unbelievable. Even Warwick is impressed."

She laughed, "So I saw."

"Being from tomorrow, did you see all this ahead of time?"

"No. It was as much a surprise to me as anyone." She wished she knew what would happen next.

"Yet you risked it nonetheless."

"I did not have much choice," she told him. "None of us did."

"Worry for you made this my worst battle ever," he confessed. "Worse than Ludford or Saint Albans."

"I should hope so." She did not want Edward to enjoy fighting. And thank goodness he did not seem to, though he was exceptionally good at it. Fighting was merely something he had to do—and do well—what he was born to, like others are born to be farmers. He lived in an age when leaders had to lead in person, putting their own lives on the line, and could not sit back comfortably ordering others into peril. She told him, "Just pray this fight is our last."

Edward smiled, saying, "I myself am very much ready for peace. War has kept me away from you, something peace will hopefully remedy. When we parted in Wales, I told you to come to me when you heard I had King Henry—never thinking you would be there ahead of me. Because of you my father can return from exile. My mother, my little sister, and youngest brothers will be set free. What can I give to repay you?" He meant it in all seriousness—now was the moment to get whatever she wanted. If she asked for the earldom of Ulster, he would vow to pry it away from his father and Owen Boy O'Neill. He was that grateful, and that in love.

"We still must get into the Tower," she told him. His family might be safe and free, but Jo and Joy were not. Seeing them alive was the reward she wanted most—right now, at least. Lands and titles could come later.

Edward's triumphant smile vanished. He told her, "I sent a warning to Lord Scales, rebuking him and holding him responsible for his prisoner's welfare, and for their lives. His lordship claims he is not holding Joanna Grey or her daughter—saying he knows not where they are."

She guessed Scales was playing games, knowing they had no proof except by magic. "Will he open the Tower gates to let us look?"

"Not yet." Edward nodded at the king and bishops. "Though now we hold the key to the Tower."

Perhaps. But that key would take time to work. He could not just sling King Henry over a saddle and set off at a gallop. The king moved slowly, even in an emergency. It had taken the whole length of the campaign to get Henry from Coventry to Northampton, something normally done in a day of hard riding. London was a lot farther off. All of southern England lay in their hands, save only the tiny part she most needed to get at. Edward shook his head ruefully. "No matter what I offer, it is never near enough." Having taken England's troubles onto his shoulders, all Edward wanted for himself was her. And all she wanted from him was the impossible.

Letting go of her hands, he reached up inside his bevor, pulling on something attached to a thread around his neck. Breaking the thread, he told her, "Here is the key to my heart, keep it until you have need of me." Raising her left hand, he slipped the ring she had given Deirdre onto her finger. She stared down at the silver rose, realizing the band had been shortened to fit her. Edward did not waste time when he saw what needed to be done.

Hearing hushed whispers from the nuns behind her, she stared at the ring. He had worn it next to his breast, through storm and battle, until he could get it back to her. "I know not what to say."

"Then say nothing." He squeezed her hand, "If love were an easy thing, every fool would have it." Edward was right: they were both so concerned with what was proper—him not wanting to force her, her not wanting to make promises she could not keep—that it left scant chance for love. Letting her hand drop, he stepped away, bowed, and then splashed back through the rain to rejoin his king. They did not even kiss.

Nuns flocked around her, craning to look at the ring. The worldly abbess welcomed her back with open arms, apologizing profusely for the rain as if she were personally responsible. Sister Perpetua looked awestruck. Novices grabbed Robyn's saddlebags, offering to show her back to her room—actually Bryn's room, but they treated her like she owned the abbey.

Bryn was not there. Instead Deirdre was waiting, eyes hollow from lack of sleep, her hair in a wild red halo—having made the muddy ride between Hardingstone and Saint Albans three times in less than a week. Deirdre's chestnut gelding gave out after the second trip, and her current horse, a dun mare, was likewise a gift from Edward. "Never did I see a man turn about so fast," Deirdre declared, "unless he was in love." Edward had been through Saint Albans, headed north past Bernard's Heath onto Normansland Common when Deirdre caught him. He spun immediately about, turning his vanguard toward Northampton, "Faster than a Kildare falcon, swooping on a sparrow. Only to get here and find you gone." Deirdre scolded her for being in King Henry's tent. "I knew as soon as I left, you would go in search of trouble."

She politely informed her serving girl that she never looked for trouble. "Trouble comes to me, without the least effort."

As if to prove her point, Collin came to call, still wearing plate armor, looking worn and weary. He told her to make free with the lodging; neither he nor Bryn needed to stay in the nunnery. "I will pass the night at my uncle's lodgings in Northampton." No surprise. Edward and Warwick would be in Northampton with King Henry, putting together the new England. Thanks to his nephew, Lord Grey de Ruthyn had gotten in on the ground floor.

"What about Bryn?" She had expected his "trial wife" to be waiting at the abbey.

"Bryn has gone to Grafton."

"Grafton?"

Collin nodded. "Duchess Wydville was in Northampton, keeping watch over King Henry while Queen Margaret took the Prince of Wales to Eccleshall Castle." If the queen had gotten as far as Eccleshall, then Her Highness was blissfully unaware of what had happened, believing her husband was still dug in before Northampton in his impregnable camp. Thanks to the slowness of the news, Margaret would get one last night's sleep as undisputed queen of England. Tomorrow Margaret would know Henry was lost, along with London, and all

England south of the Humber, leaving her to wonder where she would sleep the night after next. Robyn sympathized, having been there herself.

"As soon as my uncle's men went over to the rebel earls, Duchess Wydville bolted for Grafton, seeing the battle lost and knowing Henry would soon be in the wrong hands." A connoisseur of defeats, Collin easily put himself in the duchess's place. "And," Collin added, "tomorrow is Witches Night."

"Is that why Bryn has gone to Grafton?" She felt the witches' web tighten around her.

"Exactly. It is our best chance to get Joanna and Joy out of the Tower alive."

"How?"

Collin arched an eyebrow. "I imagine that will be a women's mystery." She stared at him, saying nothing, thinking how strange it must be for a man to grow up amid witches. Was Collin's mother a witch? Probably. His sister certainly was. And Collin was not just any man—far from it. He was Sir Collingwood Grey, knight champion and lord of Greystone, nephew to a baron, near the top of the feudal pinnacle in a land where law was made with a lance. Yet within his family he was a mere man, excluded from magical power and women's secrets as surely as the lowest stable boy. Something totally contrary to law, custom, and religion.

Aside from odd flashes of irony, Collin handled it well, acting as if male privilege did not exist, reading Christine de Pizan and staying in nunneries. Doting on his landless sister and her difficult bastard daughter, when by law he could have turned them out. Able to have almost any woman he wanted, he chose to wed a Welsh witch with less social standing than little Beth Lambert. Presumably for love, because Bryn was bound to be a handful—even in bed. Mayhap there was much to be said for witchcraft, so far as raising sons went.

She nodded curtly. "Of course I will go, if it will help Jo." Holy Hecate, it had better, because she had grave misgivings about going to Grafton. "But Duchess Wydville has shown no sign of wanting to free Jo."

"Ah, but now we have King Henry in hand," Collin reminded her. How weird that everyone's destiny was bound up in this little monk-like man in black—Jo's life, Joy's freedom, Edward's success, England's fate. Everything hung on who held King Henry. Now for good or ill, Edward and Warwick had him. "That is what Bryn has gone to tell Duchess Wydville—that we have Mad King Henry. Before now the good duchess had to fear what the queen would think, or Henry Holland, or Chief Justice Fortescue. Nor do I blame her, for they are people to be feared, dreaded by many besides the duchess of Bedford. But their power came from King Henry—now that they have lost him, they will be headed for Wales. Or France. Or Scotland, if they have a dram of sense."

She agreed, hoping Queen Margaret would take her little son home to Anjou, where she would reflect, repent, and write her memoirs—though that did not seem over likely.

"It is high time the good duchess lost her fear of them," Collin concluded, "and learned to fear us instead." On that hopeful note he left.

Watching Collin go clanking off, Robyn wished she shared his confidence. Should she try to see Edward again before Collin claimed her on the morrow? Edward would be in Northampton with King Henry—where Buckingham and other victims of the battle were slated for lavish burials. Going to Grafton meant missing the funerals and attendant tedious ceremony—no great loss there. She felt bad enough about the men killed, without actually seeing them put lifeless into the ground. Let Edward handle that. King Henry would be in his element, able to be king and still wear black, praying in Latin along with the priests.

If she did see Edward, what would she say? As Collin aptly pointed out, whatever happened at Grafton would be a women's mystery. Edward never seemed worried by witchcraft; in fact, he rather liked the idea of her being a witch, finding it exciting, just as he liked the notion of her coming from the future. Edward wanted everything about her to be special. What had he called her this afternoon? "The most marvelous thing that ever happened to me." Men in love did lose all sense of proportion. Usually that was good, unless you needed their advice.

As soon as they were alone, Edward would want to talk about love, mayhap even marriage. His mind sure ran in that direction. This was his moment—he had everything else he wanted. Half his joy at victory came from thinking now he would have time with her. The seemingly hopeless task of seizing King Henry had been incredibly convenient, letting them talk of love and trade kisses without fear of things going any further. So long as he was a knight errant on an impossible quest, getting serious was unchivalrous. One wet week in July had changed everything. Now the fantastic odds were overcome, and all the neat barriers beaten down; nothing stood between them but her feelings, most particularly her need to go home. "Happily ever after" was always the hard part.

God, did she even want to go home? What a treasonous thought! And ridiculous, as well. No one was offering her a trip to the future. Far from it, she had been a big hit here in the Middle Ages, and all sorts of folks both high and low wanted her to stay. But what if she were suddenly given the chance to go back? Right now it would be hard for her to just say, "See ya later." She fingered the ring Edward had given her; what had been a simple impossibility suddenly became a choice. He had told her to keep the ring "until you have need of me." She decided to take Edward at his word, and not go to him until she was sure he was what she needed.

Collin came for her the next day, Saint Benedict's Day—a saint who was supposed to be especially adept at dealing with issues of witchcraft—hopefully a good omen. Collin had traded in plate armor for his blue brigandine, but retained his surly attitude, a sign he was worried sick about Jo. Deirdre insisted on coming with them, determined to keep a close eye on her trouble-prone mistress. As they rode south from Hardingstone, Robyn asked Collin, "How do we get the duchess to do what we want?"

Collin smiled thinly. "Threaten to have handsome young Edward cut off her head. That should concentrate her thoughts."

"Edward would not do that." Edward claimed never to have harmed a woman, and she believed him.

"Not even for you?" Collin gave her a disbelieving look.

"No, not ever," she shot back.

"Then you are but half the woman I imagined. Or he is but half the man." Collin had never sounded so bitter before—acting as if he were jealous of Edward. Perhaps he was, though not over her. Edward had King Henry. Grey de Ruthyn would get his traitor's reward. Southern England was spared the rape and plunder promised Percy's border reivers. But Collin's sister and niece still sat starving in a stone cell. "Duchess Wydville cannot know for sure Edward is so chivalrous," Collin pointed out. "Pray do not undeceive her."

By the time they got to Grafton, it was dark. Grander and more spacious than Duchess Wydville's plush apartments at Kenilworth,

Grafton already had an air of defeat. She could see it in the servants, who were wary and unsure, wondering where the next blow would come from—and how best to dodge it. Jacquetta Wydville, duchess of Bedford, looked anything but beaten, dressed like a queen at coronation, wearing a white cloth-of-silver embroidered gown and an ermine mantle trimmed with lace and fastened with silver tassels. Silk damask streamers hung almost to the floor from a white horned headdress edged with pearls. Her eldest daughter, Elizabeth, wore Wydville red and silver. Bryn had on Collin's colors, a long Welsh dress and a blue mantle trimmed with white lace, making Robyn feel terribly underdressed in her travel-worn gold riding gown and red sleeveless jacket.

They could all have been wearing wool sacks so far as Collin cared. Going straight to the point, he demanded something be done to get Jo and Joy out of the Tower. "Lest they starve waiting for the walls to be battered down."

Duchess Wydville asked in her stiff, haughty Franco-German accent. "What makes you think I can have them freed?"

Collin laughed. "Lifetimes of living alongside the power of witches gives me a notion of what you can or cannot do."

"And if I cannot do what you demand?"

Collin's smile grew pained. "My good and gracious duchess, seeing how near you sit to the queen, the slightest failure on your part could be construed as treason."

"Nonsense," the duchess retorted.

"Really?" Collin raised an eyebrow. "Do you wish to explain your powers to a panel of Westminster judges? For I swear if you fail to satisfy me, that is what you shall do, with FitzHolland for sergeant-at-law. My uncle and I have just handed King Henry to Earl Warwick and Edward of March, a name you will know well. Young Edward will be much wroth to learn who the witch was that drew him by magic to your ship, to deliver him to his enemies. Especially when he had you in his power, and he chivalrously set you free—only to plot his death through sorcery. Remember, there is no sanctuary from charges of heresy, necromancy, and treason, as the duchess of Gloucester discovered to her regret." He quoted the ballad dedicated to Duchess Wydville's late sister-in-law, the witch who seduced the duke of Gloucester:

Farewell, all wealth and world so wide.
I am assigned where I shall be:
Under men's keeping I must abide.
All women may beware by me.

"I will see you get the cell she got, with just a popinjay for company."

"You do not dare," the duchess replied icily.

"Test me and see," Collin told her. "I am a most desperate man, totally immune to chivalry."

Duchess Wydville snorted. "That I can believe."

"Then do as I say," Collin advised. "King Henry takes his religion most seriously, being a great hater of witches and of their attempts to marry into his family. Fail me not. Or Barrister will be sniffing you over while Le Boeuf fits you for a stake. That I swear."

"And what if you do not much like the result?"

Collin made a mocking bow. "That, my good duchess, is a hazard I am well ready to risk."

"So be it," declared the duchess, "let what happens be on your head." She turned to Robyn, "There is but one sure way to truly enter the Tower."

From the duchess of Bedford's stern measured tone, Robyn could tell the plan involved her and would not be easy. She had been desperately trying to imagine a magical means for freeing Jo from the Tower. Ordinary Witches Flight clearly would not work—how weird that she now thought of out-of-body journeys as "ordinary." They always ended where they began. Somehow they had to get Jo and Joy physically out of the Tower, a far harder proposition. She could feel herself pulled toward something weird and dangerous. "What way is that?"

Duchess Wydville graced her with a smile. "The same way you came here, my dear."

The duchess did not mean by mare from Northampton; Old Lady Weirdville meant through the future. "Do you mean by going into my own time?"

"*Natürlich*" Duchess Wydville rewarded her with a stern smile. "In your proper time was it possible to enter the Tower?"

"Very possible." Millions of tourists visited the bloodstained monument every year. She herself had done it on her first day in England, and still remembered the schedule. "The Tower is open weekdays and

Saturdays nine to five, and most Sunday afternoons. Except for Christmas Eve, Christmas Day, Boxing Day, New Year's Day, Good Friday, and Sundays during the winter."

Duchess Wydville looked askance at the mention of Boxing Day, which she had seemingly never heard of. "So, if you were returned to your proper time, you could get into the Tower?"

She nodded. "Easily."

"Then the prisoners in the Tower can be freed as easily."

"How?" Was she suddenly on the verge of being returned to her proper millennium? How utterly impossible.

"That must be our mystery." Duchess Wydville nodded significantly at Collin. What would follow was not for male ears, making it time for him to go.

Collin quietly acquiesced. Leaning close to Robyn, he whispered, "Many thanks, Lady Stafford. I would be with you if I could." He gave her a swift kiss, bowed to the duchess, and departed. Too bad. She, too, wished Collin could come with her. But Bryn and Deirdre were here, to keep a watch on good duchess Wydville and her daughter. She announced herself ready, hoping it was true.

"Good," the duchess declared primly. "Let us begin." Surprisingly they began by saddling up and riding back toward Hardingstone. Halfway there, Robyn realized she was headed for the ancient ring fort at Hunsbury, where she and Beth Lambert were initiated into the coven, and where Collin stopped to pray on the way back to Northampton four days before. Clearly the duchess had done this night ride many times, leading them easily over miles of darkened fields and woods, avoiding roads, fences, and pitfalls. Reaching the ring fort, they dismounted, leaving their horses with serving women. Deirdre came with them, carrying a lamp. Robyn could hear the matins bell ringing in Delapré Abbey, calling Sister Perpetua to prayer. Hopefully some of those prayers were for her.

Demanding the duchess go over the ritual beforehand in detail, she found it much like the one that brought her to the Middle Ages. Somewhat encouraging. But this time there was only one anchor, something to take her into the future and then bring her back again. She decided on Edward's ring. Nothing else had that powerful a pull on her, and nothing else was as likely to bring her back. She showed it to the duchess.

"Good, good choice." The duchess sounded more than ever like the

Widow Weirdville. "Give it to me." Chills ran up Robyn's spine as she handed her the ring. The Duchess held it high in the lamplight, letting it shine. "This ring will take you there, and bring you back here. Keep it with you at all times, but not on your finger. When you get into the Tower in your proper time, put it on your finger and you will return at once. Lose it—or fail to use in timely fashion—and you can never come back."

"What do you mean by timely fasion?" she asked suspiciously.

"One day," replied the duchess. "Once back in your own time, you will have from dawn to dusk to get to London, enter the Tower, put on the ring, and return here. Otherwise the spell will be broken and you will remain in your own time. And be gone from here forever." Duchess Wydville made that sound like by far the most desirable alternative.

Strange. Robyn stared at the rose on the ring. Returning to the Middle Ages had never been a big worry for her. Not even a remote consideration, actually. Suddenly it was crucial to everything—to Jo and Joy's survival, to ever seeing Edward again. Once she was home, how could she even think of coming back? Telling her she could go home to stay, if she just forgot about everyone here and now seemed like cunning mental torture, pitting one part of her against another. Shoving all the spiraling possibilities out of her head, she focused on the duchess, demanding, "What happens when I get into the Tower? What then?" How was she supposed to free Joanna and Joy?

Duchess Wydville motioned to her daughter, who produced a silver box small enough to fit in her palm. It had a little lock and a tiny key. "This box contains a powerful sleeping spell. Keep it with you, and keep it closed. When you open it, everyone in the Tower but you will be instantly asleep."

That sounded good. "What then?"

Duchess Wydville arched a frosty eyebrow. "All of London is trying to get into the Tower. *Nein?*"

"True." They had been pounding the walls from Southwark when she left.

"Then go up onto the ramparts and invite them in."

Right. That sounded like the shakiest part of deal. "Why not just go to London and open the box upwind from the Tower?"

Duchess Wydville gave her exasperated look. "This is not a scent box. This is a sleeping spell that must be invoked in the heart of the Tower. In the White Tower itself. And you, too, must believe in it with all your heart."

Gingerly she took the little silver box, determined to do just as the duchess said. What other choice did she have? She had to believe. Time after time she had doubted her powers—and each time she did, it had been a disaster. This time she would give it everything. But first, she needed to leave something behind, just in case. Getting out her electronic notebook, she showed Deirdre how to work it. Witches stood around her, fascinated by electronic magic. She told Deirdre, "I want you to take this message to Edward in Northampton, give it to him only. Do you understand?"

Deirdre did. Robyn sat down, struggling to compose herself. Yet again, way too much was happening way too quickly, forcing her to make immediate heart-wrenching choices. For starters, she had to semi-trust Duchess Wydville—no easy task there. Then she had to contemplate going home, only to come back here. Looking from Duchess Wydville to Bryn, she realized that both these women had ample desire to see her gone, and small reason to want her back. Deirdre was the only one here she would miss—and who would miss her—not the duchess of Bedford or Prince Glendower's granddaughter, but the most ignoble product of an illegal union. She started to write, hoping it would not be her final entry:

Friday, 11 July 1460, Saint Benedict's Day, Hunsbury, Hardingstone, Northamptonshire.

Dear Edward,

I am about to do something desperate and dangerous. What else is new? I cannot say what it is, except that it will free my friends in the Tower. If something happens and I do not return, I want you to know that I love you—probably since that first wild day in Wales, when you wanted to know the way to Llanthony. In that one day you completely changed my life. You are smart, brave, and caring, and no doubt much too good for me. But as you may have noticed, I am not easy to please. Being smart, brave, caring, etc. . . . is not nearly enough. I will not apologize for being choosy. Love is very important to me, and huge chasms separate us. Five hundred years of history.

Not to mention our own breeding and birth. We come from vastly different worlds, and up until now, I have been desperate to get back to mine.

But now that I fear I might never see you again, I cannot face what I must do without saying how much I love you. Though you think I am bold with words, this is the one great thing I have left unsaid. Despite all our differences, I truly do love you. Quite madly, as a matter of fact. If I do not come back, it will not be because I did not try. I have your ring, and I mean to bring it back with me.

Love,
Robyn

P.S.—I am forced to put all my faith in Duchess Wydville; if this turns out ill, get hold of her. Sir Collingwood Grey will know how best to wring the truth from her.

P.P.S.—If anyone ever told me I would be going home, but meant to come back, I would have thought them seriously insane. Consider yourself complimented.

⋖⟫ Into the Tower ⟪⋗

She landed with a thud, looking about. Witches Night had turned to broad daylight. Deirdre, Bryn, Duchess Weirdville, and Her Grace's beautiful blond daughter Elizabeth were gone, along with the wax-spattered ironstone altar and all the rest of medieval England, including the turf beneath her feet. Sometime between then and now the floor of the ancient ring fort sank considerably—having been mined for ironstone. Materializing in midair at medieval ground level, she fell several feet, landing with a thump in the third millennium.

Picking herself up, she straightened her headdress, hearing the hum of traffic, smelling auto exhaust. She was home, and already finding it unfamiliar—the drop in ground level made the ancient overgrown ring walls seem higher and more dramatic. Lifting the gold hem of her gown, she scrambled up a low spot, pushing frantically through the undergrowth. Emerging from the trees she saw the modern world spread out around her, roads, traffic, tall smokestacks, power lines and many, many more buildings, stretching off into morning haze, as if her whole mad medieval adventure never happened. Un-fucking-believable. She had done it. Months in the Middle Ages completely swept away. She could no longer prove she had ever been there—not even to herself. All she had to show for her trip was a red-gold medieval gown and headdress, the handmade Northampton riding boots on her feet, and the silver ring in her hand. Pretty flimsy proof. Hardly better than pomegranate juice on her fingers. Looking down at the ring, she remembered Duchess Wydville's parting advice, whispered just as the spell took hold—"Do not come back."

We shall see about that. Right now she was home. Good and gracious Duchess Wydville had not sent her to prehistoric Antarctica or ancient Timbuktu. Pocketing the ring, she thanked Hecate, and the dreary duchess, doing a little hop, skip victory dance all the way to the roadside. Home again, home again, jiggity jog. If not home, at least back in modern Britain. Bloody incredible. She did a wild homecoming twirl alongside two lanes of morning-commute traffic. Happy to have done the impossible again. She was back. Holy Hecate, what a witch. Miss Rodeo Montana in a medieval dress.

Cars whipped down the wrong side of the road at breakneck speed, headed into Northampton. Someone honked at her. Coming to a breathless halt, she stood at the roadside in her velvet gown, leather boots, and medieval headdress, feeling centuries out of place, like Edward when he came riding out of the Black Mountains and into her life. Wondering what day it was, she glanced at her wrist—her watch said Saturday, July 12, 1460, but was not to be trusted, especially the 1460 part. And it felt too cool to be July, not in the age of global warming—currently doing wonders for the dismal English climate. She remembered the song of True Thomas, who passed forty days among the faeries, then returned to find he could not tell a lie, and that "seven years were past and gone." Let's hope not. Reaching into her gown pocket, she touched Edward's ring for luck and then stuck out her thumb.

Two cars zipped by; then a maroon Mercedes pulled out onto the shoulder, rolling to a stop right in front of her. The passenger-side window sank, and the door lock clicked open. She looked in before even touching the door, seeing who was behind the wheel—a guy, with a cell phone in front of his face. Otherwise, the oversize car yawned empty, except for the low purr of circulating air. So much metal and power used to move one man made her see why Collin scoffed at her stories about the future, people bred to ride and prize horses were not much impressed to hear how wonderful their replacements were.

Hanging up his cell phone, he invited her in, looking nice, but certainly no Edward, more than twenty years older than she, white at the temples and balding on top, with a bemused grin—not at all looking like your normal well-heeled rapist. She opened the door and got in. England was a pretty law-abiding country—nowadays, anyway. With no guns, thank God. Unpinning her headdress, she held it in her lap, trying to keep her gold skirts from getting caught in the door. Air freshener could not hide the stale cigarette smell, immediately making her want to smoke.

"Where are you headed?" He managed to make the question a comment on her costume.

"London," she replied promptly, proud to have a destination at the ready, proving she was not just wandering about the countryside in a gold-embroidered Renaissance riding gown.

He laughed, "You are headed the wrong way."

"Really?" She had assumed she could pick up the main London road in Northampton.

"M1 is just south of us. You would do best hitching by one of the entrances, a ride there would take you right into London." He had a friendly likeable Northumberland accent, not near as thick as the ones she had heard here five centuries ago. Strange how she could now tell English accents apart. Everything from Cockney to Yorkshire used to sound alike.

"Maybe you should let me out?" She hated leaving such a cushy ride right away, then having to go through the whole routine again with someone else.

"That is all right, I will take you to an entrance." He turned promptly to stay south of the Nene, keeping Northampton on the far side of the river, riding right over the spot where the battle was fought. She saw a huge Avon cosmetics building where King Henry's tent had been—a strange, jarring sight. Resisting the impulse to borrow a cigarette, she glanced at the dashboard clock. 9:43 A.M. But when? She asked the smiling guy at the wheel what day of the week it was, then the date, and then the year. Seeing him get more curious with each question.

Her watch was hopelessly off, wrong hour, wrong date, wrong year, wrong millennium. It was October 17, the same day she left. Only the day of the week was right, still Saturday. Both her displacement and her return followed on Witches Nights. Off to the west in the Cotswolds, she had only just disappeared. Widow Weirdville was probably still making excuses to Jo. Now here she was, back again, riding south through Hardingstone, headed for M1 and London. She would have to call Jo to say she was okay. And Heidi.

Duchess Wydville said she had "from dawn until dusk" to get into the Tower—but she was not surprised to get short-changed. The duchess wanted her to fail, or quit.

"You are not from around here, are you?" the driver asked.

"No," she smiled to herself, that was for sure. "I am American, from Hollywood, California."

He chuckled, "That explains the dress."

She leaped to Hollywood's defense. "Actually I got this here. The boots are handmade in Northampton, and this is a genuine medieval English riding dress." Given to her by a genuine medieval English knight.

"Remarkably preserved," he observed, in a tone that showed he did not believe her. Fine. She did not want to be believed. Better to have him think she was a flake. When she was in his place, her most charitable interpretation of Edward's story was that he was crazy.

"So are you going to a party, or a pageant?"

"Nope, just to London." Hardingstone had grown tremendously, but only the base of her Eleanor's Cross remained. She asked what happened to the cross. "Puritans did it," replied the driver cheerfully. "You know, those perpetually disapproving sorts we shipped over to you on the *Mayflower*."

How sad. Suddenly she thought of something, asking the man, "Do you speak any foreign languages?"

"Only if you count French. They forced some into me at university."

"Say something to me in French."

"Why?" He looked quizzical.

"Please," she begged, "just anything. I want to see if I understand it."

He rattled off a sentence, that she could tell was French, but other than that, nothing—the Displacement Spell was broken. She was back in her "proper" time.

"Did you *parlez-vous* that?" he asked.

"Not in the least," she replied happily. For the first time in months she had not understood someone. Other than Nest.

"Did you ever study French in school?" he asked.

"No. Never." Until recently she had shown absolutely no aptitude for languages. Unless you counted horse whispering.

"But you thought you might understand it anyway?"

"You never know."

At the entrance to M1 the Mercedes pulled onto the shoulder, and the passenger door unlocked with a soft click. She started to thank him, her mind already on the next ride, not looking forward to getting out of her warm seat, and standing on the cold road shoulder with her thumb stuck out. He asked her, "If not a party or a pageant, then what? You're wearing enough bullion to start a bank." He was not going to let her go until knew why she was wearing the gown. She could understand; look how far she had gone to find out where Edward came from.

She shook her head. "If I told you, you would never believe it."

"Try me," he insisted.

She hesitated. He looked nice enough, in a rich uncle sort of way, but she was not telling her story to everyone she met, not right away at least. She had to get to the Tower, before they dropped a net over her and dragged her off to the Royal Psychiatric Academy. "Take me to London, and I will tell you."

"What?" He looked taken aback.

"Take me to London, and I will tell you the whole story. It is a doozy, too—but I swear you will not believe a word of it."

He stared at her, cars zipping by behind his head. Then he turned to check the traffic on M1. On a cold Saturday morning the traffic headed into London looked manageable. He looked back at her, saying, "A deal."

From behind her came the soft click of her door locking, and they were off, merging into M1 traffic, headed south. He picked up his phone, calling a Northampton restaurant, changing a lunch reservation to a dinner reservation—for "Chisholm." Handing up the phone, he asked, "Where are you going in London?"

"The Tower."

"Where else?" He laughed. "But you must tell me the truth, and I will try my utmost to believe you."

"The absolute truth—but not until we are closer to the Tower. Because you will not believe me, and I do not want you turning me out two miles down the road for being a lunatic."

"Good enough. My name is Bill Chisholm."

"Robyn Stafford." Bill turned out to be married, and on a business weekend in Northampton; he was in broadcasting, BBC radio to the Midlands. Their jobs were close enough that she easily convinced him that she did work for a major movie studio.

"So are you making a film?" He looked about inquisitively, "Are we on camera now?" He did not look overly worried, speeding away from his business conference with a young woman beside him.

"This is not how we make movies," she assured him. "Not in Hollywood, anyway." Not by hitching about Northampton in costume.

"Good, because this could look wrong if it ever turned up on tape." He was flirting with her, but only flirting, otherwise he would never have told her he was married. Bill was not wearing a ring, at least not on this "business weekend." But then, her ring was in her pocket as well. "I mean, a pretty girl like you must have a boyfriend."

"Yes," she told him sadly—but by now he had been dead five hundred years. Along with Deirdre, and almost everyone else she had gotten to know. Even little Beth Lambert. Seeing the modern world whip by through a curved tinted windshield was oddly distancing. Time after time she promised herself a joyous delirium of nonstop overindulgence "when" she got back, heaped with everything she missed, starting in some super-deluxe hotel room with hot running water, cable TV, and room service, where she could sprawl in her bath, drinking peach margaritas, eating Chinese take-out, and watching first-run movies, while a hunky masseuse rubbed her shoulders and a manicurist painted her toes. Now, faced with the real thing, she had forgotten even to fall down and kiss the ground. The "real world" sliding past outside looked rather ordinary, even humdrum. How could peach margaritas compare to capturing a mad king? Or facing down a witch-duchess in her lair? Modern times just looked remarkably cluttered, full of cars, buildings, and people busily going about unexciting lives. Despite the drawbacks, medieval England was never unexciting.

South of Dunstable, Bill suggested a stop for late breakfast and coffee. She opposed it, until he came to the magic word—*coffee*. She had not had a cup in months, and had gotten absolutely no sleep the night before. Why not face the day a little more awake? Turning off M1 at Abbots Langely, just south of Saint Albans, they stopped at a little mom-and-pop eatery, where they could get "a real English breakfast, beans, bangers, and eggs."

What she wanted most was the coffee. When the coffee came, she drank half the steaming cup in one greedy gulp, amazed at how good it felt. Hot caffeine shot through her system, and the world seemed suddenly lighter and brighter. She sighed, setting the half full cup back on the table, saying, "This is the first coffee I have had in months, and I have badly missed it. I am a terrible addict."

Bill lifted an eyebrow. "Been living in a monastery?"

"A nunnery, actually." She thought of Sister Perpetua, long dead by now, along with everyone else. Hecate help her, hopefully Perpetua found someone, or at least left the nunnery. "But only for the last few days or so."

"Which nunnery?" Bill sounded anxious to hear her story.

"Saint Mary de Pratis, near Northampton." She doubted the place even existed nowadays—probably closed by the Puritans—but she had to start somewhere. How could she spend a day in her own time and not tell anyone what had happened to her. Of course she could not picture anyone believing her, but that hardly mattered. She had been through the most amazingly unbelievable adventure imaginable—she was a living witness to history. How could she not tell? Bill seemed a safe enough victim.

"What were you doing in a convent?"

"Seeking shelter." What convents were for.

"Shelter from who?" Bill asked. "Or what?"

"From Percy harbingers. Border reivers brought south by Lord Egremont."

"Lord who?"

"Thomas Lord Egremont, brother to the earl of Northumberland. I was there when he died. When he was killed." Separated from the deed by just a thin layer of tent silk, in the mud and rain outside Northampton. Two days ago at most, and now here she was staring at a plate of beans and bangers under fluorescent lights. Half-eaten eggs stared back at her. Her brain could barely contain the insane contrast, threatening to throw her into cosmic shock, making her feel like a reincarnation of herself. Thank heavens for the coffee. She held tight to her cup to keep from shaking, glad the waitress had left a pot and cream.

"You saw this lord killed?" Mention of murder brought Bill up sharp, afraid he had picked up more than a pretty hitchhiker.

"No." Thank goodness. She emptied her coffee cup and then poured herself more. "I was with the king in his tent. But I did see the duke of Buckingham's body afterwards. That was enough, believe me. I still get the shakes." Seeing Bill's puzzlement, she decided to take the plunge. "Believe it or not, I have just spent more than two months in the Middle Ages."

"You mean as in a medieval fair? Or some fantasy encampment?"

"No, as in May, June, and some of July 1460. And a few days in April." She told Bill the whole story, more or less front to back, leaving out the personal parts and women's secrets. Bill did not notice, being too busy watching his mysterious and pretty hitchhiker turn into a raving lunatic over a plate of bangers and eggs that he had to pay for. She watched Bill's eyes go wide with horror, then start to glaze over as she piled detail upon detail. He listened, at least. And asked intelligent questions. Bill knew who Warwick was, said he was called the Kingmaker—but was not sure why. Whatever the reason, it did not bode well for England; Warwick was not who she would choose to make or unmake kings.

For every question he raised, she had a ready answer. By now she knew more about life in late medieval England than anyone else on earth. She knew what London's bells sounded like in the rain, what market day smelled like, how nunnery food tasted, what it was like to come down to the castle kitchen early on a cold May morning. How it felt to ride over the moors on Witches Night under a waning moon. Bill looked both stumped and fascinated, unable to find a single hole in her incredible tale. Of course, he had no way of checking any of it, but she prided herself on her completeness. How many lunatics bothered to work out every conceivable detail? Not many, she bet. All Bill had to swallow was the magic itself, accepting that such a displacement was possible. A mighty big gulp, but here she was, living proof it had happened. "So what brought you back here?" Bill asked.

By now her bangers and eggs were history, and she was starting her third cup of coffee. Her story had gone as far as the king's capture at

Northampton, but she had not yet gotten to Grafton, Duchess Wydville, and her trip home. Suddenly, she remembered something she had missed more than coffee. She stood up smiling, saying to Bill, "Tell you in a minute. Let me freshen up first."

On her way to the loo she met a woman coming the other way, who smiled and complimented her gown, a good sign. The dingy single-stall women's room was a small slice of heaven, with a lock on the door, hot running water, and sparkling clean facilities. With toilet paper by the roll, waiting to be used. Paradise drenched with phony pine scent. She nearly cried. For the first time in months she could use the facilities without holding her breath or wondering what she dared wipe with. She could take her time, washing with warm water, utterly relaxed; even the queen and Duchess Wydville did not enjoy such luxury.

And she had Bill half-believing her. Just sitting down over a hot clean meal to tell her story was a godsend. She had not realized how badly she needed to tell someone until the words came tumbling out. She desperately needed someone to bounce ideas off, like she did with Deirdre. Or Edward. Bill was no Edward, but he was a big help, especially in ordering her thoughts. Between here and the Tower, she would pump him on what to take back with her. He seemed the practical type, who would think of things she never could. Telling her story reminded her of all she'd gone through to get this far, and how many times she gave herself up for lost. Yet here she was, back in a real rest room, something she had thought never to see again. Rinsing her face in wonderfully warm water one final time, she went back to the table.

Finding Bill gone. She stared at his chair, thinking he might have gone to the men's room. But his coat was gone, and there was money by his plate, enough to cover the meal and a bit of a tip. Through the window, she saw an empty parking slot where the maroon Mercedes had been.

Easy come, easy go. She thought she had been totally convincing, but she merely convinced Bill she was crazy. Everyone in the little eatery stared at her, wondering why the well-heeled guy she was with had abandoned her, leaving her standing there in her outlandish gold medieval gown. Her headdress was in the Mercedes, headed back to Northampton. But no matter how curious they looked, she knew none of them really wanted to hear her story—Bill proved that. She had only to open her mouth to turn herself from a person of interest to an object of pity, or worse. All by telling the simple truth. So much for being True Thomas. Or finding someone to share her troubles with.

Calmly finishing her third cup of coffee, she added a couple of King Henry's silver pennies to the tip and then strolled out to the edge of the parking area and stuck out her thumb.

Cars whizzed past. This close to London it took more than a gold-red gown to get a ride. She had felt that if she just got back to her own time, everything would be easy. Compared to the Middle Ages, she lived in a millennium of plenty, dedicated to instant communication and immediate gratification. Problem was, to carry on a successful conversation she had to pretend that the biggest most amazing thing in her life had never happened, becoming just another ditzy American in medieval dress.

Another car pulled out of the pack. No Mercedes this time, a lime green Toyota with a patch of primer gray on one fender. The guy behind the wheel looked like a student, with dark hair and a scraggly beard, not much older than Edward. He asked, "Which way are you going?" sounding like he was willing to go any way she wanted.

"To London." She nodded at M1.

"Sure, no problem," he replied, and she got in, finding it even harder to fold her gown into the little Toyota. Duchess Wydville never had to deal with Japanese subcompacts. "Where in London?"

She straightened her gold skirts. "The Tower."

"Cool." He shifted into gear. "You are dressed for it. Where did you get that gown?"

"You do not want to know." This time she really meant it—this guy only thought he wanted to hear her story.

"Probably," he admitted, admiring her gown. "No story could be as good as the one I am imagining." That's what you think. She let it go at that, not wanting to be dumped out on Bushey Heath. Right now this guy was happy he picked her up, glad to take her wherever she needed to go. Better to leave it that way, though it meant shutting up about the biggest thing that had ever happened to her. Finding home so inhospitable was a shock.

Nor could she blame it on the Brits. Everyone here had a cheery greeting for her, and guys were glad to go out of their way driving her about. Hitching in Hollywood was not nearly so user friendly. But wherever she was, no one was going to believe her. Or if they did, it would be for all the wrong reasons.

Edward never doubted her. Nor Deirdre either. Maybe it was the medieval belief in miracles. Though a lot of medievals were not what she would call broad minded. Look at FitzHolland. Or Le Boeuf, for God's sake! Edward and Deirdre had that youthful sense of wonder, where the amazing was still possible and a woman from the future was someone to be listened to. It helped that Deirdre was raised on fairy tales, and Edward had a fantasy upbringing in Ludlow Castle—both safely beyond the reach of public education. She no longer felt so proud of coming from an age that had outgrown miracles.

She never got the name of the guy in the lime green Toyota, but he was genuinely friendly and enjoyed dropping her off at the Tower, in her gold gown and crimson sleeveless jacket. Thanking him, she adjusted her skirts staring past the gaping tourists. Yellowed tree-lined walls faced the sidewalk. Within them, the upper stories of the White Tower looked out over the City. That was where she had to get to, the heart of the Tower.

But first, some shopping. Right now she had a chance to dive into one of the modern world's commercial capitals and come out with whatever she could carry. And who knows when she would come this way again. Every dress she ever made, or got as a gift, or borrowed permanently got a little inner pocket for her folding money and VISA card—which went with her everywhere—to have left them behind would have been admitting she was not instantly ready to go home. Now vigilance and needlework were vindicated. Money was no object, up to the limit on the VISA card—no sense saving credit she might never see again.

Curious to see more of the modern city, having lived in the medieval one, she walked up Bywater to Great Tower Street, then up Eastcheap and Cannon Street all the way to Saint Paul's—drawing stares and greetings on the way. Londoners and tourists liked seeing a bit of history go strolling by, even if they did not know why. She barely recognized the great church when she came to it, in part because Saint Paul's had been completely rebuilt, but mostly because it was dwarfed by the modern city. Cathedrals were just not as grand surrounded by miles of concrete and big buildings. On her way, she looked into every shop, trying to fill her huge mental list of things she missed in the

Middle Ages. Buying a sturdy bag that went with her gown, she stocked up on trivial necessities like Tampax and extra underwear, a box of plastic lighters, little flashlights and batteries, a toothbrush, dental floss, flea bomb, lotions, shampoo, batteries for her electronic notebook, five pounds of coffee, a silver thermos, several bottles of water, and a nifty hand-sewing kit with all the extra gadgets you could never get in the Middle Ages, plus an old-fashioned refillable ink pen and a waterproof notebook, topped off by a bulky but precious four-pack of toilet paper. And of course chocolate bars, something alarmingly lacking in Medieval England. At a pharmacy she bought some over-the-counter antibiotics and the most powerful pain killers British law allowed. Being in England, she was not even tempted to buy a gun, but she did buy a high-pressure can of the nastiest bug spray she could find.

She spent most of her remaining credit at a jewelry shop, investing in flashy gemstone rings, some gold coins, and a gold necklace that she could take apart to sell the links. But her most fateful and important purchase was in a bookstore, where she picked out the thickest, most detailed paperback she could find on the Wars of the Roses. King Henry stared out at her from the cover. She agonized about even opening it—if something horrible was going to happen to Edward, she did not want to know. Yet this book might be the most valuable thing she brought back from the future.

Gingerly, she skipped over the table of contents, which might tell her things she did not want to know, leafing through the pages, looking at nothing but dates. Finding the part that covered the first half of 1460, she read it over, trying to judge the book's usefulness. All the big events were there, Edward and Warwick's return from Ireland, the landing at Sandwich, and the march on London. The trip she and Edward took to Burges was not mentioned, but there was a detailed description of Baron Rivers, Sir Anthony Wydville, and the duchess being taken prisoner to Calais in January—apparently lifted from one of the Paston's letters. A whole slew of Paston letters seemed to have survived, making her wonder if any of them mentioned her. Flipping to the index, she found a long list of Staffords, none named Robyn.

Closing the book, she considered alternatives. Just having it in her hand was scary. It frightened her to think that she had only to thumb through the index to find out when Edward would die, or whom he might marry. And what did it mean that she was not in it? Was she too insignificant? Or headed for an early demise and an unmarked grave? If something was in this book did it mean it had to actually happen? Shakespeare had been incredibly wrong about Falstaff. Maybe the third millennium was wrong about the Middle Ages. Or the Wars of the Roses. And could the past be changed? Had her presence already changed it?

She put the book back on the shelf, but could not bring herself to let go of it—the book was too potentially valuable. If she left it behind, she felt sure that somewhere, sometime, it might mean life or death to know what would happen next. When that time came she would remember having this book in her hands, and bitterly regret not buying it. Blaming herself horribly.

She bought the book, stuffing it far down into the bottom of her bag. She did not have to read it, but buying it preserved her choice. By now it was well into the afternoon, and the Tower would be closing soon. Using up her folding money, she treated herself to a final third-millennium meal at an Indian restaurant, gorging herself on flaming hot curry, chapati, melon slices, fried milk balls, and a dozen other dishes not much found in medieval England. At the end of her "last meal" she nervously lifted a few instant coffee packets from the table, already fearing she would be doing without. Stuffing the foil packets into her gown, she found a public phone in sight of the Tower, calling Jo's number in the Cotswolds.

Joy answered. When she gave her name, the girl shouted gleefully, "Robyn, you are back! We thought we had lost you."

"Yes." She smiled at the child's enthusiasm. "I am back. Can I speak to your mother?"

Jo came on the phone, saying, "Oh Robyn, I am so happy to hear you have returned. I hope you have not been harmed."

"No, I have not been harmed." Actual physical harm was the one thing that had not happened to her. Yet.

"Where are you?" Jo asked.

"In London, just outside the Tower." She could see the tops of the White Tower from the phone booth.

Jo's voice dropped. "I see."

"Do you?" Robyn asked. "Do you know where I have been?"

"Somewhere in the Middle Ages?" Jo hazarded.

"Yes, 1460, to be precise." And she was on the verge of going back. "Tell me the truth, did you know this would happen?"

"No," Jo sounded very much like she meant it. "I did not know what would happen to you."

"But my arrival in England was not a complete surprise?"

Jo sighed, "No, not even close. We have all been waiting for you—Collin and I have—ever since we were kids."

"Waiting for me?" Even after all that had happened, it seemed so patently absurd. Jo and Collin were both older than she, so she would have been at best a baby, a hemisphere away in Montana.

"Yes." Jo spoke slowly and deliberately. "Ever since we were children in Greystone, we have known your name. Robyn Stafford, Hollywood, California, appeared on our Ouija board when we first learned about our past lives. For years all we knew about our previous selves was that we were last reborn sometime in the Middle Ages, and that Robyn Stafford from Hollywood had played a huge role in our medieval lives. It was a puzzle. How could someone from modern California matter so much in the Middle Ages?"

How, indeed? "So Collin came looking for me in Hollywood?"

"Apparently. He did not warn me ahead of time. I went to Greystone for his birthday party, and suddenly there you were, Robyn Stafford in the flesh. And Collin had not only found you, but started an affair, as well. I would have taken you in if your name were Betsy Ross—but for Robyn Stafford I would have done just about anything. I know now that I owe you a great debt, having something to do with the Tower."

She stared past the phone in her hand at the turrets and battlements of the White Tower poking above the trees. Being a witch, Jo could never give her a straight answer. "A great debt" that had "something to do with the Tower." She felt like Lady Macbeth, trying to separate prophecy from self-deception. "So, why did you send me to Wales?"

"That first Witches Night after Collin's party, I had a vision of you walking along the Welsh border, above the Golden Valley, on the way to Llanthony. I did not know what you would find there, but I had to send you."

"Why?"

"Visions are blessings, and meant to be fulfilled—if possible. I saw no harm coming to you. And you looked happy, hiking along. Almost at peace. I honestly thought it would do you good."

"You might have warned me," she reminded her, still smarting at being misled.

"These were witches' secrets," Jo reminded her, "and you were not an initiate. And I did not think you would just disappear. Besides, would anything I said have prepared you for what really happened?"

"Not in a million millennia." Nothing could have prepared her.

"What exactly did happen?" Jo knew she had vanished, headed for the past, but that was all. Plus the date she had just given Jo—1460.

"Well, for starters, I have been gone three months. Even though it was only a few hours to you." She told her story again, or at least as much of it as made sense, concentrating on Jo and Joy, their lives and family. Jo was intrigued to learn she was a niece to Lord Grey de Ruthyn, and that Joy's father had been duke of Somerset. She was less pleased by the Duchess Wydville's betrayal, and sobered right up by the news that she and Joy were left to starve in a Tower cell. Even the news that Robyn was about to enter the Tower in a do-or-die attempt to save her did not exactly lift Jo's spirits. Jo soberly asked if Robyn was sure of what she was doing.

"Sort of." If she thought too much about this, she might end up taking Duchess Wydville's advice and "not come back."

"You do not have to do this just for me and Joy," Jo reminded her.

"Never fear, I am not." She was not going back just for Jo, though were it not for Jo she would be taking a totally different route.

"Well, witches' instinct says you will come out well. My vision had you walking free and happy; I cannot believe it could lead you into harm."

Let us hope so. She said her good-byes and then talked for a while with Joy, telling the girl how her necklace got them out of Berkeley Castle. Joy was ecstatic and then crushed to hear her newfound friend—and "oldest ever companion in adventure"—was going back. It was touching. Joy was the one person who positively pleaded with her not to go, insisting she promise to come back. She swore she would; then she hung up.

Hanging on to the receiver, she smiled at the tourists staring at her. Fortunately, no one needed the phone. She considered calling her own phone, to see if Bryn still had it. But what would she say? Besides, Collin might have it by now, and she had less to say to him—much preferring his medieval replacement. If you are going to be a rotter, at least be good with a lance.

Instead she punched an international number. Checking her watch, she saw it was six-thirty Saturday morning in L.A. Perfect time to catch Heidi at home. She called collect. Heidi's sleepy voice answered, "How didya get this number?"

"It is me—Robyn. Did I wake you?"

"Hell, no—it's Saturday." Heidi's voice came awake. "I'm just going to bed."

"That's what I hoped."

"Changed that ticket for you." Heidi sounded proud, too bad she would not need the flight.

"Remember that earl?" she asked.

"Sure, the one you are dumping Collin for." For Heidi all this happened in the last few days, not months ago.

"I think I am going away with him."

"Good for you." Heidi sounded happy. "Glad to see you finally finding your wild side."

"Far away," she told her.

Heidi grew serious, sensing trouble. "What do you mean?"

"I mean I may not come back."

"How come?" Heidi went from serious to worried.

"Can I tell you something totally crazy. I swear it is true, but you are the only person who might believe it."

"Sure, shoot." Heidi was fully alert.

"This earl lives in the Middle Ages—in 1460." She could hear Heidi fumbling with something over the phone. "And I have been there."

"Been where?" Heidi asked, distracted by what she was doing.

"To the Middle Ages. With knights and castles, troubadours and everything, masked balls, outrageous feasts with really funky food. I even met a king, and practically had to hold his hand in battle."

"Shit," Heidi laughed at the other end of the line, "English hash must be as good as they say."

"Wish it was that, but I am stone sober—though they drink beer and wine like water back there, breakfast, noon, and night. Had to take to herb teas just to stay level. I know it sounds insane, but it happened. Now I have to decide whether I am going back. If I do, I may never see this millennium again." Or anyone in it.

Heidi did not answer; instead there was a click on the other end of the line, followed by a sharp intake of breath. That crack about hash was a tip-off. Heidi was clearing her head with some smoke. Exhaling heavily, Heidi asked, "So what are the Middle Ages like? I mean, you know, is it like Mexico—only more so?"

She laughed. "Sure, picture Mexico, without the cars, or highways, or TVs, or resorts."

Heidi took another toke and then asked, "What's left? Burros and churches?"

"Pretty much, and people." People were what she was going back for. "Except for London and towns like Northampton and Calais, England is one big green barnyard dotted with really huge churches. But it is a fascinating place, raw and elegant at the same time. And there is always something to do, either making your own clothes or growing your own food. You get to ride horses every day and hear live music every night. With balls, pageants, and parades, masquerades, bonfires, and midnight dancing, and Witches Flights on weekends. Folks drink beer at breakfast, and sleep three to a bed."

"Could be cool," Heidi admitted.

"So what do you think?" she asked. "Should I go back?" Even if it is forever. Jo expected her to go, and thought it would all come out well. But that was Jo. Jo always believed in doing right by others—and look where it got her.

Heidi took a long drag on her joint. "There is really only one question here. And we all know what it is."

"We do?" She saw so many questions she could not list half of them.

"Sure," Heidi insisted, "only one thing matters. Do you love him?"

Heidi hit it, as usual. That is what it came down to. Did she love Edward enough to take this wild plunge into another world? "Yes, I think I do."

She had to come home to know it. Until now she had been obsessed with getting home—correcting this huge cosmic mistake—which meant putting Edward five hundred years behind her. Now that she was here, and had her free choice, she already missed him. Having Edward all to herself, free of strife and politics was what she looked forward to most. Never seeing him again was obviously not an option, which meant she had to go back, and soon, before she lost her nerve.

Heidi took another drag. "Well, remember me when you are a countess."

"Sure," she promised, then added, "I will miss you."

"Me, too." Heidi already sounded far away.

"Give my regrets to the studio." She could not think of anything else to say.

"With pleasure," Heidi chuckled. "But I am not looking forward to breaking in a new boss lady."

They said more good-byes, but she hung on to the phone, not wanting to break the connection, adding, "I love you, Heidi." Better to say it now than leave it unsaid.

"You, too, girl." Heidi hung up.

People lined up to tour the Tower applauded her appearance, thinking she had to be part of the show. By now she felt like she was; a genuine bit of the history these tourists came to see. When the Tower turned its guns on the city for the first time—July 4, 1460—she had seen the sparks sail through the night, hitting the rooftops like great exploding comets. And if everything went as planned, she would be responsible for London retaking the Tower. Buying her ticket, she did a pirouette for the crowd, followed by the adventure of going through the Tower's airportlike security in a gold embroidered dress.

Untangling herself from the metal detectors, she passed through the squat Middle Tower, crossing the filled-in moat, entering the outer ward through the Bywater Tower. Here the inner curtain wall, studded with towers, curved away in two directions, ringing the inner ward and the White Tower. The tour route ran along the south wall, past the entrance to Traitor's Gate—the old water gate to the Tower— and then turned to enter the inner ward through the Bloody Tower's huge portcullis gate.

Stepping out of the shadow of the Bloody Tower, she saw the White Tower rearing up before her, ninety feet high, soaring over the trees along Tower Green, where Lady Jane Grey died. She went around to the entrance on the far side of the White Tower, which in olden times was really painted white, but was now a grim gray with white trim. Cemented with mortar tempered by the blood of beasts, the White Tower was the oldest royal residence in Europe, older than the Kremlin or the Vatican, older than the Louvre, and far older than Versailles. So far as princely prisons went, only the Castel Sant'Angelo in Rome was older. Modern flights of steps led up to the ancient entrance.

Here she stopped, staring about. If all went as planned, this was her last look at the third millennium. Tourists in sunglasses and polyester jackets, and white-haired Britons in wool and tweed listened intently to tall tales from Yeoman Warders in seventeenth-century costumes. Heads kept turning to gawk at her framed in the entrance to the White Tower. People smiled at her, as if they wanted her to tell her story, too. Sorry folks, you had your chance. A strange last sight, but it would have to do. At least she was in regal company. Anne Boleyn, Katherine Howard, and Lady Jane Grey were failed queens who got their last look at the world a few feet from where she stood, before kneeling for the headman's ax. Women far preferred inner ward executions, avoiding a public spectacle—letting them play their final scene for a select audience.

Unlike them, she had a choice. She could quit now, and walk away a winner. She was alive and healthy, and reasonably sane, and she had gone on a marvelous journey to another time. She could thank the fates for such a gift and then get on with the rest of her life. By far the most sensible thing to do.

Sort of. To stay meant living in a world that would never believe where she had gone and what she had done. Like many a Tower martyr, she could live a safe "normal" life only by denying what her heart knew to be true. That falsehood would hang over everything she did, forever after. She would not condemn herself to living a lie. If it was so damned essential she come back to this millennium someday, at least now she knew she could. She just had to make herself witch enough to do it.

So be it. Time to do the time warp—again. Pulling Edward's ring from the pocket of her gown, she lifted her gold hem and mounted the steps to the first-floor galleries with their magnificent collection of hunting bows and jousting armor. Again heads turned as she entered. She pictured headlines in British papers tomorrow—MYSTERY WOMAN DISAPPEARS IN WHITE TOWER, or SURPRISE APPEARANCE BY GHOST OF ANNE BOLEYN. It was comforting to know that whatever explanations were offered, no matter how wild or scientific, they would all be totally wrong. She would become one more mystery in the Tower, a little joke on the "real" world that refused to believe her. Unless, of course, nothing happened; then the joke would be on her.

Saying a short prayer, and willing herself back with every bit of her being, she slipped the ring onto her finger. Instantly the crowd filling the great armory vanished, along with the displays of armor, and the lights and air-conditioning. She found herself in a dank, dark hall, dimly lit by narrow firing slits. Dust motes danced in thin shafts of summer sunlight falling on the stone floor; from the low slant in the sunlight it looked to be late afternoon. Everything had that musty medieval stone church smell. Welcome back.

Swiftly she searched through her pocket, finding the silver spell box Duchess Wydville had given her. Kneeling on the stone floor she placed the box in front of her and got out the tiny silver key. Now was when she had to purge herself of any doubt—hard to do when Duchess Wydville was her sole guarantee the sleeping spell worked. How could she not doubt the good duchess? She had only one true hold on the witch-priestess, and that was Edward. Duchess Wydville feared him—and with good reason—Edward was forgiving in victory, but would be merciless toward treachery. Harm someone he cared for, and Duchess Wydville could not conjure up a more dangerous or implacable foe.

So she concentrated on Edward, willing the spell to work, reminding herself of the mystical bond between them. The bond that had brought her across time and space, from the third-millennium Cotswolds, to a sailing bark off the medieval Irish coast. Now the magic would bring them together for good. She said her prayers, kissed the silver key, and then inserted it in the lock. Picturing her reunion with Edward, she turned the tiny key. This was the act that would bring them back together.

With a click, the silver box sprang open. It was empty, but that did not matter, it was her determination that counted. Now everyone in the Tower but her was asleep. And she was fairly exhausted herself, having eaten two full meals after going several centuries without sleep.

Rising slowly, she left the box where it lay, lest she disturb the spell. All she need do now was go to the outer wall and call to the besiegers. Londoners would come swarming in, and the Tower was taken. The sole door to the White Tower was off a guard chamber, the same door through which she entered five hundred years hence. Reaching the guard chamber, she peered inside. Four men were there, all fast asleep, one slumped over a table, the others lying on mattresses spread along the far wall. The door to the Tower stood open, and she could see the sunlit Inner Ward, looking strangely empty. No tourists. No Yeoman Warders spinning yarns. No sign anyone was awake. So far, so good. Edging toward the open door, she took care not to wake the sleepers.

And ran right into two men coming up the stairs. She stared in horrified surprise at a bluff blond ruffian in a red brigandine studded with gold nailheads, wearing a visored sallet and Duke Holland's livery. Clean-shaved, and carrying a longbow, he looked as shocked to see her as she was to see him. With him was Le Boeuf, beef-blood beard and all. And neither of them was asleep, or looking the least bit drowsy.

⊰⊱ Dismal Eve ⊰⊱

W*hat are you doing here?"* Le Boeuf demanded, showing off his horrid gold-wire dental work.

She had no good answer. What was Le Boeuf doing here? Wide awake—looking ungodly ugly and suspicious—when he should be anesthetized. She put so much effort into the spell that she could hardly believe it failed. Had it all been just a ruse by the duchess— but to what end? Aside from merely doing her ill. She asked, "What day is it?"

"Saturday, my lady," replied the bowman in Lord Holland's livery. "Saturday, the twelfth of July, yesterday was Saint Benedict's Day, and tomorrow is the Dismal Day of July, which makes today Dismal's Eve." He would have gone on to name the hour, season, and year, happy to turn her question into a conversation.

Le Boeuf cut the bowman off. "She is not a lady—she is a witch. And a spy. Go tell FitzHolland we have her." Taken aback, the friendly bowman shut up, sorely disappointed to find the forward young woman in red and gold was not to be flirted with—clearly the Tower under siege suffered from a shortage of unattached young women. He disappeared up the spiral stairs in the corner of the guard chamber. She had not needed some smiling bowman to tell her tomorrow would be dismal—if she got to see it. Saturday the twelfth. That meant she had returned half a day after she left, landing in the one spot where she was sure of a hostile reception, well ahead of all possible help. Edward was in Northampton with the king, and Heaven alone knew how long it would take to get Henry to London. Collin was a bit closer at Grafton, and unencumbered by a king—but still at least a day away from London. And neither as yet knew of her plight, leaving her very much on her own for the foreseeable future.

FitzHolland came briskly down the steps, breaking into a gleeful grin. "Lady Stafford, how lovely—I cannot imagine anyone I would rather have here with us."

God, here was someone she never wanted to see again. His gleeful smile made her shiver, clearly she was the best thing that had happened to FitzHolland in weeks. The last fortnight had been a nightmare for these men trapped in the tower. First the rebels landing at Sandwich, then Kent rising up, and London throwing open her gates to the earls, letting them lay siege to the Tower. She could hear the boom of guns across the river, pounding on the south wall. And the news from Northampton would be equally bad. Having a new woman to torment must be their one big boost. FitzHolland beckoned cheerily, "Come, Lord Scales would see you right away."

How lucky to be popular. White-haired Lord Scales saw her in the White Tower's high-galleried great hall on the second floor, looking like an aristocratic vulture roosting in an abandoned royal hall. Kings of England had ruled from here—one had even been deposed here, putting Henry's grandfather on the throne. Lord Scales kept less formal state, just himself, an ensign, a couple of clerks, and a trio of genteel thugs wearing Duke Holland's livery. Bowmen guarded the door. Clearly she had brightened Scales's day, as well. "Truly wonderful to see you, Robyn Stafford. What on God's great earth brought you here of all places?"

What, indeed? And how come you are not comatose? If these men were not staring at her, she would have sat down and cried. How could this be happening? Minutes ago she was utterly safe, applauded by third-millennium tourists, listening to Yeoman Warders spin their lies. Now she was trapped in a hell of her own making, having trusted in her overblown powers and Duchess Wydville's sleeping spell. Half of King Henry's KGB was here, including Scales and Hungerford, the lords responsible for the rape of Newbury, along with Le Boeuf and FitzHolland, and some of the most hardened of Duke Holland's henchmen. What an absolute idiot—home free, and she threw it away. "Come," Scales insisted, "you must have a reason for being here?"

She had to say something. Luckily they could not know her role in

Henry's defeat. Summoning all the self-assurance she could muster, she smiled warmly at Lord Scales. "I have come to offer you all a royal pardon."

"Pardon?" Scales acted like he had never heard the word. "For what? From whom?"

"From King Henry." It was two days since the battle of Northampton, and word must have just reached London, amid a welter of rumor and hyperbole. She had to use that somehow. "A free and clear pardon for firing wildfire onto his royal capital and for conspiring with the traitors who held him captive."

"What traitors are these?" Scales sounded skeptical.

She rattled off the names of the most noble dead at Northampton. "Lord Egremont, Duke Buckingham, Viscount Beaumont, and John Talbot, earl of Shrewsbury. All of whom paid the ultimate price for preventing King Henry from seeing his loyal lords."

"His loyal lords?" Scales fixed her with a cold hard glare. "Who might they be?"

She looked surprised, as though the names were common knowledge, "Why the earls of Salisbury, Warwick, and March. Two days ago I was in King Henry's tent by Northampton, and witnessed the reunion between King Henry and his earls. His Majesty was so filled with joy he dispatched me immediately, to carry the marvelous news to London, and his loyal lords in the Tower." Robyn struggled mightily, putting her case in the best possible light, emphasizing she lay under the protection of King Henry and politely pointing out that noblemen far greater than Lord Scales had died opposing the new powers that be. At the same time, she gave them the welcome news that they need not face treason trials, and could retain their lands and titles—so long as they did her no harm.

Scales smirked. "If King Henry sent you to carry royal commands to me, His Highness is madder than I think." He was not taking the bait. Worse yet, his lordship's willingness to call King Henry mad to her face meant she would not be around to tell of it.

She reminded Scales, "King Henry will soon be in London, and you may hear it from His Majesty himself, until then I have the king's protection"—working *king* and *His Majesty* into the sentence as many times as she could, showing she had royal favor. Henry was proud of seeing her through the battle of Northampton, and considered her under his special care.

His lordship's smirk broadened into a smile. "Pray tell, how did you get into the Tower?"

Here he had her. Her heart fell, knowing she could not answer without admitting to witchcraft. She shrugged, saying, "This Tower is not so secure as you think."

"She is a witch"—FitzHolland spat it out—"who escaped from a locked cell in Berkeley Castle by sorcery."

She appealed to Scales, who was just a sadist in silks, not a sergeant-at-law out for revenge. "What does it matter how I got here, when I come offering peace and Good King Henry's mercy?"

Her struggles amused his lordship. "We are a fortress under siege," Scales pointed out, "it matters very much how you got here." For Scales this was a repeat performance—ten years ago he had been penned in this same fortress by John-Amend-All's rebels. Scales had saved himself by handing over Lord Saye and waiting out the storm. Now he had no king's treasurer to give up, nor was London going to take arms and drive the rebels out. And after Northampton, no king's army would march south to save him. Retribution hung heavy over both of them. "Is there some secret passage into the Tower?" Scales asked. "One even I do not know about?"

She said nothing, knowing any answer would only drag her in deeper.

"Are you a witch?" Scales asked softly. "Did you enter the Tower by magic?"

Again she said nothing. Despite Lord Scales's pleasant tone, this was the only question that mattered. She could not be drawn into admitting she was a witch. Jo long ago told her most witches were convicted by confession. Police methods here and now were way too rough and ready to really "prove" anything so complex as witchcraft. Without confessions, witch trials became a welter of hearsay, speculation, gossip, superstitious argument, and animal evidence. Fortunately confessions were not always easy to get, since under English law torture could only be applied with a royal warrant, signed by the king. And King Henry was not going to be signing any warrants against her. Not with Edward watching over his shoulder.

FitzHolland ticked off her supposed crimes, running from mundane to ridiculous. "On Saint Mark's Eve you escaped by magic from Berkeley Castle, aiding another witch in flight."

Actually she got out with a credit card—but the truth would do her little good, and lies would only make her look foolish, leaving her with nothing to say.

"On May Eve you danced with witches."

More silence. They must have gotten that from the women at Greystone. She pictured women leaping over the May Eve embers, hand in hand, shouting their wishes for the future. Hers, at least, came true.

"You enticed women and girls into games of cards where aces and jacks beat the king, subverting the natural order. Secretly inviting treason."

She pictured those same women forced to give absurd evidence before these men, hoping none held back or suffered for her sake. She was convicted ahead of time, making the actual charges inconsequential. This stuff was all trivial anyway, hardly scratching her accomplishments. Clearly they had not talked to the O'Neills. Nor was there mention of Jo and Joy or of Duchess Wydville, or her role in taking the king.

FitzHolland finished off with a sop to his half brother Admiral Holland. "And on the first of June you conjured up an ill wind to treasonously defeat Duke Holland at sea."

How could he leave out inadvertently seducing a nun? These men did not know even half her crimes, and just meant to burn her on general principles. She stubbornly held her tongue, reminding herself she had the right to remain silent. Keeping her treasonous contempt for them locked in her heart, along with her love for Edward, and her women's secrets. Without a warrant from Mad King Henry, they could not make her talk—not legally, at least. So far, she had heard nothing that had to come from Jo or Joy, though she knew they were in these men's hands more than a month. If they could keep silent, so could she.

"Have you naught to say to these grave charges?" Lord Scales plainly liked playing cat and mouse with her.

"I try to be a good and honest daughter of the Church," she told them. "King Henry himself can testify to my piety." She was, in fact, tons more religious than when she first arrived. And far more Christian than these fiends incarnate.

Scales eyed her shrewdly. "If you are so devoted to God's truth, tell us how you got into the Tower?"

"Before God and all the saints, I swear I know of no way into the

Tower that would allow your enemies in." By now she wished to Heaven she did.

"Not good enough." Scales enjoyed rejecting her pleas. "You must tell how you got in the Tower." Legal or not, she knew they would make her suffer for her silence—and if she told them what they wanted, she would suffer even more cruelly. Scales clearly delighted in her dilemma, and could not wait to have her convict herself out of her own mouth. She chose the lesser evil, saying nothing. So long as she kept silent, the law was with her, for however much that was worth.

Smiling broadly, Scales nodded to FitzHolland. "Take her below and show her the instrument." FitzHolland and two thugs in Duke Holland's livery led her back down the same spiral stairs she came up, the only way between floors in the old Norman keep. Descending past the first floor she felt the stones close in around her, shutting out air and daylight. Her skin crawled in horror at the cold, dank darkness ahead. Lamplight danced on flint, chalk, and Kentish rag, bound by mortar mixed with the blood of beasts. How many prisoners had gone down these steps before her? She thought of Glendower's little granddaughters—Bryn's cousins and Mortimer heirs—disappearing into the Tower.

Her steps faltered, and she stopped halfway down, unable to force herself farther, frightened by the clammy darkness. Pleading, she told FitzHolland, "You have no right to do this."

"Really?" FitzHolland planted a hand in her back and pushed. "We shall see."

She stumbled forward, only just keeping from falling. At the base of the stairs, vaulted cells supported the massive weight of the huge stone keep above. Big barrels of wine stood along one wall. Rolling the barrels aside, Holland's men uncovered a secret cell with a thick wooden door. FitzHolland produced a key, turned it in the lock, and pushed the door open.

Rats and roaches scurried for cover. In the center of the cell she saw a black wooden table with a windlass at one end—Duke Holland's Daughter. FitzHolland made a mock bow, inviting her to enter and inspect the torture rack. She entered the cell, deathly afraid they would hurt her, but knowing pleading was worse than useless. Showing fear would only convince FitzHolland that torture was the right choice, and pain could wring whatever he wanted out of her. She had to hoard her fear, saving it for a moment when it might do her some good.

FitzHolland patted the rack affectionately. "This gives voice to the dumb, cures deafness, and converts the most stubborn heretic." Lifting the straps and shackles used to bind the victim to the rack, he asked her, "What say you? Shall we see how it fits?"

She shoved her arms deep into her gold sleeves, holding herself together as best she could, refusing to look at the rack. "You dare not harm me," she told FitzHolland. "I have King Henry's protection—to lay hands on me is treason." Or so she hoped. Medieval England could never be accused of coddling criminals; hangings, floggings, and burnings were gala social events. She had seen brands on men's faces, and hands cut off—but secret torture was abhorred. Being borderline sadists did not make these folks stupid. There was a big difference between wanting to see criminals entertainingly punished and letting the government snatch people off the street to mistreat at its leisure. Resort to secret torture numbered among the many things that made King Henry's court so widely hated.

FitzHolland reached out, seizing her chin in his hand, twisting her head around hard, making sure it hurt, forcing her to stare at the rack. "Look at it, you ignorant witch! Do you really think I would not dare harm you?"

Tears blurred her sight, until she could barely see in the dim lamplight—still he kept her face twisted toward the rack. Holland's men laughed at her struggles, saying things like, "Stupid slut. Useless from the waist up. Cry all you like, but you are going to stretch."

Letting go, FitzHolland turned and left. Holland's laughing thugs left with him, taking the light, leaving her in darkness with the rats and the rack for company. Soon as the door closed and the lock clicked, she heard the scrape of claws on stone. Desperate to get her feet off the floor, she reached out blindly and found the rack. Pushing the shackles aside, she scrambled up atop Duke Holland's dreaded Daughter—the only bit of furniture in the pitch-black cell. She could hear them rolling the wine barrels back up against door. FitzHolland had learned that locked doors alone would not hold her.

Sitting hunched atop the horrible machine, she put her head down and sobbed. With her tormentors gone, she did not have to be brave. What a hellish mistake this was—she should never have left the third millennium. She had been shopping in London, gorging herself on melon slices and fried milk balls, getting rides whenever she stuck out her thumb. That should have told her something. Now she was sitting atop a torture instrument in a rat-infested cell, waiting to entertain a pack of murderous sadists. What a dimwitted imbecile. Even Duchess Wydville warned her not to come back. What good did it do Jo and Joy to have her trapped in the Tower, as well? She was sure by now the duchess betrayed her. Setting aside all her doubts, she had prayed with an open heart for the sleeping spell to work, she had wanted more than anything to have everyone safe and to be with Edward. She had thrown herself open, trusting in the universe—but it was just an empty silver box. Duchess Wydville's warning had been a final conscience-saving gesture. Assuming Her Grace had a conscience. What a cold, brisk, arrogant bitch.

Stupid, stupid, stupid—how could she have trusted the duchess at all? Now she would die for her stupidity, deserving whatever they did to her. Robyn Stafford chump of the century. Maybe the millennium. No surprise that she did not make the history books. She should have known from the first FitzHolland would win. The FitzHollands and Duchess Wydvilles of the world always won. Because they cared nothing for others and killed without regret, even with pleasure. Faced with people like them, ordinary people had no hope, going about, working hard, helping out others, becoming willing victims. Even sending themselves to the Tower. She had come to them in peace and forgiveness, and these men's immediate impulse was to have her hurt and killed. Londoners said it was ten years ago today that John-Amend-All died in a sheriff's custody. Happy anniversary.

Wiping her eyes, she looked about, seeing nothing but absolute blackness. She was in a windowless stone room, buried beneath a fortress with walls fifteen feet thick—ringed by two more walls and a moat. Secure and then some. Holland's men had taken her bag containing everything that might make conditions bearable, like her flashlight and bug spray. Or those bottles of water. She had nothing but herself and her clothes. Her cell door did not even have one of those little barred windows to let in light and air—she was in a real-life dungeon cell, without the normal Hollywood amenities. Not even a proper cell, really, just a stone box to hold her until they had time to torture her. Alone and in the dark, utterly exhausted—having by her own figuring gone centuries without so much as a nap—she curled up atop the rack, where the rats could not get at her, crying herself to sleep.

For the first time since being sick in Calais, she awoke not knowing where she was, or even what century she was in. All she knew was that she was cold and lying in dark, on something hard and uncomfortable. Stiff and aching, she rolled over. And nearly tumbled off the rack onto the rat-infested floor.

She saved herself by seizing one of the shackles, bringing her instantly back to what passed for reality. Sinking back down onto the rack, she looked at her watch. She had not reset it since returning to the past, and could not make much sense out of the glowing digits. Did being in the Dark Ages mean you gained or lost an hour? Half-awake and thoroughly confused, she was suffering from serious time lag—though the tiny light was comforting.

Lying in the dark, trying to decipher the digits on her wrist, she heard a scrape and muffled rumble. Someone was rolling the wine barrels aside. That must have been what woke her. Horrified, she listened intently, hearing bootsteps, then voices, then a key turning in the lock. How could this be happening so soon? They were coming in—and it was too much to hope they were bringing dinner. She had no time to prepare herself. Mary help me, do not let this happen. Stripping off her watch, she felt around, hanging it on a nail under the rack. Then she sat up to face them—saying a hurried prayer to the Holy Virgin who saved women even from the stake—glad for what little sleep she had gotten.

Lamplight stabbed at her eyes. Black shapes filled the doorway; then the lamp entered the cell, casting huge dark shadows against flint and chalk walls. Lord Scales's gold gown and flowing sleeves shone brilliantly beneath a halo of white hair. FitzHolland was with him; so were a couple of Holland's men. And worst of all, Le Boeuf; they would not be bringing him unless they meant to hurt her badly. Tears stung her eyes. Seeing her sitting up on the rack, FitzHolland laughed, "Here is a witch who cannot wait to get started."

Since they had driven off the four-legged rats, she swung her legs down onto the floor and stood up, looking as composed as she could with tears in her eyes. Just because they had her alone in a dark dungeon did not mean the fight was over—in fact, for her it had just begun. Rebellions are fought in prison cells and at the execution block as often as in the open field. Ahead of her lay a battle of wills more desperate than anything that happened in King Henry's tent by Northampton. She was gravely outnumbered, and they wanted what she had in her head. Scales meant to have the truth out of her at any cost. So she would have to give him some of it, but not all of the truth, and not right away. And she had to mix in plausible lies.

"Now is the time to talk," Scales told her, primly adjusting his snow-white cloak. "You must tell us how you got into the Tower."

Telling them would brand her as a witch, but she could not think of a decent lie. She could only repeat her plea for peace, sounding awfully hollow in such a hellish place—even to her. "King Henry has promised you all full pardons if you freely open the Tower. Fighting can cease immediately, with no need for any more harm." Resistance was ridiculous, the rebels had King Henry, and London, and all the surrounding counties, even command of the sea—everything except the Tower.

"Hold her," Scales ordered, signaling to the pair in Duke Holland's livery. Hard male hands seized her, pinning her arms, hurting her wrists. How horribly unfair, to be faced with five armed men, any one of them stronger than she—all intent on seeing her suffer. She withdrew into herself, trying not to feel their hands on her. Le Boeuf stepped up, his gold-wired grin gleaming hideously in the lamplight. He started undoing the buttons on her sleeveless jacket.

She instinctively shrank from his touch, but FitzHolland stood behind her, holding her shoulders, keeping her from backing away. He whispered in her ear, "That day of punishment I promised is finally here—first this, then the fire."

He was enjoying himself. And she could see Scales savoring the cruelty of what they were doing. Rebels might have London and the surrounding counties, but Scales and FitzHolland had her, and they meant to indulge themselves. FitzHolland hated her. And Scales wanted to hurt her. Leaving not a lot to choose between the two of them. Pleas for peace and decency made no impression; far above such petty concerns, both Scales and FitzHolland were from noble families, confident of royal clemency—no matter who won. Or what they did to her. Somehow she had to shake that confidence. Remembering Collin's oath to bring down the duke of Buckingham—which hardly seemed possible when he made it, on the run in Wales—she looked straight at Scales, telling his lordship, "You will not get away with this. Harm me, and I swear before Mary who is Mother to all, you shall suffer grievously."

Le Boeuf laughed and slipped the jacket off over her arms; then he began unlacing her gold gown, fingering her breasts through the fabric, happy he was finally going to get to abuse her, something he must have wanted to do since the first moment they met in Widow Weirdville's cottage. Scales graced her with a sanctimonious grin, saying softly, reasonably, "Come now, we do not mean to harm you. Yet you must give us the truth."

Alas, the truth was that she was a witch. And she doubted her ability to straight out lie like a lord, especially under torture. Lord Scales vastly enjoyed her dilemma, knowing she could only avoid pain by admitting to crimes with even more horrible punishments. This was the moment Scales had longed for since her first day in the Middle Ages. That hanging and quartering on the way to Berkeley Castle—delightful in its own way—had been merely the beginning of their relationship. Now he would get to hear her condemn herself to death. Stripped to her linen shift, Holland's men hoisted her onto the rack. Scales himself strapped her ankles to the windlass cords, seeing that the straps fit snugly. Straightening up, Scales left her arms free for the moment. "This is your final chance. Tell me how you got into the Tower."

Sitting shivering atop the rack in her thin shift, she shook her head. "What matters how I got here? I have hurt no one, and have meant you no harm."

"That is not enough," Scales warned. "You know what will happen if you refuse to answer."

Weakly she nodded her head, looking up at men's faces, thrown into hard, cruel relief by the lamplight, all staring at her, and all happy: Scales smug and smiling, FitzHolland gleeful, Le Boeuf excited, Holland's men eager to see her stretched out on the rack. From the very first she let these men know she did not respect them, and in fact considered herself far above them, flouting authority, speaking her mind, and telling extravagant lies. Fear and hurt were the only holds they had on her, and they meant to make the most of it. "How did you get into the Tower?" Lord Scales demanded. "This is the last I shall ask."

"By magic," she admitted, looking straight at Lord Scales, telling them what they most wanted to hear.

"So you confess to being a witch?" FitzHolland smiled triumphantly, eyes alight, already picturing her burning.

Again she nodded. "Yes, I am a witch." For better or worse, she had put herself in Hecate's hands. Strange indeed, since before coming to the Middle Ages she had never been a very spiritual person. She had not found religion until she was persecuted for it. Now she believed with all her body and soul, so much that she would tell even her worst enemy—particularly if the alternative was torture.

"Told you she would talk," Le Boeuf crowed in triumph. "Witches always do."

"Why did you come here to the Tower?" Scales seemed genuinely puzzled—what reason could she possibly have for putting herself in his power?

"I told you why," she answered softly, conserving her strength. Here comes the hard part. "To put an end to the fighting," she told them. "To have peace. And to offer you all a royal pardon." That was true, but she could not let them know her most important purpose; any mention of freeing Jo and Joy would merely drag the two of them into the questioning. Bad as this was, that would make it infinitely worse—if they hurt Joy in front of her, she would go to pieces.

Men in fancy livery looked down at her in amazement. Scales shook his head, saying, "Surely you did not think you could just talk us into laying down our swords and throwing open the Tower?"

"That had been my hope." One of her hopes. No point in mentioning the sleeping spell, which had not worked anyway. She never meant to harm them, just to end the fighting by putting them to sleep—"innocent sleep, that knits up the ravell'd sleeve of care . . ." When they awoke, Henry would have happily pardoned them.

Scales seemed genuinely astonished. "Who aided you in this mad godless endeavor?"

Now came the worst part. She knew they would want her to name others, and there were people she desperately needed to protect—Jo and Joy in particular, since they were already in these men's power. If she gave up names too easily, they would just demand more. She had given herself up already—since they would have forced that confession out of her anyway—saving her strength for this. She pleaded, "Please do not make me tell, for I do sorely fear her."

"Fear who?" Scales demanded.

"I dare not say." She shook with very real fear, knowing what had to happen next. Now she had to let them hurt her, or they would not believe her answers.

"You will when you fear us more than her." Scales nodded to Le Boeuf. "Rack her."

Gleefully, Le Boeuf grabbed her hands, jerking her back down onto the rack, shackling her wrists above her head. Unable to move, she stared at shadows in the cell's chalk ceiling, saying a silent prayer to Hecate who stood by women in their hour of greatest need, in death and in childbirth. And to Mary, Mother of Mercy. She must make Scales really want this answer, since it was the only one she had to freely give.

Le Boeuf slowly turned the windlass, pulling her limbs straight. She willed herself to go limp, letting the ropes take hold of her body, stretching her out. If ever there was a moment to be out-of-body, this was it. But she could not just drift off into bliss and let them rip her body apart in frustration. She was not ready to be all spirit, not if she could help it. She had to let them hurt her. That is what they had come to do, what they had eagerly anticipated. Up to now, she had bested them. Twice she humiliated FitzHolland and Le Boeuf, and she had escaped from Scales on Saint Mark's Eve. Now finally they had her. If she did not give them this excuse to hurt her, they would surely find another one.

Strain on her limbs turned to excruciating pain. She screamed for them to stop, but Le Boeuf tightened the windlass even more. She screamed again, even louder. Forced to let go, she rose above the pain, her spirit hovering just out-of-body until Le Boeuf relaxed the ropes. As she settled back down into her aching body, Lord Scales and his ghoulish companions grinned down at her; that would teach her not to think herself better than they. "Enough, enough," she whispered, "I will tell."

Relaxing the windlass, they waited expectantly, eager to hear the name. Robyn rolled her head to the side, again looking straight at Lord Scales, willing him to believe. "I was aided by Her Grace Jacquetta Wydville, duchess of Bedford. Her Grace cast the spell that let me enter the Tower unseen."

It spoke volumes for Duchess Wydville's reputation that none of these men leaped to her defense. Holland's men exchanged significant glances, having something to tell their duke. FitzHolland seemed smugly satisfied, as if he must have long suspected the duchess, who had a dubious past and was his half brother's rival. Le Boeuf stood waiting, eager to work the windlass. Scales merely asked, "Who else?"

Sighing, she lay her head back against the rack. There was one other name that went with the duchess. "Her eldest daughter, Elizabeth Grey of Groby."

Again no one seemed surprised, though beautiful blond Elizabeth was daughter-in-law to Lord Ferrers and lady-in-waiting to Queen Margaret. Since King Henry had been betrayed by Lord Grey de Ruthyn, they were willing to believe the worst of Ruthyn's female relations. One of Holland's men snickered, "All the best bitches are witches."

Scales nodded sagely, then asked, "And who else?"

Closing her eyes, she shook her head. "No one." Scales had no way to know Bryn and Deirdre existed, so there was no need to enlighten him. She imagined herself trying to explain Nest to them, the silent six-foot Welsh armed nurse, who spoke in tongues on Witches Nights. There were some truths even Scales was not ready for.

Lord Scales considered her answer, then asked, "What about the witch Joanna Grey?"

Feigning surprise, she opened her eyes wide, shaking her head. "No, she did nothing. Joanna and her daughter were taken more than a month ago by these men." She nodded at Le Boeuf and FitzHolland. "I have not seen her since—they would know better than I what Joanna has been doing."

Scales stared hard at her. "What if I told you Joanna Grey was here in the Tower?"

She let her head drop back. "Since your lordship says so, I will believe it. But the only people I knew to be in the Tower were your lordship, and the lords Hungerford, de Vesci, Lovell, de la Warre, and the earl of Kendal, and the duchess of Exeter. And I made this magic on Witches Night at Grafton with Duchess Wydville and her daughter Elizabeth—nothing you do to me now will put Joanna Grey there."

And they believed her. She could see Scales relax, his attention starting to wander. Holland's men whispered between themselves. She had alerted them to a magical conspiracy at the very heart of their cause.

With King Henry in rebel hands, they would have to fall back on the queen—and now they knew she confided in witches. Jo and Joy were out of it, at the cost of giving them the names of Duchess Wydville and fair Elizabeth. And of course, her own, as well—but that hardly counted, since they thought her guilty from the start. Best of all, she did it without them actually tearing her limb from limb.

FitzHolland spoke up. "You were seen often in the company of Edward, earl of March. Have you been aiding him by witchcraft? Did you give him a favorable wind on the first of June? Did you plot with him to take this Tower?"

"No, of course not." She shook her head wearily. This was the other name she had dreaded hearing. "Lord Edward does not know I am a witch, or he would not hold me so close."

"She is lying," FitzHolland declared, looking toward Le Beouf, who gladly seized the windlass handle, anticipating the order to hurt her.

She tried to prepare herself, eyes closed, letting go of her body, thinking of Edward. He would not care if she named him. To spare her even a moment's pain, Edward would happily hop up and take her place on the rack. Yet she hated these men, more than she ever hated anyone. They were murderers many times over, and abusers of women—who thanks to a quirk of fate and a mad king were running the country when she arrived. She was happy to have helped bring them down, even if it cost her life. They meant to kill her—no matter how she answered—so how could she accuse someone she loved, just to satisfy them? Even when that someone was big and strapping, and well able to take care of himself. She felt the ropes tighten.

"Stop," Scales ordered. She opened her eyes in surprise. Ropes relaxed, but when she fully reentered her limbs, they felt like they were on fire.

FitzHolland turned to Scales, unable to believe what he heard. "But she lies. You can see it. She hides things harmful to Edward of March. There is a vast conspiracy of witches against the king."

Scales arched a bushy white eyebrow. "And do you think the earl of March may lead this conspiracy?"

"He may," FitzHolland insisted stubbornly. Scales was just a sadist, but FitzHolland had the family male insanity.

Scales smiled. "If young Edward of March is the anti-Christ, I am afraid he has already won. Set the witch free for now."

Great, though she hated being called "the witch." It was never very healthy to be referred to in third person—as in "the witch." Or "the prisoner." Or "the victim."

FitzHolland tore her straps off in sulky vengeful fashion, being none too gentle on her wrists and ankles, hissing, "Never fear, witch, we have not finished with you."

Nor I, you, she thought, struggling to sit up, barely able to use her limbs. At Sudeley Castle she had winced to see FitzHolland lying hurt upon the tilt ground—glad he was not killed—he would never get that from her again. Next time, she wanted him dead. Sitting atop the rack, she rubbed her wrists and ankles, trying to bring life to tortured limbs and cold fingers. Seeing her shiver, Lord Scales loosed the snow white cloak from his gold embroidered shoulder, draping it over her, showing he, too, had not finished with her. As Scales pulled the cloak snug about her shoulders, they stared at each other in the lamplight, an odd intimate moment between torturer and victim. Scales smiled a kindly, older man type smile, saying, "You did well. I have seen grown men fall to groveling at the sight of the rack—for all the good that did them."

Fond reminiscence from Lord Scales, who was so happy he had to prolong the moment with chitchat. Complimenting her performance. His lordship just could not get enough of her. Hecate help me, she thought, I'm going to be his favorite victim. Lord Scales's attempts at being comforting came off like a scary old uncle you were not supposed to get too close to. Still it said something for the Middle Ages that even sadists had to keep up appearances. After all, he had tortured her for the best of reasons—to preserve the crown and serve religion—that Scales thoroughly enjoyed it was a mere fringe benefit.

She sat on the rack, wrapped in his cloak, nursing her hurt limbs, breathing methodically, while Holland's men wrote out a confession for her to sign. As they did, she noted a familiar odor in the cell, faint but unmistakable, the dank metallic smell of male sex. Someone had really liked the show. She herself had not found it in the least arousing. Despite all the whips-and-chains "erotica" on video, real dungeons were a ghastly turn-off. At least for her. But the guys she was with sure had a time of it, chatting happily as they wrote out her confession, expressing pious hopes for her future salvation. As if she had a future—the confession they wrote implicated her, Duchess Wydville, and Elizabeth Grey of Groby in enough crimes to hang half of London. When the time came for her to sign, her fingers were so weak Scales had to help her hold the quill.

Soon as she signed the confession they left, taking her gown, boots, and jacket, leaving her in blackness with just the linen shift and Lord Scales's cloak—not bothering to roll the barrels back against the door when they left. After what they had done to her they no longer seemed to fear her magic. Weird in a way, since until now they had not known for "sure" she was a witch. But seeing they could hurt her, and make her cry and beg, reassured them immensely. Male egos can be remarkably easy to please.

Happy to be alone, she did her best to relax. Unbelievable as it sounds, things could have been horribly worse. She wiped away tears with the cold, numb back of her hand. She had come through her first torture session with all her toes and fingers intact, and without implicating anyone she cared about. Closing her eyes, she lay back on the rack, proud of her acting—before a damned hard house. About the worst audience she ever faced. She would have taken a bow, but she could barely sit up. Standing was not an option. Her biggest fear was that she had been too good, and Scales might want an immediate encore. On that happy thought, she said her good nights—thanking Hecate and the Virgin, and wishing a pleasant sleep to Edward, and to Jo and Joy whose cell must be somewhere close by. Then she curled up in his lordship's cloak and returned to sleep, the Bard's blessed balm for damaged minds and hurt bodies.

⟶ Traitor's Gate ⟵

*S*he *awoke cold and hungry,* and crawling with fleas, wishing to Heaven she had her can of bug spray. Hours dragged by in total darkness. Sitting in a pitch-black Tower vault turned out to be so utterly boring, she actually began hoping someone would come for her. Not for another torture session, mind you. She did not want to repeat her starring role as an S&M heroine anytime soon, but some mild interrogation might be nice—Scales or FitzHolland could at least take the time to sneer and gloat over her, adding a little insult to injury—giving her someone to talk to. It was not like her captors had a lot to do, being prisoners of the Tower themselves.

Finally, she heard boot steps, then a key in the lock, and the door opened. Blinded by lamplight, she instinctively pulled the cloak tight about her, drawing her hands and feet inside. It turned out to be merely one of Duke Holland's men, bringing the prisoner wine and bread for supper, or mayhap breakfast. Two trips through time, then Hecate knows how long in a basement cell had totally thrown off her time sense. She asked Duke Holland's man, "What day is this?"

He looked curiously at her, saying, "Today is the Lord's Day—the thirteenth and the Dismal Day in July." Soon as he said it, she saw he was the same man she asked for the date when she arrived back in the past—the talkative fellow who had been with Le Beouf, and went to fetch FitzHolland—but not one of the ones who helped strip her for the rack.

"Thank you again." She smiled wanly, squinting at the light. "Being down here is very confusing. Could you tell me the hour, as well?"

"Morning," he told her. "Not much after dawn."

So her wine and bread was breakfast. Sunday morning meant she had slept half a day, from late afternoon until early morning—with one ghastly nightmare in the middle. Her torture session must have taken place late Saturday night, done on Dismal Eve in order not to abuse helpless women on the Lord's day. It might have been noon for all she knew at the time. Duke Holland's man continued to stare at her, saying nothing. Pretty, bedraggled prisoners must be an intriguing novelty, especially in a fortress under siege, cut off from sweethearts, wives, or favorite whores just over the wall in London. Figuring if he wanted to look he ought to pay for it, she said softly, "It would mean a lot if you could bring me some well-boiled water."

Surprised at the request, he nodded, but made no move to leave.

"And maybe a blanket," she added, not sure how long she would have Lord Scales's coat. Nodding again, he turned to go.

"And a chamber pot," she called after him. Her first sip of wine had gone straight to her bladder. Her guard got away before she could come up with further requests. At the moment her needs were enormous, if this makeshift cell was to be made livable. Fumbling in the darkness under the rack, she found her watch and reset it for SUN 7-13-60, making a best guess at the time.

Holland's man returned with a big steaming kettle of water, two blankets, a bucket to use as a chamber pot, and a big piece of hard cheese. Blinking at this huge bounty, she thanked the man profusely, then knelt down, using the light and hot water to wash her hands and face. Then she poured some of the steaming water into the wine, warming and diluting it. Holland's man watched in puzzled wonder and then asked, "Are you really a witch?"

She nodded. "But not an evil one. My name is Robyn Stafford."

"I know." He nodded. "You are the earl of March's whore. I am Matt Davye." He did not mind giving his name to a witch, especially one he thought had loose ways, which showed how hard the witch hunter's task was, when even his own men could not be trusted to be merciless on women they liked.

"Thank you, Matt Davye." She smiled up at him, her clean face no longer tearstained. "If ever I can do you a favor, I will. And when this siege is over, I will testify you did me no harm." It did not hurt to remind Matt Davye that he was surrounded by a vengeful city, and any man wearing Duke Holland's livery might need friends to speak for him. Matt Davye merely said good-bye and left, taking the light with him. Which was okay, because she desperately had to use the bucket—too bad it had to be in the dark.

Then she sat wrapped in her new blankets, sipping hot weak wine and nibbling cheese, thinking about Matt Davye. How far would he go to help a witch in distress? She had asked for a blanket, and he had brought two. And she had not even asked for the cheese. Could it mean he was kindhearted? Or guilt stricken? Or in love? Hard to say. Any man who did unasked favors for a witch and whore must have pretty mixed motives. Trying to read something special into a spare blanket and a bit of cheese, showed how far her expectations in men had fallen.

That was the absolute tip-top of her day. She thought they might take her out for Sunday services, but confessing to witchcraft apparently ended any chance of salvation. Sunday in the Tower turned out to be a long wait in the dark—living up to the thirteenth of July's reputation as a Dismal Day. She thought about all the illustrious prisoners who had been lodged in the White Tower—King Richard II of England, King John of France, David King of Scots—knowing her own stay would not likely be so memorable. Not letting her out even for Sunday Mass seemed particularly ominous. At Mass she would have been seen by the priest and any congregation. As it was, aside from Matt Davye, the only ones who knew she was in the Tower were the men who tortured her—those with the least to gain by letting her live.

But there was always the bright side; she had not been raped—another twist in the medieval mentality. She had been horribly mistreated for what any sane person would consider trivial offenses, but thanks to their weird sense of chivalry, she was fairly safe from being molested. She had not even been strip-searched for witches' marks. Any bold knight with a string of bastards to his name might frequent whores or force not-so-willing peasant girls, but would never lay hands on a "captive"—that would be breaking the knightly rules. Lord Scales happily anticipated seeing her bound to a stake and set on fire, yet would be incensed if some man-at-arms sneaked in ahead of time and lifted her shift. It would be an affront to the sense of moral superiority that justified mistreating her. Just as King Henry triumphantly delivered her untouched to a nunnery, Lord Scales aimed to bring her unmolested to the stake, wringing whatever good times he could from tormenting her along the way.

Hopefully she would not be making that trip anytime soon. Buried in her confession was an insurance policy of sorts, one she had taken pains to put there in believable fashion. She was their only living witness against Duchess Wydville—a woman the Hollands hated—that alone would tempt them to keep her around, aside from any amusement she offered Lord Scales.

On Monday, Matt Davye returned with more wine and bread—but no cheese. He offered to empty her bucket, and she thanked him repeatedly, both when he took it, and when he brought it back. She felt like a bit of an idiot, trying to seem warmly intriguing to someone emptying her toilet bucket. But when he came back with the clean bucket, he had another hunk of cheese. And he left the candle, proving Matt Davye did care.

She could hardly wait for tomorrow. Especially with nothing else to do that day but watch the candle burn down and listen to rats scurry about. To pass the time, she tried to remember poems from Jo's book of Christine de Pizan—that great defender of women and lover of men—the book FitzHolland burned with her white rose inside. She found her medieval French coming back to her:

Whenever I see these lovers
casting tender looks
and trading tender glances,
laughing with joy, and drifting off
to play their own special games,
It would melt my heart!

For because of them I remember
the one from whom I am parted,
and for whom my heart hungers
to bring him back to me.
But my sweet love, my kind friend,
is somewhere far away.
For him I mourn so deeply,
It would melt my heart!

Christine de Pizan certainly knew her stuff, and could be very clear-eyed about relationships, particularly for a poetess—loving men even when she hated what they often did to women. Christine did not expect women and men to be saints, but hoped they could be partners, even condoning flat-out adultery, so long as it was done with love:

God! Everyone complains too bitterly
about these slanderous husbands,
so jealous, snarling, and wrathful.
But not me, I never complain,
having a husband to my liking—
good and fine, and never against me.
Wanting nothing but enjoyment,
He scolds me when I sigh.
And is pleased to have my lover amuse me
when I choose someone besides him!
Nothing I do is doleful,
And everything I do pleases him . . .

An interesting comment on the state of medieval marriage—but not much help in her current predicament.

Tomorrow came and went, without anyone coming to feed her. Once, in the morning, she heard men outside, but all they did was roll the barrels back in front of the door, making her nervous and hungry. Her most private horror was that the door might never open again, leaving her to die of thirst alone in the dark. Which made burning seem humane.

Wednesday—according to her watch—and still no one came, worrying her even more. She feared they had just decided to leave her to die, like Lady de Braose, or Glendower's granddaughters—a convenient way of putting to death women and little girls, who would evoke sympathy on the scaffold. She snacked on some two-day-old bread she had been saving. Cheese was a mere memory. On Thursday morning she finished her last bit of bread, spending the rest of the day in black, hungry monotony—giving her plenty of time to think, and to get adept at killing fleas in the dark.

Robyn had long given up cursing herself for coming back. What was the point? She had been given the chance to turn her back on Edward and this whole mad, magical adventure—sent back by Duchess Wydville, just as she had wanted. And with a warning, "Do not come back." But she had come back, because she had unfinished business, and because she refused to live in psychic exile, with an unbelievable adventure locked in her head. She chose to see that adventure to its end, and if it ended with her starving to death in the Tower basement, so be it. But she would not give up. She would go down fighting, meeting fate on her own terms, not running from it. Tomorrow was Witches Night, somehow, she would use that to get away. Or at least get word to Edward.

No one came on Friday, either. Small surprise. She had gone beyond hunger, to giddy fatigue, the medieval diet with a vengeance. She could feel herself getting thinner. So she spent another day in the dark, lying on the rack, conserving her strength, sipping the last of her boiled water, reciting her prayers, and checking her watch. She saved one swallow of wine for Witches Night. Only one Christine de Pizan poem matched her mood; the one that went:

> **Alone am I, locked fast in my chamber;**
> **alone am I, without my love.**

When her watch chimed the witching hour, she knelt on the rack, with no candle, and the rats for an audience, saying her prayers, solemnly drinking her swallow of wine. With so little body left, she had no problem leaving it, floating off into darkness. And bumping into the cell walls. She could float about in blackness fine enough, but could not seem to get out. It was like her attempts at Witches Flight on the way to London; the same heavy dank walls stopped her, only this time she was beating on them from the inside. And there was no Hela here. No magical magpie to show here the way out. She prayed for someone, anyone, to guide her.

Faintly she heard her name being sung through the stone, as though from far away. Encouraged she redoubled her prayers, hoping some-one had heard her. As she prayed the singing got louder, coming closer, close enough that she could make out words:

> **When Robin came to Nottingham,**
> **Serenity withouten lain,**
> **He prayed to God and Lady Mary**
> **To bring him out safe again.**

Dressed all in scarlet and singing happily, John-Amend-All strode straight out of the wall, perfectly visible even in blackness. He made a sweeping bow, saying, "My Lady Stafford."

She smiled and nodded, saying, "We must stop meeting like this." It seemed they only met when things were most desperate, at that ambush in Wales, escaping Berkeley castle, and penned aboard the *Fortuna*.

Straightening up, the scarlet archer sighed, "I fear this will be the last time we meet. For I have come to say good-bye."

"Good-bye? Things cannot be that bad." Or so she hoped.

"They are for me," he replied. "I am ten years dead, almost to the day. So now I must be off to meet my Maker—and not beforetime, if you ask me. My business here is done; the Wheel of Fortune has come full circle. Ten years ago we were beaten, betrayed, and mas-sacred, but now our cause has triumphed. Edward of March is vic-torious, and has returned the king to London, and to his people—no small thanks to you."

"He is? Here in London?" Her heart lifted, hearing help lay just beyond the Tower wall. "Can you take me to him?"

John-Amend-All looked surprised. "Take you to whom?"

"To Edward." She would rather go in body, but she would settle for going in spirit.

"Shoo?" He shook his head. "Through these walls? Fifteen foot thick and mortared with beast's blood?"

"That is what I was hoping." Praying for, actually.

"M'lady, this is no leaky ship in the Irish Sea. This is many feet of flint, rag, and solid chalk, half-sunk beneath Tower Hill. And there is a spell on these walls, to stop any living soul from passing. Luckily, I myself am dead."

She sighed. "Then what have you come here for?" Aside from raising false hopes in her.

John-Amend-All smiled. "Why, to say good-bye. We have been through a lot together, have we not? And I have grown much fond of you. You have that quality—you know, people *like* you, often at first sight. I did. Edward, too. And women, as well—look at Jo and Deirdre. Children, too. You must have noticed."

"Yes," she admitted. "My latest conquest is Lord Scales." Currently loving her to death.

"There, see, I told you. 'Tis a rare and wonderful gift, and ought not be wasted—comes from you being so caring and open yourself." John-Amend-All glanced about, as though he could see through the blackness. "Sorry for all this, though. Looks fairly horrible. They tried to drag me back here, but luckily I died of wounds on the way, thank Jesus for that."

She could see he was getting set to go. There was one hope left. "Will you take a message for me? Will you tell Edward where I am?"

John-Amend-All nodded absently. "If I can, lass, but as I told you, my time here is near up. So I will not make any promises, except to say good-bye, and good luck, and never despair." Turning about, the scarlet archer sauntered into the blackness, singing as he went:

> **Little John called up the jailor,**
> **And bade him rise anon;**
> **He said Robin Hood had broken prison,**
> **And out of hit was gone . . .**

So much for Witches Night. John-Amend-All had been freed, but not she—she was still among the living, and only death could set her free. She settled back into her thin, famished body, overcome with despair. Not even magic could save her. She had lived the last two days for Witches Night. Now what? What was she going to live for tomorrow?

If there was a tomorrow. Clearly this was why she was not even a footnote in the history books—because she died alone and friendless in the Tower. Never marrying the earl of March, never living long enough to be noticed by the chroniclers. Weak with hunger and heartache, she closed her eyes to the blackness, slipping into a hopeless stupor.

At the crack of dawn, the lock on her cell door turned for the first time in days; then the door swung open. Light flooded the cell, bringing her blinking out of her coma. After days in the dark, it took forever for her eyes to adjust. "Ho," a cheerful male voice called out, "this hole stinks to high heaven."

She heard FitzHolland's laugh, "Lady Stafford, you are looking lovely as ever."

God, what a grotesque dream. Shading her eyes and squinting, she made out Lord Scales standing right in front of her, holding an overripe strawberry under her nose. "We thought you might be hungry."

For once she did not care where the food had come from, or how poorly it was washed. She ate it right out of Scales's hand, and the strawberry seemed to explode on her tongue, sweet and wet, thrilling her down to her toes. She genuinely thanked him.

"Here, have another." Scales held out an even bigger one. She took that one, too, thanking him again, knowing she was in the hands of one really sick fuck. Scales had kept her in the dark for days, sans food and water in a foul cell, terrified she was being slowly put to death. Afraid she would never see light or air again, shattering her faith in life, and fate, and in herself and in her spellcraft—making her even doubt Heaven's mercy. Just so he could surprise her by handfeeding her strawberries in the morning. Some sick stupid joke. Shaking with hunger, she ate every strawberry he gave her, feeling more than ever like she was torturer's pet. Lord Scales laughed at her eagerness, saying, "Come, save some for your friends. I have brought a pair of acquaintances to break their fast with you. It cannot be much fun penned here day and night, all on your own."

He stepped aside to reveal Jo and Joy standing behind him, thin but alive. Elated to see them, she did her best to hide it, settling for a surprised smile. Scales was smart enough to read a poker face, but if she showed too much glee, they would use it against her—hurting them to get at her. She acted happy to see her friends alive, no more, no less. Jo greeted her graciously, "My Lady Robyn, how lovely to see you again. It must be months since we last met."

"Centuries, it seems." For them it had been two months, almost exactly. Two months ago today she had been setting out with Collin, headed for the Welsh Marches, wondering how she would survive in the Middle Ages without Greystone. Now she knew.

Happily playing lord bountiful, Scales gave out bread, cheese, wine, fresh pippins, and more ripe strawberries. Also some small tart oranges, the first she had seen here and now. Taking his cloak, which she was using for a comforter, he departed, chatting pleasantly with FitzHolland. Scales was having the time of his life, alternately loosening and tightening the noose. Fascinating as this cat-and-mouse stuff was to Scales, it merely pissed her off. She supposed it was meant to reduce her to a clinging, pleading wretch, killing her spirit before they killed her body. Given time, it might even do that. But in the name of God, did the man not have better things to do? He was in a castle under siege, the court's last remaining toehold in the capital, and he spent his time playing mind games on prisoners. No wonder King Henry's government foundered. There was a studied incompetence in everything they did—the court had long ago given up trying to govern the country, just as Lord Scales had given up holding London for Mad King Henry. Instead they used King Henry to cloak their private indulgences, feeding their passions for lands, titles, money, or victims— whatever their pleasures might be.

As Scales and FitzHolland departed, Matt Davye set down a steaming kettle, saying, "Here is boiled water. Be of good cheer—the Tower is back in King Henry's hands." He took up her stinking bucket and disappeared. So the Tower was back in King Henry's hands. Then why were they not free? The obvious explanation was that no one knew they were there.

Washing for the first time in days, she ate greedily, at the same time furiously figuring out what to say to Matt Davye when he brought the bucket back. By the time she heard boot steps coming back, she had a neat little speech worked out, promising a reward, pardon, plus her eternal gratitude just for carrying a simple message. She was prepared to seal the deal with a kiss, even a French kiss, if necessary. So long as it got him headed the right way. But the man who brought the bucket back was not Matt Davye. It was another of Holland's men—one of the ones who tortured her—setting down her bucket without saying a word. Nor was she tempted to try out her speech on him, much less offer a kiss.

As the lock clicked shut behind her, she prepared for another day in the dark. Then a softer click came from behind her, and light leaped out. She turned to see Jo lighting a candle with her lighter.

"Where did you get that?" she whispered, barely believing it was safe to talk.

Jo pointed to the big bag Robyn had bought in London, lying open alongside the rack. "FitzHolland left that here. I saw your firestick inside." Must have been while Scales was feeding her strawberries.

She heard something bump against the door, followed by scraping sounds as the heavy wine barrels were wrestled back into place. Once again she was barricaded in, but this time with food, and light, and company. Making an incredible difference. Fishing through her bag, she found a flashlight and turned it on. Joy squealed happily at the sudden flood of light, the first sound she had made so far—Lord Scales and FitzHolland had been keeping the girl unnaturally quiet. Joy asked, "What sort of wand is that?"

"The Kmart sort." She searched through her treasure bag, shoving aside the Tampax, toilet paper, and antibiotics, finding her can of industrial-strength bug spray. The bag had been opened and searched, but it all seemed to be there—with two notable exceptions, all her gold and jewelry was missing, and so was her paperback history of this century. Figures. She used the bug spray on her ankles, pleased to see the fleas go leaping off.

"Oh," Jo objected, waving her hand before her nose, "that smells horribly rank."

"Sorry," she apologized for the artificial reek of insecticide, "it has to, or it would not faze the fleas." Medieval England might be a perfumed barnyard, but was remarkably free of industrial carcinogens. Washing the bug spray off her hands, she propped the flashlight in her lap and ate ravenously; all her food inhibitions starved out of her. Between bites she told Jo what had happened since they parted—her trip with Collin through the Welsh Marches, meeting Bryn, various misadventures aboard the *Fortuna*, her stay in Calais, the march on London, then Northampton, and her Witches Night with Duchess

Wydville. "She must have betrayed me. I did the spell as she said, wanting with all my heart for this to be over."

"As does everyone with a dram of sense," Jo agreed.

"But not Duchess Wydville," Robyn reminded her, "or the spell would have worked."

Jo reluctantly agreed, hating to speak ill of another witch, "Duchess Wydville could not just turn the Tower over to the queen's enemies. I wager she hoped you would not even come back to test the spell."

Robyn nodded. "She told me not to come back."

"Yet you came anyway." Jo's dark eyes gleamed in the flashlight beam, hollow from hunger, on the verge of tears. Robyn could only remember Jo crying once before, that day at Greystone when she got Joy back. Jo wiped her eye with a square of toilet paper. "You are amazingly loving and brave."

"Idiotically so," Robyn agreed, attacking one of those tart little oranges, ripping the skin with her nails. So far she had done nothing but add another witch to the Tower collection.

Jo's tale was shorter; she and Joy were run down by FitzHolland and Le Boeuf just beyond Gallop Wood, then taken past the burning Greystone to Ebrington, and held there for a couple of weeks, until Scales came and took them to London. "The duchess gave me over to FitzHolland to stay in Queen Margaret's favor, putting a spell on the Tower, keeping me from calling Collin for aid. Until you got through." That magical coup that had yet to really pay off. "In the beginning it was not so terrible," Jo decided. "We were treated like hostages they might exchange. . . ."

"They fed us then," Joy explained. "And let us out in the air."

"But when the rebels reached Southwark, Lord Scales acted enraged—"

Joy corrected her mother, "He went berserk."

"Yes, well." Jo thought the term strong. "I do suppose he meant to starve us—but after you came on Witches Night, he relented."

Robyn supplied the reason: "Edward warned Scales personally that his lordship would be responsible for any prisoners in the Tower, naming you and Joy in particular. Scales denied he was holding you, but must have got the message."

"So, do you love him?" Jo asked softly.

"Who? Scales?" The thought horrified her—though you were supposed to love your enemies. FitzHolland was merely bigoted, hateful and stupid. Scales relished evil for its own sake.

"No," Jo laughed, "Lord Edward."

"Oh." She sucked on an orange slice. "Does it show?"

Jo nodded. "Most women do not customarily call Lord Edward Plantagenet, earl of March, *Edward*—nor do they speak so easily of his affairs. Not unless she knows him well."

"Yes," she admitted, "I do love him."

"And he, you?"

"So he has said." More than once.

Jo's stern features lit up in the flashlight beam, breaking into a smile. "I hope the two of you are happy." Her daughter's name showed how she felt about her own affair with a duke.

"So do I." To be really happy, she had to get free—love was for the living. Her flashlight cast stark shadows on a shining circle of flint and chalk just behind Jo's head, making it seem like yet another gothic slumber party, huddled under blankets in the dark, eating chocolates by flashlight, drinking bottled water, telling scary stories and comparing boyfriends.

Being an accomplished witch, Jo read her thoughts. "Now that the Tower is in the king's hands, Collin and Lord Edward can come for us. We might be freed in a moment."

"Maybe, if Collin and Edward can find us." She shined the flashlight at the blank cell door. "Holland's men have pushed heavy barrels against the door to keep it hidden. You could comb the White Tower from turret to vault without ever seeing this cell." And that was just the White Tower; the fortress as a whole had dozens of towers and gatehouses, plus numerous buildings, halls, and chapels, riddled with rooms and basement cells. Not a cheery thought. As the day wore on, no Collin came. Nor Edward either. But as days underground go, this was by far her best, with food and friends, and clean water, and light when they wanted it. They talked, made shadow puppets, and went through her treasures from the future, playing with the refillable ink pen and sewing kit, jacklighting rats with the little flashlights, and making cat's cradles out of dental floss.

Long after night fell outside, she heard the scrape of heavy barrels being manhandled aside, unblocking the door, followed by a key turning in the lock. Dousing the flashlights, Robyn waited, her most precious new possessions hidden on her person—just in case. Praying fervently for it to be Edward.

Slowly the door swung open. Not totally blinded this time, she made out a dozen men in loose hooded robes, though she could not distinguish faces. Maybe not Edward, but for a moment it looked like they had been rescued by monks. Until one of the monks spoke up. "My dear Lady Stafford, would you and your guests be pleased to join us?" It was FitzHolland.

Lord Scales was with him; so was Le Boeuf, making a horribly unlikely man of God. Matt Davye stood with his hood thrown back, holding two spare robes. He offered them to her and Jo. Robyn took hers, wondering to herself, What is all this about?

Sensing the question, Scales told her, "We thought you might be pleased to take a walk. It must be tedious, spending day after day locked in a tower basement."

So let's all dress up like monks and skylark around the Tower at night. She did not believe that for an instant. Scales and FitzHolland would not be midnight masquerading as monks unless something desperate was afoot. But she went to lengths not to show it, thanking them extravagantly, acting the perfect airhead, as if she really thought they were doing it for her. Her bag slipped easily under the robe, which was cut for Friar Tuck, not a half-starved female. Jo donned her own robe and took Joy's hand; then they all set out up the spiral steps. Robyn fell silent; the first part of getting away was to let them forget you are there.

When they got to the White Tower entrance, she stepped into the open for the first time in a week, sensing dark empty space spreading in all directions, reaching up to the stars. Thank Heavens. She breathed in cool dark night air, remembering when she never expected to take another breath above ground. Since returning to the Middle Ages she had seen nothing but the inside of the White Tower, nothing but blackness and stone walls, not a single peek at London, not an inch of countryside. Instead of being back, she felt trapped in some ghastly extended nightmare that was grotesquely resisting her best efforts to make it go away. The latest episode had her dressed in drag—as a monk, no less, skulking among other phony monks across the Tower's inner ward, headed for the black yawning gate in what these people called the Garden Tower, but later generations named the

Bloody Tower—the same way she entered the touristy twenty-first-century Tower.

Beyond the open portcullis gate they crossed the narrow outer ward, going straight to the Tower's water gate—called the Traitor's Gate, because prisoners sent downriver from Westminster entered through it. This could only mean they were fleeing the Tower. Lord Scales was not the type to dress everybody up like monks and go night boating on the Thames merely for the thrill of it. He lacked that sense of whimsy. This meant he had lost the Tower—or expected to lose it in the morning—and was making his escape, taking his most valuable prisoners. But taking them where?

Two small boats waited in the lamplight at the base of the gate-house stairs, lapped by black Thames water entering through the open water gate. FitzHolland ordered Jo and Joy into the nearest boat. She moved to join them, but Lord Scales caught her arm, saying, "Come Lady Stafford, sit with me. This night is dark and wet, and having you near is always cheering,"

Smiling, she did as Scales asked, doing nothing to attract attention. She sensed a crisis. A moment was coming when the forces would shift to her favor. She had to know it when it came, and be ready to act. Lord Scales was engaged in that most delicate of military operations, retreat in the face of overwhelming odds. He needed everything to go without a hitch. The man who starved her in a stone box and liked watching her being pulled apart now wanted her to be sweet and docile. She let him to think she would be, to keep his mind off her. Being a man, Scales did not question her obedience, even expecting sympathy for his predicament. "Thank you, I have much to do. Having you here is a great comfort."

She could believe it. Scales had lost the Tower but he still had her, to abuse at his leisure. At least it kept her alive for now. Hoping Lord Scales had indulged himself once too often, she noted dry stonework above the waterline—the tide was coming in. So Scales aimed to escape upriver, which meant running London Bridge in the dark, a rather risky business, but there was nothing for him downriver—just an unfriendly fleet and hostile country along both banks. Upriver he could hope for sanctuary at Westminster or even escape to the north, or to some Welsh castle with a sympathetic lord.

She settled into the stern, striving to be inconspicuous. Monks climbed aboard around her, unshipping the oars, in not very seaman-like fashion, rocking the boat and complaining, "Stop splashing, this water is colder than a nun's cunt." Maybe they were just nervous—she was.

Scales took the tiller, his men pushing off with their oars. Fitz-Holland's men did the same, and both boats nosed out the water gate onto the broad dark river. Which Robyn found to be remarkably crowded, especially upstream, as Saturday night traffic passed between London and Southwark, backlit by the lights of London Bridge. London was celebrating the return of the king, and looked likely to be up late. Boats passed on either hand, most rowed by professional boatmen, though one boat full of drunk party-goers was thrashing about in midstream, trying to get to Southwark by rowing both ways at once.

Striving to avoid the revelers, Lord Scales ran afoul of a cargo wherry coming the other way. Telling his oarsmen to back water, he waited to let the wherry past. Boatmen called out to them, "Ho! Who are you? Why do you come from the Tower?"

Scales had his answer ready, "We are brothers from Saint Katherine's by the Tower . . ."

Here was her moment. Her hand closed on her flashlight, as she called on her carefully hoarded courage, praying to Saint Joan—the teenager who beat Lord Scales in battle, long ago on the field of Patay. Leaping up, she pulled back Scale's hood and flicked on the flashlight, shining it full in their astouned faces, blinding them. "A lie!" she shouted. "A lie! See, it is Lord Scales, escaping from the Tower! Stop him in the name of King Henry!"

⊷⊜ Baynards Castle ⊜⊶

*C*haos erupted around her on the dark water, a wild melee of flailing oars and colliding boats. Boatmen yelled curses and cast things at her boat. Scales squinted in white-faced astonishment, straight into the blinding flashlight beam. Behind him, phony monks blinked and shaded their eyes with mailed hands. Beyond them Robyn saw white splashes on black water as boats thrashed toward the light. One of

Holland's pseudo-monks lunged at her flashlight arm, nearly upsetting the boat. Her hand had already found the bug spray; jamming it in the villain's face, she pressed so hard she broke the plastic button. "Here's for hurting me."

Insecticide spray shot through the flashlight beam into his face, sending him howling backwards in shock, mailed hands covering his eyes, throwing the boat the other way. Shrinking back into the stern, she held the flashlight and bug spray in front of her, protected by surprise and the products of far-off techno-civilization.

Another boat banged into hers from behind. Boatmen swarmed aboard, shouting threats and stumbling over one another. One landed atop Lord Scales, propelling both of them into a noisy tangle at her feet. Lifting her legs, she swung them around, clicking out the light as soon as her feet found the other hull. Ducking her head, she dived into the dark bows of the neighboring boat. Curled in a ball, she heard men leap over her, emptying the boat—one going crashing in the water—sending the boat she cowered in spinning backwards, despite dismayed shouts from the tiller.

Sitting up, she saw only one old man in the boat, clinging to his useless tiller, clearly surprised to be sharing his boat with a woman in monk's clothing. Wild splashing and frenzied shouts faded into the darkness, leaving them alone from the moment. "Who are you?" the old boatman demanded, acting dangerously excited. "How in heaven's name did you get here?"

"Robyn Stafford," she replied, deciding not to bug spray the surprised boatman. "Lady Robyn Stafford," she added, hurriedly giving herself a title. "I was a prisoner of Lord Scales in the Tower. Please put me ashore at once. There is silver in it for you."

He stared at her, trying to gauge her offer of silver—her monk's habit must not look promising—then he peered into the surrounding blackness. Shouting had subsided, and from the sound of things most boats were making for shore. Heaving an exasperated sigh, the old boatman tied down his tiller, picked up a pair of sweeps, and started rowing rapidly toward the lights of Southwark. "Why were you a prisoner?" he asked. "What was your crime?"

She shook her head, watching the lights come closer. "No crime at all, aside from wanting peace, and wishing to see the Tower back in King Henry's hands."

He snorted suspiciously. "Any fool wants that."

She nodded gravely. "And now we are likely to have it." Seeing he would get nothing sensible from her, the boatman redoubled his efforts, splashing industriously toward shore. She searched the blackness for sign of FitzHolland's boat, still holding Jo and Joy. No trace of them showed in the night. She doubted FitzHolland would try to run London Bridge in this uproar. Nor was returning to the Tower much of an option. FitzHolland would be headed for Southwark, or drifting downriver trying to slip past the fleet. If he was not already drowning in his armor. Southwark wharves loomed out of the night; they were approaching the south bank of the Thames, just below Bankside and the Bridge. She felt the little boat bump against a dock crowded with people, and the boatman called out for someone to take his line.

Rough hands caught the line, tying the boat to the wharf, then reached down to pull her up. She scrambled onto the dock, thanking the men who helped her ashore, managing to disengage from their friendly grip. They would have gladly kept helping her, right into a tavern, followed by who knows what. Sorry guys, maybe some other time. She was free, happy to feel the wet boards against her bare feet. Safely out of the Tower, and back on the friendly streets of old London town. Or at least old Southwark—a short walk from her little river-view room at Falstaff's Place. She felt like doing another victory dance right there on the dock, but restrained herself. There would be time for celebration later, once she found Jo and Joy, and Edward.

Throwing back her monk's hood, she looked about the crowded dock lit with lamps and torches, seeing no sign of Jo, or anyone from FitzHolland's boat. Drunken loiterers caroused with local fishwives and sailors from afar, drinking, singing, and celebrating Saturday night, and the return of the king to London. Across the street from the dock stood a waterfront inn, and a long line of houses leading up to London Bridge. Between her and the Bridge reared the tall square tower of Saint Mary Overy—Saint Mary Over the Water, in clipped London slang. She could hardly believe how familiar it all felt. Men stared at her in mild amazement, calling out drunken endearments, saying, "Here's a handsome young monk." Or, "Where is your apron beauteous goose?" Southwark prostitutes—Winchester Geese—were not allowed to wear aprons, to keep men from propositioning market women and housewives. And on a riotous Saturday night any woman without an apron was likely to be accosted. One of the drunk sailors who had helped her up onto the dock pulled at her sleeve, "Come pray with me pretty monk; I have been a long time at sea." Someone else offered her a tankard of ale, telling her to drink to the return of the king.

Shaking her head, she slipped from the sailor's inebriated grip, dodging the tankard and heading up the street toward the church, saying, "I go to Saint Mary Overy to give thanks." Hoping they would mistake her for some sort of cross-dressing pilgrim.

"What about my silver?" asked the suspicious old boatman.

She told him, "Edward, earl of March will reward you."

He looked askance, as if that were a fanciful way to escape without paying. Why not tell him to get it from the king?

"Really," she insisted. "Present yourself at Grey Friars. . . ."

"But he is at Baynards Castle," declared the boatman.

"Baynards Castle, then. Go there and present yourself; tell them you helped Lady Robyn Stafford escape from the Tower, and you shall be well rewarded. Now I must go and give my thanks."

Another sailor grabbed at her, but she was too quick. "What do you give thanks for, pretty monk?" he called after her.

Life, love, and freedom. She said it to herself, glad to leave the friendly drunks behind her, heading briskly up the street toward the church by London Bridge. Saint Mary Overy was where Jo or Joy would go if either had managed to escape FitzHolland in that watery melee. Hoping to find friends waiting, she lengthened her stride.

And ran smack into FitzHolland, standing square in her path, having doffed his monk's robe, wearing the livery of a king's sergeant-at-law over a coat of chain mail. The grinning bastard was not even wet. He laughed mockingly, "This is no monk. She is witch and a whore. And my prisoner."

Stepping back, she saw a half-dozen of Holland's men were with him, all of them wearing King Henry's livery. Jo was there, too, still in her monk's habit, loosely held by Matt Davye. What really kept Jo in check was Le Boeuf, who had Joy in one hand and his bare bollock knife in the other, fully ready to cut the girl's throat if her mother got out of hand. "Come with me," FitzHolland commanded, reaching out to seize her.

Hollywood training took over, stepping swiftly out of reach, she shouted, "No! Do not touch me." The women's self-defense mantra flashed through her head; when a man tries to grab you in public, be assertive, resist loudly, attract attention, make it clear you do not know him—not strictly true in FitzHolland's case, but the principle applied. "Stop, let me be," she yelled. "This man is a murderer!"

Boatmen looked up. So did drunk stevedores, pasty-faced apprentices, and pleasure-seeking sailors. Revelers from London, fresh off the Bridge, heading for taverns and brothels stopped in their tracks to stare at the mad woman in monk's drag crying *murder*. FitzHolland stepped closer, saying loudly, "She is a crazed witch. Pay her no heed."

Her heart fell, finding her new freedom suddenly gone. How wretchedly unfair. FitzHolland meant to have his way by sheer force of arms, betting no one in the drunk and happy throng would go up against a sergeant-at-law backed by a half-dozen men in armor. Nor did her case look good—a wild, unkempt woman wearing a monk's robe, facing armed men in King Henry's livery. Somehow she had to appeal to this Southwark crowd; if FitzHolland got hold of her, and shut her up, she was finished. "These are Lord Scales's men from the Tower," she shouted. "And they mean to do murder."

"Nonsense, I am a king's sergeant-at-law," FitzHolland protested. "This witch woman is my prisoner, and her punishment will be decided by law, in court. Interfere, and you side with the Devil, tempting a similar fate."

"He is Duke Holland's bastard brother," she shouted to the perplexed crowd, knowing how roundly Duke Holland was hated in London. Aside from a sailor off the *Fortuna*, not a single face looked familiar in the mostly male throng. Not the crowd she would have picked to appeal to—drunken medieval strangers looking for love on a Saturday night—but she had no choice. This was the jury she must win over. At least she spoke their language, easily slipping into a clipped London accent—FitzHolland had to make to do with law court English and his native Devon. She pointed at FitzHolland, trying not to sound shrill—she had to come off as convincing, not crazy— "These men are from the Tower garrison, the same ones who threw fire on the City, seeking to escape justice."

"Ridiculous," FitzHolland retorted, hand on his sword, furious enough to cut her in two. If he laid hands on her now, that torture session in the Tower would seem like a pleasant late-night romp.

"It is Holland's bastard brother," a boatman called out. "I carried him to Westminster."

"And his executioner," added an apprentice, pointing to Le Boeuf. Duke Holland's readiness to hang merchants and apprentices for trivial offenses had not made him popular. But Le Boeuf himself was a something of a celebrity—renowned for his cruelty on the scaffold. "Tell it to Le Boeuf," was a common curse in Southwark.

More people piled out of the tavern—drawn by the commotion, adding to the ring of faces around her, looking excited, curious, or puzzled—drunken peddlers mostly, and their women, real Winchester Geese who began clamoring for Le Boeuf to "Let the little girl go."

"She, too, is a witch," FitzHolland retorted frostily, looking like he had never been so insulted in what must have been a long and touchy career.

"And I, too, am a whore," a woman shouted back, "so do not give yourself French airs." Her customers laughed. Prostitutes in Southwark practiced a lawful trade, protected from abuse by pimps or customers, making them very free to speak their minds. With them was the innkeeper, anxious to see what had happened to his customers. Since licensed brothels could not serve liquor, his was an illegal establishment, and he looked properly nervous facing an angry sergeant-at-law.

FitzHolland's fingers were flexing on his sword hand. Given an excuse, he would cut her down right here at the dock and stand over her body, sword in hand, daring anyone to do something. She heard boatmen behind her tell how she had shown them Lord Scales, "His lordship would have gotten safe away, had she not shouted to us. She raised her hand and a blinding light shone on Lord Scales's face. We thought her an angel, now it seems she is but a witch."

Luckily they had not seen the bug spray. Making her pitch higher and more personal, she called clear and loud to the crowd, "Send word to Edward, earl of March. I am Robyn Stafford of his household. He will speak for me."

"Edward of March?" The tavern keeper looked askance at her wild appearance and weird costume. Well fed and well dressed himself, he wore a colorful velvet doublet and feathered hat—a respected neighborhood leader, catering to his patrons' every bodily desire—even if that meant bending the bishop's law. "Do you mean Duke Richard of York's young heir?"

"Yes, Edward, earl of March." Or even Warwick, for that matter. Any of the rebel leaders would love to lay hands on FitzHolland and his merry men, but Edward was the one she desperately wanted to see. "Edward will speak for me."

"She is Edward's darling," a whore called out. "She rode in with him the day Lord Edward entered the city." Her girlfriends all agreed—trust your local strumpets to know who was dallying with whom. None sounded envious, just excited, "She was with Lord Edward even when he took the king at Northampton. They came together from Calais." They clearly thought it romantic, happy to see a harlot make good.

"Aboard his lordship's own ship, the *Sparrow*," added a sailor. "She lodges at Falstaff's Place," a baker's boy called out in a reedy voice. Others shouted out times and places that they had seen her—on the march to London, at Saint Paul's, riding over the Bridge with Edward. Robyn had not realized how well known Edward's lady was—no one sounded scornful of her, or envious, just glad to know someone so close to a national hero, happily basking in her fifteen minutes of fame, not caring if it was ill-gotten. She felt touched.

"She is a witch," FitzHolland insisted, seeing his authority mocked.

Whores and boatmen jeered. "A good witch, I ween," came from the sailor off the *Fortuna*. "Who saved us from the wild Irish."

"And who owes me for bringing her here," that was from the old boatman, still hoping to see his silver.

Robyn braced herself, knowing things were balanced on a knife edge. FitzHolland had lost the crowd, but he still had force to fall back on. Movement in the night air caught her attention. Flickering through the torchlight, shadowy wings flashed above her head. She glanced at Jo, mouthing the words, "Be ready." Reaching inside her bag for the bug spray, she prayed to Hecate, begging not to have this end in bloodshed.

Hela dived out of the darkness, directly at Le Boeuf's eyes, wings beating, claws out, screeching like a banshee, catching the executioner by surprise. Like everyone else, Le Boeuf had been looking at her and FitzHolland, never seeing Hela coming. Shrieking in alarm, he batted at the black bird, slashing blindly with his bollock knife.

As soon as Le Boeuf let go, Joy ducked under the flailing knife, dashing over to Robyn, cheered heartily by the crowd. Grabbing hold of the monk's robe, Joy practically buried herself in the folds. Reaching down, Robyn congratulated the girl, "Well done. We are almost home."

Hela flew in raucous circles around Le Boeuf's head, cawing triumphantly just out of knife range—imitating a human horse laugh.

FitzHolland immediately protested, insisting, "She, too, is my prisoner," pointing a steel finger at the girl cowering behind folds of fabric. "Hand her back to the law."

"Too bad, bastard," a wag called from the crowd. "Tell it to Le Boeuf."

"That may do in Devon," a Londoner shouted, ridiculing his West Country accent. "But thanks to God we are in London town." Southwark, actually. She smiled at how this drunk Londoner fresh from a brothel bed sounded like Lord Sudeley standing before his castle in godly Glouscestershire—all Sudeley had lacked was slurred speech and Cockney accent.

Stroking the terrified child, she told FitzHolland, "You are the one who must face the law, for holding the Tower against King Henry and throwing fire on the city."

"Lies," FitzHolland retorted not too convincingly, most of it being true.

"Let Edward of March decide," she shot back. "He will know the truth of this. I claim his protection." Heads nodded in drunken agreement. Everyone wanted to see Edward dragged into this, and maybe King Henry, as well, making it a Saturday night Southwark would not soon forget. Winchester Geese took up the chant, "Let Lord Edward decide. Let Lord Edward decide. . . ." Their patrons joined in.

Seeing he would get no help from the crowd, FitzHolland nodded to Le Boeuf, who quit batting at the bird and put his knife to Jo's throat. Stepping forward, FitzHolland reached for Robyn with a mailed hand. "Do as I say, or the child shall see her mother die."

Chilled at the man's ruthlessness, she stepped back. FitzHolland meant to win by force, taking them in front of everyone, trusting in edged steel and the king's livery. "No," she insisted, "let Edward decide." Southwark loudly agreed.

From above and behind her came a familiar voice, calling out, "Yes, let Edward decide." She looked behind her, seeing the black flank of a horse whose booted rider had forced a path through the crowd—it was Caesar. Edward sat atop him, bareheaded, wearing his murrey and blue, looking idiotically happy, given the circumstances. Collin was with him, as well, also ahorsed.

Edward was instantly recognized, turning the chant to cheers. Southwark had gotten what it wanted. She had demanded to take her case to the popular young earl of March, and now their hero appeared. Bending in the saddle, Edward slung a strong arm around her waist, lifting her onto Caesar's black crupper, sitting her down side-saddle. At the same time he managed to pry Joy's hand off her robes, helping the girl scramble up onto his lap. Another neat bit of horsemanship, which further impressed the crowd. Looping her arms about his waist, Robyn leaned against Edward's back, resting her head next to his, ridiculously happy herself—given the circumstances. FitzHolland still had armed men at his back and a knife at Jo's throat. Edward was not even wearing armor, and his sword hand held Joy in his lap. They were defenseless, protected by nothing but Edward's habitual audacity, and the love people bore him. She whispered in his ear, "I am so ungodly happy to see you."

"And I, you." Edward twisted about in the saddle and gave her a quick kiss.

Southwark cheered their kiss. Edward turned back to FitzHolland, sounding more like a man on his honeymoon than the leader of a mob, saying "Gentle sir, this is indeed a matter for the law, so let us proceed in fair and charitable fashion. Surrender yourself, your men, and your prisoners into my protection. Or accept dire consequences."

FitzHolland glared at him. "Consequences, my lord? I am a sergeant-at-law to King Henry." Edward was unarmored, with a little girl sitting in his lap. FitzHolland had armed and desperate men at his back, and one prisoner left to bargain with.

Edward's calm voice turned serious, nodding toward Le Boeuf, still holding his bollock knife at Jo's throat. "Killing a woman is plain murder. Doing it in breach of the king's truce could easily be construed as treason. As a sergeant-at-law, you can tell me the penalty." Everyone within earshot knew the horrific penalties for treason. She had seen Le Boeuf administer them on her very first day here and now.

"My lord, these women are witches," FitzHolland warned. "Aid them, and you imperil your own immortal soul."

Edward thanked FitzHolland for his pious concern—"but it is my immortal soul, and I may best judge its peril."

Collin nudged his horse through the crowd, sword in hand, with Hela preening herself on his mailed shoulder. "Worry more about keeping your own body and soul together." Unlike Edward, Collin had come wearing steel, armed and ready to do battle for his sister. Tavern patrons shouted encouragement out of second-story windows, hoping to see a Saturday night duel from a safe distance—cheering Sir Collingwood Grey by name over the heads of the crowd. He had taken first prize at the last Westminster tourney.

Edward rose in the saddle, speaking not just to FitzHolland, but also to the armed men with him. "Good sirs, the choice is with you. Surrender and submit to King Henry's justice—or die. Either here on this street, sword in hand, or on the morrow before a jeering mob atop Tower Hill—for I swear that all you will gain by resisting your king is a poor night's sleep." For a recent rebel in exile, Edward was remarkably cool about wielding the king's authority. Yet from his earnest lips it sounded convincing. Seeing no contradiction between loyalty and rebellion, Edward merely wanted to have King Henry's England run right from now on. And he was naturally generous enough to give even his most hardened enemies one last chance to repent.

FitzHolland glumly studied the hostile Southwark throng. His position was hopeless—Edward might show mercy, but the crowd would not, and the most to be gained by fighting was a particularly gruesome death. Reluctantly, he slid his sword back into his scabbard. Le Boeuf let his knife drop, as well. Matt Davye walked Jo over to Collin and then let her go.

Squealing with delight, Joy slid out of Edward's grip, alighting alongside Jo, flinging her arms around her mother. Jo herself looked spent, wearing her monk's robe and a dazed expression. Robyn guessed Jo had been ready to die, sacrificing herself so Joy could be saved; to have both of them be alive and free must seem totally unbelievable. Collin swung out of the saddle to comfort his shaken sister.

As he did, Edward told him, "This man is yours, if you want him," pointing to FitzHolland, still armed and waiting, wearing King Henry's lions and lilies on his armored chest. Tensing, Robyn feared the fight might not be over.

Collin already had a mailed arm around Jo's waist; he glanced at FitzHolland. "No other man ever did me so much hurt. But I have never yet killed a man, except by mischance—nor have I ever much wanted to. I would not change that for Gilbert FitzHolland. Let the law have him. Justice will no doubt be harder on him than I." Collin had his family back; wanting just to enjoy that feeling, he could not be bothered with revenge. She did not blame him. Why put everything at risk to kill FitzHolland when the law would likely do it for him?

"So be it." Edward turned back to FitzHolland and his not-so-merry men. "Put down your arms, in the name of King Henry. Or add treason to the charges against you."

She relaxed as the last hold-outs from the Tower laid down swords, axes, and knives. At last, it was truly over. London was theirs, and the Tower, and King Henry, and as much of England as they cared to claim. FitzHolland was the last to put down his sword, but when he did, it got a lusty cheer from the citizens of Southwark—who surged forward to take charge of the prisoners now that they were disarmed. Laying her head back on Edward's shoulder, she whispered in his ear, "Thank you for saving me."

"Saving you?" Edward laughed. "I saved Gilbert FitzHolland. If he had so much as touched your sleeve, those good people would have torn him apart."

She sighed, supposing it was true. "Then thank you for saving me from that."

Seeing FitzHolland about to be dragged away to the clink, or worse, she lifted her head, shouting, "Wait! See if he has a book on him!"

Edward twisted in the saddle, asking, "A book?"

"Yes, a printed paperback, with King Henry's picture on the cover. It is mine. He stole it."

Edward had them haul FitzHolland over, and Collin found the paperback tucked into a boot top. Looking quizically at the glossy cover and King Henry's picture, he handed it up to Edward, saying he had never seen a printed book before, "And never imagined they were so small."

"Even the letters are tiny," Edward flipped through a few pages and then handed it to her. "You should have seen the map she had when we first met in Wales."

"Yes"—Collin grinned up at her—"my lady Stafford has so many surprises."

FitzHolland fixed her with a malevolent grin, making her wonder if he had read any of what was in his boot. Hopefully not. FitzHolland was the last person she wanted looking into the future. Taking the book, she stuffed it deep in her carrying bag, not wanting to say where it came from or what it contained. She was almost ashamed to have it—another of those weird witchy secrets separating you from men. But so long as she had the book, she would never find herself wishing she bought a readable history of the period.

Right now she did not give a fig about the future, just wanting to savor the moment, to hold on to Edward, happy to have come through everything safe and whole. Absolutely amazing. Dumb luck, or a sign she made the right choices? She whispered to Edward, "How did you find me?"

He smiled over his shoulder at her. "How could I not? First came that scarlet archer, invading my dreams, swearing it was for the last time. He told me you were in dire need, and would be by the church of Saint Mary Overy in Southwark . . ."

Holy Mary, John-Amend-All had come through for her; she must remember to light him a candle.

". . . By the time I was dressed and at the Bridge, there was Collin saying his sister had called to him. Crossing the Bridge we met a madly cawing magpie, a sign Sir Collin put much faith in. And the bird led straight to Saint Mary Overy, and to you. It is enough to make a man believe in witchcraft."

And she had thought she was alone, with barely a friendly face in sight. Spirits in the night had watched over her, spreading the alarm and summoning aid, spooky but effective. She felt a thrill of satisfaction surge through her, lifting her up and lightening her heart. Despite disaster after disaster, they had done it. How happy to be the darlings of fate, watched over by Heaven, knowing your cause is just and then seeing it triumph. Looking about, she saw the old boatman staring wide-eyed up at her, finally convinced he had carried Lord Edward's lady. She pointed him out to Edward. "That old man brought me safely here. Please see he is rewarded."

Edward called the fellow over, got his name, and told him, "Come on the morrow to Baynards Castle, and I will see you get your due." Glad to see his silver materialize, the boatman bowed and vowed to be there.

Happily paying her debts at Edward's expense, she offered up her room in Falstaff's Place to Jo, proud of her first chance ever to play hostess to Jo Grey—in this or any millennium. Collin hoisted Jo, then Joy onto his horse, and they set out, Collin walking, while she and Edward rode ahead, parting the cheering throng.

At Falstaff's Place they got a similarly enthusiastic welcome from tenants and household staff. Light spilled out tenement windows onto the street, shining in the puddles. Word had come ahead of her, and Deirdre met her at the big open gate. Introducing her Irish maid to

Jo, she told Deirdre, "Lady Grey and her daughter will be needing my room."

"So you will not be sleeping here tonight?" Deirdre sounded crushed. She must have been praying hard to her heathen spirits for her mistress's safe return.

Robyn reached down, letting Deirdre seize her hand, saying, "Apparently not." She felt dead beat and horribly dirty, unable even to remember when she had her last bath. But she had not so much as let go of Edward since they were reunited—except to stuff that Wars of the Roses book back into her carrying bag. She desperately needed to be alone with him. Just the two of them, without the fate of England hanging over their heads.

Deirdre understood, cradling Robyn's hand against her cheek, then kissing the fingertips. Letting go, the serving girl helped Jo and Joy dismount; then she showed them through the gate and into the manse. Seeing his sister and niece in safe hands, Collin bowed to Edward, saying, "Your lordship, I am again in your debt. Forever sorry for siding against you, and thinking to deliver you to your enemies."

Edward dismissed the apology. "You owe me nothing. You served your king, better even than he deserved. How could I hold that against you?" With her head resting beside Edward's, she could hear his happiness, genuinely glad to call Collin a friend. Such natural generosity made Edward all the more appealing, and she tightened her hold, feeling his strong hard waist through the fabric, pleased that for once he was not wearing armor.

Collin did another bow, this time to her. "Lady Robyn, I am doubly in your debt. This is the second time you have brought my family back together—if ever you are in need, I am yours to command."

She did not doubt it. Thanking him, she reached down her hand—which Collin kissed. Then he begged Edward leave to see to his family, which Edward readily granted—and Collin was gone. Watching him vanish into the crowd by the gate, she knew there would always be a link between her and Collin, and since they manifestly could not be lovers, they had best be friends. Strange how she had to go half a millennium to find that out.

All at once, she was alone with Edward—if you did not count the street full of adoring onlookers. He asked over his shoulder, "Have you ever seen Baynards Castle, my father's London home?"

"Only from a distance," she admitted. Baynards Castle was a stern row of towers rising right out of the river, upstream on the London side, at the southwest corner of the city wall—like the rest of his father's holdings, it had been "in the King's hands" until now. "Never from the inside."

"Capital," Edward declared happily. "I must show you how I am having it remade."

"Must you?" It seemed an odd moment to show off an unexpected bent for interior decorating.

"Absolutely." The boy brimmed with enthusiasm. "You could not imagine a moment more opportune. Come, I swear you shall love it."

With that, Edward took his leave, working the crowd one final time. As Caesar turned about to go, Deirdre came dashing out the gate, a clothes bundle in her arms. Doing a little bobbing bow, she offered up the bundle, saying "Clean night clothes, and a gown for the morrow, m'lady Robyn. An' slippers for your feet."

She took the clothes, knowing it must have been miserable for Deirdre, abandoned among Saxons, fearing never to see her mistress again. Deirdre did what passed for a proper Irish curtsy and then turned to go wait on Jo. Robyn called to her in Gaelic, and Deirdre came running back. Shifting her clothes to her knight's lap, she bent down, taking her excited maid's head in both hands and kissing her on the lips. "Thank you, truly. Please care for my friends tonight."

Deirdre beamed. "You came back to me, m'lady."

"Yes, I did." For better or for worse.

Deirdre curtsied again, turned, and was gone. Who would have thought having servants would be so personal. She shook her head in rueful wonder—not three months in the Middle Ages and she already had people totally depending on her. She retrieved her slippers and clothes from Edward's lap. He told her, "You are lucky to inspire such love."

No mean compliment, coming from someone loved by half the nation. Seeing Deirdre run out barefoot and unasked, with slippers and clothes for her mistress pleased Edward more than having London aldermen fawning on him—the very sort of thing that made Warwick question the boy's sense of priorities. "Yes," she agreed, holding tight to his firm middle and to her change of clothes. "Most lucky."

He set off again to more cheers from the crowd, headed for his father's castle on the London side of the river. "Though not so lucky as I," he added over his shoulder.

"Why not?" What was wrong with her luck? It felt damned miraculous at the moment. She had survived everything the Middle Ages threw at her—serving it back hard so far as Scales and FitzHolland were concerned.

He reached back, patting her knee. "I am luckiest, since I finally have you alone, not needing to share you with anyone." Funny, she thought that was her good luck, having Edward all to herself—with no derring-do needing to be done, no desperate fights against daunting odds, no invasions to plot or kings to capture. Nothing more harrowing than a castle in dire need of redecorating. How incredible, just the two of them, riding up Long Southwark toward the lights of London across the river, getting friendly waves from whores and happy drunks.

This gay little spell lasted as far as the stone steps of Saint Mary Overy. By now the Saturday night crowd had thinned; those that remained were gawking at a naked white-haired body sprawled in the light, a pale bloodied old man, freshly beaten to death. She got a brief horrified glimpse of the battered face before looking away—Lord Scales.

"How terrible," Edward turned Caesar toward the Bridge, trying to shield her from the sight. "It is shameful to see him lying so." One of Edward's most endearing traits was his knack for seeing good in everyone, showing compassion for those who most folks thought better off dead. She had sworn to Holy Mary she would bring Scales down—as he got set to hurt her in that horrible cell—and now he lay dead on the steps of Mary's house in Southwark. She was glad she succeeded, yet she had not wanted the old man stripped and beaten to death. Or stretched on his own rack, which Scales probably would have enjoyed. But Lord Scales sitting in a cell somewhere, contemplating his sins did sound nice. Maybe make him a monk in a cave on some rocky island off the Irish coast, with no one to torture except himself. The citizens of Southwark were not so forgiving.

"He stood godfather to me," Edward told her softly, "in Rouen, when I was born."

"Lord Scales? Your godfather?" She could barely believe it.

"Certainly"—Edward nodded sadly—"and until these last months he had always been good to me. Even now, he was only doing what his king wanted."

And enjoying the heck out of it. Now she knew why Scales stopped racking her when he did. Much as Scales might enjoy seeing her hurt, he did not want his godson implicated in witchcraft—especially when Scales was relying on Edward for a pardon. She nodded silently, not wanting to say what Scales had done to her, in fact trying to put it completely out of her own head. She would think about it tomorrow, and maybe even tell Edward. But she meant to give herself one full night of triumph—reliving her shame and horror would have to wait.

Caesar's hoofbeats turned hollow as they started over London Bridge. Edward steered his black charger around the breaks in the Bridge, saying, "We must get this roadway repaired." And they could. Right now, they could do almost anything—within reason—even fix the ten-year-old potholes left by John-Amend-All's rebellion. She closed her eyes and listened to the hollow hoofbeats, clumping out a tune:

> **London Bridge is falling down,**
> **Falling down, falling down.**
> **London Bridge is falling down,**
> **My fair lady . . .**

How long since she'd had a bath? She could barely remember. As danger faded, the mundane world returned. She felt totally drained and incredibly dirty. Her current visit to the Middle Ages was a sanitary nightmare. Fortunately, she now had her mini-pharmacy with her, and new-bought underwear; but most of all, she desperately needed a bath. And clean food. And sleep. Weariness brought back old doubts and fears—what was she really doing here? Jo was back in the bosom of her family, so was Collin, who had Bryn as well. While she was still adrift hundreds of years from home. She held hard to Edward, resting her head against him, listening to the hoofbeats:

> **Build it up with needles and pins,**
> **Needles and pins, needles and pins,**
> **Build it up with needles and pins,**
> **My fair lady . . .**

City guards waved them through, giving an inebriated cheer for the heroic young earl and his lady, riding sidesaddle and barefoot in a monk's habit. Her costume drew knowing snickers—it had been that sort of a Saturday night. At the London end of the Bridge they turned away from the light and noise of the Fish Street inns, heading up Thames Street, past darkened wharves and warehouses, and huge halls belonging to Fishmongers and Vintners, and the fortresslike Steelyard, headquarters of the Hanse merchants. Ship's boys and sailors shouted greetings. She was going to have to get used to being cheered wherever they went. Already it made her feel less alone.

At the uppermost end of Thames Street, by Saint Paul's Wharf, Baynards Castle rose straight out of the southwest corner of the city walls. Guards in Edward's murrey and blue saluted him at the gate, ushering them into a narrow, irregular courtyard surrounded by tall stone walls and towers, topped with starry black night. Stable boys hurried up, bowing before their lord, helping them dismount, and taking charge of Caesar. Men in Edward's livery took her carrying bag, and the clothes bundle Deirdre had given her. She would have to get used to being waited on as well. Feeling she suddenly had nothing to do, she stared up at the stars; after months of rain and a week in the Tower, this was her first chance in a long time to just look at the night sky. Edward came to stand beside her. "Are those the same stars as in your future?"

"Yep, the same ones I counted as a girl growing up in Montana." Stars and constellations remained the same—it was everything else that was different.

"Since the stars are the same, come see my surprise." Edward sounded almighty eager to lead her into the castle hall, impatient to show off his new town house. Whatever his surprise, he was immensely proud of himself, prouder even than he had been kneeling in King Henry's tent at Northampton. Too bad she just felt tired and dirty. The big rectangular hall had a walk-in fireplace with a huge kettle steaming on the fire. Hopefully that meant boiled water. Otherwise the high hall was fairly empty, with trestle tables stacked along one wall and the duke of York's falcon-and-fetterlock banner done in silver on cloth-of-gold hanging above the mantel. Like the castle's bare inner court, the hall was an impressive underused space, rising up toward the carved-wood hammer beam ceiling—plain but full of promise. No wonder Edward was desperate to redecorate. He led her up stone stairs at the back of the hall, worn from centuries of use and splashed with water. At the top, light and heat poured out of an open door, along with the smell of roses. Letting her hand drop, Edward made an elaborate bow, ushering her in with a broad smile. "Here you are, my lady. Comforts from the far-off future—all for you."

His infectious happiness already had her forgetting how bedraggled she felt. Stepping cautiously over the high wooden threshold, she looked to see what comfort of the far future Edward was so tickled to recreate. Naturally it was the lord's bedroom he led her to, with thick carpets, carved oak chests, and tall sculpted windows looking out on the darkened courtyard. Before the white-and-gold canopy bed stood a huge wooden vat, wafting rose-scented steam up into the vaulted ceiling. Liveried servants were industriously pouring in more hot water from heavy cauldrons. Her clothes and carrying bag sat neatly stacked atop a chest, along with soap, towels, and her electronic notebook. Amazed he could so readily read her mind, she asked, "How did you ever manage this?"

Edward patted the tub. "Knowing your superstitious fondness for bathing, I put this here against your return. When I went out tonight to search for you, I ordered it filled."

"Before you even knew you would find me?" Now he was the one foretelling the future.

His hand went to her shoulder, drawing them closer together. "I knew I would find you. I had to." He was the charmed lad who always got his way.

Almost always. She could think of one thing he very much wanted but had not gotten. Looping her arms around his neck, she asked, "Does that make you a sorcerer, too?"

Edward whispered, "I wish I were a sorcerer, so I could be sure of keeping you here."

Amen. She, too, wished she had the power to keep them always together—this centuries-apart business got really old. "I told you I would return," she reminded him. And here she was—as promised—though at times she herself had not believed it would happen. "And I am afraid I will be here with you for the foreseeable future."

Next she knew, they were kissing, buoyed by a rapturous sense of freedom. Forget time, forget rank—so what if he was a teenage earl from the fifteenth century. She was going to be from the fifteenth century, too—for the foreseeable future. What mattered was that he was brave, resourceful, and loving. Look at this amazing bath he prepared.

Their kiss ended with a rap on the door, still standing wide open.

A servant in murrey and blue had brought wine, cheese, fruit pastries, fresh vegetables, and boiled water—all favorites of hers. Setting down the silver tray, the servant bowed and withdrew, discreetly closing the bedroom door. They laughed guiltily. Liveried servants knew how to behave, even if young earls in love did not.

Edward poured for both of them. She found the wine perfect, rich and fruity, barely fermented—so much medieval wine tasted like bottled vinegar. And it went straight to her head. Tipsy from wine and fatigue, she could not take her gaze off the scented water in the tall wooden tub. By now the bath was full, and just seeing the steaming water lying still as glass in the tub loosened knots in her neck. She tested the water with her hand, finding it pleasantly hot.

Now was the time. Drawing her monk's robe off over her head, she handed it to Edward, who stood holding the robe, looking her over. Barefoot and bedraggled, wearing just a stained shift, she told him, "I must look a mess."

"You do, indeed," Edward smiled broadly. "A most lovely mess."

Men can be so easy to please. Sometimes. She thought of her desperate attempts to please Lord Scales and shivered—but you cannot judge a whole sex by the likes of Lord Scales and Le Boeuf. Too shy just to hand Edward the white shift as well, she climbed half-dressed into the steaming tub. Warm clean water caressed her skin, washing away the feel of days and nights in a filthy cell, dissolving the knots in her neck, along with her shyness, lifting the wet dirty shift up to her waist. Pulling it off over her shoulders, she let it float away. Smiling, she crooked her finger, inviting Edward to come closer.

He stepped up to the edge of the tub, looking most handsome in his very own murrey and blue, resting his palms comfortably on the rim, pleased by what he saw—considering all they had been through, it had taken an unconscionably long time for him to see her naked. Centuries, in fact. She asked her bold knight errant, "What about your bath?"

Edward looked puzzled, "My bath?"

"Yes, your bath. Is there another tub filled for you?"

"Why no, there is not." Edward had clearly not seen the need. She was the one who had spent days in a filthy dungeon. He had been out with Warwick and the boys in God's clean air, escorting King Henry back from Northampton, entering London in triumph—yet again. How could he have gotten dirty doing that?

She matched his innocence, blandly saying, "Then I suppose you must use this one."

"Must I?" For a moment he seemed confused over whose bath this was.

"Yes, you must." This was the Middle Ages, where you rarely got to bathe alone. She reached up and began unlacing his doublet—probably not the proper protocol for undressing an earl, but for once she would have things her way. "Come, I swear you shall enjoy it."

Edward's eyes lit up and his smile widened. "If I must, then I must." Not too terribly disappointed, he helped her undo the doublet, then stripped away his shirt, kicking off his boots, and rolling down his hose, looking more handsome nude than he was on horseback—which was saying a lot. Her tired body tensed with anticipation. Edward fished out her sodden shift, then climbed in next to her, sending a swift spasm of desire shooting from nipples to groin. Edward laughed, "You make me feel like Sir Lancelot rescuing enchanted Princess Elaine, held naked in her high tower and perpetual boiling bath."

And he was supposed to make her feel like this was a fairy tale. Funny how folks here and now thought it more important that she was an enchantress, and lady to the earl of March, than that she came from the far future. The third millennium meant nothing to them. Supremely confident that Merry Olde England was far superior to her high-tech tomorrow, all they wanted from the twenty-first century was her. As if to prove it, Edward pulled her to him, bringing their bodies into wet, thrilling contact. He sighed heavily—"Here is what I hoped and longed for."

"Is it?" Reaching around, she locked her arms behind him, pressing them closer together, skin against skin, until she could feel his body from breast to knees. "Is this really what you wanted?"

"Of course"—he smiled happily—"do you know I spent the whole day searching for you?"

"You did?" After all that happened in the Tower, on the Thames, and in Southwark, she had never thought to ask how his day had been.

"As soon as we had the Tower, Sir Collingwood Grey and I searched it from top to bottom. Lord Scales claimed you were not in the fortress, and by day's end I very nearly believed him." He looked utterly devastated to have been so wrong. "I went through the White Tower from the topmost turrets to the chapel vaults. And every tower on the curtain as well, thinking I might have to have to take the place apart stone by stone to find you. We finished off by torchlight, and I was getting my first bit of sleep when that scarlet archer woke me." She saw that behind his whimsical bravado Edward had been worried sick, despairing of finding her, since there was no real proof any of them were in the Tower. It was Lord Scales's word against that of admitted witches—not the sort of testimony you could use in court. Edward asked, "Where did Scales have you secreted?"

"In the vaults of the White Tower, behind a great line of barrels." She felt her calm slipping as unwelcome memories crowded in on her.

"I saw those great heavy barrels, but they looked like they had been there since King William built the place."

"There is a secret cell behind them." With that she started to cry, clinging to Edward for support, unable to stop huge sobs welling up from deep within her, shaking her whole body.

"What is wrong?" he asked. Clearly this was not what Edward expected when he climbed into the tub. What a ditz she was, surviving the Tower, escaping from Lord Scales, facing down FitzHolland, and then going all to pieces in her bath. Between sobs, she told Edward everything she had meant to hold back—about being in the cell, and what they had done to her, how her soul had been stripped bare, and how she despaired of ever getting out alive, of ever seeing him again. Feeling much the worse for wear, she started to pull away, horribly ashamed, sickened by what the men in the Tower had done to her, mocking her, hurting her, forcing her to play up to them, confessing to ridiculous crimes—just because she wanted to live. Mortified to have ruined Edward's romantic moment, she tried to retreat back into herself, hiding from all that had happened. But he would not let her go; full of youthful strength, yet amazingly tender, he held her tight, soothing the sobs out of her, saying her name over and over in her ear, "Robyn, Robyn, I do love you so."

She stifled her tears, saying simply and stupidly, "You do?"

Edward brushed wet hair out of her eyes. " 'Tis true, my lady, when we opened up the Tower and you were not there, nothing else mattered. It was you I wanted, not the Tower or London, or King Henry, or my earldom of March. Victory had no meaning, and triumph had no glory, not without you to share it—the way you shared my trials and exile. I have loved you dearly since that day we first met in Wales."

She smiled through her tears. "You mean when you thought I was a boy?"

"Even then," he admitted. "I thought you the prettiest, smartest boy I had ever seen, able to read magic maps and to speak boldly and curtly to an earl in armor, without a trace of fear—I very much wanted you for my friend and companion." He kissed her full on the lips, then added, "Usually I do not fall for pretty boys I meet on the wayside, so imagine my happiness when I found how badly I was mistaken."

Her smile widened. "Imagine mine, when I found out you were not mad." Or at least no crazier than any man in love. Her whole life turned on the moment that John-Amend-All's black arrow thudded into the sod at her feet. Terrifying her senseless at the time, but instantly transforming Edward from a wandering lunatic in armor into a bold engaging boy, in love with life and honor, and with her. When the bath started to cool, Edward lifted her wet from the tub, with water streaming off her in warm silken threads onto his carpeted floor. Taking up a pair of towels, he dried them both off, then carried her naked to his canopy bed.

Lying in his arms under clean white feather bedding, she could not believe how long she'd denied herself, holding close her heart, afraid to open up to love and life, ignoring the call of her dark innermost core, that secret dangerous self that wanted not just Edward and Edward's love, but Edward's world as well, with its pomp and grandeur, and closeness to the land, its peril and adventure, its prayer and spellcraft. Nestled in darkness, she instinctively fitted her body to his, astonished at how their flesh seemed to fuse together, until she could barely tell what was her and what was him. Shuddering with pleasure, she felt lips kiss her throat, then the curve of her neck, and finally whisper in her ear, "Now you must marry me." Good thing she believed in natural childbirth.

⊷ Betrothed ⊶

*E*dward *did not believe in wasting time.* Nor did Robyn, once she knew what she wanted, so they were betrothed the following Tuesday, the twenty-second of July, Saint Mary Magdalen's Day—one day short of her three-month anniversary in the Middle Ages. Saint Mary herself was a prostitute saved by Jesus, so her day was considered a lucky one for making illicit unions legal. Kneeling next to Edward in a shaft of sunlight, she said her own vows in Baynards Castle's sumptuously decorated chapel, at a private ceremony before a tall priest and a gold gem-encrusted altar. Feeling like Juliet being secretly married to her teenage Romeo by Friar Laurence, she added some Shakespeare to her vows:

> **They are but beggars that can count their worth;**
> **But my true love is grown to such excess,**
> **I cannot sum up half my sum of wealth.**

But this plush private chapel was nothing like Friar Laurence's plain little cell, and she was dressed like the Princess Bride in a blue-and-silver gown, and wearing a silver circlet in her hair. Edward wore his earl's livery. Deirdre attended her, while Joy and Beth Lambert held her train. Jane-Beth was newly fostered into the Grey's growing London household. Her parents were delighted to see her situated with a noble family, especially one so close to the earl of March. Greys also gave Robyn away; Jo, Collin, and Bryn acted as her surrogate family, bearing witness to her betrothal. Collin wore his blue-and-white colors, with her kiwi-green Minnie Mouse scarf on his sleeve.

No one stood up for Edward, not so much as a squire. As a belted earl, he was assumed able to defend his own interests. Part of the reason for a private ceremony was to keep his engagement secret, confirming Robyn's rights without alerting Edward's family and enemies. With his father still in Ireland, and his mother just released from custody, the family could not take the shock of their eldest son and heir promising himself to a penniless witch from California. Edward said he had to tell his father face-to-face; no secondhand report could ever make it sound like good news. Like Juliet, her love must be legalized in secret, lest it fuel the feuding families. But secret or not, the betrothal was binding, and neither could break it without the other's consent. By marrying Edward she would become countess of March, and when Edward's father died, she would be duchess of York—just like Fergie. Which meant she was taking England's most eligible bachelor off the market, never a popular move, especially among the high nobility. Warwick, for one, would be furious.

That was Warwick's problem. She saw a new age dawning, where love and freedom counted for more than rank and station. Those that did not accept it risked being trampled in the rush, like Duke Buckingham and dear kindly Lord Scales. For once everything was going her way, and whosoever opposed her and Edward did so at their own peril. Warwick had best beware.

Collin came to see her before the ceremony, while the women and girls were getting her ready, saying he had an engagement gift. Wearing a blue cloak trimmed with ermine, he had one hand hidden from sight, promising her, "A good omen for a happy day."

She sat down with him in an alcove window seat overlooking the castle courtyard, where they could have a bit of what passed for medieval privacy. He asked if she was as happy as she looked.

"Marvelously so." She meant it. She was marrying the man she loved, magically trading a Hollywood life that had been going nowhere for a wild new world, unimaginably alive and exciting. She had the friendship of the king, and the foremost young nobleman in the kingdom to marry, plus the love of London.

Collin grinned at her enthusiasm, happy not to be losing her to the future, saying he must soon return to the Cotswolds, to begin rebuilding Greystone, with Bryn at his side. He had ridden out to Greystone from Northampton before joining King Henry in London, to inspect the manor's charred stonework. He planned to have a roof up before autumn to keep out the rains, "so work may go on through the winter."

So a lot of folks hoped. She guessed that across the West Country, families great and small would be returning to sacked or forfeited homes, praying the peace would last so they could get their farms ready for winter. Those who had taken their homes were now on the run themselves. Collin's nosy neighbor, Chief Justice Fortescue, who first set FitzHolland on the Greys, was no longer chief justice, or even a neighbor. He was headed into exile, along with Queen Margaret, Duke Holland, and the most diehard members of the court party. FitzHolland himself was awaiting trial in the Guildhall before the citizens of London, along with Le Boeuf. Victory is seldom so complete. Sitting with Collin on the sunlit window seat, she could not help remembering their first meeting at Berkeley Castle, when she had been the confused and terrified stranger and he had been the cool, confident Sir Collin, sizing her up. "What did you think of me," she asked, "when we first met?"

Collin considered, then answered, "I saw a pretty but hapless witch, newly snared by FitzHolland. And hoped you might be useful, assuming you could somehow be saved."

She thanked him for his concern. "Why did you think I was a witch?"

He shrugged. "Everyone did. And you are one, are you not?"

"But, I was not one then," she protested.

Collin grinned. "As any witch knows—*then* and *now* can be somewhat slippery terms. Besides, you had that air."

"And was I useful?" she asked demurely, confident she had been, but nonetheless wanting to hear Collin say so.

"More than I ever thought possible," he admitted.

And now she was going to become his social superior, marrying into the same nobility that had found Collin's skill and loyalty useful—but seldom worth rewarding. She told him soberly, "Everything I have, I owe to you. If you had not taken me in, I would now be dead, or worse."

"I doubt it," Collin scoffed, nodding at the carved stone alcove around her and the castle court below. "You have done astoundingly well for a friendless stranger from the far-off future. Which is why I am giving you this back, now that you no longer need to keep it hidden." Drawing his hand from under his fur-trimmed cloak, he produced a badly burnt bound manuscript by Christine de Pizan. Half the heavy cover was gone and most of the pages were singed, but the heart of the manuscript had survived. Pressed between the half-burned cover and the title page was a white rose.

Gasping in surprise, Robyn stared at the rose that had brought her here, pressed flat, with petals missing, but still the same flower she mooned over on the train back from Abergavenny. Or rather the one she would moon over, five hundred years from now—as Collin observed, *then* and *now* were often hard to keep straight. Carefully, she closed the book and gave Collin a kiss, thanking him for "being my champion, when I most sorely needed one."

Collin touched the Minnie Mouse kerchief on his sleeve. "I still have your favor. If Lady Robyn ever needs another champion, she need only let me know." He bowed and left her to the women.

All the hurt and resentment she once had for Collin was long gone, lifting a huge weight from her soul. She was glad to be sharing this world with him, not as lovers or enemies, but as dear friends and allies. And she very much needed such a friend and champion, for she was embarking on a fantastic voyage through uncharted waters. Robyn Plantagenet. Witch-countess. Friend of the king. Married to one of the foremost earls in the land, who sat on the Royal Council and stood to inherit a dukedom—none of his manors and castles had plumbing, of course—but still a splendid catch. All in all, Countess Robyn could use a sturdy champion, and she could hardly do better than Sir Collingwood Grey.

Weird how this society naturally spun webs of personal dependence. She was linked to the Greys through Collin, and to the Mercers Company of London through her sister-initiate, Beth Lambert. When she wed Edward, she would become cousin by marriage to the Nevilles. You could not live here and now without making family connections. She was even linked to Duchess Wydville, through the Greys of Groby and the coven, but she would not be joining the Bedford household anytime soon.

Despite Collin's dire threats, Duchess Wydville was beyond the law's reach. No one died from her betrayals, so she could not be charged with murder through witchcraft. Technically, Duchess Wydville had committed treason by betraying their attempt to take the Tower after they had the king. But with more nobles coming over to them every day, trying the duchess of Bedford for treason on magical evidence was not the message they needed to send to the upper nobility, not when they wanted her husband for the reconstructed Royal Council. Besides, it was Duchess Weirdville who brought her here—twice. And she owed the evil old sorceress something for that.

Witchcraft was another matter. Jo was determined to form a new coven, for which they already had a nucleus—sort of. It would be a coven relying heavily on novices and ne'er-do-well witches from the future. Still, it was a start.

After the betrothal, she dragged Edward up to Baynards Castle's topmost tower to look out on London lazing in the summer sun. On one side lay the walled city, with its warren of streets and alleys, and forest of stone steeples. Beyond the walls, past Holborn and Smith-field, green hills rolled off to the north and west. On her other side the Thames flowed beneath London Bridge, past Southwark and Bankside, as broad as an arm of the sea. Life seemed utterly perfect—given she was in the Middle Ages to begin with. But who said you could pick your century? Besides, she had already lived through the absolute worst medieval times had to offer, short of actual death or mutilation, which might happen anywhere, any time, even in the third millennium. This was an age without AIDS, handguns, auto wrecks, or plane crashes—like the one that killed her parents. And sooner or later everyone died, if only to be reborn. Leaning on Edward's arm, she told him, "I foresee wonderful times for us."

He laughed, "Do I have your witch's word on that?"

"You do, indeed." She was not that sort of witch—except on occasion. As she said it, she thought of the paperback history hidden among her things, and the temptation to look ahead. Were the Wars of the Roses really this short? Would Northampton be the end of it? There had been fighting on and off since Saint Albans, five years ago, which seemed like time enough to her. She had such a horror of reading something terrible—with no way to stop it—she would just have to keep the book as her insurance policy, and go blindly forward, buoyed by an unaccustomed wave of confidence. "Everything will go well. We have the king, we have London, and we have peace. . . ."

Edward smiled ruefully. "At least no armed opposition."

"Most folks will settle for that." Everyone she knew was sick of fighting, only wanting to get on with lives that were hard enough already.

"Peace can be as difficult and dangerous as war," Edward warned. "Forbye, we must now convince our enemies through reason, instead of merely beating them into submission."

Too true. Somehow they must hold the kingdom together, uniting both factions, loyalists and rebels, Lancaster and York, red rose and white, while undoing decades of misgovernment. "At home," she told him, "we have a permanently divided government—with two parties that roundly hate each other, without even being related. But we settle it with votes, women's as well as men's."

"A wise system," Edward decided, confident he could win an election even easier than a battle—particularly if women voted. Edward was not averse to learning from the future, when it seemed useful. "We, too, have our votes." He meant the Mother of Parliaments, soon to be called by the victors. "When King Henry summons Parliament, we will have a friendly commons and clergy, and most lords will accept the new Royal Council. Those lords who do not are already headed for Scotland, or for France."

Along with Queen Margaret and the infant Prince of Wales. She hoped Queen Margaret had the good sense to keep on running—all the way back to Anjou. In exile, Queen Margaret and the six-year-old prince of Wales became a distant discomfort, hanging about some foreign court, at someone else's expense, giving other people problems. Margaret did not worry her as much as threats closer to home. Soon she had to testify at the Guildhall, against FitzHolland and Le Boeuf, and in favor of Matt Davye—with Warwick for a judge, a real stretch role for the former thief and pirate, and aspiring kingmaker. She warned Edward, "Warwick needs to be watched."

"So he must be," Edward admitted, looking out over the city, well aware of Earl Warwick's faults. "But not now," he begged, "not on our betrothal day."

Too true. Let Warwick watch over himself for a while, it was their day. Edward worked closely with the touchy earl of Warwick, but she was the only one outside the family he fully trusted—in fact he trusted her so much he wanted her in his family. Edward was big on family, a loyal son and loving older sibling. She admired that sense of rootedness and family love, wanting some of it for herself. Wind off the river blew hair across her face—uncut for three months and getting too long to be contained by a simple silver circlet. Edward reached out a bare hand to brush it aside. Fingers touched her cheek, and she turned to kiss them. "Do you miss the other London," he asked, "the one paved over from Dartford to Windsor?"

"No." She did not miss the great sprawling impersonal third-millennium metropolis, wonderful as it was. She liked this compact little London, wedged within its walls, its skinny crowded houses facing dirty cobblestone streets—the London whose people rallied to her against FitzHolland, where she could not go fabric shopping without drawing smiles and greetings. Or cheers when she was with Edward. "Not in the least."

He looked gravely at her, happy to have her, but still concerned by all that she was giving up. "And your home in Holy Wood, will you miss it, as well?"

"Not Hollywood, either." Not much anyway. Pretty unbelievable, considering that when she first arrived here on Saint George's Day, she had been so full of indignant moral superiority, appalled even to be in such a benighted unsanitary century. But by now she felt swept up something gigantic, staking her heart on a mad, impractical, unscripted love, one that had turned her life inside out and upside down. Glad to be making history instead of movies, she gloried in her strange new life, and in the dangerous power to see wrongs righted and justice done, to make magic work and virtue triumph—even at the risk of life and limb.

Maybe not everyone was meant to make it in the third millennium. She had certainly given it her best. She pictured herself in the far, far future, walking out her troubles in Wales. Standing on the grassy windblown ridge above Llanthony, watching Edward ride up, both irritated and intrigued by this handsome boy in armor—wondering if this were some weird cosmic joke, or a fairy tale gone awry. But it was no joke, and no mistake. And now she stood looking out over old London from a castle wall, living the fairy tale, trusting in love to see her through, against all logic and reason, happy to have found her era.